the
TURNCOAT

the
TURNCOAT

T.J. London

Book 3 in the Rebels and Redcoats Saga

The Turncoat

by T.J. London

Copyright © 2019 T.J. London
All rights reserved
ISBN: 978-0-578-49670-2

First Edition

This book is a work of fiction and does not represent any individual, living or dead. Names, characters, places, and incidents either are products of the author's imagination or are used fictionally.

Edited by Kathe Robin
Cover design by Steve Miller of www.LookAtMyDesigns.com
Copy Editing by Jo Michaels
Proofreading by Tia Silverthorne Bach
Interior formatting by Gaynor Smith
all of Indie Books Gone Wild

Published in the United States of America

It is within these pages that I found justice...

Books by T.J. London

The Rebels and Redcoats Saga:
The Tory
The Traitor
The Turncoat

Foreword

The Turncoat is historical fiction, so while the story is a creation of mine, and there are some liberties taken with times and locations, my goal was to be as accurate with my historical details as possible. Some of the language in the story may be harsh and politically incorrect, but it's reflective of the times we were living in, and for accuracy's sake, I've tried to stay true to that. Details about the Oneida Nation and the Iroquois Confederacy is extensive and vast; however, some of it is still missing as theirs was neither a written history nor does a true tally of their numbers and losses during the American Revolutionary War exist. I did the best I could with the historical references I had, drawing on many resources, and what I couldn't find, I tried to create as accurately and respectfully as possible. The story of John and Dellis is fiction, though it takes place on the backdrop of real events—and with real people who are often overlooked when discussing the founding of our nation. The goal of my stories is to provoke the reader to question the version of history we know and seek the truth, for only then will we, as a nation, learn from our mistakes and begin to truly heal.

Fort Stanwix was renamed Fort Schuyler in 1776, but to avoid reader confusion, I continued to call it Fort Stanwix throughout the series.

Table of Contents

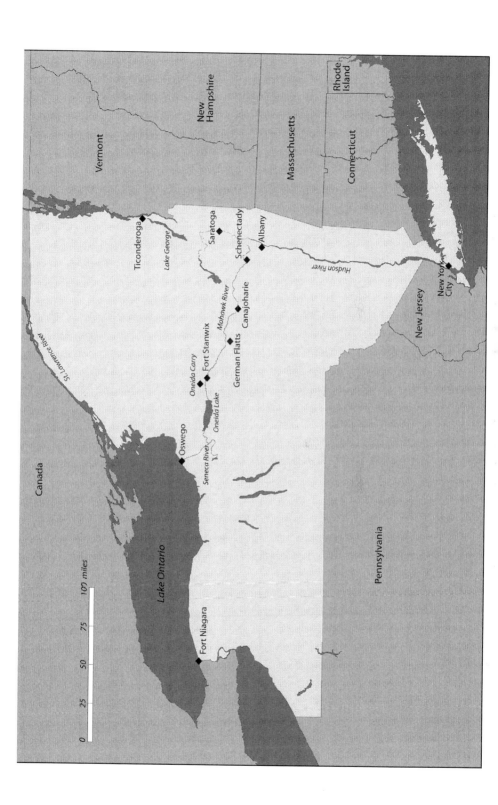

Chapter One

Fort Stanwix, New York, June 1777

*K*arma, the gun… Justice, the bullet… Judgement passes, transgressions are exposed, you get what you deserve. Hot metal passes through flesh and bone, tearing out all that is you—ripping out the memories you longed to forget. You, the empty shell, the one you created with grasping avarice and self-indulgence and now are forced to reckon with.

"Face him, John. Look at yourself! Do you see him? Do you?"

John stared into the mirror with loathing; a handsome face and an angel's smile—the Devil's lapdog—staring back.

"Do it!"

The steel barrel against John's cheek was cold yet, oh, so comforting True power was in his grasp; to live or die was his to decide, much like a god. Justice, for once, held tightly in his fist.

One second more and the pain would be over, his story encrypted in the destroyed matter and stain of blood that only he could read. Unequivocal truth. There would be no mask, no reagent, no letter to decode his tale. He would appeal his case to the Devil himself, and fall prostrate at his feet.

"No mercy to be found here," the Devil would say.

John laughed.

1

"Pull it, dammit! Pull it! Coward. You could give the damned order, but you lack the stones to do the deed to yourself."

Better to murder some innocent women than lose his precious, useless life: a Viscount's spare heir, a debtor, a lecher.

A traitor.

"John," she said, in a breathy whisper.

Rubbing the metal against his cheek one last time, he turned the end of the barrel to his temple and pulled the hammer back to full cock. The clicking sound set his heart aflutter with excitement.

It was time.

If there was no God, no Hell, then at the other end of this was sweet oblivion and a peace no drink or woman could afford him. No longer a victim of his vices. Freedom. A gambit he was willing to take.

"Lie to me, sweet justice; tell me it will be over soon."

He squeezed his eyes shut, a spasm in his finger, as he started to pull.

"Justice... John..."

John Carlisle looked towards the heavens, allowing the azure sky and healing sun to drown out the memory of that pitiful, defeated drunk paying homage to a steel barrel and a lead ball.

I am not that man anymore.

Damn Karma, yanking him back into the past. She could go to the Devil and fester in perdition's flames before John would relinquish his soul to her.

I'm the master of my destiny now: Captain John Carlisle, an officer, a spy in service of His Majesty, and an Oneida.

Hiding amongst the ferns and brush of the forest floor, John eyed native spies—*one, two, three*—scouting Fort Stanwix as it stood peacefully on the cleared grounds of the Oneida Carry. They were Mohawk; their distinctive scalp locks adorned with brilliant red and blue feathers were like beacons, making the braves easily visible in the pale olives and brilliant greens of the forest. Trespassers in Oneida territory, though the tribes were brothers in the Great Iroquois Nation. But not for long. By the will of the colonists and the British, they'd trampled on a three-hundred-year-old confederacy, fracturing the fragile peace between the tribes—and John was one of the puppet masters pulling the strings. But one good turn deserved another, and by Fate's sleight of hand, he had become an Oneida: Just One, a name given to him for bringing justice to their sworn enemy Roger DeLancie.

The Mohawks started their advance towards the fort, their eyes greedily fixed on the target, muskets in hand. John's first instinct was to shoot them down; from his vantage point it could easily be done, but he hesitated, his finger resting on the trigger. *Steady. Steady.* The Mohawk were his allies, loyal to the British and enemy to the Colonists. Such was his deliberation at that moment and the dichotomy of his inner turmoil; the woman he loved—his obsession—was Oneida and a colonist, but the King was John's sovereign, and his soldier's duty and honor was sworn to the crown.

The sun apexed in the noon sky, sweltering heat causing a bead of sweat to roll down John's forehead into his eyes, but he ignored it; the Mohawks' owl-like hearing would pick up the slightest movement, even a pin dropping into the grass. Looking up at the trees to his right, John spotted Anoki, his musket aimed, and on the left, in the brush, Great Bear's grotesque face could barely be seen as he fingered the trigger of his musket.

Taking a deep breath, John counted, *one... two... three...* and then let the air out in attempt to quell the miasma of impending doom that pervaded while he waited for the signal. His hands shook, the wooden stock resting against his shoulder, his eye gazing down the line of the barrel.

Can I do this? Should I? There was no more time to consider; Anoki nodded, cocked his musket, and fired. The crack of the gun discharging sliced through the languid silence of the forest as the Mohawk closest to John dropped, the other two racing off into the trees towards Wood Creek. Aiming, he cocked his muzzle loader and then pulled the trigger, sending a ball whizzing through the air and into the calf of his target with pinpoint accuracy. The brave limped but didn't stop, bolting through the forest. John gave chase, unhindered by the ten pounds of steel and wood in his hand, his soldier's training making him deft and skillful, navigating the hilly terrain with the grace of a cat.

A shot of adrenaline coursed through his veins; the thrill of the chase, in accord with the blazing heat, making him lightheaded, like inhaling a heady mix of whiskey and tobacco would. Just ahead, he spotted one of the Mohawks racing up to a canoe docked on the muddy shore of the creek. John stopped abruptly, pulled out his pistol, and aimed, zeroing in on his target.

It was Roger DeLancie's former right-hand man and scout, Eagle Eyes.

The giant Mohawk grinned. "Come and get me, traitor."

"By all means." John steadied his breath and pulled the trigger, but the Mohawk dodged swiftly, the ball dropping into the water with a plunk and a spatter.

"Damn!" John let out a barrage of expletives, watching his old adversary row up the river and out of range, recognizing the look in those onyx eyes: unabashed hatred. Their private war wasn't over. The Mohawk was on the hunt for vengeance, and it was blood he craved—John's blood.

Turning back to the woods, he stopped, the sounds of heavy breathing coming from a few feet to the west, over his shoulder. *Damn!* He had no rounds left, both his musket and pistol fired. Throwing down the useless weapons, John pulled out his knife and tomahawk, ready for some hand to hand, just a little skirmish to work off the extra adrenaline from facing Eagle Eyes. Fisticuffs was John's specialty—next to aiming a pistol.

With each step, the shallow breathing got louder, the rapid pace guiding John to his target. When he stood at the feet of the injured Mohawk, John held up his weapons for his adversary to see, an inducement to stand down.

"Why are you here?" John demanded.

The brave smiled defiantly, his bright, white teeth flashing against black and red paint smeared on ruddy, dark skin.

"What do you want?" John yelled, that time in *Kanien' keha*, Mohawk dialect.

"You, John Carlisle," the brave replied and then whipped a hunk of dirt in John's face.

Too stunned by the answer to react, the caustic debris landed in his face, burning his eyes and obstructing his vision. Reflexively, he rubbed them, further adding insult to injury, his eyes watering profusely. Pushing the advantage, the brave rolled on his side and reached for his tomahawk, taking several swings at John's ankles. Through blurry vision, he managed to dodge the blade, jumping left and right, and then threw himself on top of the brave, pinning him to the ground.

"Who sent you? Was it Butler?" John grabbed the native by the collar of his shirt, slamming him into the ground. "Who are you working for?"

Eagle Eyes rarely worked alone, a notorious thug for hire, and a tenacious one at that. Someone put him up to it.

John held the blade to the brave's neck, letting him feel the sharp edge, giving him a moment to reconsider his next move, a soldier's courtesy. "Tell me."

The Mohawk defiantly put up his chin, offering his neck, so John dug in, blood trickling from the small slice. "Tell me, now."

"Just One, stop," Anoki yelled from behind. "He'll admit nothing."

John froze, trepidation giving him pause, until Anoki stepped up with warning in his dark eyes. Against every instinct, John sheathed his blade and stepped back.

Anoki grabbed the Mohawk's arm and pulled him to his feet. "You're trespassing on Oneida land. Now, you'll answer to our chief, spy."

John glanced over his shoulder at the river; Eagle Eyes was barely in sight, rowing against the current. *Damn.*

"What will Joseph do with him?" John asked.

"We'll take him to the Colonel at Stanwix. They'll use him to negotiate with the Mohawk."

"Lot of good that will do." He shook his head despondently. The situation was hopeless. The Mohawks were fiercely loyal to the King's cause, and the Oneida had thrown their lot in with the colonists. Brother against brother.

But am I not a King's man and an Oneida?

Damned divided loyalties.

Bending down, John grabbed his musket, hooked his pistol back on his hip, and then started towards the village. The longer he walked in the tranquility of the forest, the more shattered it appeared as memories seeped into the present; around him, the innocent lay bleeding in the grass, and the outstretched hand of a woman reached through the forest to find him. *"Justice... John."* His haven, his shelter from the storm, had been breached. Eagle Eyes was back to settle old scores, and war was the inevitable recourse.

John could hide no longer. Karma had come for him.

Viceroy raced through the woods, the *clomp, clomping* of hooves on the dirt path bringing John ever closer to the only place he ever belonged: home, the village, Dellis.

When the forest broke and the trees parted, he could see the wooden stockade of the Oneida village, smoke billowing from the quaint little cabins within. Crossing the threshold, he dismounted and led Viceroy to the barn, setting him up in a stall next to Dellis's mare, feeding and brushing both of them. Stopping for a moment, John looked around, ignoring how his horse nudged his master's back, wanting more gentle ministrations and an extra carrot or two. Though the building was new, the original one blown to bits six months prior, it was still the place his nightmares were fed—the place he was tortured. Looking down at his wrists, where the scars from the shackles that held him prisoner were still vibrant, he was reminded of all that had come to pass.

A captain. A spy. A prisoner.

And now an Oneida.

Shaking off the memory, he patted Viceroy's soft, silky nose again and gave him the spare carrot that was stuffed in John's side pocket.

"Just One?" Joseph entered, interrupting the quiet reflection.

"Yes?" John smiled upon hearing his native name. Just One. A rather ironic turn of phrase, yet in a way, fitting; yes, he'd brought justice to the Oneida by killing their enemy, Roger DeLancie, and freeing their men from Fort Niagara, but it cost John the proof that would've cleared his name and expunged his record. "What is it, Joseph?"

Their relationship had transformed from one of distant regard to friendly, almost fatherly, since John had rescued Dellis and the Oneidas. He turned to the chief, noticing the concern etched in the deep creases of Joseph's brow and cheeks.

"There were three Mohawk spies near Fort Stanwix. We shot one, and one got away; the other, Anoki should've brought back to you for questioning."

Joseph nodded, a furrow drawing his long, jet-black brows together. He looked tired, older, the strain of impending war weighing on him, further aging him in a moment's time. "That's not the reason I came to see you, Just One."

"Then what is?" John already knew the answer, for it was the very same conundrum he'd been contemplating for a month, since he'd returned from Niagara.

"You're using our village to hide from the world." Then, with a cock of the brow, Joseph added, "Rather successfully."

Squeezing both eyes closed, John tried to shut out truthful words. Yes, he was hiding; at first, trying to recover from his injuries after battling DeLancie, and then later because John wanted to indulge in a moment's peace in his beloved's arms. But his wounds were healed, and Dellis was his wife in the tribe. There was no excuse; well, except the one he was avoiding: His duty as a soldier in service to the Crown.

"I know, Joseph. I know." John shook his head despondently.

Confiding in another human wasn't something he did easily, but Joseph was the closest thing John had to a father—a wise and experienced man. Turning, John looked into his confidant's onyx eyes and relented.

"Since I left Bristol, I've known no home save this village and The Thistle. I'm torn. I care for Dellis and all of you, yet I'm a soldier; that's my duty, my sacred honor." John let out a breath, glancing down at the ground, while he dug his toe into the dirt, kicking a patch of it.

"You cannot have your foot in both worlds, Just One. You must choose."

Yes, but how?

"We'll understand, no matter your decision." Joseph's voice was stern, as always, but there was a hint of tenderness, newfound and comforting, so unlike the austere military talk John was accustomed to. "Dellis is another matter you must settle. She'll never leave our village. Lily was an adventurous soul, like the wind, always wanting change, welcoming it, but Dellis is of this earth, strong and immobile once she loves something. She's lost so much. If you're to be a part of her life, you must be her safe place, her shelter. You must give her a foundation to grow on, like a tree, with deep, strong roots. That's the promise you made when you took her as your wife."

"Yes," John replied, knowing it was true. Dellis needed stability; too much of her life was spent in chaos—most of it because of his actions. He couldn't ask her to give up her life for his. No, the choice was his to make. And the sacrifice.

Resting a hand on John's shoulder, Joseph gave an encouraging shake, from father to son. "Your friend is here. Lieutenant Clark. He's waiting for you in your cabin. Confide in him."

"Thank you." John walked out of the barn, desperate to leave the truth, and the decision, behind for another day.

The village was alive with activity, Skenandoa and Kateri sitting neatly in the shade sewing while the warriors practiced at their fighting techniques, the clanking of metal against metal ringing in the little valley. The trees had grown to full foliage, towering over the village, allowing only little beams of sun to peek through the canopy and land on Wind Talker, who was sitting with his eyes closed, chanting reverently to the heavens.

It was beautiful. And so damned fragile. Suddenly, everything in John's life, everything he loved, was being threatened. *But what to do about it?*

As he walked back through the stockade, Ho-sa-gowwa, the village's youngest and most diligent guard, waved, his face lighting up with a friendly grin. Gone were the days of standing at musket point, waiting to be admitted under suspicious eyes; John was welcomed with open arms at every dinner table. When they made him a member of their tribe, the Oneida took him into their hearts without apprehension, and he went willingly.

Upon sight, Kateri ran up to him, bright eyed, two long, thick braids hanging down to her shoulders, resting on the doeskin of her tunic. "I have a gift to welcome you to our tribe, Just One. I hadn't finished it yet when you went through the ceremony; forgive me for being late with it." Her sweet voice was breathy and winded from the sprint.

"Don't apologize." He smiled, scanning her lovely face; little beads of sweat dotted her brow, and wisps of her hair stuck to her forehead. She looked lovely and dewy from the summer heat, like a rose in the rain. "What is it?"

She hesitated and then handed the gift to him, her cheeks blushing prettily. It was a bracelet made of rows of tiny purple and white beads, intricately woven together, forming little diamond shapes in each color.

"You made this?"

Kateri nodded, practically bubbling over with excitement.

"Will you put it on me?"

He noticed how her blushed deepened, her hands shaking as she tied the cord around his wrist and then arranged it neatly. When she pulled his cuff over the bracelet, she held onto his hand for a moment. "Do not distress yourself, Just One. You'll find the answers you seek."

Somehow, she always knew what was in his heart, from the first moment they met, when he saved her life and sent her running into the forest for protection. Since then, a unique bond forged between them, not love, but devotion, like kindred spirits in life. Helping her was the first step on his road to redemption, and he was forever grateful to her for starting him on his way.

He grasped her hand in his own and kissed it gently. "Thank you, Kateri. I will treasure this."

She smiled, touching his hair, tracing her fingers over the braided locks down to the trinkets Dellis had given him so long ago. Kateri's onyx eyes were so deep, so dark, like a window into her soul; within them, he saw unyielding trust. "You'll always come for us, no matter what choice you make."

"Yes." Her faith in him was humbling, and something he desperately wanted to be worthy of. "I must meet my guest; forgive me?"

She nodded, releasing his hand, but her words resonated with him on his walk through the village. Did he already know the answer? Was he just fighting the inevitable?

"Clark, what brings you here? Where's Smith?" John placed his musket on the gun rack next to the door and then removed his pistol from his hip and deposited it on the table, placing his tomahawk and knife nearby.

"John, are we disarming a brigade?" Simon snorted as he watched John remove his many weapons and ammunition. "Or the whole damn fort?"

"Feels like it sometimes." He laughed.

It was good to have his closest friend back. After taking a few weeks to recover, John sent Clark to Oswego to retrieve Agnes, and their collective belongings, and bring everything back to The Thistle. It had become their home, and John knew Clark felt the same.

"Smith went with Captain Forster and the rest of the light company to Oswegatchie."

St. Leger's battalion is finally on the move. The first words spoken about the war as reality further slipped into John's quiet haven. "And Agnes?"

A smile lit up Simon's round face, fine lines crinkling the corners of his coffee-brown eyes. "She's at The Thistle. Thomas already put her to work, and I daresay she was excited about it. She was cooking up a storm by the time I left."

"Dellis will love having her for company. I think they became rather close in Oswego." Agnes was as cherished to John as any sister could be, his only solace after the loss of the baby when Dellis was too embittered to share in their grief. "Those two have much in common. They'll need each other when we're away."

"Yes." Clark nodded.

"You care for her, don't you?" Not long before, Simon had butted his nose into John's personal affairs, so it seemed only fitting that he should return the favor by asking a few questions of his own.

Clark guffawed. "John, do I get to accuse *you* of impertinence now? Will you warn me that I'm making a bad decision by falling for a former slave and remind me of all the challenges we'll face?"

"No." John shook his head, though the thought had crossed his mind. *What will it be like for my friend, a white British officer, with a former slave for a wife?* Society would forever shun the couple, their adversity so physically obvious, unable to be hidden or denied. But was not his relationship with Dellis just as scandalous?

"I'm happy for both of you. Agnes is lovely and kind, and a damn good cook—which is rather important!" Then, after a long pause, he added, "And we don't choose the ones we love."

"Amen to that." Simon grinned, ear to ear. "Now, take this letter so I can get back to her right quick."

John recognized the handwriting immediately. It was a dispatch from Carleton—orders no doubt. Taking the missive, John unfolded it and sat down at the table to read. It was encoded as a series of three numbers separated by periods, each grouping representing a page; a line; and finally, a word. At the bottom of the paper, Simon had already done the translation, using Blackstone's *Commentaries on the Laws of England 5th Oxford Edition*, Carleton's chosen decoder.

I have sent orders to Major Butler to prepare a group of Indians to serve in consort with His Majesty's Battalion under the command of Lieutenant Colonel St. Leger. He is to meet with and appoint leaders for this contingent which will serve under his direction until the time has come to advance. You are to report to Major Butler and assist him with preparations. I know the two of you will be capable of conducting and managing this group until such time as they are needed.

John walked to the hearth and threw the letter into the smoldering embers, watching the paper crumple up and turn to ash.

"You can't ignore that letter, John. This is what you've been working for, what *we've* been working for. If you help Butler create this native army, and we defeat the Rebels at Stanwix, your reputation won't matter anymore. The past will be buried where it belongs. You'll have the accolades you seek and St. Leger singing your praise. Hell, you could even be promoted. Think about this. Carleton is all but handing you everything you've wanted. Don't waste this chance."

He looked back at Clark, noting the graveness in his expression. "I know."

"John, I know what vexes your mind, but you have more leverage on this side, and with Carleton and Butler as your allies. Here, you have a real chance of helping the Oneidas, more than if you join ranks with the colonists. You'll always be seen as a former British spy to the rebels. A traitor who'd turn on his own."

"I agree," John replied, solemnly.

"I saw Lord Tomlinson when I was in Oswego; there's still no sign of his wife." Clark sat at the table, pouring some cider from a small steel pitcher and sipping it. "We have to find her. We have to force Alexei to give her up."

"He won't do it." John rubbed his forehead and huffed out a breath, the reality of his predicament closing in on him like a noose tightening around his neck. He pulled at his neckerchief, loosening his collar. "If Alexei wouldn't give her up to free his own men from Niagara, then he definitely won't do it to help me."

"What do we do now?" Clark asked, looking into his glass before taking another sip.

"I have to find the woman before we leave for Oswego or it'll be my neck. And the last thing I want is Miles going after Alexei; there'll be no mercy afforded. Alexei is just a misguided zealot; he'd never hurt the woman."

Turning back to the table, John looked out the window at Kateri, teaching one of the village girls to sew; both of their lovely, ebony heads were turned down, their eyes focused on their work. There was such peacefulness in the picture they painted, yet it was a façade, war just on the brink, their tranquility soon to be a fleeting memory.

"I saw Eagle Eyes today." He looked back at Clark. "He and two other Mohawks were spying on Fort Stanwix. I managed to take one of them down, but Eagle Eyes got away."

"And I assume the Oneidas took the other spy right to Gansevoort?"

John nodded.

"John, what are you doing? You can't continue to blur the lines. You have to make a decision."

"I know, but not today." He'd allow himself one last day of peace with Dellis before he had to tell her the truth—before he had to put on his red coat once more.

Chapter Two

The warm summer sun felt heavenly on her bare shoulders, contrasting sharply with the brisk chill of the river water lapping and pooling around her legs. Dellis smiled, lifting her arms to the heavens and lathering up with a zesty lavender soap bar. It smelled like a garden in springtime: fresh and floral yet invigorating.

Holding her nose, she dunked her head, rinsing off the soap, ebony waves of hair flowing around her in the cool stream. When she resurfaced, she heard a crackle of tree branches and then a crunch of leaves underfoot. Smiling, she lathered up her tresses again, never once turning to investigate; only one person would breach her private sanctum and watch so boldly: her soldier, her Just One.

"I hear you." A hint of mischief in her voice matched the smirk on her lips.

As if on cue, he stepped from the trees. "My Artemis, where's your bow and arrow? Aren't you afraid you might be set upon by thieves or the unsavory types that lurk in the woods?" There was humor in his mellifluous baritone and a bit of challenge.

"Who? Rogues? Spies? The British?" Then, with a quizzical cock in her brow, she turned to face her leering perpetrator. "Or perhaps just a rogue British spy?"

A grin started from one corner of his kissable lips and spread to the other until he opened up with a laugh. "Touché, my love. I've been caught. But what will you do to me now that I'm a defenseless prisoner? Will you finally take that crop to me? I've been very bad indeed."

So much suggestion in those words and that damn twinkle in his eyes. He was more enticing than a man had a right to be. And he knew it. "Don't tempt me, husband."

Her feeble rebuke only spurred him on. "Hum: spy, redcoat, scoundrel, husband… Which one would you like me to play in your boudoir tonight? Or we can try all of them, one at a time?"

"Oneida?" She threw down a challenge, waiting to see if he'd take the bait.

Again, he let out a laugh, his sapphire-blue eyes following her as she slowly rose from the water, his breath audibly catching when her nude body was fully exposed. Dauntless, she stopped for a moment, letting him look his fill. Blue flames licked from his gaze, making her hotter than hours spent basking bare skinned in the summer sun.

Dellis purposely took her time toweling off, knowing how he liked to watch her, his eyes the conduit to unquenchable passion. And oh, how she reveled in it. She amazed herself, bold where once she was afraid of being touched, much less admired, by a man. Yet, when it came to John, she wanted every last bit of his attention. It was decidedly his fault; he'd made a brazen tart of the lady she'd once been.

The sun had streaked his dirty-blond locks, leaving flecks of gold that sparkled when the rays shined down on him. A devil in angel's clothing. The braided trinkets she'd woven into his hair weren't pulled back in his queue but tucked behind his left ear. She loved how he wore his hair looser, giving him an unchained, slightly reckless appearance, unlike the coiffed, tailored soldier of yesterday. She'd refitted her father's muted-blue linen waistcoat and matching breeches to fit her husband; the collar of his white shirt was open at the neck, exposing the top of his chest, a hint of a scar just barely visible under the purple and white wampum necklace. His whole aura had changed since he'd returned from Niagara; he was more at ease in her world and with the man he was—her John, not theirs.

"The water looks cold." His eyes feasted on her breasts, her nipples pebbled and erect, ready and waiting for his hands. Where he was concerned, they had a mind of their own.

Taking a deep breath, thrusting her chest out a bit, she smiled. "Why don't you find out for yourself?"

"As temping as that offer is, I must refrain. There are things we have yet to discuss, my love, that can no longer wait." His tone was contrary, no more amusement, yet the look he was giving her implied something totally different was on his mind, the bulge in his breeches further confirming her suspicions. "Dellis, we must speak of the inevitable."

She shook her head. "No, John."

When he tried to open his mouth, she put two fingers over his lips, shushing him.

He grinned underneath her fingertips, the little wrinkles in the corners of his eyes rippling the sun-kissed silk of his skin. "While I'm a dutiful soldier, and try to always follow orders, this time, I'm going to have to break protocol. General Carleton has sent for—"

Mustering up the most authoritative look possible while standing nude as the day she was born, Dellis replied tersely, "You're being insubordinate. Keep this up, and you'll be reprimanded, Captain."

John's eyes widened, and then he chuckled. "I don't believe you. You're all chatter. What has a man got to do to make you follow through on your threats? Perhaps I'll keep nattering on and hope for better things. What say you, my love?"

She laughed at the cock of mischief on his brow. The man was irresistible.

"I'm your prisoner. Pick your poison?" His hand slid down her waist to gently caress her hip, sending a fresh surge of warmth between her thighs, leaving her with slick, wanton results.

"Huh? Perhaps I'll make you get down on your knees and beg for my favors or force you to watch as I bathe, yet not allow you to take part."

Resting a hand on her hip, she looked down her nose at him, trying to appear stolid and prim like a general. "What do you think of that?"

Once again, his eyes grew impossibly large, but that time, he said nothing, just swallowed like a starving man waiting to feast.

"What was that look for?" She laughed, enjoying the silky sensation of his hand curving around her hip to her bottom. To her surprise, he delivered a little smack to her backside and then another one, his brow lifting with suggestion.

"I find it amusing that you think any of that is punishment." John smiled and then nudged her closer to him. "I guess I'll have to take my reprimanding like a man." His hooded eyes focused on her lips, the tone of his voice dropping an octave as he continued. "As I started to say earlier, General Carleton has sent orders for me to return to Oswego…"

Stepping even closer to him, she placed her hand on his chest, feeling his warmth through the fine linen of his shirt, his heart quickening against her palm. "John?"

"Yes, goddess?" He smiled and then prattled on. "I have a duty to my men; they're waiting for me. And there's the matter of Miles's bride, and oh, yes, the war these damned ungrateful colonists started."

Running her hand down the flat planes of his stomach to his hips, she grasped the waist of his breeches, pulling his body towards her.

"I'll have to—"

"I don't want to talk about that!" she yelled, and with one hard yank, she pulled him into the water, both of them submerging into the icy depths with a loud splash and a curse to the heavens.

When they surfaced moments later, he gasped. "Bloody hell! I never learn."

"Always be ready for a frontal assault, Captain." She laughed, watching him brush wet locks out of his face, his usually full, pink lips turning blue over chattering teeth. "I warned you."

"Yeah, but I was hoping for better things." He grabbed her arm, dragging her to him. "What about the crop? You promised."

She couldn't help but laugh; he sounded like a wounded child who'd been reprimanded.

"You weren't bad enough, but you *were* in desperate need of a bath."

"Oh, really?" Wrapping his arms around her, John submerged, bringing her with him. When they surfaced again, he whispered in her ear. "Am I bad enough now?"

Dellis yelped, trying to break free, but he dunked her until she could take no more, the icy water giving her a chill. "I give. You're horrible," she said, her own teeth chattering. "And you still stink."

When he brought her up the final time, he wrapped his arms around her; the wet linen of his shirt pressed against her breasts while the heat of him emanated through the cold fabric, warming her world and her heart.

"I'm a scoundrel, aren't I?"

Instead of volleying a well-placed witticism, she spoke the truth, her heart aching for him already. "I don't want you to go, John."

When he looked away, she touched his cheek, drawing him back to her. "This is your home now. Don't you see that?"

"Dellis, we've been through this. It's not as simple as that. I can't just walk away from my duty."

Pulling away, she stomped out of the water and started to dry off. With her back turned, she tugged and fisted the piece of linen, wringing out the excess water. *Why is he doing this?* Didn't he understand that they'd never work if he stayed with the British?

Damn men and their honor.

Tears welled in her eyes; she sensed him behind her, felt his warmth, and then his arm wrapped around her waist, his lips close to her ear. She heard him inhale, his face buried in the wet hair at her nape. "Dellis, please, don't fight me. I have to do this."

Grabbing his left hand, she raised it to her lips, kissing his palm and then pressing it to her heart. He grasped the column of her neck, his face still buried deep in her hair, their bodies molded together as one. She could feel him trembling against her, his inner turmoil tangible in the rigid steel of his arms. He didn't want to go. There was some comfort in knowing he was fighting it, too.

"When will you leave me? And when do you return?" She needed to know; her heart demanded answers, though her head knew the truth: there were no guarantees.

"I'll come back to you. I promise" was the last thing he said before she found herself in his arms, being carried to an ancient willow tree. The world tipped sideways as he lowered her to the grass, the long jade branches like curtains blowing in the breeze around them, providing their own clandestine retreat.

"Tell me something, anything?"

His lips stopped hers before she could ask again. When his tongue touched hers, she moaned and pulled at his waistcoat, desperate to feel his skin against hers, while he worked the buttons of his front fall. She needed him immediately, inside her, using his lips and his body to chase away the fear that ruined her perfect world. "John?"

"I *will* come back, my love."

But when?

"Marry me before I go, in a church, before God. So that everyone knows you're mine," he whispered against her lips so quietly she thought she'd imagined it. Only the wind could utter such sweet words so softly. "Now. Today. This week."

She didn't respond, unsure what to say. Was he in earnest or just caught up in the moment? When they said their vows before the tribe, she always assumed God was listening. Who performed the ceremony mattered not; it was about the intent. Her mind raced with all the reasons he was asking that of her, and yet she desperately wanted it, too. Yes, she did—more than anything.

John backed away, searching her face. "Dellis, did you not hear me? I want to get married in a church. Officially. If anything happens to me, you'll have what you're due as my wife, as the wife of Captain John Carlisle. And if we're legal, my family can't deny you my inheritance." His eyes were asking, almost pleading, with her, and hidden deep in sapphire blue was fear—fear of rejection, of her saying no, but not of what he was implying. His death. She pulled his lips to hers, afraid to answer, the thought of losing him so painful the words lodged in her throat next to her full, aching heart. *What if he* was *killed?* No, she couldn't think of it.

Suddenly, he was between her thighs, her legs wrapped around his waist, his blunt warmth perched at her opening, caressing her slick folds like steel against silk. He was waiting for her, brushing her lips with his own but not indulging, teasing her with turgid passes over her soft skin, readying her for his inevitable dominance and that blissful moment of submission. She thrust a knuckle between her teeth, fighting the urge to scream out "*please*" and offer him anything he wanted to just give in. It was too much emotion all at once. The elation of marrying him again; the fear of losing him; and oh, the aching need to be filled with him. To be one. Body and soul. Husband and wife.

Still, the words were kept captive, held down by tortuous pain and blooming passion.

"Marry me again?" His lips touched her ear, a tender graze of his tongue sending a jolt of lightning to her core and lush ripples through her sex.

She quivered with anticipation, reaching for him, but he held fast, gliding back and forth ever so slowly, until she let out little, high-pitched gasps of desperation. Then he whispered, so sweetly, "Don't you want me, my love?"

Her heart ached for that needy little boy that desperately wanted to hear the words. So tender was his heart that her silence could render him broken. She reached up and touched his cheek, her thumb tracing the strong points and smooth contours of his upper lip until he closed his eyes and drew his brows together painfully. Yes, she'd marry him. She already had once. *How can he not know?* She'd do it every day of her life if he asked.

But what would become of them?

The words finally broke free, breathy and ardent. "Yes, John. Yes." Her heart spoke for her head. Damn the consequences and all her fears. "I want you."

He groaned, and with a surge of his hips, he thrust deeply, sliding inside so perfectly she whimpered when the tip of him touched the base of her womb. *Have mercy.* The sensation of him was thick and filling, the two of them becoming more one with each passing moment. His ardent hands spread her legs farther, and then he leaned back, affording her a decadent view of lean, long abdominals flexing as his slick, turgid manhood advanced and retreated with the masterful grace of a swordsman at play. His eyes were squeezed shut, a mask of pain and pleasure on his face, though he moved slowly, drawing out their bittersweet lovemaking with each stroke until she was crying out his name. It was a miracle he was able to control his passion, steeling himself, mind over body, to prolong their pleasure, taking her to the edge once, twice, three times, until she could fight it no more, ecstasy crackling through each and every fiber of her being. She screamed his name again, gripping him tightly, each ripple of her muscles asking—no, begging—for him to join her as her world exploded into fractals of light. And he did. There was no shudder of release, no quickening of his pace, just her name on his lips and their eyes locked while his hips languidly pumped his essence into her. For a split second, she was sure she could feel his heartbeat deep inside, and then with sweet surrender, he fell limp into her arms, and whispered, "mine," into her neck.

Forever.

After moments of gentle, loving caresses and fevered kisses to his forehead, he reemerged, wrapped his arms around her, and rolled onto his back. She smiled against his chest, listening to his still-quick breaths, feeling his heart slow underneath her cheek as he drifted away.

"Mine," she said, quietly, repeating his sweet, boyish sentiment. Yes, he was hers, and nothing could separate them, not her family or the military… Not even the war. "My John."

How could John do this to me? Had I not kept my part of the bargain? Women. Sex. Money. Information. Everything he wanted, she'd given him, yet he handed over his soul and his love to that savage whore.

"Mrs. Allen?"

Celeste sighed and looked up at the man who so resembled the one in her daydreams, the one she longed for. "Lord Carlisle, shall we pay a visit to your brother?"

Gingerly, she ran a hand over her stomach, smoothing down her dress, a bit of nausea still lingering from a bout earlier in the morning.

"Your services are no longer needed. I asked you to bring me to my brother, and you needed safe transportation. I'd say we've both been paid satisfactorily." Gavin Carlisle's familiar blue eyes roved over her attire. She'd chosen her favorite emerald-green dress, with the low-cut bodice, knowing how absolutely tantalizing she looked in it.

"Wouldn't a united front put a bit more *fear* into your brother?" She stressed the word, hoping to invoke his accord. "The enemy of my enemy is my friend?"

Gavin leaned into her, his eyes shooting icy daggers.

Wow, does he look like John. They both had that same cantankerous, angry glare, but did Gavin make the same incredible expressions when he was in the throes of passion? That was the important question.

"You, my dear, are nothing but an opportunist and whore. I know not how you managed to sink your talons into my brother, but you'll not make a fool of me. I'll deal with John alone and be on my way."

He was so much less pliable than John, and sadly, with no vices to exploit. Perhaps it was the *Lord* in Gavin? Though they looked almost identical, the two men couldn't be more different. Well, until lately. John had become rather obstinate, much like his brother. *Does love make all men into such boring fools? Or is it the lack of making love?* Celeste let out a laugh, imagining John trying to bed his skinny little quim. *Boring.*

"You'll find John at The Thistle tavern with his native whore, Dellis McKesson." Standing up, Celeste pointed out her window towards the west side of town. "Just up the street; you can't miss it. Look for the most worn-down, white, two-story house you can find. It's practically a hovel."

Gavin grabbed his fine felt hat, smoothed his hair back, and then placed it on his head. "Goodbye, Mrs. Allen."

She nodded. "The pleasure is truly all mine."

Once the door slammed, she turned around and let out a snicker. It could still work to her advantage; alliance or not, Gavin was bound to stir up trouble. "Oh, John, I almost feel bad for you."

Now to deal with the other issue at hand. Walking over to a sad little mirror, she examined her face, taking a moment to apply a daub of red to her lips and a bit of powder to her cheeks and décolletage. She placed the diminutive sea sponge back on the dresser top and closed her pot of lip rouge. Giving herself a onceover, she was satisfied with the exquisite, stylish woman that stared back at her. She needed to look her best for her next meeting.

Grabbing her small, blue-and-white-brocaded purse, she practically skipped out the door and down the steps, ready to mesh out a bit of evil. Lilith on the prowl. The Silver Kettle was bustling with activity, but Celeste barely took notice; the local backwater cliental was completely beneath her. She had a more important person to meet: James McKesson.

Chapter Three

"I expect this from Dane, the loathsome traitor that he is, but how could you do this to me, Stephen? We're brothers." James shifted his gaze back to his middle brother, utterly dumbfounded. "I've been good to you, paid for your schooling. This is how you repay me?"

"What you did put our whole family at risk." Stephen stepped between James and their youngest brother, Dane, preventing fists from flying. "Don't you see? We'll all pay for this."

"It's you who's the traitor, James!" Dane yelled, grabbing Stephen by the arm, trying to push him out of the way, but he held fast. "We're all His Majesty's subjects; now, George will think we're on the side of Charles the fool. We'll lose everything."

"This wasn't about our family, please. You turned me in to suit your own purpose," James said, with conviction. "This is to repay me for throwing you out. Which you deserved."

"I did it to protect us, to protect Mother from your treachery. What would she say if she knew you'd take up arms against our King? You used our family money to support a liar who'd dare to lay claim to the throne of England."

James shook his head, his temper rising. "Make no mistake, Dane; you did this out of jealousy, grasping and wanting what's mine to inherit. I'm the oldest, and you couldn't stand that." His youngest brother was silent, but the look in his *eyes said James had hit on a bit of truth. "Don't you see? They'll punish us all for this."*

"No, they'll punish you," Dane spat back. "The King's men are coming to take you away, brother. And I'll be here to watch."

"No!" James yelled. Panic set in; he had to get away, to protect Helena. There was no way he was going to the gallows. Grabbing his overcoat, he ran to the staircase, a sudden pounding on the front door alerting him that the soldiers had arrived. He touched his neck, feeling the noose tighten, and swallowed the pit in his throat.

"Helena," he whispered to himself, knowing he had to leave his beloved wife and their unborn baby behind or face certain death.

"James?" Helena's sweet voice, gilded with her native Russian accent, tugged him back to reality. "Husband."

"Forgive me. I was just thinking." He turned back to his desk, looking at the pile of papers lying in disarray. Somehow, he'd find a way to replace the supplies he owed Butler.

Damn Alexei; it was because of his ineptitude that everything was stolen by DeLancie. Once again, Alexei had proven himself a failure; first a sickly, useless young boy and then a self-righteous upstart who only cared about the Rebel cause. But without him and his Oneida thugs, there were no supplies, no income. No mere farm could yield the type of money that selling stolen arms to the British and the colonists could.

James needed his son and those damned Oneidas.

To make matters worse, James's cash flow had all but dried up when Dellis discovered he'd been stealing the installment checks Dane was sending from her father's inheritance. After all, it was James's birthright, stolen by his brothers; he merely saw it as paying himself what he was due as the rightful heir.

"Wife, why are you here? You should be at The Thistle."

"Since Dellis took in that darkie, she no longer needs my assistance. I tried to convince her that running The Thistle wasn't as easy as it seemed, but she insisted." Helena sat down in the wingback chair across the desk from him, her eyes scanning his papers curiously. "There's nothing I can do."

"What about Stuart?" he asked, glancing up at her. "I know he's been sleeping here for the past month."

"He and Ruslan have joined the Tryon County Militia; they spend their days doing drills at the fort. Why do you ask?"

"Well, Dellis can have him back if she's so damned independent. And she can pay us all the money I spent to keep The Thistle open."

He had no use for Stephen's children; they'd been a burden since the day their father died.

"Where's Alexei? I haven't seen him in over a month." Helena paused, clearly choosing her words with caution. It was a conversation James didn't want to have, for it would inevitably lead to an argument. She was far too soft on their son. "James, what have you done? Did you quarrel with him?"

James clucked his tongue and looked up at his wife, worry etched in her brow and in fine lines bracketing her bow-shaped lips. "You already know the answer."

"James, he's your son." She shook her head, pain turning her blue eyes glassy and red, tears brimming. "Why do you do this to him?"

He hated her tears, and that he was the source of them, but it was time she faced the truth. "Because Alexei is a failure at everything he puts his hand to. Since the very beginning, he's been—"

"Don't say it!" She got up from her chair, turning her back to him. "You blame him for what wasn't his fault. You've always blamed him."

James followed her, grabbed her shoulders, and forced her to turn around. "This *is* most definitely his fault. Now, I have to find a way to recoup my losses. I owe Butler. And now that we no longer have the extra money coming in, we're in a bind. John Carlisle knows the truth about us."

He locked eyes with her, trying to appeal to her head and bypass her much-too-soft heart. "You need to find a way to get back into The Thistle. I'll handle the rest."

Tenderly, he wiped a tear from her cheek and then kissed where it was. She was his reason to be, his love; everything he did was for her. The money, the house, all of it, was to replace what was rightfully his and stolen from her. She deserved to be the Duchess in McKesson house, not that scandalous whore his grasping youngest brother married. But that opportunity was gone, the future cruelly ripped from James's hands, and he had to protect their little place in the world before it, too, was taken away. "Helena, love—"

Before he could finish, the servant girl, Mariah, walked in, clearing her throat to make her presence known. "Sir, I'm sorry to interrupt."

Releasing his wife, James backed away, reining in his passion. "What is it, Mariah?"

"There's a Mrs. Allen here to see you. She's brought one of the savages with her."

What's that woman doing in German Flats? He'd warned Alexei not to try and negotiate with her; she was a whore and an opportunist.

Damn.

"Escort her in." He nodded to his wife. "Leave us."

"Agnes, I've missed you so." Dellis ran into her friend's outstretched arms so the women could kiss cheeks and hug. They'd forged a tight bond after the baby's death, Agnes's kindness and encouraging words the salve needed to start healing the wounds left behind. "I'm so glad you're here. I promise you'll be very happy at The Thistle. John will be so glad to see you."

Agnes's smile lit the room, and everything about her was brightness and sunshine, from her even, white teeth and flawlessly beautiful ebony skin to the curls popping out from the scarf tied neatly around her head. She needed no adornment to be pretty with her full cheeks; wide, round face; and huge brown eyes that smiled under long, arched brows. Even her simple, threadbare, overworked, beige dress and petticoat did nothing to distract from her cheery, natural grace.

"Come, sit." Dellis pulled Agnes to the table in the corner of the kitchen and sat down across from her. "Would you like some tea or something to eat?"

"No, miss, I'm fine." Agnes looked around, inspecting the surroundings, her eyes widening upon seeing the giant hearth in the corner. "I thought grand houses such as this had separate kitchens."

"There's one out back; it used to be the summer kitchen, but now I just use it for laundry. During the winter, this keeps the house warm, and it's easier when it's only me doing the work."

"Where's the Captain, miss?" Agnes leaned forwards, looking around Dellis towards the dining room. "Surely he's somewhere eating with such a bountiful kitchen?"

Dellis giggled. Agnes knew him so well. If John wasn't working on his maps, then he was somewhere drinking tea and stuffing his face full of cherry tarts. "Agnes, you must call me Dellis, and I do think it's time you start calling the Captain by his name. I know John would agree." Dellis reached across the wooden table and clasped her friend's hands, squeezing them gently. "You're so dear to us both."

"All right." Agnes gave a curt nod of agreement. "But not when we're working in the tavern. It wouldn't be fitting."

"I can live with that." Dellis understood the desire to keep up pretenses; it made explanations easier. "But remember, you're an employee of my tavern and will be treated as such. You must tell me if any of my patrons harass you; they'll no longer be welcome."

"Thank you."

Dellis smiled. It was so good to have a friend, another woman she could talk to, especially one who knew John. There were times when a woman needed another woman's counsel; so often she only had her aunt, and their relationship didn't lend well to exchanging confidences.

"I brought your dresses and shoes with me from Oswego. I put them up in your room on the bed." Reaching into a dress pocket, Agnes pulled out a small red velvet box and handed it to Dellis. "And this…"

Running her hands over the velvet, she savored the soft material against her fingertips for a moment before opening the lid. It was the garnet choker John bought her. She pulled it out of the box and held it up, admiring the blood-red jewel as it winked in the sunlight. Only John could've picked something so lovely and so perfect for her.

"You should wear it," Agnes said, grinning. "I know it would make the Captain happy."

Nodding, Dellis tied it around her neck, feeling it rest at the notch of her breastbone. In a small way, it was like having him close to her, a bit of comfort she would need when he was away. "I have some good news; the Captain asked me to marry him before he leaves for Oswego. We already said vows within my tribe, but he wants to make it legal."

Agnes jumped out of her seat with zeal and wrapped Dellis in a tight hug. "Oh, I'm so happy for you."

"And," Dellis said, practically vibrating with excitement. "I'm with child again."

"No! Have you told him yet?"

She shook her head. "No, I haven't. I just realized it yesterday. I plan on telling him after the wedding." When John told her earlier that he was leaving, she was too overcome with emotion to confess her news, and after losing their son, she was hesitant to get their hopes up. The possibility of being with child again was still something of a miracle.

"He'll be thrilled." Agnes gave Dellis another affectionate squeeze and then pulled away.

"I hope so. It'll be hard letting him go once he knows." The reality of him leaving had opened a wound that was still too fresh to acknowledge. He promised to stay for another couple days, until they were married and he'd given her a proper wedding night, but it wasn't enough. It would never be enough. She wanted more.

"So, where's it going to be?"

"Here in the parlor. Agnes, you and Simon must witness. I'll ask Father Squires if he'll officiate, but if he can't, then we'll have to settle for vows over the anvil by our local blacksmith. I know Hugh would help us; he's a dear friend, and when he met John, they seemed to get on well."

With their wedding being the untraditional sort, her heritage and lack of parents to give her away, they might have to settle for hand fasting. But as long as they had papers, it was legal.

"Agnes, I know you use to do Mrs…" she trailed off, unable to speak that vile woman's name even for a second. "*Her* hair. Would you be willing to do mine?"

"Yes, of course!" Agnes clapped her hands exuberantly. "And I'll make you a spice cake, and there will be dinner, and of course, I'll decorate your bedroom." She cocked a brow suggestively, making them both burst into laughter. "This will be fun."

Dellis nodded, her excitement replacing a bit of the pain of his leaving. "I want lots of candles in our room. I don't care if they cost a fortune. We'll buy every beeswax candle we can find, and flowers, yes, lots of flowers. And I'll wear the new dress John bought me and look like a proper lady for him."

They clasped hands again. "You don't need any of that. You know he doesn't care."

Maybe not, but she wanted to show him that she could fit into his world just as well as he fit into hers, a proper lady, the wife of a captain.

"So, tell me, what has you beaming so bright?" Dellis asked, changing the subject. "I know it has nothing to do with working in my tavern, though I'd like to believe it."

She already knew the answer; John had told her earlier Clark and Agnes were in love. The thought of two people Dellis dearly loved being happy pushed her looming sadness aside.

"Simon has asked me to marry him." Agnes smiled, dimples forming in her full cheeks.

"And you said yes, of course?" Dellis hugged her friend again.

"Actually, I said no at first; the idea of a white, British soldier marrying a former slave is preposterous. Well, it just isn't fitting."

Dellis pulled back, looking Agnes in the eyes. "Please, tell me he convinced you otherwise? Isn't fitting, that's nonsense. Love is a precious gift; who cares what anyone thinks?"

John had taught Dellis that, loving her in spite of her heritage and in the face of her ruin. Yes, love was precious indeed.

"Agnes, we won't worry about any of that now. You must let me and the Captain return the favor and have a wedding for you here! He'll be so thrilled—"

The side door swung open abruptly, letting in a rush of hot air, followed by Alexei, who was clearly exhausted, the usual hollow of his cheeks more profound, several days' growth of dark hair on his chin and jaw. It looked as if he hadn't changed in weeks; his linen shirt was stained at the collar and in several places on the front, and his buckskin leggings were soiled with mud he was tracking on her shiny, clean floor.

Dellis went to give him a hug but stopped when she got a whiff of him. "Alexei, while I'm glad to see you, I'm *not* glad to smell you." She wafted her hand in front of her nose, trying to rid the air of his foul stench. "Good Lord! Did you bathe in a swamp?"

"And it's good to see you, too, cousin." A sarcastic grin lifted the corners of his mouth while he eyed the fresh, fluffy biscuits on the counter.

Alexei, much like John, had one thought in the early morning, and sure as the sun came up, her cousin would be ready and waiting at seven a.m. with fork and knife in hand. "Sit. I'll make you something to eat." Dellis pointed to the empty chair next to Agnes. "Alexei, this is my new employee; her name is Agnes. She comes highly recommended, and she's quite a good cook."

Giving Agnes a wink, Dellis walked to the counter and started prepping tea for the three of them. In her cupboard, she had a bit of John's East India tea left over and a little jar of herbal tea, a mixture of dried berries and chamomile. Saving the fine tea for John, she grabbed the little jar and put a large helping of it into her father's china teapot, the aromatic scent immediately filling the air, further brightening her mood.

Alexei pulled out the wooden chair and sat down. "Can you pack me some food, enough for five days? I don't have much time; we're leaving tomorrow, once Thomas Sinavis and his men arrive."

"Where are you going?" She poured boiling water from the hearth into the teapot and placed the lid on top.

Alexei reached for the counter, his impossibly long arms stretching just far enough to snatch a biscuit. "I don't know if I should tell you, what with the company you've been keeping as of late."

Grabbing a few scones and a couple biscuits from the counter, she prepped the tray with milk, sugar, blackberry jam, and some butter. "You're being ridiculous; even grandfather trusts John enough to confide in him. He helped them catch a Mohawk spying on the fort yesterday."

Alexei reached onto her tray before she could put it on the table and pilfered another biscuit, stuffing it into his mouth. The man ate more than two horses, yet he was still lean and fit as a stallion. Dellis shook her head incredulously. *Must be nice.*

"There are spies everywhere now. It's only a matter of time before the British come. Schuyler has asked Thomas Sinavis to travel to Canada and do some reconnaissance of his own. I'm going with him."

"Do be careful, Alexei." A chill raced down her spine, evoking ripples of goosebumps on her arms at the mere mention of war. The two men she loved most in the world were on opposite sides, and her people were caught in the middle, such was her sad state of affairs, with no remedy in sight.

Dellis dug though the cupboards and quickly packed some provisions, wrapping them in a piece of linen for his haversack. "All I have ready right now is venison jerky, biscuits, and some cheese. But I'll give it to you."

Will, her new dish boy, sauntered into the kitchen carrying a large tub full of soapy water, setting it on the wooden stool next to the counter. It was upon Alexei's recommendation Dellis hired the boy, and part of her was starting to regret that decision. Will was quiet and cantankerous, and he never had a pleasant thing to say to anyone. Alexei owed her a favor, and his firstborn, for taking on such a project.

"Will?" Dellis called the boy's name, but he ignored her, more interested in snatching a biscuit and eating it. His eyes intently followed Alexei, shooting angry, sharp daggers in his direction. No matter, there was work to be done, and quickly, as the breakfast crowd was due any second. "Will, can you go into the cellar and grab a pitcher of cider for Alexei?"

His cherubic face registered a scowl as he pointed at the counter. "I have all those dishes to do before customers start coming in for breakfast. You get it for him."

Before Dellis could give the insubordinate young buck a piece of her mind, Alexei got up from the table, grabbed the boy by the seat of his pants and his collar, and lifted him off the ground. "You don't talk to Dellis that way. She was kind enough to give your sorry, unwanted arse a job and a place to live."

"Put me down, you dumb oaf," the boy yelled.

Alexei lifted the boy up higher, staring him down with those hawk-like blue eyes. "Someone should wash out that mouth of yours."

To everyone's surprise, and humor, Alexei dunked Will's head into the tub of soapy water, swishing him around a few times before pulling him out by the hair. "Is it clean yet?" Alexei looked the boy in the eyes and then repeated the actions.

Will yelped and howled with the high-pitched cries of one who had yet to come of age.

Dellis put a hand over her mouth, stifling a laugh.

"Apologize to my cousin, now!" Alexei yelled, holding Will's face up for Dellis's inspection. The poor boy looked like a drowned street rat with locks of dirty-blond hair dripping in his face and the front of his shirt plastered to his chest, but to his credit, he didn't relent. She admired his spirit; having been punished by Alexei herself, she understood the depths of Will's conviction. When Alexei wanted his way, he was an absolute brute.

"Oh, you want to be difficult. I can be difficult, too." With that, Alexei dunked Will's head again, holding him under for a few seconds longer.

When he came up, he vomited a mess of soapy water into the tub and then coughed and gagged, his hazel eyes full of rage when they caught sight of Alexei.

"Cousin, I think he's had enough." Dellis rolled her eyes and shook her head. Both of them were behaving like brats. "You've made your point."

Agnes got up from the table and walked into the bar. "We have some patrons in the dining room. I'll see to them."

"Thank you." Dellis turned her attention back to the first act of a rather brash comedy playing out in her kitchen, and on her floor, which had become a soapy mess. "Can I get back to work?"

Alexei released the young man, giving him one hard shove, sending him sliding across the wet floor and landing at Dellis's feet. "Don't ever disrespect my cousin again, and clean this mess up." Pointing one long finger, Alexei continued. "If I ever hear of you talking to her like that again…" Then he lifted his hand high as if he'd offer up a swift smack. "Understand?"

"Alexei, stop." Dellis touched her cousin's arm, trying to calm him.

The look in the boy's eyes changed from anger to hurt, tears welling up, a quiver in his bottom lip.

"Come on, take your stuff, and get going. I'll help Will clean up this mess."

Alexei hugged her again, but his blue eyes stayed focused on the young man who was already on his hands and knees mopping the floor. "Careful what you tell your Redcoat lover, cousin." Alexei's words were clipped and low. "You've already felt the sting of that wasp."

Dellis took a deep breath and closed her eyes, trying to shut out the truth in his words. Historically, yes, John had used her, but things had changed; they were together, and he'd never turn on her again. No, it was just more of Alexei's blustering. "I love him, Alexei. He's my husband."

"I know." He nodded. "But be careful what you trust him with. I don't want you to get hurt."

It was too late; John had already captured her heart. And soon, he'd run away with it. Again.

"Please, go now, before I throw you out."

Alexei would always think the worst of John, no matter what. It was about overinflated male pride. The world worked in shades of grey, but Alexei functioned in black and white, good and evil, rebel versus redcoat; he naïvely only understood dichotomy.

"Take care and be safe." She stood on her tiptoes and kissed his cheek. As the door slammed behind him, Will stood and raced out the door after Alexei, dust flying everywhere. Through the door, she could hear the two of them bellowing at each other like old horns, and tears, lots of whimpers and tears coming from Will.

Getting down on her knees, Dellis mopped up the rest of the water from the floor with a rag and then rested back on her haunches, inspecting her work. "What a mess. I should make them both come back and clean this."

As she leaned over again, Agnes walked into the kitchen, her eyes wide and glassy. "Dellis, there's someone here to speak to you."

"Who is it?" Dellis asked, finding the blank expression on her friend's face worrisome. "Is something wrong?"

"I think you should see for yourself," Agnes replied, with the awe of someone who'd just seen a ghost.

Chapter Four

Removing her apron, Dellis smoothed her stray hairs back and adjusted her dress, fixing the tucker that had fallen loose from her bodice. "Agnes, can you finish cleaning up and check the bread in the oven?"

When she stepped into the dining room, a ray of sun peeked through the window, shining directly on her guest, masking his face in shadow, though his form was undeniable. It was John. What sort of game was he playing at? Clearly, he and Agnes were up to something.

Dellis chuckled, ready to go along with whatever game they were playing. He looked so handsome, the sun casting shadows over his face, accentuating his profile: high forehead, long nose, defined cheekbones, and the little cleft in his chin. *Cleft in his chin?*

On closer examination, Dellis realized the man was slightly taller and not as broad as John. He wore a worsted suit of green fabric, with socks pulled up to his knees, and polished leather shoes adorned with shiny brass buckles. His overcoat was intricately brocaded at the cuffs and on the facings, the edges trimmed with gold cord. John would never wear such a garish outfit, always preferring an understated, yet elegant, fashion. The man she was approaching looked more like an over-adorned peacock or one of those British dandies she'd read about. The only thing he was missing was the powder in his hair and tight curls above his ears.

Stunned, she stopped dead in her tracks only a few feet from her mysterious guest and shook her head, doing a double take. He removed his hat and bowed to her; his well-coiffed hair was much darker than John's, and on the man's pinky, a garish, gold signet ring glimmered in the sun's rays.

"You must be Miss McKesson?" he said, in almost the same mellifluous baritone as John, only the accent was more pronounced.

"Yes" was all she could muster up, her eyes transfixed on her visitor.

"Lord Carlisle, John's older brother." With a grin that lit up his face, he bowed again, elegantly. "At your service."

Carlisle? John's brother.

Yes, it was definitely him. They were almost twins—same striking blue eyes, same full, kissable lips, straight brows, and high forehead—though Gavin's smile lacked the fine lines that bracketed John's mouth, and there wasn't even the slightest hint of naughtiness tugging at the corners. But the man was handsome, devastatingly so; her heart fluttered just as it did every time she saw her beloved.

"*Lord* Carlisle?" She blushed, feeling suddenly embarrassed for staring so long. John never told her his older brother was a lord. "You're definitely John's brother, of course; forgive me, I was just struck by how much you look like him."

Gavin flashed her a sardonic grin, but again, there were no lines around his mouth that infectiously spread to the corners of his eyes. "I wouldn't know. I haven't seen my brother in ten years. And you may call me My Lord."

"Of course," she said, nodding, feeling like a child being scolded. "I assume you're looking for John. He's not here at the moment."

A sudden, sharp pain shot through her abdomen and then dissipated quickly. Dellis pressed a hand to her stomach and smiled; just early pregnancy pains, the baby's little reminder of its presence.

"May I wait?" He gestured to the table, pulling out a chair for her. "I'm sure you must be busy, but would you join me for a drink? I'd enjoy the company."

"Of course; forgive my rudeness." She took the seat he offered, watching as he sat down across from her, leaning back and stretching out his legs leisurely. And just like that, the wealthy, cultured Lord seemed at ease in her humble tavern. Another trait he shared with John, a relaxed elegance that allowed him to fit in wherever he went—a bit of brio sprinkled with élan.

Behind her, the door opened; Ruslan and Stuart bounded inside, leaving dirty tracks on the way to the kitchen, both of them chattering away. As if he smelled brimstone and sulfur, Stuart stopped abruptly, fixing his gaze on Gavin as if spying the Devil in brocade fabric.

She huffed out a breath of frustration, watching a stray piece of hair fly out of her face. The last thing she needed was Stuart's antics.

"Excuse me for a moment." As Dellis started to rise, Stuart flashed her a knowing grin and then scurried into the kitchen like a rat after a hunk of cheese.

Crisis everted. Thank Goodness. Taking a seat again, she turned her attention back to her guest, curious about his sudden appearance. "How did you know John was here?"

"I have ways of keeping tabs on my brother."

His answer was purposely ambiguous; he was hiding something. John once told her he wasn't welcome at home; if that was the truth, then what provoked his elder brother's sudden appearance?

Agnes set a tea service down on the table and started to pour for them, giving Dellis a sidelong glance and a wink of reassurance. "This is Agnes; she's a friend of mine and the Captain's."

Gavin rolled his eyes up towards the pretty maid and then back to his cup, dismissing her with palpable disdain. Clearly, that was where the brotherly resemblance ceased; John would never disrespect another person, no matter their color or race.

Lord Carlisle picked up his cup of tea and sipped, one pinky extended straight in the air like an elegant woman at court; another way in which he differed from John, who usually gulped his tea and inhaled his food with little decorum. "How did you come to know my brother?"

"The Captain and his men were my lodgers for a time."

"A British spy and his men welcome in a tavern in German Flats? No, there's more to that story, I'm sure of it. I know about my brother and his clandestine pursuits. And this area is notoriously loyal to the colonists." Gavin hesitated, though his eyes purposefully roved down her form. "And for a lady such as yourself, an acquaintance with a man like my brother would be pernicious to your reputation. Unless, you and he…"

He did not…

The man was being downright impertinent, yet doing it so politely any outrage on her part would seem ill-mannered. Dellis could feel her temper rising at what he was implying, but there was more than a hint of truth to it, and that pricked her conscience.

Over the top of her cup, she said, "As you've already assumed, John was undercover, and the rest is between him and me and is not up for discussion." With a curt grin, she took a sip.

"My brother is a master at the art of deception, so you've learned, and he's just as adept at using women to get what he wants." Gavin leveled those familiar sapphire-blue eyes on her, cocking a brow suggestively.

Another difference ticked off the list, John always used his charms when questioning, never for intimidation, a tactic that notoriously raised her hackles. *Time to set him right.*

"Don't mistake me for a simpleton. I'm well aware of John's past. But you will *not* speak ill of him in this house, regardless of the history you share. John is welcome here, and for now, so are you. Don't challenge this unless you wish to face the barrel of my musket when I escort you out."

Gavin raised his eyebrows, clearly taken aback by her brash show of force.

She held back a laugh; obviously, he wasn't used to a woman putting him in his place.

You're in my world now, Lord something-or-other.

After a moment's silence, his scowl transformed to a smile. "I can see why you transfix my brother so; you're both beautiful and bold, something I'm sure he's not used to, nor am I. It's refreshing."

That caught her off guard. She didn't expect him to retreat from the fight and then offer a compliment, and one so earnestly delivered. Her face flushed. "Thank you," she replied into her cup, looking up at him though her eyelashes.

With an all-too-familiar twinkle in his eye, he continued. "I understand your uncle is Admiral McKesson. I know His Grace; we're acquaintances."

She couldn't fight the excitement that bubbled up in her chest. Just the mention of her dear uncle relieved the palpable tension in the room. "I haven't seen him in two years. When did you speak to him?"

"Last year when we discussed the trouble my brother had gotten himself into—"

Before Gavin could finish, John stormed into the dining room like a tempest ready to level a town, his heels pounding on the wood floor. "Don't say another word to him, Dellis. He's not welcome here."

The look in John's blue eyes was foreign to her: pure ice, cold and unyielding, and so uncharacteristic of him. He was enraged like she'd never seen him before, his nostrils flaring, his shoulders thrown back pompously, all puffed up and full of pride.

Gavin put down his cup and stood, their eyes meeting over her, both men posturing for a fight.

Dellis rose, placing herself between the two men, her arms outstretched. "Calm yourself, husband; we were just chatting."

John cast a dismissive glance at her and then turned his attention back to his brother. "There's nothing you need to hear from him. He's only come to start trouble. Isn't that right, *My Lord*?"

"Trouble?" Gavin cocked a brow in challenge, his voice dripping with disdain. "No, brother, trouble is your expertise; mine is, sadly, to fix the messes you leave behind. That's why I'm here, to fix the problems you've caused Carlisle Shipping."

She looked back at John, his expression stony, though his hands were clenched at his sides, a telltale sign he was barely maintaining control.

"How did you find me?"

Gavin grinned, a snicker pushing its way out. "Your whore brought me here."

Dellis swallowed painfully at the mention of her old adversary and rival for John's affection. "You mean Mrs. Allen, don't you?"

Gavin nodded. "Should I tell her about the supplies you stole from me, brother? Or would you rather I tell her why we no longer speak? Perhaps she'd like to know why our mother still curses your name whenever it's mentioned?"

"Dellis, you need to go," John said brusquely.

"No, John. Whatever he has to say, we'll hear it together." She tried to take his hand, but he pushed her away.

"Dellis, please, leave now. This is between my brother and me."

He was desperately trying to hide something from her. *But what?* Nothing his brother said would change her love for him. Nothing. Hadn't she proven that already?

Reaching for him again, successfully, she squeezed his hand, trying to assuage him with her touch and then her words. "I'll hear what he has to say. Trust me, my love."

The dining room was eerily silent. Thankfully, the customers had left, save Stuart and Ruslan, who sat at the bar eating and watching with rapt amusement and an occasional snort.

Dellis turned her back to John, though her hand still held his, and looked up at Gavin. "What is it that you want?"

"He owes me twelve hundred pounds plus interest for the supplies he stole from me." With clenched fists, Gavin leaned in, getting dangerously close to her, his voice dropping an octave. "And if I don't get it, I'll personally escort you to prison where you'll rot, brother. It'll take months, nay, *years* to repair the damage you've done to my company."

Dellis closed her eyes, pain stabbing behind each orb. So that was how John got the supplies to trade with her village; he took them from his brother? It all made sense. "John?"

She eagerly awaited a rebuttal to the accusations, but he was silent, awkwardly so. How could this be? John always had an explanation, his

41

quicksilver tongue ready to talk himself out of a corner faster than one could blink. But that time, he was disturbingly mute. She turned to her beloved, glancing at the face she so adored, and pleaded. "John, say something?"

Gavin shook his head. "Miss McKesson, he says nothing because it's true. There's no denying it. Perhaps I've saved you from further associating yourself with a debtor who's sure to see prison walls. You managed to escape once, John, but not this time."

"Escape? What does he mean?" She wanted answers, but John offered her nothing, just stone-cold reticence.

"My baby brother was bound for debtor's prison after gambling away what little money he had. Our father paid off the debt and put our company into ruin. He died in a boating accident with our younger brother, trying to recoup the losses. Mother still blames you to this day. When she heard you'd once again gambled with Carlisle money, she was determined I see you sent to prison."

Dellis's heart thundered in her chest, uneven breaths forcing their way out of her lungs. "John, is this true?"

Their eyes met over pregnant, painful silence. He swallowed and then nodded. "Yes."

Dragging his gaze from her, he went after his brother again with angry, hateful words, yet he didn't deny what Gavin said. "You pompous ass. What do you hope to gain by saying this in front of her? This quarrel is ours. She's innocent."

"Call it repayment, brother. She deserves to know what kind of man she's associating herself with: a debtor and a drunk who'd steal his own brother's wife."

"No!" she yelled, turning on Gavin. That lie she would not abide. *It has to be a lie.*

"No, it's true, my dear. My jealous little brother slept with my betrothed, and when he found out she was carrying his child, he dismissed her. Later, he boasted to me about their affair, only after we were married."

"That's not how it happened," John said, suddenly calm, a lazy grin starting from one corner of his mouth and spreading to the other. "I broke with her when she told me she wanted to end your betrothal." With a confident, obstinate nod, John pointed to himself proudly. "That's right, she wanted me, not you. Face it, brother, she preferred my skills to yours. Besides, there's no proof that child was mine; I wasn't the first one to open Isabella's door."

"John!" Dellis yelled in outrage. She could hardly believe what she was hearing, much less the smugness of his tone.

Gavin cast a sympathetic glance at her, but she waved an angry hand at him in dismissal. "Clearly, my brother has yet to inform you of his past escapades. I'm sorry you had to hear it this way."

"Don't you dare! You care nothing about hurting her. This was your plan all along." John tried to push his way towards Gavin, but Dellis put her hands on her husband's chest, shoving him back. "The money is only part of this, and you know it; this is payback for old transgressions. This is about your pride. Well, I'm more than willing to face you on the field, brother—pistols at dawn. And I'm a far better shot than you."

"Then a duel it will be." Gavin advanced, the two men clashing around Dellis like soldiers on a field.

"No!" She threw her hands on both of their chests, and with a grunt and a heave, pushed them apart again. The thought of losing another person she loved to a duel brought on palpitations and most assuredly a slew of grey hair. "I won't allow it. I forbid you, John."

"Dellis, this is my affair, not yours. Stay out of this." John tried to yank her out of the way, but she fought back, slapping his hands away. He was behaving like a raving lunatic.

"John, there will be *no* dueling."

Once again, he looked down his nose at her, bringing on a fresh surge of outrage and a burning desire to slap him upside the head.

"Both of you are behaving like spoiled children," she said through clenched teeth. "This is my tavern, I make the rules here, and you've worn out your welcome, My Lord, or whatever I'm supposed to call you. Please, take your leave now, and you may return to discuss your grievances with John when both of you can conduct yourselves as gentlemen. Not before." With a curt nod, she finished. "Good day to you."

Dellis glanced up at John, narrowing her eyes, a silent warning of what was to come.

Grabbing the hat from the table, Gavin jammed it on his head and stomped to the door. "Fine. No duel. Yet. But this isn't over, brother. I'll take the money out of your hide if I have to."

When the door slammed, Dellis looked at John, dumbfounded; for the first time, she wasn't sure if she actually knew the man, her husband and partner. Only hours before, he'd been a stormy, tender lover in her arms, but right then, he was behaving like an overbearing ass.

"That was none of your business." His voice was so low she could barely hear him.

Releasing her pent-up fury, she let him have it, full force. "What's come over you? How dare you speak to me in my own home as if I were some insignificant woman! You forget yourself, Captain."

Grabbing her arm, John hauled her up against him, their bodies pressed together intimately and charged with passion. "Will my wishes always be second to yours? I asked you to let me speak with my brother privately. Wife, does not a husband deserve respect, too?"

She leaned into him and met his gaze with an imperious one of her own. "I think you forget that in my tribe, it's the woman who counsels the man, and if he doesn't do as suggested, he's removed from his post."

"Removed from his post?" There was a tremor in his voice and a challenge in his eyes; yes, he was daring her to fight back, but she refused to be goaded into an argument with a hot-tempered knave. She wanted her John back, and then they would speak.

Realizing that, he released her, taking a step back. He was suddenly calm, almost aloof, but she knew better; it was a façade, his steely ability to control his anger further infuriating her like a door being slammed in her face.

She wanted a piece of him, and smugly, she went for it. "Husband, huh? Not if you keep behaving like an overbearing ass. I think you forget this is my house, and I make the rules. If you don't like that, then there's the door." With that, Dellis stormed out of the dining room, knowing she'd thrown down the gauntlet on their relationship and their love.

"Mr. McKesson will see you now, Mrs. Allen," Mariah said, opening the door to the study.

It was about time; making Celeste wait fifteen minutes in his rather garishly decorated parlor, with only Eagle Eyes as company, was just plain bad manners. She didn't like waiting, nor did she particularly like frustration; it was bad for the complexion. Wrinkles were already starting to mar the delicate skin at the corners of her eyes and her once-smooth forehead—not something a woman could take lightly at her age, especially when beauty was her greatest commodity.

She motioned to Eagle Eyes, and they followed the servant into James McKesson's study. As expected, it was just as plush as she remembered, though again, a bit garish for her taste. Just because one could embellish didn't mean one should. Every inch of the blue walls were covered in something, from bookcases to pictures, and even maps, giving the room a busy, cluttered appearance. The alcoves were packed to the brim with fine, leather-bound books, almanacs, and encyclopedias. All the furniture, chairs, tables, and the large desk that dominated the center of the room, were Chippendale, with ribbon-laced backs and smooth curves of the rococo style. The rich, dark, mahogany wood looked sumptuous against the large Oriental rug that covered the shiny, well-cared-for wooden floors. Nothing said success like a library, and that room was no exception, gaudy as it might have been.

The maid made a hasty retreat, her small, blue eyes darting back and forth as if she feared a reprimand for lingering. James McKesson, though a devious man, seemed far from violent—perhaps Celeste had been wrong about him. *One could only hope.*

James stood and gave her a curt nod, his eyes flashing up to Eagle Eyes for a split second. "Mrs. Allen, what can I do for you?"

He was incredibly handsome for his age, rich, dark-brown hair, only lightly dusted with grey in a few places; high, razor-sharp cheekbones; and a strong jaw that locked in place when he was cross. His perfectly-straight, full brows accentuated his piercing blue eyes, giving them a fierce, hawk-like quality that made one feel like prey when he focused on them. He was exceptionally tall; if she had to guess, about six foot two, his shoulders so broad she couldn't see around them, and he was fit—*my, he is fit*—his perfectly tailored brown coat and waistcoat fitting him like a second skin.

"You never answered any of my letters. I was hoping it was just an oversight on your part, but when a response never came, I began to feel a bit, shall we say, slighted?" Celeste smiled, taking a seat in the chair across from his desk. Looking over her shoulder, she waved towards a chair against the wall; Eagle Eyes followed her direction like an obedient lapdog, though he was a wolf in disguise.

"Mrs. Allen, my intention *was* for you to feel slighted." James sat down in his wing-back chair, his hands resting on the arms, giving him the aura of a king or a god on a throne. "I have no need of you, and even less so now that DeLancie has been dealt with."

From behind, she could hear Eagle Eyes stir at the mention of his former superior. She considered getting the native riled up; it might be fun to see him unleash his fury on McKesson, but better to save that for later.

"Are you so sure?" Celeste crossed her arms over her chest and sat back in her chair, getting comfortable. Cat and mouse was her favorite sport, and she relished the idea of playing with such a worthy adversary.

"You're just wasting time, trying to provoke my curiosity. I see through your games already. Now, tell me what you think I need from you, Mrs. Allen. So I can be done with you once and for all."

Time to drop the bait.

Have a little cheese.

"Well, if that's how you feel, I guess there's nothing I can say to prove my usefulness." Shrugging, she added, "I'll just find John myself. After all, he's here in German Flats. It can't be that hard. Oh, and from what I understand, he's looking for a woman, one who disappeared with a substantial dowry and Butler's shipment."

Wait for it. Wait for it.

Celeste rolled her eyes towards the ceiling while she tapped her foot lightly, giving him a chance to get caught up. Men could be rather slow on the uptake, and he was a decidedly stubborn mouse. "It couldn't have been you who stole it? Oh, that's right, from what I've heard, you're out of commission. Perhaps it was someone you know who took the shipment and the dowry? Oh, and the heiress?"

"How do you know this?"

Caught. She bit her lower lip to hide a smirk.

Now to play with him. Men were so easy, especially the ones who believed themselves above intrigue.

"Wait, my friend. Not yet." She waved to Eagle Eyes, who'd gotten up and started to leave. "John's looking for the woman, and he owes a great deal of money to his brother. It's only a matter of time before he finds her and the stolen goods. From what I understand, it was a group of Oneidas that took her. And being that you're no longer in business with your son, you were clearly not the benefactor of that important shipment or her fortune."

Putting her finger to her lips, she pursed them sweetly. "Wait, weren't you the one who paid off DeLancie and Butler to look the other way when this all started?" She grinned, ear to ear, once again flawlessly executing her plan.

Time to bat the mouse around a bit.

"Oh, yes, now I remember how it went. When Stephen caught on to your scheme, you sent DeLancie to that little Oneida village and had him burn it to the ground, but only *after* he murdered your brother and his wife and had his men deflower your niece."

She grimaced, a tremor of disgust flowing through her body at the mention of John's native whore. "Hmm, it's funny, the only other person who knows that whole story, and is still alive to tell it, is John Carlisle."

James shot Celeste an icy glare. "What do you want?"

Now to swallow him whole.

"My friend here also has a bone to pick with John. Not only can he get your supplies back, but he can put an end to Carlisle as well. No one needs to know about your involvement."

"And how do you intend on doing that?"

Grinning, she reached over his desk, pulled the top off his fine crystal decanter, and poured herself a drink. "I assume you were so caught up in our discussion, you forgot to be polite. But not to worry, I'm not offended. I can pour for myself."

Taking a sip, she held back a gag—Scotch whiskey, disgusting drink. No matter how fine it was, it still tasted god-awful.

"Please, continue, Mrs. Allen," James said, watching her sip her drink.

So tasty, that poor little mouse.

He was impatient for her answer, a good sign he was sufficiently caught, and rightly so, for she held him in the palm of her hand. "Well, my friend, Eagle Eyes, is now in the employment of Major Butler. Part of his job is to seek out enemy spies and bring them to justice. Apparently, John Carlisle has become rather close with the Oneida. As a matter of fact, Eagle Eyes witnessed John helping his Oneida friends capture a spy loyal to His Majesty earlier today. Also, Schuyler has sent a group of his own spies up the St. Lawrence to do reconnaissance, some of which are Oneida. Eagle Eyes would be more than willing to deal with John and these Oneida at the same time, with the full consent of Major Butler. For all we know, John may even lead us to your son, the woman, and the dowry. This can all be done clean and neat, and once that poor woman gets back her fiancé, you can say you had a hand in her rescue."

James quietly scanned the papers on his desk, looking disinterested, but she knew better. "What do you want from me?"

Brilliant. So brilliant. "I want to open another business in Philadelphia. I can't return to Manhattan, and though Niagara is profitable, it's far from my taste in society. I need a new investor."

Celeste got up from her chair and walked around the desk, resting her hip on the sumptuous wood, and then leaning forwards, affording him a view down her heaving bodice. "What I'm looking for is a partner."

His eyes skimmed her breasts, but there was no stirring in those icy-blue orbs, not even a smolder of passion. *Damn.*

"I'm sorry, Mrs. Allen; my wife wouldn't approve of infidelity, and Russians have been known to be just as violent as savages. I'd suggest you retract your proposition. I don't mix my business with pleasure."

Celeste shrugged nonchalantly and then got up. "Fine, I can find someone else who'd be interested in the information I have. Perhaps your younger brother Dane would pay for such enlightenment? From what I understand, he was trying desperately to prove who murdered his brother. It shouldn't be hard to get a letter to him."

Quick as a flash, James was out of his chair, grasping her wrists, squeezing them painfully tight. Celeste fought back as tears welled in her eyes, but he held fast.

"Don't you dare try to play me. I have no need of your favors, woman. If I decide to work with you, it'll be on my terms, not yours."

She laughed, despite how her heart fluttered nervously in her chest. "You've already made up your mind."

"Never threaten me again." He hissed through clenched teeth.

She loved how his blue his eyes narrowed when he was angry, the muscles in his jaw flexing, and how he towered over her, dominating her. He was all man, and one she'd like to sink her teeth into. With a smile, she reminded herself that it was inevitable. No one could resist her, not even that great titan.

He released her abruptly.

"Do we have deal?" She slid her hands up his lapels, feeling his strong chest and all that decadent, pent-up frustration against her palms. "You'll invest in my venture, and I'll see to the business of getting your money back, and of course, dealing with John Carlisle and his Oneida friends."

Standing on her tiptoes, bringing her lips within an inch of his, she looked into his eyes and grinned. "We can save the other part for later, when you want it bad enough."

Chapter Five

John stood at the window, looking out on the dirt road, the gravity of the day's events weighing heavily on his mind. After ten years, his brother still brought out the worst in John. Five minutes in the man's presence and John was back to the quick-tempered, jealous little brother, throwing mud and picking fights in the back yard. And Dellis; he groaned, remembering the look of pain in her eyes when his brother told her the truth about the affair with Isabella. How would John ever explain it?

At first, he was livid with Dellis for putting her nose where it didn't belong, but as the day went on, her silent treatment, the most potent weapon in her arsenal, had worn down his resolve. Breaching her impenetrable wall of anger was damn near impossible, so he'd learned. He couldn't stand for her to be cross with him; the ache in his chest and the frantic need to make things right were new sensations to him. He had nothing to compare it to. His feelings for her were still so foreign and unsettling.

Making love to a woman was easy, but loving her was so much harder.

Damn, she was frustrating and headstrong, refusing to do his bidding and then calling him out in front of his brother. The very traits that John loved most in her were rather insufferable when turned against him.

He heard her come up the stairs, the hallway dark, only a flicker of candlelight glowing from the room across the hall, and then quietly, she strolled into their room, wearing only her shift, her silky, dark hair loose to her shoulders. She pulled the covers back on their bed, climbed in, and then drew the curtains shut, ignoring him.

The silent treatment. Have mercy.

There was no use fighting the inevitable, so he relented, throwing up the white flag in defeat. "My love, I know you're angry with me. I'll make no effort at trying to seduce you into forgiveness. I surrender." When she peeked her head out from behind the curtains, he grabbed his kerchief from the desk and waved it in the air. "See my white flag? Now, have at it, I'm ready for a direct assault. But remember, you're attacking an unarmed man."

He scooted behind the wing-back chair at his desk, making a point of protecting his cock from her aim, and then put up his fists, ready to block.

Getting out of bed, Dellis walked over to him; his goddess, barefoot, the candlelight drawing attention to her heavenly silhouette through her diaphanous shift, distracting him for a moment, but he rallied, reassuming his defensive position.

"I'm ready." He noticed her smirk of satisfaction despite the valiant effort she was making to show her anger.

"Are you afraid I'll harm you?" She cocked a brow, her glance below his belt making him grow impossibly thick.

He nodded sheepishly, adjusting himself behind the chair.

"Your family assets are safe for now, husband. I'd be more concerned about your pretty face."

With that, her right hand came up, landing a well-placed slap to his left cheek, sending his head whipping to the side.

"Finally, you reprimand me?" He smiled through the sting, his cheek burning like the devil. *Damn her right hook.*

"I'm not playing, John. How could you keep something as serious as this from me?"

"My love." He held his breath for a moment, praying for patience and the gift of tactical words; provoking her would only make it worse.

"I wasn't sure how to tell you. Besides, it's irrelevant now. What happened with Gavin was part of my past, but it's not who I am today."

"No, John." She shook her head, her glossy tresses falling into her eyes.

He reached up and smoothed a stray lock behind her ear, his hand sliding down to cup her cheek.

"Why didn't you tell me about the money you owed? Are your problems not mine, too?"

He nodded, running his thumb over her porcelain skin, memorizing every curve of her sharp cheekbone. She was so beautiful, otherworldly so; there were moments when he could hardly believe she was his alone. "I should've told you the truth—about all of it. I just didn't want you to see what kind of man I used to be. I'm ashamed of him. Do you understand?"

"You don't need to hide from me. I love every version of you, even the frustrating scoundrel I met today." She smiled, turning her face into his hand, kissing his palm, sending painful jolts to his heart.

Stepping closer, he looked into her eyes, letting himself get lost a bit in their dark beauty. "Dellis, there are times when you must trust me. I know we haven't talked about this, but that night you disappeared… I asked you to let me handle DeLancie, but you didn't; you put yourself at terrible risk, and men were killed because of it. Today, I asked you to leave us and let me speak with my brother, but you persisted. Both times, you prevented me from doing what needed to be done—from protecting you. I know you're used to taking care of yourself, but that's my job now. In your tribe, do the women not allow the men to make war when necessary?"

"Only after the matrons have agreed to it." Her lips turned up into a smirk, a twinkle of determination glinting in her eyes. "I'm so used to protecting myself. It's hard to give yourself over to another person's safekeeping, even to such capable hands as yours." She took both of his hands in her own and gently kissed the scars on his wrists, sending a shiver of desire chasing its way down his spine. "I need you to be honest. You're always keeping secrets."

John closed his eyes, trying to shut out all the things that burdened his conscience, truths yet to be revealed. "I want to tell you everything. I do."

Some secrets were better left forgotten, for her sake and his.

"Did you love this woman... Isabella?" she asked, a quiver in her voice.

"I've loved no woman except you." Never had he spoken truer words. "Nor will I ever, save a daughter you give me."

Her eyes softened, turning glassy. "Why did you do that to your brother?"

"Because I was jealous, and I wanted to hurt him. It's as simple as that. Isabella was beautiful, but she held no fascination to me, except that Gavin loved her." The shallowness of that statement gave him pause. How low he'd sunk to hurt his brother; he was right to be hateful.

"Was—" He could hear her choking on her words, tears welling in her eyes. "Was the baby yours?"

"She said it wasn't, but I have no way of knowing for sure. She would've said anything to save her relationship with Gavin, and when the baby died, my brother annulled their marriage." He drew in a deep breath and blew it out, trying to relieve his raw nerves. Confessions were never his strong suit, but lying wasn't the answer. He owed her the truth. "The sad thing is, my brother loved her."

Reaching up, John brushed a tear from her cheek. Another one shed because of him. "I'm sorry."

She sniffed, rubbing her eyes dry with her sleeve. "What else aren't you telling me, John?"

"Come with me," he whispered, taking her hand, leading her towards the bed. Climbing under the sheets, he rested his back against the mahogany headboard, drawing her into his arms. It was selfish, but he needed her comfort, the key to unlocking his black, troubled soul. She snuggled into his chest, her cheek resting against his breast, her arm wrapped around his waist. Under the brocade yellow canopy, with the curtains drawn closed, they were in their own safe little world, an oasis of love he could drink from and forget what awaited him. Heaven.

Taking another deep breath, he started, recanting everything he knew about her Uncle James, the letters John found, and the truth of how her parents were murdered. She listened quietly then glanced up, the innocence in her dark eyes tapping into his overburdened conscience. "And that's where I came in. General Howe gave me this mission, I took the supplies from my brother to trade with your tribe, and it was happenstance that I stumbled into this situation. But there's more."

He leaned down and placed a kiss on the top of her head, breathing in the lavender scent of her hair, losing himself in glossy tresses. "When you saw me again in Oswego, I was on a mission for my friend, Lord Tomlinson, to bring his betrothed back to Niagara. She was travelling with a large dowry and a shipment for Major Butler to trade with our native allies. The ship never made it to its destination, and the woman and everything that came with her disappeared. I believe Alexei and his men are responsible."

She looked up at him again, her eyes widening. "Why do you think that?"

"Because her chaperone said she saw an unusually tall native with blue eyes and fair skin when the woman was captured. When I was imprisoned at Fort Stanwix, I challenged Alexei to give her back in exchange for Great Bear, Anoki, and Ho-sa-gowwa. He didn't deny that he had her, but he wouldn't trade her for your men. After we rescued you, and I was taken back to Fort Niagara to meet with Butler, the only way for me to arrange the release of your men was to give him Dane's and Stephen's correspondences. While they further cleared me of fault in what happened to your village, they implicated Butler and DeLancie. The only way the Major would agree to let your people go was if I destroyed the letters."

"You gave up the chance to prove your innocence to save our people?" she asked quietly.

"Yes."

Leaning up, she kissed him, her lips as soft an angel's wings. "Thank you. I know what that cost you."

He closed his eyes against the pain she evoked, hating himself for the truth he'd yet to confess. "Don't thank me yet. I received word that Lord Tomlinson holds me responsible for his missing bride. I diverted resources he lent me to try to find you when you went missing. Somehow, I have to convince Alexei to return her and the dowry to Miles, or I'll be held responsible."

"Oh, John, Alexei's leaving tomorrow for Canada. There's no way you'll catch him."

Damn. "Alexei's my only chance. I've got to find a way to reason with him. This charade of your uncle's making, we're all victims of it—including Alexei."

She shook her head against his chest. "I don't understand what makes one hate their brother so much."

"It's complicated," John replied with conviction. "And where your Uncle James and his brothers' arguments are concerned, I can't answer. While I'm gone, you must be careful of your uncle; he's capable of anything." Tipping her chin up, he looked into her eyes, needing her to heed his warning. "His hatred for your father and brother runs deep, and it clearly extends to you and Stuart. Please, don't provoke him. Promise me."

"I promise."

"Dellis, you *must* listen to me."

She nodded. "I am."

All he could do was pray that she kept her word. Her impulsive nature and need for justice made her rash, her reason always deferring to emotion—which usually meant trouble for everyone around her.

"What will you do about the money you owe Gavin?" she asked. "I could write to my Uncle Dane; it would take a while, but I know he'd help us."

"Out of the question!" John shook his head. He'd take money from no one. "I have some investments that are due to pay out. They'd more than cover the debt." The thought of seeing Celeste again made his stomach turn, but it was his only option, save begging for help from his new wife's family. No, that he couldn't abide; his honor wouldn't allow such a thing. "By the way, I saw Stuart today."

"I know. He was here." She placed her head back on his chest, her hand gently caressing his side, lulling him with her gentle ministrations. "Thank goodness he kept to himself. I was afraid he'd try something, especially when he saw you."

Stuart's hatred of John was a wound that hurt her deeply, and he knew it. There were no words of comfort to offer her; pregnant silence lay upon them until she finally spoke. "Is there anything else you need to tell me?"

John opened his mouth to speak but then shut it abruptly.

"John?" she whispered, glancing up at him.

"No, no more secrets to tell." He squeezed her, finding comfort for his tortured soul in her soft, supple arms and delightful curves. "You'll still marry me even though I'm an overbearing ass?"

She smiled at her earlier sentiment. "Yes."

Then, out of nowhere, something popped into his mind. "Dellis, I just thought of something; you've never told me what your Oneida name is."

"Why do you want to know?" She laughed. "The only person who calls me by it is my grandfather. I don't particularly like it."

"Oh, you *have* to tell me now." He desperately wanted to know that one last secret of hers. "Tell me, please, or I'll make one up, and then you'll really hate it."

Rolling her eyes, she relented. "It's Fennishyo." The sound of her native name rolling off her lips was like a whisper on the wind.

"That's Seneca, isn't it?" He repeated it quietly, trying to translate it. "Fennishyo."

"Yes, my great-grandmother was Seneca; it was her name. It's tradition to pass on a family name after a loved one has died. It's a way of keeping their spirits with us."

"Beautiful valley. That's what it means. Right?"

With a nod, she leaned up on her elbows, giving him a clear view down the front of her shift. The crevasse between her creamy breasts drew his attention as they pressed together, his mind wandering to all sorts of wonderful things he could do to her beautiful peaks and valleys.

"How appropriate." He gave a lopsided grin.

"No good can come from that look, Captain Carlisle." She shook her head. "John, promise you'll give me at least two more days, and then you can leave. Give me this one thing."

"I'll give you something else, too." Grabbing her hand, he placed it between his legs, letting her feel how much he wanted her.

She rolled her eyes, yanking her hand away. "John!"

He relished her look of outrage, knowing it was a finely tuned act. His sweet angel could turn into a demanding temptress in a split second; so much the better, for he knew well how to conjure her passion.

Trying to coax her, he rolled her onto her back, wrapped her silky legs around his waist, and thrust his hips into hers, teasing her with his want.

"Let me put this bed to good use; our guests can wake up to you screaming my name." Bringing his lips close to her ear, he mimicked her voice, even the guttural tone it took on during their lovemaking, "*Oh, God, John, don't stop.*" Grinning, he said, "Any time a woman says *God* and *your name*, in the same sentence, it's a good thing."

"You're incorrigible," she said with mock outrage, swatting him away, pulling her legs from around his hips.

"And you love it." He laughed loudly.

She pushed him away, but he persisted, burying his face in the valley between her breasts, breathing in her lavender scent, his hands fondling the tender, twin peaks until they hardened.

Grabbing a handful of hair, she yanked his head up, forcing him to look at her. "First of all, I haven't forgiven you for your dastardly behavior, and second, you have to wait for the wedding night. After all, I'm a lady."

"Well, if you're not going to let me partake, can I at least watch?" He raised an eyebrow in suggestion.

"You'd like that too much." She grabbed a pillow and hit him in the face with it.

"Touché, my Fennishyo," he said between kisses, imagining her acting out his fantasy in that beautiful valley.

"Agnes, can you see to the guests? I need to take a break for a minute." Dellis sat down at the wooden table in the corner of the kitchen, taking a moment to catch her breath. Since getting up that morning, she'd been running nonstop, trying to cook breakfast and wait tables while working on wedding plans. Together, she and Agnes still had to make a cake, plan a supper, and decide how they were going to decorate the parlor for the ceremony.

The dining room was full for breakfast; the hash and biscuits with coffee had become a favorite of the local townspeople and was a good deal for merely a couple of pence. Dellis just had to get through the morning; once midday hit, things would slow down, and she could start working on her plans.

Agnes pushed the door open from the bar to the kitchen with her backside, leaning in quickly to grab a pot of coffee from the counter. A concerned look crossed her face. "Are you all right?"

Just like the previous pregnancy, Dellis was tired, normal daily work tapping every last bit of her energy, plus the added stress of planning a wedding in one day.

"Just tired, and my stomach isn't right." She gave Agnes a weak smile of assurance. "The smell of fried potatoes and ham aren't helping me either. I don't think I'll ever be able to eat them again."

"Nonsense. Why don't you get some fresh air? I can navigate these rough waters for a while." Before she shut the door, Agnes snatched another plate of biscuits from the counter. The noise of customers chatting and knives clanking on plates resonated through the house. Dellis was grateful for the continued surge in business, but right then, she needed a little peace and quiet.

On the table was the day's mail, a letter addressed to Captain John Carlisle on the top, and underneath, one of the letters she'd sent to her Uncle Dane, returned unopened. *Damn the British blockade.* Once again, her correspondence had fallen victim to it.

"Will, can you put this on the Captain's desk?"

The boy meandered up the back stairs just in time to drop his bucket full of water, give her a haughty look, and snatch the letter from her hands. Apparently, Alexei's attitude adjustment had lasted only twenty-four hours; Will was back to his obnoxious self.

Dellis looked around the kitchen and sighed. There was so much to do it was overwhelming: there was butter to be made, biscuits to roll out, and prepping of the dinner stew for the patrons. Exhausted, and a bit lightheaded, she poured herself a glass of cider and took a sip, the cold, spicy liquid taking the edge off the June heat. The pain in her side from the day before had returned, and more frequently, only then she felt it radiating into her back. *Perhaps I lifted something improperly yesterday?* Yes, she'd moved barrels in the cellar; it always put her back out.

Finally feeling well enough to get back to work, Dellis stood and carried the pitcher and cup to the counter. As she bent to pick up Will's carelessly discarded bucket of water, a stabbing pain shot though her side, taking her breath away. "Goodness."

Quickly, she walked back to the table, sat back down, and wrapped her arms around her waist, holding on until the pain subsided again. It was going to be a long nine months, and it was just beginning.

Just as she tried to get up, Stuart came barreling though the side door, almost running into her. "Stuart, what has you in such a hurry?"

He flung around and pointed his finger at her in accusation. "I know you plan on marrying that Redcoat. I won't allow it."

She purposely hadn't told her brother about the wedding; he wouldn't attend, and he'd never approve of John. Though it broke her heart, it was the best thing for all of them if Stuart stayed away.

"I forbid it, Dellis!" Stuart snapped in her face.

Right as she started to tell her brother to mind his own business, Ruslan walked into the kitchen and tugged on Stuart's sleeve, trying to pull him back into the dining room. "Leave Dellis alone; she's busy right now."

"No!" Stuart yelled, shrugging off his cousin. "That Redcoat hurt Mother. He attacked our village."

Dellis's heart ached for her brother; in his own deranged way, he was trying to help, but he was wrong, terribly wrong. "Stuart, you don't get to forbid me anything. Besides, John didn't kill Mother. That was Roger DeLancie. None of this was his fault."

But that wasn't entirely correct. Stuart knew the truth; he saw John the day he and his men came to the village, perhaps even heard him give the order he was forced into by his superior.

"You must let this go, for my sake. Please, reconsider."

Gently, she pushed a lock of her brother's messy brown hair out of his face, smoothing it behind his ear. Even with a patched eye, he still reminded her of their mother, same deep-set eyes, same wide face with high cheekbones, and when he smiled, it was like a ray of sunshine in the day. *Lord, how I miss Momma.*

"I won't let him use you like they did, sister. I'll stop him this time. I won't fail." Leaning into her, he whispered in a low, dangerous tone, "I'll kill him and his Tory brother."

Dellis grimaced. There was no reasoning with Stuart; their fragile peace found in desperation at DeLancie's camp had sadly ended. Wrenching free from her brother's grasp, she gave him a warning, and one he best heed.

"You need to leave. Now! There's nothing to be done. I married John in the village weeks ago. This is just a formality to make it legal. And if I remember correctly, Stuart, you're no longer welcome in this house." Looking over his shoulder at Ruslan, she nodded. "Get him out of here."

"This is my house, too, sister. I'll see he gets his. Redcoat bastard!"

Dellis ignored Stuart's vitriolic shouts; she was done trying with him.

"Don't worry, Dellis, I'll keep an eye on him." Ruslan grabbed Stuart's arm and dragged him out of the kitchen.

She shook off their argument, determined to get the dinner stew cooking so she could get back to her happy plans. *Nothing is going to spoil the day.* As she started towards the counter, the pain started anew, like a knife stabbing her lower abdomen, forcing her back into her seat. She breathed through it, trying to focus.

"I'll kill him," Stuart ranted, pushing his way back into the kitchen. "That Tory will get his."

"Stuart, stop," she said, closing her eyes against the pain.

"Are you all right, Dellis?" Ruslan rushed over to her, ignoring Stuart's rants.

She looked up into her handsome cousin's blue eyes and nodded. "Yes, women's issues. None of your concern. Now, get him out of here."

Dellis waited another minute, the pain ebbing enough to where it was tolerable. Yes, it was most definitely going to be a long nine months. Sighing, she got up again. The pot on the hearth started to boil over, spewing porridge into the fire, smoke billowing into the kitchen. As she walked over to tend it, pain shot through her stomach again; she dropped to her knees and let out a loud groan.

"Dellis, are you okay?"

When she looked up, Will was beside her, his arm wrapped around her waist for support.

"I don't think so." She choked out the words, her hands on the floor, trying to steady herself while she bore down into the pain.

"Just stay here. I'll get help." The boy stood and ran through the door into the dining room.

She stayed on her hands and knees, her stomach pitching with each powerful jolt of pain.

"Please, God, don't do this." She prayed, though she knew it was already too late; tears welled up in her eyes, and one dropped on the floor where she could focus on it. "No."

What only took seconds seemed like hours; next thing she knew, Agnes and Simon were on their knees next to her.

"Get John." Dellis groaned, collapsing on her side, the pain too unbearable to fight any longer. "He went into town to talk to Father Squires."

"Don't worry, lass, we'll find him." Simon picked her up effortlessly, wrapping her arm around his back.

She kept her face buried in his neck as he carried her through the dining room full of patrons. Only when they were on the way up the stairs did she lift her gaze to find concerned eyes following her assent, Agnes in tow behind.

As Simon gently laid Dellis down on the bed, she realized her shift and skirts were wet and clinging to her legs. "I'm bleeding." She groaned, looking up at Agnes. "I want John. Please. I'm losing the baby."

Chapter Six

John spent most of the morning looking for Alexei, but knowing his aptitude for escape, he was halfway to Canada and beyond anyone's reach. The man had the rather irritating ability to disappear like a specter in the night, leaving not a trace or footstep behind. It was only a matter of time before Miles called John to the table for his actions, and he had nothing to say in his own defense. Things were getting desperate fast. He needed to get back to Oswego. Immediately. But first, he promised Dellis a wedding, and then he could deal with everything else. It was only two more days.

John stopped when he reached the little white church and cringed at his first sight of the cross atop the steeple—not a favorite place of his to visit. He and God hadn't been on good terms for a while, but for one day, they could make a truce on Dellis's behalf. He walked up the wooden steps and opened the door. *Go ahead, God. Do it now.* John craned his neck up to the sky in challenge, but to his surprise, the heavens didn't open up, nor did a bolt of lightning strike him down where he stood. Perhaps there was a truce.

Father Squires agreed to marry them and wrote out a marriage license with no objection. "I knew Dellis's father. He'd be happy to see her marry such a fine gentleman, Captain Anderson."

"Thank you," John replied, wincing at the sound of his *nom de guerre*. It seemed odd to still be referred to as Anderson; he'd come so far with Dellis, no longer playing at deception, but the whole ruse was still necessary. If the townspeople found out he was a British officer, they'd tar and feather him and brand Dellis a Tory.

"I'll come to The Thistle tomorrow at eleven."

"Perfect." John shook hands with the priest and then rushed out of the church, rolling up the license and stuffing it in a breast pocket. *Now, to find Dellis a gift.* With what little money John had, he could ill afford jewelry or a trinket, and knowing her penchant for frugality, she'd be upset with him for spending anything. But he wanted to do something for her.

Thinking for a moment, an idea popped into his head, and it was a good, inexpensive one. He ran into the trading post, purchased some paper, charcoal pencils, a goose feather quill, pounce, and a pot of ink. The only place he knew in town that had a decent-sized mirror, besides his bedroom, was The Silver Kettle. He didn't relish the thought of spending an afternoon fending off Jussie's advances, but it wouldn't take him too long to do what he needed to, and it would be a wonderful surprise for Dellis.

As expected, The Kettle was bursting at the seams with people. He took a seat at the end of the bar next to a rowdy group of drunks but strategically across from the mirror that sat over the back counter. Looking into it, he made note of the shape of his eyes and where they sat in relation to his forehead, and then where his nose stopped over his lips. Turning his attention back to the paper, he picked up a charcoal pencil and started to sketch a picture of himself, glancing in the mirror several times, trying to get the details and spacing correct. He remembered how comforting it was to have the miniature of her when they were separated. Knowing they'd be parted soon, and having nothing else to give her, it seemed the obvious choice.

Thankfully, he was an excellent artist; his skill at mapmaking was second only to his hand at freestyle. Since he was nine, he'd been able to draw, his early talent catching his father's eye, starting with a few maps of the coastline, and then eventually duplicating all of Carlisle Shipping's maps, several times over.

John anticipated being a bit out of practice, having been unable to draw for a long while. Maps were easy, lines and distance, so pure and unfeeling, but a portrait required emotion and a deep discovery of one's subject, something that had been lost to him since the massacre at the village. But it seemed Venus was being generous, love inspiring him to once again take up his pen and regain his absent skill.

So focused was John on his sketch that he didn't notice Jussie when she sat down next to him, putting a tankard full of ale on the bar top close to his hand.

"That's quite good. Will you draw me next?"

He looked up, seeing first her forearms resting on the bar and then her breasts pressed against his arm, almost spilling over the top of her dress. She was grinning from ear to ear, her bright blonde curls peeking out from her cap, framing her wide, round face, making her look like a doll.

"Thank you for the compliment," he replied, admiring his work so far. "Perhaps next time I can draw you, but tonight I'm in a bit of a rush; this is a gift."

"For Dellis McKesson?" Jussie rolled her eyes when she said his beloved's name.

"Yes, as a matter of fact. It's a wedding gift."

She leaned back, crossing her arms over her chest, her eyes narrowing. "I'd think twice before you pledge your life and your fortune to that whore. You'll regret it."

"I think not." He refused to listen to more of her nefarious banter, all of it jealous gossip spread by her, infecting the townspeople against Dellis. "And from now on, I'd rather you not refer to my wife as a whore."

Jussie shrugged and crossed her arms over her chest. "Patrick learned his lesson." She motioned with her head towards the opposite side of the bar where Armstrong sat, talking to one of the patrons. "You will, too. Soon enough."

"Forgive me, but I'm very busy." John turned his attention back to his work, grateful when she walked away, but he could hear her voice carrying over the noise as she chatted out their conversation with Armstrong.

Much to John's chagrin, Patrick walked over and sat, tankard in hand, grinning like a cad. Putting the pencil down, John waited for Armstrong to start blustering like a pompous idiot, as he notoriously did. His eyes trained down at the picture John was drawing and then back at him.

"Will you sign that *from your lying husband*?"

John held back a laugh; the man was behaving like a lovesick dolt with a unrequited crush. "Dellis is none of your business, Armstrong. You saw to that when you jilted her."

"You're rather embellishing your looks, and the picture is surprisingly devoid of a few important details." Patrick grabbed the charcoal pencil and placed it on top of the paper. "Where's your red coat and your captain's adornments? One would almost think you were just a privateer and not a British Spy."

"Not so very different from you, am I?" John smiled, though his eyes narrowed. "Only my cover wasn't blown in the line of duty, and I did win the lady's hand and her favors. So much for amateurs; espionage is a game for pros. You'd do well to keep your distance from Major Butler and Fort Niagara; rumor has it he's looking for a Rebel spy in our ranks."

Patrick's nostrils flared, his fair skin flushing with anger. "You told Butler?"

John shrugged nonchalantly. "Be glad I warned you; otherwise, it could've been the noose for you. Call it noblesse oblige and a wedding gift to your former betrothed."

John could already see the wheels turning in Patrick's head, preparing his smug rebuke. *So predictable.*

"I could tell this whole room who you really are. They wouldn't hesitate to hang you right outside this tavern. Shall I? I'd love to see you on the other end of a noose."

"You could do that, but Dellis would never forgive you. And more than anything, you want her for yourself." John sipped his drink and then put it down, running his finger around the rim of his tankard. "So, by all means, tell them who I am. I dare you."

Patrick smiled, casting a glance to the other side of the busy dining room. John followed the gaze, and much to his dismay, sitting at a table near the window, dressed in her finest green silk taffeta, was Celeste, her dark hair perfectly coiffed, an elegant string of pearls resting on her neckline.

"I don't have to do anything; she'll do it for me." Patrick leaned in, his voice just above a whisper. "From what I understand, she has a few things Dellis might like to know. What say you, Carlisle?"

"You're not innocent in the ways of Mrs. Allen either, my friend." John cocked a brow, advancing the argument instead of retreating. He refused to lose to a jealous fool, especially a Rebel one. "Just a hint: trying to ruin me in Dellis's eyes will only make her think less of you. Is that what you want?"

"It's only a matter of time before you get yours, Carlisle," Patrick said smugly, pointing a finger at Celeste. "And that one's sure to come collecting."

John chuckled to himself, looking back at his sketch. "You have no idea how much I've paid for my association with that one." He inclined his head in Celeste's direction. "Now, if you'll excuse me, I'd like to get back to my work. I plan to give this to my wife after our nuptials tomorrow."

"She deserves better than a sketch of a lying scoundrel." Patrick hissed, and then he rose from his chair.

John ignored the taunt and put the finishing touches on his picture before looking it over. Satisfied with the result, he folded it and stuffed it in his breast pocket next to the marriage license.

After putting his writing tools and parchment in his haversack, he spotted Stuart and Ruslan walking in the door. Trying to avoid them, John went in the opposite direction, around the long wooden tables full of people, and past where Celeste was sitting.

When she saw him, she got up quickly and grabbed his arm. "Aren't you going to say hello, John?"

Taking a deep breath, he gave her a sidelong glance then rolled his eyes. "I have nothing to say to you."

She reached for his hand and placed it on her stomach. "Well, I have few things to say to you."

"Stay away from me." He yanked his hand away and then walked to the door, knowing she was fast on his heels. "I want no part of you, save the money you owe me. And if I don't get it, I'll send someone to collect."

"John, I'm with child."

He stopped abruptly, his back still turned to her. The raucous noise of the bar around him was drowned out by the nervous thundering of his heart. "That's a new one even for you, Celeste." He turned around to face her. "But the chances of that are very slim, and you're rather good at preventing such things."

"It's true, John. And knowing what you do about me, you realize I'd never let an unwanted child remain, and I want this one very much."

John searched for the truth in her hazel eyes and the lines of her face, but there was nothing hidden in her countenance, just frank honesty. "This is another one of your games to get back at me. Wasn't encouraging DeLancie to go after Dellis enough? Or lying to me after you forced me to…" He stopped midsentence and shook his head. "There's no way you could say it's mine for sure. I'm just one of many."

"I don't like what you're insinuating." Celeste countered. "Besides, who would I lower myself to sleep with in Niagara? I've yet to find a capable replacement for you."

John scanned the busy dining room frantically, searching for answers in the plaster and panels but finding none. "You'd lie to further twist the knife into me; you've done it once already. I don't have time for this."

Finished with her games, he turned his back and opened the door, desperate to get away from her before she could say more. As expected, she didn't hesitate, coldly delivering the words that rocked the very foundation of his world, threatening to topple it.

"Perhaps Miss McKesson would be willing to hear what I have to say?"

John stopped abruptly and turned around just in time to see her smile, that dangerous malevolent grin of Mephistopheles when he's ready to throw a trump card. "Would your little tart still love you if she knew the truth?"

The woman was diabolical; how John hadn't seen it the first day they met was confounding. Yes, in his drunken, drugged haze, he sensed the danger in her; yet instead of running away, his broken, tortured soul embraced it. *Damn that naïve fool.* He'd signed on the dotted line in blood, without a second thought, and paid for it ever since.

"A truce, Celeste; our business together is finished. Enough of this folly. Keep my money, leave this place, and we'll part ways forever. Please, let us both move on."

But pleading one's case to the Devil always falls on deaf ears. John should've known better.

She let out a malignant laugh, tossing a curly lock of her chestnut hair over her shoulder. "No, John. This is no folly. Deny it all you like, but you can't ignore this." Celeste grabbed his hand again, putting it on her belly, letting him feel its firmness, the slight protrusion a painful reminder of Dellis's swollen womb just before she lost his child.

Reality hit him like a punch in the face; he drew in a sibilant breath as waves of nausea, potent as being caught in a storm at sea, threatened. Pulling his hand away, he threw open the door and rushed down the steps.

But she stayed on his heels, her voice carrying through the busy street. "It's your child, John! Yours!"

"Stay away from Dellis!" he yelled over his shoulder and then continued his long strides, trying to put some distance between them.

John craned his head down, pulling the brim of his hat forwards, trying to avoid eye contact with the villagers. His argument with Celeste on a busy street was quite an intrigue and was sure to stir up all sorts of drama. Rumors spread notoriously fast in small towns yet lingered on forever. If he hoped to make it his home someday, it was best if he drew as little attention to himself as possible and try not to provoke suspicion, for both his and Dellis's sake.

As John crossed the narrow dirt street, Will came running up, frantically trying to catch his breath.

"Captain, come quick. Miss Dellis is sick," the boy said between pants.

"What's wrong?" John's heart raced. Dellis was never sick.

"I don't know. Miss Agnes sent me to find you. I've been searching all day."

John ran towards The Thistle, leaving his conversation with Celeste buried in the past where it belonged, with all of her lies.

"Oh, John." Celeste chuckled, walking back into The Kettle and slamming the door behind her. "Run back to your whore, but you can't hide forever." German Flats was a very small place, and oh, how famously rumors spread in such close society. Why, with the show they'd put on in the street, the villagers were sure to be talking already.

She placed a gloved finger to her lips and smiled. *Should I wait for the rumor to get back to John's whore or just take matters into my own hands? Better do this myself.* She refused to leave things to chance, and she relished the opportunity to see Dellis McKesson's face when she heard the truth.

"Mrs. Allen, that was quite a scene you just put on. But for whose benefit?"

When she turned around, Patrick Armstrong was standing at the bar, looking resplendent, his brilliant, olive-green eyes sparkling with mischief. Suddenly, she was hungry for a man; pregnancy had given her passions a surge, and she'd been sadly devoid of company for a month.

"As you know, I always have a plan. Why don't you join me for a drink?" She walked back to her table gleefully, lifting her skirts with dainty precision, and then smoothing them in place once she sat down.

Patrick followed, taking a seat across from her and motioning to Jussie to fill their drinks. "What did you say to Carlisle to provoke him?"

She smiled, sensing an impending cockfight; sadly, it would be fought over the wrong woman. "Wouldn't you like to know?"

"Actually, I would." He watched Jussie pour them each a tankard of cider, waiting for her to walk away before he continued. "You tell me what you said to him, and I'll tell you something rather interesting he told me."

"Fine. I thought his lady might find it rather interesting what occurred between us in Oswego. He didn't much care for that." Fanning out her arms, like a maestro to an orchestra, she said, "Now, it's your turn."

"He's to marry Dellis tomorrow."

"Really?" She noticed the furrow in Patrick's brow as he sipped his drink. "Then I shall have to act quickly."

He drew in a breath, his eyes narrowing on her. "Stay away from Dellis; focus on Carlisle."

She snorted, shaking her head. Oh, yes, she forgot how frustratingly smitten Armstrong was with his former betrothed. That wouldn't do at all. "If I remember correctly, you and I have had our own shared moments."

He winced and then buried his face in his drink.

Coward.

"I'm sure once I've enlightened her to John's infidelity, she'll coming running back to you for comfort. But don't you think she'd find you just as repugnant if I told her about *our* previous intrigue?"

"What do you want?"

Celeste cocked a brow in salute to her own ingenuity. How easy it was to play men, always thinking with their cocks and never their heads. "Nothing, as a matter of fact. Once I have words with Dellis, by all means, comfort her, take care of her, just keep her far away from John."

"What else do you want? I know there's more to it." He put his tankard down and sat back in his chair, stretching out his legs.

She admired the long, corded muscles straining against his biscuit-colored breeches, his slim hips resting against the chair. The maroon jacket and waistcoat he wore drew attention to his green eyes and reddish-brown hair.

"Actually, now that you say it, there *is* something I need." Lifting the glass to her lips, she took a sip of the tart, spicy cider. Delicately, she wiped her lips with her napkin and then folded it on her lap, noticing a bit of pink stain from her lip color. Satisfied that she'd made him wait long enough, she said, "I need you to tell me where Alexei McKesson hid Lord Tomlinson's bride and her dowry."

"I don't know. Alexei never told me about her, and I didn't ask."

She shook her head. *No lying.* "I find that hard to believe. No matter. I suggest you find out, or Dellis is sure to learn a bit more about you."

Before she could continue, a ruckus started at the bar, the noise interrupting her train of thought. DeLancie's little street urchin was banging his metal tankard on the bar top like a drunken savage. "That's the Redcoat; that's him who just left. He's the spy who's going to marry my sister."

The man next to him stood, tugging on Stuart's shirt. "That man told us not to eat here. He paid us to go to The Thistle and never come here again."

Celeste turned back to Patrick. "Isn't that Stuart McKesson?"

Patrick nodded. "Sadly, yes; the boy is a loon."

Intrigued, she turned her attention back to the young man's display, watching intently. There was opportunity there; she just had to wait for it.

"We need to get the militia boys and show him how we deal with Redcoats in this town," Stuart yelled. "Anyone care to join?"

"Aww, have a drink, Stuart, and be quiet." The man next to Stuart poured some ale into his tankard and pulled him down into his seat. "He can't be all bad; he paid me a lot of money. And he wasn't wrong, The Thistle does have better food, and your sister is a pretty thing."

Jussie walked over to the two men, her voice low but still audible. "Are you telling me that John Anderson is a Redcoat, and that he paid you boys to go eat at The Thistle?"

"You mean Captain John Carlisle." Stuart provided, all too eagerly.

"Yes, ma'am." The burly, filthy man chimed in. "We only started coming here again because you reduced the price of your drinks, but we still have breakfast and sup at The Thistle."

Celeste laughed to herself. It looked like John was soon to have even more trouble on his hands. "Well, that was entertaining; where were we?" She rolled her eyes skywards. "That's right, you're going to find out where Lord Tomlinson's bride and the dowry are. Yes, that's just what you're going to do. And I'll deal with John."

Celeste got up from her chair, putting the napkin on the table and then adjusting her skirts. "I suggest you visit The Thistle in another day or so; Miss McKesson will be in need of your comfort by then."

As she walked by the bar, Stuart started yelling again, banging his fists on the bar. "That's her; that's his whore. She can tell you he's a Redcoat. Ask her."

She smiled to herself and then promptly turned around, ready to put on a performance to bring down the house. "It's true. We were supposed to be married, but then he disappeared without a trace. I thought he was just a merchant, but it turns out he's actually a British spy. Now, I'm with child." She gently touched the corner of her eye, making it water on demand. "He left me for Dellis McKesson. I'm sure that's why he paid you to go to her tavern. Rumor has it they're spying together."

Catching her by surprise, Stuart got in her face; the smell of alcohol and rotten teeth wafted in her nose, forcing her to take step back. "My sister is no traitor; don't you lie about her."

"I wouldn't dream of it," Celeste countered, placing her hand over her nose, trying to block out his stench.

Stuart turned back to the bar, grabbing his tankard. "She's right about the Redcoat. He *is* a spy. And before you know it, he'll have the whole bleeding Redcoat army at our backs."

There was a fire brewing in Stuart's coal-black eyes, if only she could stoke it.

"We have to stop him!" the man sitting next to Stuart yelled.

Jussie pointed one of her chubby fingers at both of them and said, "Perhaps the whole town needs to know we have a Redcoat spy and his Tory whore in our midst."

"Oh, and don't forget about his brother, Lord Carlisle," Celeste added, sticking a verbal poker into the burning wood.

"Yeah!" Stuart yelled, his ire stoking to a blaze.

All too easy. She stifled a laugh, instead feigning illness. "Excuse me. I'm still distraught from my earlier meeting, and in my delicate condition, this has all been too much. I'm going to my room." Celeste slowly climbed the stairs, listening to the conversation on the way up.

"We'll take care of him and that McKesson whore," Jussie said, slamming her tankard down on the bar top.

Chapter Seven

"Dellis!"

She heard John shouting her name frantically from the hall and closed her eyes, fighting back tears. How would she ever tell him?

"My love? Where is she? Dellis!"

"She's in the bedroom," Clark said, his voice muffled though the door.

"What happened? Simon? Agnes?"

She couldn't hear either of her friends' replies, only her beloved's sweet, mellifluous baritone pleading for answers.

When she opened her eyes, John was standing at the foot of the bed, his face wan, arms already outstretched, a haven of safety ready and waiting for her.

"Dellis, thank God." He rushed to the side of the bed and sat down, grabbing her hand, placing a soft kiss on her palm while his eyes searched her face. "What happened? What's wrong? The boy came running down the street; he told me you were sick."

She wanted to be strong, knowing how it would devastate him, but she just couldn't; one look into his beautiful blue eyes, and the tears started to fall. "Oh, John, I lost it." The words came out bitter and full of pain; all she could do was repeat them. "I lost it."

There was no need for explanation; the pain that creased his brow and darkened his eyes told her he understood with certainty. "Dellis? No."

He reached for her, and she went willingly, wanting nothing more than to be held in his strong, capable arms and succumb to her pain. "I was going to tell you after we got married. It was your surprise."

He rested his chin on her head, enveloping her completely in his embrace. "You're safe. That's all that matters now." His voice was low and soft in her ear, a healing salve to her wounded heart. "I know this won't make it right, but I promise we'll have another."

"No, John." She ached all over, tired and limp, like a wrung-out, wet canvas, but the pain was gone, and with it their child. Her heart felt like it was going to crack open in her chest. Tears turned to sobs as she buried her face in his breast, soaking the fine linen of his waistcoat. "Don't you see? I'm ruined."

She could feel him shake his head, and with a gentle kiss to her forehead, he murmured into her hair. "You're not ruined, my love. What happened before was because of DeLancie, and this was just one time. I don't need to tell you that these things happen."

"No." She looked up at him, the inevitable truth on the tip of her tongue. "John, I *am* ruined. I never told you because I didn't want to believe it was true. And when I got with child last time, I thought maybe my father was wrong."

"What are you talking about, my love?" Tension and concern turned his melodious voice brittle. "I don't understand."

Pulling away, she took in his beautiful face; creases of worry strained his brow, confusion widening his eyes.

She managed to choke out the words. "When the soldiers..." Then she had to stop and take a moment to compose herself as a flood of tears started anew. After several deep breaths, she rubbed her eyes and tried again. "When the soldiers used me, one of them said something about not wanting a savage bastard with his family blood roaming the woods. When he finished, he hurt me. He did something to me." She couldn't bring herself to say it. Tears started again; the horror of that moment as fresh and real as if it were only a day before. "I fought back, kicking and screaming, when he, he…" Still, the words wouldn't come, but from the expression of pain on John's face, he understood; though the horrific truth of it was unimaginable. "There was so much blood, and the pain lasted for days. At one point, I had a fever. I was so sick. My father told me he feared I was ruined permanently. And since then, things that are normal for women haven't been for me. Do you understand?"

It was embarrassing and demeaning to have to discuss such matters with a man; women's problems were beyond a husband's concern, but it was the only way to make him understand.

John fisted his hair and whispered, "My God. No. The thought of anyone hurting you like that…" He stopped midsentence, the pain in his eyes mirroring the anguish in his voice. "My love."

She sniffed, holding back tears. "The first night we were together, I never considered we'd make a child. I didn't think it was possible. And as my time progressed, there were problems, pains, lots of them. When I went to DeLancie's to find Stuart, I was already losing the baby. Now this…"

Dellis swallowed, waiting for him say something, but he didn't—stunned silent with devastating truth. He searched her face, as if trying to comprehend all that she'd revealed, but still, there were no words. How she wished she could read his mind, hear the myriad of thoughts he was contemplating. His silence was daunting. She could wait no more.

"John, if you marry me, you'll be giving up your chance to have children."

"No!" he yelled, finally shattering his reticence with one simple word.

But no, what? No, I don't care? No, I can't marry you? No, I can't live without having children?

The suspense was killing her, the seconds ticking by like hours until he finally cracked the silence with the sweet serenade of her name.

"Dellis." Gently, he pushed a stray lock of her hair behind her ear, his hand cupping her face. "My love, listen to me. Listen. To. Me."

She nodded, her eyes misting with tears.

"You must believe that anything is possible. After all, the fact that you and I are together is nothing short of a miracle. It can happen again, and it will." Such conviction in his voice, how she yearned to believe he could see into the distant future.

"John, you don't understand how sick I was. How badly he hurt me. He... He shoved... Oh, God." She wanted to tell him what that man did to her, but she couldn't; the words wouldn't come, stuck painfully in her throat. Even when her father had asked her what happened, she couldn't speak of it. Stuart had to be the one to tell the gruesome tale. It was the one burden she could never relieve herself of, never. And for three years, she'd buried it deep, trying to deny it—until then.

The tears started again, her heart no longer able to hold up against the pain. She grabbed onto John's waistcoat, that simple fabric her lifeline as she submerged into the depths of grief.

"This happened now for a reason. It's punishment for not telling you the truth sooner. Now you'll be free to marry a woman who can give you children, a woman who fits in your world, not some poor, disgraced half-breed."

His body tensed against hers; she could feel him fighting his own inner turmoil, though his arms tightened around her like protective steel bands, drawing her ever closer. Gently, he lifted her chin, his thumb wiping tears from her cheek. "I'd rather spend one hundred childless years with you than marry another woman and have whole brood of sons and daughters. You're not negotiable in this life. Not for me."

"It will matter later." She sobbed. "When years have passed and all those around us have families, and we have nothing."

"We won't have nothing—we'll have each other. And just because you can't give me a child of your body doesn't mean we won't have children to light up our lives." Holding her face in his hands, he looked into her eyes, making her heart transform from an empty vessel of grief to a receptacle full of his love. "You're my wife. And together, we'll find a way."

But could they? She could barely see past the hour, and in another day, he'd be gone. A Redcoat—enemy of her tribe—and there would be war.

"We can put the wedding off a day, until you're back on your feet again; then Father Squires will come, and we'll be married. I already have the license. I can wait to leave. After that, we'll have the rest of our lives to figure this out. Say yes, Dellis."

Brushing her lips with his own, he whispered against them. "Say yes, my love, my Fennishyo."

She nodded, resting her forehead against his. "Yes, Captain."

He kissed her again, softly on the lips and the forehead, and then reached into his breast pocket and pulled out a folded piece of paper. "I was going to give you this after we wed. But I think you could use a present now."

He handed it to her and watched as she carefully unfolded the crisp paper, turning it right-side up so she could examine it. "This is incredible; who drew it?"

It was a sketch of him, the likeness so true to form she was in awe. The artist had managed to capture her favorite smile in action, paying attention to how his eyes wrinkled in the corners and the lines that bracketed his lips. His thick, luxurious hair was pulled back, looser, how she liked it, just as he wore it then.

"I drew it," he said in a voice steeped with pride and a bit of hubris.

"You did?" She looked up at him, completely astonished. "I knew you could draw, I've seen your incredibly detailed maps, but I had no idea you did portraits."

He smiled, a genuine grin of appreciation for her compliment, not the usual, mischievous tug at the corner of his lips. "When I was a child, I used to sketch anyone I could find who'd sit for me. My father realized I was quite good and put me to work at Carlisle Shipping; that's how I ended up making maps. It's been a long time since I drew myself or anyone else."

"Why?"

He hesitated, letting his gaze cast down at the picture in silence.

Is he afraid to tell me?

"John?"

"When I draw a portrait, I need to close my eyes and recreate the person in my own imagination, visualize them as I see them. Since that day at your village with DeLancie, I lost the ability to focus my mind." Inclining his head towards the picture, he added, "Every time I tried, I ended up drawing pictures of the women, so I stopped, at least, until today."

Dellis nodded in understanding, interlacing her fingers with his. "You're very talented, John."

She couldn't take her eyes off the picture. Once again, he surprised her. Would she ever know everything about the fascinating man that was her lover?

"Though I think the artist might've been a bit generous with your looks."

"A portrait's all about artist interpretation. That's what I see in the mirror."

When she looked up, he was grinning suggestively, that roguish tug returning. She shook her head at his teasing and gave him a wink.

"Do you like it? Truly? You're not disappointed that I couldn't afford to buy you something?"

Folding the paper, she pressed it to her heart with both hands. "It's the most wonderful gift I've ever received. I'll treasure it." Handing it to him, she said, "You must sign it."

"All right." He walked to the desk, dipped his quill in the ink pot, and scratched out something on the paper. Sprinkling it with pounce, he shuffled it around the paper and then blew it off before handing the picture back to her.

All my love,
Your most obedient husband, Captain, the Hon. John Carlisle
20th June 1777

Upon reading the words, she burst into great gales of laughter, but then exhaustion crept up on her, compounded with the events of the day.

Too weary to fight, she reached for him again. "I'm so tired. I know you have much to prepare for your journey, but will you stay with me until I fall asleep?"

John plucked the picture from her hands, placing it on the nightstand next to the bed. He removed his frock coat and lay down next to her, patting the sheets. "Come."

She snuggled into his arms, resting her cheek on his breast, breathing in his sandalwood and spice cologne, letting him completely drown out her senses until she was totally submerged in him again. Just as she closed her eyes, she finally found the courage to ask the question she'd long tried to avoid. "John, there's something I never asked you because I couldn't bear the answer. But I think now is the time…"

"What is it, my love?" he whispered into her hair, placing a kiss as light as an angel's wings on her forehead.

"What was our baby's name?" Suddenly, she needed to know very badly. "Our little boy; did you name him?"

Without hesitation or even an intake of breath, he replied, "It was Stephen." Then he rested his chin atop her head. "Stephen Carlisle."

"Thank you for telling me." Closing her eyes, she remembered the little bundle in her dreams, the one she handed over to her father's beloved care, and smiled. "Stephen."

When Dellis woke several hours later, she was alone in their bed, tucked neatly under the counterpane; the curtains were slightly pulled back, allowing the moon to cast its silvery light over the crisp, white sheets. Rolling on her side, she pulled the other curtain back; the slightest flicker of candlelight could be seen coming from the room across the hall. John always was one to burn the midnight oil. He'd probably fallen asleep at his desk, writing missives and looking over his maps.

Carefully, she climbed out of bed and tied her robe around her waist, pulling her dark hair from the collar. She tiptoed across the hall, the old wooden floorboards creaking and protesting with each step, no matter how quiet she tried to be.

Pushing the door open, it was just as she expected, John lay with his head resting on the desk, papers strewn underneath him, his quill neatly standing in its little brass pot. Locks of his silky hair had fallen onto his face and the paper underneath him, exposing the trinkets neatly pulled back and braided into his long queue. He looked so peaceful, she hesitated to move, content to just waste away the hours watching him sleep.

As she got closer, she found things weren't as serene as they appeared. His hand rested in his lap, an empty decanter in his fist, and on the floor was a broken glass and a puddle of dark liquid staining the blue area rug.

Leaning down, she could hear his sleepy breaths bringing the pungent, spicy scent of whiskey with each swish and puff. Gently, she brushed the hair off his cheek; his eyelids were closed but noticeably swollen and red. Spread out all over his desk were his precious maps. His compass lay open, pointing north towards the door, but that wasn't what he was working on when he fell asleep. His cheek lay atop a picture. She carefully pulled it out from under him and held it to the candle that still burned on his desk.

It was her; she was asleep, but it wasn't at The Thistle in their bed, it was on the cot in her village. The picture was beautiful and so lifelike, his artist's rendering precise all the way down to the minutest detail. She looked peaceful, though her face was marred with dark shadows; bruises and cuts littered her forehead and cheeks. Her body was covered in a large cloak—his cloak.

It dawned on her what he was drawing; it was a picture of her from the first time he saw her. The day the regulars came to her village.

"Oh, John." She choked painfully, running her hands over his silky hair, brushing it from his face. He was reliving those horrifying moments again because of what she told him—because of the baby.

John stirred under her hand, lifting his head, a stray lock of hair falling into his eyes; he brushed it back haphazardly and looked around. "Dellis?"

He was still drunk, his usually crisp accent slurred, her name a guttural roll off his tongue. "My love?"

She offered a hand to him. "Come to bed with me."

He nodded, his head falling forwards, his hair shielding his face from her. She got on her knees in front of him, taking notice of his bloodshot eyes and the creases in his brow that were so deep, as if etched in stone—torture's pained expression.

"I'm sorry," he said, smoothing his hair from his face. "I didn't mean to do it. I didn't want to hurt you. I had no choice."

"I know, John. I know." She took the decanter from his hand, placing it on the table, and then stood, putting his arm around her neck so she could assist him. He buttressed himself against her side, his body strangely loose as if he'd crumple to the ground if she let go.

"Don't be sorry; it wasn't your fault. You didn't do this to me."

"But she made me do... I had no choice... I had to find..." He mumbled more unintelligible words in response, his head hanging forwards as they slowly walked back across the hall to their room. He was so heavy against her she strained with each step to keep from collapsing under his weight. When they got to the bed, he landed on the sheets, limp as a doll, and started snoring again, his face turned away, giving her a glimpse of his pain-etched brow.

Knowing his preference for sleeping in the nude, she carefully removed his boots and socks and then his shirt and breeches. Pulling the covers over him, she took off her robe and climbed in next to him, drawing him into her arms. He readjusted himself, burying his face in her neck, his left hand resting on her flat, empty belly, caressing it gently.

She closed her eyes against the tears that threatened. Yes, it was so devastatingly empty. *Again.*

Dellis turned her face to his, her cheek resting against his forehead while she brushed his hair out of his face. Suddenly, she felt the wisp his eyelashes, as light as dove's wings, flicker against the sensitive skin of her neck and then precious drops of tears.

"Dellis, I promise I'll give you another," he whispered, each word choked out between sobs.

"I know you will, John. You've always given me everything I want," she replied, stroking his hair.

"Don't ever leave me." Was the last thing he said. After, he was unearthly quiet save the sounds of embittered weeping, his strong, powerful frame trembling in her arms. He hid his emotions so well, but they were deep and strong, and when they tore through him, it was like a river cutting through a rock, leaving behind a permanent ravine in his soul.

"Rest, John. I'll be here when you wake," she whispered in his ear.

He was fitful in his sleep, mumbling and thrashing, crying out her name, until she pulled him back to her breast like a child and whispered sweet words of love in his ear.

Chapter Eight

Dellis woke to the sounds of retching, and between rounds, an occasional curse. She rolled over to find John with his head hanging over the side of the bed, heaving into the chamber pot.

"Are you okay?" She rubbed his back, trying to help him, the muscles in his sides visibly straining with each painful spasm.

"No…" He shook his head, audibly gagging when he tried to speak. "But you don't have to stay here and take care of me. Pissing through one's teeth after a night of drinking is a solitary affair."

She couldn't help but chuckle, in spite of how miserable he sounded. "I've seen you sick before, if you remember?"

John rinsed out his mouth and then rolled onto his back, throwing his head on the pillow. His hair was drenched with sweat, and his normally sun-kissed complexion was pasty white with a tinge of green. "Well, that time, it was your fault."

Dellis got up, poured some water in the washing basin, soaked a piece of linen, and then wrung it out. Gently, she placed it on his forehead, wiping down his cheek to the base of his neck, leaving a moist trail wherever she touched. How she hated seeing him like that. Her strong, virile John laid weak and vulnerable with sickness.

"Why did you do this to yourself?"

He cocked a brow, though his eyes turned away from her. "Because I'm weak compared to you. My love, I envy you; your strength is a force of nature."

Wanting to soothe him, she turned his cheek, forcing him to look at her with those beautiful blues. "You're the strongest man I've ever known. It makes me sad to see you drink yourself into a state."

He winced, her words striking a chord within.

"I used to fill the decanters in this room when you were a lodger; I know how much you drank, and when I saw you that night at Mrs. Allen's house, you were drunk then, too. You were also smoking something. I could smell it on your breath."

"Opium," he said flatly.

She gulped down her unease. *Opium.* Once it got its potent, euphoric hooks into a person, it ruined even the strongest of men. "Do you smoke that often?" she asked, though she feared the answer.

"I used to. I was longing for you that night. Wanting to forget."

Her heart skipped a beat and several after; he looked so handsome and vulnerable in his confession she could barely draw breath. "This need to drown yourself has been going on for a long time, hasn't it?"

"Yes," he said, shamefully. "Since I was in my teens, but it got worse after what happened in your village—and when we're separated."

It must've been difficult for him to admit his weaknesses to her; she reached for his hand and gave it a gentle squeeze. "I've seen what over drinking has done to my people and my brother. I couldn't bear if it happened to you."

He swallowed hard, closing his eyes. "I'm sorry, Dellis, for being weak—for all of it."

"Don't apologize. I want to help you." She turned his hand over, tracing thin lines from the base of his fingers down to the scar at his wrist. Such capable, strong hands, long, dexterous fingers that could fight so bravely, draw proficiently, and touch her with such tenderness. She drew his palm to her lips, giving it a gentle kiss. "What happened to me wasn't your fault."

When he turned away, she palmed his cheek, forcing him to look at her again. His eyes were red and bloodshot, strain making the lines in the corners and on his forehead deeper. He looked so very tired, as if he'd aged ten years in a moment.

"It. Was. Not. Your. Fault."

"They haunt me day and night. Even now, when you're so close. I'm never free of them. When I was released from prison, I tried to drink myself into oblivion, but it didn't work. One night, I held a gun to my head, but I lacked the courage to pull the trigger. The barrel was at my temple; the cold steel was strangely comforting. I sat there for hours, trying to convince myself to just end it. But I was a coward. I wanted to do it, but I couldn't. And when you held the gun to my head, I wanted you to pull the trigger. Part of me wanted to die and be free of this wasted life."

"No." Her eyes welled with tears, imagining John in such a state of despair that he'd take his own life. Leaning over, she took his face in her hands, drawing him closer. The thought of holding him still and cold, like her father, caused her breath to catch painfully. "Your life isn't wasted. Do you hear me? Please, don't ever say that again."

He nodded, his eyes cast down shamefully for a moment before he spoke. "You need not worry. I can't face the idea of being parted from you."

He was quiet, but she could sense the millions of thoughts flooding behind those twin sapphire gems.

"We'll have another child. I believe it, and I believe in you." With her words, his expression softened, his long, straight brows pulling together as he tenderly searched her face. Her heart swelled with love right at that moment. "That we're together is nothing short of a miracle. To me, that means anything is possible."

He nodded serenely and then let out a groan. Clutching his abdomen, he rolled over again and hurled the contents of his stomach in the chamber pot. "Bloody hell!"

Once more, she rubbed his back and pulled his hair from his face, watching him strain painfully.

From over his shoulder, she said, "Well, with you like this and me abed, I guess we'll need to postpone the wedding."

When finished, he rinsed his mouth again, and then rolled over, wiping his lips with his forearm. "Absolutely not; you'll rest, and I'll spend the day helping Agnes get things ready. This is nothing. I've gone into battle with it coming out both ends."

"I really didn't need to know that." She closed her eyes in disgust, trying to ignore the visual he'd painted for her.

He burst into laughter. A little bit of mirth did wonders for both their spirits, the mood already lightening, lifting the pervasive cloud of melancholy.

"Well, it's true. Preparing for our wedding while hung will be far easier than trying to surprise a group of continentals with your guts ready to explode. The smell alone is enough to expose your position."

She laughed so hard her eyes started to water. "Goodness, John. There are some secrets of yours I'm happy not to be privy to, and that's one of them."

John threw the covers off and sat up, giving her a view of his nude torso and long legs. Like a shy maid, she blushed when he noticed her eyeing him. "Perhaps next time, I'll draw you a nude." He paused, his eyes widening, a sly grin spreading from cheek to cheek as if he'd come up with a brilliant idea. "Now, that's a thought. I'll draw you a nude so you can look at it when we're separated and..." He winked.

"You're incorrigible!" She slapped his chest, feeling herself grow hot from the insinuation. How quickly he went from being raw with emotion to downright naughty. He was back to himself again, those emotions locked up behind his steel walls, masked with jokes and bravado.

"Do men really say such things to their wives, or are you just an oddity?"

"I don't know. I've never been married before." He said it with such seriousness, she had to laugh. "But if these last few weeks have taught me anything, I'd hope it was that between us, no conversation is forbidden. You tell me what you want and what you need, and as your husband, it's my duty to give it to you. No matter what it is." Another little smirk started in the corner of that delicious, kissable mouth and spread all the way to his eyes. "And I should be able to do the same."

Good Lord, he's trouble personified.

Dellis rolled her eyes, crossing her arms over her chest. "You'd like that entirely too much, John Carlisle."

She loved the intimacy of the moment and his playful sense of humor. It was a shame to have to interrupt it, but there was much to do, and the breakfast crowd would be coming within an hour.

"I don't need to stay in bed. I'm right as rain. You stay here and rest?"

"Absolutely not, *you* are to stay in bed for the day. I'll get up. Besides, rest is for a weaker man; a little hair of the dog, and I'll be fighting fit." His voice was so full of braggadocio she rolled her eyes skywards again.

"Breeches." John pointed to a navy pair on the floor; she leaned over the side of the bed and picked them up, handing them to him. He stood and pulled them over his lean, powerful thighs, fastening the buttons, her eyes drawn to the flat planes of his stomach, following the bit of light hair on his naval and the scar that dipped below the waist of his pants. "I'll get cleaned up, and then I have few errands to run. I'd wanted to wear my uniform when we married, though I think under the current circumstances, I'll settle for my navy suit. I'll make sure it's cared for."

"I see your point," she replied, unable to avert her gaze as he adjusted himself through his breeches, his erection thick and straining against the fabric proudly.

"My love"—his voice was muffled as he pulled his shirt over his head—"it's more fun undressing me and then watching me dress, isn't it? It's rather like rewrapping a gift after you've already enjoyed it. We can reverse this process if you like. Just say the word."

Heat emanated through her body and pooled at her core, making her melt with desire. Wanton thoughts of him on his back while she rode him wildly popped into her head, but she shook them off. He was provoking her purposely, like the persistent scoundrel he was.

Suddenly, his expression changed, a furrow of deep thought etched in his brow. "Dellis, should we not postpone our wedding after what happened yesterday? Not that I want to, but…"

Always her attentive lover. There was such tenderness and concern in his voice her heart threatened to burst from it. But he was right; physically, she wasn't ready. And the thought of letting him go, not knowing when he'd return, and not making love to him, was downright painful.

"Perhaps you're right." She nodded, her eyes cast down, trying not to let him see her utter disappointment.

But of course, he did. John finished tucking his shirt in his breeches and then walked over to her and lifted her chin.

She couldn't help the tears that threatened, trying to sniff and blink them away, but it was no use.

He caressed her cheek with his thumb, catching a tear as it descended, wiping it away. "It means that much to you?" he asked, his voice low and tremulous with emotion.

She nodded, but she was unable to put words to her pain. What if he never came back from the war? What if he was killed? Her body ached for him already, pervasive thoughts adding to the urgency of the moment.

"You flatter my ego that you desire me so." He let out a little laugh, but the look in his blue eyes was serious. "I'll still make love to you; we'll just have to be a little creative."

"I'll leave it to your ingenuity." She stopped, unable to hold back a laugh when he raised his eyebrows suggestively. "No good can come from that look, Captain."

He clasped his hands, rubbing them together vigorously, a maniacal grin lighting up his face. "Oh, the mind wanders."

Dellis rolled her eyes. "You're entirely too satisfied with yourself."

"I am, and you will be, too." With that, he leaned in and placed a kiss on the tip of her nose. "But for today, we shall both rest; an extra day will do us both a world of good, and it can only serve to improve my stamina. Consider that an added incentive to do as I say, my love."

She shook her head as he roared with laughter. The man was incorrigible.

After a day abed, Dellis was chomping at the bit to do some work, with the wedding at noon and a breakfast crowd due, it was too much for Agnes and Will to handle alone.

John left early in the morning to run errands, so there was no one to tempt her into lounging idly under the soft linen sheets and waste away the day; she was ready to get up. Dellis rolled out of bed, dressed quickly, and then walked down the hall towards the servants' staircase.

It was her wedding day. *Again!* That thought brought a smile to her lips and a peppy kick in her step that would've turned into a jig if she weren't already halfway down the little winding staircase.

When she opened the door at the bottom of the stairs, the summer sun's rays peeked through the windows, shining a lemony bright beam in her eyes that said, "good morning," and she embraced it with a sigh. No matter what had happened, the loss of the babe and John's inevitable departure, she'd live for that one day. That perfect moment.

But her happiness was short lived, for when she rounded the corner into the kitchen, her aunt appeared out of nowhere, spewing words of venom. "Tell me you're not going to marry that man! He's a disgrace! You can't marry him. I won't let you."

"Auntie, this is none of your affair." Dellis countered, taken aback by her aunt's sudden, unprovoked attack. "How do you know about it, anyway?"

"Stuart and Ruslan told me."

There was commotion coming from the kitchen: shouts and high-pitched yells. Dellis pushed past her aunt only to find Uncle James trying to wrestle letters from the much smaller Will's hands.

"Excuse me, Uncle, that's my mail."

James McKesson backed away, releasing the letters and the dish boy.

"Will, take the mail upstairs and put it on the Captain's desk. After, can you please see to our guests? Find out what they'd like for breakfast. I'll clean up the kitchen."

Once Will was gone, Dellis turned back to her uncle, unleashing a touch of her pent-up anger at him. "I'll thank you to not frighten my dish boy. And just so you know, I've found no mail addressed to you in weeks. I'm not sure what you're looking for, but it's not here."

"Where's Alexei?" James demanded. He was trying to intimidate her, but she wasn't afraid of him—not anymore, and she wanted him to know it.

Planting a hand on her hip, she tartly replied, "He left for Canada yesterday. I don't know when he'll be back. Now, if that's all you came for, please, leave. I have much to do."

Her uncle seized her arm, squeezing so hard she yelped. "You'd do well to respect me, Dellis. I'm still family."

Yes, sadly, he was. And he should be the one walking her down the aisle in the place of her dearly departed father. But that would never be. And since she'd learned what part he'd played in her father's death, she longed to confront her uncle and demand the truth from his lips, but it wasn't the time. Someday, she'd make him pay for what he did to her family and to John.

Wrenching her arm free, she tamped down her passion, allowing good sense to pervade. "Please, leave now, both of you, and don't come back. Ever."

She peeked around at her aunt and then back at Uncle James, making sure they heard the earnest words. With that, the pair disappeared, slamming the door behind them, leaving Dellis in blessed, peaceful solitude.

Yes, someday, she'd make him pay.

Nothing would keep John from enjoying the day. Nothing. It was his last night with Dellis until when, he knew not, but at least once they were officially married, she'd be protected should anything happen to him.

Death was a possibility, a chance he risked every time he put on his red coat and took up his musket, but it never used to worry him, almost daring the Fates to try and smite him. Since Dellis, everything had changed. He had a home, a wife. That drunken fool holding a gun to his head never could've predicted such undeserved bliss.

There were things he needed to get from the local store for his travels before he went to get Father Squires. Malcolm, the owner, greeted John upon site, the two of them exchanging pleasantries as he looked around for what he needed. When he was finished, they said a cordial goodbye, his sac full of food for Viceroy, more parchment and charcoal pencils, and a new shaving blade.

With swagger in his step, he walked towards the church, throwing his shoulders back, indulging in the feel of contentment for the first time in years as he nodded to the locals that passed by. He was home. And it felt good. The sun was full and bright, a cool breeze abating the sweltering heat, making for a pleasant summer day. A perfect day. Visions of Dellis with a dark-haired babe at her breast wandered pleasantly through his mind, warming his heart, making him smile. It would happen someday. He just knew it. A fanciful thought indeed, and one he'd do his damnedest to see come to fruition sooner than later.

He skipped up the front steps of the church and burst through the doors, confident the truce with God was still in place.

Much to John's chagrin, Gavin was sitting at the end of a wooden pew, looking stolid and prim, while he examined his nails.

"Surely God is outraged to have two sinners such as us in his house." John quipped, walking up to his brother. "What did this poor church ever do to earn the presence of such miscreants?"

"Don't patronize me, John; it's you who specializes in cardinal sins. That alone should've had you cast out upon entry, if God was actually vigilant." Gavin stood, doing a worthy job of looking down his nose, though he was only an inch taller.

"Tell me, brother, what's brought on this sudden need for spiritual nourishment? Surely, it's not to provoke me, for your efforts are wasted."

John volleyed the taunt back into Gavin's court, the next verbal jab was his to take.

"I heard you're marrying the McKesson woman today. Does she know what she's signing herself up for: a life of poverty with a debtor and notorious philanderer who's bound for prison?"

John shook his head, holding back a laugh. That was Gavin, smug with a side of condescension; he never changed, not one bit.

"But there's still hope for her. I understand your friend, Mrs. Allen, has a secret or two to share."

"I'd be careful of that one if I were you," John said under his breath, trying not to cause a scene in a house of God by bringing up Lilith.

"Women are your weakness, John." Gavin smiled. "But Miss McKesson is different. She's special to you, and if she does, in fact, become your wife, everything that is hers will be yours. Actually, you're already as good as married, living together as you do."

"Leave her out of this, Gavin." John knew exactly where his brother was going with that statement. "Dellis has been through enough."

"I'm sure I could wring fifteen hundred pounds out of that tavern of hers. She may even have to give it up if you can't pay. What say you, John?"

John closed his eyes, trying not to think about the repercussions of such an act. Dellis had lost far too much because of him. "Celeste has my money; take it from her."

"Oh no." Gavin shook his head. "This is your mess, brother, not mine, and I'll get my money back, one way or the other."

After what happened the day before, John couldn't bear the thought of facing Celeste again, no matter how badly he needed the money. "Leave Dellis alone. I'll get the money for you." Putting a hand to his forehead, he rubbed his brow, trying to ease the ache behind his eyes. "Just give me time."

"Finally, you realize who has the upper hand here." Gavin boasted. "I leave for Albany tomorrow. Either you have it then, or we duel; you choose, brother. Send word to me before the evening is out. And there will be no seconds, just you and me, and one of us doesn't walk away."

"Are you sure you want to do this?" John asked, cocking a brow, seeing advantage in his adversity, a chance to pluck at his brother's pride. "There's only one thing I do better than firing a pistol, and we both know your former wife could speak on behalf of that."

"I'm not joking, John. I'd enjoy putting a bullet in you." Gavin turned and started for the door. Over his shoulder, he said, "Don't try me."

John watched his brother walk out of the church, smug and full of self-righteous indignation as if he were holding all the cards and about to double his money.

Damn.

"Captain, are you ready?"

When John turned around, he found the priest waiting in his dark habit and white collar with a Bible in hand.

"Yes." John nodded.

Once again, reality peeked its nosy self into his perfect world through Gavin and snatched John's happiness away. Had he been selfish wanting one pure, untainted day? Was he not entitled to just one? No. He'd not allow it! First, he'd marry Dellis and give her the wedding night she deserved, and then, the world could come crashing down around him. The Devil take it all.

Together, Agnes and Dellis rolled the dough for biscuits and cut them out with metal rings, prepping for the breakfast crowd. They worked in unison, side by side, like she and her mother used to, slicing up potatoes and sausage for the morning hash and then kneading bread dough on the flour-covered countertop. When the oats were simmering in a cast-iron pot over the fire and the bread was in the oven, Agnes gave Dellis an elbow. "You need to get dressed. You only have two hours."

Looking at the clock, she let out a gasp of delight. *It's time!* Together, they ran up the stairs to her room, both of them prattling on with excitement like two birds chirping on a tree branch. She stripped down and pulled on a brand-new pair of baleen stays over her favorite gauzy shift, the one John gave her when they were in Oswego.

Agnes pulled the strings tight while Dellis watched in the mirror, admiring how the new shape accentuated her narrow hips but displayed her large bosom to her advantage. A grin tugged at her lips as she remembered John nimbly tying up her stays a few days before, raining kisses down on her neck as his hand occasionally found their way to her breasts between working the strings. Somehow, he managed to tighten her stays just right before he tore them off again and they made love in a pile of her undergarments.

With a snicker, she leaned over and pulled her silky white stockings up to her thighs, tying the maroon ribbons in a bow to hold them in place. Grabbing the wool-stuffed bum roll off the bed, Agnes tied it at Dellis's waist and then adjusted the quilted maroon petticoat overtop. They used a couple of tapes to draw up the skirt in the polonaise fashion, making it look full and puffy in the back. The last thing she put on was the deep-maroon gown, which fastened together in the front, end meeting end perfectly, synching together, giving the bodice a smooth, flat appearance. At her elbows hung some beautiful, delicate, white lace, the finishing touch to the dress, giving it a polished, elegant look. With excitement, Dellis slid her feet into the gorgeous, maroon brocaded shoes, the one-and-a-half inch heels making her feel tall, unlike the flat leather ones she wore daily.

Agnes pulled Dellis's dark, silky tresses off her neck so she could tie the garnet choker in place. "Have you thought how you want your hair?"

She grinned; the dress fit her perfectly, no longer tight in the waist or the bodice. The last time she'd worn it, she'd just lost their son and was still carrying a bit more weight. "What do you think?"

Agnes started to play, twirling the silky strands up into different styles. "I think it's best if you keep it simple."

Dellis agreed. "I defer to your wisdom and expertise."

"Hmm." Agnes looked in the mirror, tilting her head side to side. "I have an idea."

An hour later, Dellis was dressed and ready. Looking at her reflection, she let out a giggle; it was perfect: the dress, her hair, everything, perfect. Agnes had arranged Dellis's hair so it was twisted up to one side of her face and then hung down in large, fat, glossy curls. The last things she did were to use some of the black kohl she bought in Niagara to line her eyes and daub a bit of red on her lips.

"Miss, there's a woman downstairs for you," Will said from behind, standing just inside the doorway, admiring the show with a twinkle in his eyes.

Dellis turned around and smiled. The boy was actually being helpful and kind, taking care of the patrons as she prepared. A pleasant change for her perfect day. "Who is it?"

"She didn't say, but she has some flowers for you."

Dellis shrugged, looking back at Agnes and grinning. Maybe it was a surprise from John? "Tell her to meet me in the parlor."

"Oh, Agnes." Dellis hugged her dear friend. "Thank goodness I have you here. I wish you could've been with us at the village. It was just as beautiful."

"And it will be today! I'm so happy for both of you."

After giving her hand a squeeze, Dellis carefully navigated her large skirts down the narrow servants' staircase. Her heels clicked on the wood steps, the added height making her have to stoop even more to clear the low ceiling.

When she reached the bottom of the stairs, she was too excited to go slow, rushing into her father's parlor, ready for her surprise. "Whatever you've planned for me, John, I know I can't—"

But it wasn't the surprise she anticipated.

Mrs. Allen was waiting, wearing a decadent, navy-blue gown, looking elegant and prim, a spray of colorful wildflowers in hand.

Dellis stopped dead in her tracks, like hitting a brick wall suddenly. "Your timing is impeccable, as usual. I'm beginning to think it's premediated. What can I do for you, Mrs. Allen?"

Celeste flashed a grin and handed Dellis the bouquet. "I understand congratulations are in order."

Dellis took the bouquet and discarded it on the table, unwanted. Surely flowers from Lilith were tainted with bad energy.

Mrs. Allen looked around, her pert nose wrinkling in disapproval as she eyed the parlor. "But where's the groom? Where's John?"

What game is she playing? Any moment, the devious scheme hidden up her sleeve to spoil the day would reveal itself in all its crowning glory.

Dellis was ready, refusing to give an inch to the malevolent, black-hearted woman. "He's getting the priest. Now, if you'll excuse me, I have to finish getting ready."

Just as Dellis turned to leave, Celeste put a hand over her mouth and let out a pretty excuse for a gag. "Forgive me. I haven't been feeling well, morning sickness. I know you understand."

No, she didn't! Dellis turned back around, rolling her eyes. "Try some ginger root; it'll help."

"That's kind of you." Celeste smiled, her hazel eyes twinkling mischievously. "But, you see, part of the reason I feel so under the weather is because of guilt."

"Really, guilt?" Dellis had to stifle a laugh. "I'm not a priest, and I don't think there are enough Hail Marys to cleanse you of sin, but you're welcome to use our priest for confession after we say our vows."

"How unkind of you." Celeste clutched an imaginary string of pearls at her neck with outrage.

Dellis rolled her eyes again at the woman's overdramatic gesture.

"I'm trying to help. I couldn't live with myself knowing you married John under false pretenses."

A laugh burst from Dellis's lips, forcing her to put a hand over her mouth to stifle the impending gales that threatened. "Oh, please, no more lies, Mrs. Allen. But really, this performance of yours is enough to bring down the house. Surely you're playing to the second balcony."

"But it's true." Celeste rubbed her stomach, exaggerating each stroke as if her belly were enormous, though it was barely noticeable through the layers of satiny fabric. "When you ran away from John, he was angry and distraught. And you and I both know that frustration and longing can often send a man into the arms of another woman."

The nerve of her, insinuating such things, but it was all for naught; Dellis didn't believe a word. She shook her head with incredulity. "Careful, your evil's showing." She pointed to the hem of Celeste's skirt, and the woman actually glanced down to check, to Dellis's utter delight. "John would never take comfort from you."

"On the contrary, he thought you left him. Why, you disappeared like a puff of smoke. *Poof!*" Celeste fanned her fingers out in the air, acting out the picture she painted with wide-eyed innocence, but then her lips turned up into a malevolent grin. "You forget, John was mine first, and he always comes back to me because I can fulfill his needs."

Dellis's heart raced, a pit forming in her stomach. *Is there truth in Mrs. Allen's words?* No matter how she wanted to deny it, a miasma of doubt infected her steely confidence, damaging her faith in her beloved.

But nothing could've prepared her for what Celeste said next, thoroughly ruining Dellis's world and her beautiful dreams of the future.

"See, I find myself enceinte, but the problem is, when I told John, he dismissed me. Well, I couldn't live with myself if he married you without confessing the truth. You know how he conveniently forgets these little details."

The wind rushed from Dellis's lungs as if she'd just taken a fist to the gut. Somehow, she managed to rally, but painfully so. "You're a twisted, evil woman, and you'd do or say anything to hurt me and John. I know it was you that provoked Roger DeLancie to attack me, and I know whatever you made John do, it was out of force."

"Me, a woman, force John into lovemaking?" Celeste shook her head, the condescending *tsk, tsk* noises she made further stoking Dellis's rage. "The fault is your own, Miss McKesson. You practically pushed him into my arms by leaving him like you did, and John has a rather voracious appetite when it comes to women. Besides, he's never been one for the pristine, virginal type. Though from what I understand, you're far from... Shall we say, chaste?"

The tirade that threatened broke loose, and Dellis unleashed the inner hellion in all her rage-filled glory. "Coming from a woman with your reputation, that might actually be a compliment. Now, get out of my house!"

Her shout drew Simon and Agnes from the kitchen, both standing in the parlor door, awestruck.

"Get out!"

"Agnes." Celeste smiled, her gaze shifting back and forth between Dellis and the maid. "So good of you to find my missing slave."

"I don't work for you anymore." Agnes hissed through clenched teeth. "Now, you best be getting out of here; this is a tavern, and we don't want the patrons thinking we have a vermin problem."

Celeste smoothed out her dress and offered up a crisp curtsey. "Good day, Miss McKesson. But do yourself a favor; ask John about my meeting with him the other morning. Ask him. I'm not surprised he didn't tell you about it himself."

Dellis turned her back on Celeste and her ugly, hateful words, but it was too late to shut out the revelation of John's betrayal—Lilith's sting striking Dellis's heart with pinpoint accuracy.

"Out!" Agnes yelled, grabbing Celeste's forearm, yanking her from the parlor, and pushing her into the hall.

Dellis clenched her fists at her sides, keeping her back turned until Mrs. Allen was out of hitting distance, fearing what might happen if she came in range. The room was stifling hot under layers of constraining fabric and silk taffeta. Dellis put her hand on the wall, trying to steady herself, to slow her rapid decent, but the rug had been pulled out from underneath her—and she was falling. Fast.

Then she heard it, that beloved voice calling her name like an angel's song.

"Dellis, my love?"

When she turned around, John was waiting for her in his beautiful, elegantly-tailored, navy suit, with his arms outstretched, beckoning her to come to him. He looked incredible. His hair was pulled back tightly, accentuating his tanned, handsome face and high cheekbones with a smile that lit up his eyes, making them look brilliant blue.

She was speechless, unable to find words or form coherent thought, and then suddenly, the color red flashed before her eyes. Navy suit. Navy! His suit was made of the same damned fabric that was used to make Celeste's dress, the color and brocaded style matching to perfection.

With a grin, he said, "You look good enough to eat! Are you ready, my love?"

That green-eyed hellion within Dellis was unleashed once again, bringing with it all the fury of a woman scorned. "You bastard!"

Chapter Nine

"A rather impressive house you have, brother. I never imagined a simple country doctor could accomplish so much." James walked up the steps of his brother's new home and into the front parlor. The spacious room was exquisite with blue-and-white damask paper lining the walls, the maple floor shining so brightly, James could almost see his reflection in it. Handsome, mahogany Chippendale furniture decorated the room; a wing-back chair and beautiful matching fire screen sat before the fireplace. A giant, blue, oriental area rug, detailed with sumptuous gold cord, sparkled in the afternoon sunshine, catching his eye. "Or was it my inheritance you and Dane stole that paid for all of this?"

"James, we lost everything because of your actions. It was only recently that Dane has been able to reclaim what belonged to our family."

He looked around, noticing every nook and cranny of the front parlor, down to the Chinese porcelain dishes on the table and the crystal decanter full of fine sherry. "And you seem to be reaping the benefits. I assume Dane lives at McKesson House then?"

Stephen nodded. "It's time we put an end to this. We're brothers, and mistakes were made on both sides. Can't we start over, forgive each other?"

James laughed. "So self-righteous, yet you live the life of a king, and I'm reduced to squalor in a one-room cabin. Do you feel no guilt in the part you played?"

"*Brother, I'm more than willing to give you some of my inheritance, all of it, if we could make this family whole again.*"

With a shake of his head, he replied, "That won't do, Stephen. I'm no charity case, especially when it's my own money you're bestowing on me."

"*James, you went against our King. I can't undo what's already been done. This house was a gift from Dane, but I'd give it to you if we could be brothers again.*"

He chuckled, though his heart ached, as if their betrayal had been fresh and not fourteen years prior. No, there would be no forgiveness. "I'll see your precious Thistle burned to the ground before I grovel at your feet, Stephen."

Suddenly, he heard a cry, and Lily walked out of the hall carrying a little dark-haired girl, her eyes red and puffy, tears streaming down her cheeks. As they got closer, he noticed, hidden in his sister-in-law's skirts, a dark-haired boy with huge blue eyes staring up, his two fingers, wet and sticky, stuffed in his mouth.

"*Oh, sweet Dellis, don't cry." Stephen cooed, taking the little girl, holding her in his arms, trying to soothe her. "Brother, have you nothing to say to your niece or Alexei?*"

James shook his head, looking down in disgust at the pathetic, sickly excuse for a child; the boy scooted further into his aunt's skirt trying to hide. The last thing James needed was a weakling for a son. Russians were known for their resilience and strength, yet Helena had born one son who died of measles and another with weak lungs. But Dellis, a half-savage, half-Scot girl, was strong with a loud, lusty cry that matched the whooping calls of her native ancestors.

"*James, what happened to Jamie wasn't Alexei's fault; all the little ones were sick, Dellis included.*"

"*And Alexei got it from those damned savages you care so much about. It almost cost me my wife; Helena barely survived. He's just as responsible as those vermin." James leveled his eyes on his son, pointing at him. "You look well enough, boy; time for you to come home and start learning your place.*"

"*No!" Alexei yelled, running back to the kitchen, his little breeches falling down to his knees on the way.*

Dellis started to howl again, her black eyes fixed on James as if she could read his mind. As if she knew how he despised his son… and her.

How dare Dellis talk back to me? Just like when she was young, her defiant, black eyes and that loud, lusty voice were wailing in anger. After all James had done to protect her and her brother, yet she still disrespected him.

Throwing the door open, James stalked into The Silver Kettle, the fetor of burned food and sweaty, unkempt bodies wafting into his nose. The staggering warmth inside the tavern accentuated the foul stench, making him want to gag. How the business stayed open and actually attracted clients was confounding.

James walked up to the bar, trying to avoid the ruckus taking place at the tables.

Multiple games of dice were being thrown while a pile of money sat in the middle of the long table, as two men stood, nose to nose, posturing over it.

"What can I get for you, sir?" Jussie asked, mopping the countertop with an old, dirty rag.

"Is the owner here? I have whiskey to sell, and I'm looking for a buyer."

"Why don't you talk to your niece over at The Thistle?" Jussie shot back smartly, putting a hand on her hip.

James shook his head. "That's none of your affair. Just get the owner."

She flashed him a knowing grin and then slid a tankard of ale across the smooth wooden bar top. He grabbed it and took a quick sip.

"My father's in Albany. I'm running the tavern for now. How much whiskey do you have?"

"About four hogsheads of…" James stopped and glanced over his shoulder, eyeing Stuart and Ruslan sitting amongst the group chatting. "Excuse me for a moment."

Leaving the ale at the bar, James walked over to the table and grabbed his younger son's collar, pulling him up from the bench. "What are you doing here? You should be at home, bailing hay."

Ruslan panicked, mumbling a barrage of "ums" and "ahhs" before he finally got the words out. "We're here with the militia boys. We finished drills, and now were having a drink."

"Where's Alexei?"

Ruslan shook his head. "Don't know. I haven't seen him in days."

Stuart turned around and lifted his glass in salute to his uncle. "Have a drink with us. Ruslan and I are just having some fun until it's time to get the Redcoat. We're going to make him ride the rail, or tar and feather him. Not sure which." Stuart chugged his drink with gusto, a trail of liquid dripping down the front of his shirt. When his tankard was empty, he slammed it down on the table and offered up a cheeky grin. "Or maybe we'll have the bastard do both."

"What Redcoat?" James asked.

Before Ruslan could respond, Stuart interjected. "John Carlisle. It's because of him Dellis won't let me come home. But we're gonna take care of him. Promise."

James clucked his tongue. *So the boys and the militia are going to go after Carlisle?* Rather convenient. Poking his son in the shoulder, James said, "Ruslan, keep me informed."

His son nodded. "Yes, sir."

Suddenly, all the clamor at the tables ceased, the men focusing their attention on the woman descending the staircase like a queen into court. It was Mrs. Allen, and she spotted James immediately, her face lighting up as she gently glided over to him, turning every envious man's head in the room.

"Well, Mr. McKesson, it's a pleasure to see you again."

She was terribly overdressed for the locale, purposely making a spectacle of herself in the backwater bar. It was the attention she craved. And though she was attractive, and her clothing was expensive, she looked gaudy. The navy dress she wore was too dark for her complexion, her hair was beyond ridiculous with the newly fashionable high roll, and there was too much color on her cheeks. She looked like the painted whores he remembered from the French court.

"Mrs. Allen." He nodded to her, taking her hand and kissing it.

"Mr. McKesson, always a pleasure." He noticed a little sparkle in her eyes, her lips curving into a smile.

"I understand the gentlemen have discovered two Redcoats staying at your niece's tavern. I hate to say, but it does make her look like a Loyalist. And we know the locals aren't particularly fond of Tories. If I were you, I might be concerned for her safety."

Jussie brought Stuart and Ruslan another drink, her voice rising above the noise. "That Redcoat bribed my patrons to frequent his Tory whore's bar. He was spying on all of us. But we know what to do with him!" She turned to the crowd and pumped the air with her fist. "Right?"

"Yeah!" the crowd yelled.

James grinned. Celeste was ingenious, devious, and useful—if he could keep her at arm's length. "You did this, didn't you?"

Her eyes widened innocently, though the smirk on her lips suggested otherwise. "The conversation had already been started by your nephew and his friend here. I just further supported what they already knew."

James tugged on Stuart's collar, getting his attention. "When are you planning on doing this?"

Stuart shrugged. "Maybe later, when it's dark, so he can't get away. I know my sister will try to protect her lover, but we'll catch him."

Celeste gestured to the young man. "It was I who suggested they wait 'til dark. John's notoriously good at getting away, and I suspect he'll be rather occupied this evening and unsuspecting. After they're done softening him up, you can do what you want with him."

"Mrs. Allen, I didn't give you enough credit."

With a shake of her head, one glossy curl dropped over her shoulder, resting against her breast. He allowed himself one peek at her ample bosom, of which she noticed instantly.

"Now you're willing to take me seriously," she said suggestively, cocking a brow.

Misery acquainted a man with strange bedfellows indeed.

"Let's see how this plays out."

Grinning, she said, "Well, then take a seat, act two is bound to be just as entertaining."

"Dellis, my love, are you ready?" John raced through the dining room with excitement, ignoring the curious glances of the onlooking patrons. "Come, she's in back." He gestured for Father Squires to follow, rushing through the bar into the kitchen and then into the yellow parlor.

When Dellis turned around, his breath caught in his throat. She looked stunning; the maroon gown he'd bought her in Oswego made her ivory skin look luminous, and her dark hair hung over her left shoulder in large, silky curls that caught glints of sunlight peeking through the windows. When she looked up, her eyes were wide, confused, and then they narrowed, focusing on him—with rage? *No, it can't be.*

"You look good enough to eat," he said, grinning suggestively. He was suddenly famished for her. Perhaps they'd skip dinner after their nuptials and head right for their bed. The thought of removing every layer of that dress, piece by piece, and tasting every inch of her, was foremost on his mind.

"Are you ready, my love?"

"You bastard!" She ran at him, her fists pounding into his breast with such force his heart skipped a beat. "How could you!" Her dark eyes were red and bloodshot, tears brimming her lids; she pulled back her hand and took a swipe at him, like a feral cat in the woods, catching him across the cheek with her nails, leaving bloody track marks.

"Dellis, what's wrong?" He reached for her hand, but she yanked it away forcefully and then turned to their guests, her words coming out between labored breaths.

"Father Squires, you may leave; we won't need you today."

"My love, what are you doing?" John's eyes narrowed with abject confusion. "I don't understand."

"Agnes, Simon, please, leave us and close the door." When both hesitated, she practically growled. "Now!"

Stunned silent, he waited until the door clicked shut, and they were finally alone, to speak, and then he did so cautiously. "Dellis, tell me what happened? I want to know."

She turned back to him, her head bowed as if she couldn't bear to look at him. "How could you, damn it?" She choked out, and then repeated it, each time pounding her fists into his chest until her words became a heart-wrenching howl, and he could no longer draw in breath. "How. Could. You."

She knew. Somehow, she knew. But there were no words, only unadulterated fear.

"Say something, you bastard! Say something!"

But he couldn't; his heart stuck in his throat, holding the words captive. How did one confess such a betrayal—on their wedding day, nonetheless.

"Fine!" When she started to walk away, he yanked her into his arms, burying his face in the silky curls at her nape. She smelled like an English garden, with hints of lavender and vanilla, and she felt like Heaven, with the fine silky fabric and her soft hair caressing his cheek. *God, how I love her.* "Dellis, I'm sorry. I didn't have a choice."

She tore at his arms, digging her nails in, leaving more bloody tracks that stung, but he refused to let go, desperation giving him the strength to endure.

"You're a liar. Don't you dare tell me you didn't have a choice."

"Dellis, you ran away. I couldn't bear the thought of DeLancie hurting you again. Celeste was the only one who knew where he was."

Her eyes grew impossibly large with outrage. "So you made love to her? Forgive me, but I find fault with your twisted logic." She elbowed him in the stomach, breaking free from his grasp and rushing to the door, but he caught her before she could get away, hauling her up against the wall, pinning her back to it with his body.

"Dellis, you must listen to me." He begged.

She fought to get away, twisting and pushing at him, but he held fast, desperate to hold onto their perfect world if only for a moment longer. "Dellis, please. When you disappeared that night, I searched everywhere for you. Agnes remembered seeing Celeste with Roger DeLancie; that's why I went her. I was desperate to find you."

"And that's when you put your cock in her, right? The temptation was that great. I know I lack her skills, but you could've waited longer than a day!"

The pure venom spewing from her lips gave him pause, the wind knocked from his lungs, and only breathless, painful words would come out. "Is that what you believe? After all I've done to prove myself?" He released her, feeling suddenly defeated. "Have you no respect for me or my love for you?"

"She's with child, John!" Dellis yelled in his face, her eyes boring a hole through his.

"It's not mine." He shook his head. "I don't believe her. Celeste would say anything to hurt us."

Dellis lifted her chin defiantly, her words taking a stab at his heart. "It doesn't matter what you believe, because I do."

No! He had to make her understand. It didn't happen like that. It wasn't making love or an act of passion; it was desperation, pure and simple.

"Dellis, I interrupted it. I didn't give her my—" Her hand connecting with his left cheek stopped him midsentence, and then, like rapid fire, her palm kissed the other cheek with a loud *smack*! Back-to-back hits sent his face whipping in both directions.

"Dellis." He pushed through the pain and tried again, but she interrupted him with more words full of vitriol.

"Don't you dare tell me the details of your sordid affairs. If I remember correctly, you weren't too overly cautious with me, either. Perhaps she's just the first of your many jilted lovers to turn up with one of your bastards. Better I know now."

His ego smarted, the truth tearing at his very core, cutting him deeply. It wasn't that simple nor that sordid. She gave him too much credit.

"You know that's not true, my love," John fired back. "I admit I haven't always been careful, but I swear the child's not mine."

"Liar!" She slapped him again, landing her palm against his right cheek, his teeth jarring together painfully.

John winced, his tongue starting to bleed from biting it. "Do you feel better now that you've hit me? Is the frontal attack over? Now will you listen to what I have to say?" No good would come from their angry rants; he needed to regain some semblance of control on the situation, and then they could talk like adults.

"Save your attempt at condescension; you're not the voice of reason." She snickered, though her beautiful dark eyes were red rimmed and full of pain. "And don't act like you're the wounded party, John—*you* did this to us. You were going to marry me without telling me the truth. Again!"

"How could I tell you that after what happened to our baby?" When she turned her back on him, he raised his voice, trying to breach her impenetrable wall of anger and find that sweet, loving woman he knew was locked inside, imploring her with the painful truth. "Answer me. You underestimate how the loss of our child affected me. I was suffering, too."

"From a guilty conscience," she muttered under her breath then reached for the door handle.

"My love, I didn't know how to tell you. We were both hurt"—he paused and corrected himself— "still hurting." But she said nothing, leaving him stunned by her frosty demeanor, a totally uncharacteristic side of her never before revealed. Yes, she'd been angry with him, she'd even been reticent, but deliberately cold—never. "I don't know what else to say."

"I don't want to hear any more of your excuses. Just leave, now." With that, she whipped the door open and raced out of the parlor, starting down the hall.

Fear gripped his heart; the farther she got away from him, the more distant their blissful future became. "No, Dellis, no!" he yelled, chasing her to the servants' staircase.

She slipped through the door quickly, slamming it shut and then bolting it. Panicking, John ran though the kitchen, the dining room, and up the front stairs only to see her slam their bedroom door, the bolt clicking as it locked in place.

"No!" Pounding his fist on the door, John yelled into it. "Dellis, you're acting like a child. You owe me a chance to explain. Please, let's just talk this out."

But he was met with silence, the wooden door her forbidding surrogate; turning his back to it, he slid down until he was sitting on the floor. "If you love me, you'll listen," he yelled, resting his head on the wood. "Please."

Still no response.

No, dammit. No!

John banged the back of his head against the door several times, anxiety fueled with adrenaline driving him to desperate measures. *Bang. Bang. Bang!* He felt no pain as his head bounced off the wood, the knife stabbing at his heart circumventing all other sensations.

"Dellis, yes, it was wrong of me to not take precaution the first time we made love; I admit that. I was selfish and caught up in the moment, but I swear to you, I have no children save the two we made together. Please, open the door and let me explain."

There was so much he needed to make her understand. He felt like a caged animal, ready to tear off his own skin if she didn't relent. He turned and pounded his fist against the door, once, twice, three times; with each hit, the stress slowly dissipated into the wood. The door jarred in its frame in protest, but still never opened.

He buried his face in his palms, hopelessly. "Dellis, please?"

But still, irrevocable silence.

On and on it went. The minutes passed like hours, and her solitude continued, no words, not even weeping, could be heard through the door. Still, he remained steadfast in his faith in her—she'd open the door. *She loves me.* Both of them were stubborn, passionate people, prone to temper flares; they'd fight it out, and then they'd make love one last time before he left. *That's how it will go.* Yes, she could be feisty, even truculent when provoked, but there was no way she'd let him leave to go to war without making it right.

Yet the clock ticked relentlessly, seven o'clock, then eight, but the door never opened.

When the sun finally set, reality reared its ugly head, and John could wait no longer to deal with the issue of his brother and their impending duel. He got up and walked across the hall, penning a letter to Gavin and sealing it. The thought of Dellis having to sacrifice her house because of John's mistakes was too much to bear on top of everything else. No, *that* he could make right.

Upon hearing heels clicking on the wood floor, John glanced up from his letter; it was Will, his round, cherubic face looking somber. "Captain, what about the wedding? We're all still waiting."

John shook his head with defeat. "There'll be no wedding. I need you to take this to Lord Gavin Carlisle at The Silver Kettle; you're to wait for his response."

"Yes, sir," the boy said, nodding.

When Will was gone, John opened the letter on his desk. It was from Butler, also encoded using Blackstone's *Commentaries on the Laws of England 5th Oxford Edition*. John pulled his volume from the desk drawer and did a quick translation.

You're to proceed with haste to Fort Niagara. I'm preparing a meeting for Irondequoit Bay on July 16th and after at Oswego with the Six Nations. You're to assist me with negotiations and act as an interpreter. I assume that you secured Lord Tomlinson's wife and the significant dowry and supplies she carries with her. They will be needed for our negotiations with the natives.

Folding the letter, John dropped it on the desk and walked back across the hall, taking up his lonely vigil once again.

"My love, I have to leave soon," he said quietly, resting his forehead on the door, imagining her in the same position on the other side. "I don't know when I'll be back. Please, talk to me. I can't bear leaving you this way. You don't have to forgive me. I just need you to listen."

He stared the door down, willing it open with all of his might, never hearing Agnes when she came up the stairs and approached him. Only when she put her hand on his shoulder and patted it gently did he look up.

"Captain, you need to get some rest. You have to leave early."

He shook his head; there was no way he'd go to bed, not when there was still a chance Dellis might relinquish her sanctuary.

"She'll open the door, I know it. She just needs time." His voice sounded brittle and strained from fighting against tears that burned his eyes and stung his throat.

Agnes sat down next to him and held his hand, neither speaking a word, but the incessant quietude must have worn on her, too, for she got up and started down the hall. "I'll be in my room if you need me."

He nodded, too overcome to speak. When the door to Agnes's room shut, the hall fell into silence again—painful, unyielding silence, and hopelessness where once there was love.

An hour later, Will returned, letter in hand. "He'll meet you at dawn, just outside of town, on the north side of the river."

John reached into his pocket, pulled out two pence, and handed them to the boy. "Thank you."

"I'm sorry, sir," Will said quietly and then excused himself.

John waited the rest of the night, sketching little pictures, trying to pass the time until the placidity of darkness finally ended with the crow of a rooster. It was time. What was supposed to be the best day of his life had turned into nothing short of a nightmare come true. And now he was off to duel his brother. Karma had thrust out her palm, demanding payment of all John held dear.

Quickly, he packed his belongings and then penned his last words to Dellis. There was so much he wanted to say yet couldn't; his feelings didn't belong on paper, etched in black, unforgiving ink, but delivered from his lips directly to his lover's ears. But that time had passed. He sealed the letter with wax and affixed his stamp, placing it on the desk where she'd see it. Reaching into the top drawer, he pulled out the wampum necklace that belonged to Dellis's father and tied it on, stuffing it under the collar next to Kateri's cross.

Walking across the hall, John rested his hand on the door, praying one last time that Dellis would relent with just a kind word or a glimpse of her beautiful, dark eyes around the edge of the door.

"I'm leaving, my love." But still, he was met with silence as cold and forbidding as the wood door between them. His heart sank into the bottomless pit of pain that gripped his soul, broken and bereft of her love. "Goodbye, my Fennishyo," he whispered, before he walked away.

So this is surrender? Once again, Karma had sunk her claws in deeply, and Justice slammed the door in his face.

Chapter Ten

Dellis woke the next morning to the twittering of birds, the morning sun just barely peeking through her windows. Her body ached from lying on the wood floor; the door, her stalwart support, was pressed up against her back. As she pushed herself up, she found John's picture on the floor beneath her, his brilliant eyes staring back at her, that boyish grin tugging at her heartstrings.

He was gone; she didn't need to open the door to know it was true. The pounding had ceased, no shouts or pleas to further shut out, but what remained was a hole in her heart and gut-wrenching loneliness. She could still hear his voice carrying through the wood, full of anger and sadness. *"If you love me, you'll listen."*

She'd wanted to yell back, but no words came out, only strangled yelps from deep within her soul, and tears, lots of them. *Could it be true? He had no choice?* No, it didn't make sense. How could a woman force him to do such a thing? The facts just didn't add up. He was just giving her another one of his carefully crafted excuses, more subterfuge to keep her believing.

She closed her eyes, running a hand over her empty womb again. The thought of that diabolical woman giving John what Dellis couldn't was too much to bear.

"She'll open the door. She just needs time."

Such devotion; he had so much faith in her. Yes, it was wrong to slam the door in his face, rage and jealousy getting the better of her, but the thought of another woman touching him, loving him, drove Dellis to madness. She just couldn't look at him and not see that malevolent woman making love to him, kissing him. *John—my John.*

Dellis folded the picture and pushed herself up slowly, ignoring the protesting cracks and pops of her back, and on heavy limbs, she walked across the hall. His belongings had been cleared from the room, and the desk that was once littered with his maps and pens was cleaned. The only thing left was a note, addressed to her, resting against a solitary brass candlestick.

Picking up the letter, she cracked the seal and opened it slowly, unsure of what she'd find in his last words to her. The first paper was a sketch of him, sitting profile with his back to the door, his knee drawn up with his hand resting on it. The rendering was so precise, she could see lines of worry etched in his brow and around his mouth, a look of sadness marring his countenance. Underneath was a letter, penned in his beautiful handwriting.

My love,

You need not worry that this letter contains an explanation of my actions. Your reticence has shown me you don't wish to hear what I have to say. But in your silence, you've prevented me from a proper goodbye as I leave for war with no assurance of when I'll return. All I can give you are these written words as a declaration of my love for you. I know you've set your mind against accepting it, but I pray you can't convince your heart to do so.

I wish you safe.

John

Walking back to her room, Dellis changed out of her wedding gown and back into her dark-brown stays and muted-blue petticoat and fixed her hair neatly under a cotton cap. She pinned her apron in place and then tucked her kerchief into her bodice, readying herself for work. The façade of normalcy was back in place. That was how she did it, how she'd always done it. But how would she cope with losing everything again?

God, help me be strong.

When she walked back across the hall, she saw little flickers of light on the horizon through the windows, but it wasn't happy rays of sunshine. Coming up the dirt road towards The Thistle was a crowd of people carrying lanterns and torches, some of them with pikes and pitchforks. As the mob neared, she could hear shouts rising above the rabble.

"Get the Redcoats! Let's tar and feather the bastards!"

"Oh no!" Her heart stunned in her chest and then thrummed with an irregular rhythm of terror. At the head of the pack, carrying a burning torch, was Stuart, and next to him was her cousin, Ruslan.

John.

Dellis raced down the stairs; as she passed through the dining room, a brick flew through the window, throwing glass in every direction, shards of it piercing her cheek. "Simon! John!"

When she reached the kitchen, she found Agnes already up, kneading dough, while Will, elbows deep in hot water, cleaned dishes and hummed a merry tune. They had no idea what was coming, or they wouldn't have looked so calm. "Agnes, where's John and Simon?"

Agnes deposited her dough on a tray and wiped her hands on her apron. "Dellis, my goodness, what's wrong?"

"There's no time to explain." She huffed between labored breaths, pointing to the window. "There's a mob outside. They've come for John and Simon."

The noise from the crowd finally reach the kitchen, another brick flying through the window, landing on the floor with a big *thud* and then cracking into muddy pieces.

"Where are they?" Dellis yelled frantically.

Agnes visibly swallowed, a portent of her fear. "Simon's in the barn. The Captain left already."

"Oh my God! We have to find him!"

"He's meeting someone near the river on the north side of town at dawn," Will said from behind.

"Who's he meeting? Who?" Dellis ran up to the boy and grabbed his shoulders, shaking him vigorously. "How do you know this?"

A rock flew through the kitchen window, hitting Dellis in the back, throwing more glass in every direction.

The boy yelped, a tiny shard cutting his right cheek, a slow trickle of blood starting. "Oh my God! They're going to kill us!"

"They don't want us! We have to help John and Simon," Dellis replied, sounding more confident than she actually was. "Will, tell me what you know."

The boy stammered fearfully, his eyes tracking back and forth, searching for answers, while the shouts of the mob echoed in through the broken window. "Last night, he asked me to take a letter to his brother at The Kettle and wait for a response."

"What did Gavin say?" Panic set in, her worst fears playing out: a meeting at dawn, outside of town, near the river. *Oh God. A duel.*

"Tell me what he said!" Dellis yelled, giving Will another hard shake.

The shouts were getting louder, reverberating through the kitchen, further adding to her fear. The three of them were trapped together in a crucible at the mercy of an angry mob with a taste for blood. It could only go one way if John was found.

"Will, you *must* tell me."

"The Captain was to meet him near the North side of the river, and they wouldn't need seconds."

"Oh, no." She gasped. "I've got to stop them. I've got to warn him."

Simon rushed in the back door, musket in hand. "Dellis, where's John?"

"He's gone to the river to duel his brother. You need to leave now, and we have to figure out a way to convince that mob that you're not here."

He shook his head. "It's not going to work. They'll burn this place down before they stop."

"No!" Not her house. She bit back the fear that threatened to consume her, fighting it with every fiber of her being. Rational thought was the only thing that would see her through. Taking a deep, calming breath, she tried to focus on one thing at a time. "I can reason with Stuart and Ruslan. I'll go talk to them."

"Lass, that's not going to work with an angry mob." Simon stopped her before she could make for the door, his eyes scanning the kitchen. "Do you have any weapons here?"

Dellis nodded. "I have three pistols upstairs"—she looked around the kitchen then grabbed one of the large knives off the counter—"and this."

Clark laughed and took it from her. "Well, let's not hope it comes to that. Get your pistols and meet me down here."

"Simon, what are you going to do?" Agnes asked, digging through the drawers, pulling out every knife, fork, or utensil that could be used as a weapon, even an ugly-looking iron hook. From under the counter, she pulled out a copper pot and a cast-iron pan, putting them both on the table.

"I'm going to ride off towards the river and hope they follow. Dellis, you're the only one besides me who can ride fast enough if they decide to chase. You wait until I leave and then sneak out and find John. Tell him to meet me at sundown on the old military road north of the dock on Wood Creek."

"What about them?" Dellis looked back at Agnes and Will. "The mob will brand them Tories for giving aid to Redcoats."

"Don't worry, he's just a dim-witted boy, and I'm your slave. We don't know nothin' about nothin'," Agnes said with a pronounced accent. She winked at both of them, ready to play whatever part she could—even belittling herself—to help. "With Dellis gone, and you and the Captain nowhere to be found, it'll look like you abandoned us."

Dellis's heart swelled with love for her dear friend. "Agnes, I can't leave you like this. If anything happened to you or Will, I'd never forgive myself."

Simon nodded at Agnes, their eyes meeting tenderly, a silent understanding passing between them. "Lass, she can handle this. We need to go now. I'll ride by the front of the tavern and draw the riders away; you find John."

Dellis watched as Simon kissed Agnes, his fair skin a stark, yet beautiful, contrast against her ebony cheek as they embraced one last time. How devastating for the two lovers to have to part that way.

Dellis ran up the servants' staircase, grabbed the three pistols she kept hidden upstairs, checked that they were loaded, and then rushed back to the kitchen.

Agnes took the knife from Simon and grabbed the frying pan from the kitchen table. She cocked a brow and turned to Will. "I'm not going out there alone. You best be taking something, because you're coming, too."

The young boy's eyes widened, but he nodded and picked up an iron poker from the hearth and a pot. "I'm with you."

Dellis's eyes teared up. *How can I leave them alone to face that mob?*

"Don't start crying, Dellis. We don't have time for blubbering." Agnes chided.

Dellis hugged both of them quickly and then nodded to Simon. He took one last look at Agnes and ran out the back door towards the stable.

"Don't you worry about us; just find the Captain." Agnes started through the bar into the dining room, Will following behind; both of them armed and ready. From Dellis's vantage point, she could see Agnes bravely facing the crowd from the front porch, her voice rising above the noise.

"There ain't no Redcoats here. Just me and da boy, and we both servants here. You best be leavin'."

Stuart ran up the staircase, shaking his torch at Agnes. "I know he's here. I saw him yesterday with my sister. I'll burn this house down around you before I leave."

Agnes pushed him back, holding her knife up to his face. "They ain't here, and if you set fire to this house, you'll be burning nothing but two servants and your papa's dream. Don't do it, Stuart."

Dellis took several gulps of air, watching as her brother looked through the windows, searching for John and Clark. Suddenly, she heard the *clomp, clomping* of horses' hooves pounding on the dirt as Simon raced past the crowd towards the woods.

"There they go!" one of the men yelled.

The riders took off after Clark like hellhounds in pursuit of the righteous.

It was her moment; no time to stay and watch. Sprinting to the stable, Dellis saddled and mounted her mare, kicking her into a sprint, throwing up a cloud of dust in her wake.

It wasn't the first time she'd made that ride—history in repetition; another day, another life, repeating itself with startling accuracy. Visions of her father lying in the dirt flashed before her eyes, and her arms ached, cold and heavy, with the remembrance of his dead weight. No, she refused to lose another person she loved to ten paces and a bullet.

Honor be damned, and John, too, if I get my hands on him.

She looked over her shoulder several times, but thankfully, no one was following her. *God be with Simon!* If they caught him, they'd surly lynch him. Poor Agnes and Will; Dellis's heart ached for them, facing the crowd alone. She said a silent prayer for her friends and her house.

The rhythmic clomping of her mare's feet racing across dirt and the sounds of birds singing sweetly was a strange dichotomy to the frenzy of the moment. Dellis rode down the hill to the river basin, pushing her horse as fast as she could when she reached the low, even ground. In the distance, she could see the outline of two men, giant willow trees surrounding them, and lush green grass underfoot framing the scene that was about to play out. She reached for her pistol, and then suddenly, a gun went off with a loud *pop!* The shot echoed in the valley, reverberating in her ears, followed by earth-shattering quiet.

Dellis swallowed. There was no second shot. There. Was. No. Second. Shot.

"Oh, God." She leaned up on the balls of her feet, pushing her mare hard. As the two men came into better focus, Dellis saw a puff of smoke floating in the air, and then one of them fell to the ground.

"John!"

"One!" the brothers yelled in unison, taking their first steps towards an irrevocable conclusion: one of them would die.

John inhaled deeply, trying to slow his racing heart; it was far from his first duel, but he'd never considered facing his own brother at the end of a barrel.

"Two!"

Will Gavin actually pull the trigger? Will he really kill his own brother over money? Yes, he would, and that thought made John's stomach grumble nervously. *How have things gotten this bad?*

"Three!"

Gavin is a terrible shot. His aim is as notoriously lacking as his skill in the bedroom. So John had been told by Isabelle, and Maria, and Josephine, and… *He always pulls to the right, so if I shift to my right a bit, I might actually survive this, but if I hesitate, the ball will strike my breast and puncture a lung. It'll all be over.* To die there, on the field, before he could make up with Dellis, was unthinkable, and even worse, it would be by his brother's hand. No, someone with John's skill as a marksman should go down by a more proficient adversary.

This I can't abide.

"Four!"

Ravens just flew overhead; that's a bad omen in Oneida folklore. What does that mean?

"Five!"

Why wouldn't she listen? Women! It all started because of women. Isabella. Celeste. Dellis. Damn his overzealous cock; it was always getting him into trouble.

"Six!"

I'll miss having Dellis in my arms and the way she screams my name before she comes. He could almost hear the little whimpers she made when he was just pushing inside her. *Incredible.*

"Seven!"

Focus, John, focus. Bullets. Gun. Death. Duel. Think duel.

"Eight!"

Will she miss me? Will she forgive me when I'm in a pine box? Is that what it will take?

"Nine!"

Taking another deep breath, John glanced at the pistol next to his head and pulled it to full cock as his finger gripped the trigger. *Remember to shift to the right when you turn around.*

This is it.

Just as he started to yell, "ten," John heard the echo of a woman's voice carrying on the breeze; a familiar lament calling his name. *Why now? What does it mean?* He closed his eyes, letting her cries fill his ears.

Justice, is this your will, for me to die in petty duel?

"Ten! Present!"

Goodbye, my love. He'd never see Dellis on the other side, for he was surely bound for Hell. "Dellis," he whispered her name, the last word he'd ever speak, and then he whipped around, extending his arm straight up to the sky, but holding his fire.

I will not *shoot my brother.*

Pop! Gavin's gun went off.

Time stopped, everything around John ceased to move, and he froze, suspended in the nihility of space. Smoke puffed from Gavin's pistol as the ball burst from the barrel, moving through the air in slow motion, the seconds ticking by like hours. The woman's song crescendoed, drowning out everything around John, his focus keen on the ball that whizzed towards him, its terminal target. He glanced at his brother, unabashed fury in Gavin's eyes as he held his pistol steady, watching, waiting for the bullet to strike.

Gavin really did it. He pulled the trigger.

A hatred born of youth's jealousy and pride's need for revenge had come to a head: Brother destroying brother, Rebel against Redcoat, Mohawk destroying Oneida, all one in the same, and in it all, John played a part.

As the ball neared, he dodged to the right with just enough time to clear the bullet from his chest, but it lodged in his left upper arm, the force taking him down to the dirt.

"John!"

He heard a familiar, beloved yell and hoofbeats coming from the east.

The pain was like fire moving through his left arm, the blood spattering out, soaking his linen shirt. He grabbed it, trying to stop the bleeding, the searing pain spreading into his shoulder, his fingers tingling all the way to the tips. Taking a long, calming breath, allowing reality to sink in as time started anew—he was alive!

"Damn you!" Gavin yelled, throwing himself on top of John before he got a chance to roll out of the way.

They both fell back in the dirt, John's head smacking the ground, eliciting a groan and stoking his fury. *The bastard is really going to fight this out to the death.* Grabbing Gavin's jacket, John drew his brother down so they were face to face, an inch of crackling space and years of untapped hatred between them.

"Gavin, stop! You took your shot. We're even."

"I'll see you in Hell!" He threw a punch, forcing John to dodge far to the left.

"I'm better at this; are you sure you want a fight?" He was more than willing to serve up some fisticuffs, courtesy of His Majesty's training and years of bar fights, at Gavin's expense. "This is over; you missed."

But Gavin wouldn't relent, slamming John into the ground again, more blood pouring from the wound in his arm.

Tightening his hold on Gavin's lapels, John rolled them over and straddled his brother's waist. The moment was long overdue; it was time to punch the smug off His Lordship's face.

John cocked his fist and landed a blow on Gavin's nose, blood spattering from his nostrils, staining his snowy white cravat. "Gavin, don't make me kill—"

Suddenly, there was the loud *pop* of a gun, and both of them stopped abruptly and looked up.

It was Dellis, looking dangerous and beautiful all at the same time, and like an angry woodland goddess, she threw her pistol to the ground and jumped down from her horse.

"Stop! Both of you!"

With that, she pulled two more pistols from her pockets and aimed at both men, fingering the triggers.

Releasing Gavin, John stood, grabbing his bloody arm. "Dellis, stay out of this."

Gavin took the opportunity to land a well-placed blow on John's nose. The pain, like a hammer, reverberated into his ears, causing his left one to pop as his eyes watered. He could taste the blood pooling on his lips, its metallic flavor all too familiar.

"I've got a bullet here with each of your names on it. Keep it up," she yelled, cocking both guns, the clicking sound echoing in the valley. When Gavin rolled his eyes, Dellis lifted one of the pistols and aimed at his face. "Are you a gambling man? Care to make a wager on my skill?"

John shook his head, warning his brother to back off. Having faced the barrel end of Dellis's pistol twice before, John had no desire to find out if the third time was a charm. Knowing his luck, and the state of their relationship, she'd aim for his balls.

"Dellis, enough!"

"Call your woman off, John. This is between us."

"I'm no man's woman. And right now, you're not endearing yourself to me, brother-in-law." Her black eyes burned with intensity, but there was also challenge hidden in their depths, and he knew better then to cross her in the heat of the moment. Instead, he put his hands up, surrendering the fight.

Satisfied with his submission, she turned to Gavin. "I have two shots here, and from my count, you have nothing to bargain with but your life. You threatened my house and my husband; that hasn't exactly endeared me to you. Care to try me?"

When he finally put his hands up in defeat, John let out an audible sigh of relief.

"I've seen the damage of hatred between brothers firsthand." Her eyes narrowed on John, making him feel like an ill-behaved child. "How could you do this, John? How could you?"

"Dellis, I—"

She waved off his attempt to explain. "We don't have time for more lies or excuses. There's a mob at The Thistle, and they're looking for you and Simon. You've got to get out of here."

"Mob? What do you mean?" His mind was still reeling from the shot to his arm and the realization that his brother came with intent to kill. John clasped the wound tightly, blood oozing down his hand, staining his sleeve.

"You, stay there!" Dellis pointed the gun at Gavin in warning.

She ran to John, reaching under her skirt and ripping a piece of fabric from her shift. The little flash of her shapely calves would normally have sparked a bawdy comment from him, but he held back. It wasn't the time.

Carefully, Dellis examined his arm, her eyes staying noticeably cast down, avoiding any connection with him. "The ball is stuck near the bone. We don't have time for me to take it out. I'll bandage it, but Simon is going to have to care for it as soon as possible.

She tied the linen around his arm, pulling it tight and padding it with the kerchief she pulled from her bodice. "Simon will meet you on the old military road where it enters Wood Creek at sundown."

He could smell her lavender scent, tormenting him and drawing him into her mystical world that he longed to drown himself in. "Dellis, I need to talk to you," he whispered. The prospect of death and the heady sensation of having her near heightening the moment, sending him into a frenzy. "Please." He closed his eyes, breathing her in again. "Please, I beg you."

But she was cold and immobile. "Save it, John. You don't have time, and I don't have the fortitude. A mob is about to destroy my home, and Agnes and Will are alone with no one to defend them."

"Let the mob have him; a bullet is too easy," Gavin yelled, walking towards them.

Dellis held both pistols up, cocking them again, and aiming. "Don't tempt me. You're both in danger. They're looking for Redcoats, but a Tory will do for a drunken, angry mob just as well. I can throw you to the wolves if you like?"

"Agnes, my God." John gasped. He had to do something, Agnes was his dear friend, and she'd been so good to him. He owed her. "I'll go back with you. I'll let them have me." The mess was of his making.

"And ruin everything they sacrificed themselves for? No. You've done enough." Dellis shook her head, her dark eyes finally meeting his with a cold, empty stare. For the first time since they met, he couldn't read her. It was devastating. "Leave now. I'll go back and help."

She turned to Gavin. "I'll lead you to one of our secret roads; you can take it to Albany. You'll be safe there. I'll see that you get your money."

John puffed up. The money was his affair, and he had it in his mind to tell her so, but the angry glare she gave him shut him up in an instant. Instead, he mounted his horse, Viceroy fussing as John adjusted himself in the saddle. His arm burned, the blood oozing from the saturated binding, running down his arm. He was already starting to get lightheaded; at that rate, he wouldn't last long on the road.

Dellis glanced up at him once, giving him a curt nod. "Go, John."

He hesitated, wanting a moment more in her presence. "Dellis?" He could hear the desperation in his own voice.

"Go!" she yelled, unmoved by his plight.

With that, he took off, Viceroy racing down the path towards the forest and farther away from the woman John loved.

Chapter Eleven

Damn John, how could he do this? A duel? He knew what that meant to her. Her temper flared, considering the stupidity of an act that condoned two individuals shooting each other to show who had the bigger stones. *How is that honorable?*

Men.

She rode up to The Thistle, her gut churning in anticipation of what she'd find, but to her surprise, the crowd was gone. Their plan worked; the mob must've followed Simon. *God help him.* She prayed he was able to meet John at dawn so they could both get away safely.

It was eerily quiet though her heart thundered in her ears. She took slow, deliberate steps up the stairs to the front porch; glass littered the wood planks, the two front windows broken and the door busted down, but thankfully, her house was still intact.

"Thank you, Papa," Dellis whispered. There was no doubt in her mind he was watching from Heaven, determined to protect his precious home and her. She walked inside gingerly. The dining room was empty, the tables and chairs knocked over, most of them destroyed like discarded rubbish. Her father's beautiful, blue-and-white china plates and tea set lay broken on the floor near the bar. All her whiskey, including her finest scotch, were gone—stolen by the mob.

Dellis walked into the kitchen, awestruck at the mess she found. "Agnes? Will?"

The kitchen was ransacked; all the dishes had been pulled from the cupboards and lay in a broken heap on the floor; her cooking utensils were gone, nowhere to be found. The cauldron she kept full and bubbling in the hearth was turned over on the floor, the day's stew a brown, wet mess, smoking on the smoldering embers.

"Agnes? Will?" Dellis picked up the pot and hung it on the crane and then poured some water on the hearth.

"Out back!" she heard Agnes yell, the distance making her voice faint.

"Oh, thank God." Dellis raced out the back door and down the steps.

Agnes peeked her head out from the little storage shed and waved Dellis over. "Come quick. I could use your help."

Dellis let out a sigh of relief. *They're safe!*

Inside the little shack, Will sat next to the hearth, weeping; on floor at his feet was a bucket of steaming hot water and a pile of linen. He was covered head to toe in feathers, his hair and clothes plastered to his body from thick, sticky pine tar.

"Oh my." Dellis gasped and then stopped Agnes when she reached for a hot rag. "No hot water; that won't work. Agnes, we need to get some cold water from the well. It's the only way to stop the burning and solidify the tar." Dellis got down on her knees in front of the boy, grasping his hand. "You'll be all right. I promise."

Will trembled, his slight body hunched over, holding himself tightly. "Okay" was all he mustered up between sobs.

Dellis grabbed two buckets off the floor and ran outside to the well, Agnes following.

"Thank God you're safe," Dellis said, drawing the bucket up from the well and filling the two she brought with her. "Tell me what happened."

"Did you get to the Captain in time? Where is he?"

Dellis could hear the desperation in Agnes's voice, and as usual, her first thoughts were of John. Dellis couldn't help but feel resentful—the whole debacle *was* his fault, yet Agnes seemed more worried about him than anyone else, even her beau.

Dellis put her aggression aside and acknowledged that she, too, was grateful for John's safety. "Yes, he's fine. Gavin shot him in the arm, but he's all right. He rode off to the meeting place."

"Thank God!" Agnes's voice was full of relief. "The men on horseback followed Simon, but the rest of the mob ran through the house, searching for the Captain. They destroyed everything downstairs, but thankfully, they didn't do too much damage upstairs, just knocked things over and made a mess. When they couldn't find anyone, they accused us of being Tories. They held me down and grabbed Will." She sniffed, her great brown eyes turning glassy. "The poor boy; they beat him with a crop and then tarred and feathered him and carried him on a rail into town. They tried to put him in the stocks, but luckily, Mr. Armstrong stopped them just in time."

"Patrick?" *Thank God for small favors.* Patrick, being the town magistrate's son, was above reproach; if he said the boy wasn't a Tory, the crowd would surely listen. "Where is he?"

"He helped me carry Will out here, and then he said he'd go back inside and start cleaning up the mess."

They carried the pails of water back into the shed, filling the giant wood tub that sat in the middle of the room. "Will, I know this is going be cold, but it'll help stop the burning, and it will make it easier for me to remove the tar."

The boy nodded but kept his eyes cast down, little sniffles escaping from his taut lip. "Come on now, let's get in."

Will stood slowly and walked over to the tub, feathers flying off him, wafting around the room like snowflakes. He had pine tar everywhere: in his hair, down the front and back of his shirt, and it had even oozed down his breeches, the fabric adhered to his buttocks from sitting. And there were feathers all over.

He sneezed loudly, more of the downy fluff flying up in a great white blizzard.

Dellis stifled a laugh, hiding an unintentional smile with her hand. The poor thing looked pitiful.

Carefully, Will put one foot in the water, then drew in a breath, squeezing his eyes shut as he climbed the rest of the way in. With a yelp, the boy submerged up to his shoulders, his teeth already starting to chatter. "I can't do this!"

When Will tried to scurry out of the tub, Dellis grabbed his arms, pushing him back under the cold liquid. "You need to stay in for a few minutes until you cool off."

Once again submerged, he sat with his head down, pouting, refusing to look up.

Dellis could only imagine how humiliated and miserable the boy must've felt. Grabbing a bucket, she dipped it in the water, filled it, and then poured it over his head, trying to rinse his hair. "I'm so sorry, Will. I don't know how I'll ever repay you for what you've done for me."

"Why didn't you talk to him?" the boy whispered between chattering teeth. "He waited for you all night."

She sensed an undertone of anger in his voice—clearly the boy had taken John's side. *Men! They always stick together.*

Rinsing Will's hair again, she replied, "Talking to the Captain wouldn't have changed what happened."

Will's eyes rolled up towards Dellis and then back down. "I think you behaved poorly towards him. He's your husband."

Dellis found herself taken aback by the boy's stern rebuke, but after what he'd been through on her behalf, he'd earned the right to voice an opinion. "Maybe I did behave poorly, but there's more to what happened between the Captain and me than you know." She sat down next to the tub so she could get a better look at Will's face. "And though I respect your opinion, this is my affair. For now, we'll worry about you." Holding out her hand, Dellis said, "Now, let's get you cleaned up."

He took her hand and climbed out of the tub. "I don't feel so well." He groaned and then crumpled into her arms like a sack of flour.

"Agnes! Help!" She held on to Will, awkward as it was, slowly lowering him to the earthen floor. His forehead was hot to the touch, his arms and legs still burning under the tar.

"Agnes, get all the tallow we have, and bring some linen and whatever we have left to drink from the house." The poor thing was overheating; the hot summer air combined with the thick, adherent pine tar, trapped in the warmth in spite of the bath.

"We'll have to get you out of these clothes."

When she tried to pull his shirt over his head, the boy woke immediately and grabbed her hand. "Don't touch me."

"Will, that shirt is ruined, and I need to get the tar off your skin. Now, take it off." Dellis grabbed the hem, but he slapped her hands away.

"No."

He was acting bizarre; perhaps he was just shy? The poor thing had to be terribly frightened and miserable. Appealing to him, she tipped his chin up so she could see his eyes. "The skin that's under the tar is damaged, and the heat is locked in by all that sticky stuff overtop. If we don't remove it, your burns will progress."

Rubbing some of the pine tar from his cheek, she waited patiently for him to reconsider the situation, and then slowly, he backed away and removed his shirt. To her astonishment, the boy's chest was wrapped in a thick layer of linen bindings; the pine tar had oozed underneath, adhering the fabric to his skin.

"What are these bindings for?" she asked, their eyes meeting, but Will was silent. With his round, cherubic face and full cheeks, she'd always assumed he was just a young boy on the verge of becoming a man, but on closer inspection, she noticed his dark, tapered eyebrows, how they arched over pretty hazel eyes; the fullness of his lips; and his tiny, slight build. Will wasn't a boy.

He was a woman.

Will nodded—a silent confession for Dellis's eyes only.

"I understand." She carried on as if she hadn't just learned the poor woman's dark secret. "We still have to remove the bindings and get you cooled off. If you jump back into the tub and clean off, I'll see that you're properly covered."

Grabbing a knife from the counter, Dellis cut the bindings away, slowly peeling them off, layer by layer, the poor woman gasping with each gentle pull on the fabric until it was finally removed. Will was covered in pine tar underneath both breasts and in the crevasse between, blisters already forming, sure to leave a permanent scar on the tender white skin.

One could only imagine how it must feel, that area so sensitive to touch on a good day.

"Are you in pain?"

The woman nodded, her eyes cast down.

"I'll get you some whiskey, it'll help. Why don't you sit on the cot, and I'll put some cool compresses on your chest."

Outside, Agnes was already walking up with a bucket of tallow and a basket full of linen. "Are there any spirits left?"

"No, the mob took them all," Agnes replied, handing Dellis the supplies. "And after you use that, we'll have nothing for making candles."

Things were just getting worse by the minute—and complicated, very complicated. "I can't worry about candles right now. That's the least of our problems." Puffing her cheeks, Dellis looked around, trying to think of a place where she could get more whiskey. Will was going to need something for the pain. "Agnes, is Mr. Armstrong still here?"

"Yes, he's upstairs cleaning."

"Ask him if he could get us a bottle of spirits. Anything will do. I just need something to help her with the pain. Ah, him." She stuttered, remembering the woman's cover wasn't yet known to Agnes.

"Of course, and I'll get to work on the kitchen after."

Dellis grasped her friend's hand and gave it a squeeze. "I was so worried about you. Thank God you're safe."

"I'm worried about my Simon."

"I know. I'm sorry." Hugging Agnes close, Dellis's heart ached for her two friends, so unfairly separated without a chance for a proper goodbye.

What about John? Anger didn't circumvent her concern for him. His arm was bleeding when she'd sent him on his way. If he didn't get that bullet out soon, the wound would fester. Her heart raced; she closed her eyes, drawing strength from the knowledge that John and Simon were seasoned soldiers. They could take care of themselves.

Agnes lifted her head, a tear rolling down her cheek, but she smiled and wiped it away. "The Good Lord will see the Captain and Simon safe. I know he will. Shame on me for second guessing God's greatness after how he protected us today."

Humbled by her faith, all Dellis could do was nod in agreement. How was it possible that Agnes had so much conviction in God and love after all she'd been though? *What's my excuse?*

When Dellis opened the door to the shed, Will was sitting on the cot, her arms wrapped around herself, teeth chattering together, making a rhythmic, clicking noise.

"I'm going to use this tallow to try and remove the tar. Let me know if I'm hurting you."

Grabbing a bar of the white greasy stuff, Dellis smoothed it over Will's arm, gently using it to help soften the hardened tar. The first few pieces of the black, icky stuff finally came off, exposing red, blistered skin underneath. The burns on her breasts were the worst, the bindings holding in the heat of the tar, compounding the injury. Will cried out, the delicate skin peeling away, leaving red, raw flesh exposed.

It was a slow, laborious process, and Dellis carefully tried not to remove any more of the sensitive skin, though she was only modestly successful. The whole time, she had to tamp down her curiosity, keeping her questions to herself. It was none of her business, no matter how intriguing the whole situation appeared.

Agnes peeked inside. "How's it going?"

When she started to open the door, Dellis jumped up and blocked Will from line of sight. "Things are going okay out here, just slow."

"Mr. Armstrong said he'd stay a little longer and help me with the kitchen and the dining room."

"Perfect. We'll meet you inside when we're done."

"He sent to his house for cider and some plates for us to use, and thankfully, our bread is still good. I'll get another pot of stew on the fire, and we'll have something to eat right quick." Agnes grinned. "My father always said, 'The only thing that stands between you and a good supper is the Lord,' and it's not Sunday, and I already said my prayers. A bunch of local drunks aren't going to keep us from our evening crowd."

Dellis fought back tears, her heart bursting with love for her friend's devotion. "You get started, and I'll meet you in a bit."

It took another hour of rubbing and peeling to remove the rest of the pine tar, and by that time, both women were wrung out and ready to rest. Unfortunately, Dellis had to cut Will's hair; the tar had knotted and snarled up her blonde tresses and refused to give in, even with brushing. The woman's eyes misted up when she ran a hand through the short, uneven mess.

"I'm sorry about your hair, Will, but if there's any bright side to this, no one will suspect you now."

With that, Will buried her face in her hands, letting out loud, gut-wrenching sobs. "I'm so ugly."

Dellis drew the girl into a hug, offering up a shoulder for comfort. *The poor thing.*

"He'll never love me like this. Never."

Tucked into Stuart's unused bed, Will rolled over on her side and wept into the pillow.

Dellis ran her hand over the poor woman's forehead, trying to assuage her. "Rest now, and I'll bring you something to eat."

The woman sniffed and nodded but kept her gaze focused on the wall. As Dellis got up from the bed, she turned back and said, "Thank you for what you did for me."

Will buried her face in her hands, her body trembling, as quiet cries turned to loud gut-wrenching sobs. "He'll never love me now."

"Don't say that. You were so brave; how could he not?"

Surely, the mystery man would be proud if he knew how bravely Will defended The Thistle and survived the mob to tell the tale.

But she shook her head against the pillow. "How could he bear to look at me this way?"

Dellis, better than anyone, understood that type of grief; it was private and inconsolable. Bravery meant little to most men. A woman's beauty and virtue were all she had to her credit, and losing either of those meant rejection and life as an unwanted spinster. *Damaged goods by no fault of her own.* Yes, she understood that.

Closing the door, she walked up the servants' stairs to check on the state of her bedrooms. Patrick managed to put everything to right; even her bed was set and the papers stacked on the desk. John's office was also tidied up; she went over and leafed through the papers he'd left behind, making sure everything was accounted for. On top of the stack was the picture he drew of himself, sitting in the hall waiting for her the night before he left.

She carried his papers back to her bedroom, putting them in the top desk drawer and locking it for safekeeping. Better to let things rest for a while; her wounds were still too fresh to contemplate.

When she got to the bottom of the staircase, she found the broken windows already boarded up and the front door back on its hinges. Between Agnes and Patrick, they'd managed to get the dining room cleaned, and both were already serving guests filing in for supper. Thomas, the bartender, who'd been taking some time off to nurse his ailing wife, was behind the counter, pouring drinks for a few patrons sitting at the bar.

The kitchen had also been cleaned up, a Dutch oven hanging from the iron crane, bubbling over the fire, and bread already in the bake oven. Dellis opened the cupboards to find a stack of red and white porcelain dishes she didn't recognize, her father's precious tea set and dishes cleaned up and discarded.

When she turned around, Patrick was standing behind her, his bright, olive-green eyes regarding her with sympathy. "I brought the plates and a pitcher of wine from my father's house. I even managed to get a few hogsheads of good Scotch whiskey."

Unable to control herself, faced with the trials of the previous few days, she started to cry. He opened his arms to her, and she went willingly. "Patrick, how will I ever repay you for all you've done? If it weren't for you, who knows what would've happened to Will and Agnes. And then cleaning up my house and the plates."

"Shh," he whispered, stroking her hair. "You don't need to repay me. How I've longed to be of some use to you, Dellis." He was so warm and strong, the feel of his chest against her cheek and his arms wrapped around her was soothing. She just needed a sturdy chest to lean on and strong arms to hold her, even if only for a moment, and then she'd take on the world again.

He pulled a kerchief from his pocket and handed it to her. She blew her nose and then balled the linen in her fist. Taking a deep breath, she looked up at him and smiled. "I *will* find a way to repay you."

"I assume Carlisle and his friend got away unscathed, and you've been left to clean up the mess." Patrick's voice dripped with disdain. "How could he leave two helpless women and a boy to handle that crowd?"

Dellis pulled away, Patrick's condescension bringing her back to painful reality. "John was already gone by time they got here. He knew nothing of this."

She poured some water into the iron kettle and hung it over the fire to boil. Tea would do her some good.

"Where did he go?"

She shook her head, in no mood for more male pride or green-eyed jealousy, having contended with enough for one day. "I don't wish to discuss this further."

"You're protecting him, in spite of everything he's done to you." Patrick walked towards her, his six-foot frame and the hearth at her back preventing her from escaping. "Why?"

"What do you mean 'after everything he's done to me?' What do you know?" She stared him down, wanting an answer.

Patrick hesitated, his confidence turning to unease.

He knew. Dammit, Patrick knew.

"You know what I mean, Dellis. He kept company with Mrs. Allen."

"Kept company?" Dellis laughed, shaking her head at his attempt to be modest. "That's what it's called now?"

"Dellis, that's not the only thing he did." He grabbed her arm when she tried to push her way past him. "He told Butler I was a spy. He ruined my cover."

Everything seemed so miserably humorous. She snorted, hitting the breaking point of her poor, frazzled nerves. "Of course he did. Well, at least he warned you instead of letting you return and face the gallows. He didn't even offer me that much." She laughed again and then put a hand to her neck, the noose of John's betrayal tied tightly and painfully, making it hard to breathe.

"You didn't marry him, did you?" Patrick demanded more than asked, his eyes searching hers. "Tell me you didn't marry him."

"*Now* you care, Patrick? Now?" She tried to push him away, but he wouldn't let her, his gentle but firm hands holding her close. "You're three years too late."

"Dellis, did you marry him?" His eyes were pleading with her, but she was numb, unmoved by him, beyond pity.

"Yes, we exchanged vows within my tribe, and my people accepted him as one of us." She stopped, waiting for him to bluster with outrage, but he said nothing. "I know you don't consider my tribe anything more than a bunch of savages; our traditions mean nothing to you. But to myself and John, it was as good as a standing before the Holy Father."

"Dellis, don't put words in my mouth. I'm here because I still care for you, and I want to help."

She was taking her anger at John out on the wrong person. All Patrick had done since breaking their betrothal was try to make amends. He didn't deserve her rebuke. "I'm sorry. I know you mean well."

Grabbing the kettle from the fire, Dellis placed it on the counter and then prepared a pot of tea with leaves from the cupboard. Letting them steep, she leaned against the counter, taking a moment to just catch her breath.

When the tea was finally ready, she put the pot and four of the new cups and saucers on a tray, arranging them carefully. "I'm going to take some tea out for Agnes and Thomas. You're welcome to join us, though sadly, I have nothing to feed you just yet."

"This will do just fine." His face lit up with a smile, the red in his hair shining brilliantly against his fair skin.

Dellis picked up the tray and followed him out to the dining room. Carefully, she set everything down on the bar top and poured some tea for the four of them. "Thank you, all of you, for what you've done."

They sat quietly, sipping their tea, the events of the day like an ominous cloud hanging over them, and then together, they cleared out what was left of the patrons, set one of the tables, and sat down for supper.

Dellis listened as Patrick and Thomas exchanged commentary on the war, something about General Carleton, General Burgoyne, and a man named St. Leger. Next to her, Agnes chatted about feeding the breakfast crowd in the morning and wondered where they could get cheap supplies quickly. But Dellis was in a daze, suddenly exhausted, emotionally and physically. It was truly the day that would never end.

At least she was surrounded by people she loved and trusted; that was more than she'd ever had in the past when the world came crashing down. But she was tired, so very tired of it all: the war, the fighting, and not knowing what was coming next.

Chapter Twelve

Celeste jumped and clutched her neck as the door to her room flew open.

Patrick stomped inside and slammed the door, his face as red as perdition's flames. "Was that your plan, to set a mob on The Thistle? I thought you were just going after Carlisle?"

"And good day to you, Mr. Armstrong." She flashed him a smile and then continued pouring her afternoon tea. "Care to join me, or are you too full from your evening with Miss McKesson? I assume that's where you were."

"I want none of your games." He gave her a sidelong glance, those olive-green beauties eyeing the bodice of her dress, sending a surge of heat straight to her core.

Sipping her tea, she smiled over the rim, relishing his weakness, all men's weakness. "It's no game. I delivered the lady to you as I promised." She wiped her lips with the napkin on her lap and then placed it on the table as she stood. "Now, it's time for you to keep yours. Where's Alexei McKesson keeping the woman, and where's the cargo?"

He was silent, though rage leeched from his every pore, spilling out into his scrunched-up brows and clenched fists. "I don't know where Alexei put the woman."

Celeste placed her hands on the facings of his coffee-brown jacket, slowly inching them up his chest and then linking them around his neck. "You must know something?"

She heard his sharp intake of breath, indicative of his inevitable submission to his baser needs. Reaching into his pocket, he pulled out a letter, holding it up between them. "I found these on Carlisle's desk when I was cleaning up The Thistle."

"What do they say?" She massaged his neck gently, noticing how his eyes closed, resisting yet enjoying her gentle ministrations. He was putting up an admirable fight, but it was futile. No man could resist her charms, well, except John; perhaps that was why she wanted him so.

"They're orders to return to Niagara. He's working with Butler to unite a native fighting force for the British. Apparently, Lord Carlisle and John dueled earlier in the day; he was shot, but he got away and left for Niagara."

John was alive; that was promising. "What else do I need to know?"

Patrick pushed her hands away abruptly, taking a step back. "Don't touch me."

She rolled her eyes at his feeble attempts to deny himself the pleasure he was so obviously longing for. But he'd give in eventually. "What else did the letters say? Or do I tell our dear Miss McKesson that this baby could be yours? I'm sure that would send her right back after John. Not exactly what you want, is it?"

He laughed, though it was contrary to the dangerous look in his eyes. Yes, she'd definitely found his tender spot. "It's not mine, and stay away from Dellis."

Celeste shook her head, letting mirth turn up the corners of her mouth. "Oh, you and I both know it's possible, and Agnes saw the room after you left. It was—*after all*—her office."

Patrick relented, though with much bravado, huffing out a breath and thrusting a hand in his hair, pushing it from his eyes. "There's a man named Merrick who's been helping Carlisle look for Alexei. They've set a trap for him in the port of Oswego."

"See? That wasn't so hard." Things went so much better when he remembered who was in charge. "Anything else?"

"There was a letter from Lord Miles Tomlinson. He's looking for his wife, Wilhelmina Parkhurst. Apparently, John diverted resources provided by that man to help save Dellis." He was silent for a moment, the muscles in his jaw working. "Alexei has gone with Thomas Sinavis to spy on the British; after that, he was headed to Oswego to get more supplies. The woman isn't with the Oneida; they frightened her, so Alexei put her elsewhere. I assume she's here in German Flats."

And once again, Armstrong didn't disappoint.

"She's here?" Celeste clucked her tongue, an idea brewing. "If Alexei isn't on good terms with his father, and he couldn't take her to his village, where else could he keep her? Who does he trust most, if not you?"

She could tell Patrick was already following her lead, his head shaking vigorously. "No, Mrs. Allen."

"No? Whatever do you mean, no?" She asked, wide-eyed and innocent. "I haven't said anything."

"You want me to spy on Dellis."

She touched the tip of her nose with her index finger and then pointed to him. "Spot on. You're in the perfect position to do it. She trusts you. You're her knight in shining armor, her Sir Galahad come to the rescue." Celeste cocked a brow, almost laughing at the pathetic picture she painted. "And from how I see it, you don't have much of a choice."

He let out a self-deprecating laugh, his Adam's apple twitching nervously in his throat. "Fine. Do what you will to Carlisle, but stay away from Dellis. That scoundrel blew my cover; he ruined my mission."

Celeste liked the fear in his voice; he was taking her seriously. *Finally.* "By all means, go. Be with your precious Dellis before the British attack, and you're needed at the Fort." Giving him a languid onceover from head to toe, she stopped when their eyes met. "And find out where the woman's hiding. If you do that, Miss McKesson will never know about the two of us."

"What will you do with the information?"

They were so close, she could smell his woodsy cologne mixed with his own manly scent. She breathed him in, desperately wanting a bite. "All you need to know is that I'll make sure John never finds his missing heiress."

"You must really hate Carlisle."

She almost laughed at the utter ridiculousness of that statement. *Hate John? Hate. John.* "On the contrary, Mr. Armstrong. I love him, and I want him back."

When Clark arrived, John was barely coherent, the loss of blood and sweltering heat rendering him weak and lethargic, his legs like rotted wood beams threatening to cave at any moment. Simon tried to remove the ball from his friend's shoulder but was unsuccessful; it had embedded itself deep, near the bone, held in place by thick, obstinate tendons. The only choice they had was to go to the village for help.

After Skenandoa removed the bullet from John's shoulder, she dressed the wound and then saw him fed and set up in the cabin.

He rested in the bed he'd shared with Dellis not five days before, pondering their future while trying to regain his strength for the pending journey. It was strange to be there alone, his beloved's effervescent spirit everywhere from the drying flowers hanging above the table to the jars full of herbs she used to treat the villagers. It even smelled like her, lavender and vanilla, sweet and herbaceous, yet fresh as a spring morning. If he closed his eyes and took a deep breath, he could almost get a whiff of her venison stew bubbling in the hearth and hear the scratching of porous stones as she ground dried corn for meal. But it was quiet, the bed cold and so very lonely.

After their wedding in the village, the little log cabin had been like a private haven where they spent hours making love and playing at being husband and wife. He could still see her when they said their vows; she was exquisite. His blushing bride.

In her buff-colored doeskin dress with her inky-black hair in one long braid to her shoulders, she looked like an innocent maid, no sign of his brazen virago who set fire to his bed the night before. She handed him a small basket of linen shirts and buckskin leggings and a pair of intricately decorated moccasins. "Just One, I promise to be a good wife to you. I'll care for your home and your children, feed and clothe you, and when you're unwell, I'll care for you."

He noticed a twinkle in her eyes as she said her vows. She'd already done all those things for him and so much more—she taught him to love.

With a grin, John handed her his basket; inside was a trove of baked goods, corn cakes, and bread that Kateri had prepared for him to give. And at the bottom of the basket was a dagger, the one she took from him months before. "I promise to be a good husband to you, Dellis, and provide for you and our children. I promise to give you children to be part of this community, care for you when you're ill, and protect you when you're in danger."

John said every word with the truest heart; he'd love and care for her always, and more than anything, he wanted to give her children to fill her arms, to nurture from her breast. Protecting her, that was another matter. He stifled a laugh, remembering all her direct assaults and his feeble attempts at blocking her. She was fiercer than any warrior or soldier he'd faced in battle.

After their vows, they each held an end of the wampum belt in the presence of Joseph, Great Bear, Rail Splitter, and Skenandoa, who stood in for Dellis's mother and Matron of the Bear Clan.

When the ceremony was finished, there was a large banquet and ceremonial dancing. Together, the newlyweds lead the revelry, taking part in the dance, until finally, it was time for them to leave for their marriage bed.

John carried Dellis to their cabin, and they made love all night. He called her wife, and she called him husband as they lay in each other's arms, praying the world would never catch up with them.

But it did.

When John woke the next morning, he dressed and ate quickly, his arm still throbbing like the devil but once again viable. Before he left the cabin, he penned Dellis a quick letter, leaving it on the table with the bullet that had been removed from his shoulder. Joseph and Great Bear met John at his horse, both of them looking concerned.

"Just One, be safe," Joseph said sternly, like a chief to one of his warriors. "I know you'll have a care for our interests when you go back to the Great Father's men."

"I will. I promise." John was in earnest when he pledged to protect and defend the village as a member of their tribe. Those people had given him the only true home he'd ever known.

"Keep an eye on Dellis for me," he said, putting his knapsack on the back of Viceroy's saddle, fastening it in place.

Simon showed up next to John presently, dressed and ready to leave.

Joseph nodded. "As husband, that's your duty to Fennishyo."

Yes, it is. John bowed his head in contrition and then nodded. "I'm sorry to ask, but Dellis is unhappy with me, and rightly so. I haven't been a good husband to her."

"Were you protecting her? Were you honoring her?" Great Bear asked, provoking John to rethink all his actions up the present.

If it was only that simple.

"I was trying to," John replied. "But I failed."

Great Bear's scars had finally healed, pink and white connective tissues, weaved together like an intricate web, stretched from the top of his forehead all the way back to the base of his skull. He looked frightening, like a ghoul from a childish nightmare, in stark contrast to the gentility of his nature.

"Just One, it's about your intent not your success. You're a good husband. Perhaps it's Fennishyo who's not being a good wife to you?"

"I don't think she sees it that way." *Not in the least.* "Take care, both of you." John shook their hands, offering up one last warning for his conscience's sake. "I know you're aware of what's coming. I urge you to protect yourselves, even if that means helping Schuyler. St. Leger won't hesitate; it's only a matter of time."

John looked around one last time at the familiar faces of his adopted family and sighed. *Will I ever see them again?*

"God go with you, Just One. I pray you find the answers you seek. Remember, you're Oneida wherever you go." Joseph's farewell was warmly given though ominous in its delivery. Something was coming; the great chief felt it, too.

"Thank you," John replied, mounting his horse.

Standing together, the villagers waved goodbye, watching John leave. He took one last look back, a strange feeling in the pit of his stomach. And then he heard it: a sweet, sad song carrying on the sultry summer breeze; it was so soft and melodious, lacking its usual persistence, more like a dirge or a requiem.

"Justice, John."

Chapter Thirteen

"Will, it's good to see you up and around." Dellis eyed the forlorn young woman as she sauntered into the kitchen and took a seat at the table. The poor thing looked tired and defeated. "How are you feeling?"

Will's hazel eyes darted around as if she were lost in the forest at night; large bags underneath spoke of no sleep and tear-filled hours. She wore a cocked hat, covering her extremely short locks, the exposed skin above her collar red and excoriated from tar burns that would surely leave scars.

"Agnes will get you some breakfast. There's clabber on the counter if you're hungry right now. I have to travel to my village today, and I'll be gone until tomorrow. If you feel up to doing a little work, you can, but you don't have to."

Dellis finished prepping biscuits, placing them in the bake oven. Carefully, she removed the lid from the pot hanging over the fire and stirred the cornmeal porridge she'd prepared earlier.

"Thank you," Will said, pouring some tea from the pot sitting on the table. "I appreciate you keeping my secret."

Dellis rested her hand on the woman's shoulder, willing a little comfort to her. "It's the least I can do after what you did for me. And when you're ready, you can confide in me."

It was good to have yet another woman around. There was strength in numbers, and that included the emotional sort, not just the brute kind. "We women have to stick together—the three of us."

"Can I trust—" Before Will could finish, Agnes walked into the kitchen, her hands full of candles.

"Look what Mr. Armstrong sent over, and they're all beeswax."

"Well, the house will certainly smell lovely; at least, until we're back to tallow." Dellis took the candles and put them in the storage pantry.

"He gave us this, too." Agnes held up a small bucket of white, greasy lard, just what they needed to start dinner.

"I'll have to thank him when I return. I need to get going." Dellis removed her apron, hung it next to the door, and then grabbed her bonnet from the hook. "I'm going to take some of the leftover bread from yesterday and the dried venison so I have something to eat. Oh, I picked strawberries yesterday. We can make tarts when I get back."

She packed her knapsack full of provisions and then tossed it over her shoulder. "Thomas will be here any minute to take care of the bar." She turned back to Agnes before opening the door. "I'll be back tomorrow."

Stopping, Dellis glanced around her kitchen, taking one last look. Her house was safe. *Thank God.*

She saddled up and took off, the early morning sun just starting to rise, hues of pale pinks turning to brilliant blues, spreading out over an endless sky. Part of her wanted to ride out towards the sun and follow it west, leave everything behind, but too many people depended on her, and she'd never run away from a fight in her life. No, she'd face it all—head on—like her father taught her to.

The long ride to the village was a blessed reprieve from her cares and gave her time to clear her head, the unseasonably cool morning air seeping into her lungs with each breath, relieving her frazzled nerves. When she arrived at the village, it was aflutter with activity; several of the women were on their knees, grinding corn, their bodies moving rhythmically as they worked, the clicking and scraping noise of the stones rubbing together like music to her ears. Just inside the stockade, the men were hanging fish, and stacks of corn were being laid out for the summer sun's gift of preservation through drying.

Ho-sa-gowwa greeted her at the gate, as usual, welcoming her in with a smile and a nod. "Dellis, you've come at a good time. Rebel soldiers were captured near the fort by spies who'd slipped past our scouts. They were some of our brothers, Mohawks. Almost a dozen men were murdered, and a few were taken prisoner. Joseph and Rail Splitter are leaving for Oriska to meet with the Colonel's men."

There was no more respite from reality, her deep-seated anxiety burgeoning considering what she learned about the war from Patrick the night before. "What about Alexei? Is he here?"

The young brave shook his head. "No, he's not returned."

Her grandfather and Rail Splitter stood outside their cabins, talking, both wearing scowls, and she knew why. The spies had trespassed in the Oneida woods, and her people would have to explain to the Colonel why they failed to catch the intruders—the first sign of inner-tribal fighting.

Although her grandfather and Han Yerry had pledged their support to General Schuyler, as a whole, the Oneida tribes were still divided in loyalties. Her village and Oriska allied with the colonists at Stanwix, but the other Oneida castles, Old Oneida and Kanonwalohale, held fast to the Confederacy's neutrality. With the British on the move, time was running out for all of them, the last granules of sand falling through the neck of the hourglass.

"What will you do?" She looked at her grandfather, noticing how his scowl deepened upon seeing her. "Are you and Han Yerry going to meet with the Colonel? What about Thomas Spencer from Kanonwalohale? Is he going to join with us?"

"Dellis, this isn't for you to discuss." Joseph snipped, reprimanding her like he did when she was a little girl.

But she refused to be talked down to; her position as clan matron gave her the right to council and an opinion. "Grandfather, I'm a Matron of the Bear Clan. I deserve to know what's going on."

He countered with silence and a frosty expression, and then took her hand. "Dellis, we must speak alone. Come with me."

She let him pull her towards his cabin, but she was concerned. He was acting strange, his unusual coldness bewildering.

Once inside, her released her hand and turned to her. "You should sit."

"Grandfather, what's going on?" Unaccustomed to his churlish demeanor, Dellis hesitated, trying to understand. *Have I done something wrong?*

He pointed to the small wooden chair in the corner, directing her, once again, like a misbehaving child.

She sat down slowly.

As is if launching an attack, he started at her. "Just One was here yesterday; Skenandoa removed a bullet from his arm."

Dellis breathed a sigh of relief. "I must thank her."

"As your husband, it was your duty to care for him. Where were you?"

Suddenly, she felt this growing need to defend herself. *Why is everyone siding with John? First Agnes, then Will, and now my grandfather?* "I had to leave him; there was a mob threatening to burn down Father's house. Two of my friends were alone, trying to protect it."

"No!" Joseph waved his arms in the air aggressively, as if trying to slice it in two. "He was in need of your tending. It was your marriage vow to care for your husband when he was ill. You disrespected him."

"Grandfather, I have my reasons. He was *not* a good husband to me. He betrayed me. Are you on his side now? Am I not your granddaughter?"

Joseph was quiet, yet his anger was tangible through the silence, his black eyes regarding her with disappointment.

Dellis swallowed her pride, feeling childish and deserving of his reprimand. "Was he all right?"

"Yes, and his last words were of you."

She nodded, closing her eyes. *He's safe.* A weight she didn't know she'd been carrying was suddenly lifted, her breaths coming more easily than they had in days. "What happened today?"

"Dellis, that's no longer your concern." There was command in his voice; not the usual sweetness of her grandfather, but the order of her chief.

He walked to the door and called for Rail Splitter. When the ancient sachem arrived, her cousin, Skenandoa, was following close behind.

Dellis got up from her chair and gave her cousin a hug. "Thank you for caring for John."

"Just One is a warrior," she said in her sweet, soft voice that reminded Dellis of her mother. "He was fine."

Dellis couldn't help but smile upon hearing John's Oneida name, a reminder that he, too, was one of the tribe and trying desperately to fit in her world. It was so easy to forget in the heat of the moment.

"The bullet was deep, but I got it out. He lost a lot of blood, so we made him stay for the night and rest."

"Dellis," Rail Splitter said her name firmly and then met her eye to eye as if addressing one of the warriors. "It's been decided by the matrons of this village and the chiefs of our tribe that you'll be replaced in your role as Matron of the Bear Clan."

"What?" Blindsided, she grabbed onto the chair in front of her, trying to steady herself. "I don't understand."

"Skenandoa will take over, as the next oldest woman in the Bear Clan." Joseph looked over Dellis's shoulder at her cousin and nodded.

"But I don't understand." Dellis's eyes darted back and forth between her cousin and their grandfather, but neither spoke, further provoking anxiety. "Why are you doing this? I feel like I'm being ganged up on by a pack of wolves."

"You haven't kept your duty to this village. Instead of using good sense and putting your people first, you let passion lead us into a battle that wasn't of our making. When questioned by me, you refused to listen to my counsel. You're always blustering like wind, never listening and advising as your role intended. We look to matrons to lead us, to give advice; yet you, Granddaughter, have set a poor example. This was decided by the women of the Bear Clan and agreed upon by the chiefs and matrons of the Wolf and Turtle clans."

Tears welled in her eyes, turning beloved faces blurry. He was disappointed in her. That was what he was saying. She could hear it in his voice, anger and despondency, where normally there was hope and optimism. "Do I not get to defend myself? Does no one want to hear my side of the story?"

"You've done enough talking, Fennishyo. Now, it's time you accept the decision of our people." Joseph clipped, in a voice like ice.

Suddenly, anger gave her courage where she'd normally be reserved. Defying her grandfather was something she'd never done until that moment. "Roger DeLancie threatened me, Stuart, and all of you here in the village. That man killed my parents, he attacked me, and I lost my baby. Does that not matter? He was trying to turn our brothers against us. I was acting on behalf of all our people. I'm a true clan matron."

How can this be happening? Her whole world was falling apart. Again. "Why now? Why didn't you tell me this when I returned last month?"

Rail Splitter and Skenandoa excused themselves, leaving Dellis alone with her grandfather. The silence in his cabin was as thick and ominous as a cloud of smoke billowing over the forest. Tears broke loose, burning her eyes, but she wouldn't wipe them away. She wanted him to see her pain. She wanted him to know how his decision devastated her.

"Is this because of John?" she muttered, her voice sounding nasal from crying.

"No, Dellis, this has been on my mind for a while." He walked to her and placed his hand on her cheek, cupping her face in his leathery palm. His fierce black eyes softened, his scowl relaxing, allowing a gentle smile to surface. "You've been through too much for any one person to bear. All you can do right now is lash out and fight like a wolf in a cage. That's all you've ever been able to do. When you stop fighting me and fighting life, you'll see that this is for your own good, and for the good of our people. I'm relieving you of a burden too great to carry—but not forever, my Fennishyo."

"I don't understand." She held his hand to her cheek, tears grazing both of their palms.

"This is a difficult time for our people. War is coming. We must have clear minds and hearts when it comes to making decisions. I'm not telling you that you're not to be present in negotiations and when our council meets, but now, you must listen and learn. You must make peace with all that has happened to you. Only then can you make a good clan matron and a good wife to Just One."

Joseph leaned in and kissed her forehead. The tenderness of the moment brought on a fresh surge of tears. "A good wife and a good clan matron must listen and lead with life's wisdom, and you're gifted with more than most."

When she finally got the courage to look up at her grandfather, she found tears in his eyes, something she'd never seen before, not even when her grandmother died.

"I want you to have peace, Fennishyo. They're gone, your mother and father, Lily and Healing Hand. They'll never come back no matter how you fight. And Just One is a brave and a true warrior who'll care for you if you just stop pushing him away. But that will never happen until you find peace. You're your own worst adversary; if you keep fighting, you'll drive everyone away."

His next words were so profound Dellis was rendered speechless, the truth cutting to her very core.

"Or was that your goal, to drive Just One away so he didn't have the chance to leave you on his own?"

The cabin was quiet—a long, protracted silence that he finally ended with a terse command, not to be ignored. "You'll do as I say, Granddaughter. Don't defy me."

She nodded. Her head accepted the situation, though her heart could not. At least, not yet.

"I'm to meet with the Colonel at Oriska; we must provide condolences to the colonists and discover who's responsible for capturing their men. Will you be here when I return?"

"Yes." Though she didn't want to be. Her one safe place, her shelter from the storm, had turned to ruin in a matter of minutes.

"I think it's best you go back to your cabin and rest. For now, you'll only see anger and frustration. It takes time and separation to see truth."

After a kiss on the cheek, she left, the short walk to her cabin made frustratingly long by humiliation and the knowing glances of her village family. Dellis pushed the door open, dreading the quiet and solitude, a stark reminder she was truly alone. She sat on her cot, looking around, remembering her mother standing at the table, tying up herbs for drying, her father coming in and wrapping his arm around her waist, kissing her cheek.

Father would know what to do; he always did. *How I miss them.* The pain was like a knife, sharp and brutal in her chest. Closing her eyes, she conjured her dear father, blond, handsome and so perfect.

"Papa."

"Dellis, when you fall down, you must get back up again. Just as the sun rises every morning, so do we. Yes, it may be night for a time, but the day always comes."

She could see his great blue eyes wrinkle in the corners and his cheeks lift with a big, hearty grin—that beloved face she'd never look upon again.

"Yes, Papa."

"That's my brave lass." He laughed, leaning in so only she could hear him. *"That's good, stubborn Scot's blood in you. It'll make you tough as steel and resilient as stone. That's where you'll draw your strength from. Remember that. But you must learn to listen and be calm; that's where your mother's native blood comes in. It'll give you the wisdom of life to guide when I'm no longer here for your counsel. You have the gifts of both our people, and they'll see you through in the worst of times."* With a light tap on her nose, he stood and grabbed his haversack, throwing it over his shoulder. *"Now, I'm going to see to my patients; you wait here until I come home, and then we'll go fishing and I'll tell you the story about how your Uncle Dane and I travelled the seas in his great ship, the HMS Boudica."*

"Yes, Papa."

"Yes, Papa." Her words melded with that innocent little doe-eyed girl who'd forever be waiting for her father to come home.

"I love you, Papa."

It was a three-day journey to Niagara across vast, unending forest that yielded only when the great stone fort was in sight. Passing through three different Iroquois tribal lands meant John and Clark were constantly on guard for an ambush or spies looking to take captives, and two British officers would fetch a healthy ransom. At night, they slept in shifts—one taking four hours to rest while the other kept watch. And while John lay awake, looking up at the black velvet sky full of stars, he contemplated all his mistakes with painstaking repetition. There were too many to count; he was a creature of vices too often indulged and never denied.

Coward. He should've done it. He should've told Dellis the truth about Celeste. *Now, I'm serving a sentence with no end in sight.*

When he and Clark arrived at Fort Niagara, they proceeded across the parade ground to the Officer's quarters located at the rear of the fort, facing the water. The great stone building was unchanged, John's room left surprisingly empty despite the influx of officers. It could only mean one thing: Butler was expecting John, and it wouldn't be a happy reunion for either of them.

He threw his haversack on the cot and removed his hat. "Unpack only our clothing, and make sure both of those are stocked with plenty of cartridges." He pointed to the bed where the leather box he usually wore on his hip was lying. "I have no doubt once I speak with Butler we'll be travelling again."

Since John had last seen the Major, not only had their superior, General Carleton, been supplanted as commander of the Western Expedition by General Burgoyne, but Butler's old rival, Colonel Daniel Claus, the former

Deputy Superintendent of the Canadian Indians, had been appointed Superintendent of the Western Expedition. Colonel Claus held a notorious grudge against the Major, calling him an "illiterate interpreter." That put John and Butler in a tenuous position, at the mercy of an adversary who was potentially working against them for his own betterment. John shook his head. Once again, politics superseded the common goal in the British Army. Could they not just make war on the Rebels?

"Captain Carlisle, I'd hoped you'd have good news for me." Major Butler stood, tension leeching from the fisted hands at his hips. "You were supposed to bring back Lord Tomlinson's wife and our supplies. St. Leger will be leaving for Buck Island soon, and he'll be expecting news of our negotiations with the native allies. Those missing supplies were to trade with our Seneca friends at Irondequoit Bay. I don't need to remind you that without General Carleton's help, both you and I are subject to the whims of Colonel Claus."

"But what of the intelligence I collected? Didn't you send it to General Carleton?" John demanded more than asked, and surprisingly, he wasn't rebuked for his insubordinate tone.

Butler held back with chilly resolve.

"Major, are we really going to put our fortunes behind a native contingent? Plying them with rum, guns, and powder won't buy allegiance; they're notoriously unreliable. When faced with their Oneida brothers, the Mohawk and the Seneca will refuse to fight. This is a fool's errand."

"Captain Carlisle, are you aware that General Howe will no longer be sending his forces to meet us in Albany? He's turned his attention towards Philadelphia. We need the natives to fight for us." Butler pounded his finger on the desk, further making his point clear. "We have no choice. The majority of our men have been sent with General Burgoyne to take Ticonderoga."

John shook his head in disbelief. "Does St. Leger realize that Stanwix is ready and waiting for our assault? Has he not seen the maps I drew and the estimates of its refortification? Schuyler and Gansevoort know we're coming, and they're preparing. There were at least five hundred men garrisoned at the fort, a full battalion. They know the access through Wood Creek will block our advance. Their native allies are all over the St. Lawrence, watching us. If Howe isn't meeting us, then we're finished. Stanwix can hold a siege, I promise you."

Butler laughed, his dark eyes narrowing on John. "Who'd believe the words of a disgraced spy? Howe choosing you in the first place was rather suspect. We all questioned the logic of his actions. You were once a promising officer, but you have a penchant for drinking, and your history with DeLancie was a taint on our ranks. The only reason you're still here is because Admiral McKesson protected you; otherwise, you would've faced the gallows." Butler sat in his chair, leaning back casually. "I have to admit, you showed a bit of promise initially, but then you played friend to the Oneida, acting in complete opposition to everything I was trying to accomplish." Butler flattened his hands on the desk and leaned in, stressing his point. "Let's just say I've been keeping you busy so I don't have the Admiralty on my back. Carlisle, you couldn't even handle the simplest of duties; all you had to do was escort a woman to her husband."

"Major, you know what I was dealing with."

"Do I?" Butler asked, cocking a brow.

John's stomach churned, his face growing hotter one degree at a time as his temper rose to a boil. Without any witnesses, it was Butler's word against John's. He knew burning the letters would come back to haunt him, but it was the only choice he had to save the Oneidas.

"You should've kept your focus, John, and stayed away from this other business."

"I had no choice. DeLancie came for me." With Butler's blessing, too, John wanted to add, but he held back; pointing the finger at his superior would only make the situation worse. "But I still completed my mission. I brought the intelligence to you. I was in Fort Stanwix. Who better to tell you its fortifications?"

All the work John had done, the sacrifices he'd made, were for naught if no one believed him. He bit his lip, fighting the urge to lash out.

"We have our own spies that have said the opposite. Carleton saw both reports and passed them along with his recommendations. Clearly, no one puts much faith in your intelligence."

"What do you believe?" John asked, barely controlling his rage. "You know the territory as well as I do, and news travels fast, especially to your desk."

Butler clucked his tongue stoically. "My job is to unite the Six Nations and prepare the largest fighting force of natives this country has ever seen. And you're going to help me do it. We're in this together now, our fates strangely entwined. If there's any truth to what you say, then it should add all the more urgency to our combined cause, and it can only reflect well on both of us if we show up prepared."

"You believe me."

The Major remained nebulously silent, though his eyes confirmed what John knew with conviction—Butler believed it, but no one else did. It had nothing to do with John's ability. The only reason he still had his commission was to placate a duke who spoke on John's behalf for telling the truth about Stephen McKesson's murder. All of it was a ruse, a slap in the face.

"Why don't you defend me to Carleton? Why don't you tell him it's true?" John demanded, knowing he'd passed into insubordination.

"Carleton has been slighted and pushed out of his position by Burgoyne, and I find myself at the whims of Daniel Clause. No one is listening to either of us. They've formed their own opinions and will act accordingly. We have a job to do. We'll bring St. Leger his native fighting force, ready and well equipped. Now, find the supplies, and be at Irondequoit Bay with them. I could give a damn about the woman. You're dismissed, Captain."

"Yes," John replied. His future in the British military, and his fate, was tied to Butler's; they'd rise together or fall as a pair. The man who'd used and betrayed John had become his partner. *What a strange twist of fate.*

Clark was waiting in the hall outside Butler's office with two letters in hand. "These are for you."

John took both from his friend, cracking the crimson wax seal on one and reading it quickly.

"From the look on your face, the meeting didn't go well."

John rolled his eyes and then finished skimming the correspondence.

"Who's it from?" Simon asked, looking around the stone halls while he waited for John to finish reading.

"Miles. He's in Oswego, and he wants to meet with me." Things were getting worse by the minute. "He's threatening court martial for what happened with his wife."

"Damn, John, what do we do?"

He shook his head, his hands fumbling with the other letter, his nerves getting the better of him.

Captain,

I have good news for you. We've spotted a certain thief on Buck Island and have tracked him as far as Oswego. I'm here with some of the Eighth, keeping eyes on him, waiting for his next move.

Smith

"What does it say?"

Shaking the letter, John glanced at his friend, grinned, and then took off down the hall. "Would you believe, as much as the previous letter was our demise, this one is our savior?"

Clark ran behind, trying to catch up. "I don't understand."

"Smith found Alexei; he's in Oswego." John threw the door to their quarters open and starting repacking his bags.

"We've only been here a few hours. Can't we stay the night?" Simon rushed in.

"No, we leave now. This can't wait." John didn't look up from his packing, just kept at it, making sure he had enough food for the journey and plenty of cartridges prepared. "If Adam has Alexei in his sights, then perhaps Merrick does, too. If we can catch Alexei, maybe we can reason with him."

Simon's eyes widened as if he'd just heard John spout off like a drunken fool. "That's not going to happen. What are the chances he hasn't given everything to Schuyler? And even if we do catch him, he won't confess willingly."

"Then we'll force him to comply, Clark, or he faces the noose." John threw down his bag, frustration getting the better of him. *Damn my luck.* It would serve the whole expedition, and St. Leger, if they failed. John tried to warn them. He'd done his job, yet because of his reputation, no one would listen. The only hope he had of salvaging the mission at that point was Alexei.

"Compliance or not, those supplies and the dowry are as good as gone."

Simon was right, and Butler needed goods to entice the natives into battle. That's really all he cared about, and Miles's wife was irrelevant; well, at least to Butler.

John stopped packing, pondering the situation, searching for inspiration in the face of impending defeat. Out the window, he could see blue waves crashing on white, sandy beaches, the sun twinkling on the water like beautiful jewels—sapphires on porcelain skin, just like the necklace Dellis wore the night she confronted him at Celeste's brothel.

"I've got it!" An idea hit him like a fish tugging at a line.

"What?" Simon stopped packing and threw down his bag. "Have you been drinking and I didn't know it? The least you could do is share."

John rolled his eyes and went for the door. "I'll be back. Be ready; we leave the minute I return."

He ran down the narrow hall, pushing past sweaty officers returning from drills as they rushed in the opposite direction towards their barracks. At the end of the hall, he stopped abruptly and knocked on Butler's door. "It's Captain Carlisle again."

When permitted, John pushed the door open, racing inside, barely able to control his zeal. "Major Butler, I have an idea."

"What's that?" Butler lifted his kettle from the fire and poured himself a cup of steaming black coffee. The smell reached John's nose, sweet and robust, making his already nervous stomach grumble.

"We need something to trade with the Seneca to get them to join us, correct?"

Butler nodded, taking his first sip. "Stating the obvious, Carlisle?"

John let out a chuckle, dumbfounded that he hadn't thought of that solution before. "What about luxury goods?"

"What do you mean?" He had Butler's attention, the major's cup stopping on the way to his lips, suspended in midair.

"I mean rum, madeira, jewelry, furs, clothing, linen. Luxuries." John smiled when Butler nodded in agreement; finally, he was following along. "We can give them those things. Mrs. Allen has a merchant here in town, someone who deals in luxury goods. She was able to host that gathering during the winter, and her establishment provides regular entertainment for our officers. Either her supplier is bribing someone in our ranks to traffic his goods down the St. Lawrence, or they're coming by way of the Royal Navy under the Provincial Marine."

John racked his brain for a name, and then it came to him; he pointed into the air as if pointing at her. "Mary, Mrs. Allen's assistant; she'd know. If we find Mrs. Allen's supplier, we can buy on credit, money backed by the Crown."

"That could work," Butler said.

John gave himself a mental pat on the back for his ingenuity.

"Carlisle Shipping should be able to provide you with rum and Madeira. They have one of the few licensed ships that can travel the waterway. Captain Denny works for my brother. I can get word to him when I return to Oswego."

"That doesn't fix the problem of ammunition and guns. We'll need them to supply the natives."

"I'll deal with our thief and, hopefully, find Lord Tomlinson's bride and the supplies. But we may need to tap into what's coming in from Oswegatchie, or perhaps you can get word to General Carleton? He might be able to help us on the side. Carleton needs us to succeed, and this is how we do it. Both of you have faced unfortunate slights at the hands of your superiors. Here's the chance to prove them all wrong."

Butler's nostrils flared, a tinge of disgust surfacing at his political predicament. "I'll handle the issue from this end. Get word to your contact in Oswego, and send me notice of what you're able to procure. I'll see you at Irondequoit, Captain."

"Yes, Major." John walked out of the room and breathed a sigh of relief. He bought himself time, but eventually, he'd have to deliver.

Dellis rubbed her sore eyes and brushed the stray hairs from her face, her head throbbing like she'd drunk too much the night before. Crying had a way of making one feel relieved when doing it but miserable the next day. It was morning already. She sat up slowly, the sunrays shining through her window, casting an ethereal glow over her family's cabin; a crick in her neck smarted and pulled as she stretched. When she lay down the night before, she had no intention of falling asleep, but her burdens were too heavy for her tired shoulders to bear a moment longer, and she succumbed.

Damn. She'd slept through her grandfather's return from Oriska, and she knew she'd have to nose around to find out the details. Actually, it was probably better that way; had she been present when Joseph returned, her instincts would've pushed her to ask questions and try to give counsel—and that was no longer her duty. *So, now what?* She needed to be steady and listen more, so her grandfather said. *Why is everyone always sticking their noses into my life?* She never asked for advice. Since her parents died, she'd done just fine without all the unwanted intervention. First Alexei, then John, and then her grandfather—three proverbial pots calling the kettle black. *Who are they to give me advice on behavior?*

On the table, she noticed something bright and silver, the sun's rays dancing over it, casting a reflection on the wall. It looked like a musket shot. Underneath the trinket was a letter for her; it was from John, his distinct penmanship immediately recognizable. The piece of parchment wasn't folded or sealed; she picked it and the little metal ball up and started to read.

My Love,

Skenandoa was kind enough to retrieve the bullet for me. I think it was lucky having missed my more vital parts, and thankfully, the ones I'd miss (and you would, too). I give it to you for luck. I pray that Agnes and your precious Thistle are safe from the mob. Please, take shelter when the army comes, I couldn't bear the thought of something happening to this village, my home, or you, my wife.

Your loving husband,
John

She held the shot between her fingertips, rolling it around, feeling the smooth roundness of the steel against her skin. She couldn't help but laugh at John's devilish wit; his letter, while unassuming, still had a tinge of his traditional bravado. When she closed her eyes, she could see the ever-present twinkle in his sapphire blues as he contemplated what to write; his quill in hand, and nearby, a little pot of ink.

Folding the letter, she shoved it in her pocket, dropping the bullet in next to it. When she stepped out of the cabin, it felt again as if every villager were watching her, sidelong glances and whispered words under her breath were being had, though they pretended to ignore her. She threw her shoulders back and thrust her chin up; better to face them all than continue licking her wounds in silence. Her grandfather was inside his cabin, sitting at his table, eating a bowl of corn mash and talking with Rail Splitter. When she opened the door, Joseph gave her a weak smile and then waved for her to enter.

"Good morning." She nodded to both men.

"Come, Dellis, eat something." Joseph pointed to the little wooden bowl sitting on the table. She walked over to the hearth, lifted the top of the cast-iron pot, and spooned herself a steaming helping of corn mash.

She sat down, lifted the spoon to her lips, and blew on her steaming breakfast several times before finally starting to eat. It was so good, sweet and a bit savory, the salt and butter a decadent mix, but what she loved most was the texture: slightly gritty and thick in consistency.

Rail Splitter stood. "I have much to do. I'll speak to you later, Joseph."

There was no doubt in her mind, he left so she could have another "talking to" by her grandfather, but instead of chiding her, after the sachem left, Joseph sat quietly, eating his mash.

Their ceasefire went on for several minutes, both of them shoveling food into their mouths as she fought the urge to bust through the uncomfortable silence and defend herself. When she could take it no longer, she volleyed first, asking the question she knew her grandfather was anticipating.

"Will you tell me what happened at your meeting last evening, or am I not privy to that any longer?"

"Dellis," he said, brusquely, his eyes still fixed on his bowl. "Did you listen to a word I said yesterday?"

"Yes, but can I not ask?" She put her bowl down and dropped her spoon in it.

Joseph let out a heavy sigh and then shook his head. "Fine. Five men were captured; four were scalped and one was butchered. Unfortunately, one of the men taken captive was an officer with vital information about the fort."

She swallowed, a burning pit forming in her stomach. "Do they know who did it?"

Joseph shook his head. "We arrived late, as they were taking the captives away. There were at least forty men in the woods; John Oteronyente was seen among the spies."

An illustrious member of the Mohawk tribe, his presence was indicative of their brothers' support for the British. "They passed through our lands unseen, our scouts blind to their advance." He glanced down at his breakfast, his face long and forlorn. "It was a great failure of our promise to the Colonel."

"What now?" Dellis stood and refilled her bowl and then her grandfather's.

"Thomas Sinavis should be back soon with information from the west. Han Yerry and I will travel to meet with him. We need Kanonwalohale on our side."

"May I go with you?" She paused before adding purposefully, tactfully, "To listen."

Joseph said nothing; the verdict was still undecided—she sensed that in the way he clenched his jaw. Their trust was irrevocably damaged, and that hurt her terribly. "There's to be a meeting between the Seneca and Major Butler soon. Fewer of our brothers are holding on to neutrality. Joseph Brant has been rallying men to his side; he was in Unadilla with two hundred warriors and challenged Honnikol."

"Honnikol? You mean General Herkimer?" Her grandfather was using the native name given to Brigadier General Herkimer of the Tryon County Militia and friend of the Iroquois.

"Grandfather, Joseph Brant has become rather arrogant now that he has the British backing him. The General has always been a friend to the Iroquois. I'm surprised Brant would be so foolhardy towards an ally, even if Herkimer is working with the colonists."

"Brant is bold indeed. When facing the General, Brant listed the Mohawk grievances against the colonists. He claims the confederacy covenant was with the Crown, and the colonists have gone against their King."

"And us, too, for that matter." She stopped there, resisting the urge to say more. The longer she stayed in the village, the harder it became for her to remain silent. It was time for her to go—before she permanently damaged her relationship with her grandfather and her friends. "I have to leave; please, let me know if anything develops. And if you see Alexei, tell him I need to speak with him."

Her grandfather started eating again, his face relaxing, his brows drawing back from their tense furrow. "I'll send word to you when we're planning to travel."

This is a good sign. For now. "Thank you, Grandfather."

As she turned to leave, Joseph cleared his throat, making her stop, and then in a quiet voice, mellifluous with meaning, he said, "Failure is the greatest teacher, Fennishyo. She wants you to learn something. Listen to her."

Dellis nodded, though her heart hurt too much to see wisdom in her humiliation.

There were so many things she wanted to say, a war of ideas waging within, but she held back. Her voice had been silenced within the village. A submissive posture forced on her when it was time to advance and be aggressive.

"You must listen and learn. You must make peace with what has happened to you, my dear one."

But why is that so damned hard?

Chapter Fourteen

When they arrived at Merrick's little, two-story, blue house, it was just as they left it, John's spare uniform and the rest of his clothing cleaned and neatly kept, awaiting him. He washed, shaved, and changed quickly, making ready for his next meeting. He could delay no longer, it was time to face Lord Tomlinson.

"Do you want me to go with you?" Simon asked between mouthfuls of thick, gluey oats.

John curled his lip and pointed to the bowl. "Those are terrible."

Simon snorted and then stuck his spoon in the gloppy mixture, both men glancing at each other with wide-eyed surprise when the utensil stood straight up on its own accord. "John, when both of us take notice of food, it means we've officially been spoiled. I miss my sweet Agnes's buttermilk biscuits."

John rolled his eyes and chuckled.

Simon's words and lurid grin dripped with innuendo. "How does Merrick put up with this poor excuse for food?"

"He's a sailor. If you can survive on victuals for months, you can eat anything. Salt pork and hard tack, and that sludge they get off the boiled meat. Yuck." John groaned, his gut mocking the consistency of lead, full with a mixture of trepidation and Merrick's innkeeper's oats. Her cooking was perfunctory at best, a far cry from the heavenly dishes he was used to at The Thistle. What John wouldn't have done for some of Dellis's ham and potato hash and a strawberry tart. His stomach grumbled painfully from withdrawal. "I need to see Miles alone."

"Will you face the court martial, John?"

He shrugged, casually undermining his looming fear. "I don't know. I'll worry about that when the time comes."

Putting his hat on, he gave himself a onceover in the mirror, examining his uniform for any signs of wear; only the elbows looked a little threadbare, but otherwise, he looked every bit an officer. He turned to his friend and pointed to the desk. "See that those correspondences get to Butler. Today. If you don't see me in a few hours, come find me in the gaol. I take my leave."

"Good luck, John," Simon said before the door slammed.

In the two months since John had last visited Oswego, the population of the sleepy little village had more than doubled to that of a bustling city. It was a safe haven for Tories escaping the tension in the Mohawk Valley, and the meeting place from which General St. Leger would launch the western prong of what was to be a three-pronged attack on New York that included Burgoyne's advance from Quebec down to Albany and Howe's advance up the Hudson River. Only, according to Butler, Howe was no longer going to be a part of the plan; he'd gone after a more illustrious prize: the seat of the Continental Congress in Philadelphia.

Fort Ontario was a British outpost located on high ground on the east side of the Oswego River, one of a few remote forts, including Fort Oswego and Fort Niagara, remaining on the St. Lawrence waterway. It was rebuilt after the French war in the modern European style: a five-point star shape with castmates, a dry moat, earthwork and timber exterior, and barracks enough for five hundred men. Several hundred feet past the outer walls, there were square-shaped redoubts for advanced defense of the fort.

As John walked through the main gates into the parade grounds, he passed rows of canvas tents and soldiers practicing their drills, cleaning their guns, and prepping for the long trek to Stanwix. Militia companies with their uniquely colored uniforms, white, blue, and green, contrasted against the brilliant crimson of the Regulars. Native contingents stayed in one large, isolated territory, far to the other side of the fort, Brant's Mohawks among them, eyeing the soldiers suspiciously while they readied for war. It was to be a combined fighting force, the brigade consisting of both native and regimental soldiers, yet neither fully trusted the other. The whole area had an atmosphere of a powder keg ready to blow; there was too much sitting around and waiting, disorganization adding to the rising tension. Lack of activity notoriously irritated the natives. The officers often tried to bribe and placate the braves with alcohol, only adding drunkenness to the mounting frustration and distrust.

But it wasn't John's problem to solve the mismanagement of the British Army, and he'd said his piece many times about using a native fighting force. He could see errors everywhere he looked and had a deep sense of foreboding about the impending battle. Yes, the warriors were an asset to the army, brilliant tactical fighters, but they could be just as much of a liability when their patience ran out.

John shook his head. After ten years serving in Niagara and with the natives, no one would heed his warnings; his poor reputation silencing his hard-earned political savvy.

"Lieutenant." John stopped behind an officer running drills with his men. "Do you know where Lord Tomlinson is? I need to speak with him."

"I'm busy at the moment. You wait," the Lieutenant yelled over his shoulder, continuing on with his drills. "That was slow! We load, aim, and fire in less than a minute. Ready!" The soldiers responded in unison, pulling cartridges from the boxes at their sides.

John's temper flared. He had it in his mind to see the Lieutenant get twelve lashes for insubordination. "Lieutenant, is that how you address a superior officer?"

The officer whirled around, his eyes widening upon seeing the glimmering gold epaulette on John's right shoulder.

"Captain, excuse me," the Lieutenant said penitently. "Lord Tomlinson is in the officer's barracks." The soldier pointed to the northwest casemate, a small, wooden cabin attached to the interior wall of the fort structure.

"Lieutenant, show respect, or you'll be on your hands and knees cleaning barracks with your tongue." John gave his terse reprimand and then went on his way, letting out sibilant expletives as he crossed the grassy field. He might be the most controversial, polarizing figure in the whole British Army, but he'd earned his rank, and damn it all, he'd shove it down every disrespecting throat if need be.

"Impertinent fool." He grumbled.

The blazing summer sun and the lack of shade further added to his agitation, his wool coat and layers of clothing plastered to his skin with sweat. He watched some of Brant's Mohawk braves loading their muskets and sharpening their knives, realizing how advantageous it was to wear only leggings and a loincloth. How many times Dellis tried to get John to wear native attire; had she asked then, he surely would've relented, and not just to indulge her fantasy.

When John reached the casemate, the sentry stepped in front of the door, chin down, shoulders back, waiting to be addressed.

"Captain Carlisle to see Major Tomlinson."

"Wait here." The guard opened the door and disappeared inside.

After a few pensive moments of looking around and trying to ignore a bead of sweat that rolled down John's nose and hung there persistently, the door opened and he was admitted. The room was dark, his eyes taking a moment to adjust from the midday sun, though he caught a whiff of fresh-cut wood, crisp and pungent like a wintery forest. As everything came into focus, he found the room was, in fact, made of eastern white pine, from the walls and tables to the bunks, and even the ceiling panels. Adorning the back wall was a great stone fireplace that also served as a hearth; inside, two pots, suspended from an iron crane that extended the length of the fireplace, hung over smoldering embers. Cast-iron sconces flanked the two small windows that were on the opposite wall from the fireplace, and from the ceiling, a crude iron candelabra hung, bringing additional light to the room. In the corner were two sets of bunks for the officers to share, each with a thick, cotton-stuffed mattress and blankets that were ten times nicer than the rest of the battalion could boast. It was the barrack of a lord, immaculate and luxurious by military standards, definitely not what a humble captain and his first officer could ever hope for.

Lord Tomlinson sat behind a crude wooden desk, writing, his quill making scratching noises as he finished his letter, never once looking in John's direction. "I'm almost done, Captain. Be patient for a moment."

When finished, Miles poured pounce over the paper, shaking it a few times before blowing the fine powder into the air, and then he folded the letter and affixed his seal with wax and a thump of his brass stamp.

Finally turning his attention to John, Miles said, with a hint of condescension and a dash of ire, "It took you long enough to get here. Explain yourself."

John offered up no apology, though protocol technically demanded it. What was good for the goose wasn't necessarily good for the gander, but the Lieutenant from earlier needn't know that. "Miles, I had to report to Major Butler before I could come to you. I do have my own assignments."

Lord Tomlinson stood and walked towards John, taking slow, deliberate steps, until the men stood face to face. His friend was shorter by at least three inches, yet he had the innate ability to appear taller; perhaps that was what title and rank did for a man, making him larger with pride what he lacked in stature.

"I should have you taken in front of the court marital. This is dereliction of duty."

John looked down, using his height to his advantage. "If that's what you wish, my friend, then so be it. But I promise you, I'm doing all I can to find your wife."

Miles eyed John, a dark onceover that hinted of malice. Survival was the strongest of instincts, and John's sensed something duplicitous in his friend's nature. They'd known each other since childhood, were playmates as boys and drinking mates as young men, but friendships often ended when rank and duty coincided. They'd become soldiers, and time and experience had changed them, taking them down different paths. Miles's commission was handed to him on a silver platter; John had to fight tooth and nail for everything he had, and there was honor in that fact, though few in the elitist class of the British Army recognized it. Serving in the harsh environment of the frontier, and the trauma of life under Roger DeLancie's thumb, had hardened John, turning a pampered, spoiled youth into a seasoned officer.

"Are you really looking for her, or are you, once again, just pursuing your own ends?" Miles's nostrils flared as if he smelled something rancid permeating from John's direction. "Where's my wife? And where's my money?"

"I have my suspicions. But I don't believe she's in any danger."

"You had one job to do, that was to see her and the shipment safely to Niagara. Instead, I find you chasing after your latest paramour who's gone missing. I trusted you, John. We *are* friends, but my patience is wearing thin." Miles's voice dropped an octave, his dark-brown eyes turning coal black with fury. "Find my wife and my money, or face the court. And we both know your reputation can't afford to take another hit."

His threat bore down on John, like Atlas with the world weighing on his shoulders. Miles was formidable, and he had the teeth and fangs to bite back hard: money, power, and rank.

"I *will* find her."

"Good!" Miles backed away, his demeanor lightening suspiciously. "I have a guest who's come a very long way to meet with you."

"Who?" John asked. A rather unusual change in his friend's demeanor—first, threatening a court martial, and then playing introductions as if the men hadn't just argued over something as grave as his wife's disappearance.

Lord Tomlinson opened the door and said something to the guard before shutting it again. "After I met your lady this spring, I sent word to His Grace about our little tête-à-tête. It seemed he was here in the colonies; rather fortuitous, don't you—"

Before Miles could finish, the door flung open and in walked an old friend. A welcome one.

"Merrick?" John shook his head, fearing his tired eyes were deceiving him.

"John!" Merrick stepped into the office, looking larger than life in the Royal Navy tunic of a rear admiral with gleaming gold epaulettes at his shoulder and fancy trimming on his cuffs and facings. In his hand, he held a black hat, also trimmed in gold; his typically messy red hair was pulled back tightly and plaited into a queue, tied in place by a fine black bow.

Miles gestured to Merrick and then to John. "May I introduce, Rear Admiral of the Blue, the Duke of McKesson. Your Grace, this is Captain John Carlisle of the King's Regiment, Light Infantry division."

With a bit of merriment and a mercurial grin, Merrick thrust out his hand. "It's good to see you again, my friend."

Still confused, John shook the duke's hand, fumbling with royal protocol. "Ahh...Your Grace; it's an honor."

Merrick laughed, loudly and heartily, then threw his hat down on the desk. "I know it's rather strange rolling off the tongue, John. I confess it was much harder to become an admiral than a duke and, sadly, far less glamourous sounding. I know the ladies find duke much more intriguing. Don't you think?" He laughed and then elbowed John. "But there's no need for formality between friends; call me Merrick, as you always have."

John played along, though inside, he was still utterly confused. How was it possible that the wind-tossed sailor from Oswego was Dellis's illustrious uncle? Another slap in the face on Fate's behalf, but at least it was in John's favor.

Merrick turned to Miles, and with an authoritative look, he said, "John and I have much to discuss... privately. Please, leave us."

With a curt nod, Lord Tomlinson walked to the door, though he was clearly irritated at being excused, outranked, and out-nobled by his guest. Before Miles opened the door, Merrick made a request.

"Can you have one of your ladies bring refreshment and some tobacco? My friend here has had a long journey." Then, with a wicked grin, he added, "Only the best."

"I'll speak with you later, John," Miles said tersely, obviously unappreciative of being dismissed so thoroughly and quickly.

Once alone, John waited for Merrick to speak, unsure what to say since his true identity was revealed. It was because of him that John survived the gallows yet faced the disdain of his fellow officers. Merrick's protection was both a blessing and a curse simultaneously. Once again, John found himself in a strange reality, so much revealed to him that he never knew was hidden.

"I think I put old Tomlinson's nose out of joint. He's always has to be the prettiest, biggest peacock in the room. What? What?" Merrick laughed and then pulled at the fabric of his sleeve. "And this uniform notoriously does the trick. If it weren't for protocol, I'd wear tarpaulin and linen every day; this tunic itches, and it's hot as Hades in the summer. The Duchess, on the other hand, loves all the pageantry and flash." He pointed to the gold epaulettes at his shoulders and the cording at his wrists and then grinned suggestively. "Women love uniforms, titles, and all pageantry. But a happy wife makes a very happy husband, don't you think?"

John nodded in agreement, though he questioned whether Dellis found any pleasure in seeing him in crimson and gold and what that signified.

"John, speak. It's not like you to be so reserved."

Merrick seemed the same: humorous, brash, and worldly; the only thing that had changed was... Everything. The dynamic of their whole relationship had suddenly shifted from partners with a mutual goal to unsuspecting savior, experienced mentor, and... friend?

"Your Grace—" John started.

"Please, don't call me Your Grace; it's not necessary, and it puts too much distance between us. We're friends." Merrick removed his navy tunic, throwing it over the back of a chair. "And it's bloody hot in here; please, make yourself comfortable."

He took a seat behind the desk and threw his feet on top of it rather unceremoniously. "Army men are so overindulged. It took me until I was a Captain to have even half this space." John followed Merrick's lead, glad to remove the wool tunic and let some warmth out. "Isn't your name Dane?" Not exactly the first question John wanted to ask, but it seemed an easy way to start a conversation.

Merrick leaned forwards and rubbed some dirt from his shiny black shoes with his thumb. "My India usually keeps me looking proper; thankfully, she's not here, or I'd get an earful. I'm really just a humble sailor who belongs on a ship. This uniform and all this formality are just to keep up pretenses." He eyed his shoe for a second and then eased back in the chair. "And, yes, you're not entirely wrong. My full name is Dane Merrick McKesson. But a name can be a curse, and so mine was for a long time. Now, I'm called Merrick out of habit. I think you understand what I mean. The name John Carlisle isn't frequently spoken with much acclaim."

"Yes," John replied. That, he knew all too well.

"Enough said about that nonsense."

Looking more closely at Merrick, John could see the resemblance to the McKesson family, all of them having razor-sharp cheekbones and straight, tapered eyebrows with a long, narrow face. But unlike the rest of men in the family, Merrick was under six foot in height and had brilliant, almost garish, red hair. His shorter stature didn't diminish his intimidating presence; his innate swagger and aristocratic air, unusual for a privateer, made sense for a duke and an admiral.

"You still look confused, my friend; how about I start by asking the questions?" The corner of Merrick's mouth turned up, forming an edgy, dangerous grin. Though he tried to diminish himself with self-deprecation, Merrick wasn't a man to be trifled with, and he wanted John to know that. "How's my sweet Dellis?"

Before John could answer, two of the camp women entered carrying rum, two tankards, and a tray full of food.

"Here are your cigars," one of the ladies said, opening a small wooden box, flashing Merrick a peek of the long, cylindrical indulgences. "After your refreshment, Lord Tomlinson has paid for us to keep you company for the night."

Merrick clucked his tongue, glancing at John. What once would've been a welcome diversion for the evening no longer interested him.

He shook his head. "Thank you, but that won't be necessary; please, keep the money. His Grace and I will be fine with just this and a light supper later in the evening."

The woman nodded, her eyes cast down, looking forlorn at his kind rebuff. A duke and a captain would be an illustrious catch indeed and sure to pay out well.

"Was that for my benefit? Because I'm Dellis's uncle? I'm familiar with your reputation, John. I'm assuming my niece is, too, and has accepted it." Merrick cocked a brow.

Accepted it? A laugh bubbled up in John's throat at the thought of Dellis accepting any of his old vices. "No, she'd never accept such things, and chasing skirts is for a younger, drunker version of me. The thought of another woman is… inconceivable now." He remembered his last days with Dellis, making love under the willow tree, the way she consumed his soul each time he touched her. "Bedding a woman is easy sport, but making love to one is something quite different. It ruins you."

"Aye, it is." Merrick reached for a raspberry and then popped it into his mouth. "I spend months away from my wife, and by the time I return, I'm like a traveler in the desert who's found an oasis. I can barely come up for air." Then, with a raise of his eyebrows, he said, "And she loves it. But I've found that rum can be a decent stand in, or at least it numbs me enough so I forget."

Merrick poured them both a tot and handed one to John. He swirled the dark liquor in his glass then looked up. "I have a weakness for overindulging. I promised Dellis I'd abstain."

Merrick lifted the glass to his nose, smelling the liquor, and then opened the little wood box and picked out a cigar before offering John one. "We all overindulge in the service of His Majesty. It's inevitable. I've been promising the Duchess I'd abstain, too, but she's not here, and I'm not expected to perform tonight. Now, shall we salute and keep this just between us?"

"Bottoms up." Finding little fault in Merrick's logic, John clinked glasses and downed the spicy liquor. The initial calm that always came with a drink permeated his veins, drawing him into the warm, familiar place that he only found in the bottle.

When Merrick poured another drink, John threw it back quickly, reaching again for that elusive moment of nihility before it was gone and he was one with his demons again.

What did the woman want? James sneered, looking down at the letter in his hand. Her fine feminine script was in complete contrast to her cold, calculating demeanor, and of course, she kept the letter nebulous; the goal was to get him to come to her. It was all part of her plan to draw him into her lair and sink her claws in deeply.

My Dear Sir,
Meet me in my room at The Silver Kettle.
CA

James threw the letter on a tray and lit it with a candle, watching the paper smolder and turn to ash. Grabbing his hat, he stalked out of the house and mounted his horse, riding off towards town. It was one of her ploys, another little game to try and weaken his resolve. Business was never enough for that type of woman; she had to have it all: money, sex, control. But her ultimate goal was power. He'd known plenty of women like her back in England. Having played the courtly games of love amongst the wealthy and privileged, he could give just as good as he got.

As expected, when Mrs. Allen opened the door to her room, all her attributes were on display; candlelight illuminated her curvaceous form through the gauzy, diaphanous fabric of her shift. Her chestnut locks hung down to her shoulders, fat, shiny curls gently resting on her bosom, drawing attention to their lush fullness.

James laughed at her solicitous attempt and pushed past her, taking his first steps into her inner sanctum. "Put a robe on. This isn't a social visit, Mrs. Allen."

"Are you sure you want me to do that?" She rested one of her dainty hands on his jacket, fingering the lapel and then trailing down to his waist.

"You're welcome to service me, but I'm not in the position to return the favor." He pulled her hand away abruptly. "Let's just get that out of the way."

He relished the change in her expression from a sultry, heavy-lidded glimmer to wide-eyed outrage, her dark, inky pupils turning to perfect points.

"Mrs. Allen, have you never had a man be so direct with you? I highly doubt that. And your innocent act is wasted on me; you're no blushing maid on her wedding night," he said tersely. "I have no interest in you save the information you bring. You're industrious, I'll give you that, but you're also more trouble than you're worth. That's what all your other suitors have failed to realize." He stepped closer to her, loving the frustrated scowl on her face. "Tell me, have I spoiled your plans?"

She backed away, grabbed her blue silk robe off of the bed, putting it on, and tying it around her waist. Pulling her hair out of the neckline, she turned to him and smiled. "On the contrary, I've dealt with plenty of your type." Under her breath, James heard her sibilant mutter: "Churlish with a side of brute."

"Now, what do you have for me?" He pulled a velvet sack from his jacket and shook it so the coins clanked around. Her eyes widened like a dog spying on an old soup bone; she reached for the little bag, but he snatched it away, holding it up high above her head.

"Tell me!" He commanded, as if he were giving orders to his pet.

She crossed her arms over her chest and rolled her eyes, no longer indulging his game. "Alexei is in Oswego procuring more supplies, and the British are holed up in Fort Ontario waiting for St. Leger, which makes it a proverbial gold mine for your son—if he doesn't get caught."

"Good." James nodded. Yes, she could be helpful when properly motivated. "What else?"

"About a week ago, The Thistle was ransacked by the local militia, looking for Redcoats. Your niece has been branded a Tory sympathizer. If it hadn't been for the magistrate's son, they would've burned the house down."

Now we're getting somewhere. "What happened to Carlisle?"

She grinned. "Both he and his friend got away before the mob could get to them."

It was all good information, but not what he needed. "Did you learn anything about the woman?"

"No, not yet. What are you going to do?"

"I have business to attend to. I'll be leaving town tomorrow," James replied. His plans were none of her concern, and the less she knew, the better.

"Can I make a suggestion?" she asked, cocking her brow.

"Go on."

She was plotting again; her acting was so predictable he could read her every tell.

"Take my friend Eagle Eyes and his men with you; he's very useful, and he has a personal gripe with John Carlisle and the Oneida. Should you run into them, it will look like nothing more than another native skirmish in the woods. Why, Butler may even thank you for such a deed."

Occasionally, at best, there were flashes of brilliance delivered by her calculating female mind. Occasionally. James actually liked that idea; she could be fastidious when it came to planning.

"Have him come to my house at dawn tomorrow. I leave for Niagara then. Now, if you'll excuse me." He put the velvet pouch in her hand and gave her a curt nod of good riddance.

"While you're there, I encourage you to visit my place in The Bottoms. See what a good investment you made with your money."

When James turned to leave, Celeste grabbed his coat, trying once more to draw him under her thrall. He knew what was coming; she was making her move. With a grin, she slowly dropped to her knees and started working the buttons of his front fall.

"Have you never met a woman who found giving just as pleasurable as receiving? But then you've had the same wife for so long you've probably forgotten." She glanced up at him suggestively, her tongue slowly running over her lips, moistening them to a tart, dewy red before she leaned in to take her first lick.

That was one department his beloved was sorely lacking in.

"You can do that all you like," James replied, watching her head move up and down as she went to work. No matter how hard she tried, he'd never give her what she wanted. Control—that was her weakness—and she'd just lost it.

Chapter Fifteen

When Dellis reached the stable, she quickly brushed the dirt and sweat off her mare, furnishing her up with some water and a bucket of oats. Slowly, Dellis walked around the front of The Thistle, picking up a few dead branches and a discarded piece of paper that littered the landscape, trying to keep the grounds neat and tidy. A gentle breeze swept between the giant maple trees that flanked the house; their limbs reached over like hands, offering blessed shade from the blistering summer sun. Stopping for a moment, she sighed, looking up at the boarded windows, jagged, angry bits of glass still jutting out from the frames. Somehow, she'd find the money to get them fixed. Surely her father up in Heaven was having a fit; he was always so attentive to his precious house.

As she took the steps, the mail courier approached and handed her a letter.

It was the first time in days she'd received mail; only the letter wasn't for her, it was addressed to John, and it used his real surname, not his pseudonym. She flipped the envelope over, running her finger over the wax seal, debating whether to open it. *What if it's from Mrs. Allen?* She crumpled the letter in her fist, trying to forget her wedding day and the matching navy fabric John and Mrs. Allen wore as if they were the intended couple.

Damn him. But good sense won out where anger pervaded; he could be in trouble and the missive Dellis's only conduit to him.

She cracked the seal and opened the letter. It was from Gavin, his scrawl-like writing a stark contrast to John's more elegant, round, copperplate style. Slowly, she walked up the steps, so intent on reading that she bumped into a gentleman tacking an angry-looking notice full of oversized words on the front door.

"What's this?" She snatched the paper off the door, tearing the top where the tack fixed it in place. He ignored her and started down the steps.

"Excuse me, what's this?" She held up the paper, shaking it in the air impatiently. "This is my tavern, and I'd like to know what you think you're doing?"

The man turned around, and with an air of superiority, he replied, "Miss, you've been accused of harboring and assisting British soldiers in your establishment. By order of the town magistrate, your tavern has been closed and your property confiscated. There'll be a trial today at three o'clock."

"That's in an hour!" Dellis's shook her head incredulously. "I don't understand. Who's accused me of this?"

"You may face your accusers in court. Just like in Westchester County, we don't take kindly to Tories, and we know how to deal with them. If you're lucky, you'll only have to give a Test Oath and your tavern can reopen."

Dellis swallowed down the lump in her throat. Test Oaths were used to force Tories into swearing allegiance to the Colonies, but they could also be used to take away businesses and justify imprisonment, or even death, if broken, or if one was suspected of sympathies to the King.

"Have mercy." Still in shock, Dellis walked in the front door and sat in the first chair she could find before she fell down. Taking a deep breath, she reined in her emotions before she had to face Agnes and Will. Distressing them would only make matters worse.

Unfolding the letter in her hands, she read it quickly.

My dear brother,

Since you've selfishly denied me the pleasure of a fair duel, I consider our negotiations also notwithstanding. You owe me the sum of 1500 pounds, that's the 1200 plus interest. If I don't get the money before I'm due to leave for England in a month's time, I'll see you in debtor's prison and your properties confiscated.

I remain, &c.,

Carlisle and Kenyon

She put the letter on the table, her head dropping into her hands. *How is this all happening at once?*

"Did that man tell you about the court order?" Agnes asked, her arms full of plates as she cleaned up the bar.

Dellis heard words coming from somewhere, yet she couldn't find the source, nor the answers, too embittered to speak. Grabbing the missive off the table, she walked upstairs to her room and shut the door, wanting to lock the world out and deny its existence. In a matter of weeks, everything that was important to her had been stripped away: first the baby, then John, her role in the tribe, and then her house—it was too much.

But no matter how she willed them, the tears wouldn't come. And what good would they do? She refused to let anyone take away her father's house. They'd have to burn it down around her before she'd give it up. If she was to go before the magistrate, then so be it; she'd face her cowardly accuser in court and say her piece.

Walking across the hall, Dellis unlocked the top drawer of John's desk, put Gavin's letter in with the rest of documents, and then closed it. Quickly, she used the basin next to the bed to perform her daily ablution. She readjusted her hair and placed a new kerchief in the neckline of her dress, making sure she looked appropriate for court. Appearance was essential when facing a town full of judgmental men who thought of her as only a woman—actually less since she was half native and notoriously debauched.

When Dellis came back downstairs, Agnes and Thomas were sitting at a table, chatting over cups of coffee.

"Do you want one of us to go with you?" Thomas asked, looking up from his beverage.

What to do?

Dellis nodded. Her energy tapped by the mounting events of the previous two days, she sauntered to the table and poured herself a cup of coffee, hoping it would rejuvenate her. "Yes, both of you, please come. I'm going to need all the help I can get."

"Of course." Agnes reached over, giving Dellis's hand a squeeze of much-needed support. "This is my home, too, and I'm not going to let anyone take it away from me. I've nowhere else to go, so here it will be."

How she loved Agnes's stubborn spirit; it gave Dellis the extra boost she needed when it seemed nothing else could.

"All right then." She looked down at her father's table, the grooves of age in the wood reminding her of the lines in his beloved brow. At least she was no longer alone; he'd seen to it through the friends sitting next to her, proof of his unending love. "Go get Will, and we'll walk down to the courthouse. Better to be early than late."

While they waited for Thomas and Will to return, Agnes said, "What will you tell the magistrate about Simon and the Captain?"

That very question had been on Dellis's mind since she tore the letter from the door. "I'll tell them the truth. We had no idea they were spies until after they left."

"But what about your relationship with the Captain? What will you say?"

"I haven't figured that out yet. To be quite honest, I was hoping something would spontaneously come to me, but at the moment, I'm so overwhelmed, I don't know what to do."

Once Thomas and Will were in the dining room, Dellis took one last look around, swearing to herself that she'd return victorious. No, she couldn't possibly lose so much, God was surely not that cruel. The paint might be peeling, the plaster molding on the ceiling darkened from soot, and the wooden floors scuffed beyond repair, but it was her home, and she'd fight to the death to keep it. For all of them.

After several drinks and indulging in a tray of delicacies, John felt more at ease. He'd yet to expound on his situation or ask the plethora of questions that loomed under the surface; instead, he simply exchanged jokes and pleasantries with Merrick.

He sat back in his chair and puffed his cigar, the tip glowing red when he inhaled. "John, tell me about Dellis. Is she well? I miss her so."

John, taking a long draw off his own cigar, held the sweet smoke in his mouth for a moment and then blew it out, the tobacco helping him expunge a bit of tension. "She's written you several times; if you've longed to hear from her, why have you never written back?"

"If only that were the truth." Merrick poured them both a tankard of ale, sliding one across the table to John. "I've been writing her almost every month for the past three years. What's most disturbing is that I was sending portions of her father's inheritance to help her and Stuart. What you say further confirms to me that James has been intercepting my letters."

"When I first came to The Thistle, Dellis was bordering on destitute." John smiled, pleasantly diverted by memories of home, the smell of her cooking, the decadent bed in his room, and the promise of her being there when he woke in the morning. "Despite her predicament, she's managed to carry on, and quite well. I've never met a more determined woman, though your brother has worked very hard to undermine her."

He puffed his cigar again, enjoying how the tobacco combined with the rum circumvented his anxiety—blissful relaxation for the first time in days.

"Before we go there, how are you and Dellis? You're going to marry her and make a proper lady of my niece?"

Caught off guard, John coughed up smoke, choking on Merrick's boldness. He certainly got to the crux of the matter, though he sat back, sipped from his tankard casually, and puffed his cigar as if he hadn't asked the most serious of questions.

"Of course," John said between coughs, the smoke burning his throat. "We're not together right now." An understatement if he'd ever heard one, their last moments together still fresh in his mind. "But I married her within the Oneida tribe. I consider her my wife, though the law may not."

With a laugh, Merrick kicked his foot across the desk, hitting John in the lower arm. "You scoundrel; you didn't even ask her next of kin for her hand."

"Actually, I did. I asked her grandfather and the members of her clan." John tapped the end of his cigar, dropping his ash in the tray.

"It's strange twist of fate that you should marry her. But I remember you not so long ago brooding in your ale over an unexpected parting. Is this still the same problem?"

"No." He paused, taking a moment to decide how best to proceed; it was, after all, Dellis's uncle and surrogate father, and there were some things that shouldn't be discussed with family. "Everything seems to be working against us: this war, our past, my past. When I left, she wouldn't speak to me."

John drank deeply from his tankard, drowning himself in the hoppy brew, his heart feeling like it was being squeezed in a vice from want of her. Pushing his cup away, he waved off Merrick when he went to pour more, better to stop before turning mawkish.

"It's the worst torture when your wife has closed her heart to you." Instead of Merrick's merriment and humor of earlier, there was something grave with understanding about the words. "My darling India has forsaken me before, and the only cure for her disdain was time."

"Your wife's name is India?" John asked. "Rather exotic."

"It's my pet name for her, and she prefers I call her that."

There was sentiment and adoration in Merrick's voice, true love's endearment. It was fitting that Dellis's Oneida name should mean beautiful valley; she was the most beautiful, peaceful thing John had ever known.

"India is a jewel, the ruby in my life. And like me, she has a fiery spirit that leads to ferocious arguments and decadent, heated reunions."

"I understand." John could get behind that. He lifted his tankard in salute. Lovemaking after a fight was his favorite, blissful and wanton, especially when Dellis was in the wrong.

"Don't distress yourself, my friend; you'll work it out. Time heals all wounds. If not, a well-placed smack on the bottom works, too. And don't think I haven't done it to the Duchess, though it defeats the purpose when she enjoys it."

John covered his mouth with his fist, coughing out more smoke as he laughed. "Why are you here, Merrick?"

"I suppose I owe you the truth, after all you've done for my family. It's fitting that my niece's hand now belongs to you, poetic justice that only Shakespeare himself could've penned."

Justice? No, it wasn't justice, it smacked of Karma's sleight of hand. John snorted, taking a sip from his tankard. "Not quite sure about that."

"Where to start? It's a long story, which, I'm afraid, reflects good on no one." Merrick sighed.

"My brother James inherited our family title, and a considerable fortune, along with McKesson House, when my father died. My father supported King George the first during the Jacobite uprisings in seventeen-fifteen. You can imagine that wasn't popular amongst the clans, and it earned us a reputation as traitors. James was a Scotsman through and through, and though he was favored at court, and with King George the second, my brother always wanted to get back into good graces with the other Scottish lords. When he was on his Grand Tour, he fell in love with a Russian diplomat's daughter—"

"Helena." John provided.

"Yes." Merrick nodded. "The tour took him to Italy, where my brother payed court to the Old Pretender James and his son Charles and even made alliances with them, seeing a chance to earn back our family reputation. James agreed to support the Jacobite uprising, sending thousands of pounds and allowing Charles to use some of our land to prepare his men. When Culloden was lost, King George was swift with his reprimanding of the Scots and anyone who assisted in the uprising. Out of fear for our family, Stephen and I exposed James's treachery to the authorities, but it was too late; we were declared traitors, our lands confiscated, and our fortune and title revoked."

"It all makes sense now," John said. "Why he was angry with Stephen… and you."

"There's more." Merrick held up his hand. "James escaped to New York and then later sent for Helena while Stephen and I were forced to reckon with the irreparable damage the scandal caused our family. Many years after, when I was an officer in the Navy, Stephen joined the crew of my ship; we travelled to the colonies, and we tried to reconcile with James, but it was pointless. Stephen, ever the peacemaker, wouldn't give up. He stayed behind, even followed my brother north to the frontier."

"That's how he got to German Flats," John said.

Merrick nodded. "For personal reasons, I won't discuss how our family title and lands were returned, but suffice to say, it eventually happened, though James and his children were disinherited. I imagine, when he found out, he was rather furious."

"And that's why he went after Stephen, isn't it? He couldn't get at you." John had already put the dirty little pieces of the puzzle together. All the killing, all the anger… In the end, it boiled down to nothing more than revenge and a family squabble over money.

"Not entirely. He's tried to get at me and has been rather successful. Twice, I've caught my brother stealing and selling weapons; at first to the French, during the war, and now, to the colonists. But he was also stealing from our side. While I served on the Navy Board, I found out James was falsifying my name on licenses for privateers, granting them passage down the St. Lawrence. He was stealing from our ships in New York and Boston and then selling everything back to us on the frontier."

"So he was playing both sides of the fence?" John shook his head with incredulity. "But far enough away to not be caught." *Brilliant.*

With a nod, Merrick continued. "One of his ships was eventually boarded, and they found documents with my name on them. Currently, there are only ten privateers that have licenses to travel the St. Lawrence, by order of the Vice-Admiralty of New York. James was making money selling fake permits with my signature, knowing that as a member of the Navy Board no one would ever question me. But the worst part is that some of the goods on these boats *were* authorized by me, for Stephen to trade with our native allies. It was just another place that my name was on the paperwork. When James realized I was on to him, he turned his focus to Stephen, and that's where you come in."

"No need to recant my tale of woe. I lived it firsthand," John said sarcastically, though he found the whole situation far from humorous.

"Of course," Merrick replied. "James hates all natives because they attacked German Flats; even though the Oneidas warned the villagers, and they chose not to listen. Forty men and women were murdered, over one hundred and fifty were captured, James's farm was destroyed, and several of his workers were killed. Right after, the measles went through town; first Alexei and then Helena fell ill. Jamie, my brother's oldest son, died. My brother never forgave Alexei for it, nor the natives."

There was one piece of the convoluted puzzle Merrick had yet to reveal, and John could wait no longer for the answer. "How did you find out about me?"

"After Stephen died, India lost another child. I was distraught, having lost so much I held dear in such a short time. India begged me to bring Stephen's murderer to justice. It was the one thing we could do, a sliver of power to hold on to when everything else was beyond our control. Stephen and I had long suspected James of treachery, and I was convinced he was responsible. When I arrived at Niagara and started asking questions, your name came up as second-in-command under Major DeLancie. Carlisle Shipping is a very important supplier to the King, and your father was a dear friend to me."

"You knew my father?" John interrupted. "How? Through the Navy?"

Merrick offered up little, leaving John with more questions than answers. "He did me a favor when I was down on my luck. And though your father was dead, I'd never had a chance to repay his kindness. So I took up your case on his behalf, and the more I researched the matter, knowing what I did about James, the worse it all looked. I requested your reexamination by the judge advocate; only that time, you told the truth. Roger DeLancie and I go way back. I'd seen him in action before, and your account of his demeanor was decidedly accurate. Once your testimony was given, I made your superiors promise they'd send you back to your men. It was my fault I never followed up on what actually became of you."

"What would you have done had I not changed my story? Had I lied again?" John was fearfully curious what his friend would say.

"You would've hanged," Merrick replied, flatly, with no remorse.

A long drop and a quick stop.

John put his hand on his throat, abrupt truth and realization of death so close giving him pause.

"So, now you're here. I assume to catch James," he said, quick to change the subject.

"When you and I met, I didn't know who you were; it was only through our discussion that I discovered your true identity, and then I wasn't sure if you'd keep my secret. I had to stay hidden from my brother. I was trying to catch Alexei in the act; then, I could put pressure on him to help me implicate James."

"I hate to state the obvious, but if James is a wanted traitor, why don't you just have him arrested?" It seemed an easy enough option, especially with Merrick's lofty position.

"My brother has many friends in high places, and they're powerful men who made a fortune because of his dealings here in the colonies. If he goes down, they, too, could face reprimand. It would cause a scandal, and one that would further prove the corruption of our system and add fuel to the colonists' fire."

"Alexei is here in Oswego," John said, a plan coming to mind. "We can catch him and put a stop to all of this. You and I."

Merrick's grave face returned to its former jovial expression, his lips turning up in the corners. "My men already have eyes on him. We're just waiting on him to make a move. Will you help me?"

Merrick poured them both a tot and slid one of the glasses across the table.

"I owe supplies to Butler, and I must return Lord Tomlinson's wife to his safekeeping. Alexei is my only hope."

"All right then." Merrick picked up his glass, holding it in salute. "To justice."

John clinked glasses. "To justice." He paused, considering what that meant to him. The end. Peace. "Finally." That word brought with it an exhale, a breath long held since the day he first faced the court martial.

He threw back his shot and placed the glass on the table, upside down.

"Now for our plan." Merrick puffed his cigar with a grin.

Chapter Sixteen

"Major Butler, you have a visitor." James could hear the guard speaking through the wooden door. After years of keeping a healthy distance from anything related to the military, it felt oddly familiar being in the thick of it again. Had James not been betrayed by his brothers, he might've had a brilliant career as an officer and then moved on to serve in the House of Lords. He never wanted to be a farmer or a privateer, both jobs beneath his station, but when destitute, one either rises to the occasion or is crushed by the elements. Failure wasn't an option.

When the door to Butler's office opened, James rose to his feet and gestured for Eagle Eyes to follow. Major Butler stood behind his desk, his dark, bushy brows furrowed. It wasn't a meeting either of them had looked forward to with any sense of pleasure.

"Don't sit, McKesson." The Major waved his index finger at both James and Eagle Eyes and then pointed to the door. "You're both leaving now."

"Butler, I have no desire to be in your presence either, but we have arrangements that must be discussed."

"No, no." Butler shook his head emphatically. "When DeLancie died, you and I ceased to have any arrangements. I'm surprised you dared to venture out of your lair; none of your associates are around to cover for you any longer."

"You can run, but you can't hide, Butler; just because DeLancie is gone, you aren't absolved of your sins." James leaned over the desk, meeting Butler eye to eye with an icy gaze. "You forget—"

"You were paid for goods, but you failed to deliver." Butler interrupted. "I could have you arrested right now, call it theft. I'm sure His Grace would pay a great deal of money if I delivered you to him."

James didn't take the threat of his younger brother lightly, and Butler had just as much to fear from Dane, having played a part in covering up their venture. "You don't want my brother getting involved in this if you know what's good for you. If Dane finds out that you knew about Stephen's murder and said nothing, he'll have your head. You freed DeLancie, and you've been looking the other way while we all profited off this little venture. It's only now that an eye has been turned on you that our business is inconvenient."

Butler struck back quickly, and with force. "McKesson, there are only two people who know the truth and would actually gain something from talking, your son and John Carlisle, and neither of them have reason to protect you. But myself, on the other hand, it would serve neither of them to expose me, especially Carlisle."

Pointing at Eagle Eyes, waiting patiently in the corner like a benevolent king, James said, "Give me time. We'll get your supplies and deal with my son and Carlisle."

"No, you're out of time." Butler shook his head. "I've no need of you anymore."

To their surprise, Eagle Eyes relinquished his solitude and spoke. "I can bring you more of my brothers, Major. You need us."

Butler's gazed flashed to the giant Mohawk, wheels turning behind those dark, beady eyes. "What do you get out of this?"

James remained silent, curious as to what the notoriously diffident native would say on his behalf.

"Revenge."

Nothing surreptitious about that; Eagle Eyes was still bitter about the loss of his mentor, and that worked to James's advantage.

Butler cocked a brow, affording the Mohawk a look of appreciation. "Vengeance is a powerful ally. And for more of your brothers, I'd be willing to negotiate."

"We'll go after my son and his Oneidas and take back what's ours." James added.

"That's all fine and good, but before you do that, I have a suggestion, one that might help relieve you of some of your obligations to me." Butler sat down and pulled some papers out of his desk, digging through them until he found what he sought. "There's a woman in The Bottoms who runs an establishment that the officers frequent."

"Celeste Allen." James provided.

"Precisely." Butler handed over a piece of paper containing a list of merchants and suppliers that delivered to Niagara through Carlisle Shipping and other licensed privateers. "There's a man named McKenzie; he supplies Mrs. Allen with the luxury goods for her establishment. Perhaps you can persuade him to sell to us; of course, with the backing of His Majesty's government to cover the cost."

James tossed the paper back on the desk. "Luxury goods? I thought you wanted guns and ammunition?"

Butler nodded. "That's why you'll go after your son and get my weapons back. But for now, I need something to trade with the Seneca at Irondequoit. Rum and furs will do nicely."

"What about Carlisle?" James asked. That man was a mutual thorn in their sides, and it was time to silence him for good. Before he exposed everything.

"Captain Carlisle is currently on a mission for me, locating something he lost. No need to worry about him now."

Carlisle was looking for the woman. "Where is he?"

"Oswego."

It all made sense. Carlisle was going after Alexei and the woman, which meant James could kill two birds with one stone.

Easy enough.

195

"Come, Eagle Eyes. We have work to do." James put his hat back on and nodded to Butler. "I'll have supplies for you by tomorrow."

The county courthouse was in Johnstown, but a small, local case such as hers would be held at the church in German Flats and be officiated by the town magistrate, Patrick's father.

Dellis cringed at the prospect of seeing the man that had once treated her like a daughter, the very same one who separated her from her betrothed three years before. They'd not spoken since that day, and he always turned the other way when they passed on the street; she was permanently tainted goods, and he was a man of position, unwilling to sully his name with the likes of her.

As Dellis walked up to the steps of the little brick building, some of the locals were already filing inside ahead of her. She eyed them suspiciously, wondering which of her friends, neighbors, or former patients of her father would do such an odious thing to her.

Will, Agnes, and Thomas followed close behind, the three of them wan faced and wide eyed. The Thistle was their home and their combined livelihood. *What will happen to them if I lose my house? Where will we go?*

Father, please, help me. How she wished he were there. He would've known what to do.

The church was much too small for the crowd that adjourned, the pews ready to tip from the weight of so many bottoms, and the white-washed walls buttressed those who waited in the standing-room-only section at the back. It was like a crucible that threatened to burst, the room charged with anger and fear, made worse by the smoldering heat four open windows couldn't negate. Just in front of the altar, a large, cherrywood desk had been set up where George Armstrong-Jones, the town magistrate, sat down.

Dellis and her friends took their places on the bench nearest the front of the room. She glanced over her shoulder several times, looking back at the townspeople she once called friends; leering eyes and looks of disdain were afforded to her while they whispered under their breath. It had a bit of theater about it, an auspicious event for the sleepy town: a scandalous woman harboring a British spy and his men, clandestine meetings, and passing missives. Oh, the drama. She'd given the townspeople something titillating and salacious to talk about in their mundane lives, a good show for their amusement; yet, once again, she was the object of ridicule, her life up for judgement by jealous transgressors. No man was free of sin, but they'd burn her for hers. The town pariah.

Patrick walked in, his warm smile and kind green eyes a welcome sight as he made his way up the aisle and sat on the bench, taking her hand and giving it a squeeze. Not so very long before, the thought of a man touching her was terrifying, but since John, she'd learned to find comfort in their strong hands and warm embraces, a reassurance of her own inner fortitude. When she turned back to the magistrate, his eyes were following the interlude between her and his son with skepticism.

"Patrick, perhaps it's not such a good idea for you to be here." She pulled her hand from his.

"Nonsense, I'll speak on behalf of you and your friends. I'm the magistrate's son; who better to stand up for you?" Patrick took her hand back and squeezed it again.

"Thank you." She looked down at her aged, muted-blue petticoat and picked a piece of lint from the fabric while mentally preparing herself for the inevitable. She'd have to speak about her relationship with John in public for the first time. Something so personal and intimate was meant to be private, between two people, and theirs was a convoluted story, easy to misinterpret from the spectator's position. But from within, after all the deception fell away and the truth was revealed, they were quite simply star-crossed lovers just trying to hold on as forces around them pulled in all directions. *But can I denounce him to save myself?*

Overcome with emotion, she put her face in her hands, praying the earth would open up and swallow her whole. *Why is it now that I miss him most?* John could always talk himself out of a corner. A bit of his silver tongue would serve her rightly in her predicament, and tactical diplomacy was something she notoriously lacked, finding verbal swordplay tedious and disingenuous.

"Miss McKesson, please stand," the magistrate said, his voice carrying over the crowd, causing a hush.

Dellis stood, her stomach churning, threatening to crawl its way up her throat and choke the words back.

"Yes, sir," she said quietly. She glanced over her shoulder; the entire room was silent, watching her with accusing eyes, shaking their heads in disapproval. In the corner, she spotted Stuart and her cousin, Ruslan, regarding her curiously.

Looking back at the magistrate, she swallowed back her fear, waiting for him to address her.

"You've been accused of harboring a British spy in your tavern and helping him gain intelligence about Fort Stanwix. It's also been brought to my attention that you were helping him try to recruit our townspeople to the British cause." His voice was stern; his familiar, olive-green eyes leveled on her, hard and cold, lacking sympathy for her plight. "What do you have to say for yourself?"

"Sir… sir," she muttered, fear making her mouth dry and sticky. "I'm no spy, nor am I a Tory, and anyone who says different is lying. Just like my father, I'm loyal to this community and have done my utmost to care for the people within it. At the time these men arrived at my inn, I had no idea they were British soldiers. I was under the impression they were merchants who'd come to trade with the local tribes. It was only later that I learned the truth about who they were."

"Liar!" a female voice shouted, further provoking Dellis's fear.

"No!" She shook her head but resisted the urge to look back and see who yelled. "I'm not lying. Truly, I didn't know."

"But after you learned the truth, you allowed them to come back and stay at your inn, and both of them were able to slip away with the assistance of you and your staff. And I have it on the word of one of our witnesses that a marriage license was prepared for you and John Carlisle, who we've learned is actually one of His Majesty's spies."

"Who are my accusers? Can I not face them directly?" She demanded. Very few people knew John's true identity, much less his real name; it had to be someone close who betrayed her.

"All right." The magistrate nodded, waving to the crowd. "Please, step forwards."

To her utter shock, Stuart stood and walked towards her, followed by Jussie Simpson and two gentlemen Dellis recognized as patrons of The Thistle. She trembled as her beloved brother faced her; his unpatched eye, the very same one that use to look at her with love and kindness, was black with hate.

"Stuart?" She gasped, her heart kicking wildly in her chest. "How could you do this?"

His stone-cold gaze shifted to the magistrate and then back to her, though Stuart's expression remained stoic, hardened to her plea.

"My sister's been boarding that Redcoat and his men since the wintertime. I told my cousin Alexei he was a spy, and I tried to tell her, but she wouldn't listen." His brow lifted suggestively, bringing with it a wide, toothy grin. "She was too busy spreading her legs for him."

"No!" she yelled, as the crowd erupted in loud jeers.

"*Whore! Tory Trash! Damned Loyalists!*"

She heard the shouts, like something out of a nightmare, surreal, yet in fact, it was her reality. *What have I done to deserve this?*

"That Lobsterback put me in prison when I discovered he was a spy. He did it to keep me quiet."

Forgetting that it wasn't John on trial but her, she went after her brother with words full of vitriol. "Did you tell them what you did to him, Stuart? Did you tell them how you tortured him and killed one of his men? Did you?"

"He's a Redcoat; he got what he deserved." Stuart sneered, his good eye narrowing on her, the patch on his left eye gapping, exposing a bit of marred flesh. "I told you I wouldn't let you marry him. I warned you." Stuart turned his attention back to the magistrate. "I've been unable to live at my home for the past eight months because my sister has been fornicating with that spy."

Dellis's heart sank in her chest. *How has it come to this?* Not two months before, she and Stuart held each other, comforted each other, as Roger DeLancie terrorized them both. Stuart had saved her life; he helped Alexei and John save her.

"Miss Simpson, please, come forward," the magistrate said, his voice rising once again over the rumbling crowd.

As if on cue, Jussie showed up center stage, one hand on her ample hip, her shoulder cocked back with attitude. If she put her nose up any higher, Dellis swore the woman would contract a nosebleed from sheer elevation. "I always suspected Miss McKesson was a Loyalist. We've all heard the rumors about her and the Redcoats at her village. Apparently, they all got a turn."

Dellis fought back a reply, the crowd stoking up again like a fire that was vigorously tended, blazing with laughter and jeers.

"Redcoat Whore! Wasp!"

Jussie stared Dellis down, as though daring her to say something, but she couldn't; it would only make her look guilty and defiant. With a cheeky grin, Jussie continued. "Thankfully, Patrick was able free himself of such a woman before it became a blight on your good reputation, sir."

"Tory! Tar and feather her!"

"Be quiet, everyone!" the magistrate said tersely, glaring at the boisterous crowd. When they quieted down, he finally spoke again. "That's immaterial, Miss Simpson. Please, just tell us what you know."

"The Redcoat we're speaking of introduced himself to me as Captain John Anderson. He frequented my establishment several times during his stay in German Flats and even kept company with one of my lodgers on one occasion." Jussie stopped briefly, a snicker pushing its way through her lips. "He did offer for me a few times, but I turned him down. I always sensed there was something not quite right about him."

You wish. Dellis rolled her eyes, remembering how shamelessly Jussie flirted with John and how deliberately he snubbed her.

"Are you jealous, Miss McKesson, that your beau would make an offer for me first?" Jussie thrust her chin up defiantly, and she grinned. She was clearly enjoying her moment of prominence, *immensely*. But there was no truth in what she said, and it was irrelevant to the case at hand.

Ignoring her taunt, Dellis went after Jussie with truth. "Where's your proof? I've heard you accuse Captain Carlisle of nothing more than being suspicious. How does this have anything to do with me or my establishment?"

Jussie pointed to the two scruffy-looking men standing behind her, the ones Dellis recognized as patrons from The Thistle. "This is Frank Slatterly and Jacob Mercier, regulars at The Silver Kettle. Why don't you tell the magistrate, and Miss McKesson, why you're here?"

The shorter of the two stepped forwards and removed his hat, revealing a balding scalp and a mane of scraggly dark-brown hair. "One night, when we were walking into The Kettle, that tall man, the blond one, he stopped us and put a little satchel in my hand. He told us that he'd been made sick from the food in The Kettle and to go eat at The Thistle. He told me that the food was better, and the owner was easy on the eyes."

"What was in the bag, Frank?" Jussie nudged him with a sparkle in her eyes. "Tell them."

"It was six pence." Jacob looked around at the crowd and nodded. "And we ain't the only ones he paid off. Right, Jedidiah?" He pointed to a white-haired gentleman sitting in the back corner of the room.

"That's right; he paid me a tanner to bring my friends with me to The Thistle." The man stood, hat in hands, and nodded.

Suddenly, it all made sense; that was why her business picked up so quickly during the winter, and that was why The Kettle was struggling. John had bribed villagers to frequent her tavern. *Damn him.* Yet her heart skipped a foolish, love-laden beat. *Damn his corrupt, misguided, wonderful, tender heart.*

With that thought in mind, Dellis bolstered her courage and turned back to the magistrate, ready to plead her case. "What does this have to do with me? I've heard you accuse Captain Carlisle of bribing locals to eat at my tavern, but that's it. That isn't a crime, disturbing as it may be. And this still doesn't prove that he spied on any of you, nor does it prove that he was trying to recruit our townspeople to his cause. You have no case here."

"He's been spying on us. He drew plans of Fort Stanwix. I know because I stole them from his desk." Stuart pointed to himself, grinning satisfactorily. "You're only standing up for him because you're tupping him."

"That's true," a familiar female voice chimed in from off stage. The slow click of heels on the wood floor rang out, and the faint scent of brimstone wafted into Dellis's nose, sending a chill down her spine.

The Devil take the hindmost.

Turning on a heel, Dellis stared directly into the cold, calculating eyes of Celeste Allen. Lilith personified.

"He's a spy. I know because he used my establishment in Manhattan to collect intelligence for the British," Celeste said, making her assent up the aisle to the magistrate's desk, wearing her finest pink frock with her hair piled in a high roll, looking like a proper society lady. "Once the British took over the city, he stole money from me and turned me in; now, there's a warrant out for my arrest, so I can no longer go home. I'm with—"

Patrick stood, interrupting her. "I'm a friend of Miss McKesson, and I've known her for a very long time; there's no way she'd be a party to spying. She's no Loyalist. The only thing she's guilty of is perhaps naiveté and having an over-generous heart."

"If this is, in fact, the case, then why did Miss McKesson still allow him to come back once she knew his true nature? And you can't refute that only days ago John Carlisle procured a marriage license for the two of them." Celeste's eyes shot daggers at Dellis with the skill of a proficient.

"I'd also like to speak on behalf of my niece," said a sweet voice in the wings.

Dellis turned towards the crowd as her Aunt Helena stood, her light eyes surprisingly full of sympathy.

"My husband and I are good, upstanding citizens of this village. At the time Captain Carlisle took up residence at The Thistle, I was working with my niece. I was the one who allowed them to stay as lodgers and obtained their fee. Neither I nor my niece had any idea they were spies. The Captain and his men always behaved as gentlemen; they never asked, or insinuated in any way, that they were anything less than the merchants they claimed to be."

"That still doesn't change the fact that Miss McKesson knew he was a Redcoat and allowed him to return!" Celeste yelled, once again stoking the ire of the crowd.

"Tory whore!"

"You intended to marry him. What does that say about you? It was only when you were caught by the mob that you helped him escape; otherwise, he'd still be here, under our noses, spying on all of us." Celeste directed her attention to the crowd, pointing her tapered fingernail at them, allowing it to slowly track back and forth. "And now, we know the British are coming. Ticonderoga fell only days ago; the next place they'll strike is here, at Fort Stanwix, and she led them to us."

"No!" Dellis screamed, trying desperately to connect with the crowd, but no one would meet her gaze. "I'd never help the British. I, more than anyone in this town, have reason to hate them. They destroyed my village and murdered my parents. And they ruined my..." Dellis looked back at Patrick, his eyes softening—their betrothal a tragic casualty of the war. "I know what people say behind my back, that I'm a whore, that I sleep with Redcoats. If all of that were true, then this entire case would be damning indeed. But it isn't."

It's so much sadder.

Dellis took a deep breath, reaching for that inner well of strength that seemed perpetually full, but it was dry. There were no words. Her hands shook, the roar of the crowd rising in slow motion, shouts of "Whore!

Trollop! Loyalist!" biting at her like little gnats, penetrating her thickened skin and gnawing at her heart.

She glanced at Agnes and Will, standing in the front row, watching her, their hearts in their eyes. Those two were all Dellis had left, and she refused to see them on the streets. She swallowed down the bitter pill of pain stuck in her throat and turned back to the crowd, ready to do battle no matter what it cost her.

"I was raped by the soldiers that came to my village; I did *not* go willingly to them." She looked at Stuart, his head bowed, avoiding her truthful gaze. "It's a cruel lie that's plagued me since that day, and it cost me everything: my betrothed, my reputation, and my chance at happiness. My father loved this town just as I do. He even cared for many of you when you were sick. Captain Carlisle came to my tavern undercover, that's true, and eventually, I did learn his real identity. But he also saved the people of my village and protected me from a madman that was trying to kill us. Was I planning to marry him? The answer is yes—because I love him."

Dellis focused on Celeste, drawing courage from her outrage. "And he loves me. Yes, he's a British soldier, and I may not agree with all that he's done, but I can love a person and not like what they are."

"Miss McKesson." The magistrate interrupted. "If you married him, then as your lord and husband, his beliefs become yours. If he's British, then so, too, are you."

She laughed to herself. *Utter nonsense.* Men knew so little of the thoughts and feelings of their wives. How many women greatly disagreed with the political beliefs of their husbands? Rumor had it even General Gage, a British officer, had a defiant Rebel wife.

Turning back to the magistrate, Dellis took a deep breath, ready to face the music. "If you wish to punish someone, then so be it. Put me in the stocks, tar and feather me. I don't care, but don't punish my workers for this. Don't throw my servants out on the streets. You've already damaged my house and beaten my poor dish boy—who did nothing more than protect his home. Leave them out of this."

"Father, please. Don't do this." Patrick begged. "I know you never approved of our betrothal, but don't let that cloud the truth of what's happened here."

"What happened here?" George Armstrong-Jones raised his voice so that it bounced off the walls, silencing the muttering crowd. "Based on the testimony of your aunt, I believe that you didn't know Captain Carlisle was a spy when he initially lodged at your inn. I don't know what to make of him paying off some of our locals to frequent your establishment, but it's clear to me that you had no part in that either."

Dellis nodded, penitently.

"However, after you discovered his true character, you did allow him and his men to stay in your establishment, and you did intend on marrying Captain Carlisle. Based on the evidence provided by your brother and Mrs. Allen, the Captain spied on Fort Stanwix with the intent of delivering the information to the British. This smacks of collusion, and that, I can't absolve you of, nor have you provided proof to refute this claim. Because I was friend to your father, and he saved my life when the Pox struck, I'll give you this one concession. You may keep your house, for now, but you're no longer allowed to operate as a tavern or an inn. Your business is officially closed as a warning to others who may feel inclinations towards the Crown. That is my final judgement."

Dellis swallowed; the pain like ground glass in her throat made it impossible for her to speak. Yes, she still had her house, but not for long if she couldn't work. It was prolonged torture, like the slow removal of a bandage from a festering, open wound.

Stuart stood before her for a moment, bitter silence between them, then he smirked and walked away. She'd never forgive him; it wasn't just a betrayal directed at her, it was against their parents, too.

Dellis spied a devilish grin on Celeste's face before she picked up her voluminous skirts and left the courthouse, Justine and the rest of the town following.

Dellis grabbed Agnes and Will's hands, and the three of them walked together through the doors into the summer sun. The crowd shouted obscenities, but the trio held their heads high, walking back to their home together. Their sanctuary.

"Whore! Tory slut!" the crowd yelled.

Someone threw an egg at Dellis, the shell cracking and leaving a gooey mess on her skirts, but she carried on. The three of them said nothing during the short walk back to The Thistle, still hand in hand, clinging to each other for support. When they reached the top of the steps, she opened the door, waiting for her lady friends to go inside, Thomas slowly following behind.

"Dellis, don't you worry. We'll find a way to pay the bills," Agnes said.

"Thank you." Dellis closed the door and then bolted it tightly, praying it would hold up against the mob if they returned.

Bills? She couldn't even think about bills right then.

Agnes grabbed Dellis's hand, trying to pull her towards the kitchen. "I'll make some coffee, and then we can figure out what to do next."

She shook her head, pushing a stray lock of hair behind her ear with a trembling hand. "I just need to be alone. But the three of you, please, eat something."

Slowly, she walked up the stairs to her room, the great, mahogany, four-poster bed was empty, waiting for her to throw herself upon it and weep out her cares. But she didn't. She couldn't. She was done playing the victim, the whole persona she'd carried for years wearing thin on her nerves and her all-too-broken heart.

Turning around, she walked across the hall to John's office and unlocked his top desk drawer, pulling out the picture he drew for her. When she unfolded it, his smile was the first thing she saw and then those extraordinary blue eyes.

"Damn you, John."

God, how she wished he was there so she could wail at him, scream at the top of her lungs, and slap both his smooth, kissable cheeks. He bribed those men. *Oh, the scoundrel.* She'd smack the smile off his face and then throw him down on her bed and take that much-wanted crop to his backside, making sure he wouldn't sit for a week. It was as if he were looking out at her through the paper, a sheepish smirk of guilt with a tinge of smug. *Bastard.* But his gambit saved The Thistle. Those customers were the reason she was still in business. Only he would do something so foolish—and so incredibly sweet.

Damn that man for turning her life upside down and then escaping when things went to Hell—and damn herself for needing him. He wronged her, betrayed her in the worst possible way, but still, she wanted him so much.

The door opened behind her, but she didn't turn to acknowledge whoever it was. She was in no mood to talk. Suddenly, strong arms were around her, and a warm chest was there to press her cheek against. She turned into him and held on, taking whatever comfort she could get.

"Dellis, Carlisle caused this mess, and he left you to clean it up." He placed a kiss on the top of her head, his hand gently stroking her back, relieving some of the tension that knotted the muscles from her neck all the way down her spine. "I know I wasn't there for you before, but I am now. If you let me be."

He reached down and pulled the picture from her hand, dropping it on the desk. "*I'm* the one that's here with you."

Dellis rested her hand on Patrick's chest, feeling his heart kick quickly and then speed up.

"I knew I could make you feel better," Patrick whispered, stroking her hair. He reached down and flipped the paper over. "You don't need that anymore."

Chapter Seventeen

"**B**urn the village, and find out where those weapons are by any means necessary!" DeLancie raged.

"Major, there's nothing but women and children here; these are farms. The barn is empty." John pointed to an old, dilapidated, wood building just beyond the village stockade. "I've looked everywhere; they've either moved everything, or they have a better hiding place. There's no point to this." His voice cracked with fear. "It's sheer brutality. These are our allies; we need them."

"Our allies? Our. Allies." DeLancie shook his head, a laugh gilded with demented merriment escaped him. "They're not our allies. They'd turn on us in a second if someone could offer them more. Don't you forget that. I've learned that lesson the hard way."

"Major, let's find the men. We can go to Oriska. We can question them." John searched for some way to change DeLancie's mind, anything to prevent mass murder from ensuing.

"I've given you an order, Captain. Burn it. And make those native whores talk. You, of all people, know how to persuade women."

The next thing John knew, there was gun barrel in his face, point blank, cold steel pressed to his forehead.

"It's either you or them, Johnny. What's it going be? I know how you love life. Spoiled fool."

DeLancie cocked his pistol, the resounding click *of the hammer pulling into place the last sound John would ever hear. "Give the Goddamned order now or meet your maker. Do it."*

Turning around, John looked on as his men ran into the native cabins, dragging the rest of the women out at gunpoint. He walked towards the camp, taking a deep breath, mentally shutting off his emotions, like blowing out a candle. "Find out where the supplies are, by any means necessary. If you have to, kill them. Kill them all. Then burn the village to the ground."

"Johnny, I knew you were too much of a coward to take the bullet. He who wishes to fight must first count the cost."

Ignoring his superior, who was stalking behind like a feral cat following a mouse, John walked to one of the women being questioned and said, "Tell us what you know."

With a pistol to the back of her head, she glanced up at John, her dark, beautiful eyes pleading. "Help us, please. We know nothing. We're innocent."

"I believe you." John winced, knowing she spoke truth. "But sadly, you'll all die." His words came out stone cold, betraying no emotion, because he felt none. He couldn't.

"Do it." He nodded to his man; the cock of a pistol resounded as John walked passed her.

"You'll pay for this."

And then she screamed the words as the pistol went off.

"Dellis!"

John woke abruptly, sweat pouring down his forehead, drenching his hair, his linen shirt plastered to his skin.

"Dellis." He groaned, rolling over on his right, expecting her to be there, but she wasn't, just empty sheets and the cold loneliness of his bed. How he needed her, if only to wrap his arms around her and find one fleeting moment of respite against her breast. He shook, his body involuntary trembling; wrapping his arms around his bare chest, he tried desperately to comfort himself. There'd been no sleep for him for over a week, just endless nights of wakefulness, rendering him unable to concentrate on anything save being with her. He was so tired; all he wanted was rest. But they persisted. The voices.

"Justice… John…"

With each passing moment they were getting louder until they were screaming in his ears. He fisted his hair, pulling at it, wanting to tear out the memory like ripping a page from the book of his brain.

"Dellis," he whispered to himself, feeling the pieces of leather still braided into his hair, her trinkets tied back at his nape. He remembered the very moment she gave them to him, their torrid lovemaking that preceded it, and after, one incredible night of rest in her arms. It was the first time he'd known peace in years.

Closing his eyes, he took a deep breath and lay back against the sheets, conjuring Dellis lying nude in his bed, her arms open—his angel, his goddess. Suddenly, the heady sensation of having her near washed over him, bringing with it a calm that circumvented all the fear. His heart slowed, and his loins started to ache, desire like the warmth of the sun radiating through his every pore. She was so real he could almost touch her. His body begged for her, desperate and yearning with the uncontrolled ferocity of a youth just becoming a man. If he tried hard enough, he could smell lavender oil on skin so white it rivaled the sands on a Caribbean beach.

He gave into it, sweet oblivion, allowing the dream to be real. One second of peace.

But it was over as fast as it started, so damned, achingly brief, the sad cries of the Sirens starting again, blowing through the window, calling his name. *"Justice…John…"*

"Damn!" he yelled, covering his eyes with his palms. "Go away!"

There would be no peace for him. Not on that night. He was doomed to a life sentence of paying for his crimes. How would he bear it without her? He'd never considered she wouldn't take him back. But in the in the cavernous, placidity of night, he wasn't so sure.

Throwing the sheets off, John rose and washed his hands and face in the basin next to the bed. The sun had yet to come up; better to work than fight a losing battle. Besides, brooding in the quiet would win him nothing. He refused to surrender his will to the specters of the past. It was just his conscience getting the better of him since he'd gone back to doing his duty. Yes—that was it—he was just feeling guilt for working in opposition to the Oneidas.

Pulling on his breeches and retying his hair, he sat down at his desk and started to work on plans for his travels to Irondequoit and then read through his stack of correspondences.

Once finished, he threw down his pen and looked into the dark of his room; he swore he saw dark hair blowing in the breeze and the flicker of candlelight in black, fathomless eyes. There she was, but it wasn't the ghosts that haunted him, it was Dellis. He picked up his charcoal pencil, pulled out a piece of paper, and started to draw, losing himself in the lines of her face. Conjuring her.

So intent was he on his drawing that when Merrick came in an hour later, John barely noticed the man's presence. Only when the servant entered with the breakfast tray did John look up from his work.

"I can't believe it's been a week, and still, there's no sign of Alexei. My men tracked him to Oswego. Five shipments came from Oswegatchie, yet still nothing. What's he waiting for?" Merrick huffed as he pushed his hand through his coppery locks, rumpling them.

"I understand your frustration." John shook his head, looking down at the picture he was drawing, running his fingers over the charcoal, smudging it to add shading. "Alexei has slipped through my fingers countless times. He's smart."

"What are these?" Merrick reached over and grabbed some of the papers from the desk, scanning them.

"I made maps of the port of Oswego and Fort Ontario. The X's are all the places Alexei has been spotted in the past; the O's are the places we've looked. There's no pattern to any of it. He's disappeared like a damned ghost—as usual."

John turned his attention back to the picture he was drawing, chewing his lip. After several failed attempts at a portrait, that one was no better. Much to his frustration, he could never seem to get Dellis's eyes right, unable to capture that otherworldly look. Having tossed away all his previous attempts, he drew from dreams of her, reminiscing on their first night together, and started anew. With a scratching noise, he glided the charcoal pencil across the paper, letting his memories guide his hand.

"John?"

But he was too entranced by the picture to answer.

Carefully, he outlined the curves of her breasts, paying homage to the milky dunes and dusky peaks with careful strokes, showing how they swelled and pillowed with arousal. And there, in the valley between her breasts, he ran his fingers over that place—his favorite place—and smudged the charcoal again, adding depth. Slowly, he extended the pencil lines, sketching her torso, long and sinewy, sloping down to her hips and her long, silky legs. He remembered the way the candlelight cast shadows on her, like a beautiful nude goddess in his bed. Her fear was so great, she turned from him, the picture capturing that look; those enchanting dark eyes looking away, gazing at the wall, her high, sculpted cheekbones in shadow, a slight furrow in her brow.

"What are you drawing, John?" Merrick glanced over John's shoulder.

He flipped the paper over and laughed. "Something an uncle should never see."

"What?"

He flashed the picture just quickly enough for his friend to understand and then turned it over again.

"Yes, quite right." Merrick shook his head as if trying to unsee what he just saw. "But I know that type of obsession, John."

"Yes."

Merrick's observation was astute. John was obsessed.

Fatigue set in, and his eyelids grew heavy; resting his head in his hands, he closed his eyes for a moment. Just as he started to drift off, he heard the pop of a musket firing and jumped in his chair, looking in every direction.

"You'll pay for this!" The woman's cries reverberated in his ears, and then another musket went off. Again, he jumped, placing his head in his hands.

"John, it's just musket drills. What's going on? You look terrible," Merrick said, his voice full of concern. "Have you slept?"

John glanced up and shook his head. "I don't sleep."

"I've seen this behavior before in my men after battle," Merrick said calmly, sipping his coffee. "Nightmares. Sleeplessness. Drinking. You have all the signs."

"Signs of what? I'm a soldier; battle is what I'm trained to do." John rubbed his eyes and then his cheeks, trying to bury his raw emotions under a stoic mask. "I wouldn't make a very good Captain if I couldn't engage as such. I'm just overtired."

"It's not the battle that does it to you. It's the fear. The aftermath. You're afraid of something. Tell me what troubles you." Merrick's gaze was direct but not without sympathy.

Perhaps he does understand.

"Since that day in the village, I have visions of Dellis's grandmother and the dead women; they call to me almost every night." John felt ridiculous confessing such a thing, but it was the truth. "Only when I was with Dellis did they relent. As long as she was there, I could ignore them, get back to sleep. Since we've been parted, they've started again."

Merrick nodded knowingly. "You blame yourself and needlessly. John, you were forced to give that order; the fault lies with DeLancie. You'd never have done it unless under duress."

No. He was so wrong.

John shook his head vehemently. "That doesn't absolve me of anything. Yes, I was forced to give the order, but it was I who walked away as they shot a woman who pled for mercy. I stood there and watched as they dragged women and children out of their homes, defiled and murdered them before my eyes. DeLancie held the gun to my face, but I still could've said no—"

"Then where would Dellis be? And what of the people you saved? They'd surely have died if DeLancie gave the order himself." Merrick persisted like a lawyer pleading a case to a judge. "Don't forget, you admitted your fault in court, you killed DeLancie, and you protected the village later; doesn't that count?"

"I was there when your brother was murdered. Stephen looked me in the eyes and told me I was a disgrace to the uniform I wore. And he was right. I could've stopped that duel, somehow, but I didn't." John ran his hands through his hair, nervously pushing it out of his face. "And know this: I would've lied, like the rest of the men in my unit, if I hadn't hated myself so much I wanted to die. It wasn't bravery; it was cowardice. I was hoping they'd hang me. I wanted it."

"John you can't continue to beat yourself up over this. It's fruitless and unwarranted." Their eyes met over the table, true concern softening Merrick's traditionally icy gaze. "You'll never get over what happened. I'm sorry, but you won't. Absolution is beyond your ability. You're a man of conscience and integrity; those qualities, while gifts, are also curses. All you can do now is learn to live with it. That's what soldiers do."

"Dellis lost a baby before I left. When she was raped, the soldiers, *my men*, used her terribly. It was my order that resulted in this. Your brother, Stephen, believed it permanently ruined her chances of having children." John fought against the pain in his chest, his eyes watering in protest. "I hurt her, though I didn't do directly." He sniffed, resting his forehead in his hand. "It's Karma's way of paying me back."

Merrick leaned across the desk and grabbed John's wrist, forcing him to look up. "The world doesn't work that way. There's no such thing as checks and balances. You had no way of knowing this would happen."

John took deep breath and then let it out, releasing some of his pent-up tension. "There's a woman claiming to be carrying my child. It devastated Dellis when she found out. She pushed me away. I know it's because she fears I'll be childless if I stay with her."

Merrick drew in a deep breath, his head moving in a slow nod of understanding. "My wife was raped and beaten by French pirates. They treated her like an animal and scarred her permanently. Since then, we've lost all six of the children we've made. I know the pain you're feeling, my friend. Nothing is worse than looking into the eyes of the woman you love after she's lost a child."

John nodded, remembering Dellis's sad, empty gaze when he ran his hand over her empty womb.

"I don't love my wife any less because of her inabilities, and I know you feel the same about Dellis. Cruel men took from our women what was theirs to gift." Merrick's head fell forwards, his voice low, full of pain. "Women are soft, our haven for serenity and light, yet they're also so strong. The victims of men's vitriol, forced to always stand behind their husbands, yet they're as necessary to us as air and water. Man cannot create man alone. Why we defile our partners in this world, the ones God created to love us, makes no sense."

When John looked up, he found Merrick's icy-blue eyes had turned to water, the whites red and glassy.

"You didn't do this to her, my friend. You don't get to claim responsibility for everything. There's no room for martyrdom in this story."

"The child isn't mine. I swear."

"Don't explain yourself to me, John. You're a just man. I'm sure you had your reasons."

"I did." John paused, trying to clear the bad taste of Celeste from his tongue. "And I'd trade everything, my reputation… my life, if I could see Dellis hold our child in her arms. It's strange. For so long, I couldn't imagine having a wife and child, and now, I can think of nothing else."

Merrick nodded. "I'm sorry for both of you. Perhaps, in time, her aunt and I can offer her some comfort. For now, all I can do is try to help you."

"How?" John asked, taking a deep breath.

"By convincing you that it isn't ghosts that haunt you but your past. You must learn to face what happened and accept it. Learn from it, but don't live in it, or it will ruin you… and her."

Merrick sipped what was left of his coffee, a weighty silence between them, until he finally spoke again. "And there's one other thing I can give both of you."

"What's that?"

The sadness in Merrick's eyes was replaced with a glimmer of hope. "James's children can't inherit our family estate, and because of Stuart's issues, he's incapable, so Dellis is my only heir. Ours is an ancient Scottish title that can be transferred through a woman. Everything that's mine will be hers."

John locked eyes with Merrick.

"And yours… She'll be the Duchess of McKesson. My dearest Stephen will have his justice, and you'll be able to tell all those who wronged you to go to the Devil."

There was a tinge of satisfaction at the idea of throwing a powerful title in the face of John's naysayers, but was it what Dellis would really want? She was above money, save the necessities of life, and she loved her home and the village. Wealth and a title seemed frivolous when it came to her.

"What say you, John?"

"I just want to see her happy for once." He glanced down at the picture, drinking her in one last time before he carefully folded it and placed it on the desk. "I just want to know that when I go home, she'll be safely waiting for me."

The idea of having a home was so foreign to him; he couldn't fathom what it would be like to return to a place where he was always wanted. Welcome. Wherever she was, that was home.

"All the more reason we must catch Alexei and put a stop to my brother. This is James's fault. All of it."

John grabbed the map from the table, looking it over. "We've searched everywhere. Alexei's not here. I have to leave tomorrow for Irondequoit Bay. I was supposed to have more goods to trade with the Seneca, but I've managed to accomplish absolutely nothing since we've been here."

"Maybe I can help with that." Merrick clucked his tongue, his eyes rolling to the side. "If you can wait a day, we can bring what extra shot and gunpowder I have in storage. It's not a lot, but it'll work. I can ask the quartermaster if there's anything we can spare. My men and I will escort you to Irondequoit. Besides, it's time I had words with Butler."

"Thank you. I'll take whatever you can give me," John said. "But that still doesn't solve the Alexei problem."

"No, it doesn't," Merrick said.

As he got up from his chair, John stood and they shook hands. "Thank you, Merrick."

"You're welcome." Merrick started for the door and then stopped and looked back. "I'm guilty of many sins in this life and many failures. But if I can help another human in pain, they were all well served."

Their eyes met in mutual understanding. Only someone who'd seen death and destruction delivered by his own hand could have such a pained expression. The man had demons. And just like John, Merrick lived his life trying to free himself from them.

James pushed open the door to the two-story, Georgian-style house, stepping into the lavishly decorated foyer. Already, there was music in the air, the sound of a fiddle and a piano playing in unison; the candles in the Moreno glass candelabra over the foyer were lit, casting diamond-like sparkles on the white walls and shiny wood floor. In the red parlor to the right of the foyer, some of the women were preparing for the evening's festivities; one was leaned over, tying up her stockings with a neat little bow above the knee, another was applying rouge to her cheeks with a cotton puff full of brilliant red vermillion. When Eagle Eyes stepped inside, his upper lip curled, and his dark eyes glanced around, taking in the surroundings as though mapping out a plan. James sensed trepidation from his traditionally stoic companion; there was something about the place that innately bothered the Mohawk.

An elegantly dressed woman in a fine, crimson, silk gown that extended out a foot on each side walked into the foyer to greet them. "Gentlemen, we're not open yet. Give us an hour, and we'll be more than happy to provide you with services."

James smiled, admiring her creamy white skin, contrasting sharply against the brilliant red of her bodice, her full breasts brimming the edge perfectly, rising and falling with each breath. Her chocolate-brown hair was piled high on top of her head in neatly arranged curls, adding to her already statuesque height, while her dark, kohl-lined eyes regarded him with curiosity.

"We're not here for your services, miss, though I thank you for your hospitality. I've come to inquire about a man named McKenzie."

"I don't know anyone named McKenzie." Her eyes darted towards the door and then over to one of her ladies—the woman was lying, her tell rather obviously delivered.

Good for him—bad for her.

"Oh, I disagree." James persisted, flashing a grin. "He's the one who supplies you with your luxuries and indulgences. How else would you come by such finery in Niagara?" He waved his hand skywards, gesturing to the chandelier hanging above the foyer.

"Sir, I'm going to have to ask you to leave." The woman stepped back, lifting her chin defiantly. "Besides, we don't serve his kind here." She flashed a haughty glance at Eagle Eyes, her lip curling in disgust, mimicking the Mohawk's disdain.

"Really, you don't serve his kind?" James turned back to the brave and asked, "What do you think of that, Eagle Eyes?"

The giant Mohawk nodded and then opened the door, allowing four other tribesmen into the foyer. One of the women standing in the red parlor gasped, the rest turning around immediately in response. Their fear was tangible, white skin turning ashen at the sight of buckskin-clad natives, with tomahawks at their belts and fierce looking scalp locks, walking in the front door.

James grinned.

"Eagle Eyes, why don't you and your men pursue the ladies? Show them that you're gentlemen." With lightning speed, James whipped a jagged, rusty-looking knife from his hip, pulled the woman into his arms, and held his blade to the column of her neck. "While I give you a chance to reconsider my question. Now tell me, where is McKenzie?"

With a lick of the lips, Eagle Eyes stalked into the parlor, the rest of the warriors in tow like beggars ready to feast—heartily. One of the women screamed and tried to run, but Eagle Eyes reached out his large, powerful hand and yanked her back, and with one swipe, he tore the silk fabric of her bodice like paper, exposing her stays. She screamed again as he threw her on the ground with a resounding *thud* and pounced on her like a jaguar on prey. They landed on hands and knees, his deft hands fighting her off as he pulled up her skirts, exposing her creamy thighs, and tore off his loincloth, thrusting himself into the woman from behind. She kicked and flailed underneath him, trying to crawl away, but it only further provoked his fury. He pulled out his knife and held to her neck. "I'll kill you, woman, if you don't stop."

Still holding a hostage at knife point, James looked on as Eagle Eyes used the woman violently, fast and hard, ramming into her while she wailed and fought beneath him. He finished with a satisfied groan and then flipped her on her back and held the knife to her throat. "This is for Mrs. Allen." Adjusting his grip, Eagle Eyes plunged the blade into her tender flesh, metal kissing wood on the floor beneath her. The woman stilled, a loud gurgle bubbling up from her throat as blood spewed forth and then rolled down her cheek.

In one fell swoop, the rest of Eagle Eyes's men descended on the remaining women like vultures, brutally raping and murdering the lot of them. The screams of the innocent resonated in James's ears, but they didn't pierce the frozen wasteland of his heart.

He leaned over, whispering in his hostage's ear, "Now, have you changed your mind, or would you rather join your ladies?"

The woman nodded, her eyes like saucers, following the braves; her fair skin wan, making her rouge stand out in comical red circles. "McKenzie works at the trading post here in The Bottoms. I don't know if he's in port currently. He was working with some of the officers in Oswego."

"Where do you keep your supplies?" James asked, turning away from the violence playing out in the red parlor. He'd had enough.

Suddenly, there was a high-pitched wail, followed by a strange ripping noise, like tearing wet canvas. James looked over his shoulder; Eagle Eyes was scalping one of the women, slowly yanking her hair back as he removed the strip of flesh from the bone.

James's stomach pitched, forcing him to turn away again. "Tell me, or I'll let them have you."

But the woman refused to submit.

"Eagle Eyes!" he yelled.

The Mohawk looked up from his most recent kill, his eyes leveling on the woman like a hawk on its next meal.

"No, please. No!" She shrieked. "It's in the room just off the kitchen. Everything is there for you. Take it." James yanked her back, her body trembling against his, tears welling in her eyes. "Take everything in the house, just please, stop."

"I just might do that." Looking over his shoulder, James barked out his orders. "Take everything of value you can find."

Eagle Eyes motioned for his men to follow him. The torture had stopped, but James could find not one of the women left alive; their dead, scalped corpses haphazardly discarded on the fine red and gold Oriental rug. "Now, show me this room, woman."

James released her abruptly, pushing her down the hall with one hard thrust. Tied up in layers of skirts and accoutrements, she landed on her hands and knees, her body hitting the floor full force. Frantically, she rolled over, scooting backwards on the shiny wood, retreating towards the kitchen.

"What's in these rooms?" James tried the handle on one of the doors, but it was locked. "Open it!"

He yanked the woman to her feet, holding his knife to her back. When she hesitated, he dug his blade into the tender flesh between her shoulder blades, puncturing the fine scarlet fabric with the rusty tip, a little trickle of blood running from the wound.

With a gasp, she relented, opening the nearest door. It was an office, elegantly decorated in fine, white damask wallpaper and mahogany furniture. Over the fireplace was a great mirror gilded with a gold metal frame. "Where's Mrs. Allen's safe?"

The woman stopped abruptly, shaking her head. "I don't know."

"Surely you don't want me to have Eagle Eyes convince you?" James leaned in, nose to nose with the woman, his blade between the two of them. Her eyes crossed glancing at it, and then a tremble started in the corner of her lower lips, spreading all the way across her mouth until it was quivering like ripples on the water. "Where's her safe?"

"I think it's behind one of the paintings," she muttered through sobs.

He walked over to a garish picture of the English countryside and tried to lift it, but the painting didn't budge. He tried the two others, finally finding the safe behind the one just above her desk.

"Open it."

That time, the woman didn't hesitate; she did as he said, stepping out of the way for him to inspect. The safe was full of money; he didn't have time to count, just reached in and filled his haversack. "Is there any more in this house?"

"No, sir," she replied, shaking her head. He could read the truth in her fear. She'd learned her lesson—and rightly so.

"Show me the storage." He followed her down the hall, into the large kitchen at the back of the house. On the counter was enough food to feed thirty people: chocolate warmed in a metal tureen, smoked salmon arranged neatly on a tray, venison, meat pies, and an array of elegantly prepared desserts. His mouth watered just looking at it—but that wasn't what he came for. In the corner of the room was a door; she unlocked it, reached for a lantern from the kitchen counter, and handed it to him. What he found inside the pantry was a virtual treasure trove of luxuries: several hogsheads of rum; bottles of whiskey; casks of wine, including Madeira and Claret; chocolate blocks from Spain; and opium—lots of it.

James grinned, running his hand over one of the rum barrels. "Thank you, Mrs. Allen."

He turned around and walked back to the foyer; Eagle Eyes and his men had already ransacked the rooms, and a pile of furs, silver plates, and silk fabrics were stacked on the floor. On one of the fine Chippendale tables was a small wooden box; inside, he found silver and gold jewels, little service bells, and other valuable trinkets and fobs.

"Get the cart; we'll load this up through the back door. Also, we need to clean out the pantry."

James walked back to the kitchen, turning his attention to his gracious, compliant host. "I'll let you go now, but if you speak a word of this to anyone, my friends will find you." Shaking a finger at her, he threatened her one more time for good measure. "If you cross me, my men will scalp you, and then they'll gut Mrs. Allen. Her death will be on your hands. Do you hear me, woman?"

He grabbed the bodice of her dress, yanking her against him, her eyes widening with fear. "If you don't believe me, I can persuade you otherwise."

Using both hands, James tore the front of her dress open, exposing her stays, her bountiful breasts heaving the rim. She screamed when Eagle Eyes walked in behind them, his roving eyes finding her.

"Should I let him do it?" James asked, looking over his shoulder at the Mohawk and then back at her.

The woman shook her head, her brown eyes glassy with tears. "I won't say anything. I swear it. Please, let me go."

James released her, throwing her across the floor where she landed in a heap of crimson fabric. "Now, get out of here, whore. Run! Run! And don't ever speak of this again."

The woman stood and bolted out the back door as quick as a lightning strike. He turned back to Eagle Eyes and laughed. "Empty it out. Take everything. Leave nothing behind."

James stood at the top of the back steps, watching as the men cleared everything from the house and loaded up the cart. When they'd stripped the house of all its valuables, he grabbed two lanterns off the counter and threw them on the floor, the glass shattering to pieces, fire quickly igniting on the wood. There was a container of whale oil on the floor near the counter. James opened it and poured the contents on the brewing flames, creating a blaze.

Walking out the back door, he watched the fire climb its way up the outer walls, the flames greedily consuming the clapboard. "Mrs. Allen, I believe our business is now completed. But thank you for services rendered." He adjusted himself, remembering the exquisite job she did sucking his cock.

"Eagle Eyes, have your men take this stuff to Butler; we'll find McKenzie."

The trading post was only a couple yards from Mrs. Allen's house, facing the dock. The smoke from the fire billowed into the dusky sky, suffocating the soft hues of pink and purple with weighty black clouds that hung over the little village. James could hear the commotion as the locals rushed to the brothel, trying to put out the fire, buckets of water being carried up from the shore, heading in the direction of the blaze. He grinned as he banged on the door to the log cabin, but it was deserted, the shutters pulled closed and the door locked tightly.

James waved the natives over. "Fortune favors the bold, my friend," he shouted, watching as Eagle Eyes kicked in the front door. They walked inside, the aroma of pine and gunpowder mixed with tanned leather permeating the store. "Look around. There's sure to be a hiding place here, probably in the ground. Get down on your knees and look."

The wood shelves on the back wall behind the counter were full of linens, blankets, snowshoes, and some leather moccasins. Hanging from the ceiling were several well-made leather saddles, stirrups, bridles, and other necessities for horses. Also dangling from the rafters was a large piece of dried beef jerky and some long, tasty-looking sausages. Just what one would expect at a trading post—but no luxuries.

"McKesson," Eagle Eyes said, in his haunting, deep voice.

Hiding under the counter, wide-eyed and trembling like a mouse caught in a trap, was a slight elderly man dressed in a linen shirt and buckskin leggings. Grabbing him by the arm, Eagle Eyes yanked the man out of his hiding place.

"I know there's more. Where are you hiding it?" Eagle Eyes thrust his blood-stained blade in the man's face—persuading him. "Or I'll let you have a taste."

With that, the Mohawk lifted the knife to his lips and licked a little of the blood from the tip. The man gasped and pointed to the floor in the corner.

James got down on his hands and knees next to the Mohawk and pulled back the wooden floorboards, exposing a secret hiding place. Inside was another dragon's hoard to match what James found at Mrs. Allen's house. It was full of luxury goods, and to his delight, gunpowder and several guns, specifically British Long Pattern Muskets with their distinct forty-six-inch barrels and brown wooden stocks.

"Hello, Brown Bess," he said, lifting one and pretending to aim at the scared shopkeeper. It was an elegant weapon, a 0.75 caliber smooth bore with a range of almost one hundred yards; the ten pounds of steel and wood felt good in James's hands. *Power.* His fingertip practically sparked upon grazing the trigger.

Putting the musket down, he leaned over again, searching the cubby. At the bottom, he found a small cherrywood box; inside was a pair of dueling pistols, lying in green velvet, with a plaque on the outside that was inscribed: *Major DeLancie 8th Regimen of Foot, In gratitude, Captain John Carlisle.*

"Well, what are *you* doing here?" he asked and then handed the box to Eagle Eyes. "Perhaps you might like to have this."

The Mohawk grabbed the box and stuffed it under his arm. "What now?"

James shrugged. "Let's empty the place out. After we turn this over to Butler, you leave for Oswego to find my son."

"What do want me to do with him once I find him?" Eagle Eyes asked.

"Kill his Oneida friends, and bring him to me with whatever booty he's stolen." As James started out the front door, he stopped abruptly, rethinking his plan. "Actually, rough him up a bit, but don't kill him. A little painful persuasion might do my son some good. Am I understood?"

Eagle Eyes nodded.

"Now, finish up here."

When James stepped outside, he could hear a sudden gasp and then a deathly gurgle as Eagle Eyes slit the shopkeeper's throat, and not a second later, the Mohawk appeared, carrying casks of wine from the building. *So damned efficient.* James marveled at the Mohawk's ability to be so taciturn yet kill with such violent efficiency.

Well, at least James no longer owed Butler, and what was found in Mrs. Allen's safe—that was no one's business. *Now, to deal with my son and John Carlisle.* After that, there'd be no more witnesses—no one who knew the truth about James or his secrets.

Chapter Eighteen

Irondequoit Bay was located approximately eighty miles west of Fort Niagara on the east shore of Lake Ontario. The long, narrow inlet was surrounded by marshy lowlands which were ripe with bugs and croaking frogs in the smoldering heat of summer; a layer of slime, rich, olive green, lay like an untouched blanket on the stagnant water's surface. It took a half day's travel by boat to arrive; Merrick's expertly trained sailors steered the two-masted schooner through the rough waters of Lake Ontario with Royal Navy prowess. The inclement weather worked against them; rough, choppy water jostling the boat back and forth with five-foot swells coming from dead astern as the men tacked downwind with the sails, moving with grace that only a team who'd manned a ship of the line in battle could possess.

Below deck, John listened to some of Merrick's plans while choking back a wave of nausea and the previous night's victuals. The *Mal de mer,* which plagued John his whole life and ruined his chance of ever working for his father's shipping business, once again reared its ugly head, John's stomach pitching furiously with each roll of the ship. The last thing he wanted to do was embarrass himself and his regiment in front of a bunch of Royal Navy sailors. His pride smarted as he imagined himself with his head in a fire bucket, retching, while the Navy blues laughed over his shoulder.

When the ship dropped anchor inside the bay, John breathed a sigh of relief and then raced to the deck, determined to be the first one on the bateau, escorting the supplies shore. Already anchored and waiting were two other Royal Navy Schooners, likely carrying men and cargo from Fort Niagara on behalf of John Butler and General St. Leger. Clark and Smith rowed with John to shore while Merrick and his men waited on board. The Admiral was determined to keep his presence a secret as long as possible, maintaining his advantage over Alexei and James. Once Merrick revealed himself, word would surely get out about his unexpected appearance and would travel back to German Flats, and James, at breakneck speed.

On what little bit of dry land that could be found, camps were already being set up; British army tents to one side, and the natives on the other, conveniently segregated. Their meeting wasn't about friendship, it was about war and mutual need. The Seneca brought their wives, children, and their most esteemed sachems along with forty western native tribes. As the largest tribe in the Six Nations, the Seneca were fractioned off by location and loyalties, and all were present for the meeting—including the pro-Loyalist Allegheny and Genesee settlements, and the lake area people, who were notorious neutralists. The challenge fell on John and Butler to find a way to unite the powerful, yet conflicted, tribe and bring them to the British cause—turn them against their brothers.

Each man must go his own way. John shook his head with consternation, an all-too-familiar theme in his life. It wasn't about Dellis's village or his shared past with her people. *This is my mission, my duty.* His career was the one thing he could hold on to, the culmination of his life's work, and if he succeeded, he'd be rewarded—a promotion, accolades. *Finally respected.* The Seneca were also the most powerful tribe in the Six Nations, and the elder brother of the confederacy; where they went, the rest would follow. He could do it. Yes, he'd find a way to bring them all together.

For three days, before the opening of the council, the Seneca were treated to every indulgence. John and Clark, under orders, were to provide the natives with all the luxuries they required and show them to the stock should they need to obtain more—and they did. Cattle were slaughtered, and a great feast was prepared with all the food and drink one could want. Rum flowed as plenty as the ocean, bringing with it drunkenness and chaos, fights breaking out randomly as the warriors became more inebriated. It was a feast of avarice, all designed to lure the natives into British hands like the Devil's contract after a night of unearthly pleasure—and the natives went willingly, naïvely. Even the women, who were notoriously distant and untrusting of the white man, joined the festivities, indulging to their hearts' content.

Major Butler arrived three days after the Seneca and immediately requested John's presence. "What have you brought me, Captain?"

John rattled off his list of procurements proudly. "Ten barrels of rum, eight casks of wine, fifteen barrels of powder, and ten boxes of shot." Pausing for a moment, he stepped out of the tent and motioned for Smith and Clark to bring in some of the goods. "Also, we brought some furs, skins, and scalping knives that were confiscated from other tribes, and some copper pots and kettles."

When Simon placed a barrel of gunpowder in front of the Major, his eyes lit up. "This is good, but where's the woman? Where's the shipment?"

"Were you able to find Mrs. Allen's supplier? Did you get access to her shipments?" John pushed, ignoring Butler's initial question, trying to avoid the topic as long as possible.

"Yes, the ship carrying that cargo should be here any time now. They followed us into port." John watched Butler lift some fabric from a large leather trunk and carefully start unrolling it. When he pulled the last piece of linen away, it revealed two long wampum belts, one John recognized as the Great Old Covenant Chain; the two rows of white beads alternated with three rows of purple, representing the treaty between the Six Nations of the Iroquois and the Crown. The other belt was smaller and less infamous, though it also signified a treaty with the Crown.

John looked down at the bracelet on his wrist, the one Kateri gave him—it was an exact replica of the Covenant Chain. He pulled his cuff down over it, trying to shut out the significance of the piece.

"What do you intend to do with those?" John asked, watching as Butler lifted the intricately woven belt and examined it.

"*This* is the key to getting the Seneca on our side. This will remind them of their duty to King George."

There was awe in the Major's wide eyes and in the way he ran reverent hands over the delicate beads as if they were the finest Chinese porcelain. He seemed giddy. Drunk with power. "Where's the woman and her dowry?" He demanded, carefully placing the belts on the table and covering them with the linen wrap.

"I'm working on it."

"Captain, Major," Clark walked in, acknowledging both men with a stoic nod, though John could sense his friend's trepidation. All three of them were on edge; the whole council, and the Western Front, depended on them being able to unite the native tribes. The Seneca alone had the potential to double St. Leger's fighting force with their five hundred men, and Burgoyne's whole plan depended on defeating Stanwix and reconnoitering in Albany.

"The Seneca arrived three days ago, and we've seen to their temporary needs. They're ready for the opening protocol of the council. Major, I could…"

John stopped in mid-sentence, his jaw dropping as Eagle Eyes walked into Butler's tent; behind him were several men with arms full of casks and crates. "Major, the goods you requested."

Their eyes locked as Butler opened one of the wooden crates for inspection. "This was from Mrs. Allen's supplier?" the Major asked, looking up at Eagle Eyes.

"Yes, sir."

John recognized some of the things inside the crate: damask curtains, a silver service bell, ostrich feathers, and a Murano glass vase tucked safely at the bottom, protected by a pale-pink satin petticoat. All of it belonged to Celeste. While an opportunist, Celeste was also notoriously covetous of her belongings, and specifically her business. Her servants would never willingly give those things away.

"How did you get these?"

Eagle Eyes cocked a brow, a sinister grin tugging at the corner of his mouth, exposing some of his black, rotting teeth.

Stolen. All of it.

John knew it just as surely as he knew all her women were dead. His stomach churned as he thought of those poor innocents.

"What does it matter how he got them, Carlisle? Mrs. Allen felt the need to donate to the cause after all the business we've provided her." Butler closed the lid on the crate and pointed to another one sitting just inside the tent flap. "What's in there?"

"More of the same, plus furs. We also brought rum, wine, whiskey, and some opium."

Butler pointed to Eagle Eyes, shaking his finger with excitement. "This is how you get the job done. I sent our Mohawk friend here to collect from Mrs. Allen, and he delivered. You, on the other hand…"

John shook his head. "I'm working on it. I have my men out looking for the woman. It's only a matter of time."

"That's what you always say, Carlisle." Butler walked up to John, their eyes meeting, though he was a few inches taller. "I grow tired of your failures."

He inclined his head towards the cargo being brought into the tent. "It was my idea to reach out to Mrs. Allen, and I brought plenty of my share for this council. This is far from a failure."

Butler clucked his tongue, his gaze darting from John to Eagle Eyes. "Perhaps I should send my friend out looking for our heiress?"

That wasn't a good idea; Eagle Eyes would surely hurt the woman. "I'll find her, the supplies, and her money." John worked to control his frustration; it served him better not to be divisive. "I'll find her."

"You're running out of time, Carlisle."

Butler put on his hat on and stomped out of the tent, leaving the Mohawk and John alone in hatred-charged silence.

Eagle Eyes walked over slowly, each step as precise and methodical as a dance, until he stood before John, towering over him. Sliding a hand down his side, John fingered the pistol at his hip, waiting for the native to make a move.

"So the traitor has returned?" Eagle Eyes said, his deep, gruff voice sending a chill down John's spine. The Mohawk was notoriously a man of few words, and when he spoke, it was usually the last thing one heard before they met their maker.

"So now you're with Butler?" John laughed. "Do you realize he did little in the way of protecting your old friend?"

"I'm not here for Butler."

John believed it. Eagle Eyes was loyal only to himself and his pocket, nothing more than a hired thug who moved from person to person, depending on who could pay the most.

"Probably a good decision on your part. Butler's not going to pay you for services rendered. He's only interested in the war."

"But his goal and mine are on the same course." Eagle Eyes stepped closer to John, forcing him to look up. "And he brought me to you…"

Out of the corner of his eye, John could see the Mohawk fingering the tomahawk at his hip, his thumb gliding over the top of the blade and then rubbing back and forth until the skin split and blood dripped down the silvery metal.

"You're not as fast as me." John ran his hand over his pistol, making sure Eagle Eyes saw the gesture. "And you know I'm just as good with a blade. You're welcome to try me. Size doesn't necessarily mean success."

Eagle Eyes grinned. "I'll get you when you least expect it, Carlisle."

"The thing about working with DeLancie for all those years… it makes one really good at surviving. Anticipation is something I do very well."

"That's good, because you deserve to suffer, long and hard, and so does your Oneida whore and the rest of those traitors. Joseph and Han Yerry will pay for going against the Confederacy."

Eagle Eyes stared John down for a moment and then turned and stalked out of the tent, their faceoff ending in a stalemate. Both of them were products of DeLancie's tutelage, and since the mentor was gone, the students would destroy each other like wolves fighting to be the leader of the pack. John breathed a sigh of relief, but he knew better; he'd been put on notice. Eagle Eyes was coming. But when?

Celeste walked up the steps of The Thistle, taking care not to catch one of her satiny heels on the nails sticking up from the rickety wooden steps. She smiled, noticing the little sign on the front door that read *CLOSED*. Having made it her goal to see the place permanently shut down, it was more than a satisfactory result, though she would've preferred John's little tart living destitute on the street, or perhaps whoring herself for some pocket change. Celeste giggled at the thought of Dellis McKesson turning her first trick with a man. *Does the woman even know what to do with a man? What does John see in her?* Celeste rolled her eyes. *Such a waste.*

She knocked on the front door, but no one answered. As she went to remove her white glove, she found a splotch of dirt stuck to it. *Damn.* In her current state of affairs, she had neither another pair of gloves, nor the money to purchase more. Grabbing the handle, she pushed the door open and walked inside.

The dining room was quiet, the tables empty and moved to the corners of the room, and the old wooden chairs were stacked on top of each other, out of the way. The faded white walls and scuffed floors looked like something she'd seen in the lowliest taverns on the New York docks.

"Hello?" she called, walking towards the bar, but no one responded. Slowly, she made her way past the counter and then under the archway into the kitchen. It was quiet, the whole place deserted, yet the counters were full of food: biscuits, pies, a pot bubbling over in the fire, and bread rising on the counter.

"Hello?"

She heard noises coming from the hall, through a door cracked on the right that led to the dingy little parlor she remembered from her previous visit. Much to her chagrin, when she pushed the door open, instead of finding long faces and the sad interlude she expected, there was a happy gathering taking place. Her traitorous former assistant, Agnes, was sitting at the table, chatting with the dish boy and another gentleman Celeste didn't recognize. Patrick Armstrong sat next to Dellis, both of them laughing heartily as they sipped from little porcelain teacups. Their fête of merriment included a card game which they were all playing.

"Mrs. Allen." Dellis dropped her cards and stood. Once again, her attire was atrocious, her muted-blue dress and brown stays looked like something a common wharf doxy would wear. And that beautiful, shiny black mane, her one positive attribute, was tied in a chignon at her neck instead of being neatly arranged in a fashionable high roll.

Why, John, why? Celeste would never understand his infatuation with the woman.

"Miss McKesson," Celeste said, giving a curt nod.

"As you well know, my tavern is permanently closed, and Captain Carlisle isn't here. Please leave. Now."

A stern rebuke. But it only provoked her more. If a catfight was what the little tart wanted, then Celeste was more than willing to deliver.

"Actually, I came to speak with you." She winked at the ragamuffin dish boy when he looked in Dellis's direction. "Forgive me for interrupting your revelry, but it's important."

Dellis cocked a brow, crossing her arms over her chest, her stance smacking of impertinence. "Really? Well, I have nothing to say to you, so please, leave."

When she turned her back, Celeste grabbed Dellis's arm, forcing her around. "I think you might want to listen to me."

Patrick stood abruptly and planted himself between the two women.

He's afraid of what I'll say. Good. A little fear would serve him rightly. One word from Celeste, and all his chances with his precious Dellis would be over in heartbeat.

"You need to leave," Patrick said. "You're not welcome."

"Is that right?" Celeste grinned, eyeing Dellis. "So, now he speaks for you. I wonder what John would think?"

Before he could open his mouth, she pushed her way around him. "Fine, we can talk in the other room." Putting her hand on Patrick's sleeve, she said, "I can handle this, but thank you." The disgusting sweetness in the woman's voice made Celeste want to heave. She gagged audibly when Patrick took Dellis's hand and kissed it lightly.

"Come with me." She inclined her head towards the doorway.

Celeste followed through the kitchen, under the archway, and into the dining room. Once in private, Dellis whirled around, a fire brewing in her dark eyes.

Now to stoke it.

"I see no need to keep up pretenses, Mrs. Allen. You and I aren't friends, nor are we in polite society." With her arms akimbo and her stance fixed, their eyes met. "What do you want?"

Celeste smiled. *Oh, this is going to be fun.* How she wished John were there to see it.

"I need to find John. I wanted to talk to him about the baby. I'm concerned about its welfare, especially if its father is keeping company with scandalous women. I don't want it to be born with the stigma of bastardy."

"Just stop!" Dellis yelled. "You don't care a wit about that baby. All you want is John. Though I think he might have something to say about the matter. I don't remember him mentioning you when he left town."

"You've moved on rather easily. I'm surprised." Celeste put a gloved hand to her mouth, bracketing it, and whispered, "I'd be more careful about the company you keep. You never know who you can trust." She stifled a laugh. *Time to plant the seed and watch it grow.* "Armstrong, really?"

Dellis let out a snicker, her head shaking. "Oh, my goodness, you didn't really come here to tell me that, did you? Of course, it's so clear to me now. What was I thinking? You must be so bored now that you've completely ruined me. What *will* you do with your wasted life now that you've taken everything you possibly can from poor, unfortunate Dellis

McKesson?" She started to laugh hysterically, the loud, brazen cackle of the demented.

Celeste found herself rather taken aback. Something wasn't right with the woman. She was as crazy as her lunatic brother.

"Mrs. Allen, you needed to get one last jab at me because you have nothing else to do. Consider yourself successful; you've managed to put a wedge between me and John; you've seen to it that my business is closed; and soon, I'll lose my house because I haven't the money to pay the debt owed to Gavin Carlisle. You've won." She put her hands down, crossing her wrists so Celeste could see them. "Clap me in irons and have me taken to the gaol. That's all that's left. There's nothing else you can take from me but my freedom." Suddenly, Dellis's crossed wrists were being shoved in Celeste's face, forcing her to take a step back. "Do it! Do it! I dare you. Have them tie me up and take me to the gaol. I belong there for the thoughts I'm having about you at this moment."

Dellis leaned in closer, their eyes locking. "You're a miserable, spoiled, frustrated woman. But no matter what you do, no matter how hard you try, you can never hurt me again. I won't let you. And I won't let you hurt my friends. We'll survive in spite of you. Now, get the hell out of my house. My father is rolling over in his grave thinking I'd allow such rubbish in his home."

She grabbed Celeste's upper arm, yanking so hard she lost her footing and stumbled, trying to keep up. Stopping abruptly, Dellis opened the door and pushed Celeste through it with one hard shove.

"Good Day, Mrs. Allen." The door slammed in her face so hard the paint on the frame cracked.

Celeste brushed the filth off her pale-blue dress and righted her sleeve. *The nerve of that crazy woman, dragging me out the house like a piece of unwanted chattel.* Perhaps Celeste would take Miss McKesson up on her suggestion and have her escorted to the gaol for assault, or for lunacy. It would serve her right to be locked up permanently for *non compos mentis.*

Throwing both shoulders back, Celeste gave the dilapidated old house a onceover and grinned. "I'm not finished with you yet."

As she turned to leave, Patrick Armstrong stepped out from around the corner of the house, blocking her path. "Just what did you think you were doing?"

She threw her head back and laughed. "Oh, this is fun. You've come out here to protect the lady. How gallant of you. I bet she wouldn't find you so noble and knightly if I told her you fucked me on a desk to find out information for her cousin." Making for the steps, she threw down the gauntlet with a sibilant sound. "What say you? Shall we find out?"

Patrick grabbed Celeste's arm, pulling her towards the side of the house, but she wrenched it free, affording him one hard slap to the right cheek, a red handprint forming instantly. "Keep your hands off me."

"Stay away from Dellis; you've done enough."

"Have you found out where the woman is?" Celeste leaned into him, her voice low. "We had a deal: I deliver Miss McKesson to you, and you find out where my missing heiress is. I've kept my part of the bargain, but I find your efforts severely lacking."

"I'll find her. Just give me time." He backed away, smoothing his loose hairs. "In the meantime, keep your distance."

"I'll do no such thing." She put her hands on her hips, leveling her gaze on him. "You forget who makes the rules here. And you seem to forget I have nothing to lose, but you, on the other hand—"

"You're the most..." He fisted his hands at his sides.

She watched him fight back what he really wanted to say—but oh, how she wished he wouldn't. She wanted to hear him call her *"evil"* or *"conniving."* Men loved to say those things about her. Why, John alone had created his own dictionary full of insults she deemed endearments. Men were so deliciously vulgar when backed into a corner. But she still wielded the sword, just like justice, and Celeste had come to collect.

"You're running out of time, and I'm running out of patience," she said, relishing the look of frustration in his olive-green eyes. "Think of me like

236

Karma. I always revisit your sins upon you—and eventually, you'll pay. If you don't believe me, ask John. I'm sure he can fill you in on the details."

Tossing a loose lock of her silky brown hair over her shoulder, she picked up her skirts and walked away, enjoying the anger that emanated from Patrick's furrowed brow. Unable to resist a challenge, she provoked him as she walked away. "Test my patience. I dare you."

Dellis looked out the window, watching Patrick and Mrs. Allen chat. Their interlude had the appearance of a conversation, yet Dellis sensed an argument. The pair spoke quietly, but they leaned into each other aggressively, and occasionally, changes in octave made their voices carry through the window. She admired him for wanting to defend her honor; he was such a gentleman. A little chivalry extended in her direction was an uncommon courtesy, and she would've been remiss to turn it away. But it was pointless arguing with Celeste Allen; she wasn't only malevolent, but persistent beyond reason. How John ever became associated with her exceeded comprehension.

John. Dellis shook her head despondently. She couldn't think about him without breaking down, and crying would do no good. After he left and her grandfather had taken away her position as a tribal matron, she was sure she had nothing left to lose. *Was I ever wrong.* But the truth was, she could sit and brood about it, or she could rally and start over again. Her destiny was her own; she was beholden to no one.

Since losing the baby, she'd been so damned emotional, wanting to strike out at everything and everyone around her. Inner turmoil brewed, fueled by adrenaline and pain, that was quick to ignite with the slightest rebuke or word of advice. Even when she and John quarreled, it was as if a demon was inside her, and just like that, it was loose, spewing venom. That was why she slammed the door in his face; she couldn't control the rage. She'd never hidden behind a door on anyone. It was cowardly. Even throwing Mrs. Allen out, it was unlike Dellis to let someone burrow beneath her skin. She remembered the feeling after she lost her first baby. *Is it grief that drives me to behave like this? Self-preservation?* Probably a bit of both.

Failure is the greatest teacher, so her grandfather said, and there was a lesson to be learned in all of it besides patience and listening. But what was that?

When Patrick appeared again, he looked tired; lines she'd never noticed flanked his lips, his eyes strained with worry. "She won't come back."

Dellis shook her head, her eyes closing against the ache forming behind them. "Yes, she will. She won't leave until she's thoroughly ruined me and John. The woman's sick."

"You and John?" Patrick asked, brusquely. "Does that mean you want him back?"

"Stop, Patrick." It was none of his business, especially a man that knowingly left her devastated when she was most in need. He was no angel in her eyes, but he loved trying to make John the Devil.

"Dellis, we have to talk about him."

When Patrick reached out to touch her cheek, she backed away. "*We?* What do you mean *we?* There is no *we.* And John isn't a topic that's up for discussion. While I'm grateful for all the help you've afforded me, please, don't misunderstand our relationship as anything more than platonic."

"I know you're as fond of me as I am of you. I know I failed when I broke our betrothal, but we've gotten so close lately. Don't shut me out."

He was genuinely pleading with her, so much sorrow in his eyes, but still, her heart was cold to him. "Patrick, I can never get over what happened between us. I'm sorry, but that's the truth."

"You can't, or you won't?" Quick as a flash, he pulled her into his arms, his lips finding hers for a deep, gentle kiss. He pulled away for a second, speaking into her lips. "Tell me you don't feel this."

She didn't fight back or struggle. His lips were sweet and soft, and when his tongue touched hers lightly, she met him halfway. It felt good to be held close, her body missing the intimacy, the power, of being in a man's strong arms—but she couldn't fool herself, he wasn't the one she wanted. While his kiss was tender and his arms comforting, it was so very simple: she didn't love him.

When Patrick released her, she looked into his eyes, her heart aching for what she had to do. He needed to hear the truth. "Patrick, you're so sweet and good, but you need to stop this."

"It's because of him. There's no hope for me?" There was finality in his words and bitterness in his voice. "You can't forgive me for the mistake I made, but you can forgive a man that lied to you, used you, and then cheated on you—a man responsible for the death of all those you hold dear. How? I don't understand."

"It's not that simple." She shook her head. Nothing about John was simple. Nothing. It was complex, and scary, and so very difficult, but... "I never said I'd go back to him, nor have I said I'd go back to you. For now, I need to focus on just being me, alone, by myself. I need to learn to stand on my own two feet again. After that, who knows what will come. But my mind is set upon this course."

"What will you do?" Patrick asked, the pain ebbing a bit in his countenance, his face softening.

"I can still cook and sell things at the town market. Agnes is rather good at sewing, and I make candles and butter and all sorts of things. We'll find some way to sell our wares, and perhaps then, we can make enough to keep going. I don't know if it'll work, but I have to try."

"And I'll be right there beside you to help." He added.

"Patrick..." She started to argue and then stopped. There was no use; he was in earnest, and she was in no mood to fight. "I appreciate the help; thank you."

With a nod, she walked back into the parlor, knowing he was following. If anything, he was persistent. And she was grateful for his help; without him, she could never have repaired The Thistle after the mob came.

"Dellis, is everything okay?" Agnes ran over, her big brown eyes searching Dellis's face.

"I'm fine, though I came pretty close to hitting Mrs. Allen."

Will laughed. "Well, she would've deserved it. And I'll be damned if I wouldn't want to see it. Perhaps next time, I'll do it for you."

"Thanks, Will." Looking around at her friends: Patrick; Thomas; Will; and dear, sweet Agnes, Dellis sighed. Thank God for her makeshift family. They kept her going.

"Why don't we finish eating, and then we can play some whist," Thomas said, pouring some ale into his tankard.

"We'll stay up late and sleep in until the sun is high in the sky!" Agnes added, doing a little jig.

"That sounds like a brilliant idea." Since Dellis's parents died and she'd been forced to take up running the tavern, she'd lost a bit of merriment in her life. The idea of not having to wake up early to wait tables and spend her nights enjoying company in place of prepping food sounded like a little slice of Heaven.

Yes, she'd find a way to go on. Together, they'd all find a way.

Chapter Nineteen

John stood to the side, waiting in the wings, as Butler opened the council meeting with all the bravado and élan of a seasoned Shakespearian actor taking the stage. Ever a charismatic orator, it was no soliloquy. There was no rambling; his words were powerful and explicitly chosen to remind the brother tribes of their ancient alliance with the Crown. It was about intimidation and persuasion, something he excelled at with his vast knowledge and experience with the Six Nations. After his comments, he offered the ceremonial hatchet, the sacred declaration of war, to the Seneca. It was the duty of the Iroquois to side with the King, and he, in turn, would support them with his limitless bounty. When Butler finished, the opening of the council adjourned for the night, the Seneca and the members of the local tribes leaving to attend a private negotiation. When they returned for council the next morning, the tribe stood firmly with their brothers of the Six Nations and their treaty of neutrality with the colonies.

Cornplanter, the Seneca war chief of the Wolf Clan, stood, his commanding presence unifying the group in silence. "We've made an agreement with our brother tribes and the colonists to remain at peace, and that is what we must do." He turned his dark, omniscient eyes to Butler, and said with unwavering certainty, "While we support the Great Father, we can't be a part of this war."

Chief Sayenqueraghta seconded Cornplanter's pleas for peace. "We must keep with our brothers. It's the only way for us."

The sun had just dipped below the horizon, the hues of pink and purple bursting forth from the azure waters of the lake, streaking the sky like a painting. It was cool, the scorching heat of the day relenting to a crisp summer night, the kind that beckoned John to lie under a tree and dream sweet dreams of dark hair and obsidian eyes. On that sandy beach, with the lush blue waters lapping back and forth at his boots while diamonds sparkled on crested waves, it was an affront to plan war as God was trying to remind one of the beauty of life by putting it all on display.

John turned away from the lake, looking back at the forest and the unknown darkness hidden amongst the trees. The meeting, the negotiations, they were a contrivance, a false show of power to impress because the Crown lacked the might to do the job themselves. They needed the native men; King George couldn't win without them. John felt foul and duplicitous—lying to men of peace for those who wanted war.

He scanned the council area, taking note of all the illustrious players: Cornplanter, Sayenqueraghta, Blacksnake, and Arron Hill. Each of the Seneca factions sat around the fire, partitioned by their specific villages. Standing with the other Mohawks, Eagle Eyes kept his gaze leveled in John's direction, watching his every move as if plotting the inevitable strike.

Butler stepped forwards, his expression a combination of impassive military man and reverent preacher, serene yet stoic. "Remember, the Great Father's rum is as plenty as the waters in Lake Ontario, and his men are as numerous as the sands on the shores of the great lake. We'll see to it that your families are protected while your men join us at war. Your women and children will be safe."

Waving to Eagle Eyes, Butler said, "Show your brothers what bounty is to be had by joining with King George. They'll follow your lead."

John shook his head with disgust. Once again, Butler was gilding the lily of the Crown's finances while hiding the true intentions. On cue, Eagle

Eyes and some of the Mohawks carried in a barrage of crates and barrels, carefully emptying them and distributing the goods between the factions.

One of the Allegheny chiefs stood, pointing to Butler. "Brothers, we must side with the Great Father; he has been good to us. The colonists are like unruly children lashing out at their parents."

"No! We must stay neutral!" a voice yelled from the congregation.

Stoked and ready to fight, some of the men leapt to their feet, shouting back and forth over the fire. "Yes! The Great Father will protect our land!"

The argument continued between the chiefs and sachems while Eagle Eyes and his men reached into the treasure trove and started passing out more of the plunder.

John recognized some of Celeste's furs being handed to Cornplanter, and there were silks, silver bells, beads, and jewels enough to fascinate the women and further cement the myth of the Crown's financial power. But it was all subterfuge, even King George had limitations.

"If we separate from the Confederacy, this could mean a blood war between us and our brothers. We must stay out of this fight." Cornplanter added, to which many in the group yelled and boasted against his efforts for peace.

"Major, another ship has come with the rest of our goods," Eagle Eyes said.

"Bring everything here." Butler sent his men to collect the shipment, the crates brought forth to the council site one by one. "Don't you see the generosity of the Great Father?"

As the natives inspected the goods, he walked to John and whispered, "Go get the belts from my tent."

He nodded. It was Butler's moment—his coup de gras. John made his way to the Major's quarters, lifted the two belts out of the trunk, and carried them back to the meeting place. Butler unwrapped them quickly and then lifted the Great Old Covenant Chain into the air, high above his head, and shook it vigorously, violently.

"This is the covenant between the Six Nations and His Majesty, King George the Third, the Great Father, *your* Great Father. He's lavished many gifts out of his great love and esteem for his brethren. This will be an easy victory, I promise. These traitorous Rebels will fall to the King's might. Fort Ticonderoga has already fallen; it's only a matter of time before Stanwix follows."

Butler then recited the Articles of the Covenant, impressing the Seneca and all those in attendance with his knowledge. The meeting adjourned again for the night, the Seneca still undecided on their course of action. Instead of returning to the tent, John held back, listening in on the discussions between the factions. Not surprisingly, after the presentation of the Covenant Chain, the conversation had tipped from favoring neutrality to British cause. Butler had done his job brilliantly.

When they reconvened the next evening, the whole tone of the meeting had switched, the Seneca declaring their loyalty to the crown. They appointed Cornplanter and Sayenqueraghta as their war chiefs, both men reluctant, still wanting neutrality, but following the wishes of the greater group. Butler dispersed muskets, ammunition, scalping knives, tomahawks, brass kettles, and clothing to each warrior present. To the war chiefs, Butler gave money and the promise of eight pounds sterling for each rebel scalp they brought back with them, a bounty on American scalps and their loyal natives.

John tamped down his ire, encouraging payment for scalping would only come back to haunt the British; as with the French War, once that practice ensued, it would spread like a bad infection that festered, taking innocent lives in the process.

While Butler and his men finished passing out the supplies, one of the war chiefs stood, imparting a bit of wisdom and hard truth.

"We'll make our final decision known to the rest of our brothers at the Grand Council of the Six Nations. But I warn you, not all of our brothers will join the cause of the Great Father."

"We're aware," John replied with a nod, his thoughts going to Joseph, Han Yerry, and the other Oneida. "Have you spoken with your Oneida and Onondaga brothers? Are they still clinging to neutrality?"

"The Oneida haven't been honest with their brothers." Turning attention away from the piles of furs, Cornplanter pointed to one of his warriors. "We caught two of our brothers spying on us last evening."

"Spying?" John eyes flashed to Butler, who shook his head with confusion. "Oneidas, spying here?"

Cornplanter nodded and then waved to his men. Not a moment later, four Seneca braves appeared with the two prisoners, both with their heads down and their arms bound tightly behind their backs. Throwing one of them on the ground at John's feet, the warrior yanked the prisoner's head back, exposing his face.

John shuddered. It was Alexei, his face battered and bloody, but his icy-blue eyes were full of their usual intensity—and hate.

"Who's the other man?" John's eyes locked with Alexei's for a second.

The Seneca brave pushed the other man to his knees and drew his head back. It was Anoki. His dark eyes were swollen shut, both of his cheeks bruised severely, but ever his defiant self, he kicked and fought against his gaolers. Of all places to find Anoki and Alexei, that wasn't what John had anticipated, nor was it going to be easily remedied. His mind raced, searching for a solution to the fortuitous conundrum that had been suddenly thrust upon him.

"These *are* Oneidas," Eagle Eyes said with unmitigated satisfaction. "They're from Joseph's village.

"Yes, they tried to steal from us," Cornplanter replied.

The giant Mohawk eyed the two men and started towards them with slow, methodical steps, circling his prey, ready to dive in at any moment. Butler also walked from behind, grinning; with his over-embellished nose, fleshy cheeks, and thick sloppy lips, he looked like a caricature. Suddenly, the protagonist of the play had switched roles; the antagonist was drumming the tips of his fingers together manically, staring down the unexpected guests that entered the scene and stole his renown.

"Well, well, Oneidas," Butler said, his pleasure disturbingly obvious. "Had you made your presence known, we would've asked you to join."

"These Brothers of the Standing Stone are *our* prisoners." Cornplanter insisted. "We'll deal with them."

"With all due respect, Chief." John stepped between Eagle Eyes and the prisoners, fearing Alexei and Anoki would end up scalped and the first sixteen pounds sterling paid right then and there. "Perhaps we should spare them. It will only serve to anger your brothers, and with the Grand Council coming, we might be able to leverage them to the Oneidas for their loyalty."

Alexei cocked his brow, a smirk forming at the corner of his lips. Even when faced with death, he was defiant and boastful. John admired his adversary's spirit, though a bit misguided in that moment.

"No, Captain." Cornplanter countered. "We'll deal with them as a warning to our brothers. You can take their scalps to the council and present them to the Oneidas after you pay us for each." The chief nodded to the brave holding Anoki. With that, the Seneca pulled out his new scalping knife, held it to Anoki's forehead, and started to cut, a trickle of blood running into his brow.

John's premonition rang true as the situation descended into chaos. He had to do something fast. Without a thought in mind, he threw up his hands, praying an idea would come to him. "Wait!" The Seneca warrior halted, mid cut, the blade flashing in the firelight, still pressed to the tawny skin of Anoki's high forehead. "What if I paid you to give them to us? I have more weapons, shot, even gold. Name your price."

"Why do you want them?" Cornplanter asked suspiciously, his eyes narrowing. "Are you going to negotiate with the Oneida behind our backs?"

"No, not at all. We ahh…" *Come on, John, think!* "We'll take them to the council to negotiate with the Oneidas." John fumbled, his usual finesse with words still eluding him. "Of course, in front of all parties, and naturally, we'll mention to the Grand Council your generous negotiation with the Crown, and how you wanted to prevent any injury to your brothers over this unfortunate event."

John shook his head, not his best effort, but no flashes of inspiration presented themselves in the heat of the moment. He knew the lie sounded rather obsequious, but if it worked, and the Seneca played along, he'd have Alexei in hand.

"No." Cornplanter shook his head and then made a cutting motion with his hand. The Seneca warrior fisted Anoki's hair, pulling it back, the blade slicing an inch-long cut at the top of his forehead. The trickle of blood turned to a stream, crimson red spurting from the wound.

Try again. Normally, John had a little whiskey on board for liquid courage, but that time, he was clean and decidedly less effective. *So much harder.* "Great Chief, the King has as much as rum as you can possibly want. We have boats, pelts, metalwork. Name your price." The desperation in John's voice betrayed his calm façade. The other brave pulled out his scalping blade and held it to Alexei's neck.

"Tell us the truth!" Cornplanter yelled, his dark eyes turning fierce. "What kind of deception are you playing?"

John put his hands out again, trying to halt them as the brave pushed the knife into Alexei's throat. "I speak the truth. Don't do this; I'll give you anything you require. But we need to gain the Oneida's friendship. These two men could help us do that."

Butler muttered, "What are you doing, Carlisle?"

With a sidelong glance, John whispered, "That's Joseph's right-hand man. These two are their strongest warriors. It would better serve us to use these men for potential negotiations than let the Seneca murder them."

"I don't know if I trust you." Butler sneered. "But go on."

John confidently turned his attention to the Seneca, though inwardly, a miasma of fear pervaded. "What's your price? Name it. It'll be yours."

Cornplanter waved his men off, the cutting stopping abruptly. "We, the Keepers of the Western Wall, will be in charge of your native force, and we'll decide if the brothers fight or not. The final judgement is ours to make. And I want more weapons and gold."

It was all up to Butler then. He eyed the two Oneidas kneeling at knifepoint, and after a moment of charged silence, finally nodded.

"We agree to your terms," John replied.

"And we want more horses and the promise that we'll keep our land once this war is over."

That was something John couldn't give them. A decision like that could only come from the royal governor and the King himself. The Seneca weren't afraid to ask for the moon, but John could only give them the stars, and even that would cost him a great deal.

Thankfully, Butler stepped in, taking over the negotiations. "We'll ask the governor to negotiate your terms, but neither Captain Carlisle nor myself are in the position to promise something as significant as land. We'll see that you're adequately equipped for war with horses, muskets, and powder. You'll want for nothing. As I promised you, it'll be an easy fight, made even more so if we can get your Oneida brothers to join us."

Eagle Eyes glanced at Butler and then trained his gaze down to the two prisoners. "I'll see that these two are protected until the council. You have my word, brothers."

The Seneca deliberated for a several moments, their voices at a murmur so no words could be heard above the crackle of the fire. John's heart pounded against his breast while they waited, the lengthy amount of time a portent of his failure.

Please, let this work.

Cornplanter turned back to them and nodded. "Take them."

The braves released Alexei and Anoki, both men falling on their hands and knees. John held back a sigh of relief, opting to turn to Clark and Smith, hiding his expression of pleasure. "Take these two and see that they're properly guarded."

When Eagle Eyes went for Alexei, Butler held up a hand. "Captain Carlisle's men will guard the prisoners. It would serve us better to have you here, brother."

Eagle Eyes's stony expression darkened, black, piercing eyes finding John through the towering fire—a silent warning. He'd taken his first swipe at the Mohawk in their battle to the death, but Eagle Eyes would strike back with a vengeance.

"Now, we'll finish with the council negotiations, and then we can ready ourselves for war!" Sayenqueraghta pumped his fist in the air.

John turned his back, smoothing his hair out of his face with trembling hands. His forehead was wet with perspiration, his stomach knotted and bilious. Yes, John might have found Alexei, but he was a prisoner of the Crown—and at the mercy and whims of Butler.

"Just what the hell was that about, Carlisle?" Throwing his hat down on the table, Butler whipped around, unleashing his rage. "You better have a damned good excuse for what you've done. I've no idea how we'll fulfill their demands."

Neither did John.

"I had no choice! We need those two for negotiations with the Oneidas."

"The Oneidas of Kanonwalohale and Oriska have already sided with the Rebels. They can lie all they want about neutrality. Joseph or Han Yerry will never negotiate for these two men. They're as immobile and obstinate as a tree." Butler stepped closer to John, their eyes locking. "Twice now you've gone out of your way to protect the Oneida. Whose side are you on, Carlisle?"

That was an excellent question. Butler was right. Twice, John had acted in favor of the Oneida, and from the Major's vantage point, there was no reason for it. If John told Butler that Alexei had stolen the woman and was responsible for the thieving over the previous two years, he'd surely face the gallows—a just course of action from John's perspective—but Dellis would never forgive him if anything happened to her cousin. *Dellis?* Again, there was too much blurring of the lines, allowing personal affairs to supersede the mission. It wouldn't do. *I can't go on this way.*

"Major, I'm on our side. You know this."

Butler slammed his fist on the table. "No, actually, I don't. You blackmailed me into releasing three of their prisoners, you want to negotiate for these two, and you have yet to deliver me the Oneida. I know they meet with Schuyler. I know they scout and spy for him. No. From now on, I'll handle the Oneida. You'll function as an interpreter, and that's all."

"Sir." John took a deep breath, trying to regain control of the conversation and his nerves. "With all due respect, you and I know that the natives are capricious. It's not too late to change their minds."

"That may be true, but from now on, I'll be handling all the negotiations." Butler snorted. "You had one job to do: find the woman and bring back the supplies. And now you have to come up with a way to meet the promises we made to the Seneca—and quickly. Colonel Claus surely won't give me more supplies."

The situation was rapidly deteriorating. John needed to keep a hand in the negotiations, and he had to keep Alexei safe from Eagle Eyes. There was only one way to guarantee that: Alexei's true identity would have to be exposed. A bad choice, but it was the only one John had. "Major, that's Alexei McKesson, the very man we've been searching for."

Butler's eyes widened and then narrowed to beady black holes that fixed on John. "Are you telling me the truth, Carlisle?"

"Yes," he replied. "There may be a way for me to persuade him to talk. Not only could he lead us to the woman, but he may also serve to turn the Oneida. He's invaluable to their cause, their thief who's been stealing from us."

"What a fortunate find." Butler's voice was strangely full of sarcasm and a touch of irony.

John wasn't quite sure what to make of the sudden change in demeanor.

"I'll have Clark and Smith keep watch on the prisoners while I try to negotiate with him."

"No, no." Butler shook his head. "I'll take care of guarding the prisoners. Take your men, and find the cargo we promised the Seneca. We have less than a fortnight before the council in Oswego."

"What will you do with them?" John asked, purposely bucking authority.

"None of your business, Captain. Just get the job done. Fast."

"Yes, sir." When John stepped out of Butler's tent, Eagle Eyes was waiting, ready to strike back.

"I find it rather intriguing that you volunteered to guard the prisoners. Isn't sentry duty beneath you? Will Butler pay you?" John asked, giving the Mohawk a sardonic onceover. "Perhaps it's because you've been looking for Alexei as well?"

Eagle Eyes said nothing, allowing his aggressive posture to do the communicating.

John cocked a brow in challenge, imitating Eagle Eyes's stance: feet spread wide, arms akimbo. Provoking the choleric native brought an immense amount of pleasure.

"Who'd have the money and desire to catch two Oneida thieves?" John smiled, the blurry picture becoming clear. "James McKesson. It all makes sense. Without his son, McKesson's situation fell apart?" He tapped his chin with his index finger curiously. "But how did you happen to meet him? That's the real question."

"You have an axe to grind with Alexei," Eagle Eyes replied, evading the question. "And yet you went out of your way to secure his safety."

"To negotiate with the Oneida; it's our best chance of gaining their support."

"That's a lie. You're protecting him, and we both know why." The edge to Eagle Eyes's voice was so sharp it could cut through an animal hide. "So which one of us will get to him first?" Then he smiled.

The last time John saw the Mohawk do that, he scalped and murdered a pregnant woman.

Alexei's wife.

Chapter Twenty

Since The Thistle was officially closed, and Dellis didn't have worry to about leaving early for the village, she slept in longer than usual, indulging in butter-soft sheets and downy pillows while she contemplated her uncertain future. Instead of doing upkeep on the house, Agnes and Will had taken to making candles and baking for the local market. Selling odds and ends would hopefully yield enough money to keep everyone fed, at least until winter, but it wouldn't help with Gavin Carlisle. That was a problem Dellis had yet to solve. And because she was once again *persona non grata*, there was no one in German Flats who'd hire her for medical services. The townspeople had deemed the three of them Tories, and fear of self-incrimination meant they were isolated, alone in a powder keg doomed to blow. On several occasions since the court, bricks had been thrown through the windows of The Thistle, notes had been tacked to the door, and one night, someone set fire to the stables—which thankfully, the trio managed to put out before it caused serious damage.

Later that day, on her way through town, she passed Stuart, practicing drills with his militia friends outside Fort Dayton. The moment they eyed each other, he yelled, "Redcoat whore!" and pointed to her, rallying his friends to join.

"Tory! Whore!" they yelled, chasing after her.

Digging her heels into her mare's sides, Dellis sped off, putting enough distance between her and Stuart to avoid confrontation. Once again, she was the focus of his rage; before, it was guilt, then it was because of John, but Stuart's last betrayal put an end to any chance of reconciliation. She could forgive her brother his guilt, even his hate, but not his betrayal of their parents. The Thistle was their father's home, and Stuart had jeopardized its very existence.

How has it come to this? All she'd ever known was sibling rivalry; first her father and his brothers, and then her and Stuart. What was it about McKessons that made them determined to destroy their own? Passionate nature and competitive energy couldn't be contained in one house, so it lashed out until only the strongest survived. Just like John and Gavin.

Dellis rode for several hours, the sweltering heat from the blazing sun causing her to stop several times to rest her horse and stretch. The solitude of the forest was surprisingly welcome—a moment of calm before the storm. She heard General Schuyler had ordered more soldiers garrisoned at Fort Stanwix, and they were working to block Wood Creek, hoping to slow the impending British advance downstream.

Would John come with the brigade? Knowing what he did about her people, would he use it against them? Putting her head in her hands, she searched for the answer only to be bombarded by a myriad of questions. He was the consummate soldier; how could he not be loyal to his mission? To turn would cost him everything; he'd said it before. What made that moment any different? Could she forgive him if he stayed with the regiment? There were times when she saw him talking to her grandfather and Great Bear, and she knew they shared mutual admiration. And those quiet nights when she lay in her beloved's arms and he whispered sweet words in her ear, calling her village home, she thought he meant it. Didn't he?

She arrived at the village just before sundown, breathing a sigh of relief at her first sight of the stockade. Though her relationship with her grandfather and the village was strained, it was still her refuge. *Home.* The trees around the village had grown thick and full under the adoration of the summer sun, their branches hanging over like massive hands. Giant maples with five-pronged leaves and aspens that twirled and twisted in the wind like giant friends protected her precious home from the elements. The ground was lush and green, ferns and grasses soft under her leather boots as she dismounted. Past the village, atop the hill, she could see the new barn, the trees around it burned down, new ones budding up from the earth, little saplings starting anew. Yes, it was home. She loved how different it was from The Thistle; in the village, she was isolated. Protected.

Her grandfather was in the village center, meeting with Han Yerry; around them, the villagers listened intently. "We've learned from Thomas Sinavis and his spies that the British have made a deal with our Seneca brothers. They brought out the Great Old Covenant Chain and promised much in the way of goods and supplies if they'd break with the neutrality agreement."

Dellis put her hand over her mouth, stifling the urge to interject. *Listen. Learn.*

"Chief Spencer at Kanonwalohale is right. We can't allow the British, or our brother tribes, to march over our sacred lands and do nothing. We must fight. Our chances are better with the colonists. We must act decisively," Han Yerry said, strained lines of worry creasing his brow. "We've spent much time spying and offering our services, but we have yet to fully take up the hatchet. What do you think, Joseph?"

Her grandfather drew in an audible breath and let it out, glancing at his warriors and his sachem for their approval. "What was Chief Spencer's final word on the matter?"

"He suggested we meet with the King's men and our brothers one last time at Oswego and plead for neutrality. When we're refused, then we declare ourselves. One last effort on our part." Han Yerry's words were direct, plotting their course, yet it wasn't going to be as easy as it sounded.

"You know there'll be retribution for this?" Joseph asked.

Oh, God. Her stomach knotted and churned; the inevitable had come, bloody war between brothers *and* with the British.

"We have no choice, Joseph, and we can't continue our present course."

Her grandfather nodded. "We'll go with you to Oswego as representatives of our village. And we'll stand together when the Great King's men come."

Dellis approached her grandfather and waited, biting her lip against fearful words that were already on the tip of her tongue. When he finished wishing Han Yerry and his men well, her grandfather turned to her. "You'll come with us to Oswego."

She shuddered. It was as if he anticipated her question and gave her the answer she least expected. Instead of boasting any disagreement or saying anything more, she simply nodded. "Yes, sir." Her fearful words could wait.

"We'll travel to Kanonwalohale and meet with their delegates and then on to the council together. It's the safest course now that our brothers have declared themselves."

Joseph took her hand in his and slowly directed her to his cabin. When they were inside, he closed the door and turned back to her. "You should sit down."

She did as she was told, preparing herself. When someone says to sit, it always precedes grave news, and the look on her grandfather's face indicated just that.

"Dellis, Alexei has been captured by the King's men."

"What?" She gasped, suddenly sick to her stomach. "How do you know that?"

"Thomas Sinavis. Some of his spies were with Alexei when he was caught. They have him and Anoki."

"Grandfather, the British will try and leverage them for our loyalty." She stood and walked over to him, needing to look him in the eyes, the truth would be in them, no matter what words he spoke. "What will you do?"

"I can't endanger my whole village for two men. And I won't go against the decisions of Chief Spencer or Han Yerry. Alexei knew the risks when he went out."

He was in earnest, his gaze direct and true.

"Grandfather, what about John? Maybe he can help us?" She blurted it out, trying to come up with some other option that didn't include her cousin facing the gallows.

"Fennishyo, it wouldn't be fair of you to ask that of your husband. You'd be putting him at risk to save Alexei." Joseph put his hands on her shoulders as if anticipating one of her usual, impulsive, retorts. "Just One is a warrior, and he's chosen his side. We must respect it."

Tears welled up in her eyes, but she forced them dry. "So what's the alternative? Alexei is hanged? We must do something."

"Asking Just One to help us could see him hanged instead. Are you willing to risk that?"

She closed her eyes, shaking her head. But they were out of options. John was their only hope. She was convinced. "Oh, Alexei, what have you done?" she whispered to herself.

"We'll be leaving in another day for Kanonwalohale. Prepare as much food and supplies as you can bring and rest up; we'll be travelling for a few days, and it won't be an easy ride."

She nodded. "Then it's better if I go back to town tomorrow, first thing. I have some extra food, and I'll get my belongings. Also, I have to let Agnes and Will know I'll be gone for several days. I wouldn't want them to worry."

"All right, be back soon."

"John, I want to talk to Alexei." Merrick pulled on his frock coat and grabbed his hat, thrusting it on his head. "That young man has much to explain."

"Merrick, if you meet with him, Butler will know you're here. It will spoil all of your carefully laid plans, and we've both fought hard for this moment." John prayed cooler heads would prevail and his friend would rethink his decision. "Let me talk to Alexei first. You trust me, don't you?"

Merrick nodded, but John sensed apprehension.

"I'll go now. Do you think you can help me with the Seneca? Making this deal was the only option I had to keep them from killing Alexi and Anoki."

"Let me look over my books while you're gone. I'll see what I can do."

The rain pelted John as he rowed from the schooner back to land. Quickly, he ran to his tent and changed into a dry uniform, slicking his wet hair back and tying it at the nape. His damp skin itched under the layers of linen and wool, but at least his feet were dry, and he looked regulation.

After negotiating with the Seneca the night before, John was unable to question Alexei or Anoki. Butler required everyone to attend the council closing ceremonies and finish out the negotiations. Clark and Smith assigned two of their most trusted men to guard the prisoner's tent, keeping Eagle Eyes out of proximity—at least for a while.

John walked up to the stoic sentry, guarding the prisoner's tent, and addressed him. "Captain Carlisle to speak with the prisoner."

"Yes, sir." The guard stepped out of the way, nodding.

Lifting the tent flap, John turned for a second, scanning the area for the giant Mohawk. "Where's Eagle Eyes?"

"Major Butler requested his presence. He was here earlier."

"Thank you," John replied, satisfied there would be no unwanted interruptions from his adversary.

When John stepped inside, Alexei looked up from a plate of food and smiled, a contrary expression to the danger he faced. Twisted fate had turned the tables on the adversaries; not three months before, John was a prisoner and Alexei held their collective fates in his hands, though the airy, comfortable tent was a significant improvement to the dark, cavernous bastion at Fort Stanwix. It looked as if Alexei's wounds had been cared for, a small line of stitches on his cheek peeked out from under the lock of dark hair that hung in his face. His hands were shackled together, but otherwise he was unrestrained.

"So, you've finally done it." Alexei dropped his fork and knife on the plate and leaned back in his chair arrogantly like he was the one wielding the sword. "Though I find it humorous that it was actually the Seneca that caught me, and not you, Carlisle. I always knew you lacked the stones to do the job."

"Don't patronize me." John countered, ignoring Alexei's taunting snicker—it was trite and unconvincing. "Actually, you'd rather it be *me* that caught you instead of the Crown. You wouldn't be a victim of subterfuge at my hands. Mercy isn't in Butler's vocabulary. He'll do as he wishes and cover it up neatly."

"Aren't yours and Butler's goals one in the same?" Alexei mocked, his eyebrow cocking in challenge. "And now, you'll use me to negotiate with Joseph. But guess what? He won't make a deal. You'll have to hang me."

He seemed so confident, so calm, yet John knew better, it was all a front, naïve hubris from a man who'd never paid for his crimes. He'd be wise to learn a little fear.

"You may get your wish, Alexei. Butler would love to send you to the gallows, and Eagle Eyes is just waiting for me to make a false step so he can gut you."

"So, Just One, what's your plan?" Alexei taunted, purposely using John's Oneida name, a reminder of his divided loyalties. "Justice, is that what this is? Or revenge?" Alexei stood and walked across the room, his height allowing him to tower over John by four inches. "Tell me, how did you convince Joseph to let you become one of us? I knew you were silver tongued and good at deceiving women, and maybe even Gansevoort, but a whole tribe? That takes talent."

John looked up at Alexei with the conviction of life experience, something he lacked. "You know the truth of that. I rescued those men— *your men*—that you left behind. You could've done the same but chose not to. I'd never leave my men to rot in a prison while there was a breath left in my body. That's the difference between you and I."

"Noblesse oblige from a scoundrel is laughable." Alexei cocked one of his straight, full brows again, his razor-sharp cheekbones and deep-set eyes reminding John of Dellis.

"You're a petulant boy playing at war, and now you have it. The Oneida are separated from their brothers, on the side of the colonists; that's exactly what you wanted. I hope you like what you get." Battlefields and rivers of blood flashed before John eyes, the spoils of war. So much waste. "It's not you that I want, Alexei, it's the woman. Tell me what you've done with her, and I'll find a way to see you released."

Alexei was motionless, no flinch, no change in his countenance. Perfect, unreadable reticence.

"I know you took her because of the dowry and the supplies that were on that ship. Just give me the woman, and you keep the bloody powder and guns."

Alexei stared John down, like a hawk watching its prey, but said nothing.

"I'm your last hope. You'll face the gallows if you don't tell me where she is."

"And what of Dellis? It was by your hand that I'm here. She would've understood if the Seneca murdered me, but she won't be so forgiving of you." A masterful grin spread from one side of Alexei's mouth to the other, and then he shook his head slowly. "You know this, and so do I. And that's why I always win."

John's temper rose, adrenaline coursing through his veins, making him twitchy and nervous, his fists aching to connect with flesh. He paced back and forth, searching for the answer, trying to dissipate some of his anxiety by making tracks in the ground.

Think, John.

His quicksilver mind drew off everything he knew about Alexei, looking for a weakness. It had nothing to do with the village or the Oneida.

Why would Alexei not want to return the woman? Why? And then suddenly, there was a moment of clarity. He was trying to protect her.

"She's beautiful and quite wealthy," John said, grinning.

Granted, he'd never seen the woman, but Alexei didn't know that. If Miles was smitten with her, she had to be quite a catch.

"Perhaps you want her for yourself? We killed your wife, so you take one from us. This is just retribution, isn't it? Plain and simple."

John stopped pacing and stepped closer to Alexei so they were face to face, his shackled hands between them. "I remember your wife, Mary. She was quite lovely even when heavy with your child."

"You know nothing about my wife." Alexei countered, his hackles rising, rage turning his blue eyes to ice. "Do *not* speak of her."

"What would she think of you now? Would she condone kidnapping another woman after what happened to her? Did you make the woman a member of your tribe, or did you just rape and murder her?"

John saw the flare in Alexei's nostrils, his eyes narrowing.

Now I'm getting somewhere.

"Raping and murdering women is your style, English, not mine. She's safe."

"So you do have her?" John smiled. *Finally, an admission.* "If you tell me where she is, I'll see her safely back to her husband, and you'll be released."

Alexei shook his head. "Unlike you, I wouldn't forsake my woman for duty. What would Dellis think of you if she saw you now? She loves you. How could you do this to her?"

"Don't speak of your cousin to me. You've done your damnedest to come between us, and quiet successfully on many occasions. It should make you happy to see us this way." John clipped, tersely levelling up his gaze with Alexei's.

"I helped you save her; what of that? And what about Joseph and our village? They've accepted you as one of their own. You vacillate between sides when it suits you, but know this: no one respects a man who sits on the fence. Put your flag in the sand, be done with it, and leave Dellis and my people alone. Have some honor, man."

"You know nothing of honor, Alexei. You've never had it a day in your life, so don't try to manipulate mine. You have no idea what this war cost me, what you and your father's actions have done to my life. I've paid dearly…" John stopped, the words lodged in his throat as he thought of his lost son and all Dellis endured. He hands balled into fists at his sides, his anger barely contained. "Save your self-righteous indignation for someone who gives a damn. And just so you know, I'd never forsake Dellis. Never."

He stepped back, taking a deep breath, trying to regain his composure. Then something Alexei said struck John as unusual. *Forsaken my woman? My woman.* How had he not seen it? Their plights were mirror images. Alexei wasn't merely protecting the woman—he was in love with her.

John laughed at the sudden commonalty of the predicaments. Fate's sleight of hand had turned on Alexei. Finally. "You're in love with her; that's why you won't give her up."

Alexei said nothing, but his silence spoke volumes.

John let out breath, shaking his head. He, better than anyone, understood what it was like to fall in love with the wrong woman and what one would do to protect her. "*That's* why you won't give her up. She's hidden somewhere for safekeeping."

"You don't know what you're talking about." Alexei countered.

"Oh, I do. Better than anyone," John replied. "The problem is, Miss Parkhurst was married by proxy to Lord Tomlinson. She's *married*, Alexei. She can never be yours; even if I let you go, Miles will search high and low for her. He's a viscount and very powerful. Think about it. If I return her to him, she'll be safe, and I'll tell them you helped me find her. He *will* let you go."

"No."

"Alexei, you must give her up."

"No! Would you have given up Dellis so easily?" Alexei raged, his stance fixed, posturing and ready to fight. "As I much as I loathe the thought of you with my cousin, I know you love her. You'd never give her up, not to anyone."

Alexei was right; were the situations reversed, John would never relinquish Dellis. Their negotiation was done; it was a no-win situation.

"Alexei, you're wanted as a thief, and you were captured spying. Know this: I'm your only hope, and if I don't find the woman, then I'll face the court martial. If that happens, you'll be on your own."

Alexei smiled. "Then we'll go down together. Fitting, isn't it?"

John closed his eyes, drawing in a breath full of unease. Yes, they'd go down together, but unlike Alexei, John had already felt the sting of British justice.

Chapter
Twenty-One

"Where are you going?" Agnes followed Dellis through the kitchen as she rushed around, stuffing her satchel full of provisions for the trip. She grabbed some berries from the bowl on the table and wrapped them in linen, adding them to her already overflowing haversack.

Quickly, she made a mental list of what else she needed to bring; rushing down the hall to her room, she snatched her basket of medical supplies and the bottle of whiskey she put aside for cleaning wounds. As she raced back into the kitchen, Agnes stepped in the way, halting Dellis's advance.

"Please, tell me what's going on. You've been running around like a chicken with its head cut off since you returned."

Dellis let out a sigh, turning back to her dear friend, recognizing genuine concern in her countenance. "I'm going with my grandfather to the council meeting in Oswego. We'll be gone for a few days."

"All this craziness is for that?" Agnes moved, allowing Dellis to pass, and off she went, down the hall to the pantry, grabbing a few candles.

"No, that's not all of it." She rushed back into the kitchen, placed the basket on the table, and dropped in a chair, her body exhausted from two days of riding back and forth to the village. "Alexei and Anoki have been taken prisoner by the British."

Agnes poured both of them some coffee from the kettle and then sat across the table. "What will your grandfather do?"

"The British will use them to try and blackmail us into joining the fight, but my grandfather said he won't negotiate. He'll never risk the tribe to save two men."

"Do you believe him?"

Dellis nodded, a painful knot forming in her stomach. "Alexei knew the risks when he went out spying. I know Grandfather is right, but I have to do something. I have to try."

Agnes's dark eyes narrowed accusingly. "You mean to ask the Captain to help you?"

"Yes," Dellis replied, sheepishly. "If I can find him."

"Dellis, that would be presumptuous of you; after the fight you two had, how do you think he'd receive such a request?"

"Whatever do you mean?" she asked, innocently, but her grimace smacked of guilt.

"You're asking him to take a terrible risk. He'll see it as you choosing your cousin's life over his." Agnes grabbed Dellis's hand, squeezing it lightly. "I know you want to save Alexei, but there has to be another way."

"There's no other way. Besides, John doesn't have to be the one to do the rescuing; he could just tell us where Alexei is being held prisoner. My grandfather and his men could break him out."

"You're being naïve. You need to think this through. It would hurt the Captain."

She stood, her anger rising. "What about how he hurt me? Everyone seems to forget that John is the one who wronged me!"

"And you never fail to remind us all of that fact," Agnes replied tartly.

For the first time, Dellis was taken aback. "You did *not* just say that."

"Yes, I did." Agnes met Dellis eye to eye. "Forgive my impertinence, but you're not innocent in this argument with the Captain. And you're not the only one who was hurt."

"He owes it to me and my village to tell us where Alexei is being held." Dellis huffed out a breath of frustration, throwing up her hands. "Why must you always take his side?"

Agnes's voice was low and calm, but her expression didn't soften. "This isn't about sides. I love both of you, but you seem to have a selective memory where the Captain is concerned and an unreasonable amount of forgiveness for Alexei. John has done so much for you, yet it's never enough."

Before Dellis got a chance to rebuke Agnes with an earful of "mind your own business," a sweet, feminine voice interrupted them. "Alexei's being held prisoner?"

Dellis grimaced. *Will?* When she turned around, of course, Will was listening in on the argument, her hazel eyes full of tears. "This is because of me, I know it. I have to go back; I have to find my husband." With that, she ran down the hall towards her room.

Dellis looked at Agnes, their eyes widening. "Husband?"

"Husband?" Agnes repeated, aghast.

"Stay here." Dellis rose and walked down the hall; by the time she reached Stuart's old room, Will had already emptied her drawers and filled her haversack.

"Where are you going?" Dellis closed the door behind her.

"If the British have Alexei, it's because of me. It's my husband. I just know it. Alexei warned me to stay clear of the Captain. Maybe he told Miles?"

The Captain? Miles? Inspiration hit her like running into a brick wall. Will was the woman John was looking for, Lord Tomlinson's bride. All that time, the missing heiress had been right under their noses, and Alexei had put her there. *Damn, he's good.* Only he could hide a woman in plain sight.

Dellis chuckled to herself and then let out a chain of expletives. *Damned arrogant ass.*

"Do you think this is humorous?" Will asked, clearly offended, and then raced to the door.

"Will, wait." Dellis grabbed the slight woman by the shoulders, forcing her to stop. "No, this situation is far from humorous, but if Alexei brought you here, he did it for a reason. Going after him won't help. Trust me."

"No." Will persisted and then burst into tears. "Don't you see? They're after him because of me. My husband wants me back. I can't let them hurt Alexei because of me. I just can't."

Dellis drew the woman into a hug while she sobbed out her pain. "The last time I saw Alexei, we quarreled. I begged him not to go. I had a bad feeling Miles would catch him. Oh, God, they'll hang him, won't they?"

"Don't say that." Dellis gently stroked Will's back, trying to comfort her. "If I can get word to John, maybe—"

"No, you mustn't; my husband and the Captain are friends. They're working together. I must find Miles myself; that's the only way this works. Please, let me go with you, I promise I'll protect Alexei."

Goodness, the poor thing was desperately in love with Alexei; only true attachment could make a woman so foolish and starry eyed. "Will, there's much about Alexei you don't know. Yes, he's wanted for stealing from the British, but that started long before you came into the picture. Even if you hand yourself over to your husband, Alexei will still hang for his crimes."

"I don't understand." She sniffed, wiping her nose with a small embroidered handkerchief from her pocket.

"Alexei and my Uncle James have been stealing from the British for years. My grandfather and our village assisted them until Alexei and his father had a falling out. Since then, Alexei has been spying for the colonists. Taking you and your dowry is just one of many crimes he's wanted for, and I'm afraid if you hand yourself over to the British, you could be forced to speak against him."

"We have to do something! I can't bear the thought of him facing the gallows. I can't..." True and utter desperation rendered the woman's voice brittle; she waged a tangible fight to continue. "I... love him. God, I love him."

Dellis ached for Will and Alexei. Another pair of star-crossed lovers torn apart by war. But going back to her husband wasn't the answer; Alexei hid the woman for a reason.

"Will, you must stay here. I'll find the Captain. He'll help us. I know it."

Will sniffed several times, wiping her nose again with the little kerchief. "Are you sure?"

Dellis nodded. "John's our only hope."

"What if you can't find him?"

"He's either in Oswego or Niagara. He works with Major Butler."

"But what if you don't find him?" Will persisted.

Dellis looked into Will's big, sweet eyes and considered the options. "I met your husband when I was with John. You're correct, they're close friends. If anyone would know how to find John, Miles would."

"What do you intend on doing?" Will asked, clutching the front of her shirt daintily as if holding on to a string of pearls. How Dellis never realized Will was a woman was mindboggling, such small, delicate hands, and such elegant gestures; no, she was unmistakably feminine.

"I'll go to Lord Tomlinson and see if I can persuade him to tell me where John is; that is, if I don't find him myself first."

"No." She shook her head vigorously. "Miles may seem like a kind man, but I assure you, he's violent and ill tempered. When he was leaving for the colonies, he tried to force me into consummating our marriage before the documents were signed and the proxy took place. I stayed off his advances, but he struck me. I'd be afraid he'd do something to hurt you."

"I'll be fine. No need to worry."

Dellis snorted. She'd dealt with one or two brutes in her life, and a grabby, drunken husband with love on the brain, yet she lived to tell the tale. There was nothing a little saltpeter and a metal ball couldn't put a stop to. She got up from her chair and rushed across the hall to her room, digging through her chest of drawers.

"What are you looking for?" Will asked from behind.

Dellis pulled out her pistol, a horn full of gunpowder, and little pouch of musket balls. She glanced up at the door, where both Agnes and Will were looking on with curiosity. "Where's my blue dress? The one John had made for me in Oswego."

"It's upstairs. Why do you want it?" Agnes asked.

"Because I may need to dress the part of a lady. I highly doubt a Lord would be the least bit tempted by a woman in an ill-fitting wool dress that has patches all over it. Can you run upstairs and grab it and the dress I wore to my tribal ceremony? I may need that one, too."

"Dellis, this is a terrible idea. Don't do it."

Dellis threw up her hands in frustration. Clearly, the two of them had no intention of helping her. Pushing past, she rushed through the kitchen and into the dining room on her way upstairs. As the passed the front door, Patrick walked in, his arms full of fruits and vegetables and a couple bottles of wine.

"Mr. Armstrong, please, help me talk her out of this folly." Agnes begged, taking the stuff from his arms and placing it on the nearest table.

"What folly?" Patrick looked at Agnes and then at Will. "What's going on?"

"Alexei's been taken prisoner," Will said, no longer disguising her voice. "She's going to try to find him."

Patrick shook his head as if he wasn't sure he heard her correctly. "Come again?"

"Alexei's been captured by the British," Dellis repeated, bounding up the rest of the stairs. She walked into John's room and started digging through his chest of drawers.

The door flew open, and Patrick crossed the room in two long strides, grabbing her shoulders, forcing her to turn around. "You're not going after Alexei. It's too dangerous. Let me go."

She laughed. *Now he's at it.* Why couldn't they all just support her? *Now is when I need them most.* "Patrick, you're a wanted spy. If you're caught, then you'll face the gallows with him. It has to be me."

"Dellis, stop and think for a second. Just how do you intend to free Alexei?"

"I'm going to ask John," she said with conviction, pushing free from his grasp and then starting through the drawers of the desk.

"What? You must be out of your wits. Carlisle's been trying to catch Alexei all this time. There's no way he'll help you."

She shook her head and continued tearing through the drawers, looking for John's pistol, only to remember she'd dropped it in the grass at the duel and never picked it up. Cursing her bad luck, she slammed the drawer shut and looked up at Patrick. "Of course you'd say that; you just don't want me to see him. You're afraid I'll go back to him."

"You're right, I don't want you to go back to him, but this has nothing to do with that. Carlisle will never free Alexei."

Dellis stood and dug through her chest of drawers, but her dress was nowhere to be found. Getting down on her knees, she lifted the draping blanket out of the way and searched under the bed.

"Ah ha!" She reached way under, pulled a box out, and then leaned in again, dragging out something else that was lying on the floor. It was one of John's tunics.

Carefully, she wiped the dust off his fine, red, wool jacket and placed it on the bed. The sight of the crimson fabric no longer induced fear; memories of John wearing it when he returned to the village with Samuel and the other captured braves brought a smile to her face. He was so handsome, his blond hair in stark contrast against the brilliance of the red fabric; the thought of seeing him again made her heart race, betraying the anger that still simmered below the surface.

Lifting the top off of the box, she pulled out the navy-blue dress John bought her in Oswego. It was made of the richest, most luxurious silk taffeta with a creamy-buttermilk petticoat brocaded with blue flowers, the design reminiscent of the fine Chinese porcelain in her aunt's dining room. Yes, it would do nicely.

"Dellis, don't go. Alexei will be angry with you for putting yourself at risk. Think about it."

She carefully wrapped the dress in some linen and stuffed it into a sack she could hang off the back of her saddle. "Alexei's in no position to be angry at anyone. And my mind is made up."

When she looked up, she was surprised to find Will standing in the door, her large, hazel eyes glassy with tears. "Oh, Dellis, do be careful."

"I will, and I'll find a way to bring my cousin back to you, safe and sound."

"Wait." Patrick's gaze shifted back and forth between Will and Dellis. "Bring Alexei back—*this* is the woman?"

Dellis nodded. "I hate to impose on you, but I need a favor, and you're the only one I can trust. Can you keep an eye on her and Agnes while I'm gone? Please?"

"I will," he replied, still wide eyed and dumbfounded by the revelation. Thank God she had Patrick.

Chapter
Twenty-Two

Fort Ontario New York, July 1777

"Lord Tomlinson is unable to meet with you, sir. He's left for Buck Island to escort General St. Leger to Oswego, but there's a correspondence for you. Also, Major Butler has just arrived; he'd like to speak with you today."

"Thank you." John took the missive from the courier and stuffed it in a pocket. "Is Butler available now?"

"He's meeting with Colonel Claus at present."

That was sure to be a pleasant meeting; the two men were constantly at odds with each other, vying for a superior position. But Butler had just landed a huge win, securing the Seneca to the Crown's cause, and while it was an advantageous turn of events, Claus would undoubtedly try to undermine the Major—politics and pride added fuel to their fury.

John turned back towards the parade grounds of Fort Ontario, the open grassy area occupied by almost three hundred natives and their tents. Joseph Brant, the illustrious Mohawk who'd been working on behalf of the British to unite the tribes, was present, along with warriors from the Wyandot, Ottawa, Potawatomi, and Chippewa tribes. Daniel Claus had also arrived from Buck Island, bringing more supplies to outfit the natives.

And the Seneca had returned with Butler from Irondequoit and were eagerly awaiting the Grand Council of the Six Nations.

John slowly walked to the officer's quarters, reaching into his pocket and pulling out the letter. Once inside, he took a seat behind his desk, cracked the red wax seal, and started to read.

John,

I'll speak to you upon my return concerning my missing possessions. If you fail to recover them, as promised, I'll have charges brought against you. You'll face the court marital, and you'll be held accountable. I hope it won't come to this, old friend.

Tomlinson

John refolded the letter, stuffed it back in his pocket, and then let out a laugh gilded with self-deprecation and defeat. The door to his quarters opened, but he didn't look up, his eyes fixed on the flickering candle on the desk, his mind obsessing over how the colors faded from blue to white. Simple thoughts in a moment of desperation; how easily it was to deny the inevitable when one wanted to.

"John?"

"Merrick, what can I do for you?" The familiar voice broke through frustration's haze; yet still, he didn't look up. There was something strangely comforting about the simplicity of watching a candle burn, the wax dripping down the side slowly making hard tracks. If he allowed himself to think about his eventual fate, he'd reach for the bottle, seeking liquid tranquility, and no good would come from that, for drunkenness lent itself well to insubordination and mawkishness. That was what everyone expected from him.

"What's the matter?"

"St. Leger will be here any day, and we'll be launching the western front," John replied, reality seeping into the haze. "Alexei's a prisoner, yet he tells us nothing of value, and I'm to face the court martial for Dereliction of Duty if I don't find a way to make him talk."

"What for?" Merrick sat down in the chair across the desk. "Tell me."

John ran his finger through the flame quickly; when he pulled it away, the skin had blackened from being singed. He looked up at the Admiral, blinking him into focus. "When Dellis was attacked by DeLancie, she managed to get free. I brought her back to your house for protection. DeLancie figured that out. I was supposed to be watching the port, awaiting Miles's bride's arrival. Her ship was coming, with not only a large dowry but a giant shipment of weapons, powder, and other things to trade with the natives. I utilized the resources Lord Tomlinson gave me for his wife to protect Dellis and to try and locate DeLancie. I missed the boat when it came into port, and Alexei kidnapped the woman and took all the supplies."

"Why doesn't Alexei just give her back?" Merrick asked, his fair skin flushed from the summer heat, making the freckles on his face more prominent.

"I think he's in love with her, and I'm sure the shipment has gone to the Rebels in Stanwix." John sat back in his chair, resting his hands on the arms.

"Has Tomlinson officially brought up charges against you?"

"Not yet. Miles is with St. Leger on Buck Island right now, but when he returns, I'll have to face him. The worst part is, I have no defense for my actions. I can't tell the judge advocate that it was because of Roger DeLancie; it would turn everything back on Butler. I've learned my lesson about going against my superiors. I won't make that mistake again."

No, he wouldn't. Butler would find a way to clear himself of any accusations, and John would once again appear to have turned on a commanding officer. He'd walked a mile in those shoes, and he had no intention of trying them on again.

"I could help you with this, John. Miles is my friend as well. And Butler was involved in the death of my brother. If it should come to the court martial, I could pull some strings."

"No." John shook his head. "What do you think they'll do to me?"

"You'll be dishonorably discharged," Merrick replied flatly. "Or, you could face the gallows, based on your history."

It was just as John feared. He closed his eyes against the gut punch, suddenly short of breath.

"Damn!" He resisted the urge to throw something or put his fist through the wall, his temper threatening to boil over. "Once again, I'm the victim of politics. You may have secured my freedom by helping me last time, but my reputation is still rubbish amongst my superiors. As far as they're concerned, I'm duplicitous and untrustworthy, and when I get in trouble, I have you to come rescue me." He looked down at his desk in defeat in spite of all he'd done to succeed. "I just need to own up to the truth—admit my failure. Better to face the humiliation and keep what little honor I have than spend my days in the service of men who have no respect for me."

"John, you're unfortunately not in a position of power." Merrick leaned in. "But I am. Let me help you."

"No, not this time." John persisted, feeling, once again, like Atlas, with the weight of the world on his shoulders.

"I don't blame you for wanting to take your punishment and move on. Yes, you may gain some of your honor back, but it's the coward's way out. Fight with me. Work with me. We'll find a way to get the woman back, and we'll get even with James. This has never been a fair fight, John."

It wasn't that easy. Merrick, who wielded so much authority, had forgotten what it was like to be truly ineffectual.

"It's not possible to advance based on merit and one's honor as a soldier, is it?"

"You just figured that out?" A bit of humor tugged at the corner of Merrick's lips. "This army has nothing to do with being noble or honorable—it's about power and who has the most. Leave your sensibilities at the door, and start fighting fire with fire. You don't have to earn respect; you can take it with both of your hands."

He reached out, grasping the air tightly in his fists, his eyes focused on John, full of ice and rage. "It's time to take control of your own destiny.

Stop waiting on the Fates, they have too much work to do, and you're running out of time. Make your own justice, John; don't wait for her. It's time to put all you've learned about the players to good use."

John cocked a brow. "Know thy enemy as you know yourself…"

"Where did you hear that?" Merrick demanded, his traditionally jovial demeanor turning frosty in an instant.

"It's from a Chinese tome called *L'art de la guerre.* DeLancie read it voraciously. He used the techniques in it to train our company for battle."

Merrick's eyes narrowed, his lip curing in an uncustomary snarl. "Where did he get it? I've only ever seen it in France at the École Militaire."

John was suddenly confused. Why would Merrick care so much about a book of ancient Chinese philosophies of war? "I don't know where he got it, but it was signed with the name Leveque."

"Leveque." Merrick snorted. He said the name as if it meant something to him yet gave no explanation. Then, with a shake of his head, he was back to being himself again. "Forgive me, where were we?"

"Fine, let's do this," John replied, back on topic. While there was still breath left in his body, he'd fight; he'd go down swinging punches in all directions. After all, fisticuffs were his specialty, and he'd like to bloody a few lips.

"Good." Merrick nodded, seeming satisfied with the answer. "Now for a plan, I have the supplies you promised the Seneca."

"And I have to meet with Butler later today."

He chewed his lower lip, flashes of ideas hinting in those straight red brows. "I think it's finally time I make my presence known to all parties, starting with Butler. Then, I'll have words with Alexei—persuasive words."

"You're welcome to try, but I warn you, he's intolerably obstinate when he wants to be."

"Just like his father." Merrick stood, adjusted his buff-colored waistcoat, and put his hat back on. "Luckily, I'm rather good at dealing with McKessons who are misbehaving."

Chapter Twenty-Three

"Admiral McKesson here to see the prisoner," Merrick said, addressing the guard.

"Your Grace." The sentry nodded and turned to unlock the door.

Alexei and Anoki had been separated, though both were being kept in one of the officer's quarters that had been converted to a gaol. John followed Merrick inside, the door slamming and locking behind them.

Alexei sat on the bed, his knees drawn up with his head resting in his hands. He didn't look up when the two men entered, just brushed his dark hair back and gazed at the floor stoically.

In spite of the summer heat, the room was surprisingly cool; the walls of the casemate were built into the earth and then covered in wood planks for insulation. The only furnishing in the room was a chair and small cot with a cotton-stuffed mattress pushed against the wall—again, a much nicer prison than the powder keg John was forced to wait in at Fort Stanwix, much to his chagrin.

"Alexei," Merrick said in a commanding voice, waiting for some response from his nephew the prisoner. But there was nothing. "I know you're ignoring me."

Still no response, just rebellious silence.

"Alexei, you owe me the respect of acknowledging my presence. We are, after all, family." Merrick's deep, commanding voice reverberated off the walls and then fell silent, unanswered.

Suddenly, Alexei started to laugh, his body shaking, his eyes misted with mirth when he finally looked up. "Of all people for you to ally yourself with, Carlisle, you chose my grasping, devious uncle."

"I think you've mistaken me for your father, Alexei," Merrick replied. "He's perfected the art of grasping, and he's used you to do it."

"Don't speak of him that way! You're a traitor. You turned on him because you were jealous."

For the first time, John saw cracks in Alexei's icy-cool demeanor; he seemed more like a petulant child being punished than the imperious, powerful foe that always managed to steal the upper hand and then disappear in the night.

"I know not what version of our history your father has told you, but I'm sure it's missing many important facts. Your father is the traitor. He turned against our king."

"Your king." Alexei huffed. "Not mine."

Merrick shook his head, casting an imperious glance down his nose. Though he fancied himself just a sailor, he'd obviously learned to wield the power of nobility, and his position, to perfection. Instead of his usual, jovial demeanor, he was cold and almost omnipotent as he towered over his nephew, passing judgement on his life. "As of right now, Nephew, George is still the lord of this land, and you're his prisoner."

"You turned my father in. It was because of you, *Uncle*, that he lost everything."

"It's because of your father our family was disgraced. And yes, I did turn him in, though little good it did us. We lost everything because of your father's treachery, and all of us paid dearly: my mother; Stephen; Lily; Stuart; and poor, sweet Dellis." Merrick paused, his fierce posture softening, his voice following suit, echoes of pain and sympathy replacing rage. "But so have you, Nephew; losing your wife and your child, no young man should have to do that. And now, you'll likely pay for James's sins with your life."

Merrick's gaze cast down for a moment, and when he looked up again, his eyes were glassy and moist, though there was no hint of tears. "My dearest brother thought nothing of killing his own blood, but he lacked the courage to do it with his own hands, so he set a monster upon him, and even after Stephen and Lily were dead, James persists. Don't believe for one minute that he won't turn on you. He'll leave you here to take the fall for what he's done."

John felt a bit like silent observer in a Greek tragedy; the tale of the McKesson family had all the makings: betrayal, lost love, murder most foul, and a bitter feud over money. But how hard it must've been for Alexei to find out the truth about his father, to know how terribly he'd been betrayed.

"Tell me what you want from me and be done with it," Alexei said militantly, making a good show of dismissing Merrick's impassioned words.

The Admiral chewed his lower lip pensively and then sighed, recognizing his own defeat. He'd convinced Alexei of nothing, only hardened his resolve. "I don't want to see you face the gallows for your father."

Alexei let out a laugh. "Yet you think I'll help you send my own father to them—save it, old man."

John interjected before Merrick could speak. "If you tell us where the woman is, if you speak out against him, you might be able to obtain your own freedom."

Alexei shook his head. "You forget, I'm also wanted for thievery and spying; those offenses are of my own choice, and I'd do them again to help my people."

"The Oneida are victims of your father. How can you not see that this is justice? He deserves to pay for what he's done." Merrick almost begged, once again surrendering his control to passion.

"No, I'll face my fate." Alexei faced his uncle and smiled. "And you can go to Hell. My Uncle Stephen would be alive had you not turned on my father. None of this would've happened."

"Foolish youth!" Merrick shouted. "Your Uncle Stephen turned him in with me. We did it to protect our mother and our family legacy."

Alexei trained his eyes at the wall with obstinate silence. There was no point arguing anymore; John had seen that version of Alexei, and he was as immobile as a mountain.

"Your father would see you rot in this prison before he'd take your place," Merrick said. "Chew on that for a little while."

But still, Alexei remained steadfast.

"Guard!" Merrick yelled, the door opening presently, both he and John walking into the hall. Once the door was closed, Merrick thrust a hand in his coppery locks, brushing them from his forehead with frustration. "That didn't go as planned."

John understood better than anyone what it was like to face off against Alexei. "It never does. If you don't mind, I'd like a couple private minutes with him?"

Merrick rubbed his palm over the reddish scruff on his cheek. "Do you think you'll be more successful?"

"No, but it's worth a try."

Merrick nodded and then retreated down the hall, the heels of his boots clicking on the wood floor.

When the door opened again, John stepped inside quietly, looking down at Alexei with different eyes. For the first time, John truly understood his adversary, Alexei wasn't a zealot or a fanatic, but a man loyal to his cause and his people. In truth, John envied that stubborn courage of conviction that he lacked. How many times had he questioned his own loyalty, vacillating between what he believed as a soldier and what he knew was right? How easy it must be to see the world in black and white, ignoring the shades of grey in between.

"I wouldn't trust him," Alexei said in a low, growling voice, though he didn't look up. "He's no better than my father."

John sat down on the chair next to the bed and leaned back. "I understand your hatred of Merrick and your loyalty to your father, but your faith is misplaced. I think you know that, but your pride won't allow you to admit it."

"Don't patronize me, Redcoat." Alexei clipped.

"I'm not trying to. In a way, I know how you feel. I wronged my brother terribly, and he has every reason to hate me. I know this. But no matter what, I can never say I'm sorry. It's purely about my pride, and I know it, ridiculous as it may seem. To say I'm sorry would be to admit that I knowingly committed a terrible act against my own blood. You can't accept that your uncle is right because then everything you've done in this life is a lie."

John drew in a deep breath, letting it out slowly, feeling his nerves calm with each bit of air passing between his lips. He stretched his legs out and removed his hat, running a hand over his hair. "I tried to free your wife, but DeLancie and Eagle Eyes captured her and brought her back to the camp. They murdered her before my eyes."

Alexei craned his neck up, his gaze intensifying upon mention of his lost love. It was a story he didn't know, and one John had long needed to unburden himself of.

"I'm sorry, Alexei. I'm sorry I didn't save her." His voice quivered; apologies weren't his strong suit, especially when it came to his failures. The curious irony was that he found himself confessing his sins to a man who was once a sworn enemy and actually deriving comfort from it. Fate had a twisted sense of humor indeed. He rolled his eyes Heavenward. "I begged them to release her. They scalped her while I was forced to watch. I still see her in my dreams every night."

Alexei's head dropped, his submissive posture reflecting his inner turmoil. "My brave, sweet Mary. My child. You were there? You saw her?"

"She was very brave." John remembered the way she fought, her defiant spirit reminding him so much of Dellis—mothers who tried desperately to protect their young. Tears of remembrance threatened, misting up his eyes. "Women are much stronger than we are, so I've learned."

"Dellis."

John nodded. "Yes."

"You, too, have lost a child," Alexei said, that painful truth linking the two men where once they were divided. No longer were they bitter adversaries, Rebel versus Redcoat, but two fathers that had lost beloved, much wanted, children.

"Yes," John said, exhaling.

"Dellis would already have figured out a way to get us both out of this mess, or she'd die trying."

John let out a laugh and wiped his moist eyes, knowing there was truth to Alexei's words.

"How can you turn away from her so easily? How could you choose your duty over her?"

"I didn't," John replied, looking down at his hands. "That's the problem. I never chose. I was foolish and egotistical. I thought I could have her yet keep my honor as a soldier. I thought I could find a way to get the Oneida to stay neutral or make an agreement with the King, and it would all work out."

So much unfounded hubris that one should think they could stop the wheels of war.

"Knowing Dellis as I do, she didn't give you a choice," Alexei said. "She's lost so much; she just wants to hold on tight and protect what little she has left in this world—that includes you. Honor means nothing to her; it can't. It's foolhardy, the stuff of knights and roundtables, in the face of true tragedy."

John looked over at Alexei, appreciating the wisdom of his words. "Yes, but she pushed me away also."

"Of course, better to push away your greatest weakness by choice than have it ripped from you."

John stood, turning around. He'd come to the same conclusion on his own. Dellis was afraid of losing him —so afraid that she was willing to cut off her nose to spite her face. It was another form of her notorious and effective frontal assault, aimed at protecting herself from him and the world.

"Tomlinson doesn't really want Wilhelmina; he only wants her money," Alexei said from behind. "He's in debt up to his ears."

John glanced over his shoulder at Alexei, considering his words. "How do you know that?"

"She told me. She's terrified of going back to him; he's hit her before."

Knowing Miles, John didn't doubt that to be true. "But they're already married; you can't change that."

"Yes, but he has what he wants most, her money. She's a possession to him, nothing more," Alexei said flatly. "You don't think he'll ever let her go?"

"I know Miles; he's covetous and has the ego of his station in life. He'll track her to the ends of the Earth. For now, he doesn't know you're the one who's taken her, but he will eventually, and when that happens, he'll torture you until you give her up, and I'll not be in a position to help." John turned back to Alexei, meeting his gaze. "You set me free to go after Dellis, and now I owe you. Torture ruins a man in a way that is indescribable. I don't wish that on anyone—not even you."

Alexei closed his eyes and nodded, acknowledging the truth of John's past. "I had no hand in what Stuart did to you."

"I believe that." John straightened, putting his shoulders back, reverting to his officer's role. "There's a Grand Council with the Six Nations tomorrow. And though your people are sure to not negotiate, we'll try one last time. For their sake and yours."

With that, John called to be let out. When the door opened, he turned to Alexei, acknowledging the worthy adversary and adept councilor with a curt nod of respect, something John swore he'd never do.

Chapter Twenty-Four

"Sir, you requested my presence?" John stood at attention.

Something was wrong. The Major was pacing back and forth with his hands clasped behind his back and his gaze fixed on the ground. There was a miasma of frustration about him that was new and eerily unsettling.

"I did." To add to the suspect situation, he was also being short—never a good sign. He continued to do laps behind the desk.

John caught the sidelong glance given to him and thought perhaps he could lighten the mood with a compliment.

"I heard the recent news; you're to be the Deputy Superintendent of the Six Nations. Congratulations." It was a promotion Butler had long desired and worked tirelessly to obtain. *So why did he seem so melancholy?*

He finally stopped pacing. "That title's no more valuable than the paper it was printed on. Daniel Claus has been put in command over the entire native contingent, including me. He's supplanted me in the role that I've worked for this past year all because of his political allies. General Carleton has confirmed it. I was made aware upon my arrival yesterday."

Misery loves company, and John and Butler had both become pariahs, political victims together in a den of extradition.

"What do we do now, sir?"

"Claus has moved our meeting with the Six Nations to the Three Rivers Junctions. I've already sent runners, informing the tribes to meet us at the new location."

"Why did he do that?" While the location was twenty-four miles closer to Fort Stanwix, last-minute changes would confuse the native allies who'd already left for Oswego.

"St. Leger has just arrived, and the expedition leaves in the next two days. We're to join the brigade once the Grand Council has finished. The General sent spies ahead with Captains Hare and Wilson to get fresh intelligence on the situation at Stanwix. An advanced company of natives and Lights went with Lieutenant Bird to make sure Wood Creek is passable and to establish a position. Claus has distributed all the goods I saved for negotiations with the Six Nations to Brandt's men."

That was going to be a problem, especially because the negotiations with Alexei were far from fruitful. "What do we do now?"

"We? There's no we." Butler rolled his eyes and shook his head. "This is all up to me. You were supposed to be finding my missing supplies. Many of the tribes aren't prepared for war, and this battle will be more difficult than we initially expected. As you well know, we don't have near the men or the resources we anticipated. The natives expect this battle to be easy, to spend most of the time watching as we do all the work. Now it's my job to enlighten them to our new course."

"And you had nothing to do with planting that idea in their heads?" John laughed. "So, what will you use: rum, guns, and finery? The same old ploy we used at Irondequoit? And now, we have to tell them the truth—that this will be a blood war with an uncertain outcome."

"I was given a task, and I *will* follow through." Butler snipped, flattening his hands on the desk and leaning over. "It's time for you to do your part. Where are my weapons?"

"Lord Tomlinson has threatened me with a court martial if I don't recover his wife and all the goods she traveled with. That could be bad for both of us." John knew he was poking the bear of Butler's ire, but it was time to fight back—when he was vulnerable.

"What are you talking about?" His beady dark eyes narrowed on John like he was a fly that needed to be squashed thoroughly. Butler didn't like being threatened.

Remembering Merrick's impassioned words, John reached for justice, grabbing on with both hands, ignoring the fear of authority instilled by his years of military training. "It's quite simple, Major. If I face the court martial, they'll want to know why I diverted resources. And though I did it for selfish reasons, I *will* have to mention the fact that Major DeLancie was still alive... and by whose order."

Feeling heady with power, he stared Butler down over the large desk, but instead of flinching, he laughed. "There are many that knew DeLancie was alive and I covered for him. I alone wasn't his savior. You mistake my position for one of power. We're both pawns, Carlisle."

John tucked his right hand into his bicep and fixed his stance confidently as he crossed his arms over his chest. There could be no show of fear. He held fast to a rush of daring, ready to deliver the coup de gras. "Yes, but do they know you're the one who freed DeLancie? Do they know that you armed and supplied him?"

"Believe me when I tell you there are people in loftier ranks than mine that wanted to see DeLancie alive and serving this war."

Ready for the counterattack, John smiled as the door opened and the sentry said, "Sir, Admiral, the Duke of McKesson, is here for you."

Butler's eyes flicked to John and then fixed on Merrick. As expected, he walked through the door with swagger, looking stately in a gold-adorned Navy tunic and cocked hat, with his brazen red locks neatly coiffed underneath.

"Your Grace," Butler said, sounding surprised.

John stifled a grin. How he'd waited for that moment; finally, a chance to deliver a bit of "how do you like that?" to the first of his naysayers.

"Please, sit, both of you," Merrick said in an imperious tone that John recognized as the "command" voice.

"To what do we owe this pleasure?" Butler's voice quavered for a second, though his accusing eyes turned on John.

Merrick removed his hat and sat down rather ceremoniously, lifting the skirts of his jacket out of the way as he positioned himself. He was playing the role of admiral with the zeal of an actor performing for the King. "Major Butler, I've been waiting for this opportunity for a very, very long time."

"Really, well, you do me a great honor, sir." Butler's forehead instantly dotted with perspiration, his fingers nervously drumming on the chair arm.

"This is no honor, Major. I know all about your association with my brother, James, and Roger DeLancie." Merrick paid Butler about as much attention as one would a prisoner, listing off his offenses as if reading them to the court. "I know that you turned a blind eye to my brother's thievery, and I know that you profited by keeping quiet. DeLancie murdered my brother, Stephen, and his wife, and then you armed that fiend so he could terrorize the Oneida. While you didn't directly wield the sword, you certainly sharpened the blade."

John held his breath, eagerly awaiting Butler's response.

"You'd believe the word of a traitor over mine?" Butler asked smugly, pointing to John. "You can't prove any of this. Carlisle burned the letters."

"We both know how politics work in His Majesty's military. It's my word against yours." Merrick shook his head, allowing a cruel grin of satisfaction to reveal itself and slowly burgeoning anxiety in his foe. "I'm an Admiral and a Duke. That's not going to work out well for you."

"What do you want?"

"Now we're getting somewhere," Merrick said, taking the reins of authority, forcing Butler down the intended path. "You *will* take Captain Carlisle with you to Three Rivers, and you *will* allow him to help you negotiate for peace with the Oneida."

"They've already made deals with Schuyler; this is just about formalities." Butler countered.

"I understand that, and you'll keep pretenses, show that we're trying to do the right thing by negotiating. Also, you won't tell Lord Tomlinson that

Alexei McKesson has kidnapped his wife while Captain Carlisle and I try to obtain information of her whereabouts."

"I know what this is really all about; you want that Oneida alive so you can try to manipulate your brother." Butler sneered.

Merrick didn't respond, the Major's dead-on assessment of the situation confirmed with silence.

"I have no intention of stopping you from meshing out revenge on James McKesson. As far as I'm concerned, I have one mission: to unite the tribes of the Six Nations under our flag. I want none of this. A quibble between covetous York brothers is no longer my problem. Warwick I am not."

John smirked, seeing validation in Butler's reference to the three royal York brothers, a rather poetic, and decidedly accurate, representation of the McKesson family, sans the Malmsey wine.

"Major, you *will* come to Captain Carlisle's defense should he face the court martial." Merrick's eyes mere slivers of disdain. "Do you understand?"

Butler looked at John, sardonically cocking a brow. "It would seem I have no choice."

"You're right; you don't." Merrick stood.

John and Butler followed suit.

The Admiral put on his hat as he walked to the door and then stopped and turned back to them. "And not a word to James that you saw me. Captain Carlisle, I'd like to speak with you in private."

The two men took quick strides back to John's private quarters, slamming the door when they were inside.

"That was well played," John said.

Merrick smiled, those cold blue eyes lighting up with mirth. "It felt good to finally have words with Butler. That man is as guilty of killing my brother as DeLancie and James are." Laughing, he added, "I rarely throw my rank around, but it was rather satisfying."

"Yes." At that precise moment, John decided everyone should have a duke and an admiral in their pocket for safekeeping.

"John, that was as much for you as it was for me and Stephen." Merrick threw his hat down and sat back in his chair. "I just thought of something."

"What's that?"

"What are the chances that Dellis knows where the woman is?"

John sat down slowly, stunned at the revelation—he'd never even considered it—and knowing Alexei and Dellis's relationship, it was entirely possible. "She might."

Merrick slapped a hand on the table authoritatively. "Then we need to find out."

Just as John started to speak, Kent, Merrick's first lieutenant, walked into the room with two missives in hand. "For you, Your Grace." Merrick glanced up, his eyes softening upon seeing his friend. "Is it from the Duchess?"

"One of them is."

Merrick snatched the letters, quickly identifying the one from his wife and stuffing it into his breast pocket, and then opening the other one, reading it quickly. "It's Burgoyne. I'm needed elsewhere," he said, glancing at John. "While the timing is inconvenient, I must go. Stay the course until I return. You know what to do."

Chapter
Twenty-Five

It took a half day's ride for the delegates of Oriska and Dellis's village to arrive at Kanonwalohale for the caucus. It had been a long time since she last visited, but she was always intrigued by the history of the castle and how it was founded.

The warriors of Old Oneida rebelled against the hereditary sachems who wanted to separate the Oneida people from the European way of life and return to the old religion, so the braves moved up Oneida Creek, forming the new castle, making it the seat of power within the tribe. Looking around the village, she could see how continued trade had benefitted their people; the mixture of dwellings, from log cabins to huts, were adorned with European flourishes ranging from copper pots and utensils to fine clothing and jewelry. There was also a traditional long hut that stood in the center for council meetings. The castle had become self-sufficient with cultivated farming land and pens for keeping milk cows, hogs, turkeys, and even sheep. Though formed because of the European expansion, the castle was still very Oneida in its way of life, proof their people could endure, even prosper, by making friends with the colonists.

Dellis stood next to Kateri and Skenandoa, listening to Thomas Spencer address the caucus. The half European, half Oneida was a notorious supporter of the Rebels and famous for his impassioned speech in Cherry

Valley, defending the cause of the colonists and the need for independence. Respected by all, he lived between both worlds and spoke both languages with determined grace and eloquence, something Dellis knew wasn't as easy as it seemed. A kindred spirit to her, a fellow half-breed, though he had the benefit of being a man.

"Three women were attacked near Fort Stanwix; two of them were scalped and one shot. It has caused a great panic amongst the colonists. It's time we follow through on our plans to assist the Colonel." Chief Spencer straightened his back, his dark eyes strained with the same worry that echoed in all their hearts. "We can't allow an enemy force to enter the sanctity of our borders and wreak havoc on the sacred lands of our forbearers. If we fight, we go against the neutrally declared by our brother tribes, but as you know, the Brothers of the Flint have already taken up the hatchet in favor of the Great Father in England."

Chief Spencer clasped his hands behind his back and closed his eyes, pausing for a moment of uncomfortable silence. When he opened them again, he addressed each and every chief with a steely gaze, reaching out to them personally. "We must agree on our course together. I say we fight with the colonists, for them and for protection of our land."

Chief Spencer turned to her grandfather. "What say you, Joseph?"

Her Grandfather nodded. "We fight." His beloved voice was full of conviction.

"Han Yerry of Oriska?"

"We fight to protect this land," Han Yerry said proudly, his deep voice carrying through the valley.

"Then we're in agreement." With Chief Spencer's vote, the decision was final. It was the beginning of the end. Dellis closed her eyes, fear blooming painfully in her chest. Ravens cawed overhead, their inky black wings reminiscent of Death's fluttering robes, a harbinger of what was soon to come.

"Our delegates will attend the meeting at The Three Rivers Junction and offer peace, knowing we'll be met with indifference. This will stand as our last attempt to reconcile with our brothers. I've received information from one of our allies who was with Joseph Brant in Oquaga. The Great Father's men have sent spies ahead to Stanwix, and St. Leger will join them in a matter of days. I'll take word to Colonel Gansevoort." Chief Spencer turned to Joseph and Han Yerry. "You'll speak on behalf of all of us."

Both men nodded.

The Three Rivers Junction was where the Seneca and Oneida Rivers joined to form the Oswego then emptied twenty miles west into Lake Ontario. It took another full day's ride, with all the delegates and regalia in tow, to arrive at the designated meeting place.

Representatives from all Six Nations were present, the Seneca with the largest contingent and the Oneida with the smallest. There was little time for discussion; the Grand Council started immediately as the Oneida were late and last to arrive. The bother tribes sat around the fire as if attending a Grand Council in Onondaga; at the head sat the Onondaga as the Keepers of the Fire; to their right sat the older brother tribes, Mohawk and Seneca; and on the left, the younger brothers, Oneida, Cayuga, and Tuscarora. Of the esteemed Chiefs present, there were Han Yerry, Joseph, and Dragging Spear of the Oneida; Rail Carrier of the Cayuga; and Sayenqueraghta of the Seneca. As was tradition, they opened the council with brotherhood and condolences, a show of respect for each other, as if they weren't about to dissolve their four-hundred-year-old peace at the hands of the white man, both British and American.

As the granddaughter of the chief, Joseph insisted that Dellis attend with the rest of the women and wear her finest traditional attire. Thankfully, she remembered to bring her white doeskin dress from the wedding with her. She braided her hair back and wore her mother's matching headband and choker, both made of tiny blue and white beads, intricately woven together with red trim on the top and bottom. Rarely did she dress in native attire, something she and her mother gave up, spending most of their time in town amongst the colonists and not wanting to evoke their fears. But for the evening's event, it felt right to dress according to tradition, a show of solidarity with the decision of the Oneida people. A united front. No matter how Dellis felt about it.

She let out a gasp when Eagle Eyes stepped out of the trees, positioning himself with the rest of his tribe. Their eyes connected upon first sight, a smile pursing his lips. The evil warrior made her stomach turn. How much had he and DeLancie done to bring about the fracture between the tribes? While a moment of great sorrow for all attending, Eagle Eyes looked on in triumph, the specter of his leader looming over them. That was the goal. DeLancie's endgame had come to fruition. Even in death, he still managed to triumph.

Her heart skipped a beat, and several thereafter, as crimson red broke through the dense greens and browns of the forest, Redcoat soldiers carrying barrels of rum and crates full of gifts to distribute. Bribes. Leverage for native loyalty.

"Brothers, thank you for coming." A deep voice carried over the group, causing a hush, and then out from the woods stepped a short, robust, elderly man in buckskin leggings and a forest-green coat with red facings. But what came next, Dellis never could've anticipated; appearing stage left, proudly wearing the red and gold of a British Captain, was John—their John—the slick, dangerous spy, and not her gentle, tender Just One.

Dellis's heart jumped into her throat, lodging there with an audible gasp, and the world telescoped, everything around her disappearing into a diaphanous haze—except him. He was incandescent, like a twinkling star in the satiny night sky, drawing all her attention to his luminous face.

Skenandoa and Kateri reached over and clasped hands with Dellis, buttressing her with their sisterly warmth. Desperate eyes raked over him voraciously, longing for even the slightest glimpse in her direction, needing it, an affront to how angry and painful their parting was. He was so handsome, virility wrapped up in masculine confidence with the

Devil's boyish smile like a sweet dollop of cream on top. John's thick, wavy, blond locks were pulled back tightly, leaving his sapphire eyes to be the devastating focal point of his tanned, chiseled face. And those lips. Pointed and perfect. Lethal what they could do to her. The rest of him looked splendid, too; lean and broad in his red tunic, the expert cut of his waistcoat hugging his torso all the way down to the tapered angles of his hips. He looked tall and fit next to Butler's, smaller, weightier frame, like Achilles next to Agamemnon—the proud warrior and his leader.

From her vantage point, John couldn't see her, she realized, the darkness and her location allowing her to conveniently hide yet still observe. And like the fire that burned brazenly, so did her blood, hot molten lava coursing through her veins as she watched John in his element: a soldier, a captain, and her once stormy lover with unearthly powers over her body. The sultry night air felt suddenly unbearable, beads of sweat forming at her brow and between her breasts. She pressed her thighs together as pleasure most wondrous rippled around slick, unfulfilled nihility, yearning for his sweet penetration once more.

"John." She whispered his name onto the breeze, trying to once again forge their mystical connection. No matter how angry she still was with him, it all seemed to slip away when he was once again in her world.

"Friends! Brothers!" Butler held up the giant purple and white beaded belt over his head and then passed it around the group so each of the chiefs could touch it.

John stepped forwards, his melodious baritone echoing through the forest, melting into her ears, further deepening his thrall. "This is the Great Old Covenant Chain, the ancient agreement between the King and the Six Nations. The Great Father has given you many gifts of his esteem, showing his devotion to you. Now, we ask you to remember your loyalty to him by helping us defend this land against his rebellious children."

"Will you take up the hatchet with us?" Butler asked, loudly. "The colonists are poor and without goods to supply you, unlike the King. His rum is as plenty as the waters in Lake Ontario and his men as numerous as the sands on the shores of the great lake."

The crowd was silent, each chief taking a moment to touch the precious purple and white wampum beads of the Great Covenant Chain with reverence.

"We don't want war between the tribes," John said, his voice clear and crisp in the balmy night air, her knees getting weaker by the minute. She could almost hear him whispering devotions in her ear as he moved over her, inside her, deep and potent. *"Tell me you love me?"*

"We want to keep your precious peace as brothers."

"Just One." Her grandfather stepped forwards from the group, taking the stage. The sound of John's native name must have taken him by surprise, for he flinched, his eyes darting around after seeing Joseph. Was he looking for her? "Just One, you're the first of the Great King's men to address what it would mean if the confederacy chain breaks."

"Yes." John nodded, his expression stoic, betraying nothing, but in his eyes—those eyes she knew so well—there was fear. "I know what will come if you don't stay true to your brothers. We don't want that. *I* don't want that."

"We must discuss this amongst ourselves, and our sachems and matrons must be allowed to have their voices heard." Dellis panicked when she felt Joseph's hands reach back for her. Sensing what he was trying to do, she backed away, but Great Bear, her uncle, grabbed her hand, pulling her next to him.

John's eyes glanced in her direction and then back at Joseph, acknowledging her no more than any of the other insignificant attendees. Her world suddenly flipped on its side, and she fisted her hands, fighting the urge to grab onto her grandfather for dear life. John had never looked at her that way. Never. As if she didn't exist. It was her grandfather's doing; her ire rose, a well-played gambit at her expense. No wonder he asked her to come; it was part of the plan, to have her look her best, put all her attributes on display so he could manipulate the British through John.

"All right," John replied. "Meet with your people, council with your brothers, but you only have until tomorrow. The battalion is on its way, and we must join them."

Letting Butler take over, John stepped back; that was when Dellis felt his eyes on her, cold and emotionless, a stark contrast to the sultry heat her torid fantasies evoked. But his were not the only eyes watching her. Since she stood at the head of the group, the Redcoats eyed her suggestively— murmured words and an occasional whistle shared between them. It felt a bit like being stripped naked in front of the council and having them appraise her. She threw back her shoulders, reminding herself that she was a McKesson and an Oneida, a woman who'd faced the brutality of Roger DeLancie and lived to tell the tale.

Out of the corner of her eye, she spotted Lieutenant Clark, and next to him, Lieutenant Smith, blessed friendly faces in a sea of enemies. When she glanced at Simon, he smiled and inclined his head to her with deference.

"We'll leave you now to your council and reconvene tomorrow." Butler took the Covenant Chain from Sayenqueraghta and wrapped it in a linen shroud for protection. "We've arranged for a feast; there's Ox, deer, beef, and all the rum the King can provide."

And like that, it was over; John turned his back and followed Butler towards their camp, never once glancing back, not even a nod of his head. Nothing. He was notoriously good at steeling his emotions, but she'd never seen him put on such a convincing performance.

The insignificant distance between them, a patch of grass and a burgeoning fire, felt more like unforgeable miles of storm-tossed gales. In the eyes of her tribe, he was her husband, yet he no more acknowledged her than he did any other woman present. But it was all an act, it had to be; he was always good at hiding behind locked doors, but she knew with determined certainty how to find the keys.

Once all the regulars had left the council grounds, the food and beverages were brought out by some of the camp women. For the time being, the tribes would revel as brothers, before the negotiations were to begin again and war was to be declared.

Dellis rushed to her grandfather's side, tugging on his tunic. "How could you do that to me? To John?"

"I did nothing but remind him of his obligations to his wife and to our tribe."

She snorted. "I wondered why you were so eager for me to come on this trip after relieving me of my responsibilities. Dellis who refuses to listen and is too impulsive to be trusted is only useful when you're trying to entice John. It all makes sense now." She shook her head. Once again, her family had used her to suit their purposes, first Alexei then her grandfather. "You knew John would be here. Now what's your plan? Shall I go to his tent and tempt him into making a deal for peace? Or shall I offer myself up to save Alexei?"

"That malice comes from your own guilty heart." Joseph countered with a shake of his head and furrow in his brow.

She blushed at the truth in his words.

"I've asked you to do none of those things. I care about Just One *and* you, though you're determined to fight me at every turn. I merely want to see you two reunited, no matter what side he's on."

"Grandfather, I don't know if that's possible."

The hollow look on John's face was something new, a defense she'd never breached. And was he not the one who wronged her? Why did everyone seem to forget that?

"Just One hurt me. I don't know if I can forgive him."

"He's not perfect, neither were your parents, and neither are you. No man can rise so high; they'll always fall," Joseph said. "It's a lonely life if you trust no one."

He turned away from her, disappointment in his eyes and a slump in his broad shoulders brought on by their argument. Never had she been at odds with her grandfather, not once in her whole life. Suddenly, they seemed unable to speak the same language.

Dellis walked away, uninterested in the council meeting; the outcome was already predestined. Despondency took the place of hope. What was the point of going through the motions?

It was a beautiful, peaceful night, the moon full and bright in the sky, its rays shimmering on the surface of the river with each lap and roll of the water. Slowly, she walked to her tent, listening to the chatter of the other women as they filed into their own lodgings to bed down for the night. As she undressed, she could once again feel John's eyes on her, those blue gems making her body tingle and ache in the sweltering heat of the night. He was so close, his magnetic pull drawing her to him across the distance.

Quickly, she changed into her brown stays and muted-blue petticoat, removing her headband and necklace, carefully wrapping them in a piece of linen and hiding them in her haversack. She unbraided her hair and tied it up in a chignon at her neck, pinning it in place. When she stepped out into the sultry night air again, there was music and laughter, the council revelry rising above the canvas tents. She walked through the native tents, crossing the threshold into the British camp. Silhouettes of soldiers inside their lodgings, illuminated by candlelight, could be seen from her vantage point; some of them were partaking in drink and games, others in the delights of the flesh.

She blushed, feeling like an intruder, averting her gaze back to the sentry who waited to question her. "Where are you going, miss? The native camp is on the other side of the council meeting area."

What am I doing? She should've just turned around and gone back to her tent—but temptation prevailed where reason backfired.

"I'd like to speak with Captain Carlisle." His name rolled off her nervous tongue, giving it a breathy, sensuous quality.

The sentry grinned upon hearing John's name.

"Of course. I'll take you to him." The guard turned around and started to walk at a brisk pace.

Dellis had to run to keep up, averting her gaze from the soldiers that eyed her as she passed. Occasionally, she heard a whistle or a hoot, setting her body to trembling. *What are you doing, Dellis?* Walking into a camp full of drunken regulars was the most absurd thing she'd ever done, next to showing up at Celeste's brothel; well, and going after DeLancie—that wasn't one of Dellis's most astute decisions either.

When the guard stopped abruptly, she knew they'd arrived. It was John's tent, his distinct silhouette visible through the fabric.

"Wait here."

She swallowed down her fear, though it regurgitated back up, sending her heart racing along the way. "Te—tell him my name is Fennishyo... of the Oneida."

The sentry replied, "It won't matter," in a voice full of humor, insinuation ripe in his gaze.

She drew in a breath, wrapping her arms around herself, trying to ignore the leering eyes that watched her as she waited to be admitted.

Chapter Twenty-Six

John smoothed his hair back, linking his fingers behind his neck. He expected to see Joseph and Han Yerry at the council meeting, that was a given, but John hadn't anticipated Dellis. Not that night. He wasn't ready for it. But there she was, a vision, almost too exquisite to be real, like a native goddess in doeskin, her black hair braided down her back, and the beaded headband around her forehead drawing attention to her straight, manicured brows. And oh, how her brilliant dark eyes glowed in the firelight. Just seeing her evoked memories of their wedding night, how he slowly peeled away the soft, supple, deerskin dress and then stepped back, quietly marveling at the beautiful goddess that belonged to him.

He had to force himself to look away from her, the memories so raw they tore at his heartstrings, rendering the painful organ open and yearning. Surely everyone around him could see his adoration for her written in the expression on his face like a mirror into his tormented soul. And like a moth drawn to a flame, he couldn't resist the urge to look at her, indulging in the sweet memory of outstretched arms drawing him into her world, soft white skin, and satiny black tresses—one night of pure and utter bliss.

At the council, John could hear his men chattering, her incredible beauty taking all of them by surprise. A green monster within raged and fisted his gut, threatening to break loose and tear each one of them limb from limb for looking at his prize. His bride. *His* Dellis. Like a feral animal, he'd marked her, and she was his alone to gaze upon, to indulge in.

John laughed, pulling off his neckerchief and throwing it on the table—jealously—a rather new and inconvenient emotion to his human condition.

The flap of his tent lifted, and one of the camp's sentries walked inside, addressing John. "There's an Oneida woman here to speak with you. She says her name is Fennishyo."

He drew in a breath, letting it out slowly, trying to quell his racing heart. "You may show her in; after that, you're relieved of duty."

"Yes, sir." He caught the smirk on the sentry's lips, a sardonic look in his eyes.

John held back a laugh; after years of clandestine meetings in his tent with scandalous women, once again, his behavior would be the talk of the regiment. *Only this time, for meeting with my own wife.*

When Dellis stepped inside, John stood, putting his shoulders back, trying to appear every bit the Captain in control, not a jilted lover yearning for forgiveness. But his resolve weakened under the thrall of those deep black eyes, wide and hesitant as they searched his. She looked even more beautiful than earlier, just the way he liked her: his Dellis, in her usual clothes, her hair pulled back. He prayed it was an invitation and not another rebuke. Even God couldn't be so cruel as to tempt John that way—Eve with the apple, and John her willing Adam ready to take the world to Hell with just one bite.

Drawing in a breath, John composed himself, putting on a performance even Celeste would envy. "At your service, Mrs. Carlisle," he said, brusquely. "You've come to make some sort of arrangement on behalf of your grandfather, I assume."

Dellis fidgeted with her hands, her eyes darting around before they met his, their fathomless depths starting to draw him in immediately, forcing him to look away. "John, I need to talk—"

"Dellis, you shouldn't be here." He interrupted her. The sound of her voice, the anticipation of her next words, sent his heart sprinting again, but he fought back with steely focus. "I'm sure the sentry has already spread the rumor that the Oneida have sent one of their women to entice me into a deal. A man with my reputation, alone in a tent with a beautiful native woman… I don't need to tell you what this looks like."

"John, I…" She fumbled over her words again, her bottom lip turning plump and red from being trapped between her teeth. The heat and humidity had given her skin a dewy quality; curly tendrils escaped the tight bun at her nape. His eyes followed a bead of sweat rolling down her décolletage and between her breasts to that lovely valley he longed to traipse his lips through.

After a month of not seeing her, of not knowing if he ever would, he was voracious for just a touch of her skin, a taste of her lips. If she came an inch closer, he wasn't sure he'd be able to control himself. He was ravenous, a beggar in the streets, and she was mouthwatering sustenance served up on a platter.

He closed his eyes for a moment, indulging in her closeness, and when he opened them again, it was as if time stopped. The mystical force that existed between them pulled and tugged them together like magnets, both of them speechless and defenseless against its power.

She succumbed first, taking one step and another until she stood before him, her dark eyes entreating his with exquisite tenderness and a hint of query. He gifted his own sight with a moment's glance at her beautiful neck and then dipped to the bodice of her dress, eliciting from her a blush of the palest pink that deepened to red the longer he lingered. Instead of covering herself, she let her shoulders drop back, her breasts pushing forwards like a flower in full bloom seeking the sun. Him.

She was waiting, wanting him to make a move. His ego ticked and smarted where his passion smoldered—but his head won out, steadfast and resilient. Yes. That time, she'd have to bridge his defenses.

"John," she whispered, all the sweetness and devotion in the world wound up in one word—his name. "John."

She reached out and touched the breast of his tunic, branding him with her fingers even through layers of wool and linen. His heart thundered under her palm, thumping and pounding, threatening to break through its cage like a trapped bird wanting to be free, but he backed away, out of her range, feeling his defensive walls weakening.

No cannon of love would steal his resolve. He wouldn't relent. "You need to go. Now."

"Fine," she said. "If that's what you want, Captain. I'll leave." She shrugged and then turned around quickly, walking towards the flap of his tent.

Damn. Where's the fight? No pleading? Where's that passionate temptress that set fire to my bed and smoldered for my touch? He wanted more from her. His ego demanded it. His ire rose. John crossed the tent with one stride and grabbed her wrist, wrenching her into his arms.

"You'd give up on me so easily? I know not who this woman is," he said, frustration leeching out of his every pore. "Where's my fierce Dellis? No direct assault? No temptation?"

"Unhand me." She hissed through her teeth, trying to push him away, but he held her tightly, relishing every minute of the fight; for he knew where it led—his bed, Dellis spread out underneath him screaming his name to the heavens. Where she belonged.

She let out a little gasp, but he claimed it with his lips, ravaging her mouth, devouring her with all his hunger and longing. He drank from her, his lips sucking and drawing off her like he was indulging in the sweetest orange, letting his tongue reach for every inch of her sugary nectar. She groaned into him, her lips submitting, though her hands fisted and pounded on his chest, fighting back.

John's head swam from overindulgence, heady like one too many hits off a bottle of whiskey. He came up for air only to be met with a well-placed slap to his right cheek, the sting only further stoking his fire. She was angry, and he liked it. He wanted her to yell, fight, and scream out her passion. He wanted her to punish him—wail at him—tear at his flesh while he fucked her with all the love and anger he felt. To hell with the gentleman; the scoundrel wanted out.

He'd bitten the apple, and it was decadently evil.

Burying his face in her neck, John tore at the sleeves of her shift, exposing her shoulders, his lips desperate for contact with every inch of that pagan white skin. His hands fought the bindings of her stays, tugging at the strings, wrenching the seams apart until they broke, exposing her perfect, ripe breasts.

He drew in a breath, those blush peaks were hard and read for him, two supple mounds that fit his hands to perfection. He wanted to bury his head between them, squeeze them until she screamed for him, make love to them until she was wild, grabbing his hips, calling his name.

"Dellis." He groaned, an ache building and pulsating between his legs to the point of pain.

He bent to kiss her again, but she met him with another slap, that time on the left cheek, and then pushed him away.

"Your anger feels just as good as your love," he said, gasping. "And right now, I'll take whatever I can get. It's more than you left me with."

She met his gaze, her eyes like smoldering coals, burning with passion and fury. "You won't find a willing wife to warm your bed tonight, Captain. Did you forget how you wronged me? You made love to that woman."

"Wife, you're cruel." He forced her back against the desk, his hips intimately pressed into hers. Their eyes met, their labored breaths synchronized in the moment, linking them together with an otherworldly intimacy. She belonged to him, and he wanted her to know it. That night, she'd be the one to submit, begging and pleading for his love or nothing at all.

"No crueler than you are, husband."

Husband. He let out a breath, relishing the power in that word; though darting off her lips, it sounded more like a denouncement than an endearment.

"How could you?" She demanded.

But he held back, trying to understand the true motivation of her words, not the ones she was hiding behind. "You didn't come here because of Celeste. I refuse to believe it." He reached for her skirts, trying to pull them up, but she slapped his hands away. "You came for me—confess."

"You're an arrogant brute, John Carlisle."

When she went to slap him again, he caught her hand in midair, holding it, putting her index finger between his lips, letting his tongue play over the tip. His mind wandered to all the ways she worked her magic with those wonderful hands: healing him, comforting him, stroking him, slapping him, all of them bringing on tortuous pleasure. "Tell me you want me."

"No," she replied, watching him kiss and worship her palm but not fighting back.

Releasing her hand, he reached for her skirts again, hiking them up as he lifted her onto the desk. "Do you want me to take you on this desk like some doxy? Because that's what I did to her. Is that what you want to know? It wasn't about love, Dellis. It was desperation. I was trying to find *you.*"

"So many excuses. Take your hands off of me," she said, the coldness of her voice contradicting the heat in her eyes.

"Do you want me to worship you like my wife? Tell me you love me, and I will."

Sliding his hand up between her silky thighs, he found what he so desperately sought, throbbing and swollen, her desire slick and warm, coating his fingers. She was ready for him. His head swam, imagining her tight walls clenching his shaft, her hot honey making him slide in and out with luxurious, long strokes. Have mercy, he was as deep in her blood as she was in his, poisonous and addictive—the damned apple.

"Make love to me, John." She groaned out her order. "I can't wait."

Leaning into her, he gripped her thighs, wrapping her legs around his waist, parting her beautiful valley to his questing hands.

"You're going to have to be quiet, my love." With a smirk, he said, "But I plan on doing my damnedest to make it difficult for you. I love hearing you scream my name, and by God, you will when I dangle you over the edge and demand you love me again. Every man in this camp, and in Hell, will know you're mine alone." Gently, he held his fingertip over the swollen, moist pearl, but he didn't touch, watching her eyes widen and close, her hips reaching for him, wanting him in that sweet soft place that only he could have. Her poor bottom lip played the victim of his game, trapped helpless between her teeth while she fought back gasps.

Giving in, he used his thumb to circle and stroke her in tandem with his longest finger that plunged rhythmically into her warmth until she let out little, high-pitched mewls and whimpers. Music to his ears.

"If you won't tell me who loves you, tell them," John whispered, pointing to the soldiers' silhouettes as they walked by his tent. "Say my name?"

The fact that they weren't alone only further stoked his fire. With a grin of satisfaction, he pushed a second finger inside her, stretching her until she moaned and said, "John," and then shamelessly spread her legs for him.

"I'm here, love," he whispered into her mouth, his tongue lightly caressing hers.

She tugged at his tunic, pulling it over his shoulders until he shrugged it the rest of the way off. Her insistent hand reached for the front flap of his breeches, working the buttons, the other sliding down his navel into his waistband, greedily seeking him. When he was finally free, she wrapped her fingers around him, her thumb gently tracing the tender vein from the root to the tip, making him quiver and harden in her hands, expelling some of his seed. She touched the tip lightly, rubbing it away with her fingertips, and then lifted them to her lips, tasting him.

"Wife, please." He wasn't sure if he was begging for her forgiveness or for her to stay the angry, wanton virago driving him to the brink. *Does it matter?* Like an adept pupil, she'd learned all his tricks, and she was using her fully-stocked arsenal against him. His control relinquished to her expert deflection.

Her fingers closed around him, and she started to stroke, slow, long pulls and then shorter and faster ones, matching the rhythm of his hips, drugging his mind to the point of euphoria.

"Did she touch you like this?" Her eyes sought his while her hand drew away his last vestiges of restraint until suddenly, abruptly, she released him.

Drugged and confused, he held on to his resolve by a meager thread as she leaned back on the desk, letting both her hands slide down her breasts to her spread thighs, offering up that incredible nested valley for him to take. He damn near dropped on his knees right then, prostrate to his wanton goddess.

"Did you want her as much as you want me now, John?" She demanded. "Do you love her?"

The diaphanous haze cleared, and her words struck him like ice water to the face, a thousand pins and needles piercing his heart. Feeling his desire quell, he backed away. "Do you really believe that I could make love to another woman?"

"We both know you were once lovers; how do I know you didn't go back to her?" She spat back, still beautiful and half naked, spread out on his desk. "I trusted you."

"Do you really believe I'm the same man that came to you eight months ago? Of course. I'm a spy, a liar, and a reprobate with no compunction." He shook his head, the truth so devastatingly clear. "But never the man that loves you? Never the one who'd lay down his life for you?"

He buried his face in her neck, breathing in her sweet, familiar scent one last time before he backed away. She held his heart in her hands, her grip so tight it ached and worked to beat through the crushing pain she was eliciting.

"Oh, Dellis." He groaned.

"Look at me, John." She pulled his queue back, forcing him to look into those eyes he so loved. "You were mine. Mine. How could you do that to me? The thought of her touching you..." She gasped, her eyes welling with tears. "That she can give you what I can't... Oh, God, John." She pounded her fists into his breast. "She. Is. With. Child. Your child!"

Her words pierced his failing heart. All that time, he'd longed and pined for her, and yet distance hadn't weakened her resolve, hadn't softened her heart to his pleas—to the truth.

Damn, how he loved her, but he despised her, too. She was tearing the very fiber of his being to bits. He pulled away, the distance between them an impassable river of lies and pain.

"Now you back away? You turn me down, but you didn't her?" When she reached for him again, he pushed her hands away.

He didn't recognize her, a hellion consumed by jealously, but not his tender, selfless Dellis. She was the one that slammed the door in his face and shut him out of her life without the slightest bit of explanation.

Turning his back to her, he stuffed his shirt back in his pants and buttoned them, taking a moment to compose himself, though his effort fell short.

When he turned around again, she was waiting for him, his beautiful, half-naked goddess slick and wanton with passion. Oh, how she tempted him. But he resisted. He wanted more from her than just her body. He wanted it all: her heart, her soul, her cruel, decadent love—every last bit.

"You should go," he said, averting his gaze to the canvas wall.

"Now you take the high moral ground? Suddenly my sanctimonious husband."

The tartness of her words stoked his ire to a blaze. "You came for my services, did you not?" he said in the most captain-like voice he could muster up. "And I reserve the right to refuse. I find I lack significant motivation to pursue such a task. Now, if there's nothing else you need, you should return to your tent."

"John!" She demanded.

He took a deep breath, trying to clear his head from the amorous fog that permeated his every pore. "You may leave, Miss McKesson, or should I say, Mrs. Carlisle. After all, I *am* your husband." And just like that, he dismissed her as if he were relieving one of his men from duty.

Passion's expression hardened to a chill, her eyes turning to pure ice. "Yes, but never my lord. No man controls me." She scooted off the desk, taking a moment to right her appearance. When she turned back to him, she boldly met his gaze with an imperious one of her own. "Alexei is being held captive. You must take me to him."

That hurt. He snorted as if someone poured salt on his wounds and rubbed it in with determined vigor. "I'm once again a fool." He shook his head incredulously. "Of course you'd come all this way to save your precious cousin, but not to ask the truth of me." He knew that he defended himself like a wounded boy, but he didn't care. He *was* wounded, his heart bleeding freely from the jab she took at it. Once again, she'd chosen Alexei.

"He's in trouble," she said as John turned his back to her, unable to stand the sight of her a moment longer.

"You never tire of asking for more. And like a love-drunk fool, I give it to you. I traded my weakness for drink for my obsession with you."

He faced her again, rage and pain making it possible for him to say the words she cruelly denied him. "You came to my room that night in Oswego, and finally, after all we'd been through, we made love—and it was…" He trailed off, hearing the quiver in his voice, the slight crack revealing more of his pain than he wanted. "Then you left, just disappeared without a trace. I trusted you with the secrets of my mission, wanting to prove my love was in earnest, but still, you didn't confide in me. I almost went crazy thinking DeLancie would hurt you again. Celeste was the only link I had to you. She threatened me with your life if I didn't give her what she wanted." He paused, searching her face, looking for some sign that he'd reached her, but she was reticent. "You never asked why. You just assumed that I lacked the restraint of a man in love and then denied me the chance at an explanation. How could I have wanted another woman after all that we shared?"

He stepped back, his heart lodged in his throat, making the words stick.

"Our love…" He barely managed to huff out, breathless with pain. "Our lost children…"

John ran his hand over his eyes, trying to force back the tears that welled behind the lids. "Perhaps we're not meant to be, and all these things tearing us apart are a testament to that." He choked on the words. "So this is all that's left of our love—ripped to shreds like a piece of fabric by both of us. My Fennishyo."

She was silent, the ice in her gaze thawing to water that brimmed her lids. He prayed she didn't start crying; it would weaken his already paltry excuse for resolve. Instead, she turned her back to him, wrapping her arms around herself, and it was then that she started to weep.

"Go now, Dellis, before you're found here." He ordered, fisting his hands at his sides to keep from pulling her into his arms.

She sniffed and rubbed her eyes and then raced to the flap of his tent, stopping there. "What about Alexei?"

"Alexei is safe for now. But if he doesn't turn over Lord Tomlinson's wife, he'll face the gallows, and I'll face the court martial for Dereliction of Duty," he said flatly, offering her nothing, his own heart too broken to give comfort. "This could mean the end of my career or worse."

She looked over her shoulder at him, her cheeks wet with tears. "My grandfather won't negotiate for Alexei. He told me so himself."

John let out a breath, her words confirming what he already feared. "Then my hands are tied; Alexei is a wanted thief and a spy."

"Can I see him?"

"I don't know," he replied, savoring his last moments with her though it hurt him worse than the whiplashes he'd faced at Stuart's hands.

Just as she stepped through the flap, John said, "For what it's worth, that was her price. I knew the risk I was taking, but it was the only way she'd tell me where you were." *A deal with the Devil.* "It was the hardest thing I've ever done, but I'd do it again if it meant you were safe."

That's how much I love you. But he couldn't bring himself to say those words.

When she was gone, John turned around, fighting the urge to bring her back and show her how much he missed her, needed her. But he just couldn't. He had to let her go. After all he'd done to prove his love to her, yet still, she didn't believe in him. It was devastating.

Damn that overeager, traitorous organ between his thighs, gravity winning out as it pulsated and reached for her against his better judgement. But passion alone wasn't enough to save their relationship. He needed more. *Since when did I become such a gentleman?*

Reaching across his desk for the bottle of rum, he poured himself a drink. He watched as the brown liquor sparkled and swirled in the candlelight, the crystal glass sitting on the table, waiting for him, calling for him to reach out and take it. Just one drink. Just one. Rum, his snake in the Garden of Eden, and if he succumbed, he'd surely go after Dellis, full of liquid courage, and take her hard in his bed until they were both sweaty and spent. But it would solve nothing. His hand shook as he held the glass, lifting it to his lips, smelling the strong, potent liquor, ready to lose himself in it, even if just for moment.

But it was no use. There'd be no comfort in the bottle, nor would chasing after her ease the pain of what they'd lost. He was listless. Defeated. Ravenous. All at the same time.

With a roar, he hurled the glass against the wall of the tent, watching the tumbler bounce off the canvas and land in the dirt. He threw himself down in his chair, burying his face in his hands.

Again, justice eluded him. Twice, she'd come to him under unexpected circumstances, and twice, he'd been denied the truth. Both times they'd been caught up in passion's thrall, tearing at each other against a desk, but it never came to fruition, their fire snuffing itself out with anger and lies. The story of their love always on the brink but never to come to fruition— forever just beyond his reach.

Sitting back in the chair, John started to laugh, insanity brimming in the hopelessness of his situation. Then suddenly, he realized something, a small triumph in the face of such adversity; at least he'd managed to stay off one of her direct assaults with all his faculties intact.

Chapter Twenty-Seven

The sun peeked through the crack in the tent flap, bringing with it flickers of pale-yellow beams and shadows of bright-green leaves fluttering on the breeze. Kateri and Skenandoa rested on the cots next to Dellis, but she hadn't slept a wink all night. Her mind and body were held captive in her last moments with John like a verse in a fugue, building on each layer of memories until she was almost reliving it, first his words, then his expressions, and finally, his touch. But it was the truth she couldn't escape.

No matter how she tried to play the martyr, her reasons for going to John's tent were not out of a purely altruistic need to save her cousin. No. It was about lust and her bruised pride. But when he looked up at her with those eyes, so full of love, she was drawn in, unable to put words to all she was feeling. Part of her wanted to wail at him, to tear his heart out with a knife; yet part of her desperately wanted to be in his arms, to cry out her anguish. Since the day he left, she'd been carrying around an empty case in her chest that was once her heart, absent and devoid of his love, longing for it back.

Initially, when John turned her away, she was shocked, his face registering no emotion, just cold determination. Somehow, he'd managed to shut her out abruptly, like snuffing out a candle. When she walked away, she wanted to hurt him as much as he was hurting her, but then his hand latched onto her and dragged her into his arms, and it was all over for her. The truth, full of pain and jealousy, poured out of her while he waged a stealthy, amorous war on her senses. And almost won.

The thought of that woman touching his body, kissing his soft lips, made Dellis's blood boil, a hazel-eyed monster gnawing at her heart. She could almost see Celeste's hands caressing his smooth, clean-shaven cheeks as their lips pressed together in passion's kiss. But what wrought the most damage to Dellis's heart was the idea of that woman carrying his child—a little blonde, blue-eyed babe with his lined smile. The pain was so deep and potent, Dellis wanted to scream, make him pay for his infidelity—and she did, slapping him and beating him with her fists and words. But he took it all, remaining steadfast, using his lips and his body, trying to remind her how incredible their love could be.

She wanted to believe him when he said he'd lay down his life for her, that love had changed him. And then, when he backed away, saying her native name like a sweet benediction, her heart cracked open, seeping out all the hurt she kept secret, locked inside.

All that time, her anger had been misdirected, its true target so much closer to home. *Damn her defiled, ruined body.* Her every chance at happiness had been greedily snatched away by a cruel twist of fate, and she the hapless victim to its whim. A woman's duty to the man she loved was to give him her maiden head and fill his home with children—both she could never do.

She was disgraced, defiled… broken.

Finally, when he pushed her away, she came at him with such venom she shuddered to think of the terrible things she said. His blue eyes were so full of hurt, a quiver in his voice when he said his words of surrender. *"So, this is all that's left of our love… ripped to shreds like a piece of fabric by both of us."*

"Oh, God," she whispered to herself, rolling over on her side. "What have I done?"

When Kateri rose, Dellis buried her face in the pillow, wanting to privately indulge in her anguish. Skenandoa got out of bed, too, both of them whispering to each other as they dressed and readied themselves. Dellis was grateful when they finally left, needing the solitude of her own thoughts.

Before she left his tent, John told her the only way Celeste would help him was if he slept with her. *Could it be true?* If it was, he'd sacrificed his morals and beliefs, and Dellis had selfishly refused to listen.

Throwing the covers off, she sat up, looking around the tent for her clothes. She needed to know the truth. Right then. She couldn't wait. Her impatient heart wouldn't relent, kicking and pounding against her breast in question.

Quickly, she dressed, putting on her muted-blue wool petticoat and stays, stuffing her kerchief in the neckline. She braided her hair back and quickly washed her face in the little basin full of water sitting on the table next to her bed.

Outside, she could hear Kateri talking to someone, quiet murmurs with moments of emphasis, indicative of concern. Stepping closer to the tent flap, Dellis spotted her dear friend and John conversing quietly.

"My angel, I'll do as you say. You've always looked out for us," Kateri whispered in Oneida, taking his hand in hers.

Dellis watched as John kissed Kateri's hand gallantly and then held it in his own. There was no need for jealousy at their chaste interlude; a special bond existed between Kateri and John. He'd saved her life, a debt that rendered them forever close.

"When the soldiers come, you must take the rest of the women and run. I know you want to fight with your men, but you must go. They'll bring your brother tribes with them, and retribution will be swift. Promise me." His eyes trained down for a moment and then back at Kateri, only then they were deep blue and full of concern. "I couldn't live with myself if anything happened to any of you."

"What about Dellis?" She placed her other hand on top of his, patting it gently. "She loves you."

"She'll want to stay and fight, but you must convince her. Please, do me this favor. Please. Find a way to persuade her."

Dellis's heart ached, his concern for her steadfast in spite of how she'd abused him. She wanted to reach out and pull him inside, beg him for the truth, but she refrained—it was a private moment, and she was the intruder.

"There's no favor I wouldn't grant you, Just One, but we must fight with our men. Together, we're strong; that's why we failed when the soldiers came to our camp. We were alone."

He nodded, strain etched in the little lines at the corners of his eyes, a furrow deepening the creases in his brow. "Be safe."

"You too, my angel." Kateri reached up and touched his cheek gently. "I know you'll come for us when the time is right. I've seen it." Her hand slid down his cheek to the base of his neck where his neckerchief and stock covered her necklace. "God be with you, Just One."

Dellis stepped back, pretending to adjust her dress, as Kateri lifted the flap and entered the tent. "Just One is here to speak with you."

Dellis's heart overflowed with love for her kind, devoted friend; they clasped hands, drawing comfort from each other. "Thank you."

When Dellis lifted the flap, John was waiting patiently with his back to the tent. She stepped outside, taking a deep breath; there was so much she needed to say. But where to start?

When he turned around, the look he gave her didn't invite conversation. Once again, he had on his Captain's expression, cold and detached. Authoritative.

"We must hurry. Come."

"John, I need to ask you something." The words forced their way out before she could bite them back. "Please." Desperation guided her voice, causing a brief softening in his countenance.

But empathy disappeared and stoicism returned with a frosty expression and a chill in his voice. "We don't have time."

She followed him through the labyrinth of the native camp to the British side, just barely able to keep up with his long, quick strides. He never once looked back at her nor spoke a word, just kept walking, assuming she was following.

When he finally stopped in front of one of the tents, her heart raced with anticipation. John turned to her, his shoulders thrown back, his chin up. He looked down his nose, like a stalwart soldier doing his duty and not her lover and husband. "You have five minutes; that's all I can offer," he said, pointing in the direction of the tent.

"I don't understand." *Five minutes for what?* "John, I—"

He shook his head again. "A new guard will come in five minutes; until then, Lieutenant Clark will watch the door. Alexei's inside."

"Simon," he called, and Clark stepped out of the tent, her eyes drinking up his familiar, sweet face.

"At your service, lass." Clark smiled and removed his cocked hat, holding it in front of his chest.

When John started to walk away, she panicked, grabbing his sleeve. He stopped abruptly, as if she'd burned him with a hot poker, his gaze cast at the ground. "John, about last night—"

"I took a great risk to get you these few minutes. Don't waste them."

She swallowed, her heart fluttering when his beautiful eyes met hers, softening just enough to make her believe he still cared. "Thank you."

"Go." He inclined his head towards the tent.

Without hesitation, she turned and rushed inside. Alexei was sitting on the ground, his arms tied around the tent pole at his back. He looked no worse for wear, a few cuts and bruises on his face, the blueish purple color already turning the puce, yellow-green of healing.

"Dellis, what are you doing here?" Alexei asked, giving her a onceover. "Of all the foolish, impulsive ideas… It's dangerous for you to be here."

"Alexei, we don't have time to argue." She shook her head; even when he was defeated, he still behaved like a thickheaded dolt. "Where's Anoki?"

"I'm not sure. But he's safe, at least, according to your Captain."

Dellis dropped on her knees in front of him, her eyes taking in every last cut and bruise on his handsome face. *Thank you, Lord. It's good to see him.*

"Grandfather won't negotiate for the two of you."

"Nor should he," Alexei replied. "Joseph needs to stick with Han Yerry and the rest of the tribe and support the Rebels. That's the true cause."

"Damn you, Alexei! All you care about is the cause. You'll face the gallows for this." Her chest tightened at the thought of her dear cousin hanging to his death; she could already hear the whoosh of wood dropping from beneath his feet while he dangled helplessly, gasping for air. "What about me? What about Will? What'll we do without you?"

"You know about Will?" His icy-blue eyes lit up upon hearing his beloved's name. "Is she safe?"

"Yes, for now. But when she learned that you'd been captured, she was determined to return to her husband—"

"No, she can't!" he shouted, his reticent tone escalating to frantic. "You must stop her."

"I did, but she'd only relent if I swore to her I could get you out of this." Dellis closed her eyes, trying to put in perspective the enormity of the predicament that stood before her.

"Don't tell me you actually asked Carlisle to help." Alexei's voice oozed with derision, much to her chagrin. "You did, didn't you?"

"Yes," she said sheepishly, once again realizing how foolish the whole idea was in the first place. "Alexei, why did you hide Will at The Thistle? You knew John was looking for her, and you knew if I found out it would divide my loyalties."

"You'd never turn against me. You're the most loyal person I've ever known. Even now, I know you've kept my secret from your Redcoat lover."

The smugness of his tone made her ire rise, but there was also truth in his words, and that kept her from delivering a well-placed slap to his cheek. He was right. She could've told John she knew where the woman was, but she hadn't. And her true intent on traveling with her grandfather hadn't initially been to see John, but to free Alexei.

Her stomach rolled, nausea pervading to the point of sickness. Once again, her cousin had used her, knowingly, and once again, she'd chosen him over John. *Why am I always the last to figure this out?*

"Alexei, how could you?" She choked out.

"I needed to protect her, and I knew of no other that would keep her secret. If I go to the gallows, you must take care of my Wilhelmina." Alexei's eyes softened upon saying Will's name, reminding Dellis that it was about love. He was willing to die for the woman.

"Then if you won't tell them where Will is, and Grandfather won't bargain for you, we must find another way to get you out of this horrible place," Dellis said, strengthening her resolve. "I promise you, she's as determined as I am. If she learns you're still captive, there'll be no way for me to stop her from going back to her husband and trying and make a deal."

He looked down as if searching for an answer in the dirt and grass.

"Think Alexei, think." She pressed.

He lifted his head and grinned, a lock of silky, dark hair falling in his face. "There might be a way. Yes. There actually might be a way."

"What?"

"I can't tell you, Dellis, but promise me you won't let Will come after me."

"Alexei, what's your plan? Tell me." Dellis demanded. Having been fooled too many times by her cousin, she didn't trust him, not in the least.

Cocking a brow, he said, "You're not going to like it."

She could already tell where his intent lay. "Tell me it doesn't involve John?" A sudden wave of panic washed over her.

He wasn't above ruining John in the name of self-preservation.

"Alexei, if you hurt John, I'll—"

"You'll what? So you care about him now?" Alexei huffed out a breath and laughed again. "Clearly, he's the one that brought you to me, yet you thought nothing of the danger you put him in."

"That's not true. I'm worried about both of you." She shot back, her guilty conscience taking little, gnawing bites at her heart.

"And knowing you as I do, you'll go back and beg him to release me, further endangering him."

"I hate you right now, Alexei. Only you can be so goddamned petulant when facing the noose." She squeezed her fists at her sides, fighting back the urge to punch him soundly. "I should leave you here to rot."

He laughed. He actually laughed while she was practically writhing in pain for the two men she loved, trying to figure out a way to save them both.

"Dellis, I'll find a way out of this, but it should no longer involve you. You should be with your husband and be loyal to him. That's part of the vows you pledged when you married him in our tribe." His voice softened, and when she looked up, his blue eyes were regarding her with sympathy. Suddenly, she realized that he'd been baiting her into an argument so he could point out the obvious flaw in her behavior—she belonged with John—right or wrong, Redcoat or Rebel.

"You love him Dellis, and he loves you," Alexei said with such tenderness, her breath caught. "You've lost enough loved ones for a lifetime and then some. It's your turn to be happy. Everyone will understand your choice."

"Alexei, he betrayed me," she said quietly, her eyes tearing up. "And you used me." Damn both of them for playing games with her life. And damn them both for making her love them so. How would she face life without either of them? No, she was selfish. She wanted them both.

"Dellis, I remember you saying after your father died that there was a wall around your heart that nothing penetrated. When Mary died, it was the same for me. I was numb, unable to let myself feel anything. I buried myself in the cause and in Father's desire for money and power, trying to fill the space she once occupied. But then I met Will, and she broke through all my layers of pain with her warmth and sweetness. I loved her, but still, I pushed her away. Now that I'm here, facing my own end, I'd do anything for one last moment with her. If you truly love someone, you must find a way to forgive."

Alexei's blue eyes softened, and for the first time, she saw tears brimming where she thought there was only ice. "The British are to march on Fort Stanwix any day now, and there will be battle. No one knows who will live or die. If you have a chance to be with the man you love one more time, then don't waste it. You may never get another." He let out a laugh though a tear slid down his hollow cheek. "I know it's because of him that I've been spared thus far, and no matter how hard it is for me to admit this, John *is* a good man."

As Dellis reached out to touch his cheek, the flap of the tent opened, Lieutenant Clark peeking his head in. "Lass, you have to go now."

She nodded and then turned back to Alexei, taking once last look at his beloved face. Leaning in, she placed a kiss on his forehead and then gently brushed away another tear that slid down his cheek. She prayed to God it wasn't the last time she saw her cousin.

"I love you, Alexei." Tears brimmed her eyes, blurring her vision, but she wiped them away, trying to memorize his face for whatever came in the future. "And I hate you, too."

They both laughed as she backed away.

Dellis followed Simon out of the tent, resisting the urge to look back at her cousin; if she did, she'd never leave him. Clark led her to a small, private clearing, and from his breast pocket, he pulled out a handkerchief and handed it to her.

"Dry your eyes, lass; the Captain will do his best to see your cousin safe."

She blotted her eyes though the tears continued to fall. "Simon, I need to speak with John."

"He's gone to council already, and then we leave immediately to join our regiment. He gave me an order to see you safely back to your tent, and I must follow it."

There was so much she wanted to say, but the shoe was on the other foot, and she was the one being denied his presence. It was fitting, and in a way, she deserved it, having so selfishly robbed him of his last words.

"Is there something you want me to say to him?" Clark asked, his big brown eyes softening to her plight.

Everything she wanted to say needed to come from her lips alone, or their gravity would be lost with the lack of intimacy. "Just tell him"—pausing, she conjured up words from deep in her aching heart—"tell him I pray for his safe return to me."

Clark nodded, taking her hands in his own, giving them a gentle squeeze. "I'll tell him."

She looked down while she sniffed back another rush of tears.

"Tell me quickly; how's my Agnes?"

She smiled, knowing the excitement it would bring her dearest friend to hear of her beloved. "She misses you, but she's well. Thank God I have her with me. She and Will were so brave when they faced the mob. It's because of them The Thistle's safe."

"Can you give her this?" He released Dellis's hands and removed a small gold ring from his pinky. "It's a reminder of a promise I have to keep."

She took the ring from him and placed it in her pocket. "I will."

Reaching up, she gently caressed his cheek, leaned in, and placed a kiss where her hand just touched. "Be safe, Simon. I expect you and Smith to keep an eye on the Captain."

He chuckled. "Well, that's a tall order, but we've managed so far. Now, let's get you back to your grandfather."

Dellis took her place beside her grandfather in the council, the discussions already descending into heated debate over the just course of the brother tribes. To stay together or to break the neutrality; everyone wanted something different, but none of them were willing to compromise, Cornplanter and Han Yerry were both strong with conviction that their ways were right. It was so hard to stay focused with so much weighing on her mind that Dellis failed to hear the gasps when four British sentries pushed through the crowd, dragging the fighting forms of Alexei and Anoki, and depositing them on the ground in front of the fire.

My God.

The moment had finally come. When Alexei looked up, his eyes locked with Dellis's for a moment, a silent exchange shared between cousins, fostered from their earlier meeting. Her eyes shifted to John, who was slowly walking up between his men. His eyes gently closed, and he nodded with such subtlety that it could only have been meant for her alone.

John and Alexei. Rebel and Redcoat but both Oneidas. The two men she loved most in the world were in terrible danger, and there was nothing she could do about it. The urge to scream out her pain was so overpowering she bit her lip, drawing blood, sucking on that metallic crimson drop for fear the words would burst forth unrestrained. God help her, she had to do something...

Chapter Twenty-Eight

"Joseph and Han Yerry of the Oneida," John said, officially starting the meeting.

Both men stood side by side, their dark eyes directed at Alexei and Anoki, who were on their knees in front of the ceremonial fire.

"These men were found by your brothers, spying on our meeting at Irondequoit. They're known thieves who've stolen from the King many times and have taken something very valuable from one of our lords."

John glanced at Dellis, his eyes drawn to her hands, nervously wringing at her waist. Her heart was in those great black eyes, fear cutting deep lines in their corners and in her forehead. There was no comfort he could offer her; Alexei's fate was sealed.

Much to John's dismay, Butler stepped forwards, taking over the negotiations. "If you'd agree to peace with the King and to provide us with information on the whereabouts of Lord Tomlinson's wife, we'd return them to you as an act of good faith." He stopped, giving the chiefs a moment to chew on his words. "And if you agree to work with us and your brothers, we'd bestow on you many gifts. As you've already seen, His Majesty's resources are plentiful. I promised your Seneca brethren this fight will be over quickly; the Rebels can't stand against us for long."

Joseph kept his steely gaze fixed on Butler, never once glancing at the prisoners, two powerful braves whose lives were being bartering over. "I know nothing of the woman that you seek. I can't give you that which I don't possess—that is the truth. And though you'd be returning two of our bravest men to us, the payment you ask is greater than we can afford. Forgive us if we don't trust you. We've seen the protection of His Majesties soldiers firsthand—my village, three years ago, was destroyed, our women raped and murdered." Before starting anew, Joseph glanced at John, their eyes meeting. "But we've also seen great compassion from the King's men. Acts of selfless generosity that reminded me not all men are what they seem. This decision must be our own and represent what's right for our people. It's very difficult; for it means much more than just an alliance with a King or General Washington, but the breaking of ancient bonds. Han Yerry will speak for us."

The great chief's presence was so commanding it overpowered even Major Butler's. Jet-black hair hung about Han Yerry's face, his high forehead and prominent nose giving his profile depth and character, but his most striking feature, his obsidian eyes, were unreadable. With a deep breath, he started, his low voice speaking the words they all feared.

"The peace between our brother tribes is sacred to us, and we wish to continue honoring it. We've come seeking peace only to be met with indifference. Our sachems have tried to negotiate for a common way together as a confederacy, but it's not to be, so it's for us to go our own way. We chose the course of peace, but if anyone intrudes on our land, we'll protect ourselves by any means necessary."

John swallowed the bitter pill of truth. The Oneida had given an ultimatum, an inadvertent declaration of war carefully wrapped in a passive statement. To proceed against Fort Stanwix, they'd have to cross Oneida land. War was inevitable.

"Though we'd like to negotiate for the return of our men, your price is too high. Our fealty isn't up for negotiation," Joseph said, sternly.

"Then this council is concluded." Butler spat back, his ire visible in the dark recesses of his eyes.

It was ominously quiet, no whoops or hollers as one would usually expect when a decision of the Grand Council was made.

John's gaze took a turn around the fire at the different chiefs: Seneca, Onondaga, Cayuga, Mohawk, and then Han Yerry, all quietly accepting the dissolution of their sacred peace as their confederacy was officially dissolved.

Brothers today, no longer tomorrow; an irrevocable rift permanently torn in the fabric of history—and I helped bring it to fruition.

John regretfully turned to one of his men and gave orders. "Private Mills, see the prisoners back to their tents."

"No!" an all-too-familiar female voice screamed.

John whipped around just in time to see one of the regulars reach for Alexei and Dellis rush from the crowd and throw herself on the ground in front of him. "Don't touch him!" she yelled, wide-eyed, with her arms outstretched, shielding her beloved cousin with her lithe body. "Stay away from him, fiend."

John's breath caught in his throat. He clenched his fists at his sides, fighting the urge to run out there and pull her back.

To his horror, the soldier grabbed her arm, trying to wrench her away, but she spat at him and slapped his hand away. "Stay away, Redcoat bastard. This is your fault, all of you; you did this to us. Alexei wouldn't have been spying or stealing if you hadn't forced us into this. You're always using us to suit your own ends, and so are the colonists. Neither of you have the men to fight this war, so you want us to do it for you. That is the truth; admit it!"

When the Private reached for Dellis again, John's temper flared, threatening a tirade. No one touched his wife. No one. He raced toward the guard and ripped his hand away.

"Don't," he commanded in a low, dangerous tone, indicative of murder most desperate. "Do *not* touch her."

When John craned his neck down, she was prostrate at his feet, beautiful and defiant, his wife, his beloved Fennishyo.

Her eyes were full of terror, begging and pleading with him while her chest rose and fell rapidly, drawing attention to her breasts brimming the neckline of her bodice. Part of him was so damned angry with her for her impulsiveness, yet part of him admired her bravery and devotion to her cousin. A fire stoked in John's loins, both anger and unanswered lust stirring as he looked down his nose at her; somehow, she had the power to evoke such dichotomous emotions in him all at the same time. It was confounding.

And then, as if his world hadn't already been turned askew, she did something he never anticipated; she actually got on her knees and begged. "Captain, I beseech you; please, let him go."

Wisps of her jet-black hair fell loose from her chignon, delicately framing her high cheekbones with such serene beauty he was captivated. They were all spellbound, the whole crowd entranced into a moment of silence in honor of her bravery and beauty. Her lovely, fathomless eyes searched his, pleading, while her hands drew together as if she were praying.

John swallowed the lump in his throat, unable to find words.

"Take me instead. I'll give you whatever you require." The suggestion in her words drew a hoot from one of his soldiers. John knew what it looked like, and with the camp's assumption he'd spent the night with her, it only further added to suspicion against him. "Whatever you want, it's yours, Captain."

He tamped down his rising ire, his calm façade prevailing, no matter how she'd infected his blood, sending burgeoning passion racing through his veins. She scooted forwards until she knelt at his feet, her skirts touching his boots, longing in her eyes evoking sweet fantasies of her in the same position quenching his desire. None of it was for him—it was for Alexei. That thought cooled John off instantly.

Looking over his shoulder, he nodded to Private Mills.

He grabbed her arm, pulling her to her feet; she fought back bravely, kicking and hitting him.

"Unhand me," she yelled and then reached into her pocket and pulled out a pistol, cocking it, aiming at him.

Good God, this isn't a game or one of our lover's spats that ends with her playing at violence.

The soldier released her abruptly.

Dellis backed away, placing herself between him and Alexei. "I won't let you take him. You'll have to get through me." She looked at John, desperately pleading with him. "Captain?"

Every word she spoke only added to suspicion. He could let it go no further, the situation was doomed to spiral out of control.

"Private, stand down." When the soldier didn't comply, John yelled it. "Stand down!" He glanced at Dellis, mentally pleading with her, though his words were stern. "Miss McKesson, please, lower your weapon. This will do you no good."

"Please, don't do this, my love." He mentally prayed, wishing she could read his thoughts through his eyes.

Her brow furrowed, glistening tears starting anew.

Sharp pain stabbed at his heart, knowing the anguish that drove her to such a rash act, but if he showed her the slightest bit of compassion, it could damn him and Alexei.

Her grip tightened on the gun as more and more soldiers gathered around, watching the dramatic climax of the performance play out. John prayed that she didn't turn the gun on him; if she did, his men would fire without thought, protecting their senior officer. Her boldness was admirable, but it was futile in the face of such opposition; he just hoped she understood that in her frenzied state.

From behind her, Alexei said quietly, "Dellis, don't do this." But she seemed to be incapable of hearing him, her grip on the pistol steely and unwavering.

John's resourceful mind, thankfully, didn't abandon him in the heat of the moment, recognizing there was only one way to subdue her and keep her safe from his men.

Taking a deep breath, he started. "Clark, Smith, please, will you—" But before he could utter the rest of his command, Joseph stepped forwards.

"Granddaughter, come with me. The negotiations are over. You know this was the decision of our tribe." He held out his large, sinewy hand, gesturing for her to follow. "We must leave Cloud Walker and Anoki."

Joseph's simple words were calm, without trace of reprimand, but still a stern order, and one she must heed.

John swore his heart stopped, waiting for her response; seconds ticked by like hours, all eyes directed at her, but she remained strong and steady in her stance. He swallowed, watching her expression change from one of pain to one of defeat, and then, as quiet as a whisper on the wind, she said, "Yes, Grandfather," relinquishing the fight.

To his surprise, Dellis uncocked and lowered the pistol and then took Joseph's hand, allowing him to lead her back to her people. Not once did she glance back, following him like an obedient child as her tribe walked away from the council area and their brothers.

John took a deep breath, his heart finally starting to beat again, though he was sure he'd aged twenty years in five minutes. Suddenly, he felt lightheaded and weak, adrenaline ceasing to pulse thorough his veins, its aftermath sapping his vigor.

"Captain, we'll take the prisoners back," Private Mills said, but all John could do was nod in response.

He reached out, flattening his hand on the tree near him, buttressing himself with its wooden strength. When Clark walked up, John had already anticipated what his friend was going to say.

"That was bad."

John let his head drop, trying to regain his composure.

"What was the lass thinking?"

"She wasn't, but thank God Joseph stopped her when he did."

His mind raced over all the possible scenarios that could've played out had she not relinquished her pistol. *Foolish and stupid, but still my spirited, brave Dellis.*

"It's my fault," John whispered to himself, running his hand over his hair, smoothing stray locks out of his face. "She did this because she doesn't believe I'll help Alexei."

"John, I have to tell you something," Clark said, his tone grave.

"What is it?" John looked up, his eyes drawn to the scene behind Clark.

327

The tribes were somberly disbanding, the council over, and with it, the confederacy. On the breeze, John could hear the women singing, like a dirge lamenting the end of their people, the end of peace. He turned away, unable to watch any longer.

"I overheard some of her conversation with Alexei this morning."

"Go on."

Clark chewed his lip for a second and then continued. "She knows where the woman is."

John's breath caught as if Clark had delivered a stomach punch with perfect aim. "Are you sure?"

He nodded. "Yes, I'm positive."

"Did she say where the woman was or how long she knew?" John was almost afraid to know the answer, and what it might mean for him and Dellis.

"No, there were parts of their conversation I couldn't hear."

It couldn't be true. If it was, she'd come to him the previous night knowing the truth, knowing what it could cost him, and then carried on with her dramatic display before the group when she could've remedied the situation in an instant. There were no words. His stomach pitched to the point of sickness.

"John, I know what you're thinking, but she did ask to speak with you. Perhaps it was to tell you the truth."

He shook his head. "No, she had the chance last night, and she didn't."

"Don't jump to any conclusions, not yet. You two haven't exactly been on good terms. Perhaps she's protecting the woman?"

It was possible; knowing Dellis, it was exactly what she'd do. But it hurt him, his pride pricked. "Haven't I done enough to show her that I'd understand? That I would help?"

"You'd think," Clark said, sympathetically. "But we both know the lass has a hard time trusting. Remember all that she's been through."

Simon's words tugged at John's heartstrings in spite of his anger. "Did she say anything else?"

"Only that she'd pray for your safe return to her."

He stiffened, her words contradictory to everything she'd just done. "She said that?"

"Yes."

He nodded, trying not to read too much into it. After what had just happened—and his recent revelation—words meant little. Their love was in shambles. Yes, there was passion between them, but no trust and too many lies to count.

Damn! Once again, Karma stood in the corner laughing while his life played out like a Greek tragedy.

"What now?" Clark asked.

"We join St. Leger and the rest of our men. Lieutenant Bird, your replacement, was sent ahead to make sure the Rebels don't obstruct Wood Creek."

Clark snorted. John knew how his friend disliked the man who'd taken over the position since they'd been on special mission for General Carleton. "That man's a blooming idiot. He'll be lucky if he can even find the creek. What about Alexei? Will they send him back to Fort Ontario to await a tribunal?"

"I'll figure something out. Come on, let's get packed up and move."

Before John could make for his tent, Major Butler raced up, unleashing his attack through clenched teeth. "What was that all about? I've heard the rumors that you spent the evening tupping that Oneida whore. Was this her attempt to coerce you into freeing their men?"

John bit back a rebuke; no one called his wife a whore, no matter how she behaved.

"Did you promise her something, Carlisle, if she fucked you? You're just like DeLancie, both of you with your obsession for these savage women."

"Major, she's not a whore, and there were no promises made in the moonlight." *At least not last night.* "She did come to my tent, pleading for her cousin's life, but I sent her away with our conditions. That's all that happened."

Butler gave John a skeptical onceover. "How am I to believe you? You've protected the Oneida in the past. The woman clearly knew you, and Joseph called you by another name."

"That's correct. I've negotiated with them in the past. I've never lied about that. It was Joseph's men I traded the papers for." John lowered his voice, leaning closer to the Major. "That woman is the Duke of McKesson's niece. I wouldn't dream of taking advantage of her."

Butler's eyes widened. "Apparently, you do know when to have restraint, Carlisle. Though it's a skill I never attributed to you."

John snorted, and shook his head. It must've physically hurt the Major to pay that compliment, backhanded as it might have been, for he winced.

"You did right by putting a stop to that display. Get the men together and leave today; the General will be expecting us. I'll escort the Seneca and the rest of the tribes."

Chapter
Twenty-Nine

Dellis rode quietly, shame rendering her without words—and they would've been unwelcomed anyway. After such scandalous behavior, she'd anticipated a stern tongue lashing from her grandfather, yet none came, only stoic silence and sidelong glances full of disappointment. The only one who'd speak to her was Kateri, and even that was only a casual word here or there.

On their way back to Oriska, Han Yerry sent some of their men ahead to scout the course. Along the way, they spotted soldiers and a group of natives, Mohawk and Mississauga, travelling along the creek. It was grave news; the Regulars were nearing Stanwix, and it was no longer a matter of months, but days, before the fighting started. The group stopped at Kanonwalohale to share their grave news.

Chief Spencer listened intently then spoke. "I'll send a runner to Fort Stanwix to suggest the Colonel block the river; it'll slow the British progress, but it won't stop them."

"Let me take the message to the fort." Ho-sa-gowwa offered himself up proudly.

Thomas Spencer nodded. "If you're so eager, then your feet will surely be as swift as the wind."

The young brave nodded. "Yes, my chief."

Dellis's heart swelled; though he was only in his teens, the young warrior had the courage of a man twice his age. Brave acts such as his would soon become all too common and so, too, would the repercussions.

The group rode the rest of the way to Oriska; again, she spent the night sharing a cabin with Kateri and Skenandoa, but Dellis didn't sleep, her mind too occupied with the events of the previous few days to allow her peace. When the sun's first light came through the little square window, she rose, saddled her mare, and took off for home. She was eager to see Agnes and Will, and the idea of friendly faces that didn't look at her with disappointment was further inducement. The solitude of the ride back gave her more time to reflect—obsess—over the previous couple days, and as if a fog lifted, she could see the consequences of her actions in the blinding light of day.

I've been so stupid.

She wanted to hide under a rock, her face flushing with embarrassment, remembering how foolishly she threw herself down in front of Alexei, and then, to add insult to injury, she begged John, in front of his superiors and subordinates, to take her instead. As if he could? The final decision wasn't his to make, and a woman was no inducement to release a captured thief. In hindsight, she realized how lucky she was that the soldier she pulled her pistol on didn't retaliate. So many things could've gone wrong. And what of John? Her actions undoubtedly implicated him.

Damn, that was foolish. Her grandfather was right.

The pain in her stomach intensified, churning and bubbling, threatening to burn a hole through itself. But self-deprecation would do no good, and neither would obsessing. What was done, was done, and she'd have to reap what she'd sowed.

As she rode up to the front of The Thistle, she stopped abruptly so she could bask in the glow of her precious home. In truth, it was just paint, wood, and glass windows, but what lay within was the greatest treasure: love, friendship, family. Her eyes were drawn to a large white T painted on all the first-floor windows and the front door. She shuddered, fear gripping her heart. The T was for Tory. More rhetoric from the townspeople to try and intimidate her into leaving.

As she rounded the side of the house, Stuart came rushing out the back door, his arms full of garments and books, Will fast on his heels.

"Stuart, those are my clothes, and those books belong to your sister," Will yelled in a strident, undisguised feminine voice.

"You don't need them, woman." He barked over his shoulder, stuffing his plunder in the haversack hanging from his horse.

Dellis walked her mare next to Stuart, indifference replacing pity, allowing her to be terse with him. "You may take the clothes, but the books belong to the house. They were Father's." Turning her attention to Will, Dellis said, "I can get you more clothes."

Defiant to the end, Stuart yanked the reins of his horse, trying to jump in the saddle and take off, so she pulled out her pistol and aimed at him. After the week—hell, the year—she'd had, what was one more threat to add to her list? "Brother, I'm in no mood to argue; now, give me the books back, or I'll put a bullet in your arm, and I'll take them from you."

When he hesitated, Dellis cocked the pistol nonchalantly. "You know I can do it. Put me to the test."

With martyred frustration, Stuart reached into his pack and pulled out the two books, tossing them at Will, one smacking her in the cheek.

Dellis uncocked her pistol and put it back in her pocket. "Stuart, I told you that you're no longer welcome here, and I meant it. Don't come back."

"You won't let your own brother stay, but you'll keep company with a darkie and this whore disguised as a boy?" He spat at her, his black eye narrowing, the other hidden behind the black leather patch yet somehow complying. "I saved you. I helped Alexei and that Redcoat find you. What about that? You care nothing for your brother."

His comments pricked her conscience but not enough to forgive his most recent transgressions. Their relationship was fraught with history, good and bad, but it didn't absolve him of his sins, nor did blood.

"Yes, you saved me, and I'm grateful for that, and yes, you did help John and Alexei find me, but if we're calling in old debts, then remember what I did to protect you." Her voice cracked painfully, but she continued. "I've fed you, clothed you, and maintained this house without your help these last three years since Father and Mother were killed. I've taken your slaps, hits, and angry words. And I've been the brunt of your misdirected anger for being unable to protect me and Mother." Her temper flared with each infraction listed until she could contain it no longer. "But no more! Do you hear me, brother? No more! Stay away from me and my home."

"To hell with you, sister, and your Redcoat lover!" Enraged, he hopped on his horse and sped off, kicking up dirt and grass in his wake.

She watched for a moment, her heart sinking ever deeper the farther he rode away. They'd never reconcile; she accepted it, and though she loved her brother, he was determined to fight her at every turn. Was it the destiny of all those with McKesson blood to hate their kin? Questioning would only lead her to further quandary. There was no point to trying to understand.

She turned her horse away, walking it towards Will, who was waiting patiently, though her eyes were wide and pleading.

"Did you find Alexei?"

Dellis glanced over her shoulder, making sure Stuart was long gone, before she spoke. "Let's go inside. We'll talk there."

Once her mare was unsaddled, brushed, and fed, Dellis dropped off her soiled clothing in the little shack behind the house, and then walked up the back steps and opened the door. As it always did, the door creaked and protested, the familiar sound like music to her ears. How many times her father promised her mother he'd fix that door, but it had become a pleasant reminder of times long gone and promises unkept.

From the end of the hall, Dellis could see Agnes sitting at the table in the kitchen, snapping the ends off green beans, a wooden bucket full at her feet. When the door slammed, she stopped abruptly, her face lighting up with a wide, ivory grin.

"Thank God you're back." Agnes wiped her hands on her apron and ran down the hall, drawing Dellis into a warm, bosomy hug.

"It's so good to see you." She hugged her friend tightly, squeezing her a bit before letting her go. "I missed you."

Will walked in the side door, almost knocking over the bucket of beans sitting on the floor, eliciting a curse as she sidestepped the wood pail.

Dellis laughed. "Let's go in the kitchen. I've much to tell both of you, but first, where did the T's come from?"

Agnes huffed and pushed a stray sweaty curl out of her face. "Stuart. He and some of the militia boys tried to make themselves at home. He dug through the cupboard and the cellar looking for spirits, but I moved the bottles to the hiding place under the bar. All they found was cider and some leftover mead."

Dellis was once again thankful for the little cubby that Thomas, her bartender, built under the bar. It was where she used to hide her best whiskey. On several occasions, she was forced to hide the potent stuff from her brother when he was in one of his drunken tirades. "Luckily, Mr. Armstrong showed up and shooed them all away, or Stuart would've taken all the food we have left."

She smiled, removing her kerchief from the front of her neckline, using it to daub some of the sweat from her brow. "Thank goodness for Patrick; he's been a real help."

Dellis caught sight of Will in the corner, her big, round eyes still pleading while she nervously awaited word of her beloved. "Tell me, please?"

Her desperation made Dellis's heart ache. "Alexei's all right."

Will let out a sigh as her body fell back against the wall, melting into it. "Is he still a prisoner? When will he come back to me?"

Dellis admired the woman's short, lush, blonde hair, grown out a little longer then, allowing it to curl and wave around her sweet face, making her look like a cherub. She still wore men's clothing, but there was no mistaking her as anything less than a beautiful young woman. Alexei's lover. *How am I going to tell her the truth?*

Taking a deep breath, Dellis bolstered her courage, knowing there were no honeyed words or sugar flavoring that would make the bitter pill go down easier. "Alexei's a prisoner of the Crown, but when I last spoke to him, he was safe."

"When will they release him?"

"The price was my tribe's agreement to side with the British, and"—she paused, embracing the calm before the storm for a moment longer—"information on where they could find you."

Will's eyes widened, both her hands reaching out and bracing against the walls. She looked like she was ready to faint, her skin blanching white as a sheet. "Oh, God, Miles. He's going to kill Alexei. This is my fault."

Taking Will's hands from the wall, Dellis clasped them firmly, willing hope through the comfort of human touch. "No. Alexei will find a way out of this." She said it with such conviction, she almost believed it. "My cousin entrusted me with your safety, and that's a promise I intend on keeping."

Will's big hazel eyes misted up, and she started to sniffle. "Miles will never let him go. And when he finds me, he'll still punish Alexei." She shook her head with determination. "Miles is relentless; he won't stop until he wins, and I'm the prize—me, my money, and my land. He can't have any of it unless he has me. We've yet to consummate our marriage. It was done by proxy."

Will's body trembled as she gave into tears.

Dellis enveloped her friend in a tight embrace.

Agnes came over and hugged both of them. "We must believe in the Captain; he'll find a way out."

Dellis glanced at her friend, their gazes meeting in silent appreciation for the man that brought them together. Yes, John would find a way; for once, Dellis had to trust in him.

Agnes released them, and the three women stood together, their hands linked in the solidarity of sisterhood.

"Did Alexei say anything else?" Will asked, wiping a tear from her cheek.

Dellis handed over the hanky from her pocket, watching her friend dry her eyes and then blow her nose with a loud honk. "He said he hadn't realized how much how much he cared for you until now."

Will rubbed her red nose with the little piece of linen, looking up at Dellis. "He said that?"

"Yes, he did." She nodded, putting her hands on either side of the tiny woman's face, using both thumbs to brush away tears that started anew. "Alexei promised he'd find a way out of this, and he's never broken a promise to me."

Will nodded. "I just miss him so much."

"I know."

"What about the Captain?"

"I'll tell you about that later." Dellis went to the counter and pulled some linen from the drawer. "Why don't we clean those awful T's off the house? Then we can talk more about it."

Will took the linen and grabbed the extra wooden bucket from under the table. "I'll help. I need something to keep my mind busy, or I'll go mad."

"All right." Dellis agreed. Keeping busy was an excellent idea, and from the looks of The Thistle, there was plenty to do. The kitchen was empty, the candles were burned down to stubs, and there was a pile of dirty linen sitting in a basket at the end of the hall near her room. "Let's get this done."

Grabbing the bucket and her swatches of linen, she walked through the dining room to the front porch. Once outside, the sight of vandalism on her precious house gave her pause, another example of Stuart's defiance and his disrespect for their father's memory. She sank to her knees, defeated, and just stared at the giant white T painted on her door, the very same one her father and her brother once lovingly made together.

"Oh, Father, what do I do?" She reached out to touch the door, the surrogate for her father's hand, and for an instant, their fingers touched in the diaphanous haze of sweet memory. "I wish you were here."

Those two swipes of paint were like a strike against each of her beloved parents. Her ire rose the longer she looked at the offensive mark. The T didn't represent Tory, not in her heart. It meant Traitor.

"Captain, the prisoner has requested to speak with you." A sentry brought the message.

John nodded. "I'm coming. Can you see that my things are packed and my tent is dismantled? We leave in an hour."

Grabbing his tunic from the back of his chair, he thrust his hands into the sleeves and then adjusted the fabric neatly over his shoulders, smoothing out any wrinkles. Two nights in a row he'd been deprived of sleep, and the fuse on his temper was as short as a cannon's. After Dellis's outburst, he'd spent the whole evening staring at the decanter of whiskey on his desk, willing himself not to drink it. His mind replayed every possible scenario from the night before, seeing it through to completion, yet each version led him to the same outcome. It was a no-win situation.

He opened the flap to Alexei's tent, unsure what to say to the former adversary turned lifeline. They were trapped together like flies in honey, Alexei strong in his conviction, John indecisive, and the only way out of their predicament was through each other, yet neither would yield.

"You wished to see me?" John asked, as if addressing one of his men. He had no time to play further games. There was too much at stake.

Alexei nodded. "I'll help you if you'll help me."

John clucked his tongue, skeptical of such a sudden change of heart. "I'm listening." Not so very long before, when he was in Fort Stanwix, they'd faced off, and Alexei gave John the benefit of the doubt.

"Tomlinson doesn't want Will; he only wants her money and her land. I can tell you where her dowry is. I'll give you all the supplies that were taken with her if you promise—"

"You're in no position to negotiate, McKesson." John already knew the price—Alexei wanted the woman.

"She stays with me. You'll tell Lord Tomlinson that she ran away, and I no longer know her whereabouts."

The expression on Alexei's face was grave, his brows furrowed and drawn together, but then it morphed, his eyes softening to a hazy, besotted look of love. Having pled a case in the past on behalf of love, John knew what it cost the man. Exposing one's vulnerability to an enemy was akin to opening one's shirt and allowing a point-blank shot at the heart. In a split second, one could go from being a triumphant lover to a tragic hero.

"Alexei, I'll take that information to Lord Tomlinson, but it won't make a difference. Miles is notoriously tenacious when he wants something."

"He does *not* care for her."

"I understand that, but possession, to some men, means everything." John pulled a chair out from under a small desk and sat down. "I know you understand this—your father being of the same type."

Alexei nodded. For the first time, the giant of a man looked vulnerable; his normally defiant blue eyes were strained, his head cast down, his broad shoulders slumped inward with defeat. "What about my Uncle Dane?"

"Merrick?" John questioned. "What about him?"

"If I agree to help him, to speak against my father, will he help me?"

John considered the proposal.

Alexei was, after all, the nephew of a duke. Anything was possible.

"I'll see what I can do. But we leave for the front soon; it may be too late to negotiate now."

"You must take me with you." Alexei ordered more than suggested. "I'm the only one who knows where his supplies are, and you'll certainly be attacked on Oneida lands trying to retrieve them. You need me."

"What are you playing at?" John asked, suspicious of the true intent. "Is this another trick?"

"My uncle needs me to confront my father. You've no choice but to take me with you." Alexei narrowed his eyes.

Meeting him halfway, John put a bit of challenge in his own gaze. "I don't have to do anything. You've been playing games for so long, you've forgotten that you no longer have the upper hand. How do I even know I can trust you?"

"Because I trusted you once." Alexei countered brilliantly, pricking John's conscience. "And now you owe me. You owe it to Dellis, and Joseph, and our village. We didn't start this, but together, we can finish it."

John drew in a deep breath through his nose, and then, with a nod, he got up from his chair. "Merrick has left already. The decision's mine alone to make. You're lucky."

As he walked out of the tent, he swore he heard a sigh of relief come from Alexei, the same sigh John made in bombproof when they agreed to go after Dellis together. Their fates were intertwined, just as his was to Dellis and her people. Every turn in the road, every swipe of Karma's hand, kept pushing him back to that same truth. His fate was joined with that village until justice was done. Killing DeLancie was only part of it.

Was Kateri right when she predicted John would help them? Had she seen his turn?

Chapter
Thirty

Dellis dropped her bucket and dirty linen in the kitchen and started down the hall; not halfway to the parlor, Agnes stepped in the way, hands akimbo, eyes blazing, and ready to raise Hell. "You've skirted the issue of the Captain long enough; it's time you fess up. What did you do?"

There was no avoiding an admission or the look of conviction in Agnes's eyes. She'd intuitively guessed the outcome before Dellis even left, but confessing that was going to be painful.

"I saw Clark." She prematurely perked up, hoping to entice her friend away from the issue at hand, but she was having none of it, her dark eyes narrowing with suspicion.

"While I'm glad to hear that my Simon is safe, it can wait. Come on. Out with it."

Dellis squeezed her eyes shut in frustration; the prospect of recounting the scandalous tale made her want to cringe. "Yes, I saw the Captain."

"You already mentioned that." Agnes crossed her arms over her chest, her head cocking to the side. "You aren't going to fool me, so you better start talking."

Oh, why do I have to do this now?

"Can you get me some whiskey from the cubby in the bar? I'm going to need it." Dellis took a deep breath and then blew it out slowly. "And so are you."

"Oh, this is gonna be good. I can already tell." Agnes walked to the bar, grabbed two glasses and the bottle, and returned, pouring them both a drink as they sat down.

Dellis threw hers back, the smoky liquor burning a trail all the way to her stomach, snuffing out the ache that pervaded in the pit. "John was at the council; he and a man named Butler were overseeing the negotiations."

"So, what happened?" Agnes took a sip of her drink, wincing and gagging with her first taste, and then putting the glass down. "That's dreadful."

"I went to see him at his tent," Dellis said, taking the discarded drink and throwing it back, too. No good could come from her confession.

"Of course you did." Agnes provided, with a shake of her head and a roll of her eyes.

Dellis swallowed down her embarrassment and blurted out the whole story down to the most sordid detail while Agnes listened, thoroughly transfixed.

"Oh, Dellis, what were you thinking?" she asked, finally emerging from her enraptured state.

Yes, it was a juicy tale of woe indeed, and Dellis was the foolish heroine.

"Wait. You haven't heard the worst of it." She shook her head, tears of shame welling in her eyes. "When they brought Anoki and Alexei in front of the council, my grandfather refused to negotiate for them. I was so frantic I threw myself in front of Alexei when the guards tried to take him away."

"Good Lord, woman," Agnes said, putting her head in her hands. "I need another drink, no matter how bad that stuff is."

Dellis poured Agnes another and then started again. "I got down on my knees in front of John and begged for him to take me instead. When the guard tried to pull me away, I threatened to shoot him."

"What did the Captain do?" Agnes looked up though her long ebony fingers as if she were trying to shield herself from what was to come next.

"John stayed very calm and pretended as if he didn't know me." Dellis remembered the coldness in his blue eyes, his posture of detachment and control, just like a Captain and not like a husband facing his pleading wife. "Grandfather intervened before I could make things worse. But the damage was done; I could see it in John's eyes."

Sitting back in the chair, Agnes looked around the kitchen, quietly chewing her lip. "Well, damn…"

Dellis waited for Agnes to offer up more than an expletive, but she didn't, her face a mask of stoicism and calm refection; then suddenly, it changed to a cocked brow and a sarcastic tug at the right side of her lips. "Dellis, I was going to leave my comments at *I told you so,*' but this time, I think I've earned the right to a little censure of your behavior."

"Yes, go on," Dellis said, ready to take her medicine and like it.

"What in the name of the good Lord did you think you were doing?"

"I wasn't thinking."

"No, you weren't." Agnes chided. "I thought after your grandfather relieved you of your position, you'd learn something, but you didn't. Once again, you tried to take control and ended up putting everyone at risk. It was just like the night you ran away, and the Captain and Alexei had to rescue you."

Dellis nodded sheepishly, closing her eyes. "I know. I know. I just… I can't explain it. I was desperate. The night I ran away, I had a vision that DeLancie was going to murder John. I was terrified of losing him. And when the guards came for Alexei, the same thing happened."

She finally gave in to tears. "John, oh, God, I didn't tell him about Will. Alexei knew I wouldn't; that's why he brought her here, because he knew I'd keep his secret, even from John. Why did he have to be right? I betrayed my husband to help my cousin. But how was I supposed to choose between them? Now they're both in danger because of me."

Agnes reached over and clasped Dellis's hand. "The Captain will fix this."

Dellis nodded, her eyes blurry with tears. "I said such awful things to him. I was angry with him for being with *her*, but I was angrier with myself."

The warmth of love permeated between the two women, from one to the other, with a gentle squeeze of Agnes's hand. "It'll be all right."

"No." Dellis sobbed. "No. I'm broken. I can never give him a child. And now, I've pushed him away. He told me Mrs. Allen demanded he sleep with her as payment for information of my whereabouts. And I believe him."

"It sounds like something she'd do." Agnes grabbed a piece of linen from the counter behind her and handed it to Dellis.

She blotted her eyes with the little swatch of fabric and then blew her nose. Picking up her glass, she downed what was left of her drink. "Why would Mrs. Allen do that? She knew he didn't love her. It makes no sense. Unless…"

A thought came to her, something she never even considered. Dellis chewed her nail, the motive suddenly clearer. "Agnes, what if Celeste was already with child? What if she tricked him, knowing it would put a wedge between the two of us?"

"It's very possible."

She closed her eyes, absorbing the enormity of her predicament. "That woman is truly evil."

"Yes. She'd do anything to keep you and the Captain apart. She's obsessed with him."

And I let her win. Dellis shook her head. "If it *is* his child, then it's because of me that this has happened. I owe it to John to love it just as I love him. And if it's not his child, then he deserves to know the truth."

"Mrs. Allen won't make it easy on either of you."

Dellis nodded. "Agnes, I've hurt him so badly. I don't know how he'll ever forgive me."

Agnes let out a snicker laced with more *I told you so.* "Now, it's your turn to wait."

So, the tables had turned, and Dellis was the one sitting outside the door, waiting to be heard. But what defense did she have? The moment their love had truly been tested, she'd been found wanting—unlike him.

Reaching into her pocket, she pulled out the little gold ring Lieutenant Clark gave her. "This is from Simon, a reminder of a promise he has yet to keep."

That time it was Agnes who welled up with tears, putting the little ring on her middle finger. "I love that man."

"I know you do." Dellis reached over to Agnes and clasped her hands, giving back the warmth she'd given earlier. "They'll both find their way back to us."

Agnes nodded, wiping her moist eyes.

At the end of the night, Dellis trudged her way up the stairs, her body tired and worn to the point of exhaustion. She threw back the covers on her bed and stripped down to her shift before climbing between the sheets. As she went to blow out the candle, she noticed a folded piece of paper lying on the floor. When she picked it up, she already knew what it was, her heart hammering in anticipation at seeing it again.

She unfolded it slowly until her eyes beheld that smile bracketed by lines of humor, the little wrinkles in the corners of his eyes, and his incredible presence that even paper couldn't suppress. It was as if a blindfold had finally been lifted from her eyes, and she could see everything crystal clear. *That devil woman played us both.* It was all part of a plan. Had she just listened to John, trusted him, none of it would've been happening.

She looked down at the picture one last time before folding it and placing it under her pillow. "John, I'll make this right. I promise."

Chapter Thirty-One

Grinning, Celeste rubbed her swollen belly, which was just large enough to protrude out from under her stomacher. By the time John returned, she'd be big with child, a visual reminder to him and everyone else what happened when they crossed her. No one could outplay her; she held all the cards, always flipping up the Ace of Spades.

Taking a sip of her tea, she spotted a familiar face walking into the tavern. She rose from her chair, smoothed her curls, and adjusted her dress, readying herself. It was going to require every bit of her well-honed skills.

Slowly, she approached the bar, stopping just behind the tall, virile form of Lord Carlisle, his light-brown hair tied back neatly with a ribbon, the perfect cut of his forest-green suit showing off his tapered torso to great advantage.

"My Lord, you're rather brave, showing your face here. What with the recent murder of local girls by the British savages and word that St. Leger's men are bound for Fort Stanwix, Loyalists and Tories are sure to find themselves riding the rail. You'd best be careful."

"Mrs. Allen." He looked down his nose at her and then turned back to his drink.

Insufferable snob.

Glancing across the bar, she pointed to Stuart and his militia cronies, making a ruckus while they threw darts. "All I have to do is call one of them over."

Gavin turned back to her, a dangerous look emanating from those icy-blue eyes.

Gently, she ran her hands over the shoulders of his jacket, brushing away a nonexistent piece of fuzz. "I don't think this coat would look nearly as impressive with pine tar and feathers all over it."

"What do you want?" he asked, in a low, acrid tone.

"Have you seen John?" she asked, grinning. "Ever since I told him about the baby, he's been missing."

Gavin chuckled and shook his head. "I've seen the woman he keeps with, and you're a backstreet whore compared to her. Though I loathe to give my little brother credit, I find it hard to believe he'd put his cock in you, much less his seed, if he could have Dellis McKesson."

Celeste's ire rose. Lord Carlisle was frustratingly insolent on every occasion, but still, he was nothing more than a man with his own weaknesses. *Time to put My Lord out of his misery.* "Stuart, oh, Stuart," she yelled across the bar, waving Dellis's brother over.

Celeste flashed Gavin a grin, waiting for the little vermin to make his way to her side. Stuart eyed Gavin with recognition.

"He looks like that damned Redcoat."

"That he does," she replied, taunting her foe. "Lord Carlisle, have you met Stuart McKesson?" Trying not to inhale Stuart's putrid scent, she put her gloved hand under her nose and leaned over, whispering in his ear, "That's Carlisle's brother."

Grabbing one of the bottles off the bar, Stuart slammed it against the wood, the glass breaking and forming a jagged-edged weapon that he thrust into Gavin's face. "That Redcoat killed my family and raided my village. Now, he's tupping my sister. I haven't been able to find him, but you'll do nicely in his stead. Lord, whoever you are."

Oh, this is getting exciting. Celeste stepped back as Stuart took a swipe at Gavin, forcing him to dodge.

"Stop," Gavin yelled, his hand clamping down on Stuart's wrist, holding it in midair. "I wouldn't do that if I were you."

"Hey boys, we got ourselves a blooming lord here!" Stuart yelled, eyeing Gavin.

Celeste watched as the young man's raggedy group of friends rushed over, an angry mob already posturing and ready for a fight.

She clapped her gloved hands, jumping up and down a couple times with villainous mirth. *It was so easy.*

Quickly, Gavin released Stuart's hand and pulled out a pistol, fingering the trigger. "Stay back."

"You've got one shot, *My Lord*, and there are ten of us ready to take you down." Stuart hissed.

Celeste relished the fight that was about to ensue, even more so because she provoked it. "Come on, what are you waiting for?" she asked, sticking a verbal poker in the flames.

But just as Stuart lunged at Gavin, the bartender stepped between them. "There'll be no fighting in The Silver Kettle." He looked at Stuart and grimaced. "Don't you militia boys have stuff to keep you busy? Herkimer has called you to Fort Dayton; you best be getting on."

Gavin put his pistol back in his jacket pocket and then pulled his coat down, righting himself. "Forgive me, sir. I'll leave now."

The bartender nodded, standing his ground until Gavin was at the door.

Celeste looked back at the group and said, "You're not just going to let him go, are you?"

Stuart shrugged. "We'll get him another time. He'll go to my sister's house, and we'll catch him at night when one of those three whores are servicing him."

"Three?"

"Yeah, my sister, her slave, and the one that dresses like a boy."

"What woman who dresses like a boy?" she asked, trying to make sense of his usual nonsensical banter.

"The little one." He held his hand in the air to indicate Will's height. "She ain't no boy. I caught her wearing my clothes when I went there the other day."

Celeste let out a laugh. Once again, she just had to sit and wait, and all the players came to her. She marveled at her own ingenuity. "Can you do me a favor? Get Patrick Armstrong for me, and I'll see to your drinks for the night."

The little urchin nodded. "I don't have to go far, just saw him next door at Shoemaker's Tavern."

"Brilliant." She handed him a couple shillings from her pocket and made her way next door.

As promised, Patrick was next door at Shoemaker's Tavern, sitting with his back to the door as he talked to some of the patrons. The small house turned tavern had room enough for twenty people around long wooden tables, benches flanking both sides. Much like The Silver Kettle, Shoemaker's was rustic and dark, the walls covered with dingy, faded wallpaper, age-old curtains barely shutting out the summer sun, and the smell was enough to make her gag in her delicate condition. All the frontier taverns lacked the grace and sophistication of the city she so craved; how she longed to get back to it. Thankfully, it was only a matter of time. Soon, all the players would be vying for her attention and paying her handsomely.

Celeste took a seat at the bar next to Patrick, ignoring the leering eyes of the men standing around. *Poor, backwater fools.* She rolled her eyes. Clearly, they'd never seen a proper lady before. Tossing one glossy curl over her shoulder, she intentionally purred. "So, Mr. Armstrong, have you found my lady yet?"

He turned to her, his eyes uncharacteristically bloodshot and glassy, a sly grin turning up the corner of his lips. He was drunk. Piss drunk and sloppy.

"Well, Mrs. Allen. What can I do for you?"

She placed one of her gloved fingers on his chin, turning his attention back when he tried to look away. "I asked if you've found the woman yet."

He shook his head, taking a hearty sip from his drink. "Nope, can't help you."

"Perhaps I should tell your precious Dellis that the child I'm carrying could be yours. How would you like that?" When she tried to pull his drink away, he whacked her hand in midair, sending the tankard flying across the bar.

The bartender ducked just in time, the tankard hitting the wall, ale dripping down, staining the white and green paper. "No throwing drinks, Armstrong," the elderly bartender yelled from behind the counter.

She smiled, batting her eyelashes at him. "Thank you. Mr. Armstrong is being such a brute."

"Tell Dellis whatever you like. I'll no longer be a party to your plans." Patrick hissed, his face only inches from hers. "And you and I both know that child is Carlisle's."

Throwing her head back dramatically, she let out a cackle. "Sure, whatever you think. I already figured you were weak, so I took matters into my own hands."

She held up her dainty, gloved fingers, waving them.

"What are you talking about?" he asked in a low, dangerous voice.

"Wouldn't you like to know?"

As she started to get up, his hand clamped down her shoulder like a vice, pushing her back into her seat. She yelped in pain, her eyes shooting daggers.

"Tell me!"

"The woman's been right under our noses all this time. Poor thing even got tarred and feathered to protect your precious Dellis." Celeste smiled, knowing he'd eventually catch on, slow as he may be.

"Stay away from Will and from Dellis! Do you hear me!" His fingers bit into her shoulder, shaking her with such force her teeth jarred together.

"Someone, help me," she said frantically, though grinning all the while. "He's hurting me and my baby."

When one of the patrons rushed over, trying to pull them apart, Patrick turned and planted a fist in the other man's face.

"Oh!" She gasped, touching the corner of her eye, making it water. "He's dangerous. This isn't the first time he's attacked me." *Fool.*

Next thing she knew, the two men were on the ground, rolling around on the floor, throwing punches. Wow, two bar fights in a matter of minutes; it was turning out to be a good day.

"That's it." The bartender came from behind the bar, pulling out his pistol and aiming at Patrick and his adversary. "Both of you are going to the gaol."

Celeste stepped back, trying to avoid Patrick's haphazard punches as four men pulled him to his feet. "My father is the magistrate. I'll be out of the gaol by tomorrow," he yelled as the men dragged him to the door.

She grinned. "We'll see about that!"

Once the bartender was back behind the bar, she leaned over the counter top and said, "You wouldn't happen to know where the town magistrate lives? I think he should be aware of his son's recent behavior, keeping company with Tories, and now acting like a drunken brute."

A man of few words, he muttered out what she needed to know and nothing more. "North end of town. Large white house with green shutters, next to the church." He picked up his rag and started to wipe down the counter.

"Thank you." With that, she grabbed her velvet purse and went for the door, ready to mesh out a little evil.

Chapter
Thirty-Two

"Who's pounding on the front door?" Dellis walked into the kitchen to find Agnes elbows deep in thick sticky biscuit dough.

"Perhaps it's the mail courier?"

"Well, he's rather persistent; there's no need to break down my door." Dellis rushed through the dining room to the front door, opening it quickly.

To her surprise, it was Lord Carlisle. As expected, he was impeccably dressed in a forest-green suit and shiny black shoes, but his hair had come somewhat loose, stray locks curling around his ears, an unruly thick one hanging in his face. He looked disheveled and out of breath, his cheeks red, a light sheen of sweat on his brow and above his lips.

My, how he looks like John. She took a breath, trying to slow her confused, fluttering heart that was mistaking the wrong man as the object of her affections.

"What can I do for you?" she asked, noticing how he frequently glanced over his shoulder.

"Miss McKesson, may I come inside?"

Something was terribly wrong, or he wouldn't have come to her home in such a state. But before she offered any assistance, it was time to set him straight, once and for all. "You mean Mrs. Carlisle, don't you, My Lord?"

"Yes, forgive me, Mrs. Carlisle," he said between rushed breaths. "May I please come inside?"

She hesitated, letting him sweat it out for a minute, her stubborn pride surfacing in the face of his crisis. "So that you can take my home away after I help you? I don't think so."

"Please? I'm in need of a place to hide for the moment. A group of local brigands have set their sights at catching me." His voice was quick and winded, his eyes again glancing over his shoulder a couple of times.

"I'm not the local sanctuary for Tories, and since I'm currently under suspicion, and my tavern closed because of such allegations, I don't wish to further add to the situation. Good day, My Lord."

As she went to close the door, he grabbed on to the edge, pulling it back. "Please, I beg you." His sapphire-blue eyes pled, little wrinkles forming in the corners, tugging at her all-too-vulnerable heartstrings.

This is John's brother.

That fact alone was enough to change her heart. Dellis relented, releasing the door.

"Take a seat." She pointed to the one table left in her nearly empty dining room.

He sat down, removing his hat and placing it on the table. "Thank you."

"Why have you come here?" Taking a seat across from him, she watched him smooth his unruly locks back with trembling hands, feeling a tinge of satisfaction at his unfortunate plight. "You know you're not welcome."

"What happened to your business?" he asked curiously, looking around at the empty tables.

"I was accused of being a Tory sympathizer. The magistrate closed my business indefinitely." There was a hint of bitterness in her voice purposely directed at him; Lord Carlisle's appearance only added to the suspicions already mounted against her.

"I am sorry. Truly."

Dellis shook her head; though his apology seemed genuine, it was also trite after all the trouble he'd caused. "Tell me what you want. John's not here. And if it's your money, I don't have it. So if it must be, then the house is yours, and I have no right to turn you away."

"I've no wish to throw an innocent woman from her home, nor is that the reason I'm here. I only threatened you because I wanted to my brother to heed my warning. There's a long history between John and I. One that can't easily be forgotten."

He spoke the truth, his blue eyes so like John's and just as readable. Having seen the damage caused by hatred between brothers, she felt the need to try and circumvent it, even if it was against her husband's wishes. "Let me get you some tea, and then you can explain yourself."

Dellis rushed into the kitchen, quickly preparing a tray with the china teapot Patrick loaned her and a couple of Agnes's freshly made biscuits.

"Who was at the door?" she asked, kneading bread on the counter.

"Lord Carlisle." Dellis looked down at the aged tea service and mismatched cups and saucers—a visual representation of the sorry state of her affairs. But she cared not for His Lordship's station or what he thought of her home; it was her respect the man had to earn, and not the other way around.

"Be careful of him," Agnes said flatly, her back turned as she continued kneading.

Dellis nodded. "I will." Picking up the tray, she carried it through the bar, into the dining room, and set it down on the table. Surprisingly, Gavin didn't seem to notice her chipped teacups and hodgepodge of china. He took the cup and saucer she offered and started to drink. Her eyes trained to the blue cup touching his lips; in hand, a pink saucer that went with a different set.

"Your tea is exquisite, and this is just how I like it, cream no sugar."

She smiled over the rim of her cup. "That's how John drinks it. I just assumed you would do the same."

"Of course." He snorted, taking another sip.

"You're rather alike, though I know you don't want to hear that."

Gavin put the cup and saucer down on the table, his shoulders straightening as he crossed his arms. Lean, corded muscles strained against the fine fabric of his coat, setting her heart fluttering again.

Dellis looked away, trying to set it to right.

"I knew you'd help. You were kind enough to direct me to safety even after I shot your husband."

Touché. She almost put a finger to the tip of her nose. "Am I that predictable or am I just a naïve fool?"

"You're a kind woman, clearly above frivolity and capriciousness. But I'm curious, why did you not speak to my brother before he left? Was it because of Celeste Allen?" Clearly, Gavin was well informed of his brother's state of affairs, but they were still none of his business.

"I don't wish to discuss my husband, or Mrs. Allen, with you."

Gavin clucked his tongue; she could see the wheels turning behind those lovely eyes while he recovered from her tart rebuke.

"I know Mrs. Allen. When I discovered that my shipments had gone missing, I went looking for John in Niagara, where I last heard he was commissioned. That's where I met her. I regret to say I travelled with her here to find John."

Of course Celeste had something to do with Lord Carlisle's timely arrival; it all made sense. He was just another pawn in her game of revenge.

"What is it that you want? If it's to see John dead, you'll have to kill me first. And if it's to see him in debtor's prison, I'll sell this house and deny you your pleasure. I refuse to let you, or anyone else, hurt him."

To Dellis's surprise, Gavin reached across the table and took her hand, clutching it tightly. "I now understand my brother's fascination with you; not only are you beautiful, but courageous and loyal. What man wouldn't want such a prize?"

Dellis could feel herself flush from her cheeks to her toes, having never been given such a bold, honest compliment.

"You're too good for the likes of him," Gavin said, bowing his head, kissing the top of her hand.

Her eyes feasted on his thick, silky hair, its lushness so like John's that her hands ached for a touch.

"But you would make a lovely countess."

When he kissed her hand again, she inhaled sharply, trying to fight off the lovely tingles that danced their way from his lips up her arm. He was charming, clearly a Carlisle trait, but where Gavin was candid and a bit imperious, John was guarded, naughty, and sweetly self-deprecating. Flawed to perfection.

"You're too kind, but I'm content to simply be the wife of Captain John Carlisle." She paused for a moment, the frank honesty of her words catching even herself off guard. "Or whatever version of himself he chooses to be. He's everything to me."

"My brother is very lucky, though I believe he lacks the insight to know that."

Feeling suddenly protective of the man she loved, Dellis shook her head and pulled her hand away. "You don't know him like I do. He's not the same John that left your home ten years ago, nor is he the same one I met in October." She paused again, reflecting on the man who once sat across from her in deception, a spy and a Redcoat, yet the very same one who fathered both of her children and tenderly wept at her feet with remorse for his sins. No, he wasn't that man any longer. "John has paid for his mistakes many times over, and he's truly repentant. I'm sorry you can't see that."

Gavin shook his head. "My brother sealed his fate with me years ago. This feud is of his own making. You must understand."

"I don't, and I never will. I've seen, firsthand, what hate between brothers can do; my father paid the price for it with his life. Hate each other all you wish, but if you ever strike out at John, you'll have me, and my family, to deal with."

"A threat, Mrs. Carlisle?" he asked, cocking his brow, a grin turning up the corner of his lips.

"A promise." She smiled back. "You may stay here, My Lord, until you can make arrangements to leave German Flats."

"Thank you," he said calmly, though the furrow in his brow spoke of concern. "I must warn you, Mrs. Allen is not to be trifled with. It was she who set your brother and the militia men on me at The Kettle earlier today. She's planning something. I can feel it. My instincts never serve me wrong."

"Damn that woman," Dellis said under her breath. "She's relentless."

What Gavin said about Celeste only further added fuel to the fire that was still burning from Dellis's conversation with Agnes the night before. Mrs. Allen planned all of it, her trap perfectly executed. Finishing the tea, Dellis placed the cup and saucer on the tray and stood. "I'll see you to your room, and then I think it's time I put an end to this."

Following in the footsteps of St. Leger and the entire western front, John and his men traveled the seventy miles to Fort Stanwix through the dense, forbidding forest, in the scorching heat, while mosquitos feasted on the soldiers' sweaty, salty flesh. The journey was arduous at best; the old roadway created during the French War had to be opened, a tangle of shrubs and plants covering the road, rendering it impassable to the battalion. The men were forced to cut a way through, tapping their strength and endurance, slowing the army's advance. The artillery bateaux traveled by water, fighting obstructions and narrow passages through parts of Wood Creek. As the boats neared the Oneida Carry, they found the colonists had cleverly felled trees and bushes to block the waterway and access to the dock. Soldiers, at times, had to get out on poison-ivy infested shores and pull the boats, containing three- and six-pound cannons, through rushing waters with sheer, brute strength.

Before he left Three Rivers, John put his plan into place; he informed Butler that Alexei was willing to reveal the whereabouts of the stolen supplies, as well as Lord Tomlinson's heiress, in exchange for freedom. As expected, Butler found fault with the terms, but he did relent and allow

John to bring Alexei and Anoki along as prisoners. Butler clearly held out hope the Oneida would still negotiate for their men, though John knew better.

After two days of travelling, late in the evening, as the sun kissed the horizon on August second, the British army and their advance contingent arrived at Fort Stanwix.

John held his breath as the star-shaped fort appeared in the distance, the field around it bare, the newer barracks built up just outside the walls completed. Since last he'd visited, the colonists had taken further measures to fortify Stanwix: pointed stakes jutted out from the rampart in horizontal fashion, embrasures had been cut into three of the bastions, cannons were in place and aimed at the field around the fort. And as he'd forewarned in his intelligence, and much to the General's dismay, Stanwix was garrisoned and ready for a siege.

As John directed his men to set up camp, a sentry wearing the yellow facings of the thirty-fourth regiment of foot approached. "Captain Carlisle, General St. Leger has requested your presence."

Clark snorted. "In trouble already, John?"

John shot down his friend with a fierce look. Their friendly behavior in private was one thing, but in the presence of others, it was considered impertinence. "Yes, I'm coming."

John followed the sentry through the rows of newly assembled canvas tents; around them was the banging and clanking of hammers hitting metal stakes as the camp was fast being constructed. At his feet, long trenches were being dug in the dirt to drain refuse and keep the camp from flooding. He passed the women's tent, laundry already being hung out on lines while uniforms soaked in giant tubs of steaming water like bubbling soup caldrons. One of the ladies looked up from her washing and winked at him, her ample bosom hanging over affording him an unimpeded view.

He gave her a curt nod and then averted his gaze. The last thing he needed was unwanted attention from a camp matron. He was already in deeply for his intrigue with Dellis, rumor spreading like wildfire around the camp that he'd tupped a beautiful and rather brazen Oneida.

The General's tent was the largest one at the center of the camp.

The sentry stepped out of the way, gesturing for John to enter. "You may go inside, Captain."

John glanced around for a moment, collecting his thoughts, and then lifted the canvas flap and stepped inside. The interior of the tent was decorated more for a gala or summer garden party at Hampton Court than a battle. The large cot in the corner was covered in sumptuous fur blankets; underneath, a fat, feather-stuffed mattress, the quality better than any bed he'd ever been fortunate enough to sleep in. All the chairs inside were made of rich, dark, mahogany wood and upholstered with fine maroon damask that was elegantly brocaded. On the large table in the center of the tent, a fine blue and white Wedgewood tea service had already been set out, steam emanating from one of the full cups. Hanging from the center post of the tent was a giant, cast-iron candelabra holding six lit tapers that were flickering merrily. The General stood behind a giant desk just inside the flap, reviewing a stack of field maps, his gaze fixed on the papers.

Rallying courage, John threw back his shoulders and said, "General St. Leger, sir. You requested my presence. I'm Captain Carlisle."

The General kept his head turned down to his papers, though his eyes shifted towards John, a rounded, quizzical brow lifting in question. The man wasn't at all what John expected; instead of tall and robust with a commanding presence, like General Carleton and General Howe, St. Leger looked more like a romantic hero of old with his slim build, deep-set dark eyes, and long face that tapered into a delicate, pointed chin. His dark hair was powdered, pulled back, and tied in a queue at his nape, the sides of his hair loose and waving gently about his narrow face. For his forty years, St. Leger looked well beyond his age; lines of stress and hard living creased his forehead and cheeks. Rumor had it, the General had a penchant for overindulgence with a reputation for drowning himself in the bottle, something John understood all too well. Butler, along with many others, questioned the wisdom in choosing St. Leger for such an important commission. While the General was knowledgeable and a true leader, he lacked experience in the American wilderness and with the native community.

"Captain Carlisle," St. Leger said, a hint of Irish accent accentuating the R in John's surname. "I understand you've been on special assignment for General Howe and then General Carleton, and now you work with the native contingent under Major Butler."

"Yes, sir."

"I also understand part of your duty was to investigate the status of Fort Stanwix."

"Yes, sir. I provided all the information in my report to General Carleton. I believe this is a replica of one of my maps." He pointed to the map St. Leger was reviewing on his desk. "At the time I drew this, the Northwest Bastion was near the magazine." John used his finger to direct the General's attention to significant locations. "Here's the sally port, sentry boxes on the bastions, Gansevoort's quarters, and the battery. Fort Stanwix was manned by at least three-hundred-and-fifty men then, and by now, likely upwards of eight hundred, by my estimation. They knew we were coming. I relayed all of this information to General Carleton and Major Butler. The colonists have an excellent network of spies in this area, many of them native and familiar with the local terrain. They've been tracking our movement up and down the St. Lawrence for months."

John knew St. Leger was aware of that; not a month before, a dispatch of Daniel Claus's most trusted scouts, including Captain John Oteronyente, Captain John Hare, and forty men, captured five colonial soldiers outside the fort. The information they obtained further supported John's earlier report, yet it seemed both Carleton and St. Leger ignored the warning. Their initial contingent was hardly a threat for Stanwix, only consisting of two-hundred-and-twenty regulars of the Eighth regiment and the Thirty-fourth, sixty Royal Yorkers, and a smattering of Rangers. Joseph Brant brought about one hundred volunteers, while Butler was still in route with the rest of the native party. Also in route was the main party of the expedition: one-hundred-and-sixty artillery men, ninety Hesse-Hanau Jägers, a contingent of Canadians, and two-hundred-and-fifty more of Sir John Johnson's Royal Yorkers. Without Butler's native force, that he and John had worked so hard to secure, the entirety of the British fighting force matched that of the estimated eight hundred garrisoned at Fort Stanwix—not enough for a successful siege.

"Are you aware that Lieutenant Bird not only failed to prevent the blockage of Wood Creek, which has now led to the delay of our artillery and the rest of our men, but allowed a contingent of Colonials to return to the fort with supplies, thus alerting Gansevoort of our arrival?"

John held back a chuckle. Bird was notoriously incompetent; John also warned Carleton about that. "Again, if you look at the maps I prepared, I did draw attention to locations that would need to be addressed if we were to lay siege to Stanwix." John leafed through the stack again, pulling out the map specific to the water system from Oswego all the way to the Oneida Carry. "Wood Creek is the point of exit for our boats; it makes sense that they'd block it, and they have many spies along this river just as we do. On the upper landing of the Mohawk is where the Rebels can bring supplies from other locations. There are also old roads running from Fort Stanwix east towards the other forts that can still be utilized."

St. Leger regarded John curiously but did didn't say a word.

"Sir, I'd like to make a suggestion—" But before John could finish, Lord Tomlinson walked into the tent, along with a shorter, slighter, dark-haired man. "Captain Carlisle, I believe you know Lord Tomlinson, and this is Colonel Daniel Claus, our new Superintendent of the Western Expedition."

So that was Butler's adversary, with wide-set eyes and aquiline nose that sat above an exaggerated frown, Claus looked every bit the gentleman, but with a notoriously prickly demeanor. John addressed both men, his friend looking less than pleased.

"We were just reviewing these rather telling maps and some of the intelligence Captain Carlisle has been able to provide us."

Daniel Claus smiled, dissipating his previously frosty expression. "I believe we both stumbled on the same information, Captain. It says a lot for your abilities."

"Yes," John replied, nodding, though stumbled was hardly the appropriate word after what he went through to gain such details. At least he wasn't the only one the superiors had turned a deaf ear to. What good was intelligence if it wasn't utilized?

"Captain Carlisle, you have unique knowledge of this area and the fort. You'll be quite useful," St. Leger said, appreciatively. "From now on, I'd like you to be present during our briefings."

"Yes, sir," John replied, elated at the General's endorsement. "What now?"

"The rest of our men should arrive by tomorrow, and we'll show our full strength. I'll send word to Gansevoort demanding his surrender to our superior force."

John looked over at Claus and then at Miles, neither of them flinching at the ridiculousness of St. Leger's words. Stanwix was well fortified and could handle a siege. Even at full strength, a British victory was far from assured.

"General, sir, may I speak with you alone?" Colonel Claus asked, casting a glance at John and Lord Tomlinson.

"Yes."

John followed Miles out of the tent, both of them silent, the strain in their friendship having irrevocably taken its toll beyond even quaint conversation.

"Just because you've made yourself indispensable to St. Leger doesn't mean you won't face the court martial for your failure." Miles slapped a pair of leather gloves on his thigh with a loud *snap* and walked past John.

Chapter Thirty-Three

Dellis grabbed the door to The Kettle and threw it open, and before she could even take a few steps inside, Jussie rushed out from behind the bar, right on cue for a showdown.

"No whores or Tories are allowed in our tavern." With her hands akimbo, she smiled, looking thoroughly amused with herself. "Now get out."

Dellis rolled her eyes, giving her head a gentle shake. "I have no intention of sullying the good name of The Silver Kettle with my lowly presence. I just came to speak with Mrs. Allen. Is she in her room?"

She cast a glance at the bartender, Abraham, Jussie's older brother, and nodded to him. "As usual, your brother has no trouble with me being here, so it would seem the prejudice lies with you alone, and I'm not quite sure why. I've done you no harm, Jussie. What is it about me that provokes such disdain in you?"

Dellis's frankness clearly surprised the catty woman, her usually churlish demeanor suddenly suppressed. "I... I don't know what... I..."

"No matter, it'll be yours to answer for when you meet St. Peter." Dellis winked and then walked towards the staircase.

As she started up the stairs, Dellis heard Jussie whisper, "Not only is she a Tory whore, but a Papist one at that."

Once at the top of the stairs, Dellis took a deep breath, bolstering her courage, and then pounded on Celeste's door. Dellis was doing it for John—but damn if it wouldn't feel good to finally put Mrs. Allen's nose out of joint. That thought alone gave Dellis courage; well, and the two shots of whiskey she had before she left The Thistle. When the door opened, she stood face to face with her adversary, a woman who'd wished Dellis ill and acted on it at every turn.

With a cock of the brow, Celeste smiled. "To what do I owe this pleasure, Miss McKesson?"

"It's Carlisle." Dellis countered smartly. "Mrs. Carlisle."

Their eyes locked in challenge and held fast for a long, protracted, silent moment, until finally, Celeste rubbed her slightly protruding belly, drawing Dellis's attention to it.

"Why don't you come in? It's better if I sit. I've been having a little trouble with dizziness lately." Celeste opened to door to Dellis, welcoming her into the den of sin. "I'm sure you understand, having been enceinte once before yourself."

"Twice." Dellis tamped down her ire, knowing a calm, strategic demeanor would do more damage to her adversary. "I've twice been with child."

"And sadly, you have nothing to show for it." Celeste provided with a mocking pout. "At least now John will finally have a son."

"Yes, eventually, he will, but not by you," Dellis replied, her voice sounding confident, betraying none of her inner turmoil. "The child you're carrying isn't his."

Celeste let out a mocking laugh, throwing her head back, glossy, dark ringlets falling down her back in waves. "My dear, lying to yourself won't make it go away; this *is* John's child."

"No, Mrs. Allen, it's not." Dellis stepped closer, her fists clenched at her sides. "You know it, and I know it."

"Truly, you are crazy. Does John realize that?"

She refused to let the woman be intimidating; she was nothing but a scheming opportunist who was hellbent on hurting John. With iron determination, Dellis dug deeply, finding courage in something her father once said to her. *"That's good, stubborn Scot's blood in you. It'll make you tough as steel and as resilient as stone."*

Time to flex that muscle.

"You were with child long before you forced John to bed you. Agnes told me about your previous liaisons and the company you keep. You did this to separate us. It's all a hoax."

Celeste let out another laugh, but it was less confident, her eyes widening; finally, a crack in her well-honed charade. "You don't know what you're talking about. Agnes is a liar. The baby is John's."

She was determined to play the game to the bitter end, but woe for her because Dellis had reached her breaking point. Digging into her pocket, she pulled out a knife, and with one hard shove, she threw Celeste against the wall and held the blade to her throat.

With a yelp, she stiffened fearfully, her hands splaying out, grabbing the wall. "You're mad, woman! Mad!"

"I refuse to let you hurt me or John ever again." Dellis pushed the blade into the sensitive skin of Celeste's neck, letting her feel the power of cold, forbidding steel.

A little fear will do her good.

"You've lost your mind!" She spat, wriggling back and forth, trying free herself, but Dellis held the woman in place with one hand while the other dug the knife in deeper, tapping blood.

That's for my lost little Stephen.

Celeste screamed as the blade sank into her neck, a slow trickle of crimson running down her throat to her breast.

"According to you, I'm nothing more than a savage whore who got what she deserved when DeLancie attacked me. Isn't it fitting that I should behave as one?" Dellis lifted the knife to Celeste's cheek, letting the steel rest on her supple flesh. "You seduce men with your money and your beauty, but it's false. A sham! You're nothing more than a spider who traps men in her web and then sinks her teeth in. Just like you did to John. But no more!"

Dellis pushed the blade into the skin, eliciting another strident shriek from Celeste.

"What kind of sick woman are you, attacking one who's with child?" she screamed frantically, their eyes meeting in the short, crackling distance, filled with rage and jealousy.

"I would ask the same of you." Dellis's rage allowed her to push through the pain in her gut and the tears that threatened at the thought of her lost child. "You who showed me no mercy, setting Roger DeLancie loose, knowing he'd attack me, and then using me as bait to further ensnare John. I know what kind of sick woman does that… I'm looking at her."

Celeste rallied, making a hacking noise and then spitting in Dellis's face. Ignoring the sensation of warm goo sliding down her cheek, she slammed Celeste against the wall again with omnipotent strength, a gift of adrenaline and unmitigated rage.

"That child in your womb isn't John's. Admit it." Dellis dug her blade into the woman's cheek, the point puncturing the skin, drawing another drop of blood. For an effect that would absolutely terrify her, Dellis lifted the blade to her lips, pretending to taste the blood.

Celeste let out a terrific scream, her eyes widening.

Perfectly played.

Dellis pushed the point of the blade into Celeste's cheek again and yelled, "Tell me the truth! Tell me!" Her defiant silence only spurred Dellis on; she started to cut, just a slight graze, but enough to leave a mark that would never be forgotten.

Relinquishing the silence, Celeste let out another scream then started to beg. "Stop! Stop. It isn't John's! Now, please, let me go."

Stunned by her abrupt confession, Dellis almost dropped the knife, but she righted herself and pushed the blade in more. "Whose is it?"

Celeste shook her head. "It matters not, but it isn't John's. I was with child before we were together."

Yes. Dellis mentally let out a warrior's whoop and howl. *Now to set this diabolical woman straight once and for all.*

"Had you not blackmailed John, he would never have touched you. He wants nothing to do with you save the money you owe him. Now tell me where it is!"

Celeste shook her head, her teary eyes fixed on the silver steel pressed into her cheek. "I don't have it. You can search this room, but you won't find any."

There was truth in her words; the woman was frantic and too afraid to lie.

Nose to nose with her, Dellis pushed her blade into the soft flesh one last time, deepening the cut.

That one's for me.

"If I ever see you in German Flats again, I'll finish what I started today. I promise you." And with one clean swipe, she pulled the blade away, leaving another little cut on Celeste's cheek.

For John.

And then, as quick as a lightning strike, Dellis planted the blade in the door, landing it perfectly through Celeste's earring. The woman shrieked, her eyes closing in abject terror.

Releasing her, Dellis stepped back and pulled the knife from the door. She watched as Celeste righted herself, adjusted her dress, and wiped the blood from her cheek and neck.

"You're a crazy woman."

Dellis chuckled. "Maybe. But just like you, I make it a point to know my adversary's weaknesses—and yours was to underestimate me. I'm no weak country simpleton or simpering society virgin. I'm the niece of a Duke, the granddaughter of an Oneida chief, and the wife of a British Captain. And in my own right, I own my home, I've been raped by regulars, lost two children, and survived a beating at Roger DeLancie's hands. I have no fear of you. You're nothing but an overindulged, petulant woman. And in the end, you can never have what you really want, because no matter how hard you try, John will never love you. He chose the half-breed whore to Your Royal Highness—now choke on that, Mrs. Allen."

367

Dellis slammed the door and threw herself against it, her heart still racing on nerves as raw and frayed as the hem of her old wool petticoat—but she did it. She'd did it! That diabolical woman confessed. Putting the back of one trembling hand to dry lips, Dellis let out a long sigh of relief.

"Thank you, Father," she whispered to herself, sensing his loving intervention on her behalf. "Thank you." But instead of breaking into the tears of joy that burned her eyes, she opted to laugh, loudly and heartily. The terror in Mrs. Allen's eyes was absolutely priceless, especially when Dellis pretended to lick blood from the blade; that retched woman almost fainted.

Oh, it was fantastic!

Dellis picked up her skirts and raced down the stairs, her mood too light to let even the nastiest of glances from Jussie put a damper on it.

When Dellis got back to The Thistle, she walked up the stairs and propped open the front door, allowing the breeze to flow freely through the sweltering heat of the dining room. She picked up the leftover dishes from her meeting with Lord Carlisle, carrying them into the kitchen. Agnes and Will were hanging flowers over the table to dry, a bundle of lavender lying in wait for its turn to be prepped.

Putting the tray on the counter, Dellis bubbled over with excitement. "I did it!"

"Did what?" Agnes asked, her eyes widening curiously.

"We were right." Dellis ran up to Agnes and threw both arms around her. "The baby's not John's!"

Pulling back, Dellis searched her friend's face, waiting for the truth to lighten her expression. "Mrs. Allen lied."

Agnes's full lips turned up in a jovial grin, exposing her brilliant white teeth. "I knew it!"

Will embraced both of them, resting her head on Dellis's shoulder. "How did you get her to confess?"

Dellis pulled away, a snort escaping her. "I confess, I was quite awful; you won't believe what I did."

"Come on, don't keep us in suspense." Agnes took a seat at the table, Will resting nearby.

Quickly, Dellis regaled her friends with her expert performance, still amazed at what she was able to accomplish. "It was terrible of me, I know. Truly, I'd never hurt her." Grinning, she said, "I won't deny that I relished her terror. Oh, that awful woman deserved it."

Agnes nodded in agreement. "Yes, she did."

"I think that's the last we'll be seeing of her," Dellis said, tying up the last bundle of lavender and hooking it to the rack above the table. "The only problem is, I never got John's money back from her."

"What do you need it for?" Will asked, injecting her sweet voice into the conversation.

"The Captain rerouted supplies from his brother's business to trade with my grandfather, only Alexei stole the supplies and gave them to the colonists and to our village. John's in debt to his brother because of it."

Will pursed her lips, the wheels visibly turning in her head as she glanced between Dellis and Agnes. "How much does he owe?"

"Fifteen hundred pounds. Why?" Dellis replied, curiously. Normally, she didn't make it a habit of discussing the sorry state of her financial affairs with others, but losing The Thistle would affect Will, too. Honesty was the best outlet.

"I might be able to help." Will clucked her tongue and then got up from the table and walked towards her room.

Dellis and Agnes followed, watching from the hall as Will got down on her knees and pulled some of the wooden floorboards up, exposing a hidden cubby. Dellis knew about the little hiding place; it was where Stuart used to keep his most precious toys and sweets he stole from the kitchen, but how did Will know about it?

Inside, hidden under a blanket, was a wooden chest. Dellis leaned over, taking a look as Will opened it carefully. Immediately, Dellis's eyes were drawn to the glitter of gold and silver and the sparkle of jewels. A treasure chest, full to the top, just like ones the pirates of the Caribbean were rumored to keep. Gold and silver coins; enough to fix The Thistle ten times over, and jewelry fit for Queen Charlotte to wear at court. It was a sight to behold, like something out of a fairytale.

Quickly, Will counted out some coins and handed them to Dellis. "That should cover you. It's the least I can do for your kindness and generosity. And since Alexei was the one who put the Captain in such a predicament, I think this is only fitting."

Dellis stood, dumbfounded; in her hands was the answer to all her prayers.

"How?" Was all she could muster up to ask. Her fingers closed around the coins, feeling the precious metal, profoundly aware of its true value. She could keep her house. And she and John would be free.

"This is part of my dowry. The rest of it, including my dresses and some furniture, and a pianoforte, Alexei hid somewhere. God knows where he'd stash all that." Will laughed. "He felt the money would be safest here with me, so he hid it before he left and told me where it was."

Dellis marveled at the woman, heart overflowing with love. "You've saved me and my house." Running to her, Dellis threw her arms around Will, wrapping her up in true gratitude. "You don't know what this means to me and to John. We're forever in your debt."

Will backed away, her eyes red and moist with unshed tears. "No, we're even. You protected me, and at what cost? Your relationship with the Captain."

Dellis raced through the kitchen, her hands full of coins and her heart full of hope. "I must give this to Lord Carlisle, and he can be on his way. Perhaps this will put an end to their feuding once and for all."

When she reached the top of the stairs, she knocked on the door to Gavin's room.

He opened it, and she thrust out her hands so he could see them full of glittering gold and silver coins. "This is the money John owes you and then some. Now take it, and be on your way."

Lord Carlisle grasped her hands in his, and the coins pressed between them. When he looked up, his sapphire eyes were full of warmth. "My brother is *not* worthy of you."

"You're wrong, My Lord. Quite wrong." She grinned, her eyes tearing up. "If you only knew the man he's become."

He released her hands, taking the coins and putting them on the dresser. "Will you not tell me?"

Dellis shook her head; the story was too personal, too private, to share—a miracle of love and trust born out of lies and hatred. The culmination of justice in the face of so many who were denied it.

"Perhaps, someday, I'll come to know this version of John Carlisle that you speak of."

Dellis nodded. "I hope so."

"Since I have no more reasons to remain, I'll go tomorrow. I have work that needs me in Manhattan, and then I'll return to Bristol."

Unable to resist the urge, Dellis reached up, placing her hand on his smoothly-shaven cheek. His face was so like John's, with a high forehead; big, blue, almond-shaped eyes; and a strong, defined jawline. Lord Carlisle wasn't as terrible as he originally seemed; another well-developed façade masterfully executed by a Carlisle.

"I hope you find someone to love you, My Lord."

"Perhaps I should stick around and see if I can't find myself an Oneida lady? I know of no other woman such as you in England."

Dellis grinned, knowingly. "Would you believe it was I who found John?"

"Yes, actually." He laughed for the first time since she'd met him. "How could a man not lose his heart to such a woman—even one as corrupt as John?"

Running her fingers down Gavin's cheek, she grazed the cleft in his chin and then stepped back, putting some distance between them. "I hope to see you again someday, brother-in-law."

"As do I." Gavin bowed gallantly, and then to her complete surprise, he took her hands and placed the coins back in them. "Fix your home; make it a proper place to raise your children, Carlisle children, for I have none of my own, and someday, they may be my heirs."

She looked up at him, thoroughly astonished. "Are you sure? That's the money John owes you."

"Yes." He nodded. "That's not for my brother. It's for you, kind woman."

"Thank you, My Lord."

He shook his head, and then, smiling, he said, "Gavin, please."

Dellis resisted the urge to hug him, settling for words of true thanksgiving. "Gavin, you have no idea how grateful I am. God Speed, and—" The sound of someone pounding on the front door interrupted her train of thought.

Lord Carlisle's gaze darted towards the staircase, consternation forming a crease in his brow.

"Wait here," Dellis said, handing the money back to him and rushing to the stairs. "If it's more of the locals, the last thing we need is them discovering you."

"I'll stand at the top of the stairs and listen. If you should need me, I'll come." He put the coins on the desk and grabbed his pistol off the dresser, stuffing it in his coat.

Dellis smiled. He was just as chivalrous and brave as John. "Thank you."

The pounding continued, becoming frantic; Dellis opened the door, surprised to find Two Kettles Together, Han Yerry's wife, standing at the door, her lovely face wide-eyed and etched with worry.

"What are you doing here?"

It was unlike any of Dellis's native family to enter the town proper for fear of local hostility. They'd only come if something was truly wrong.

Dellis opened the door, rushing her friend inside, looking around to make sure no one else spotted her.

The great chief's wife brushed a few stray silky locks from her face, looking around the dining room. "I never knew that you had such a nice house, Dellis."

"Thank you," Dellis replied, ushering her friend to the nearest chair. "Please, sit."

Two Kettles Together fanned herself, sweat beading on her brow and at the neckline of her doeskin tunic "Actually, I can't stay. I have to get to Fort Dayton, but I need your help. Your grandfather sent me to come find you."

Sensing the urgency in her tone, Dellis felt her own heart start to race in anticipation. "What is it?"

"The King's men have come to Fort Stanwix. At least five hundred. Some of them are from our brother tribes, and there are more making their way to the Carry. Paul Powless faced Joseph Brant and his men earlier today; he managed to stay them off long enough for the supply chain from the river to reach the fort. He's gone to Schenectady for help, and I was sent here to warn the villagers and Fort Dayton of their arrival."

"Oh my." Dellis put her hand over her mouth—the fighting had started. "What do you need from me?"

"I'll go to Fort Dayton if you can inform the local villagers. We must tell them."

Dellis cringed; her relations had soured so much with the locals, surely no one would believe her warnings. Somehow, she had to get word out. "All right. Consider it done. What about my grandfather?"

"They're meeting at Oriska, awaiting my word from Fort Dayton. When you finish, join us there. I know your healing abilities will be needed."

Dellis nodded, taking her friend's hand and giving it a squeeze. "Be safe. I'll see you this evening."

Dellis didn't wait for the door to close, already on her way to the kitchen; from behind, she could hear Gavin's heavy footsteps clicking on the wooden floor. "Agnes, the Regulars have come to Fort Stanwix. That was Two Kettles Together; she said there were at least five hundred King's men coming and more near the Carry."

"What do we do?"

Dellis glanced back at Gavin and then again at her friend. "They want me to warn the village, but no one will listen to me."

"What about Mr. Armstrong?" Will chimed in. "Everyone trusts him."

"I'll go find him." Agnes removed her apron and wiped her doughy hands off on a towel as she made her way to the door.

"I'll go with you," Gavin said, the urgency in his deep voice resonating with Dellis.

"It isn't safe. Besides, if you're recognized, the villagers may retaliate against you."

He nodded. "I know, but it wouldn't be right to leave three women to their own devices. I can protect myself."

"How can I help?" Will asked, stepping forwards, her eyes darting around at the group.

"We'll prep as much medical supplies, food, and candles as we can find. Once Agnes has returned, the two of you will go to Fort Dayton for protection and to help. I have to go to my grandfather at Oriska."

Dellis looked at Gavin, her heart softening to her once adversary turned ally. "After you return, you must seek shelter elsewhere."

His blue eyes focused on her, beloved familiar lines forming at the corners of his eyes. "I'll worry about that once the town has been warned and you ladies are safe."

"Be careful, everyone." Dellis grabbed Will's arm, pulling her towards the staircase to the cellar. "We have no time to lose."

Chapter
Thirty-Four

"Where are you going?" Smith asked, trying to keep up.

"I need to see Alexei." John rushed through the camp towards the tents where Alexei and Anoki were being held.

"Captain Carlisle to speak with the prisoners," John said, addressing the sentry on duty.

"Sir, both prisoners have been taken to Lord Tomlinson's tent."

Panic pervaded, and John looked back at Smith, apprehension shared between the two of them. "This isn't good. Follow me." John sped off in another direction without a second thought.

The two of them raced to Miles's tent, both quiet, fear looming in the air. In all that time, Miles had never addressed the situation with the two Oneida prisoners; what provoked the meeting was foremost on John's mind. Had his friend figured out Alexei's identity?

When they reached Miles's tent, Anoki and Alexei were already inside, tied back to back around the tent post, and sitting on the ground. Eagle Eyes stood in the corner, arms crossed, smug with confidence. Finally, he'd made his move.

Lord Tomlinson turned to John, flashing a look of satisfaction. "So, John, it would seem you've been keeping secrets from me. And all this time he was right under my nose to boot."

All eyes were on John; what he said then would make all the difference. With austere countenance and the skill of proficient spy, he replied, "Miles, he doesn't have the woman anymore. She ran away. I brought him so we could get the supplies and the money back. He's the only one that knows where everything is hidden."

Lord Tomlinson clucked his tongue, skeptical eyes darting from John down to Alexei and then back. "You're lying, John. But the question is, why?" Then suddenly, Miles flashed a wry grin and threw down his hat. "No matter; there are ways for me to find out the truth. And I don't need you to do it."

"Miles, this is the Duke of McKesson's nephew. If you do anything to him—"

"McKesson isn't here, is he?" He looked around the tent as if searching for their absent friend. "Neither is Butler, and Colonel Claus will find no fault in what I'm about to do. The Oneida are traitors, and these two, in particular, were caught stealing by their own brothers." Miles leaned in, his voice dropping an octave, taking on an acrid, dangerous tone. "We'll use them to set an example, to strike fear in the traitors we know are lurking in the woods, spying on us."

"What do you intend to do?" John asked, though he already anticipated the answer—torture.

Eagle Eyes waited silently in the corner, watching his well-laid plans come to fruition.

Damn that steely, industrious Mohawk.

"I'll give them to Joseph Brant and his men. I'm sure he'll find a just punishment for two traitors." Miles walked over to Alexei and Anoki and knelt to eye level. "We all know what your brothers will do to you. But to show I'm a just servant of His Majesty, I'll give you this one last chance: Tell me where my wife is."

John swallowed, a pit forming in his stomach.

With obstinate confidence, Alexei shook his head and met Miles's gaze, provoking his burgeoning ire. He grabbed the collar of Alexei's shirt, drawing him in closer for protracted silence, an effectual show of dominance, like puffing up feathers before attacking the enemy. But Alexei wasn't most men, and he wasn't easily intimidated. John knew that all too well.

"Have you touched my wife? Did you defile her with your savage seed?"

To Alexei's credit, he held his defensive posture, still unprovoked by Lord Tomlinson's vitriol. Letting go, Miles backed away, his bubbling ire adding virtual steam to the searing heat in the tent.

John rubbed a hand under his collar, catching the beads of sweat that collected.

"Have you seen the gauntlet before, John?"

"Yes." Too many times. It was one of the many Iroquois practices for dealing with prisoners—torture, but on a grand scale—and the chances of survival were minimal. His angst stoked up along with the sweat on his brow, every inch of his clothing sticking to his body, locking in nervous heat. With Merrick gone and Butler not yet arrived, there was nothing to stop Miles from carrying out his threat.

"If these two manage to live through it, I've no doubt they'll be more amenable to answering my questions."

There was no way to change Lord Tomlinson's mind, but John thought perhaps he could intimidate the man into complying. "If anything happens to Alexei, Merrick will—"

"Will what?" Miles whirled around, ripe for a challenge. "This man's a traitor to his King and a thief. The word of a duke does not override the law of the land. Treason is *still* treason." With a sharp intake of breath, his calculating eyes tracked back and forth, measuring John up and clearly finding him wanting. "You've put a wedge between myself and the Duke, and once again, you've managed to survive—even in the face of your incompetence. It would seem fortune smiles on you, but your time has come, John. You failed to do your duty, or perhaps you chose to turn a blind eye to it." Miles cocked a brow and stepped back, waving John off as though he were a bug to be swatted. "It's your word against mine. And who'd believe the testimony of a disgraced reprobate such as you?"

Miles Tomlinson was notorious for his temper and pernicious treatment once crossed.

John had seen that side of his friend before, and no good would come from trying to negotiate. Without Merrick or Butler, Alexei and Anoki's fates were sealed.

"You may be indispensable now to St. Leger, but it won't last. I'll bide my time until the moment is right, and then I'll see you pay. And even His Grace won't be able to resurrect you once I've had my way with you."

Miles would make good on his threat. Further stoking his wrath would only bode worse for Anoki and Alexei.

John stood down, submitting to his friend's authority.

Satisfied that he'd rightly warned his subordinate, Lord Tomlinson turned to Eagle Eyes. "Take them to Joseph Brant and his men. Tell them that we've given the traitors back as a sign of good will and as a lesson to traitors."

When Eagle Eyes reached for Alexei, he pulled away defiantly and yelled in *Kanien'keha*, the Mohawk language, "It's you who's the traitor. They'll take your land just as they're trying to take ours. They're using you. Don't you see that?"

Eagle Eyes smiled.

Alexei's taunts were wasted on the Mohawk.

"Say what you will, Oneida. But you'll die today, and tomorrow, it will be the rest of your brothers."

Alexei turned back, finding John one last time before being dragged from the tent, Anoki shackled and following close behind.

"Shall we watch, John? I do enjoy savages at play." Miles quipped.

It wasn't a question—it was an order—hidden under his flair for drama and a perverse sense of humor.

John would have to watch as Alexei and Anoki faced the gauntlet. They were the strongest men in Joseph's village. But could they survive when the odds were so obviously stacked against them?

Pitting brother against brother, stoking the flames of discontent to serve their own purposes. *Who are the savages now?* John wasn't sure he liked the answer to that question.

Chapter
Thirty-Five

"Will the Captain be with the battalion?" Will asked, carrying a basket full of dried venison and beef jerky into the kitchen from the cellar. "What about Alexei?"

Dellis shook her head. "I have no answers for you. I know that doesn't help."

She looked at her kitchen counter and table, making an inventory of everything she'd prepared. They'd torn up every last bit of spare linen she had for bandages, grabbed the only four bottles of whiskey in the whole tavern for washing wounds, and rounded up several spools of thread and all the needles she could find. Quickly, they wrapped up all the tallow candles they made and even the two beeswax ones from John's room. From the basement and the pantry, they took the beef jerky, dried venison, some dried fish, four loaves of bread, all the biscuits they made that morning, and rolled oats for making porridge.

For good luck, she stuffed the garnet necklace John gave her in her pocket, and in her supply basket, she hid the picture he drew her as a wedding gift.

"Oh, Will, don't forget the jugs of cider from the basement, and we have a barrel of ale left and some maple syrup. Grab that, too."

Will carried the rest of the cellar storage up the stairs, depositing everything on the kitchen floor. "What are *we* going to do once this is all gone?"

Dellis huffed out a breath, a silky strand of her hair fluttering haphazardly out of her eyes. What *would* they do? They'd completely emptied The Thistle of all its supplies; not a scrap of food or a single candle was left behind to spare, and with her poor relations in the village, purchasing more was going to be a challenge. But at least because of Will's generosity, and Gavin's kindness, Dellis had money to spend.

"We can't think about that." As if trying to convince herself, she said, "This is the right thing to do." They'd deal with the consequences when they survived what was coming—if they survived.

It was evening by the time everything was packed and ready; Dellis sat down at the table, looking at several months' worth of saving and hard work ready to be handed off to men she'd never met—men who'd accused her of being a Tory and persecuted her.

The side door opened, Patrick and Agnes walking in, both of them thoroughly exhausted. "Well?"

"We've warned everyone. Thankfully, Agnes and Lord Carlisle were able to reason with my father, or none of this would've been possible."

"What do you mean?" Dellis searched for answers in their worried expressions. "I don't understand."

"Mrs. Allen had me put in the gaol. I was drunk, and she started a scene—"

"I don't want to hear any more about that awful woman. I should get going." Dellis grabbed her haversack, slinging it over a shoulder, and then checked her pistol before putting it in her pocket. "Grandfather and Han Yerry are meeting the allied tribes at Fort Dayton instead of Oriska. Things are escalating, and fast. Where's Lord Carlisle?"

"He's with the magistrate. He sends his regards," Agnes replied. "He'll be safe."

"Good," Dellis said, nodding. *One less thing to worry about.*

She took one last look at her little family, praying it wasn't the last time she saw them. "I have to go. You two, be safe." She leaned in and placed an arm around Agnes and Will, giving them both a kiss on the cheek. "I don't know what I'd do without you two. No sisters could've been more dear."

And for Dellis's former, she could only thank the good Lord that Patrick was still in her life. What a strange irony it was that their sad parting would turn into a dear friendship she'd come to depend on. "You'll help them deliver the supplies before you join the militia?"

He nodded. "Be careful."

"Aye," she replied, pulling away and giving each of her friends' hands one last squeeze on her way out the door. Turning around, she sighed, allowing her eyes to behold the beauty of her father's home one last time.

"I'll come back," she whispered; a promise to her father but more to herself, bolstering her courage for what had to be done. *My Scot's blood will make me strong, and my Oneida blood will make me brave.* "Yes, Father, I'm the best parts of you and Mother." She held onto that statement, saddled her mare, and took off, kicking up dirt and ready to fight.

She only had to travel the short distance through town and cross the river to get to Fort Dayton. It paled in grandeur next to Niagara and Stanwix, being little better than a house with a stockade around it, rebuilt in the autumn of 1776 by Colonel Elias Dayton and his Third New Jersey regiment. Outside the walls of the fort, the allied tribes, including her grandfather, had set up camp, a bustle of activity in the scorching afternoon sun as tents were being erected and soldiers practiced their drills.

"Grandfather!" She dismounted and ran to him, taking note of his illustrious company: Han Yerry, Rail Splitter, and Wind Talker. Joining them from the other Oneida castles, the most illustrious of braves: Henry Cornelius, Blatcop, James Powless, Black Louis, and Thomas and Edward Spencer. Their native contingent consisted of Oneidas from Oriska, Old Oneida, Kanonwalohale, and her village. Also in attendance was a small group of Tuscarora that sided with their Oneida brothers and the colonists. In total, there were about sixty men ready to fight.

Dellis tapped Joseph's shoulder to get his attention. "Grandfather, what now? Why all the waiting?"

His ancient brow furrowed when he saw her, not with anger, but concern. "Dellis, thank goodness you made it here. We heard rumors that the town may have been attacked."

"No, we're all safe. But what's happening?" There was so much hustle and bustle to get ready, but everyone was just standing around doing nothing. "When do we fight?" The adrenaline surged through her veins, feeding her immortal vigor, but the longer she waited, the more of the edge would burn off, fear taking its place. "So, what's the decision?"

"Remember, Dellis, be steady and listen." Her grandfather patted her arm, trying to assuage her, but it only added to her frustration. She fingered the pistol in the pocket hidden in her petticoat, the weapon's presence somehow calming.

"Grandfather, the British have sieged Stanwix. What are we waiting for?" Was that war, standing around and talking? If that were the case, women could've been waging war from their kitchens and parlors for centuries, and been twice as efficient.

"Patience, my dear; you'll long for these calm moments when we're in the heat of battle." Again, with the patting of her arm. Dellis rolled her eyes and shook her head. She wasn't a child that needed to be placated. "Honnikol will speak soon and then we'll be on our way to relieve Fort Stanwix."

"Has anyone seen our brothers with the British?"

"Yes, Dellis, our spies have spotted Old Smoke, Cornplanter, Joseph Brant, Black Snake, and at least eight hundred of our brothers, mostly Seneca."

"Oh, my." She looked around at the small fighting force and felt the sudden withdrawal of her dauntless adrenaline as fear slipped in and took hold. "Grandfather, this isn't enough men; there aren't enough of us to make a difference. How many do the British have?"

Han Yerry turned around, nodding to her respectfully; at his hip, she noticed a long, curved sword, symbol of his rank as their war chief. "We've heard at least fifteen-hundred men, once we join Herkimer and his men, and relieve Fort Stanwix, it'll be an equal fight."

Damn fear. It seeped through her veins, tracking goosebumps up and down her arms, infecting her courage with doubt. She found fault in their leader's unfounded hubris. "My Chief, I respectfully disagree. The British are far better equipped than we are; one doesn't have to see them to know that."

Han Yerry grinned. "Yes, they might be, but they're not fighting on their sacred land with the spirits of their loved ones at their sides." And with a wink, and more arrogance, he said, "And one Oneida is worth five of their soldiers. We're quite well armed, too, thanks to Cloud Walker and his men."

Though she'd never condone it, for a millisecond, she found herself grateful for Alexei's thieving. They needed all the weapons and powder they could get, for even well armed, they weren't the British with the King's infinite well of money and power.

"You must be brave, Dellis. Healing Hand and Lily are with us today, just as the rest of our loved ones are." At the mention of her father and mother, Dellis's eyes teared up. *I'm the best of both of you.* She looked up at Han Yerry and said, "My father wouldn't want war; he was a healer—a peacemaker."

In a deep, resonant voice, the great chief countered, and rather effectively. "Yes, but he wouldn't let anyone cross our land uninvited. If he were alive, Healing Hand would be fighting right alongside us, and so would Lily. Just as you will. And after, they'd be caring for all of the injured, just as you will."

Dellis nodded, fighting back damn fearful tears. In her fanciful dreams, she'd forgotten her father's fierce loyalty to the tribe. Yes, he'd fight to the death to protect them were he alive. In a way he *did* when he gave up his life to Roger DeLancie. "I'll follow you, Chief."

"Good. Two Kettles Together and the rest of the women will be with us also; united, we're strong. Let the Great Father's men underestimate the fury of our women—you'll help us to victory."

Amongst the crowd, there were Skenandoa, Kateri, and all the other women of the village; they were listening as Two Kettles Together directed them. They were loading muskets and pistols, filling their horns with gunpowder, and stuffing their pockets and packs full of lead balls and prepared cartridges. When they'd protected their village before, Dellis had helped muzzle load muskets while her grandfather and uncle shot. It was an efficient technique and allowed them to continuously volley against their foe.

Kateri walked over to Dellis, a Brown Bess in hand, remnants of the British attack on their village, fitting that it should be used against them. "Dellis, you're coming with us?"

"Of course." She choked the words out, fear rendering her unable to project her voice above a whisper. "But we're not enough to stop the King's men."

"Dellis, don't let your fear rob you of your greatest strength. You're very brave." Kateri's words, focused and true, brought back a little of Dellis's courage that had bolted away at the first sight of a challenge. "To me, you'll always be the Matron of the Bear Clan. Embrace that role now; be fearless, and we'll follow your lead." They linked hands and hearts in the moment. "Remember, Fennishyo, it's I who saw your vision, and I've seen our victory in my dreams. I've also seen Just One with us."

"Just One?"

Before Dellis could ask about the vision, Ho-sa-gowwa rushed into the group, causing a stir amongst the warriors. She pushed her way through the lean, powerful men, red and black war paint smearing on the bodice of her dress as she grazed their bare arms.

"Speak, Ho-sa-gowwa. Tell us what you know," Rail Splitter, the great sachem, said from atop his horse, looking stolid and dignified, setting the example for their warriors.

"The field is like a vast ocean of color: red, green, and white coats of the men that follow the Great Father. They've sent word to the fort, but the Colonel inside laughs at them. The colonists have raised their flag and are standing firm. They will not relent. Now, the angry British General has burned the buildings outside the fort, and shots have been exchanged."

Han Yerry and Joseph congratulated Ho-sa-gowwa on his good work, the young man walking around his friends, taking their complements humbly yet proudly. It was quite a responsibility to be given to one so young, and he'd executed flawlessly. When he neared Dellis, he waved her over so they could speak in private.

"Ho-sa-gowwa, thank you for what you've done," she said, giving the young man his just praise. "Your mother would be so proud if she were still with us."

He blushed shyly, the slightest hue of pink softening his hard, ruddy complexion, reminding her that he was still just a boy of fourteen, yet one of the bravest in her village, and soon to be tested. They'd all be tested in a matter of hours. But it was sad to see one so young grow up so fast, to be so serious, his youth stolen the day their village was attacked. Ho-sa-gowwa lost both his mother and sister to DeLancie's men, and since that moment, the young man had been hellbent on revenge against the British, shedding his boyhood frivolity and donning a man's role in the tribe, a warrior's role. He ran a hand over his long, inky-black locks, his shy smile turning to a grim scowl. "I saw Just One and Cloud Walker."

"Where?" Her heart raced. Dellis grabbed his hand and pulled him farther into their secluded space, where they could speak without being overheard.

"Alexei is a prisoner. I saw Just One walking into the tent where he's kept."

Suddenly, hope took fear's place in her heart. Alexei was alive. *Gods be praised!* And John! "Are you going back to spy again?" She fought the urge to go after them, both so close, yet so far—a thousand men separating her from those she loved. A *thousand* men.

"Yes." Ho-sa-gowwa nodded.

Reaching into her pocket, she pulled out the necklace John gave her and handed it to the young warrior. "If it's safe, and you can get close to Just One, please, give that to him. Tell him to be safe." It broke her heart to part with the precious necklace, one of the few treasures she'd ever owned, but if it was her only means to communicate her love to John, then it was worth giving up.

"I'll find a way." Ho-sa-gowwa's dark eyes softened. "You be safe, Dellis."

"We prepare tonight, for tomorrow, we march off to war!" Han Yerry yelled, bringing on a fresh wave of whoops and hollers.

She and Ho-sa-gowwa joined the group while around her the warriors shouted with fervor, fists and tomahawks raised in the air, their lean, painted bodies practically vibrating with excitement. What they lacked in numbers they made up for in passion, for it was no barrage of men—ten-thousand warriors ready and willing to take on the British—no, it was only one hundred, if that.

Her soul ached for the plight of their little fighting force. Dellis fought back tears with a sniffle and a stiff upper lip. Bold they might be, even brave, but they were no match for the might of King George.

When John stepped out of the tent, he could already hear the characteristic whooping and hollering of the native braves: high-pitched howls, unrelenting, like a banshee's wail, a harbinger of death on the brink. The Gauntlet was ready.

The sentries dragged Anoki from the tent and untied his arms, throwing him on his hands and knees at the end of the lineup; behind him, Alexei walked slowly, dignified and reticent. Both men were shirtless and without shoes, wearing only their breechcloths.

Two lines of fifteen braves stood facing each other, consisting of Seneca, Mississauga, and Mohawk. First to face the gauntlet was Anoki; though he was one of the bravest and strongest of their village, his strength and fortitude would be tested. Even the most powerful of men went down under such a harsh beating.

John stood on the sidelines next to Miles, like a Roman Emperor and his General watching the gladiators from a plush little box above the crowd;

all they needed were scantily-clad women and drinks, and the scene would be set. Miles even brought a handful of cherries, one already stuck between his teeth while he sucked the pit out. Behind them, Eagle Eyes lurked, his commanding presence felt rather than seen. Their royal sentry was on guard.

Spitting the pit out on John's shoe, Miles popped another cherry in his mouth and pulled out the stem. "Carlisle, I know you have weakness for these Oneidas. Remember, I had the pleasure of meeting your native paramour. I know you were trying to protect these savages."

John kicked the pit off the toe of his shoe and then turned to his friend, giving him one last chance to consider his actions. "Miles, again, Alexei is the Duke of McKesson's nephew. I wouldn't do this if I were you."

Miles rolled his eyes and said, "That's *Lord Tomlinson* to you."

John clucked his tongue, thoroughly reprimanded and reminded of his place in the pecking order of society. A lifetime of friendship had ended in one moment.

"If McKesson dies, it's not by my hand, but his native brothers." Lord Tomlinson shrugged nonchalantly and then smiled. "Perhaps once he watches his brother go before him, sees what awaits, he might change his mind."

John shook his head.

Alexei's famous obstinacy was yet unknown to Miles. It seemed only right to enlighten him.

"Alexei will never yield. Never. Hence why we're in this predicament. This is all a waste, My…" Refusing to give him the satisfaction of hearing the words off John's lips, he choked them back.

"My Lord, Carlisle. You can do it." Miles laughed, giving John a sidelong glance full of mirth. "Striking fear into the heart of one's enemy is never a waste. Intimidation is the most effective form of warfare. The colonists are monitoring our every move, and so are their native allies. We're merely showing them that it's futile to resist."

Anoki's hands were tied together by a tall, intimidating Mohawk with a scalp lock bearing a plume of white and black feathers that sprouted forth from the crown of his head. That was the leader, the one who'd walk Anoki through the gauntlet. The braves in the lineup whooped and hollered in preparation, building on the burgeoning tension.

"You're weak, Carlisle." Miles clipped, spitting another pit out, his lips stained red from the succulent fruit.

"If you mean I have no taste for innocent blood, then yes, I must be weak." John shook his head out of utter disgust. Provoking brother to strike out at brother might be sport for the British, but it was about revenge for the broken Iroquois nation. It would only further deepen the rift that had been torn in the fabric of their confederacy.

As a warm summer breeze swept through the wilderness, rustling the leaves on the trees, John heard an echoing in the camp, bringing with it the faint familiar refrain of a woman singing. He turned his head towards the forest, the song of spirits calling to him again.

Justice...

"You'll regret this," he said, heeding their warning.

"I think not." Lord Tomlinson's expression was as impassive as his resolve. "McKesson took what's mine, and now, he'll pay the price. And soon, so shall you."

John snorted in response, rolling his eyes at Miles's sick sense of superiority. It was like an infection, festering and brewing, the British army just a microcosm of what existed in their society as a whole. John hated it. Hadn't his life been drastically altered by men who rendered him a pawn in a power play all because he lacked influence and social standing? But in his estimation, birthright didn't make one great, only through education and enlightenment had he truly seen the elite in men, and those, he found to be the most open minded and respectful of others. There was truth in Jefferson's words "all men were created equal."

"This should be entertaining, *John*. Remember, you're not an innocent party; much of this is your fault."

The Mohawk leader tugged at Anoki's bindings, testing them once, ready to lead him though the gauntlet at whatever pace, run or a walk, at the mercy of his torturers.

"Let the games begin," Miles said, grinning and waving his arm to commence.

There was no parade, no fanfare or sign bearer with a placard informing the crowd what was going to take place, but what Anoki faced was no less terrifying than the gladiator entering the ring to challenge a lion. And like the giver of the games, with a nod from Lord Tomlinson, the sentries pushed Anoki into the first row of braves, his leader taking only one small step. The first two warriors threw rocks at Anoki's head, both landing crushing blows to his cheeks, drawing blood that oozed on impact. He shook it off bravely, following his leader, who meandered slowly, allowing the next group of men to take direct hits, pounding on Anoki's back with loud smacks, leaving red prints on his ruddy skin. From every direction, the braves whipped rocks at him, pelting him in the face and on the body, leaving little bloody marks everywhere they hit. Next came the lashes from tree branches, whipping and slicing at Anoki's back and sides, leaving long, bloody tracks of flayed-open flesh and tender, exposed meat.

The leader took his time, forcing Anoki to go slow. Losing his patience, the brave Oneida roared, trying to push through, racing to mid-point. From below, one of the braves hit him in the back of the knees with a large branch, dropping Anoki in the dirt.

John held his breath as the men slapped and pounded Anoki into the ground, descending on him like wolves consuming an injured deer. His leader took a club and pounded Anoki in the back and then delivered one hard blow to the back of his head, blood spurting from the wound, a crimson geyser shooting into the air.

Alexei paced back and forth, yelling in Oneida, "*Hanyo Takλ'nλsa'nikulyak!* Come on, you can do it! Get up, Anoki. You're Oneida. You fear nothing. Our ancestors will protect you."

Anoki fought, kicking and flailing, as his leader yanked on the ropes, dragging the Oneida through the dirt and leaves that littered the ground as each consecutive group of braves took their shots at him.

John stomach lurched; he swallowed back the urge to vomit while every scar on his body twitched and ached with horror. Having been tortured himself, he'd wish it on no man, not even his worst adversary.

"Miles?" He gasped, but his former friend didn't hear, nor did he catch John's breach in protocol, engrossed in the proceedings with rapt amusement.

"Aren't you entertained, John?" Miles's dark eyes flashed with excitement, his voice jovial. It was like looking at Cesar himself, awaiting the moment when he turned thumbs up or down to Anoki's life.

"This is barbary." John seethed.

The leader yanked at Anoki's bindings, but he was no longer fighting back, his limp body easily dragged over the rough terrain while the braves continued taking shots at him.

"You do realize, if he doesn't complete his run, he'll have to start over again," Miles said so nonchalantly it stoked John's ire.

"If he's not already dead!" He hissed through clenched teeth.

"*Ohná:kλ' nukwa!* Behind you!" Alexei yelled above the whooping, trying to spur his friend on, but it was no use, Anoki lay lifeless on the ground. The leader deposited Anoki's motionless body in the grass at the end of the gauntlet, never once checking to see if he was still alive.

"Come with me," Miles said over his shoulder, walking towards Alexei.

The leader tied up Alexei's hands, testing the knot with a few hard tugs.

Lord Tomlinson stood face to face with Alexei, unable to look down at man of such impressive height. "You have one last chance to tell me where my Wilhelmina is."

It was silent save the roaring of John's blood through his veins and the thundering of his heart against his ribcage.

The two men stared each other down yet said nothing. Alexei tall and proud with natural, God-given strength in his six-foot-five frame, and Miles in his crimson uniform with gold adornments and a noble title, power bestowed on him by man. Had they faced each other on the field of battle, man to man, there was no doubt who would've won, but it wasn't a fair fight.

Finally, Miles cracked the silence with a laugh. "I promise you, they won't make it as easy for you as they did your friend."

Though Alexei's head didn't move, he directed his gaze at John, ignoring the taunts. No words were spoken, but John understood what he saw in Alexei's icy gaze. *Protect the woman. Protect Dellis and the village.* Once, they were bitter rivals—enemies—but at that moment, everything Alexei held dear he entrusted to John. He closed his eyes and then opened them, a silent promise to a man who faced his death. A man John respected.

"Fine." Miles hissed. "Die, Oneida."

Miles waved his hand, and the leader tugged the ropes, pulling Alexei into the first row of the gauntlet. As with Anoki, the braves threw rocks, hitting Alexei in the side of the head, one drawing blood, the others just grazing his neck, leaving bloody tracks.

John watched stoically, though his stomach churned and pitched, threatening to eat itself inside out. What would he tell Dellis? How would he explain it to her?

Once again, the leader took his time, but unlike Anoki, Alexei didn't try to run, following the pace as they moved slowly, row by row, dodging and sidestepping their blows. When one of the braves took a branch to Alexei's knees, like a tree with roots deep in the earth, he braced his feet and bent his knees against the bone-crushing hit. His tall, powerful frame was rocked back and forth, but he held fast, steady like a great oak. The leader, shorter than Alexei by at least four inches, brought the club down on his side, hitting him in the kidney. He winced yet still threw his shoulders back, pushing through with strength that Hercules himself would admire.

The braves, excited by Alexei's endurance, started to whoop and holler, one throwing a club at him, hitting him in the upper arm. The leader took another swing, his club connecting with Alexei's back, again with another hit to the kidney. He winced and coughed, blood spattering from his mouth, a sticky, scarlet stream running down his chin.

As he neared the end of the rows, John let out a breath, grateful it was almost over, and his adversary turned friend was relatively unscathed. But then he noticed some activity at the end of the line; several braves were carrying torches and filling a small pit. An extra obstacle was being prepared. Hot coals.

The last two warriors pulled out their clubs, swinging at Alexei; one landed a blow to the side of his face, the other on his injured arm, hitting it several times until it fell limp at his side.

Fearlessly, and without hesitation, Alexei walked the coals, the red-hot rocks steaming with each press of his large feet against them. He took his paces, slowly and methodically. The veins in his neck strained against his taut, sun-kissed skin, threatening to burst from pain, while his face turned the color of the cherries Miles chewed with delight.

Finally, when Alexei reached the end, he stood proud—victorious. The leader untied Alexei's hands, turning him to face the gauntlet. The braves whooped and hollered in respect for his strength and fortitude. He raised his hand and pointed to the heavens, a sign of his reverence to God for seeing him through and his prowess as a warrior of the Standing Stone.

John let out a breath of relief; his eyes trained to Anoki, who was still lying lifeless in the grass.

"Take the prisoners to their tent and tie them up!" Lord Tomlinson turned back to John and spit out another pit, that one landing on his tunic. "I'll find a way to wring the truth out of that Oneida. He *will* tell me where my Wilhelmina is. I swear it." Thrusting a still-sticky red finger in his face, Miles added, "Feel lucky St. Leger likes you, or you might have faced the gauntlet yourself."

Eagle Eyes followed behind, and in a low voice, John heard the native say, "Lord Tomlinson, I have someone I think you should meet."

Who's he talking about?

Chapter
Thirty-Six

"Clark, we have to find out if Anoki is still alive." John walked deftly through the rough terrain and canvas tents, dodging men walking in the opposite direction carrying wood and supplies into camp. Under the layers of clothing, he was soaking wet, a combination of blistering heat and frazzled nerves from watching two men be nearly bludgeoned to death. His heart still raced, and his stomach twisted like a rope into hundreds of knots; the sight of Anoki lying motionless in the grass a vision John would never forget.

"What if Lord Tomlinson finds out we went to see them?" Clark asked, fast on John heels.

"Right now, I care not. If we're discovered, I'll say we were checking their wounds."

Once to the prisoner's tent, the sentry simply stepped aside, allowing John and Clark to enter. Inside, Alexei sat on the ground, blindfolded, his arms tied behind him to the tent post, his feet also bound. Lying on a cot in the corner, arms still tied together with rope, was Anoki, his body unmoving save fevered pants and an occasional jostle of his head.

John got down on his knees and whispered into Alexei's ear, "Say nothing. I'm going to check on Anoki and then I'll come back and speak to you." Over his shoulder, John waved Simon over. "We need to assess their wounds so we can report to the surgeon."

Alexei nodded as the blindfold was pulled down.

His face was a mass of bloody cuts, black and blue bruises swelling underneath the blindfold circling his eyes. His upper lip was split at the point, dried blood caked and crusted there, turning deep, reddish brown, a scab yet to form. At the back of his head was a large bloody cut that ran sticky, crimson red down his neck, soaking the collar of his tunic. His right hand was blue and purple, all of his fingers swollen like fat sausages, unable to close or grasp.

John rushed to Anoki, taking a seat on the cot next to him. Like Alexei, Anoki's face was a mass of bloody cuts and bruises, his long, black hair wet and plastered to his sweaty forehead. He took quick, shallow breaths, reaching for precious air with every last effort of his powerful frame. John ran his hands down Anoki's sides, finding the source of his distress—a knife wound in his side. The lung was punctured; it was only a matter of time.

Leaning in, John brought his lips close to the brave's ear. "Anoki, it's Just One. Your lung is punctured; you don't have long for this world."

The brave's eyes rolled open, bloodshot and red, barely visible through his meaty, swollen lids.

"Is there anything you want me to do for you?"

"Help them," Anoki whispered through cracked, parched lips. "Help them, Just One."

"I will. I swear it." A promise to a dying man, though John knew not how he'd ever keep it.

"Joseph, Kateri, Alexei…"

"I know."

Anoki started coughing, gurgling as blood seeped between his lips and dribbled down his chin. Death tapped his strength.

John reached into his tunic pocket, pulled out one of Dellis's embroidered handkerchiefs, and wiped the warrior's chin clean.

Anoki's swollen, broken hand pointed to the silver cuff on his other wrist. "It's yours now. It was given to me for my first kill as a warrior. I'd give you my tomahawk if I still had it."

John removed the crude metal cuff from Anoki's wrist and put it on. The brave coughed again, straining and fighting, blood bubbling up and spewing from his lips one last time, and then his eyes rolled shut, forever closed.

Thumbs down. The gladiator lost.

John bowed his head, closing his eyes in reverence to the brave warrior's spirit. "Protect your people from the other side, Anoki. I relieve you of your duty to the village. Be at peace."

Tears brimmed John's lids, blurring his vision, but he fought against them, keeping his emotions in check. He walked back to the tent pole, his wrist feeling strangely heavy under the weight of Anoki's cuff—and the promise.

Clark looked up at John. "Alexei's wrist might be broken; I can't tell with the bindings. The rest are just cuts and bruises. He fared remarkably well for the beating he took."

"My back, my side, it hurts like the devil." Alexei choked out. "How is Anoki?"

John did something he always did when giving sad news to his men, he got down on his haunches and met Alexei at eye level. "He didn't make it. I'm sorry."

"Anoki was a brave warrior. He went first so that I might observe. If it were not for him, I would never have survived."

"Yes," John replied, knowing it was true.

Clark inspected Alexei's side and his back, carefully lifting his shirt, trying not to move him too much. "You have some ugly bruises on your back over your kidneys. Likely you'll piss blood for a few days, but you seem to be all right otherwise."

"What now?" Alexei asked, looking at both of them.

"I don't know. Miles won't relent. The only thing I can do is get word to Merrick; he'll put a stop to this."

Alexei let out a choked laugh and then winced in pain. "The idea of Uncle Dane being my saving grace is laughable, much less you as my ally."

"Agreed." John snorted. "How times have changed."

He stood, wiping his hands off on his handkerchief and righting his clothes. Perspiration wet his brow and forehead, plastering tendrils of hair in place. He brushed them back, the melted tallow in his hair gooey on his hand as he smoothed and coiffed himself and then pulled Alexei's blindfold back up. "I'll send the surgeon to tend you. Come with me, Clark."

Once outside, John and Clark walked slowly back to their tent, the sounds of native whooping carrying over the camp between the occasional *pop* of gunshots and thunderous drumrolls. Snipers in the woods fired at the fort, trying to take out the guards on the bastions. The forest was covered in a dark, acrid cloud of smoke from the British setting fire to Stanwix's outer barracks. Still, their efforts did little damage to the wooden fort so adeptly designed to manage the long siege.

As John and Clark reached their tent, a messenger raced up to them. "Captain Carlisle, you're to report to General St. Leger's tent immediately."

John looked back at Clark and gave him terse, quiet orders. "Send for the surgeon to tend Alexei. I'll meet you here when I'm finished. Get Smith. Hurry."

"General St. Leger, you requested my presence?" John asked, lifting the flap to the tent. Inside, he found himself in illustrious company: Major Butler, Indian Deputy Superintendent of the Western Expedition; Colonel John Johnson, St. Leger's second-in-command; Colonel Daniel Claus, Indian Superintendent of the Western Expedition; Chiefs Old Smoke and Cornplanter of the Seneca; and Joseph Brant of the Mohawk.

"Good! Captain Carlisle, we require your skills at mapmaking and your knowledge of the local terrain," St. Leger said, his Irish accent deepening with the gravity of his words.

Not so long before, John yearned for such a meeting, where his services were of dire need and the opportunity to distinguish himself was ripe—

finally, he was being recognized for his accomplishments. Yet, in the face of his promise to Anoki, with all that John knew and loved at stake, he felt consternation, his feet heavy and hesitant as he walked toward the table.

"What can I do for you, sir?" He kept his focus on the General, though John could feel all eyes on him. The energy in the tent was like a dry field during an electrical storm, quick to ignite with the slightest spark. Joseph Brant, in particular, eyed John suspiciously.

"One of our spies got word to us that Schuyler is sending reinforcements to Stanwix, at least eight-hundred men."

"Is your spy reliable?" John asked.

"Molly Brant, Captain," Butler said, glaring at John.

As sister to Joseph Brant, and life partner of the deceased Superintendent, William Johnson, she was as reliable a spy as one could hope for and very well connected.

"Well then, tell me what you need."

"Our friend here, Joseph Brant, has a plan. We need you to tell us if it's possible."

John glanced at the infamous Mohawk, noting his ruddy complexion and his strong, hawk-like features, made more severe by the traditional scalp lock that left him bald save the tuft of hair jutting forth from the crown of his head. His clothing was sumptuous: a fine, tightly-woven linen shirt dressed up with a shimmering silver gorget tied around his neck by a black silk kerchief, and underneath, a large wooden cross hanging from a silver chain. As expected, he had on traditional buckskin leggings with elaborately decorated moccasins on his feet. Allying with the King had been good to Brant, making him a wealthy man and a worthy adversary.

John addressed Brant with a nod. "Tell me your plan, Chief?"

"The colonists will be coming from the east, down the old military trails from German Flats towards Stanwix," Brant said in his low, distinct voice.

John reached into his tunic and pulled out the maps from his breast pocket. Nervously, he fumbled through them, looking for the ones he made when he was living at The Thistle. Dropping one on the ground, General St. Leger leaned over and picked it up, taking a moment to unfold it.

With a grin, St. Leger pointed to the paper. "An interesting map you have here, but have you marked off all the strategic places a man should pay attention to when in pursuit?"

"Excuse me?" John eyes widened with confusion, and then suddenly, it dawned on him what the General was referring to. "I'm sorry, sir. That wasn't meant—"

"She's quite striking." The General turned the picture, taking a moment to admire it. "Is this your wife?"

John bit back a *yes* for her protection; the fewer people who knew about his association with Dellis, the better. "A former mistress."

"One so lovely should not be former, Captain. When this war is over, if I were you, I'd remedy that situation… with haste. And the good thing is, the war *will* be over very soon." The General handed the picture to John. He folded it up and stuck it back in his tunic, close to his heart.

With a deep breath, John unfolded one of the maps and placed on the table. "Sir, this shows all the military roads from Fort Dayton in German Flats and the path through the forest to Stanwix."

John pointed to the map, drawing an imaginary line with his finger. "The best place to approach the colonists would be here." With his fingertip, he directed their attention to a little spot on the map near Oriska. "There are two ravines; at the bottom of the first one is a swamp and a small bridge, and after that, the road does a sharp climb and then turns southwest to bypass another ravine just over here." He pointed to the right of the road. "The road turns west, climbs through the woods, and then dips into another ravine and across another creek." He looked up at St. Leger and the men standing around the table observing. "This is a perfect location; you have the advantage. The colonists will be on low ground, condensed as a group, and unable to see due to the thick foliage and the slope of the road."

"This is what I said!" Joseph Brant yelled, pointing to the map. "You trust his word and not mine?"

"No, my friend," St. Leger said calmly, putting his hands up, trying to placate the volatile Mohawk. "We merely wanted to confirm it. As you can see, Captain Carlisle was able to provide us with a map we can use to better plan your strategy."

"I disagree with this whole idea. We outnumber the Rebels here at Stanwix, and we can outnumber them on the road. Why not send a parley before this turns into a bloody battle?" Colonel Johnson asked.

"I agree." Butler added, "This could turn into an ambush, and it may not be necessary. We should parley."

"You're weak fools. They won't parley! Don't you understand?" Brant yelled, his face turning red with rage. "Not a week ago I encountered Cox and some of the militia. They're preparing to fight to the death. The Oneida and Tuscarora have sided with them; surely, they'll be there, too. It's a betrayal, both by the colonists and our brothers. We must strike swiftly and now! If you're not brave enough, my men and I will go alone."

"Brant, we're just as disturbed by the actions of our brothers, but if we can try and salvage our relations, then we should," Cornplanter said, his calm voice in stark contrast to the rantings of the Mohawk.

St. Leger's eyes flashed to John. "How should we do this?"

The weight of the world had once again been thrust on his shoulders, but he held on tightly, rising to the challenge. "What men are you taking with you?"

"Colonel Johnson will lead the group with two-hundred men, consisting of rangers and some Jägers; Joseph Brant and Cornplanter will bring five hundred of their natives to assist."

John looked at the map, sizing up the attack. "I'd wait until the full brigade was between the two ravines, catch them when the rear is on the bridge of the first ravine and the front regiment is climbing the slope of the second ravine. You have the perfect locale for a frontal assault of the first regiment; hit them hard and prevent them from advancing, and they won't be able to back up or move with the rest of their men coming up the ravine. They'll be trapped in the lowland. Then, the rest of the men can attack the body of the army in-between on the high ground. Have a group on either side of the road taking shots at them. Make sure you bring Lights; you'll need your best shooters to be effective in the environment. The forest is so dense in that area that it practically blocks out the sun."

"Is this not what I told you!" Brant raged again.

"Yes, it is." General St. Leger nodded at Brant in appreciation. "Thank You, Captain Carlisle, for your information. It was most helpful."

John stepped back, his eyes scanning the map, making sure every detail he provided was correct. After a moment of quiet, St. Leger spoke. "Tomorrow morning, we strike. Colonel Johnson, you'll lead the contingent, and Brant will coordinate and plan the attack. It's settled."

With a grin, St. Leger waved for his guard to come over. "Get our servant. We need a round of drinks to toast our victory."

Brant scooped up the maps from the table and walked to Colonel Johnson, eager to get started with the planning. A heady sensation came over John, elated from having so many important men listen to him— respect him. He'd proven his value in spades to the General.

A servant woman handed John a dram, and when he turned around, everyone was waiting, prepared to toast.

"To our victory," Colonel Johnson said.

St. Leger lifted his glass in salute to John and then Brant. "To our friends, Captain Carlisle and Joseph Brant, for their brilliant plan."

John threw back his tot of fine Irish whiskey, the warmth seeping into his blood, soothing his nerves.

Putting down the glass, he walked to the opening of the tent; through the flap, he could hear whispering. It was Cornplanter and Old Smoke. "Our brothers will surely be with the colonists. We can't fire on them. They're like wayward children right now, but striking at them won't bring them back to the confederacy. We can't do this."

Chapter Thirty-Seven

"Well, well, if it isn't James McKesson," a sweet, seductive voice said from over James's shoulder.

"As always, your timing is impeccable, Mrs. Allen." He turned around in his chair, the bar at his back.

Celeste took a seat next to him, overdressed and over coiffed, as usual, her lavender dress and powdered high roll much too formal for the dining room of The Kettle. He never liked that look, not even when he was at court with socialites and noble women throwing themselves at him—hence why he fell for Helena. She was strikingly beautiful even though she wore her hair natural and kept her clothes simple, avoiding the ostentatious and gaudy look, unlike the rest of the peacocks at court.

"It's been far too long, Mr. McKesson." Celeste ran her fingers down the sleeve of his worsted chocolate-brown overcoat, stopping at the cuff where she toyed with the lace of his shirt.

Wanting none of her flirtation, he pulled his hand away abruptly. "What do you want?"

She smiled, not a sweet, innocent smile, or the simpering one of a coy debutant, but the sly grin of Lilith. "I stumbled on a bit of information I think you'd be interested in hearing. Should we go up to my room, and I'll enlighten you?"

Gently, Celeste ran her tapered fingernail over the dorsum of his hand, tracing the little veins that pushed through the skin. The sensation wasn't unpleasant, simply unwanted, like all of her advances; he found them uninspiring next to the touch of his wife. His blood boiled for Helena alone, his Russian beauty, the one he sacrificed everything for.

"Whatever you have to say, you can say it to me here. I have no desire to visit your lair again."

Celeste pursed her lips, an unattractive wrinkle forming in her brow, clearly irritated with his rebuff. He held back a laugh, relishing her frustration. Oh, how he loved disappointing her. The woman needed to learn her place; negotiation was for men, and it was a whore's job to lie on her back and fuck for a living.

"Fine. I can leave, but I just thought you should know"—pausing, she leaned into him, her lips a whisper away from touching his earlobe—"I found the woman."

A chill ran down his spine; not from the warmth of her breath on his flesh, but from sudden excitement. "Where is she?"

With a grin and a shake of her head, she let out a laugh. "You really think I'm going to just tell you after you've ignored me for so long?"

James's temper flared; her games had run their course on his thin patience. Grabbing her hand, he yanked her towards him and then pulled his knife from his belt and pushed into her side. "Where is she?"

Celeste let out a feminine gasp. "Fine. I'll take you to her."

"Yes, you will." He released her so abruptly she stumbled backwards, grabbing onto the bar for support.

"Follow me," she said with a coquettish grin, recovering quickly enough to practically skip to the door.

Celeste led him west, through town, suspiciously in the direction of The Thistle. When they stopped at the front steps of his brother's house, she turned to James and grinned. "All this time, she was right here, under your nose, and you didn't even know it."

Looking up at the dilapidated old house, James still couldn't put the pieces together—it made no sense; he knew of no other woman at The Thistle save the darkie slave Dellis bought.

Much to his annoyance, Celeste laughed as if the answer was so clear yet he lacked the intelligence to see it. "The dish boy, Will? He's not actually a boy, but a woman in disguise. Poof!" She fanned her fingers out abruptly, simulating a puff of smoke.

James shook his head. "You're mad, woman."

"I'm not. Will, the dish boy, is Wilhelmina Parkhurst. If you don't believe me, ask your nephew, Stuart. He told me yesterday that he came to retrieve some of his clothing, and she was wearing them."

"Stuart is crazy; you're a fool if you believe what he says."

Again, Celeste laughed. "He's not that crazy, even DeLancie knew that, hence why he used Stuart to capture your niece."

Sensing potential truth in her words, James rushed up the steps and pounded on the front door. The house was silent and dark, the windows closed and the shutters pulled. Kicking the door handle, the bolt cracked off the wood frame, sending the door flying open; a little tornado of dust flew into the air as sunshine lit the dining room.

"Dellis!" James crossed the threshold, rushing through the bar to the kitchen, but the house was empty. "Dellis!" he yelled, racing up the front stairs, throwing open the doors to all the bedrooms.

He stomped down the stairs out the front door. "Where's my niece?"

"I have no idea. I saw her yesterday," Celeste said innocently.

"She must be at the village." James walked to the back of the house and threw open the door to the stable, but both Dellis's horses, the mare and the stallion, were gone, and so were their saddles.

Walking back out into the road, James rushed to the neighbor's house several yards away and pounded on the door; a slight, elderly woman opened it, her eyes wide when she saw him. "Mr. McKesson, what can I do for you?"

"Have you seen my niece? I'm worried about her what with the British being spotted nearby."

The woman shook her head. "I stay away from that woman and her heathen ways."

As the old woman went to slam to door in James's face, a younger man stepped up behind her, musket in hand, a haversack exploding with food and supplies slung over his shoulder. "Grandma, who's at the door?"

Before she could speak, James pushed the door open farther and stepped inside. The little wooden house was modest inside, almost no decoration, just a large fireplace and hearth with some chairs set around it. Beyond that, he could see a small room in the back that looked to be someone's living quarters. It reminded him of the dwelling he and Helena had shared when they first moved to the frontier, and he'd be back there soon if he didn't find the woman.

"Excuse me, I'm looking for my niece; she owns The Thistle tavern. Can you help me?"

The boy was quiet for a moment, the wheels turning behind his young, dark eyes. "Patrick Armstrong and the magistrate just got word around town that the British have arrived at Fort Stanwix. All the available men were to report to Fort Dayton to join General Herkimer's militia, and the women and children followed for safety. Knowing her skills at healing and her kindly nature, I'm sure she and her workers went to help. I know I saw Mr. Armstrong pulling a cart full of supplies with him; it was probably goods from the tavern to take to the fort."

"Thank you," James replied, making his way through the door. "You've been most helpful."

Once down the steps, he walked back towards The Thistle; fast on his heels, he could hear Mrs. Allen's puffing and groaning as she tried to keep up with him.

"Wait," she yelled, but he ignored her, kicking up dust with every pound of his heels on the ground.

Celeste coughed several times but kept on him. "Stop for a moment and think; rushing into a fort will do little good. Patience. They'll come back after the battle has ceased. One way or the other, I don't anticipate the British will lay siege to a fort full of helpless women and children."

James whirled around and pointed a finger in her over-painted, over-preened face. "Mrs. Allen, you're a fool. That's exactly what the British will do, but they'll send their savages to handle the dirty work."

Celeste panted, her olive cheeks flushed with exertion. "That might be so, but it won't happen right now. Don't you see? I've given you the means to find the woman; have patience, and the opportunity will present itself."

She waved her hand, gesturing towards The Thistle. "Why don't we search the house for clues? Perhaps they've hidden the money inside?"

Though James hated to admit it, Celeste was right. Dellis and the woman would come back eventually—that was when he'd strike. As they walked back inside the abandoned house, he stopped in the dining room, remembering the last time he saw Stephen alive. Their last argument had taken place right there.

"James, let this go. Admit what you've done, and we'll find a way to move forwards from here."

James let out a laugh, shaking his head at the naïveté of his younger brother. "Stephen, I'd rather drown in Malmsey wine than pray for Dane's forgiveness. It's you who turned on me; do you so conveniently forget? Smiling, James said, "You'll pay, brother, just as I have. You'll lose everything you hold dear, just as you tried to strip it away from me."

"James? James?"

"You don't get to call me by my given name, woman." He hissed. "We're not acquaintances. We're not even business partners."

The memories of his brother and their last moments together tore open an old, festering wound. Stephen and Dane had taken James's birthright and left him with nothing. Once again, he was back to scrounging for money to keep himself solvent—searching for a missing heiress was beneath him.

"We *are* business partners." Celeste countered, stepping into his line of sight, but he ignored her. "We're in this together. I found the woman for you, and you were going to invest in my business—that's how this works."

He laughed. At least there was one speck of triumph in his rapidly crumbling world. "We can't be partners, Mrs. Allen. It's impossible."

"What are you talking about?" Her hazel eyes narrowed as she planted her fists on her hips defiantly, putting on her usual stubborn act. "What do you mean?"

"You don't have a business anymore," James said, the hilarity of her predicament forcing him to stifle a laugh, though it fought its way out as a snicker.

"What do you mean?" She stomped her foot like an angry, petulant child, her eyes shooting daggers at him.

But he couldn't contain himself, another snort bursting forth. He turned to her, purposefully wanting to see her face when he told her the truth. Finally, he could put the bitch in her place and be done with her.

"When I got to Niagara, I was expecting to find the grand establishment you boasted of; instead, it was in shambles, raided by natives. All your whores were dead, scalped and tortured, and the building had been burned to the ground. There was nothing left. And from what I understand, McKenzie fled town once his trading post was raided by the same group of natives."

Her mouth dropped open, her olive skin blanching ghostly white.

"Rumor has it, your house was destroyed by a very powerful Mohawk and his band of natives." With a grin and a wink, James said, "Butler was most grateful for your contribution to the cause."

Celeste let out a howl, lunging at him, her fingernails digging into his cheeks, drawing blood as they tugged tracks through his skin.

He grabbed her wrists and then pushed her back with just enough force so she landed on her bottom, her mountainous skirts throwing up dust when she hit the floor.

"You bastard! I'll make you pay for this."

James relished her fury, the tears of frustration brimming her lids like little drops of sunshine in his day. How dare she try to manipulate him; he was no idiot like his son or a scoundrel with an overactive cock like Carlisle. James had played every one of her games and then some before he met her.

"I'll get even with you. I know about the woman. I know what you've been up to. I'll tell the truth about you!" She seethed through clenched teeth, slamming her fists on the wooden floor.

"No one will believe you. You're finished, Mrs. Allen. You have no money, no business, and you're a woman—an old one at that—whose bloom has long since passed. Now, you're carrying the bastard child of… Who knows? You'd do well to kill that brat and start selling yourself on the streets while you're still somewhat desirable."

Reaching for a wooden bucket near her feet, she grabbed a brush from inside and whipped it at him, just missing his head. "I'll make you pay for what you've done."

James laughed at the incredulity of the situation. He stepped closer to her as she tried to get up but made no move to help her. When she looked up, her face was in proximity with his front flap. "You do have one talent working in your favor; you're rather good at sucking cock. That should earn you a bit of money." With a lift of his brow, he walked past her. "Goodbye, Mrs. Allen, and thank you for the information. It'll be most useful."

He heard her clanking around behind him, and then a poker from the fireplace flew through the air, hitting the wall next to the door. "You bastard! I'll see you in Hell!"

James turned back to her, nodded, and tipped his hat in salute. "Until then."

Chapter Thirty-Eight

The last six miles to Fort Stanwix were hellish at best, an arduous, slow advance through the humid, mosquito-infested forest. Early that morning, before the company moved out, Dellis and the women of her tribe made the militia welcome, pouring coffee and passing out porridge and biscuits to the soldiers. Amongst them, she found Stuart and Ruslan jovially resting against a tree, playing cards, tankards of flip sitting on the ground next to them. She had no words for Stuart, her heart still hardened after what he'd done, but Ruslan, ever sweet and gentle, hugged her and kissed her cheek. "Be safe today, cousin."

"You as well, and keep watch on him." She eyed Stuart, but he ignored her, pretending to retie the patch around his head and then adjusting it in place.

"I will."

Dellis wrapped her cousin up in another loving hug, praying it wouldn't be the last time she saw him.

When breakfast was finished, she readied herself, checking the pistol in her pocket and the one at her hip, then making sure she had enough cartridges for loading muskets. Orders from General Herkimer came down to Han Yerry; the Oneida were to flank the main body of the brigade, and six of their best scouts were to travel ahead and report back any news. The regiments would march in two lines: Colonel Cox and the First Canajoharie Regiment was to take the lead; next, Colonel Klock and the Second Palatine Regiment; then, Colonel Bellinger and his Forth Kingsland and German Flats Regiment, followed by the fifteen baggage wagons; and finally, the Third Mohawk Regiment as rear guard, commanded by Colonel Visscher.

As Dellis mounted her horse and took her place next to her grandfather, she looked over her shoulder at the ragtag group of soldiers and let out a breath, feeling her anxiety rise in anticipation of the march. She spotted Patrick in the lineup with the Forth Regiment; not far behind him, Stuart and Ruslan were chatting, both checking their muskets as if nothing significant was about to happen.

When the pages of history are written, will this day be remembered as a tragedy or a triumph? And will anyone know the sacrifice of my people?

If they were to lose the battle, the colonists would continue to fight, their numbers much like ants, dividing rapidly in succession, but her people, one thousand souls, a tenth of them present, would be devastated.

"Grandfather, none of these men are continentals?" she asked, glancing back and forth, taking in the mass of soldiers lining up around them. Yes, they were almost a thousand men strong, but they were unruly, far from the well-trained British Regulars she'd witnessed at Fort Niagara.

"Fear not, Fennishyo; remember, they, too, are defending their homeland, just as we are. It's what's in their hearts that counts."

Hearts and passions wouldn't fell British Redcoats or stop their notorious rapid-fire lineup that could volley continuous rounds of shot. Dellis ignored the sense of foreboding that sent chills racing up and down her spine and said a quick prayer for their safety. As she'd once told John, they were on the side of the angels, and God would make powerful their swords. *Have mercy on us.* The rhythmic *tap-tapping* of the drums sounded, rolling out the forwards march, sending the stagnant body of soldiers into motion.

"We're leaving now?" she asked as General Herkimer rode past on his beautiful white horse, looking stalwart and dignified, ready to direct the advance. "I thought we were to wait until the cannons fired at Fort Stanwix, Grandfather?"

"The General has changed his mind," Han Yerry said, riding up on his handsome chestnut gelding, shoulders back proudly, looking every bit the war chief.

"But was that not the plan? We were to wait until the cannons fired at the fort to launch our attack?" Her frazzled nerves were getting the better of her, and she was suddenly frantic, as if she were trapped in a dark, tight place with no way out. She looked around, wide eyed, goosebumps dotting her flesh, though underneath her clothes, she was sticky with sweat.

Her grandfather reached over and patted her hand. "Fennishyo, in battle, plans change quickly. We must follow the General. You must listen now."

She nodded, ignoring the unease that gnawed at her stomach; the men seemed ragged and undisciplined to her, and totally under equipped, but at least she had Oneidas close to her, the finest of their fighting force. Riding near her and her grandfather were Han Yerry and Two Kettles Together; behind her, Cornelius and Blatcop. Thomas and Edward Spencer were flanking the soldiers a little closer to the front of the line, their keen eyes on the lookout.

"It's time for you to be brave, my Fennishyo," her grandfather said sweetly, though his head remained turned away, his gaze focused forwards. Like the rest of the men, he wore only his leggings and breechcloth, his torso and face covered in red and black war paint, all of them armed with a tomahawk, a knife, and a musket. She, too, had her pistols at her sides, the knife she'd taken from John, and a musket strapped to her saddle. In her haversack, she'd brought a canteen of water and John's picture, her most-prized possession, and hopefully, a good luck talisman to see her through the day.

As they pushed off, a flock of ravens burst from the trees, inky and black, crossing the overcast sky with a shriek. All her tribesmen saw it, dark eyes glancing back and forth at each other, but no one said a word. There was no turning back.

A brigade of a thousand men does not move swiftly, so Dellis learned. The trek was slow through the heavily-wooded forest, the sweltering heat and humidity making the already-fatigued army sluggish, their ranks lazily breaking, spreading out over a mile. She was unused to the slow, laborious movements of a giant army, having only been involved in the quicksilver, ambush-style fighting of her people; so efficient were they that battles were often over before they even started. With such a large, noisy group, they were an easy target, proverbial sitting ducks for the British.

As her group descended into the ravine, blessed shade gave them relief from the sun, and slowly, the lead section of the brigade crossed the small bridge over the marshy land and started up the other side. She always loved the place as a child, a hidden valley where she could traipse through the lush green and play in the river while her mother and father went fishing. In spite of the soldiers' chatter and the noise of wagons, it was strangely peaceful, ominously so.

The middle regiments and the Oneida worked their way up the other side of the ravine, the supply wagons and rear guard crossing the bridge, the sound of ox hooves pounding on wooden boards echoing around in the valley.

Great Bear hesitated, pulling the reins of his horse, waiting for Joseph and Dellis to catch up.

"There's something not right with the forest." Her uncle's words were meant for Joseph's ears only, but she heard them. "Joseph, do you feel it?"

"I feel it." She interjected.

"*Sa-sa-kwon!*" A great shout reverberated around the earthen ravine walls, followed by a pop so loud it could've shattered one's eardrums, buckling the precious membranes with brute force.

She let out a scream and grabbed her ears, her eyes wildly scanning the trees as hundreds of muskets fired simultaneously, an impenetrable cloud of smoke making a horseshoe around the lead regiment in the ravine up ahead as hundreds of bodies dropped to the grass instantly.

Then came the banshee's wail in the form of war whooping, bringing with it the screams of the injured and those that faced the onslaught of native warriors from the front. They were everywhere. Dellis whipped her head back and forth, overcome with fear.

Men were high in the trees, over the edge of the ravine, left and right, running directly into the injured soldiers, finishing them off with tomahawks and knives. It happened so fast, she couldn't blink, fearing she'd miss something. Blood spattered in the air rhythmically as the chopping of steel blades connected with bone and flesh; screams of terror mixed with sounds of muskets popping as a massacre ensued right before her eyes.

"Oh my God, Grandfather." She gasped, pulling both pistols from her pack. "What do we do?"

"We fight," Han Yerry yelled, breaking formation and rushing forwards, leading his Oneida into the fray. Joseph followed, Thomas and Edward Spencer, and even Great Bear, advancing with their chief.

Dellis's heart thundered in her chest, fear making it difficult to form a cohesive thought. *What do I do? Where do I go?* Behind her, the rear guard was retreating, native warriors chasing after them, picking soldiers off one after another, bodies dropping into the thick foliage like apples falling from a tree.

As she turned around to head for the woods, a bullet whizzed by her, the metal searing her flesh as it skimmed across the delicate skin of her cheek. Reflexively, she dropped one of her pistols and grabbed her face, blood from the wound dripping down her hand. Her mare wasn't trained for battle; fearfully, it bucked and reared, and Dellis grabbed the reins tightly, but it threw her on the grass and bolted away.

With a thud, Dellis landed on her back, her teeth digging into her lip so hard she bit through, drawing fresh blood. Another bullet struck the ground near her, dirt flying up in the air, a metal ball just missing her leg. She grabbed her sack and pistols and scurried behind one of the trees. All around her, the staccato noise of muskets popping and the howls of the injured carried above the fray. Panic set in when she looked up and couldn't see any of her people; all the Oneida, even the women, were nowhere to be found. What happened to them?

Am I alone?

Scooting out from her hiding place, she crept through the brush as another bullet came flying from high above in the trees, striking one of the soldiers fighting on the road. She followed the path of the bullet up to an ancient maple tree flanking the road, its large, pointed leaves camouflaging a Mohawk warrior, picking off soldiers one by one with deadly accuracy. Dellis circled back, keeping eyes on him as he reloaded. Fear made her hesitate; yes, she'd killed a man before, but one never grew accustomed to it. Her finger shook on the trigger of her pistol, wood and steel in her palm, power in her grasp. The Mohawk noticed her when he finished reloading—it was then or never, either he died or she would. There was no time to think. With speed she didn't know she possessed, she took a deep breath, cocked the pistol, and fired, striking the assassin in the chest; he coughed and then fell from the branch, landing on the ground with a loud thud.

Fear and a surge of adrenaline coursed through her veins—she did it. She'd killed him. Her hands shook, the pistol dislodging itself from her grip, falling to the ground. Taking another deep breath, she dug deeply, searching for strength though tears clouded her vision.

"Be my brave, strong Dellis."

John's words invigorated her, and knowledge that she could defend her own bolstered her resolve. Yes, she *was* brave, and yes, she *was* strong. Redcoats had murdered her people and threatened their way of life, and she'd die before she let that happen again. Bending down, Dellis picked up her pistol and put it in her sack; pulling out the loaded one and her knife, she ran back towards the fighting.

"I'm coming, Grandfather!" she yelled, vaulting over bodies and spindly tree roots, bridging the distance back to the fight. "I'm coming."

From the brush, a Mohawk warrior jumped in front of her, his dark eyes narrowing as he lifted his tomahawk in the air, ready to strike. "Brothers of the Standing Stone are traitors." He lunged at her and screamed, "Traitors!"

"Like hell we are." Dodging his advance, she cocked her pistol and fired, a ball meeting its target—right between his eyes.

While she quickly reloaded her pistols, in the distance, she could see General Herkimer on his white horse, climbing the side of the ravine while he shouted orders to his men. Suddenly, a bullet came from high in the trees and struck his steed; the animal reared underneath him and collapsed. Herkimer remained in the saddle as his horse hit the ground; another bullet whizzed through the air, striking the General's leg. Racing to his side, Colonel Cox took a bullet to the head, landing dead at the General's feet.

She crouched down as another volley of arrows and bullets rained from above. She followed their trajectory back to a group of snipers hiding in the trees.

"I have to get those shooters," she whispered to herself.

She finished reloading her pistols, stuffed one in her pocket, and made a run for it. In the distance, she could see her grandfather crouched behind a large maple tree, loading his gun. Not twenty yards behind Joseph, a Mohawk warrior stalked with his tomahawk drawn, and between his teeth was a vicious-looking knife.

Dellis cocked her pistol and aimed, but before she could pull the trigger, she heard someone approaching from the left. Whipping around, she saw a flash of movement; without hesitation, she pulled the trigger, dropping a Mohawk warrior in the dirt. She turned back to find the Mohawk on the ground, her grandfather on top, his arm swinging vigorously, gobs of blood flying up as he brought his tomahawk down repeatedly into the warrior's skull.

"Dellis, come here, girl!" her grandfather yelled.

Like greased lightning, a bullet sliced through the air, hitting him in the shoulder, taking him down.

"No!" Time screeched to a blinding halt as she ran through the brush on legs made of rubber. "Grandfather!"

"John! Justice!"

John woke to the voices screaming frantically; not their usual melodious lament, but the wails of abject terror. Not only was it the women, but the forest itself was calling his name between breathy pants, screaming for justice.

His sweat-soaked shirt stuck to his chest, and glistening, fear-laden beads dotted his forehead, yet a chill ran down his spine. He brushed wet tendrils from his face and looked around with confusion. He must've overslept, the sun peeking through the flap of his tent, illuminating it with happy, lemon-colored beams. Clark and Smith were already gone, their cots set and their belongings taken.

At the wash basin, John rinsed his face and wet his hair, slicking it back and tying it in place at his nape. Utilizing the little mirror Clark hung from one of the tent posts, John quickly shaved, gave himself a onceover, and then changed into a fresh uniform. After throwing back a cup of cold coffee and downing a biscuit, he rushed out of his tent. The camp was already active; men were lined up and practicing their musket drills, long barrels aimed at targets as the Lieutenant called out orders. In the distance, Stanwix looked peaceful and impenetrable, the Rebel flag flying high above in obstinate refusal of defeat.

As John ran around looking for his men, the disorientating screams started anew, loud and debilitating, the world spinning around him. He stopped for a moment, trying to regain his composure, as pain, like a knife, stabbed the right side of his head. Closing his eyes, he covered his mouth as a wave of nausea overcame him. He choked down his morning hard tack, which was threatening to come back up right then and there.

"Captain Carlisle, the General has requested your presence."

When he opened his eyes, he found one of St. Leger's bodyguards standing there.

"Yes." John nodded, fighting the pervading brain fog. "I'll be there in a moment." He reached into his haversack and pulled out a canteen, taking a couple sips of water as he made his way to the General's tent.

St. Leger was already outside, hunched over a table, examining his maps. When John approached, the General looked up, his dark eyes bloodshot, his face blanched with fatigue.

"I see I'm not the only one who didn't fare well from our night of drinking," he said, laughing.

That was what it was. The whiskey and the piss-poor rum they drunk the night before, compounded by the infernal heat and dehydration—no wonder John felt so bloody awful and had nightmares. But he was in no position to refuse his superior, and St. Leger was in the mood to celebrate; between the two of them, they finished off a bottle and a half. Dellis would've scolded John for neglecting himself so thoroughly, too much indulgence and not enough proper fluids. He opened his canteen again and took several more sips as if she were there, staring him down with accusing eyes.

"Have Colonel Johnson and Major Butler left yet, sir?"

"Of course, before the sun was up," the General said with a grin. "We're awaiting good news from the front. Once that arrives, we'll try to engage Colonel Gansevoort again. Only this time, I anticipate he won't be so obstinate."

"Yes." John's stomach churned, nausea stoking up again from the continued pain in his head and the knowledge that his plan had gone into effect.

"Captain, will you look over these maps of the fort with me? Our plan, if Gansevoort doesn't surrender, is to go after the magazine and maybe try to dig underneath."

John reached for the parchment, turning it right-side up and scanning it quickly. Out of the corner of his eye, he caught a glimpse of movement in the forest, flashes of red and black feathers darting around in the olive-green foliage.

Keeping his head down, he shifted his eyes to the side; only that time, he saw the outline of a dark figure and the flash of silver. A gorget.

"General, I have better maps amongst my belongings. I'll go get them."

"Of course." St. Leger nodded.

John walked towards the woods, glancing over his shoulder several times to make sure he wasn't being followed. Finally, when he was on the edge of the camp, he whistled a signal he knew was used by the Oneida and waited for a response.

The forest was quiet and still, behind him was the hustle and bustle of men and the camp, covering up any sounds from footsteps or crunching leaves. Trying again, he whistled, taking slow, deliberate steps into the cavernous quiet of the forest until he was several yards away from the camp. From behind, he heard the snap of a branch. Fingering the pistol at his hip, he whirled around and aimed, the end of his barrel finding the stoic face of Ho-sa-gowwa at point blank. The young Oneida lifted his tomahawk and jut out his knife, ready to go toe-to-toe with his brother-turned-enemy if necessary.

Standing down, John put his pistol back in his belt and greeted the younger man in Oneida. "*Shekoli*, Ho-sa-gowwa. *Sata'kali:te.* Are you well? I saw you from the camp. You need to be more careful."

Lowering the blades but not putting them away, the young Oneida retreated marginally. Their situation was still ambiguous. "*Shekoli*, Just One. You have good eyes. You're Oneida. The rest of these white men are too blind to look at the forest."

John couldn't help but admire the hubris in the young brave's words— he wasn't wrong; St. Leger and his men weren't paying attention to the forest as well as they should. "So you're the spy."

Ho-sa-gowwa nodded. "And you?"

"Not right now." John admitted. "Where are Joseph and the others?"

"They've gone to escort Herkimer's men to the fort."

"What?" John's stomach bottomed out with abject horror.

"They joined Honnikol at Fort Dayton. Han Yerry was leading them." Ho-sa-gowwa put his tomahawk back in his belt loop and thrust his blade into its sheath.

Fear gripped John's heart, squeezing it painfully until he could barely draw breath. "They left today? This morning? All of them?"

"Yes," the brave replied. "Dellis and the women went, too."

"My God." John gasped, unable to find words. They were walking into a trap—*his trap*. Dellis, Joseph, Kateri, Han Yerry, all of them. He swallowed down the bile rising in his throat.

Dellis.

"What is it, Just One?" Ho-sa-gowwa asked curiously, innocently.

"They're walking into an ambush." John choked the words out, his stomach pitching, threatening to expel its contents; he paced back and forth, his nerves frazzled and ready to ignite.

"How do you know that?" Ho-sa-gowwa stepped into John's line of sight, stopping him midstride.

"Because I designed it," he replied tersely. "It was my plan."

"What do we do?" the brave asked, the timbre of his voice escalating with rising fear, further stoking John's.

"I have to warn them." John's mind raced. If the battle hadn't started, it surely would in a matter of minutes, the boulder of war rolling downhill with excruciating momentum. But how did one stop a force as inevitable as gravity? There wasn't enough time. "Stay here. Wait for my return. It won't be long. Do you have a horse?"

The brave nodded.

Just as John turned away, Ho-sa-gowwa called, "Just One."

He reached into the little pouch on his hip and pulled out a bit of fabric, something sparkling inside it. "I was to give this to you; she said to be safe." Wrapped in a piece of linen was the garnet John had given Dellis in Oswego.

Holding the precious stone in his hand, he closed his eyes, his heart taking off in a violent sprint. "Dellis, what have I done?"

"*Nλki'wah*, Just One."

Chapter
Thirty-Nine

"James, that savage is at the door; he's with a man named Lord Tomlinson. What's going on?" Helena crossed the threshold of her husband's office, staring him down with one of her famously frosty expressions. Such was the way of Russians, ever cold, even in the most smoldering of heat. But that was what he loved most about his wife, the chill, because when the ice thawed, she was passionate and fiercely loyal. Her face, though aged, was still as beautiful as the day he first saw her. His Helena.

"Wife, I'll handle them."

"It's not like you to keep secrets, husband." She walked over to him, pushing her long, slender fingers into his hair, brushing locks of it out of his face. "Have we not always been in this together? Have I not always supported you?"

"Yes, wife, but—"

"We've always discussed your business ventures. Both of us decided what to do when Stephen started sniffing around and reporting back to Dane. Did I not help you procure the money that Dane was giving to Dellis?" she said quietly, her lips a whisper from his cheek before she kissed it gently. "There's nothing you can't tell me."

James grabbed her hand, lovingly holding the tiny porcelain thing in his own. "I'm doing what I can to remedy the situation. There's no need to worry."

Though her expression was serene, he knew it was an act, Helena was fastidious when she wanted something. "What do these men have to do with it?"

Relenting, but only enough to feed her curiosity, he replied, "They may provide a way for me to obtain additional money and a much-needed alliance." He brought her hand up to his lips and smiled. "Let me do this."

"Is Alexei in trouble?" Helena pulled her hand away abruptly, the cold edge of challenge steeped in her voice. Alexei was her perpetual weakness.

Her incessant protection of their buffoon son stoked James's ire. "Don't you see? It's because of him that we're in this predicament. Had he done as he was told, none of this would've happened, and Carlisle would be dead."

"James McKesson, if you hurt my son—*our son*—I'll put a knife through your breast. Do you hear me?" She hissed through clenched teeth. "You've tormented and mistreated that boy since he was young, by no fault of his own. Jamie died because of the Pox. It was in God's hands, not his brother's. Yes, Alexei was weak when he was young, but look at him now; he's the picture of you: tall, strong, and proud. The only reason he turned to Stephen and the Oneida was because you shut him out."

Like a mother bear protecting her cub, she could be fierce, but James was the authority in his house, and no woman would dictate the law to him. He stood, using his height to intimidate her into submission. Too many years together had taken the fear from her, making her a worthy adversary; her grip on his heart was strong, and she'd clamp down when need be to hold him in check. "Wife, do *not* talk back to me."

"James, I've followed you from the palaces of my home in St. Petersburg to England, New York City, then to this God-forsaken place. I've loved you, given you children, stolen for you, and even plotted with you, but I will *not* allow you to destroy our son. I promise you, if you strike out at Alexei, I'll cut out your heart, or at least, what's left of it."

Her eyes were red with tears, but she steeled herself. She was a master at controlling her emotions. His icy-cool Russian. "Alexei is our son. *Our* son. Not Stephen's and not some Oneida chief's. He's our blood."

"Please, leave me, wife. I have guests to attend to." James dismissed her as if talking to one of the servants. There would be hell to pay for that later, but for the moment, he had bigger problems to deal with.

Helena slammed the door, the sound of her heels stomping on the floor, echoes of the fury he'd face later—and a delightful reunion once she'd admitted she was wrong—met his ears.

Cracking the door, he yelled, "Mariah, please, send our guests in."

Before he had a chance to sit down, Eagle Eyes and a tall gentleman, dressed in a British officer's uniform, walked into the study.

"This is Lord Tomlinson," Eagle Eyes said and nothing more.

"Please, sit, My Lord." James waited for his guest to take a seat before speaking again. "Now, what can I do for you?" He leaned back in his large, wing-back chair, resting his hands on the arms, taking up his kingly position on a throne.

"I understand we're both looking for the same thing; perhaps we can help each other," Lord Tomlinson said, his voice low, careful, as if untrusting the walls not to have ears.

"I'm not sure what you mean," James replied, cautiously.

"I seek my wife, Wilhelmina Parkhurst, and her missing dowry. I believe you're looking for her, too, but for different reasons. I also understand you're looking for your son."

James said nothing, holding his cards, waiting to see what Lord Tomlinson had in hand.

"I have Alexei in my camp near Fort Stanwix, and John Carlisle is with us."

That was a full house indeed. James pressed his hands together, intently; the tide had turned rather fortuitously on the conversation. "Go on."

Lord Tomlinson smiled. "Your son won't tell us where he's hidden my wife. I want her back."

"Does His Majesty not have ways to coerce prisoners into confessing? That's been my experience in the past. Has George gone soft?" James fought back a grin of satisfaction; he liked taunting the noble man. Had the fates been kinder, James, too, would've been a duke and held ranks in the military. "What is it you want from me?"

"Alexei has hidden my wife somewhere in this area. You find her, and I'll pay you handsomely and hand over your son." Lord Tomlinson ran his hand over the edge of the mahogany desk, admiring the fine craftsmanship. "I was told you had a taste for luxuries. Once upon a time you were a duke; though after your notorious fall, one wouldn't anticipate you living in such splendor. Somehow, you've managed to hide from the authorities and prosper."

"What do you mean?" James asked suspiciously. *Who is this man? A* chill ran down his spine as he contemplated the source of such information.

Lord Tomlinson leaned in, his voice barely above a whisper. "You have powerful enemies that would love to see you pay for your sins. If I do nothing, they could use your son against you."

"Have you come to threaten me?" James retorted, returning to his former posture. They were in *his* castle, and he was the lord of the land. He alone divvied out threats.

"No, but to warn you. I've spoken with His Grace recently, and when he returns, he means to use Carlisle and your son against you."

"You mean my brother?" James clucked his tongue against his teeth. That full house had turned to a royal flush, a very good hand indeed. "Dane is here?"

"Not at the moment; he's with General Burgoyne, but he will be, very soon. I can hand Alexei and Carlisle over to you before he returns." With a shrug, Lord Tomlinson said, "You simply have to find my wife and my money. You know all your son's hiding places. Surely you can find a woman."

"I can find her." James grinned. "How do I get word to you?"

"Send a messenger to the camp, and I'll come, but make haste; this battle will be over in a matter of days, and we'll be on our way to meet up with Burgoyne. After that, I won't be able to prevent His Grace from having his way."

"You'll hear from me in less than a sennight." James stood, shaking hands with the Lord. "And please, let's keep this just between us. I'll handle my younger brother."

There was no time for indecision, and at the moment, John had none. He knew what he had to do. Quickly, he ran back to his tent, grabbed his haversack, and started stuffing it full of cartridges, bullets, powder, and what maps he hadn't yet given to St. Leger. Just as John opened the small trunk at the foot of his cot, Smith and Clark walked into the tent, chattering back and forth.

"John, what's going on?" Smith asked, putting his musket down on his cot.

John stopped filling his bag and looked up at his friends. There was no time to be elegant; he'd have to say it candidly and pray his men would understand.

Putting a finger to his lips, he pulled the flaps down on his tent and tied them closed.

"John, don't close those; it's a bloody inferno in here." Clark pulled his collar open as if letting out steam.

"We must speak quietly and quickly; there's little time," John whispered, waving them in closer. "The Oneida are escorting Herkimer's advance from Fort Dayton to Stanwix. They're on their way as we speak."

"Johnson and Brant left a long time ago," Clark said, catching on quickly.

"Yes." John nodded. "The Oneida are walking into a trap—a trap of my own design. I have to warn them. I'm leaving now."

He whirled around on his heels, snatched his hat from his bed, and threw his haversack over his shoulder. Clark grabbed John's arm, stopping him before he could reach for the tent flap. "John, the Colonel and his men left at first light; even if you leave now, you're already too late."

Clark was right; in John's head, he knew it to be true, but his heart refused to believe it. He had to do something. "It doesn't matter. I've made my decision."

"Captain, do you know what this means?" Smith asked forcefully, yet his eyes were pleading. "You'll be a traitor."

John snorted. "I'm *no* Rebel, but I'll have no more innocent blood on my hands. If that makes me a traitor, then so be it. George will be less one despicable, unworthy soldier. And if they hang me, then I die a free man with a free conscience—that's an honor no one can decorate me with."

He paused, his stomach aching in anticipation of his next action. "Adam, Simon, I can't ask you to come with me. We must each decide our own fates. The choice is up to you. I won't hold it against you, but if you're to stay, then you must leave me now, so that you can't be questioned or punished for what I'm about to do."

"What about Merrick?" Simon asked. John could read his friend's thoughts through his brown eyes: confusion, concern, and a barrage of other emotions. "What about your deal with him? If you turn, you lose everything, the title, the inheritance. You'll never be able to go home."

Home. England wasn't John's home, nor was Bristol—of that he was sure. His home was being threatened, right then, as they stood and chatted; that thought spurred him on. "Merrick is a just man. He'll understand. And for myself, I'll do what I've always done, get by on my wits and my God-given talents; they've led me this far. I've lived under the favors and graces of others for too long and paid dearly for it." John knew Clark and Smith understood that better than anyone. "Merrick isn't that kind of man, but I'll never let anyone control my destiny again."

A smirk creased the corner of Clark's lips. "The money would've been nice, and the title of Your Grace."

"True." John nodded. "But this is my home now, and I must protect it."

"I'm with you, John. Without question," Clark said, already stuffing his haversack.

Smith turned his back to them, his eyes focused on the canvas wall, and after a moment's silence, he turned around again. "John, when we faced the court marital, you defended me. It was because of you Clark and I didn't face our regiment's fate. You've been more than a superior to me; you're my friend. Are you sure this is the right choice?"

"Yes." The words rolled off John's tongue with true conviction. *Finally, I have a purpose.* He wanted it more than anything. "Yes, Adam. I'm sure."

Smith stretched out his hand, offering it to John. "Then I'm with you to the end, Captain. Wherever that might be." They shook hands, their bond sealed. "Where do we start? We're fast running out of time."

"Ho-sa-gowwa is in the woods waiting for me. Clark and I will get Alexei; Adam, you get the horses saddled and ready and find whatever supplies you can. Wait for us there, and we'll ride off together towards the woods."

"We're actually in luck; with all the action going on, no one will be paying attention to one lonely Oneida prisoner," Smith said, grinning.

"Clark, we have to go now. St. Leger is expecting me back at his tent to look over some maps. It won't be long before someone is sent to find me." John's eyes flashed between his two friends, offering them both a hand to shake. "I guess this means I'm no longer your superior."

"No," Clark replied, removing his hat and holding it over his heart. "You're always our leader. 'Til the bitter end, Captain."

"'Til the bitter end." Smith conferred, taking John's offered hand.

"Then let's go." Once again, their collective fate was dependent on each other. Brothers in arms. He breathed a sigh of relief; with Clark and Smith at John's side, he could face the music—no matter how loud and abhorrent it might have ended up being.

"God speed, Smith."

John and Clark walked out together and headed right for Alexei's tent. There was one guard outside; the other, usually at the back of the tent, was thankfully absent. Smith had been right; everyone was too concerned about the battle to worry about an injured Oneida prisoner—so neglect and carelessness had become their ally.

When John walked inside, he found Alexei asleep, lying on the ground on his side, his wrists bound and tied to his ankles. John flipped his jackknife out of his boot, knelt, and cut the bindings.

Alexei roused, looking around.

John put a finger to his lips and leaned over, whispering in Alexei's ear, "There's an ambush on its way to stop the militia's advance. The Oneidas are with them: Dellis, Joseph, and the entire village. We must go now."

Alexei nodded, his sleepy eyes turning wide and fierce—and icy.

"Ho-sa-gowwa is waiting for us in the forest. Clark and I are going to get you out of here, but we have no time to waste; pretend like you're sick."

Alexei nodded again, his eyes searching John's. There was question there but not a hint of distrust. "I knew, someday, you'd choose."

"Save your boast, McKesson," John replied, brusquely. "Now, pretend like you're sick."

John and Clark each took a side and lifted Alexei to his feet, throwing one of his arms around each of their shoulders. Alexei's six-foot-five frame was heavy and awkward as they tried to ambulate him out of the tent. Once outside, he let his head lull forwards while John addressed the guard.

"This man is burning up with fever, and the wound on his side has turned putrid. We're going to walk him over to the infirmary," John said in his most Captain-like voice while trying to hold up fifteen stones worth of deadweight.

"Sir, let me help you with him." The sentry reached for Alexei's arm, but John shrank back.

"No need; he's already situated, and I fear waiting a moment longer would be to his detriment."

The guard nodded, giving Alexei, who was doing a rather convincing job, the onceover. "Let me know if you need anything."

John nodded curtly and then started to lead Clark and Alexei away from the tent.

That was easy. Way too easy. Together, John and Simon slowly ambled away, Alexei between them, walking in the direction of the infirmary. As they got farther from the tent, Alexei came alive, starting to walk briskly, allowing them to pick up the pace. From the camp to the woods was several yards of wide-open field; they'd have to make a quick run for it and discard their jackets once in the woods, their crimson tunics and gold epaulets like a blinking beacon in the night.

"Hurry," John whispered to Alexei, his injuries making him slower than usual.

Smith was waiting for them, four horses saddled, Viceroy included.

John was grateful he could take his trusted mount, cantankerous as he might be; the horse was battle hardened and irreplaceable.

"Alexei, will you be able to ride?" John asked, mounting up.

In a smug, irritated voice, Alexei fired back. "Don't worry about me, English. I'll be fine. We need to move—*now*."

"Agreed." John looked back at Smith and Clark, making sure they were seated and ready to go,

"Where's the guard watching the horses?" John turned Viceroy around, ready to lead his men.

"He decided to donate his musket, and his life, to our cause." Grinning, Smith handed a British Land Pattern musket to Alexei. "It's loaded, and here are some cartridges."

He took the premade shot and powder cartridges and stuffed them in the little pouch at his hip.

"I couldn't get you a tomahawk, but this is the knife our dearly-departed friend donated on your behalf."

"I'll get one, just give me time," Alexei said, putting the knife in his belt.

"Ready?" John asked, his heart pounding, the gravity of what he was about to do finally taking root. From that moment on, he was a traitor—a turncoat. "We follow the trail towards Oriska but stay in the woods. Everyone keeps their eyes open. I anticipate it won't be long before we find ourselves in a skirmish."

With a nod, they took off, racing towards the forest as fast as they could, crossing the open plain with ease. No one said a word; it was just the rhythmic beating of hooves on the ground and leaves crunching underfoot. There was no breeze; the summer heat was stifling, the air thick and stagnant while the sky grew overcast. A storm was threatening. The specters' chant had continued to reverberate in John's head, but their song had changed; no longer piercing, it turned low and persistent, yet ever louder the farther the men rode into the trees.

"Ho-sa-gowwa should be close by." John slowed his horse as they neared the designated meeting point, but the Oneida guard was nowhere to be found. Something was amiss.

"Keep watch," John said, searching the forest. "It's not like him to be late." Suddenly, there was a pop of a musket and a cloud of smoke coming from the trees as a bullet whizzed by his leg, tearing a hole in his breeches.

Lord Tomlinson stepped out from behind a large willow tree, Ho-sa-gowwa at gunpoint. "You didn't really think you'd get away, did you?"

"John, we've got company," Clark yelled from behind.

Four sentries stepped out from the towering trees, muskets drawn and aimed at the group.

John glanced over his shoulder; Clark was to the left, and Smith just was past him, but there was no sign of Alexei. *Have they already taken him out?*

Then out of nowhere, a bullet spiraled through the air, striking one of the sentries in the chest, dropping him instantly. Not a split second later, a pistol popped, and another one of the sentries fell dead in the grass.

Lord Tomlinson kept his gaze directed at John, the pistol still aimed at Ho-sa-gowwa's head. "Call off your assassin, or I'll blow this savage's head to kingdom come."

"Alexei!" John yelled. His heart thundered against his ribs, threatening to crack every last one of them. The clock ticked by in silence, precious time lost with every wasted second.

Alexei jumped down from one of the trees and stepped into view.

"It's my thief." Miles laughed. "John, when you decide to turn, you leave no loose ends. Or was this your plan all along?"

John looked back at Alexei, his hand at his hip, fingering something. "You left me no choice."

"I think General St. Leger and Major Butler will be grateful that I brought back their traitorous spy. But this one"—Miles inclined his head in Alexei's direction—"this one, I'll deal with myself."

Before John could reply, a flash of metal sliced through the air and lodged itself in Miles's right hand. *Alexei's knife.*

Lord Tomlinson shrieked, his pistol landing on the ground, discharging a bullet into the grass.

Ho-sa-gowwa sprinted away while Smith and Clark turned and fired on the sentries nearest them. One went down, and the other dodged the bullet and took a run at Adam, the two men landing on the ground in a heap of flying fists.

Lord Tomlinson pulled out his sword and lunged at John, catching him with a tip to the cheek, drawing blood. His pistol and musket were packed on Viceroy; the only thing he had to defend himself was the hanger at his hip. He drew it with one swift motion, and just as deftly blocked Miles's next strike; the sound of metal on metal clanked and echoed through the woods.

"Get out of here," John yelled, keeping his eyes on Miles. They circled each other, sidestepping, both their swords pulled in tightly, ready to parry. "Alexei, take the men and go. Warn Joseph."

John could hear his men mounting up around him, ready to do his bidding. "I'll meet up with you. Remember to remove your waistcoats and jackets."

Miles cocked a brow. "So sure of yourself, John?"

The good thing about a lifetime of being a drunk and a gambler, one got rather adept at protecting oneself: Fisticuffs, swordplay, and pistols—the tools of a scoundrel's trade—and John was proficient at all three.

"I'm better than you at this, Miles, excuse me, *My Lord*. You know it." John taunted, blocking the next lunge by deflecting his sword to the right. "And a one-handed fighter is always the weaker."

Quick as lightning, Lord Tomlinson lunged again. John jumped back, and with one whip of his hand, he slashed his friend, cutting him across the abdomen. The white fabric of Miles's waistcoat and shirt stained red in one long streak, following the track of the cut; it was a surface wound, but it would need to be tended.

"That hand and this cut will fester if you don't get them cleaned. I suggest you get back to the infirmary, *Miles*."

John sidestepped another thrust, parrying with his blade high and to the left. Finally, seeing his advantage, he thrust his own blade, digging the point into Miles's shoulder. He was weakening, both from blood loss and lack of conditioning; it was only a matter of time before he'd succumb.

Patience.

Digging deeply, John settled into his stance, knees bent and turned out, blade high and pulled in tightly, trying to focus on the fight at hand and not the battle that awaited.

"You're a traitor!" Lord Tomlinson yelled as John deflected a series of thrusts. "We were friends, colleagues; I gave you men to help find your native whore. I trusted you."

Seizing the moment, John lunged and circled his arm, drawing Miles's wrist down, his blade pointing to the ground. Freeing the other hand, John plunged his fist into his friend's face and ripped the sword from his grasp.

Miles landed on his knees, reeling from the direct hit.

Picking the sword up from the ground, John held it and his own with their points directed at Lord Tomlinson's throat.

"If you don't kill me, I'll hunt you down. I promise." He hissed through clenched teeth, eyeing the metal points aimed at his neck.

"I have no doubt you will." John pushed the tip of his sword into Miles's flesh, giving him another taste of cold steel. "And I'll be waiting for you."

"You're nothing, John, just a dirty Rebel—a traitor." He spat, their eyes locking.

"That may be, but I still bested your sorry, noble ass. *My Lord.*" John finished with cheeky grin. Pushing one of the blades in, the skin on Miles's neck punctured, blood oozing down the snowy white collar of his shirt.

With that, John pulled back, sheathing his sword. Quickly, he removed his tunic and waistcoat, throwing both at his old friend. "Until that day, My Lord."

Jumping into the saddle, John pulled Viceroy's reins, gave a gentle kick to his sides, and took off, never once looking back.

Chapter Forty

Never had a sprint taken so long; the distance was only a few yards, yet it carried on for miles. When Dellis finally reached her grandfather, she landed on her knees next to him. "Grandfather!" she yelled, her eyes stinging with tears as she pulled him into her arms. "Grandfather."

He'd been hit in the shoulder, the bullet lodged in the wound, the red-and-black hole standing out against war paint smeared on his leathery skin. Joseph shook in her arms, and then his eyes opened, looking around for a moment before they focused on her. "Dellis?"

"Oh, thank the good Lord." She held him to her chest, squeezing him with all the fear-laden love she felt. "Let me tie that up. I'll get the ball out later."

"You stay with me. Together, we can take out some of those shooters. I'll fire. You reload," Joseph said between pants. Her grandfather winced several times as she ripped a piece of linen from hem of her shirt and tied it tightly around his arm. She'd opted to dress in a pair of buckskin leggings and a shirt, pulling a leather tunic overtop. The extra linen at the bottom of her much-too-long shirt was going to come in handy when she needed to bind up wounds; her supplies were lost somewhere with her horse.

"Where's Han Yerry and the rest of our men?" she asked, looking over her shoulder at the battle.

It was almost impossible to see; the musket and pistol fire left clouds of smoke so dense it was as if fog had settled on the ravine, blinding both sides. The high-pitched whooping and hollering of the warriors resounded over the battle; underneath, the crack of muskets rhythmically firing; and then the final *whoosh* of arrows playing out like a demented concerto—Death's dirge.

"Han Yerry and Two Kettles Together are protecting Colonel Campbell. We need to keep our eyes on Honnikol."

Dellis grabbed her grandfather's musket from the ground and checked it. "It's still good."

Handing the gun back to him, she pulled out her pistol, her eyes directed at the General who leaned against a tree at the edge of the ravine, smoking a pipe while he yelled out orders.

"What about the Spencers or the rest of our people?"

"Thomas and his brother were taken down early after the initial attack. They fought bravely."

She nodded, remembering the two men, so full of wisdom and life, and much too young to die. "Good God, when will this all be over?"

"Dellis, my sweet, this is just the beginning." *You must be ready for it.* Though Joseph didn't say it, she knew that's what he meant. It was the new normal, their life from then on: bloody battles, brother attacking brother until one fell and the other triumphed.

Out of the smoke, Han Yerry rushed past like a demon from Hell with a knife in one hand and a bloody tomahawk in the other, hacking and slashing at anything that got in his way. The great chief planted his tomahawk in the skull of a soldier charging the General, splitting it in two. With a howl of victory, Han Yerry held up his tomahawk, his face covered in blood and thick chunks of brain matter, but he was triumphant. Next to him, Two Kettles Together fired her musket and reloaded quickly, gunning down anyone approaching her or her husband.

Joseph aimed his rifle and fired at one of the soldiers who was chasing the two potent Oneidas. He handed the musket back to Dellis so she could reload as he took her pistol and fired again.

Together, that was how they worked, two pistols and one musket; he fired and she reloaded, dropping any man that ran within their path who wasn't friend to the Oneida.

"Grandfather, should we move closer to the General?" Dellis poured powder into the muzzle of the musket, dropped the ball inside, and then rammed the swatch in place.

"Let's go, Fennishyo." He handed her a tomahawk. "One hand on your pistol, the other on your tomahawk. Don't be afraid; your parents are with us today."

She nodded, grabbing her pistol and fisting the handle of her tomahawk.

They took off, hiding behind trees, staying low in the brush, until they reached the base of the ravine close to the General's resting place. In front of them, a group of soldiers was beating and clubbing a native warrior, blood splashing into the air in a crimson shower.

One of the soldiers took out a knife and slashed the brave's forehead, and with a tug on his scalp lock, and the most heinous scream of rage, he ripped the scalp away, holding it in the air like a prize.

Dellis stopped dead in her tracks, unable to look away, her eyes having never beheld such savagery. "God have mercy." She gasped.

Then suddenly, an ominous hush fell over the ravine, followed by a distinct, hollow clicking, familiar and pleasant to her ears. It got louder and louder, reverberating back and forth between the dirt and grass walls until it filled her ears with its rhythmic song. *Click. Click. Clickity-clack. Click. Click. Clickity-clack.*

"Do you hear it?" Dellis grabbed her grandfather's arm, tugging his sleeve.

"Turtle rattles," Joseph replied, looking back her.

Someone was calling the spirits, the steady beat of the rattles carrying over the battle orchestra, making its ascent towards the heavens; then, as if God himself heard, the pregnant clouds that threatened to unleash their bounty submitted. The rain came down with the fury of Mother Nature witnessing unmitigated destruction in her sacred forest. Dead bodies littered the ground as numerous as the yellow dandelions of summer that once graced the peaceful field. And with otherworldly power, the torrential downpour washed away the blood of the dead to mingle with the river water, tainting it forever.

The havoc ceased. The soldiers and the braves pulled back to their respective sides, fearful their powder would get soaked and rendered useless for the fight.

Dellis turned to her grandfather, saying a prayer of thanks that he was safe. "While the fighting has stopped, let me see to your wound."

"No, no," Joseph pushed her hands away when she started at his bindings. "See to the others. I'll be fine."

Dellis nodded, retying the linen. "If you wish." Her grandfather was so proudly stoic in his refusal, so chief like, it would've been an insult to push. "I'll look around and see if I can help some of the injured."

"Be careful, Granddaughter, and keep your tomahawk with you."

"Yes, sir."

Dellis stuffed her pistol in her haversack and grabbed her tomahawk, slowly making her way towards the men lying closest to her. All of them were scalped, brutally murdered, and discarded in the brush—someone's husband, father, brother. So much waste. She fought back tears, covering her mouth and nose with the back of her hand, trying to shut out the putrid stench of dead bodies mixed with gunpowder. The rain had stifled the smoke; the entirety of the battlefield was revealed in all its horrific glory, a sea of the lifeless lying in the grass. Death had come to the Oneida homeland.

Is this punishment for turning on our brothers?

With the driving rain came the wind, blowing with the force of a tempest. God's fury. She found the lifeless body of Thomas Spencer lying in the grass. Getting down on her knees, she gently touched his cheek, saying a prayer, before closing his lifeless black eyes forever. "Goodbye, brave one. Protect us on the other side."

As Dellis tried to get up, her feet slipped and stuck in the dirt that had turned to thick, gooey mud. She had to work to keep her moccasins on, the greedy, wet earth trying to steal them with each sticky step. She heard men groaning from near the rear of the brigade—finally, someone she could help. Not far ahead of her, some militia men were beating one of Brant's natives; she turned and went in the opposite direction, away from the bloody fights, searching every person she encountered for signs of life.

"Dellis!"

From behind, she heard one of the men groan out her name. She walked in the direction of the noise, rolling over body after body, searching them all.

"Dellis." Again, someone called her name, but that time with a gasp followed by several gurgling coughs. She followed the lifeline towards a grouping of trees and a pile of bodies lying hidden in the brush.

There, trapped underneath the corpses, was her beloved cousin. "Ruslan, my God." He was covered in blood; a large knife wound started at his forehead, bisecting his eyebrow, running through his right eye, and ending at his cheekbone. The flesh was open and meaty, blood oozing from a wound that was already caked with mud. "Ruslan, it's Dellis. Can you hear me?"

"Cousin?" He groaned, reaching for his bloody eye.

She grabbed his dirty hand before he could touch, trying to keep him from further contaminating the enormous cut.

"I'll care for it. Can you open your eye?"

Ruslan did as she asked, but the knife wound had struck the front of the orb, a giant hematoma staining the white bloody red, a dense clot sealing the delicate surface closed. Her poor cousin would be blind in that eye if he lived through the infection that was sure to follow.

Though her clothing was thoroughly drenched, Dellis ripped away a piece of her shirt and wrapped it around her cousin's head on an angle, and then she took a piece of wet linen from her haversack and stuffed it under the binding to pad the precious tissues beneath. "Sit up, love."

She took Ruslan's arm, put it around her neck, and helped him upright. They leaned against each other, seeking a moment's comfort from simple human touch.

"Is Alexei with you? I miss him," Ruslan muttered, sounding so vulnerable and sweet, her heart ached for him.

"Dear cousin." Carefully, she brushed a wet lock of hair out of his eyes, marveling at how much he looked like his brother, yet that was where the similarity ended. Ruslan was so tender and gentle, unlike Alexei, who was notoriously cold and distant. If it were Alexei next to her, he'd be barking orders, fighting to get up and direct his men, where Ruslan was content to find peace in a fleeting moment of silence.

"I miss him, too." Taking a deep breath, Dellis asked the question her heart feared most. "Ruslan, where's Stuart?"

"He was right next to me. We stayed together; he fought with me," Ruslan said between panic-laden breaths, looking around. "He should be here somewhere." His voice cracked, fear turning quickly to terror. He grabbed her arm, tugging at her sleeve. "Dellis, where is he? I have to find him. I promised I wouldn't leave him. Dellis, I have to find him!"

"It's okay. I'll look for him." She stood, knowing not where to start. It was like looking for a proverbial needle in a haystack.

"Stuart?" she called out, turning in a circle, scanning the area. The longer it rained, the more it flooded the ravine, turning the grassy area into a marsh; within it, discarded haphazardly, were the bodies of the dead. Surely it was what the River Styx looked like: a dark, syrupy water laden with forgotten souls.

One of the men near her started to groan. Thank God there was life amongst the lifeless.

Dellis knelt down and rolled him on his back. She gasped, covering her mouth with her hand reflexively; he'd been eviscerated, his abdomen split open, slick, pink intestines exposed to air. He groaned again. She took his hand and held it in her own, squeezing it gently.

The man trembled, his eyes barely opening past a slit. "Tell Mother I love her." He started to cough, his words catching in his throat, blood spewing from his lips. Between gurgles, he managed to force the words out. "Tell her I love her."

"Have comfort. I'll tell her," Dellis whispered through tears. "Go to God, brave soldier."

She held his hand for a moment, watching death snatch away his soul. It wasn't a greedy process, death wrenching and fighting to steal his essence; on the contrary, it was slow and peaceful, the man's eyes closing on a gentle last breath. She laid him back on the cold earth, making the sign of the cross over his body.

Through misty eyes, Dellis got up and started searching again, calling out Stuart's name, but there was no response, just the rustling sound of leaves and the patter of raindrops on the ground. The wind picked up suddenly, sending a chill down her spine. Turning around, she looked up at a large maple tree, and there, high above the ground, was Stuart.

"No!" she whispered, choking on the word, and then she screamed it.

Chapter Forty-One

"Damn," John cursed, dropping his head, pulling the brim of his hat down to shield his eyes from the driving rain. He pushed Viceroy to run, leaning in low over the horse's neck, backside barely touching the saddle, while he rose to the challenge, taking the thick woods and rough road at a breakneck pace. John was late. He knew it. His spar with Miles had taken longer than planned, precious time relentlessly ticking by while they dallied about, settling old scores.

In the distance, John could hear the *pop* of muskets and the whooping and hollering of war cries; an acrid smoke of saltpeter and sulfur oozed through the forest like a plague, choking away the sweet-smelling rain. The battle was near, his soldier's senses honed to the miasma of despair and eminent destruction. He strayed off the road, dismounting quickly. Viceroy was formidable in a fight, but he'd be an easy target in hand-to-hand combat.

"It's time to make a run for it, old friend. I hate to leave you here, but this will have to do." John tied Viceroy to a tree far off the road, dropping some oats and a carrot on the ground. "Be safe, friend. I'll come back for you. I promise."

Grabbing the musket and haversack, John made for the battlefield, following the sounds, using them to draw him towards the fighting.

Between the backdrop of towering evergreens and miles of proud, spacious maples, he found what he sought: war on display in all its painted, violent glory. Lying in the grass were discarded carcasses of men: British, Colonist, Native—didn't matter—in war, one's value was lost the moment flesh met earth. He stopped dead in his tracks, unable to draw breath. It was his plan. His. Plan. Aspens quaked and rumpled in the storm winds as a whisper blew through their spade like leaves, sibilant sounds made in unison.

"Justice… John."

At his feet lay an Oneida scout, one of Han Yerry's men from Oriska. John crouched down and took the brave's knife and tomahawk, putting both in a beltloop. Adrenaline coursed through John's veins, mingling with embittered loathing directed at himself. His plan played out perfectly, but to what result?

Tell me it's not too late.

Racing through the trees, John caught sight of General Herkimer sitting with his back to a large Beech tree, the rain pelting down on him while he gave orders to the men surrounding him. Not far ahead of him, Han Yerry and his wife, Two Kettles Together, took shelter beneath a tree, standing guard over the meeting, both with muskets in hand.

John vaulted over the uneven ground, careless of making noise or being stealthy, stumbling over an occasional burly, jutting root that tripped up his dexterous feet. But he wasn't alone; from behind, he heard someone fast approaching, branches cracking underfoot in rhythmic succession. He whipped his head around, searching the trees, but the forest calmed; only the gentle sounds of raindrops pelting the leaves and soldiers chatting in the distance could be heard. Someone was following him. John could feel it. The questions were: Who? And what side were they on?

At first glance, he was a British Officer without his tunic—an easy fix if it was St. Leger's men, but a tasty prize for the Americans, who'd undoubtedly take out their grievances on his hide. But he refused to be baited. He'd come so far: from being a solider in service of His Majesty and a pampered nobleman; to a traitor and a turncoat; and finally, a free man with a free conscience.

Standing tall, John yelled, "Show yourself. I hear you."

From his left, a tomahawk took a swipe at him, catching him in the upper arm, slicing his shoulder open cleanly, and then, from out of the trees, Eagle Eyes flew through the air, both men falling in the mud.

"Carlisle." Eagle Eyes hissed through rotted teeth.

The giant Mohawk rolled John onto his back, straddling his hips, using that powerful, hulking frame to bring down a tomahawk once, twice, and then three times.

John dodged to the left, and then to the right, and then farther to right, the blade of the tomahawk hitting the earth, ripping up dirt and grass with each plunge. Righting himself, he grabbed the knife from his left boot and planted it in Eagle Eyes's thigh, stabbing repeatedly, trying to get the giant native to relent. The Mohawk ignored the jabs, seemingly impervious to pain, and then pulled a large, dirty knife from his belt.

"Your scalp will be my prized possession, Carlisle."

Eagle Eyes grabbed John by the queue and wrenched his head back. He kicked and flailed underneath but was overpowered by the sheer impervious strength of his colossal foe.

It was then that John's ears filled with a quiet lament, the woman's song calling to him. *"John..."*

"Dellis." He groaned out. The edge of the blade pierced his forehead, warm blood oozing into his eyebrows. John thrashed about, trying to free himself; with the heel of his hand, he pounded Eagle Eyes's breastbone, but like an impenetrable wall, the Mohawk would not relent.

This is it. The end. John refused to close his eyes, wanting to see his death and the man that felled him.

John let out a long breath and with it, her name. "Dellis." The last time he'd say it—her name, like the sweet song of a nightingale.

"John." The voices called him again, a gentle benediction before he joined them on the other side.

"John!" His name said again, only that time it was shouted by a man and not the angels. Out of the trees, a giant figure landed on top of John and Eagle Eyes, powerful hands wrenching them apart, sending John skidding through the dirt on his back. He rolled over on his chest, quickly pushing himself up. Alexei and Eagle Eyes were rolling in the dirt, exchanging blows, the two titans throwing punches that would rock the heavens and lay waste to the Earth. Reaching for a knife, John rushed up and plunged it into Eagle Eyes's side, eliciting a howl of rage redirected.

The Mohawk groaned and whipped around, focusing on John, giving Alexei enough time to plant his long knife into Eagle Eyes's calf. The giant warrior coughed a few times, blood dribbling from his lips, but instead of advancing, he took off like frightened deer, retreated into the forest.

John took several deep breaths and then stretched out his hand to Alexei, helping him up. "A couple more seconds, and I would've been meeting Saint Peter."

Alexei nodded. "Thank God I saved you from humiliating yourself at the good saint's feet. He would've laughed and kicked your English ass out."

John rolled his eyes. "How did you find me?"

"I saw Eagle Eyes when we stopped, and then he disappeared. He never followed us on the road, so I assumed he waited behind for you," Alexei said between pants. "I sent Ho-sa-gowwa and your men ahead, and I kept eyes on you."

"Thank you." Had anyone told John six months before his greatest adversary would later save his life, he would've said they were demented. "You shouldn't have waited for me."

"We're even now. I owed you my life, now I've protected yours."

That was an obligation John understood as if it were written in plain black and white. Fate had led him down the road to truth, and he'd taken the right path. His enemy had become a friend. John's conscience blessedly clear. It was his destiny, come what may.

"Where to now?" He pulled off his neckerchief and used it to blot the wound on his forehead and then bind his shoulder.

Alexei grabbed John's musket and threw it to him. "Follow me."

They ran to the militia shelter where General Herkimer was still making plans, a pipe jammed between grinding teeth while he assessed their situation. The General's leg had been shot, leaving him immobile, a bloody bandage wrapped around his knee saturating with each passing second. Han Yerry raced up to them, Two Kettles Together following close behind.

"You're here, Cloud Walker. How is it possible?" the great chief asked exuberantly.

"He freed me." Alexei turned to John and nodded with thanks. "You can trust him. He's here to help."

Han Yerry was silent for a moment, dark eyes piercing under tightly ruching brows, regarding John with a bit of skepticism. "Just One? That's what you're called?"

"Yes, Chief." John stood tall, showing Han Yerry the same respect shown to General St. Leger.

"Joseph will be glad to see both of you." Han Yerry added, giving John a nod of acceptance. "Once the rain lets up and the battle begins again, we must stay in groups of two, one to load and one to fire."

"Have you sent for reinforcements? What's our status?" John glanced around at the decimated battlefield and the copious dead; there was no way to tell who held the advantage.

"Honnikol has urged us to stand our ground; we'll fight to the end. He's sent men ahead to alert the Stanwix and some natives, but I don't believe anyone will come to help us."

Or could, for that matter, Fort Stanwix was under heavy siege with snipers aiming at her bastions and men trying to dig in from the outside. Gansevoort was in dire straits of his own.

John looked back at General Herkimer, leaning against the tree in his navy jacket, drenched and bloody but still fighting—still rallying his men. It would be a fight to the finish with no white flag, no parley—something Johnson and Butler hadn't anticipated. But it could be used to the colonists' advantage.

"We must go it alone. No one can come to help, at least not from the fort; they're completely under siege. It would have to come from Schuyler," John said, trying to come up with a plan. "Where's Joseph?"

"Over there in the trees with what's left of our men." Han Yerry ticked his head, directing John towards the opposite side of the road where Joseph and Great Bear rested.

"Alexei?"

Together, John and Alexei walked towards the Oneidas, Joseph's eyes widening when he saw them.

"Just One? Alexei?" The old chief embraced John affectionately, making him feel lighter, more like himself again, back where he belonged.

From behind the trees, like ghosts rising from the darkness, Rail Splitter, Ho-sa-gowwa, Skenandoa, and Kateri appeared—but no Dellis.

"Where is... Tell me she's..." Panic took over, stealing words away. John whipped his head back and forth, searching for his beloved, grabbing Joseph's shoulder. The distress must have been tangible, for Joseph patted John's arm and smiled.

"Fennishyo is safe; she's taking care of the wounded."

Dropping his head in submission, he said a quiet, reverent thanks to God.

Kateri ran to John, her bright eyes drinking him up from head to toe. "Just One, I knew you'd come. I knew it."

Yes, she'd always known John better than he knew himself; like a mirror into his soul, she could always see the truth. His truth. He bent down and kissed her cheek. "You were right."

She laughed. "Don't ever tell Dellis you admitted that to another woman."

"Well said." He snorted. Such a devastating retreat could never be lived down, especially with his wife. "Where is she?"

"Dellis is back by the carts in the ravine." Kateri pointed.

"I'll be back." He glanced back at Alexei, gesturing for him to join.

The two of them walked through the sea of bodies, keeping eyes open for each other, paired in union where once they were separated by country and ideology.

As they walked down the slope into the ravine, John heard the tormented shrieks of a woman. He would've known that voice anywhere; it called to him in dreams and spoke words of love to him in the daylight. It was the cries of his other half, his heart and soul, Dellis.

She was standing at the bottom of the hill, screaming, her arms stretched up towards a large maple tree, and there, suspended high above the ground, nailed in place by two large swords, was Stuart. The poor wretch had been scalped; meaty, sinuous flesh was exposed where his hair had been torn away, while his one black eye stared lifelessly, the other still covered in a patch.

"Get him down! Get him down!" she screamed, wide eyed, searching around for someone to help.

Alexei raced past her, reaching for Stuart's leg, trying to pull him free. *My God.*

John rushed to her and wrapped her up in his arms, turning her away from the horrific sight. In her hysteria, she fought back, not realizing it was him. "Let me go. I have to help him. Let me go!"

"Dellis!" He lifted her chin, forcing her to look up at him. "Dellis, it's me. It's John."

Her eyes narrowed, searching for the truth, and then, like ice melting to water, they softened, and once again wept a torrential downpour of tears. "John! Oh, John, you have to get him down."

He drew her in even tighter, holding her so close he was sure her slight body would break like glass. But he didn't care. If they melted together at that moment and were forever forged as one, he could live that way for the rest of his days. "My love, Alexei is here. He's going to get Stuart down."

She let out a wail, her body convulsing against his. John rested his chin on her forehead, fighting back his own tears.

"Alexei will get him down, my love." He stroked her hair, his lips touching her forehead, the top of her head, and her cheek, desperate to give her comfort while finding his own.

When John looked up, he found Alexei carrying Stuart's limp, lifeless body, and then gently bending down, depositing him at her feet. She turned around and dropped to her knees, pulling her brother's poor, tortured body into her arms.

"No!" She wailed, her body shaking like a leaf, and then she buried her face in Stuart's neck. "No, no, no!"

"Dellis, don't do this to yourself."

When John reached for her, she slapped his hand away, her eyes coal black with fury. "You did this to him, all of you." Dellis turned her embittered gaze to Alexei. "You wanted war? Well, now you have it, and this is only the beginning. How much more will we lose? He was all I had left of my family, pitiful as he may be. Now I'm alone. Oh, my poor Stuart. He never had a chance to know peace…"

John clenched his fists, aching to reach out for her, to hold her close, but in her painful rants, she'd pushed him away once again, his comfort unwelcome. Taking up the mantle, Alexei crouched down fearlessly and stretched out his hand to her, beckoning her into his arms. "Dellis, you have us. We won't leave you."

She shook her head and let out a demented, angry laugh. "I hate you. I hate you for bringing him into this. He admired you; that's why he joined the militia. It was because of you. Stuart was a coward; he would never have fought."

"No, Dellis, he was brave." Ruslan walked out from behind the tree looking tired; covered from head to toe in mud; a large, bloody bandage wrapped around his head; and his hair loose and scraggly. "He wanted to fight."

Ruslan nodded to Alexei and then John, understanding linking the three of them, for her benefit. Ruslan was the only one she'd listen to. The only innocent party. "Come with me, cousin." He outstretched his hand, giving her a weak smile. "Alexei will take Stuart somewhere safe until we can properly bury him."

Grasping Stuart tight to her bosom, she shook her head. "No, you can't have him. Stuart is afraid of the dark. I won't let you bury him." She gently brushed bloody stray hairs from his face and adjusted the patch over his eye, tending him as if he were only sleeping. As if he wasn't a gruesome corpse devoid of flesh on his scalp. "Yes, Stuart. I promised Papa I'd watch after you. We'll go fishing, and we'll finish that table you and he were making in the village. Do you remember?"

John put a hand over his mouth, forcing back words, fighting his every instinct. Grief had cruelly snatched away her reason, but he wondered if her steely resolve would hold up against one more torturous blow.

Calmly, Ruslan tried again, putting a hand on her shoulder. "Dellis, the rain is letting up, and the fighting will start again. We must take him to safety. Isn't that what you want?"

With Dellis, when emotion lacked impetus, practicality would always win out. She released Stuart into Alexei's care and then took Ruslan's hand, allowing him to lead her back to safety.

John breathed a sigh of relief, watching her beloved, defeated form walk away, hand-in-hand with her cousin. She might not have been with John right then, but by God, she was safe, and that was all that mattered.

As anticipated, the rain let up, and the fighting resumed; only that time, John, with Alexei nearby, joined the lineup to defend the colonists. John was no longer a Redcoat or an officer, but a Rebel and an Oneida, and if they were to lose the day, then he'd die alongside the brave, willful men.

Word spread that relief was coming from Fort Stanwix, a company of soldiers in light-colored jackets heading in from the west to save the day, and the men started to cheer around him. But it was too good to be true. John knew there was no way Stanwix could get men through the siege. Just as the relief company approached, three of them lunged at Captain Gardiner, stabbing him with their bayonets.

It was a *ruse de guerre*.

Colonel Johnson's men were making one last attempt to win the day by turning their distinctive green jackets inside out, pretending to be a rebel militia.

"They're British!" John yelled, aiming his musket and firing for the first time into his former ranks, taking a Ranger down.

A volley of bullets rained through the air, both sides taking turns, picking off one another's men until it was clearly a stalemate. Above the fighting, John heard a distinctive "Ooo-nah!" calling the British natives to stop. Brant and his men pulled back suddenly, retreating into the woods, leaving Butler and Johnson no other choice but to retreat.

And just like that, the day was over. The battle finished. But the colonists and the Oneida were still standing tall. With a deep sigh, John put the stock end of his musket in the dirt and looked up to the heavens. It was the end of the battle, but the war for the frontier had just begun.

Chapter
Forty-Two

There were so many injured that Dellis didn't know where to start. She turned in circles, a sea of bodies surrounding her, all of them broken and bloody, screaming for help. General Herkimer ordered that not one injured man was to be left behind. The army surgeon, Dr. Younglove, sat at the General's side, tending to him while he gave directions to evacuate. What was once a fighting force of eight-hundred men had been reduced to only three hundred; the rest were either dead or captured.

Dellis grabbed Kateri and Skenandoa, and together, they got the wounded on their feet and on the road back to Fort Dayton to be patched up. The Oxen pulled carts loaded with the injured that couldn't walk. What few horses that remained were used to pull wagons full of soldiers. Amongst it all, she saw John and Alexei helping move some of the injured men, but she didn't go to them, unsure what to say. Once again, John tried to help her, and she pushed him away—exactly what her grandfather told her not to do. Embarrassment rendered her without words; she owed John and Alexei apologies for her behavior before, but it wasn't the time or place, and there was so much yet to do.

Dellis trekked the long road back to Fort Dayton, helping Ruslan ambulate, his arm wrapped around her neck, leaning on her for support. The longer they walked, the more feverish and disoriented he became as the wound started to fester. Behind her, Han Yerry, Two Kettles Together, Cornelius, and the rest of the Oneida walked together proudly. Yet beneath it all, she sensed a looming melancholy; their losses were great, and with so few men in their tribe, they could barely afford to give up more. Having taken up arms against their brothers, the Oneida would reap what they sowed.

"I'll get you cleaned up." Dellis lead Ruslan through the main gates of the fort, his head hanging with exhaustion. Sentries inside directed her where to take him; small canvas tents were already set up on the parade grounds in anticipation of the incoming wounded.

Once he was settled on a dry cot and resting easily, she ran to find supplies, anything she could use to clean and bandage a wound. To her surprise, Agnes and Will were waiting in the newly designated infirmary, by way of the parade grounds, with all the supplies from The Thistle.

"Dellis, thank God you're safe!" Agnes and Will threw their arms around Dellis for a giant, three-way hug. Another weight off her mind: her dearest friends were safe.

"I don't have time to talk yet. Do you have more supplies and some spirits? I lost my basket with my mare."

Will reached behind her into the cart and pulled out an arsenal of medical things: linen, scissors, needles, thread, and a small jug. Dellis stuffed them in her haversack and ran back to her cousin, removing the bandage from his eye and gingerly starting to clean it. Steeling her emotions, she meticulously swabbed the blood away, remembering Stuart lying on DeLancie's bed, one eye caked over and ruined.

"I'll take care of you, Ruslan. Always," she whispered.

So intent on her work, she barely noticed that the parade grounds had continued to fill up around them, the injured lying anywhere they could find a place to rest. Once Ruslan was stitched and cleaned up, she kissed his cheek and then gently caressed it.

"I'll come back soon to check on you. Once I'm done, we'll go home."

He nodded, closing his left eye, letting his head fall back against the cot.

From behind, she heard a familiar voice gilded with a warm Scottish brogue. "Lass, it's sure good to see you."

Dellis whirled around to find both Smith and Clark standing behind her, grinning like cads. "How?"

Running up to Simon, she hugged him and kissed his cheek. Holding his face between her hands, she looked up at him through tear-filled eyes. "You're here. How is that possible?"

Reaching over, she clasped hands with Smith, giving them a squeeze.

Smith laughed. "We couldn't let the Captain go it alone. Besides, he couldn't have freed Alexei without our help."

Dellis marveled at their words, her heart afraid to embrace the truth. "I don't understand."

"John freed Alexei; we came to warn you about the ambush, but we were too late."

Dellis heard Simon's words, but still, she could make no sense of them. "John freed Alexei? You came here to warn us?"

Both men nodded.

"But that's treason." She shook her head, fearing she'd lost her wits on the battlefield. "Am I hearing you correctly?"

"Aye, 'tis true." Simon added, "But we have no regrets."

"My God." Every fiber in her being suddenly ached for John; she started to look around, determined to find him.

As if reading her mind, Smith pointed to the barracks. "The Captain is briefing General Herkimer."

"My goodness, both of you are hurt," she said, spying the large cut on Simon's hand, a bloody bandage wrapped around it. Adam had several cuts on his face and arms, his white shirt torn and reddened across the back. "Sit down. I'll see to your wounds."

Before she could turn away, Simon grabbed her hand. "Where's my Agnes?"

With a grin, Dellis was all too elated to say, "Just a minute." Then she ran over and grabbed Agnes by the hand, dragging her over to Simon.

When they saw each other, Dellis held back a squeal as Simon rushed to Agnes and kissed her so soundly it drew hoots and hollers from the men around them—along with a few outraged gasps. But the two lovers heard none of it; what place did propriety have when one had just lived through a bloody battle?

"Thank God," Agnes said into his lips, their foreheads resting against each other's.

Dellis clapped her hands and said cheerfully, "I'll let Agnes tend the two of you. Tonight, you can stay at The Thistle; there'll be clean, dry beds for you to sleep in and warm food."

"That sounds lovely," Smith said, nodding. "Thank you."

Dellis walked away, leaving her friends to their reunion while she checked on Ruslan again. He was sound asleep in his tent, Alexei sitting on the ground nearby. She knelt down, put her arms around her beloved cousin, and buried her face in his neck. "I'm sorry, Alexei. I didn't mean what I said."

He nodded. His icy-blue eyes softened, brimming with tears. "Will Ruslan be all right?"

"Yes, but I fear he's lost his eye." Dellis looked down at her cousin, sleeping peacefully as if he was at home, safe in his bed. "It's strangely prophetic that he should lose the same eye as Stuart."

"They were the best of friends," Alexei said.

It was good to have him back. No matter his cantankerous nature and divisive personality, he was irreplaceable in her life, different from John, more than a cousin, a brother and confidant.

"Yes, they were like two peas in a pod." She hesitated, working up the nerve to ask the devastating truth. "How many men did we lose?"

"There's been no word. Both of the Spencers are dead, Han Yerry was shot, and Blatcop broke his arm. Two Kettles Together has gone to spread the word of the fighting, and John is briefing Herkimer about the situation at Stanwix."

"I can't believe he did it." The words rolled off her tongue with incredulity, her mind still unable to comprehend what it meant for John— for her—and their relationship. "I can't believe it."

"He took a huge risk, and bravely," Alexci said, reading her mind.

"Yes, and as always, he came to my rescue."

He patted her arm, his blue eyes giving her that "I told you so" look that frustrated her to no end. Her cousin was a master of condescension with a dash of smug. "It's time you apologize, Dellis. You owe him that."

She nodded. "I will." Her eyes blurred with tears; she leaned into her cousin and hugged him again. "Thank God I have you back, Alexei. Don't ever do that again."

He started to laugh, but it turned into a groan, and he grabbed his sides. All the time they were talking and catching up, she never noticed his two black eyes and the bandage around his left wrist. "My goodness, what happened to you? Are you all right?"

"Yes, I'll be fine; worry about these other men." He leaned back against the stockade, buttressing himself with its strength. It was just like him to be stoic about his pain, though the wrinkles in the corners of his eyes and in his brow had deepened, indicative of his true state of affairs. Instead of pushing, she relented; he'd come to her when he needed her. "Where's Will?"

"I sent her home to prepare our rooms and get some food started. You'll see her there. Promise."

Dellis followed the path of Alexei's gaze and the incline of his head. When she glanced over her shoulder, she found John, carrying the end of a stretcher, trying to find a place to deposit an injured soldier. Turning back to her cousin, she said quietly, "I don't know if I'll ever get used to you two being friendly."

"Neither will he." Alexei laughed and then grabbed his sides again. "Go to him."

For once, she didn't mind her cousin ordering her about. Following his direction, she walked over to John and waited while he spoke to one of the sentries. There was so much she wanted to say, sweet words stuck in her mouth like a fly in honey. But where to start?

When he finished, he turned to her and wiped his brow with his sleeve; the sight of blood staining the white fabric loosened her tongue, her healing instincts taking over. "You're cut. Come with me." She grabbed his hand, pulling him behind her. Once to a chair, she sat him down and ran to get her supplies.

John said nothing, quietly watching her thread two needles, his hands clasped in his lap unassumingly. *How unlike him to be so deferential.* She wished he'd say something inappropriate or drop one of his inane witticisms, anything to lift the cloud of uncertainty between them.

Dellis's hands shook as she daubed the cut on his forehead with whiskey-soaked linen, gingerly wiping it clean. "How did you get this cut?"

"Eagle Eyes," he replied curtly.

"Is he dead?" She looked down hesitantly, waiting, until finally, his eyes met hers in a weighty, restrained silence. With the first sight of sapphire blue, her stomach took a nosedive, bringing with it a tremble that resonated all the way to her bones. *My, he is handsome.* And he'd given up everything for her.

I love you. Her eyes said the words that her mouth feared to utter, praying he could read penitent black.

But much to her dismay, John looked down at his hands, his body strangely tense. The walls were up again; he was still smarting from her most recent rebuke, and rightly so, for she dealt him a killing thrust to the heart.

"Alexei and I fought him off, but he ran."

"Where's Anoki?" She asked the question, though something inside her already anticipated the answer.

"Dead," he said, confirming her fear. "Miles handed Alexei and Anoki over to the Seneca, and they both had to run the gauntlet. Anoki went first. He didn't make it."

"Oh, my." Putting down the swatch of linen, she picked up her needle and thread and eyed the cut, trying to figure out how best to sew it closed. "Poor Anoki, and poor Alexei for having to witness such a thing."

"Anoki died bravely."

She sniffed back tears, remembering the proud, gentle brave she'd grown up with, played with—one of the many beautiful souls lost that day. "Thank you for saying that."

Dellis swore she saw John's hand start to reach for her, but then he pulled back hesitantly. Yes, he was indeed smarting from her harsh words. There had to be some way to soften him.

"Once again, I'm cleaning your wounds. It seems I'll forever be playing nursemaid to your needs."

But he was reticent as she pierced his skin with the needle, her other hand holding the gap in his forehead together while she carefully stitched the wound. Suddenly, a lock of his hair fell into his face, exposing the braids bound with her trinkets, neatly pulled back and tucked in his queue. She smiled and brushed the stray lock out of the way, her mind pleasantly diverted, remembering the last time she stitched him up in her kitchen. Dellis looked down at him and laughed.

"Admit it, Captain. I bested you."

A sparkle brightened up his eyes, the little wrinkles she so loved forming in the corners. His lips curled into a smile, bracketed by those indelible lines of humor. "You do ride my horse well. But still, I'm faster than you."

Finally, a glimmer of her John in a phrase full of his usual playful banter and sensuous innuendo; it brought a smile to her lips.

She jumped at the opportunity to counter. "Captain, you know that's not true. I believe I've taken you once or twice."

"Touché," he said, laughing. "Touché."

She rolled her eyes, sticking the needle into his flesh again, making him jump.

"Ouch! Don't I get a drink for my nerves?" John reached for the bottle of whiskey and started to pull the cork. "What about my pain?"

Dellis stopped immediately, slapping his hand away. "I don't have enough to treat your pain and all these injured soldiers. You'll have to do without." Grinning, she started back to her sewing; only that time, she turned his head so it was eye level with her bosom and stepped into him, affording a more than ample view. Surely that would keep him busy.

John cocked a brow, though his eyes stayed pleasantly diverted to the neckline of her shirt. She'd long since removed her soaked tunic, her breasts heaving over the brim of her wet stays and pushing through the open front of her shirt.

"Mrs. Carlisle, you're cruel." He lifted his finger, moving a bit of fabric out of the way so he could peek at her breasts.

She continued her work, though warmth rushed from the tips of her breasts all the way to her core, making her melt like wax under his heated gaze. There was promise in those beautiful blue eyes, and delightful mischief. She had to look away, or she'd fall into one of his premeditated traps and end up in some private corner indulging in intrigue.

"Such temptation…" he said, and though she didn't look down, there was no doubt in her mind he was licking his lips like a beggar ready at a feast.

"Behave," Dellis muttered, though she made no attempt to adjust her shirt.

Tying the last stitch in place, she rinsed the wound with some spirits and then backed away, allowing him to stand. Though they'd just engaged in playful banter, there was still that air of tension hanging like a cloud of smoke between them, pent-up words needed to be spoken, but again, it wasn't the time or the place.

"When you finish here, please come back to The Thistle; there'll be food and fresh linen for you. I've already told Clark and Smith."

"Simon and Adam? You've seen them?" John asked, his eyes widening. "They're safe?"

"Yes, a little banged and bruised, but Agnes is tending to them."

"Agnes," he said with enthusiasm. "I can't wait to see her."

A little green-eyed monster nibbled at Dellis's heart. *Is he not excited to see me?* Though he teased her, he was still so reserved, so distant. But in truth, she had no one to blame for that but herself, having slammed the proverbial, and literal, door in his face so many times he was surely fearful of being rebuffed again.

"Dellis?" A familiar voice called to her. When she turned around, she found Patrick standing behind her, already bandaged up, his right arm in a makeshift sling tied around his neck.

Unable to resist the urge, Dellis hugged him tightly. "Thank goodness you're safe."

"I heard about Stuart," Patrick said, his olive eyes alight with sympathy.

She nodded, trying to ignore the gaping hole in her heart. "Thank you for seeing Agnes and Will safely here and for helping transport all the supplies. We couldn't have done it without you."

"You know I'd do anything for you." He took her hand, kissing it fervently and then her lips, catching her by surprise.

"Stop!" She pushed him away abruptly.

Patrick, ever cognizant of John, was taking a cheap shot, trying to stoke an argument, but much to her chagrin, he never rose to the occasion; as a matter of fact, he was nowhere to be found.

Ripe with outrage, she yelled, "Why would you do that!"

"He deserved it."

She was done playing games, her nerves too tired and frazzled to deal with soothing damaged male egos. "You're awful."

Patrick flashed her a knowing grin.

Male pride. Like two dogs marking their territory, and she was the tree.

Dellis shook her head. "Well, now I have to find John and set that to right, too."

"He's going to meet with Schuyler; he won't be back until tomorrow."

Damn. She didn't want to wait a day; she wanted him then, but once again, it seemed waiting was all she could do.

Chapter Forty-Three

"Alexei, let's take him upstairs and put him in the bedroom at the end of the hall." Dellis pushed the front door open with her hip while she and Alexei carefully navigated Ruslan across the threshold.

They each took one of her younger cousin's arms, helping him slowly ambulate up the stairs and down the hall. He was exhausted and limp, yet thankfully, leaning most of his weight on his taller, stronger brother.

Dellis's own body was wrung out from the events of the day.

Once they reached the bedroom, she put one of her father's clean shirts on the bed and a basin of water, along with some soap and linen for Ruslan's ablution. "Alexei, can you help him get cleaned up and to bed? I'll get him some supper from the kitchen."

Ruslan looked up at her, his face pallid, his usually sanguine demeanor replaced with pain and weariness. "Thank you for bringing me here, Dellis. I don't want to go home yet. Mother would worry if she saw me like this."

"She'll worry about you no matter what; you're her son." Dellis kissed the top of his head, brushing his dark hair back. Suddenly, her young cousin felt very precious to her; all her family was precious, she had so little left. "Get cleaned up, and I'll bring some food up to you."

"Alexei, thank God you're back," she heard her cousin say to his brother as she shut the door behind her. It *was* good to have both her cousins back,

459

but poor Stuart; no matter their differences, a sliver of her heart had always held out hope of a future reconciliation. But that was never to be. Her eyes teared up, remembering the gory spectacle that was once her brother. *No, she couldn't think about that*, there was too much to do, and the pain was too deep to indulge. Better to focus her energy elsewhere. The night would surely come, and so would the tears.

When Dellis reached the bottom of the stairs, she could hear commotion coming from the kitchen, happy revelry full of shouts and laughter. Her heart swelled two sizes too large for her chest, overflowing with love. Once again, The Thistle was full of life and the people she loved most in the world. No, it wasn't her parents or Stuart, but it was the makeshift family she'd come to depend on.

Sitting around the little table in the kitchen, Will, Smith, and Clark ate bread and butter and drank their ale while Agnes stood at the hearth, plating up some of the oatmeal that bubbled over the rim of a cast-iron pot.

"Lass, you're back!" Simon exclaimed, getting out of his chair and giving her a warm, friendly hug. Just what she needed. "Where's the Captain?"

Dellis's too-large heart deflated in an instant; the one person she wanted to see most was noticeably absent, but she wouldn't let that spoil their celebration. Mustering up a smile, she replied, "He's gone to meet with Schuyler. He'll be back soon."

Simon gave her a hand a much-needed squeeze of support. "Don't you worry, lass. He'll come back. With all the information John was privy to, I have no doubt he'll be valuable to the General."

Dellis nodded, having never considered that explanation for John's sudden departure. So much had changed for him since he'd turned sides. Was he even considered a Captain anymore? Would anyone trust him?

As if Smith were able to read her convoluted thoughts through the crease in her brow, he chimed in with a bit of wisdom. "The Captain's good at taking care of himself. Don't you worry."

"That he is." Trying to once again embrace the merriment, Dellis pushed Agnes away from the hearth and towards the table. "You sit down and eat. I'll take care of this."

Without hesitation, Agnes sat down next to Clark and leaned in, nuzzling his neck lovingly.

"Dellis, where's Alexei?" Will asked, getting up from the table and putting her dirty plate in the dish tub.

Alexei? Will?

Dellis shook her head with merriment. How could she have been so caught up in the moment that she'd completely forgotten about Will? Grinning, Dellis picked up the tray of food for Ruslan and grabbed her friend's hand, tugging her behind. "Come with me."

They didn't even make it past the bar. Alexei was standing at the bottom of the stairs, his eyes already finding Will across the dining room like a hawk spotting its mate.

"Alexei!" Will gasped but didn't move. She was stone still, her hand over her mouth, tears brimming her eyes.

Dellis thought she'd cry waiting for the two of them to finally touch.

Unlike his usually long, hurried strides, Alexei crossed the room slowly and then stopped when he was only inches from Will. It was a private moment, and one Dellis knew she should allow them to have. Adjusting the tray, she walked to the stairs, never looking back, but letting her ears eavesdrop a bit on the way. She could hear tears and sweet, mumbled words and then silence. Surely they were kissing. They had to be. Her swollen heart demanded an answer, so she glanced over her shoulder, getting a glimpse of two lovers locked in passion's embrace.

Dellis sighed and continued up the stairs.

The last words she could hear was Alexei saying, "What happened to your hair, Willie?"

She couldn't help but smile at the tenderness she'd never associated with her cousin, gilding his deep baritone, making it melodious and soft.

Once Ruslan was fed, she cleaned up his wound and tucked him under the sheets, blowing out the candle before she left.

"Cousin, don't be angry with Stuart," Ruslan whispered, stopping her at the door. "He was confused and troubled, but I know he loved you. I'll miss him so much. He was my best friend."

Kind words her heart needed to hear; Dellis melted a bit from such sweetness. So few had nice things to say about her brother, herself included. "Thank you. I need to believe that."

"I'm sorry my father isn't kind to you. And I'm sorry for my part in it." Ruslan confessed, his voice quivering.

"Don't apologize. You've always been kind to me, but you can do me a favor."

"What's that?" he asked.

"Be closer to Alexei. He needs you. Learn from what happened to me and Stuart." If she could help mend a rift between two people in her family, one less brother fighting brother, then her loss wasn't meaningless.

"I will. I promise."

"Rest now." She shut the door and walked to the landing, listening for voices. But it was quiet.

Once at the bottom of the stairs, she found the dining room empty; everyone was together in the kitchen. As she made her way through the bar, Will came out, stopping Dellis. "There's a gentleman here to see you."

John! Dellis's heart fluttered with excitement; she pushed past Will into the kitchen, unable to wait a moment longer. But to Dellis's surprise, it wasn't John; it was her Uncle Dane.

She grabbed the counter for support, feeling suddenly lightheaded. Her uncle, as always, was larger than life, bright-red hair gleaming in the candlelight, the same McKesson razor-sharp features, and that undeniable swagger that all the men of her family possessed and flaunted to their advantage. Unlike last time she saw him, Dane wasn't wearing his Royal Navy uniform; instead, he was dressed in a finely-tailored, dark-brown suit and shiny black boots that looked brand new.

"My sweet Dellis," he said, in a voice so like her father's she choked up and started to cry.

"Uncle?"

Everyone sat at the table, quietly watching, Will at Dellis's side. Her uncle stepped towards her, and then suddenly, she was in his arms, crushed against that familiar broad chest by arms like steel bands. Unable to control her emotions a moment longer, she released the threatening tears, her head taking up residence on his shoulder.

"How I've missed you, my dear," he said through tight lips. When she looked up, she could tell he was fighting back tears of his own. "It's like seeing my beloved brother again when I look at you. I've longed for him these three years."

Through misty eyes, she scanned his face, trying to memorize every beloved line and freckle. He looked like porcelain, yet his nose and cheeks were dotted everywhere, softening his severe features.

"I don't understand. How is this possible?"

Her uncle glanced around, eyeing her guests. "Where's Stuart? I'd love to see him."

An ominous hush fell over the room.

Dellis took a deep breath and then said the words that confirmed her nightmare into reality. "He's dead."

"No," Dane replied on a tortured breath. "Stuart?"

She nodded. "He was killed today at Oriskany."

A single tear rolled down her uncle's cheek, his blue eyes turning glassy. In his pain, he evoked her father, resurrecting a longed-for beloved face with high cheekbones; straight, perfect nose; and long, tapered brows that moved with each passing thought.

"My dear, may we talk in private?"

Dellis wiped her own tears on her sleeve, a bit of dried mud smearing her cheek. "Do you mind if I change quickly? Then I'll prepare us something to eat. We can sit in Father's parlor. You know where it is."

"Of course; it'll give me a bit of time to catch up with Alexei." Dane glanced over his shoulder at her cousin.

"Did you know he was here?" she asked, noticing the look exchanged between the two men.

"Get changed, and then we'll talk, my dear. There's much you don't know."

Dellis did her best to wash up; simple ablutions would never rinse the stain of war from her flesh, but a clean shift, fresh stays and a dry petticoat were welcome indulgences. When she returned to the kitchen, Agnes was already carrying a tray into the parlor, leading Dellis's uncle down the hall. Once inside, they sat down next to each other on her father's little couch, and Agnes shut the door, giving them the privacy to talk freely.

Carefully, Dellis poured milk into his cup and then filled it with tea, remembering the rules her father taught her for proper preparation. Her uncle was a Duke and an Admiral, and part of her wanted to impress him, if only for her father's pride. Somewhere in Heaven, Stephen McKesson was watching the exchange and smiling—she knew it with a certainty unchallenged.

"Here, Uncle." Dellis handed Dane the cup and saucer, watching as he took a sip.

"This is wonderful. Thank you. It's from the East India Company, isn't it?"

"Yes, it belongs to my"—she hesitated on the word and then yielded, releasing it with pride—"husband. He's a British officer. Or at least"—she stuttered, unsure what to say—"he was."

Dane nodded. "I know Captain Carlisle. We're friends."

"How?" It was all very confusing, Alexei didn't seem surprised to see Dane, and somehow, he knew John. None of it made sense.

"Excuse me if I eat while we talk. I've been travelling all day and find myself weary for sustenance." Reaching for a bowl of oatmeal and brown bread, her uncle started to eat with the gusto of a starving man. As hungry as she was, her plate went untouched, still too in awe of his beloved, long-desired presence.

"Your father and I had long been suspicious that James was involved in illicit dealings. When Stephen was killed, what little proof we'd obtained disappeared. And though I didn't want to admit it to myself, I knew in my heart James had something to do with Stephen's death. I thought all was lost, with no way to prove it, but then I learned about a young officer who confessed to taking part in the massacre of a small Oneida village. He also claimed being present when Roger DeLancie killed a doctor, a former naval surgeon, who lived with the tribe."

"John," she whispered.

"Yes. Once he made a full confession, I gave an order for him to be sent back to his men. After that, I stopped pursing James; your aunt was with child, and I was focused on that for a while. Sadly, our boy was born too early… He didn't make it. When I finally emerged from my grief, I realized I hadn't heard from you in months. All that time, I'd been sending you money, but there were no letters, nothing."

Dellis reached out to her uncle, placing a hand on his arm. "I'm sorry for your loss, Uncle."

"I know you've lost children of your own. On another occasion, when your own wounds aren't so fresh, we'll share words of comfort, my dear. My India could give you such good advice."

"Yes." Dellis closed her eyes against the pain so raw it tugged at her heartstrings. So, John had spoken of their children to her uncle? *How unlike him.* Their friendship must be quite significant indeed for John to reveal something so personal.

"After my son's death, I was determined to find out the truth; my nervous energy and grief drove me to the point of obsession. That's when I learned about Alexei and James's little scheme they had going. Since then, I've been trying to find a way to put a stop to your uncle."

"Why all this hatred? I don't understand," she asked, taking a sip of her tea. With just a taste, she let out a sigh, the lavender blooming in her mouth underneath the smoky warmth of the black leaves, instantly soothing her raw nerves.

Putting the empty plate down, Dane sipped his tea, his eyes tracking around the familiar room reverently. "I see Stephen everywhere in this parlor. He loved the color yellow and all his medical books and journals. It even smells of musty old paper and fine leather. That was Stephen, our scholar, the smart one. The peaceful one. He was content with his books and the solitude of his own company."

Dellis grabbed his hand, trying to bring her uncle's attention back to their conversation. "Tell me, Uncle. I deserve the truth." She paused, sensing his hesitation, searching for the right words to encourage him. "I'll still love you, no matter what the truth may be."

And so he did. He confessed every sad, treacherous detail of their family feud. An argument between the oldest and youngest brother that led to the death of the one in the middle—the peacemaker, felled by those that wanted war.

"I'm so sorry, my dear, for all of it." Meeting her gaze bravely, Dane continued. "In a way, this is my fault. I set this course in motion. Had I not turned on James, none of this would've happened."

Dellis blotted her moist eyes with a napkin, trying to be strong for him. "No, if this hadn't happened, Father would never have come to the colonies, and I wouldn't be here. Uncle James is responsible for his own actions. You did what you thought was right. Hindsight allows us omnipotent vision, but we don't have that gift in the moment. We must do as our conscience dictates."

"Thank you for trying to understand," her uncle replied, drawing in a deep breath and then letting it out.

"So, what now?" she asked, unsure what to make of everything.

"I needed Alexei to help me; he was the only proof I had against your uncle. John found the letters Stephen and I exchanged, but he burned them."

"I know." Dellis nodded with understanding. "I still can't believe you've met John and that you've been working together."

"Carlisle's a good man; a bit misguided and often lacking restraint—but good, none the less."

"Yes, he is." Dellis couldn't help but smile at her uncle's decidedly faithful, and rather amusing, description of her husband. "I don't know what John will do now that he's turned."

"I was surprised he did that. You're my only heir, and by marrying you, he would've inherited my title and everything I possess. I offered him the chance to spit in the eye of those that wronged him, yet he walked away from it. As a traitor, neither of you can inherit my title or the McKesson lands."

"He did that?" She clasped her hands together over her heart, feeling it stutter underneath.

"Yes." Her uncle nodded.

Oh, John. She was speechless, his name stuck on her lips, her heart overflowing with love for his sacrifice. He truly had given up everything for her.

Dear uncle and niece sat together for hours, recounting old memories, stories of her father's childhood, and even the truth of how she met John. Once the plates were empty and fatigue set in, she rounded up the dishes and cups, put them on her tray, and stood. "I still have to wash linen tonight. Ruslan will need bandage changes, and so will the soldiers. I promised to return and help with the injured. You should get some rest, and I'll get back to work."

"Your father would be proud."

A pleasant thought to end the evening on. Her uncle followed her into the kitchen, helping her unload her tray. Everyone had gone to sleep, a cauldron of water boiling over the fire waited for her linen to soak.

"I'll be with you, Uncle, through all of this." She clasped his hands in hers, turning to him, their misty eyes meeting again. "We're together now."

Just as Dane started to speak, the side door opened, and a familiar head of dirty-blond hair peeked around the edge.

She let out a gasp of excitement. "John!"

How could his niece and the woman have just disappeared? With how Dellis preened and fawned over that dilapidated old house, it seemed extraordinary for her to leave it unattended for more than a day. He'd paid one of the local drunks a week's worth of spirits to watch for Dellis's return, yet still, James had heard nothing.

Rumor had it a battle had ensued between Herkimer's forces and the British in one of the ravines off the old military road. It was surely truth as remnants of the fighting force had started to return to Fort Dayton and their local homes. Dellis had certainly taken the woman and the darkie slave along to help care for the injured. It was just like his magnanimous niece to put herself in the path of danger, pretending to be something she wasn't. Stephen's selfless influence had wiped off rather frustratingly on his daughter, and she fancied herself a doctor, always butting her nose in where it didn't belong.

James would have to go see for himself; perhaps his spy had delved into the spirits and was too inebriated to notice Dellis's return—the likely scenario. James saddled his horse, belting the leather in place, and then put his foot in the stirrup, mounting up. The gelding fussed and fought back, unusual for such a well-trained horse. He smelled something, and then James heard the crack of a branch underfoot. An intruder. He drew his pistol, cocking it.

"I know you're here. Come out." Pulling the reins tightly to the right, James turned his horse around quickly.

Eagle Eyes stood waiting, fists akimbo, looking more dour than usual. The notoriously formidable Mohawk was injured; the large swatch of linen tied around his thigh was saturated in blood, and the one at his calf was caked with red and dirt.

"What happened?" James asked.

"Carlisle and your son got away. They joined the fight."

As expected, the Mohawk was economical with his words but managed to tell James all he needed to know. "Where are they now?"

Eagle Eyes shook his head. "I don't know."

James eyed the injured Mohawk, an uncharacteristic weariness in his black eyes. That wouldn't do. He needed to be at his strongest if he was to face off with Alexei and Carlisle.

"Come with me."

Once inside the study, James called for Mariah to bring linen and hot water. When the servant appeared at the door, she cast a fearful look at Eagle Eyes, and with pained steps, she deposited a basin full of steaming water, a bottle of whiskey, and linen on the table.

As she started to back away, James seized her wrist, stopping her midstride; the girl was trying his already over-extended patience. "Girl, where do you think you're going?"

She took one look at Eagle Eyes and then shook her head.

"I have no intention of cleaning wounds; that's women's work. Now see to him."

Mariah wrenched her arm free then ran for the door before James could stop her.

"Helena!" he yelled. "Bring that girl back in here." Damn her timidity; she'd do his bidding or be out on the street selling her wares.

Not a second later, Helena appeared in the doorway, her gaze honing in on Eagle Eyes. "You can't ask that poor girl to patch up a savage. She's terrified, and rightly so."

James looked down his nose at his wife, daring her to challenge him. "Then you'll do it."

Helena met his gaze with an imperious one of her own and then turned around, walking back towards the kitchen. "Mariah!"

The servant girl returned several moments later, still trembling, her eyes full of tears, a large, red handprint on her cheek.

"See to him, now."

On heavy legs, she walked over to Eagle Eyes and started to remove the wrapping from his leg.

"Where's Mrs. Allen?" Eagle Eyes asked, though his dark gaze was focused on the bodice of the servant girl's dress.

James snorted, remembering his last encounter with the infamous, turned destitute, Celeste. "Permanently out of our hair. Let's just say Mrs. Allen will be rather busy trying to sort out her own affairs for a while."

The Mohawk licked his lips, his eyes drinking up the young woman cleaning his wound. He trained his gaze upward, inclining his head in suggestion towards Mariah.

James nodded in approval. The savage could do what he wanted with the girl, as long as he was fighting fit and ready to deal with Alexei when the time came.

"So, Carlisle was with Alexei? How is that possible?" James asked, his mind playing out all the options to conclusion. What were the chances Carlisle turned and freed Alexei? That would be advantageous, for James would have two traitors on his hands, and Butler would be ever so grateful for their return.

"Do you know where the woman is? Tomlinson's wife?" Eagle Eyes asked.

"I do. But that's none of your concern—"

Before James could finish his sentence, he heard knocking at the front door that Helena was clearly ignoring—for it carried on, getting progressively louder. He stomped his way through the house to the door, giving his wife a disapproving glance as she sat quietly in the parlor, sewing. When he opened it, he found his spy standing there, red eyed and filled to the brim with drink.

"Sir, they've returned," the man mumbled, his breath so strong it could ignite with a spark.

"Who's returned?"

He rubbed his eyes as if trying to massage the drunkenness from his vision. "Your niece, the haughty one, and the darkie."

"Anyone else?"

The drunk paused for a moment, his eyes rolling skywards. "Don't know, but for a bit more money, I might be able to remember."

Damned drunken extortionist; that's what I get for not using my own men. Reaching into a pocket, James pulled out a few shillings and held them up like a treat for an overeager dog. "Now, was there anyone else at my niece's house?"

The man nodded, vigorously. "Oh, yeah. I saw a couple of them Redcoat officers, but not the tall blond one that you're looking for."

"What about Alexei and the dish boy? Are they there?"

He shook his head. "Nope, don't know for sure."

Damn. "Thank you. Now go back and keep your eyes on the house until I tell you otherwise." James handed over some coin and slammed the door shut. When he turned back around, Helena was glaring at him.

"James, what are you doing?" She boldly stepped in front of him, preventing his departure. "Tell me!"

Suddenly, he heard the crack of glass breaking and a loud scream. He pushed her out of the way and raced back to his office. When he opened the door, Eagle Eyes had the servant girl pinned to the ground, her skirts thrown up over her head while he rutted on her from behind like a randy dog. Mariah shrieked and screamed underneath him, her legs kicking wildly.

"Enough of that." James hissed, slamming the door. The servant girl moved away, fat tears rolling down her cheeks as she thrust her skirts down and sprinted from the room. "Dellis and Carlisle's men are at The Thistle. The battle is over."

"What do you intend on doing?" Eagle Eyes stood, adjusting his breech cloth.

"I'll deal with this."

James paced, a plan forming with each passing step. "You'll go to the Oneida village and search for Alexei and the woman. I'm sure your men will be eager to dish out a little vengeance on those traitorous Oneida while you're there."

A smug grin turned up the corners of Eagle Eyes's lips. "Yes."

"Go now; don't waste time. We want this to look like retribution for today's battle."

James laughed. Finally, he'd found a way to put an end to Joseph and his village once and for all. Once Alexei and Carlisle were found, there'd be no one left to tell the truth.

Chapter
Forty-Four

At the last minute, a decision was made to wait until the morning to travel to Albany for a meeting with General Schuyler. Another runner left earlier with dispatches describing the events of the Oriskany battle. What came next was anyone guess. Stanwix was still under siege, and the colonists were still outmanned and outgunned. Exhausted and listless, the only thing John wanted to do was find Viceroy, clean up, have a drink, and crawl under the sheets, preferably with his warming pan beside him.

It took hours of searching in the dark, unending forest to find Viceroy. Someone had untied the precious mount and let him run free. John found his stubborn, yet obedient, horse frolicking in the woods, thankfully nearby, instinctively knowing his beloved owner would come back.

John took a deep breath and mounted up. It was time to finally go home. *Home.* With a gentle kick to Viceroy's flank, John took off down the road at a brisk pace. *Home.* Once again, the word popped into his head, and with it, serenity that practically seeped through his veins, drawing out his last vestiges of energy. Soon, he'd know blessed, blissful sleep in his own bed. And in his dreams, Dellis would be in his arms, long, silky tresses resting against his shoulder. Seeing her hugging Patrick earlier, and that dolt kissing her, sent a fresh surge of adrenaline laced with jealousy through

John's veins. He was angry and possessive, the events of the day rendering him impatient for what he'd fought so hard for. His wife. His love.

Once outside The Thistle, John stopped, having never been so grateful to see something in all his life. Some of windows were boarded up, and the front door was in need of repair, but still, it was heaven.

He walked Viceroy around back to the barn, his stall ready and waiting for him. "It's good to be home, boy. I know you missed it." John brushed and fed his horse and then patted him on the side. "Thank goodness you're safe."

Taking a deep breath, John prepared himself for the unknown. Would she be happy to see him? Was it fixable, the passionate, destructive love they shared?

With hope and a bit of hesitation, he opened the side door, peeking inside. It was past three o'clock in the morning; he anticipated everyone would be asleep, but to his surprise, Dellis was standing at the kitchen counter talking to her uncle.

"John!" Her mouth fell open, but those black beauties lit up with pleasured surprise. That was hopeful.

John opened the door the rest of the way, stepping inside. "Merrick. I didn't expect—"

The words were caught in his throat, thick and sticky with guilt; he'd turned on the British, and technically, on Merrick, by letting Alexei go.

Instead of dealing out provocation, Merrick gave one of his half-cocked, knowing grins. "Don't trouble yourself, John; we can deal with those issues later."

"Come in. We're just finishing up." Dellis pulled out a chair for John and then started hustling around the kitchen, opening cupboards anxiously like a squirrel searching the ground for a nut. "I'll get you some food. I have biscuits left over and some oatmeal."

Throwing up his hands, he stopped her before she made tracks in the wood floor. "Actually, just something to drink would suffice." Looking down at his filthy clothing, he said, "I'm afraid I'll soil anything I touch, including that chair. Perhaps some water and soap, and I'll go out to the barn and clean up a bit. I know I still have some shirts left here."

With a nod, she reached under the counter and pulled out a bottle of whiskey from the cupboard. He noticed how her hands shook as she poured him a drink, his own clasped behind his back, wringing in anticipation. When she handed him the glass, their fingertips touched, their eyes meeting finally. There was so much he wanted to say.

I love you. Forgive me.

Merrick cleared his throat, interrupting their silent interlude. "My dear, I'm going to take a couple of your father's journals and retire for the night. What room can I use?"

Dellis shook her head as if clearing a mental fog and then turned to her uncle. "Use Father's room. I'll sleep down here in my old room. There's one of his journals on the desk—the one where he talks about meeting my mother for the first time. It's my favorite."

"Well then, if you'll excuse me." Merrick gave them both a nod and then exited the kitchen, leaving them alone in expectant, stilted silence.

John downed his tot of whiskey, relishing the burn that chased its way down to his stomach. *Liquid courage.* He needed it. Taking the glass back, she went to pour more, but he waved her off.

"No, thank you; too much of good thing often ends up bad, particularly with me. As you know. But the water and linen would be greatly appreciated."

"Yes." She nodded. "Come with me, and we'll get you cleaned up."

We will get you cleaned up. That had potential. Or was it just a play on words? He grinned slyly to himself. There was always room for hope.

He followed her into the dining room and over to the fireplace where there was a cauldron of hot water; she pointed to it. "Can you grab that, and I'll take the one from the kitchen."

He waited while she grabbed the other cauldron and followed her outside to the little shed that stood between the barn and the house. It was a sultry night; the humidity had waned after so much rain, leaving it cool, the sky clear and full of bright, shiny stars. Dellis opened the door to the little shed; inside was another fireplace, more water warming in the hearth, and next to it, a giant wooden bathtub. There was a small cot in the corner of the space and a table next to the bed full of soiled linen yet to be washed.

"Pour the water in." She pointed to the tub.

John looked at it skeptically and then back at her.

"What's wrong?"

"A bath?" He couldn't remember the last time he'd bathed.

Her beautiful black brows drew together while her eyes tracked up and down his filthy form. "Surely you don't believe simple ablution is going to get you clean. You stink to high heaven."

John laughed at the frankness of her statement and then poured both buckets of water into the tub. "You're not wrong."

"Now take that cauldron from the fire, fill the rest of the tub, strip down, and climb in. You need to soak, and I need to set more water to boil for my linen."

What a fantastic idea.

John grinned, aroused by the prospect of taking a bath while his domineering wife looked on. But it had to be a dream. Surely, he'd fallen asleep in the barn and would wake to Viceroy nudging his master in the back.

Being ever the obedient husband, John played along, stripping down and then submerging himself in the steaming water. It felt like heaven and hell simultaneously; every little cut and abrasion smarted and burned while his tense muscles uncoiled, embracing the relaxation that came from the intense heat. Closing his eyes, he leaned his head back on the edge, allowing the warm water to cast its spell.

When Dellis returned, she was carrying a bar of soap, and her arms were full of linen swatches. The heat made him languid, accentuating his fatigue; he opened one eye, watching her dump the soiled linen into the cauldron on the fire and then stir it around.

"John," she whispered, lifting her skirts and then kneeling down next to the tub.

He rolled his head to the side and smiled, feeling drunk and amorous. *How delightful.* "I didn't know you had a bathtub. I would've insisted we use it more often."

She chuckled. "My uncle bought it for us. When my father traveled to the Far East with Uncle Dane, he learned that water and bathing had therapeutic qualities. That was something my mother and our tribe had long since embraced, but apparently, not in the schools where my father trained."

To John's utter delight, Dellis dipped the bar into the water, lathered it up, and began washing his right arm, using her fingertips to dig into the knots in his muscles while she worked to clean the dirt away. He let out a groan, his eyes rolling closed for a moment. When he opened them again, she was intent on her work, lathering up his shoulder, working the muscles at the joint with strong, competent fingers. His shoulder ached incessantly since it had first been dislocated; the thick, sinewy fibers were constantly in knots, and it was plagued with bouts of numbness and shooting pains.

Closing his eyes again, he listened to the water slosh around as she dipped the bar again and started to massage his neck and back. If he were a cat, he would've purred; there were no words, his senses in overdrive, and he stretched, surrendering to her sweet, decadent assault.

Quietly, she unbraided the two pieces of hair close to his forehead, removing the little leather bands and trinkets, placing them on the table. "Close your eyes and lean forwards."

John submitted to a downpour of hot water and then brushed his drippy locks from his face. She glided her soapy fingers through his hair, massaging his scalp, each long pull reminiscent of ardent strokes of her hand on his cock. He couldn't stifle the groan that pushed its way out of his lips.

Was she doing it purposely, torturing him to the point of painful pleasure, or was her intent pure? He opened his eyes and looked over his shoulder at her, wanting to see the truth for himself.

But her face was serene, so meticulous and intent on her work she never once looked up. Her fingers worked the caked pomade and dirt from his tangled locks and then combed through them one last time.

"Lean forwards so I can rinse again."

John obeyed. *Once again with the orders.* Perhaps if he waited long enough, her next order would be: "Now, make love to me until I can't walk." One could only hope.

The water poured over his head again, washing away all the soap and dirt, but it did nothing to tidy up his thoughts. He fisted the water from his eyes and then leaned back against the rim, watching her refill the bucket from the hearth. She was a sight to behold; the front of her muted-brown stays was soaked, clinging to her curves, the swell of her breasts at the brim, ripe and dewy from the humidity of the cabin. She'd tied up her hair, exposing her long, graceful neck; lean, corded muscles flexed as she turned her head towards him and smiled—that smile that could melt even the Devil's heart. John reached out his hand, wanting to touch, but he pulled back, closing it.

Putting the bucket down, she scooted on her knees to the side of the tub and picked up the soap bar again. As she went to lather up his shoulder, he took a chance, his outstretched hand cupping her cheek, his thumb grazing her upper lip, tracing the two perfect points.

She stopped abruptly. Waiting.

His heart overflowed, the words rushing ardently from his lips like a river in the forest. "My love, I can take no more. If you're trying to torture me to the point of prostrating myself at your feet, then you've won. I beg you. Forgive me this one last time; I swear I'll not fail you."

To his utter surprise, Dellis turned her face into his palm, branding him with a sweet, soft kiss. And when she looked up, those arrestingly beautiful eyes were full of love so deep, he was surely lost in them.

"It is I who must beg *your* forgiveness, my husband. My John. Had I not left you in Oswego, had I trusted you, none of this would've happened."

She took his hand, gently washing it and then dipping it in the water. "Then I behaved like a child, refusing to listen to your explanation. How could I not see that you'd sacrificed everything for me? I pushed you away when we needed each other most. I was afraid. I hated myself for what I'd done. Hated myself because she could give you a child, and I could—"

John's heart ached from her tender confession. Love, frantic and wanting, pushing him to take a chance. He leaned up in the bathtub and claimed her lips, stopping her mid-sentence. She whimpered into his kiss, and he caught it with his mouth and tongue, desperate to taste every last bit of her sweetness. But it wasn't enough, her fire igniting the tinder that was his passion.

"Dellis, I need you now. I can't wait." He didn't give her a second to answer, climbing out of the tub, his body on top of hers like a wolf smothering its prey, ready to consume it. He held her down with his weight, his lips reaching for whatever flesh they could find, the fabric of her dress against his wet skin driving him wild. But it wasn't enough, he wanted more. Right then.

John reached for her skirts, pulling them up, his hand seeking the supple flower between her legs, finding it lusciously weeping and ready for him. And with one powerful surge, he buried himself to the hilt, her warmth twice as hot as the bath he'd just come from—and tight, so incredibly tight and slick, gripping him with want. *Oh, Lord, she is Heaven.*

She screamed, her eyes squeezed tightly shut, receiving his love and punishment with a passion matching his own. He wanted to own her, consume her, fuck her until she tore apart, release the beast that craved her flesh like sustenance. One more taste of that evil apple.

"I can't be gentle, my love. And I don't want to. Beg for me," John said through clenched teeth, his hips moving hard and fast as she moaned in unison, sinking her fingernails into his back, torturing his flesh. Their bodies made a wild, primitive noise each time his hips met hers, the crude slapping of wet flesh against her sweet softness. It was fast and wild and frenzied. And he wanted it harder.

"I want you to hurt like I do." Jealousy and longing made him ferocious; he ripped the front of her stays, desperate for a taste of those succulent breasts he was forced to observe but not allowed to touch. He sank his teeth into her milky mound, sucking down on her flesh until she screamed again. Her nipple pebbled and rose in his mouth; he drew off it, wanting to suck the very essence from her. He suckled and nuzzled both of them, burying his face between them until he could see nothing but that beautiful valley. He watched them bounce and lift with each of his forceful trusts, both swollen, seeking him again.

But still, he needed more. It was selfish of him, but he demanded it, his body no longer his own, the animal in him instinctively taking over. He wanted her submissive, helpless, and begging for his favors, her pleasure at his whim. He hooked both her legs over his elbows and drew her high, placing his hands next to her head, spreading her wide open for his assault. He could smell her arousal, taste her on his lips, feel her luxurious warmth clenching around him; he was drowning in her, totally submerged.

Instead of continuing his furious pace, he halted; then, with all his pent-up jealousy, he thrust himself deep and hard, but slowly, in unison with each furious statement. "You're mine, Dellis. I do this to you. I alone love you. I give you pleasure. Just me." It was childish and possessive of him to say such things, but that needy boy within smarted from seeing her kiss Patrick, and John wanted her to know it. When she sighed and reached for him, drawing him down into her arms, he groaned out his satisfaction and started anew, pumping his blade into her harder, faster, watching her eyes widen with each sharp stab, screams escaping her lips one by precious one, making him feel dominant. A wolf—his beautiful doe, yelping and screaming beneath him. He wanted to come inside her, smell his scent all over her, mark her as his own. Claimed. Forever. His.

"My wife. My Fennishyo. Mine." He demanded, pushing his furious pace, pleasure racing up his spine, making ready his hot seed for that moment of bursting ecstasy. "Mine."

But instead of relenting, Dellis reached up with trebling hands, grasping his face, and whispered, ever so sweetly, "You're mine, Just One. *Mine.*"

His willful, strong Dellis; she never relented, and he loved her for it.

The fight was over, the beast tamed—her power over his heart omnipotent. With a groan and one burst of light, he pushed himself deep and once again handed himself over to her. Slow, lugubrious strokes became his rhythm as he filled her with his essence—his love and his life forever hers. Blessed, fleeting oblivion only she could grant. And with nothing left, he fell limp into her arms, his body and mind under her spell, lost forever in dark eyes and soft, alabaster skin.

It was bliss, a moment's satiation, before the craving began anew—better than opium or any drink. He would forever want her, decadent addiction, and he hapless to her thrall. John rubbed his face against her neck, marking her with his scent, covering himself in her own.

"My love."

Finally surfacing from their interlude with ecstasy, he leaned up, taking in her sweet disarray. Her clothes were torn to shreds from his rage, her legs still hooked over his arms, splaying her while she lay wide eyed, helplessly panting, gasping for each precious breath. Submission's pose. And he took her there.

Instead of the sweet reunion he dreamed of night after night, he was rough with her, selfishly taking everything from her and offering nothing. Fearfully, his lips sought hers for a sweet kiss of forgiveness. With soft eyes and dewy lips, she responded, drawing his tongue in, languidly loving it with her own.

"Forgive me if I hurt you," the gentleman said penitently, though the scoundrel in him felt no remorse.

She wrapped her arms around him, drawing his head down to rest in that beautiful valley, miles of supple legs entwining around his waist. "You didn't."

John pressed his lips to her breast, her sore, swollen nipple, red and puckered, within his view. He lifted his limp, exhausted arm, allowing his fingers to gently thumb and caress it. "I swore I'd never take you without asking." He swallowed, conjuring up the words he needed to say. "I know I didn't pleasure you. Give me but a moment, and I'll love you as you deserve. I just couldn't stop—"

She shushed him, her hand stroking his hair. "Don't apologize; it was incredible. And to know that you still need me, want me like this…"

"Still want you?" He traced a little ring around her areola, watching the goosebumps form, her nipple pebbling even more. "Dellis, how could a man not want a woman who's just as fearless in bed as she is in life? For surely you weld my weapon better than I can, and you seat a horse with such vigor…"

The double entendre of his comments brought a smile to her lips. But instead of playing along, she was serious, tapping into the core of his never-abating conundrum. "John, my uncle told me what he offered you, and yet you turned your back on it?"

He looked up at her. She was beautifully ravished, her hair in a messy bun at her neck, her lips red and swollen, and marks littered her décolletage from his scruff. He ran his hand down her stocking-covered leg, pulling the tie loose and then sliding it down until he encountered the soft leather of her shoes. She contracted her thighs around his waist, her hips reaching for him again.

Holding back, John rested his elbows on the earthen floor, lifting himself up so he could look into her eyes. "I want there to be no secrets between us. I have things I need to confess." He didn't give her a chance to interject, purging his soul before his conscience held him back. "I helped St. Leger plan the attack at Oriskany. I instructed him on how to execute the ambush. It was only by happenstance that I saw Ho-sa-gowwa in the woods and learned that you and the village were with the brigade. When I realized what I'd done, it was then that I turned. I couldn't live with more innocent blood on my hands. I'm sorry for that, and I'm sorry that I was too late to save your brother or to warn all of you. It was my fault."

Dellis was silent, her dark eyes regarding him curiously.

"But the truth is, I had long since realized my place was no longer with the army; my reputation would forever haunt my career. And if I stayed, my fortunes would forever be at the whims of men with more money and power, and yes, even your uncle. I refuse to live on the charities of others again. I'm sorry it took me so long to come to this conclusion." He brushed a lock of hair out of her face so he could cup her cheek, his thumb tracing every precious dip and curve meticulously. "I may no longer be a Redcoat, but I'm certainly no Rebel. I don't know what I am anymore. But you deserve more than a penniless traitor for a husband. I'm wanted for war crimes now. If I'm caught, I'll surely be hanged. With your uncle's fortune, I could've given you everything you could ever want, but now that I've turned, I have nothing. I'm nothing but a marked man."

John hesitated, his gut aching in anticipation of her response.

But instead of speaking, Dellis drew him down for a long, languid kiss, her tongue finding his, molding and caressing his until he let out a gasp, his residual energy tapped by her tender assault. "John, you're an Oneida now, and you're mine. I don't need anything else in this life but you."

He closed his eyes, letting out a breath, and with it, his fear. As long as they had each other, he could find a way to go on.

"I'm sorry about your brother, my love," he said, resting his head on her breast again. "I'm so sorry."

"I know," she replied, her heart gently thrumming against his ear. "He's with our parents now."

"At peace, finally," he said, closing his eyes, sleep on the horizon and blessed blissful hours in her arms. But just as he started to doze off, he heard them: ominous voices calling his name, flowing through the windows on the wind where only a moment before, her screams of pleasure carried. *What do they want?*

With each passing moment, they got louder and louder, dragging him down deep into dreams of fire and death.

"Justice... John."

Chapter
Forty-Five

"Please, stop!" John cried out, throwing his hands up in protest. "Let them go!"

It was the nightmares. Again with tortured dreams that greedily stole peaceful repose from her beloved.

"Dellis!" His head fitfully thrashed back and forth on his pillow. She rolled onto her side, wrapping her arms around him.

"Shh, I'm here," Dellis whispered into his hair, kissing his forehead.

His skin was still moist and hot from the bath, but there were also fresh beads of sweat along his hairline. He panted, quick strained breaths that fought their way out as if he'd run a great distance in fear.

"What have I done?" John cried, his eyes still closed, his brow painfully furrowed. He curled into her, burying his face in her neck. "No, I beg you. Let them go." His pleas were like painful, pitiful groans that pulled at her heartstrings.

Everything he'd ever known, he'd given up for love of her. Of course he was still plagued with nightmares, so many years of trauma, and then the added fear of the unknown.

He trembled against her, his arms, like iron bands, wrapped around her tightly, holding on for dear life. She bent down and kissed his ear, whispering into it, "I'm here; you're safe." And with that, he relaxed, his body going slack, melting into hers.

When he was finally resting easily again, she sat up on the edge of the bed, stretching her sore, tired limbs. Looking over her shoulder, she couldn't help but marvel at him a bit. He was suddenly peaceful, lying on his stomach with his face smashed into the pillow like a drunken boy, little puffs of air swishing between his parted lips. After they made love on the ground, she managed to squire him over to the cot in the corner of the shed, hoping for more of the same treatment, but he fell asleep. Only unmitigated fatigue could keep him from his favorite pursuit—that she knew for truth.

She leaned over and tousled his still damp, silky hair. God, how she loved him; her heart threatened to burst with it.

He roused, his voice sleep softened. "I'll be ready in a minute, my love; just give me a little longer. Even a stallion must rest."

She giggled. "So ardent, my lover. What has become of my husband? You must be getting old."

"You've robbed me of my usual prowess. Age has nothing to do with it." John's eyes were closed, but she could see an impish grin turning up the corner of his mouth. "You knew what you were doing when you brought me out here, my goddess."

"Do you believe I intended malice towards your person?" she asked in mock outrage.

He shook his head against the pillow. "You're no innocent, wife. Do you deny that it was your intent to seduce me with that bath, which was both torture and heaven simultaneously, and then ravish me afterwards?"

"You have selective memory, husband. For it was you who did the ravishing." Dellis shot him a heated glance, just in time for his eye to roll open and see her do it.

"No. No. This was all *your* fault. Consider yourself successful, my love. Regard me… lying here… thoroughly tupped."

She snickered, watching him rub his nose and then fall back into his sleepy puffs.

Getting up from the cot, she noticed a pile of papers lying on the floor, and something sparkling on top of it. Bending over, she snatched them off the floor; it was her necklace, the garnet winking and shimmering in the candlelight. She smiled, grateful to have it back. The papers, as she expected, were maps John had made of Niagara and Fort Stanwix, but the last one, however, was not. She unfolded it and turned it right-side up. When she realized what it was, she blushed from the roots of her hair to the tips of her toes.

It was a nude. Of her! How accurately he recreated every inch of her body from memory, all the way down to a small scar on her inner thigh.

Dellis cast a knowing glance at him but held back a reprimand. He must've truly missed her to draw such a scandalous—and though she hated to admit—beautiful picture of her.

Putting it on the table, she looked back at him, in awe of the flawed-to-perfection man that was her husband. Removing the remains of her clothes, Dellis climbed into the tub, finally able to do her own washing. The water was lukewarm, but it still felt decadent on her sore muscles. She ached between her thighs, John's vigorous lovemaking leaving her delicate skin tender, but in a good way. As she lathered up the bar of lavender soap, she glanced over her shoulder at him, a wicked idea forming. She knew just how to wake His Sleepiness.

Gently, Dellis ran the soapy bar over her arms, enjoying the slide of it against her skin, allowing her mind to replay one her most intimate dreams of him. She started to hum *Greensleeves*, knowing the significance of that song would undoubtedly pique John's curiosity.

When she was sure he was paying attention, she gently ran her soapy hands over both of her breasts, massaging and lingering over her nipples until she heard his breath catch. He was awake. The sensation of being watched and the warmth of the water was intoxicating. Wanton. Slowly, she stroked her breasts again, moaning a little as sparks shot from the rosy peaks, sending a fresh surge of luxurious moisture to her sex. Lathering up her fingers again, she ran them down her stomach, leaving soapy tracks all the way to her inner thighs.

"Did you miss me, wife?" he whispered in a horse, breathy voice. A lusty one.

She knew what he wanted to hear. Yes, it was uncharted territory for her, and so very unladylike, but with him it didn't seem to matter. The more she misbehaved, the more he relished it.

"I did miss you, especially at night, when I was all alone." She played innocent, just feeding his curiosity a tasty little morsel. When she glanced over her shoulder, she found that his eyes were focused and hot, turning so blue they looked like brilliant gems glinting in candlelight.

"And sometimes, I wanted you so badly, I ached." She massaged her inner thighs, hesitating for a moment, her body responding to her own touch, heat building in her core.

"And then what?" he said, through barely parted lips.

Dellis let out a little groan, running her fingers between her thighs, parting her sex with nimble fingers, finding her nub of pleasure, feeling its slickness, letting it swell between her knuckles. "I'd dream about us together."

He was captivated, totally under her spell. It made her feel empowered and so incredibly brazen. She took her time, noticing how his eyes followed the rivulets of water as they caressed the dips and curves of her belly down to her legs.

Then, ever so gently, she stroked and explored herself, running her hands over her breasts again, teasing the pink peak until a moan escaped her.

"Don't stop." He gasped, his hips pushing into the cot.

She smiled and boldly relented. "You were worshipping me with that wicked mouth of yours."

The look he gave her was so hot she turned from sugar to caramel, her last vestiges of restraint burned away in those sapphire-blue flames. He licked his lips, his gaze trained on her fingers as they slid between her thighs again. "Have mercy, wife... Tell me more."

Dellis shook her head, suddenly too embarrassed to admit where her thoughts went. No lady would confess such a thing—and surely not to her husband.

"You're blushing, love; tell me." His voice was husky and persistent with want. "Please."

With his insistence, she rallied, confessing the darkest part of her fantasy. "Then I… I rode you wildly, like my horse."

"Dellis," he said on a breath, sounding like he was in pain.

John crawled off the little cot and dropped on his knees next to the tub, grabbing her hand from between her thighs and salivating over it for a moment, denying himself.

"You're like the finest sweetmeats, my love, or almond comfits. Your voice, your body, your taste… I can't get enough of it." Finally, he took her fingers in his mouth, sucking gently until he'd tasted away her arousal. "Tell me, while you were riding me, where were your lovely hands?"

She grinned, brazenly, painting the rest of the picture for him in all its glorious detail. "In your hair. Making you give me what I want."

"Oh? That was your fantasy?" He cocked a brow, his eyes widening, the entirety of her admission seeming to finally dawn on him. Reaching for her, he said, "Come to me." And she could think of nothing she wanted more.

Dellis climbed out of the tub and toweled off, allowing him to look his fill while she dried herself with painstaking slowness. When finished, she looked down at him on his knees, almost prostrate to her.

He smiled, eye level with her most intimate parts. "My beautiful valley."

"You're shameless," she said on a laugh, heady and drunk from their love play.

"I can't help it. It's just too perfect." He shook his head with mirth. "And my secret. When I call you Fennishyo, know I'm thinking about traipsing my tongue through this sweet, beautiful valley, living out your fantasy."

"Enough humor, husband; worship me." Emboldened, she grabbed his hair, fisting and tugging it, drawing him closer, and he obeyed, using his large, rough hands to spread her thighs open to his wet, wanting mouth. The first touch of his tongue was like lightning shooting through her, stopping her heart with an electric jolt. She reached back for the table so she didn't collapse from the shock of it, yet she opened up more for him.

Pulling her hands back to his hair, he glanced up at her and smiled, his lips red and glossy from suckling her. "Ride me."

She let out a scream so loud surely the neighbors, several yards away, heard it. Ripples of pleasure flowed from his mouth into her sex, so intense she lacked the decency to care if God Himself was listening. All that mattered was the man on his knees, worshipping her. And he was good at it. A proficient.

His hands grasped her buttocks, caressing and spreading her, drawing her in for more of his decadent treatment. And oh, his mouth... The perfect combination of friction: rough, relentless tongue teasing yet denying her, and gentle, soft lips massaging and coaxing her. A lick here, a nibble there, and then, *oh yes*, he'd clamp down and suckle. Her hips instinctively bucked against his mouth, reaching for more, and more, and more, until she was riding his face like a saddle that fit her to perfection.

"John, I'm so close." She groaned, tugging his hair. "I want you inside me."

"No more fantasy?" he asked innocently, and then suddenly, he let out a laugh. "But we haven't gotten to the part when you pull out the crop."

"John." She groaned. Humor was the furthest thing from her mind, yet, at that moment, he seemed to be relishing his own wit.

With the scruff of his chin, he rubbed it against that perfect little jewel and then breathed warm, balmy air into her skin, singeing her. "Are you sure I can't persuade you?" Then, like a bear greedily trying to extract every last bit of honey from a hive, he buried his face deep, plunging his tongue into her, tasting her where she wanted him most. And her body responded, melting into his lips, reaching for more.

"Yes, Dellis." He pulled back, his rough tongue licking and lapping her up, and then he took her into his mouth to savor again, threatening to shatter her into a thousand pieces.

When she looked down, she found that his eyes were closed, his lips rhythmically moving, consuming her. One of his hands held her in place, and the other was slowly stroking himself until he was swollen and slick, the tip weeping with want.

"I want you," she begged, her eyes on his manhood. "Please."

Suddenly, he stopped, pulling away, a glistening, wicked grin on his lips. "So much for the crop."

He stood, towering over her, his powerful build, as always, giving her pause. He was so lean; long muscles wrapped around strong, perfect bones, and she swore every last one of them could be seen through his sun-kissed skin. She wanted to run her tongue up each of those lovely dips and curves of his powerful abdominals, trace the line from the top of his hips down into his navel. His skin was smooth and salty, his own unique flavor, like a fine, peaty Scotch whiskey. And the scars, they made him all the more beautiful. She wanted to kiss every last one.

Grinning, he said, "I've twice been denied the chance to make love to you on a desk. Indulge my fantasy?"

Slowly, he turned her around, flattening her hands on the table, using his powerful hips and needy erection to coax her against it. "I want to show you something wonderful," he whispered into her ear, running his hands down her sides, grazing the sides of her breasts and then resting them on her hips.

"Does this position frighten you?" He pressed his hips into her backside, his manhood slipping between her thighs, the blunt, full tip kissing her moist folds ever so gently.

"No," she replied, shaking her head.

Dellis knew why he asked; after what happened to her, they'd never tried to make love that way, afraid to evoke her fears. But she felt none. Her need trumped fear.

"Are you sure?" His lips were so close to her ear, his melodious voice and steamy breath sent a shiver down her spine.

She nodded, persisting against his dubious hesitation, nuzzling her backside against his erection. Reaching her hand back, she grabbed his hair, pulling his lips down to hers. "Please, John. I can't wait anymore."

He let out a groan, but she claimed it, sliding her tongue between his lips, indulging in his heady flavor mixed with her arousal. God, how she missed him. Starved to the point of mania.

"Love me," she said into his kiss, wanting to show him with no uncertainty that she belonged to him. Forever.

"Always." Their eyes met in a kiss.

His large, powerful hands at her waist made her feel small and delicate—breakable. And he was so gentle; ever so slowly pushing inch by decadent inch until she was full and sure she could take no more of him. But to her utter surprise, he went even deeper, leaning her forwards, resting her forearms on the table, her body offering him inches she didn't know she had left. And then total, decadent possession, his hips pressed to her backside, and she was gloriously full of turgid, pulsating man.

He held deep for a moment, slowly testing her with quick, short thrusts, forcing little mewls and whimpers from her lips. It was heaven.

"I want to see you when you come." She groaned out her heart's desire while her body instinctively tightened around him, holding on for dear life; no longer the nihility of yearning, he was thick and deep inside.

"Look at me."

She glanced over her shoulder, and he was there, placing a gentle kiss on her shoulder blade and then taking a little nip of it. "Now would be a great time for that mirror in my room," he said with a naughty grin.

Her hands ached to touch him; he was so close, yet out of her reach. It was maddening. All she could do was watch, deferring to his lead.

And he was glorious in his passion, with his hands resting at the base of her neck, massaging her shoulders, the taut muscles of his abdomen flexing and cording as he pumped slowly into her. He slid his hands around her sides, palming both her breasts, toying with them.

"John." She screamed his name with each thrust, like the refrain of a song played over and over with maddening, blissful repetition. His hips moved against hers, his thumbs taunting and teasing her nipples to a painful point. He squeezed her swollen breasts together, rolling the peaks between his fingers, driving her crazy. A quick death from decadence on the brink.

"Give me your hand."

She obeyed, linking her fingers with his, letting him draw them down between her legs, taking her to that little place, the flint that sparked every time he ran his fingers over it. It was so slick and swollen, with each pass of their fingertips and each surge of him inside her, she felt herself falling further into the abyss.

"I love you," she whispered, looking back at him. Again, their eyes locked, blue flames against the midnight sky. He made sounds she'd never heard before, gasps evolving into deep, guttural groans of satisfaction. She couldn't look away, not for a second, praying it would never end.

And suddenly, it was there, on the edge, ready to consume her. Hard steel invading wet silk with fast and powerful strokes; the contrasting sensation was painful, yet incredible, too.

"I'm coming." She moaned, pushing her hips back, seeking him, faster and faster, trying to find it.

He wrapped his arm around her waist, stroking her, guiding her into passion's arms. Her body instinctively rippled and then opened up, taking him deeper until she could feel him at her womb, kissing it with the tip of his sex. And like a hot coil wound too tightly, suddenly, it broke, her body releasing with spasm after decadent spasm, her intimate muscles clamping down on him rhythmically. A shiver rolled down her spine as her head fell forwards, her body limp, exhausted, and thoroughly loved.

But he wasn't finished. John grabbed onto her hips, holding her up while he pumped so vigorously, she had to grasp the table for support. And though it seemed impossible, his thrusts became quicker and harder; lush sounds of him moving in and out mixed with passionate groans. The table rocked and protested on weak legs as she held on, accepting her lover's decadent assault like a mare in the field with her stallion mounting behind. Dellis's body was raw and sore, yet taking John ever deeper, his sex growing thicker, testing her with each stroke, taking everything and asking for nothing.

"Dellis." He panted out her name. Then suddenly, he stiffened, his hands clamping down on her hips, thrusting himself full on one last time, threatening to render her in two as he groaned out his pleasure into the night. When she looked back at him, his eyes were closed tightly, his mouth open wide, passion's expression paining his visage; such an exquisite sight she'd never forget. And the sensation of him exploding against her walls, hot and wet, pumping his life into her, was incredible—and too damned brief.

John rested his head between her shoulder blades, his sweat and silky tresses caressing her nape, his strained breaths, sweet and urgent, sending more ripples of pleasure down her spine. Again. Already. He let out a sigh, wrapping his arms around her. "Please, never leave me again."

The very words she'd just been contemplating.

"You're so quiet; are you all right?" he asked curiously, worry creasing his brow.

"I'm not." She gasped, fighting back tears of joy. "I want you inside me as long as possible. I already miss you." She leaned into him, enjoying the feel of his body curved around her—inside her—like a perfect cocoon. "I, too, have longed for you, John. Now that I have you, I can't bear the thought of being parted. And I know you must leave me. I can't—"

"Don't think of it. I'm here with you now; nothing else matters." He kissed her nape, moving her hair out of the way so he could nuzzle her ear. "My fondest wish is that you tell me in a month's time that I've given you a babe."

He was so tender, she almost cried, wanting so badly to grant his wish, fearing it would never happen.

"What if I can't?"

He caressed her earlobe with his lips, taking it between his teeth, nibbling and licking it, provoking her burgeoning passion. "Then I'll enjoy trying over and over until we succeed."

When he turned her around, she looked up at him through slow-forming tears that cloaked his beautiful face with mist.

"Dellis, you must believe anything is possible. Especially between us. That I'm holding you in my arms right now is nothing short of a miracle."

John was right; not even Shakespeare could've written such a love a story as theirs. It was destined. Fate's sleight of hand. Karma.

"When it comes to you, I believe." She fought back tears of uncertainty and then tousled the front of his hair. "You always give me what I want."

Instead of quelling the passion that he was stirring, she turned into him, wanting more. "How about we try again, right now, husband? Please?"

"Yes, wife." And with a grin that spread from the lines that bracketed his mouth to the corners of his eyes, he did as she asked, so ardently.

Chapter
Forty-Six

"Someone's pounding on the door, Helena!" James yelled from his office. His little wife was doing her best to annoy him by way of the silent treatment and was succeeding. "Where's Mariah?"

Getting up from his desk, he threw open the door to his study and stomped through the house. By the time he reached the door, Helena was finally getting up from the couch to open it. "Where's Mariah?"

"Resting." Helena hissed through her teeth. "That savage scared the wits out of her; disgusting, rutting beast, treating her like she was nothing but a common doxy. I refuse to allow him in this house again."

He shrugged her off. Eagle Eyes's behavior was abhorrent, but the native was damn useful. Turning to her, James bit back a snide remark about her "allowing" anything. He was the master of the house. "You can go now. I'll handle this."

"No," she said, brusquely. "I refuse to be kept in the dark any longer, James." With a cock of her brow, Helena threw open the front door, and waiting outside, once again, was the drunken spy.

Finally, news.

"Sir, he's at The Thistle," the man said, surprisingly soberer than earlier.

"Which one?" James asked, trying to push Helena away from the door, but she fought back, inching her way through the opening.

"I just saw the British Captain there and Alexei, too."

Yes. Finally, both of them had arrived. "Are you sure?"

The drunk nodded. James reached into his pocket, handed the drunk a couple more shillings, and then slammed the door.

Fisting her hips, Helena turned her infamous Russian rage on James. "What are you going to do?"

"Stay out of this, woman!" He pushed past her, rushing back to his office. It was time to make a move. He needed his gun. On the rack next to the door was his musket; he checked to make sure it was primed and loaded, threw the strap over his shoulder, and slung it over his back. Walking to his desk, he grabbed two pistols, stuffing them in the pockets of his overcoat.

"James, I'm not going to let you hurt Alexei. This ends here!" Though slight and small, Helena did an impressive job of blocking the door so he couldn't get around her.

"Move out of the way, wife, or I *will* move you." Grabbing her arm, he tried to pull her aside, but she fought back, grabbing the doorframe, rooting herself in place like a small but tenacious maple tree.

"No, James! Too long I've let you rough up Alexei, but no more!" She clawed the wood with her long nails, digging tracks as he tried to pull her away. "Not this time, husband."

Not this time? She'd crossed the line—beloved wife or not. "Do you dare disobey me?"

She stared him down with eyes of pure ice. "To save my son, I would, and to protect Dellis. You must stop now. No more." Then, as if on cue, she softened, her graceful hand reached up to cup his cheek, but he slapped it away. "James, Alexei is your son, too. *Our son.* Have we not all paid enough? There must be another way out of this."

"Move out of the way!" He pushed her through the doorway with such force she landed on the floor in a billowing pile of pale-blue skirts.

"No!" With determination to match his own, she pushed herself up and ran at him, trying to yank the musket from over his shoulder. He reached back and slapped her hand away, but she persisted, both hands on the barrel of the gun, trying to tug it free.

"Helena, don't defy me!" She'd crossed him for the last time—with that, he grabbed her arms and threw her against the door.

With a loud *thud*, her head bounced off the wood, but she continued to fight back with all the fierce loyalty of a mother protecting her child. "I won't let you hurt him or Dellis! I know you're going after that woman. I heard you talking to Lord Tomlinson. You made a deal with him to exchange her for Alexei and Carlisle. Stuart told me she was hiding at The Thistle. I won't let you do this."

"You won't let me?" James's eyes widened. No one told him what to do, not even his wife. He cocked his arm back and struck her, the dorsum of his hand connecting with the fine porcelain of her cheek.

Her body slammed against the door, rocking in its frame, and then she crumpled to the ground in one small, dainty little heap. She lay motionless, like a tiny, discarded china doll.

James stepped over her carefully, avoiding her expensive skirt, and then turned back for a moment, watching her move, painful little gasps escaping her bow-like lips. He'd never struck her before. It was something he was loathe to do, but she'd gone too far. "I'm sorry, my dear," he said with regret and then went on his way.

Once in the barn, he grabbed a torch, lit it, and then mounted his horse and took off towards the west end of town. Towards The Thistle.

A solitary rider in the night with evil intent; the shadow of his horse followed him like an ominous ghost, waiting to see him do Hell's bidding. Never did James think it would go that far. A murderer come in the night to kill every last one of them in their beds. They'd driven him to it: Dane, Stephen, Alexei, and even Dellis. It was time they all paid. Brother against brother. Like the three sons of York with destruction in their wake.

When James arrived at The Thistle, it was dark and quiet, the candles snuffed out for the night—more's the pity, for he had a key to the house and the gift of surprise on his side. Walking up the steps, he unlocked the front door, pushing it open slowly, listening to it creak and protest on rusty hinges.

With methodical steps, he walked inside the dining room, his pistol raised and half-cocked, the torch still in his other hand. Suddenly, time ceased to exist, and the past melded with the present; Stephen, bold and full of life, stood before him, Dellis in his arms as a little girl, and Alexei at Stephen's feet.

He held up an arm, stopping James midstride.

"Brother, let this hurt between us end now. I made a mistake. I regret it more than anything in this world."

Pleading? Dane and Stephen never heard James's pleading when they sent the King's men to take him to the noose. No, there would be no forgiveness.

"You'll pay for what you've done, brother. In this life or the next." James growled through clenched teeth.

"I've already paid with the loss of your love, my dearest brother," Stephen replied, with glassy eyes that matched the ones of the little cherub-like girl in his arms, save the color. "Tell me what I can do to mend this rift in our family? Please? I beg you."

James stared down at his son, who pitifully sucked his thumb and tugged on his uncle's breeches. Stephen leaned down and patted the boy's long, dark hair as though placating a little dog.

With disgust, James grabbed Alexei's arm, yanking the boy away. "You made your decision long ago. Now live with the consequences."

"Stephen, you brought this on yourself," James said quietly to the apparition that stared him down. "And your family."

With that, he walked through the memory, ignoring the pained look in the eyes of his brother. It was too late for forgiveness. Much too late.

With purposeful steps, James searched the bar and then the kitchen. From the hall, he heard noises, first a feminine voice and then the deeper tones of a male. A familiar one. Alexei.

With the barrel of the pistol, James pushed the door to Dellis's room open, but it was empty, the bed neatly set and untouched. Across the hall from Dellis's room was Stephen's parlor; James walked through it, his upper lip curling in disgust at the sight of the shelves full of books—precious, useless journals that his brother coveted like the Bible. He'd made his dream come true, becoming a successful doctor, while James had cruelly been denied his own future: a chance to be a great soldier, a duke who was respected and admired. All of it gone. And so Dane lived off the fortune and title that was once James's birthright.

I'll burn it all down. Yes, I will. They can all go to Hades together.

As he neared Stuart's room, the noises got louder, the rhythmic sound of a bed squeaking and banging against the wall, interrupted by interludes of feminine gasps and male moans of pleasure. Perfect timing.

The door to Stuart's room was closed. Grabbing the handle and pulling the latch, James slowly opened it, and as expected, he found Alexei on top of the woman, rutting like a randy stallion in the field. Both of them heard the door open and stopped abruptly, looking back at James in surprise.

He let out a laugh. Lifting his pistol, he aimed and pulled it to full cock, staring down the barrel at his son, point blank.

"Father, what are you doing?" Alexei lifted his hands in surrender.

The room was dark, his torch illuminating it just enough so James could see the outline of his son's face and the whites of his eyes. Slowly, James trained the barrel of his pistol down towards Alexei's heart and fingered the trigger. His fear was so tangible it could be seen in the darkness, but he didn't move; instead, he just stretched out his arms, valiantly protecting his woman.

"I should've done this a long time ago." Without a second thought, James pulled the trigger, the bullet dislodging with a *pop* and a puff of smoke, hitting Alexei in the right upper chest.

Stunned, he fell back against the woman, who was on her knees behind him. She screamed frantically, wrapping her arms around him and drawing him into her chest. "Alexei! No!"

"Father?" Alexei gasped through stunned, labored breaths. "Why?"

"Because you were always weak." James reached for the woman, yanking her arm, trying to pull her out from underneath Alexei's large, hulking body.

"Don't touch her." Rallying his strength, he jumped from the bed and came at James, fists flying and charging like a bull. He swung the torch, catching Alexei in the side and setting fire to the curtains above the bed. They went up in flames instantly, catching the wall on fire, licking brands greedily climbing up to the ceiling, consuming the wood and plaster.

"Will, get out of here!" Alexei yelled and then took another swing at his father, a massive fist connecting with his cheek.

There was no way he could win at fisticuffs with his giant, god-like son, outsized and outmatched, but what James lacked in brute strength, he made up for in firepower, pistols and a torch to his advantage

He swung the torch again, bashing Alexei in the side of the head, dropping him to his knees and then took the blunt end of the pistol and whipped him across the face several times until he fell deathly still on the floor. Leaning over, James took several chopping hits, making sure his son was down and would never get up again. Pulling the other pistol out, James cocked it, and with a *click,* aimed at the woman. She put her hands up, though her eyes stayed fixed on Alexei's motionless form.

"If you scream, I'll shoot him in the head. Stay quiet, bitch." James thrust the barrel in her face.

Will nodded. Great, salty tears spilled from her eyes for his useless, waste of a son. James snorted, grabbed a shirt from the ground, and threw it at her. "Put that on, now!"

She pulled the shirt over her head slowly, her eyes still focused on Alexei, blood pooling underneath him, staining the floor.

"I love you, Alexei."

James shoved the pistol in his pocket and grabbed her arm. "I'm sure your husband would take offense to that!" He yanked the woman over Alexei's body while she fought back, her arms outstretched, reaching for anything she could grab on the way into the parlor. "Alexei!" she screamed. "He's your son! How could you do this? Alexei!"

"Shut up, whore!" James stopped abruptly, pulled back his hand, and slapped her so hard she fell limp in his arms. There was no time to waste; the flames had already started to consume the back side of the house, blocking their path down the hall. The only exit was the front door.

Grinning, he brought the torch down on his brother's precious bookcase full of journals, watching them crackle and then burst into flames. "I promised you I'd see this house burned down before I groveled at your feet, Stephen. Well, I never grovel, and you're cold in the ground."

James dragged Will into the kitchen, swinging the torch back and forth, setting fire to everything in his path. He grabbed the whale oil lantern from the kitchen table and threw it on the ground, tossed some of the linen from the hearth on top, and then lit it with the torch. The makeshift lamp ignited, the fire spreading immediately, setting the wood cabinets ablaze. "And now, everything you love will burn with your precious house."

Once in the dining room, he grabbed some of the bottles of whiskey from under the bar and threw them into the kitchen, the flames exploding with a gust of wind, shattering the windows.

Dropping his torch, he yanked the woman around so he could get a look at her. She stirred, shaking a little before she opened her eyes, blinking several times. *So this is the prize everyone is fighting over?* She was small, like his Helena, with a large, round face and pretty hazel eyes. Nothing special— hardly worth the fuss, but to him, the woman would bring a fortune.

"How could you do that to your son?" Will yelled, her eyes tear filled. "What do you want with me?"

"Miss Parkhurst, I've come to take you back to your husband."

When she let out a gasp, James laughed. "I wonder what Lord Tomlinson will think when he finds out you've been fucking my son?"

Chapter Forty-Seven

John held Dellis in his arms, unable to sleep for fear of missing a moment of being close to her. She glanced up, her fathomless black eyes shining with love that could melt even the coldest of hearts. His goddess. His wife.

"What are you thinking?" she asked.

He grinned devilishly. "The desk was everything I imagined it could be and so much more. Ready to try it again?"

"You're incorrigible." She rolled her eyes Heavenward and then planted a kiss on his lips. "Here I thought you were going to say something sweet, like you're glad we're back together or how much you love me." She looked serene and totally delectable in her exasperation, and he loved every minute of it. Her glossy hair hung down her shoulders; her breasts pressed against his chest with maddening softness; and oh, the feel of her long, silky leg thrown over his. From then on, he'd savor all the little intimacies, take nothing for granted, for that was the stuff he missed most when they parted—and parted they would be, eventually.

"I'm overjoyed that we're back together," he said into her lips. "Enraptured to have you in my arms." Then he rolled over on top of her, pressing her into the little cot. "Will that suffice, my only love?"

She gave him a sidelong glance filled with suspicion, an impish grin forming at the corner of her lips. "And don't you forget it, or you'll find yourself sleeping in the cold."

He knew where she was going with that, and it was time to put her mind at ease. "My Lysistrata, no need to hold back your favors, consider me un-rideable save your beautiful bottom; though, I confess, I'm a bit disobedient. All the more reason to bring your crop to bed."

She let out a laugh. "Exactly so!"

He kept his witty retort to himself, instead, grinning suggestively, letting her imagine where his thoughts were roaming to, but she said nothing; their banter ended, and his fears started up again. What was he going to do? He had no money, no connections. How would he provide for her?

Leaning up on his elbow, he looked down at her, drinking in the sight of her flushed cheeks and sleepy disarray. "Dellis, I'm—"

Without opening her eyes, she put her finger over his lips, silencing him. "I know what you're doing; you're worrying again."

"Aye," he replied against her fingertip, the word coming out with all the pent-up tension that had been building in his breast.

"Stop," she said, finally opening her eyes. "It's been paid."

"What's been paid?"

"Your debt to Gavin." With her fingertip, she traced the shape of his lips meticulously as if she were drawing a picture.

"How?" He shook his head; the debt was a fortune, a sum beyond anything she could raise on her own—1200 pounds plus whatever interest Gavin added to it.

"Would you believe Will gave me the money? She's the missing heiress."

John shook his head, trying to make sense of what Dellis said. "Will is Lord Tomlinson's wife?" That obnoxious little dish boy who always sneered at John whenever he was around. He laughed out loud considering the sheer ridiculousness of the situation.

With a nod, Dellis said, "Yep. Alexei had her dress like a boy and hid her right under our noses. The poor thing got tarred and feathered by the mob; that's when I figured out she was a woman, but I didn't know who she really was until recently. She gave me the money when things were looking desperate."

"Once again, I tip my hat to your cousin's ingenuity." John snickered. "And apparently, I owe this woman a debt of gratitude for saving our house."

"*Our* house. I like the sound of that." Dellis leaned in and kissed him soundly, her tongue making a delightful study of his. With a sigh that sent little shivers down his spine, she said, "By the way, I got rid of our friend, Mrs. Allen, too."

"I find that hard to believe." The mere sound of Celeste's name turned those marvelous shivers to a painful chill. That woman was diabolical— Lilith personified. "Well, don't keep me in suspense."

"You underestimate me, husband." Dellis grinned ear to ear. "Have more faith."

"I do, my love. Remember, I too, have been on the receiving end of your frontal assaults plenty of times and felt the sting." He let out a laugh, ready for her to recount her tall tale. "But do go on."

"All right," she said, cracking her knuckles as if she were preparing for a fight. "So…"

He marveled as she confessed her plan and how she executed it flawlessly. In the past, he'd never attributed acting to his beautiful wife's repertoire of talents, but he stood corrected. When she'd finished telling her story, he shook his head incredulously; it was nothing short of a comedy, worthy of Shakespeare, and she was the fierce, bold Katherina.

"I can't believe you threatened to cut Celeste if she didn't confess that she was lying about the baby."

Dellis's eyes cast down sheepishly, a hint of red illuminating her cheeks. "I did. And I confess, I relished her terror. She deserved it for what she did to you."

"To us." John interjected, reminding her that it was both of their lives that had been hijacked by Celeste's evil plan.

"To us. Yes, John." Dellis leaned up and kissed him sweetly. "She's forever out of our lives."

He breathed an audible sigh of relief, so loud and thorough, she smiled.

"That's quite a story." Never again would he underestimate the strength and ingenuity of this woman he so loved. She was braver than any soldier he held the line next to. "I'm sorry you had to go through that. Did Gavin say anything?"

She replied, matter-of-factly, "Actually, he did; he gave me the money back and offered me a position as the next Lady Carlisle."

"What?" The green-eyed monster reared its ugly head. He looked away for fear she'd see the rage bubbling up in his eyes. He'd find Gavin and put a bullet in him at first chance.

Snickering, she pulled John in for a slow, drugging kiss that thrust his fears away and made his knees weak. "I said, 'thank you, but no.' I want only to be the wife of John Carlisle. No matter whom you become, I want only you… nothing more." Then she kissed John again, her words warming his heart, soothing the savage beast within.

"Why did he give you the money back?" Surely, his brother had a reason for it; Gavin never did anything without an ulterior motive.

"Perhaps I charmed his softer side, just like I did to you not so very long ago." She kissed the tip of John's nose innocently, yet the Devil was in her eyes. "And I have hope, someday, you two will reconcile. Anything's possible."

John snorted. "That might be true, but where my brother is concerned, I think we've found the one exception to the rule."

"Oh, John, please." She gave him a look that made his heart hurt. Erasing years of anger and fighting would take more than an apology and a handshake to remedy. A man's pride was just as potent as any grudge, neither to relent easily.

"Get some sleep; tomorrow will be a busy day." He purposely changed the subject; he could take no more of her kind words about his brother, jealousy surfacing anew.

After a kiss, John rested on his side, drawing her back to his chest, their legs curved against each other, fitting perfectly together like two spoons lying in the drawer. He lay awake, watching her until she dozed off, her body soft against his, her bottom nesting itself into his hips. Running his hand over her belly, he dared to dream sweet dreams of her round with his child again.

He closed his eyes, drawing in a deep breath of contentment to take him off to sleep. But just as he started to fall away, he heard a loud *pop*, like a musket firing, and then a howl. And it was close, too close.

"Dellis, wake up." John tapped her arm, rousing her.

"What is it?" She looked sleep softened, her tired eyes barely opening.

"I heard a gunshot and someone yelling." He rose quickly, looking for his clothes. "Where are my breeches?"

"I put them to soak," she replied, getting up from bed and pulling on one of her clean shifts from the laundry. "There are some of my father's leggings and a breech cloth in that basket near the hearth. And the shirts on the table are yours you left behind."

John dug through, finding the buckskin leggings and breechcloth, putting them on, and then pulled a shirt over his head. "Well, it would seem you've managed to succeed at getting me bare assed in buckskin."

"Never doubt my tenacity, husband." With a grin, she turned her back to him, offering her stays to tie.

"A wise man would never." Once dressed, he tied his hair back, smoothing it out of his face. "My musket is in the stable with both of my pistols. I'll get them; you stay here until I get back."

When he opened the door, a thick gust of black smoke wafted into the little shed. One whiff of the caustic air made both of them cough.

"John? No, tell me it's not what I think."

But it was. The Thistle was on fire.

"Cover your mouth with this." He grabbed a piece of linen from the table and handed it to her.

Dellis watched him tie the swatch around his face and then followed suit. When they stepped outside, both of them stopped abruptly, looking up in awe. Like perdition's flames, billowy and voracious, the fire had consumed the beautiful old house as if it were a soul of the innocent accidentally fallen into Hell.

John pointed at her. "You stay here." His words were purposely forceful, and then he took off running towards the back steps; as expected, she followed him anyway.

"Dellis, I told you to stay back!" he yelled above the crescendo of flames and cracking wood—Hell's symphony.

"John, everyone is sleeping upstairs, and Alexei and Will are in Stuart's room. You can't get them all out on your own!"

She was right. He needed her help. *Damn.*

"Do you have a ladder?"

The flames had consumed the kitchen and the back side of the house, climbing up to the second floor. It was only a matter of minutes before the rest of the house would ignite. The servant's staircase was likely impassable, but maybe not the front one that led upstairs from the dining room.

"Come with me, John." Dellis waved him on, both of them running back to the stable. On the wall, high above the stalls, hanging horizontally, was a ladder. She pointed to it. "Can you reach it?"

He turned one of the feed barrels over and climbed on top, pulling the old wooden ladder free. It was rotten, the wood aged and worn past safety, but it was all they had. Together, they ran back with it. John hoisted the ladder against the house at the window farthest from the flames.

"You hold on. I'll go up."

"John, I haven't seen Alexei and Will come out. Someone has to go in downstairs and get them."

Deciding in a split second, John pointed to the door. "I'll go after them; you climb the ladder. Wake Simon. He'll help get everyone upstairs out. The front staircase should still be passable."

Dellis nodded, her eyes focused on the fiery main floor John was about to enter. "Oh, John, be careful."

He kissed her quickly and then rushed to the well, rolling the bucket up and dousing himself with the water. Quickly, he ripped the hem off the bottom of his shirt, dunking it in water, wringing it out, and then exchanging it for the dry one around his mouth and nose.

Before he ran up the stairs, she yelled to him, "John, please, be careful!"

He nodded, throwing the back door open. A gust of smoke blew directly into his face, blinding him. John coughed several times as more caustic air filled his lungs, irritating and tickling his throat, causing spasms in his chest. The whole hallway was ablaze. Dellis's room was already burning, her four-poster bed like kindling in a campfire. Stuart's room was on the other side of the parlor, but it, too, was engulfed in flames. John could go no farther.

"Alexei!" he yelled, but no response.

It was gut wrenching to watch the fire turn what was once their safe haven into a fiery inferno. All of Dellis's father's precious books and furniture destroyed. Panic gripped John's heart; he yelled again and then continued down the hall. The kitchen was full of black, blinding smoke, his eyes watering in protest, further disorienting him. He reached his hands out, feeling around for anything he could recognize; taking another step, his foot encountered something large and immobile lying on the floor.

"Alexei! Will!"

John got down on his knees beneath the smoke, trying to see through teary eyes, his hands feeling around until they found what they sought. It was a body. He leaned in to get a better look. It was Alexei.

Rolling him over, John slapped Alexei's cheek a couple of times, but he didn't rouse. "Damn."

There was a bullet wound in his right shoulder and a large cut on his forehead. John looked around, but there was no sign of Will, the billowing smoke limiting his vision to only a couple feet. With as much strength he could muster, he dragged Alexei's hulking form through the kitchen towards the dining room, stopping for a moment in the bar to breathe.

Painful coughs choked their way out of John's lungs while he searched around, trying to find a way to escape the blaze.

As he reached down to grasp Alexei's hands again, John heard a loud *thunk*; simultaneously, a sharp pain bloomed at the back of his head. He'd been struck. He reached back to grab his assailant, but he was struck again; *thunk*, metal met bone with a crushing force. He could feel the warmth of blood oozing down his neck under his collar, a throbbing pain spreading from the source and radiating forwards, causing his head to feel like it would explode any second. His stomach pitched with robust nausea; he gagged and groaned, fighting the urge to vomit. Reaching out into the billowy smoke, he tried to snag his assailant, but it was no use, another loud whack resounded, bringing with it more pain. The room spun around him so fast he lost his footing, his cheek smacking the wooden floor so hard his head bounced once before it landed, and with a grunt, he succumbed to blackness.

Chapter Forty-Eight

"Wake up, wake up!" Dellis pounded on the window with all her might, the glass threatening to break with each hit. The flames were already climbing up the sides of her precious house, grabbing the wood with greedy hands, turning it to smoldering embers.

The ladder came painfully close to the fire; it was only a matter of time before it, too, would ignite, the rotted wood perfect kindling. When no one responded, she used her fist on the window, hitting it several times until the glass finally gave way, spewing into the bedroom. She unlocked the window and opened it, climbing inside. The room was already full of smoke, a gust of it billowing into her face; she coughed several times, her lungs protesting the hot, irritating air.

Smith was lying on the floor in a heap; she got down on her knees next to him. "Adam?" He roused a bit, his eyes rolling open. "You need air." She helped him to the window, hanging his arms over the ledge, encouraging him to take breaths. "Get some air. I have to find Clark and Agnes."

Rushing down the hall, she frantically pounded on all the doors, screaming everyone's names until finally, one flew open; Simon and Agnes both raced out, half dressed.

"Oh, thank God!" Dellis exclaimed, looking at both of them. "We have to get Ruslan out of here. There's a ladder at the window to Smith's room."

509

"What about the stairs?" Clark asked, between raspy, heavy coughs.

"We could try them. Smith isn't well; you're going to have to help him." Suddenly, it dawned on her, there was one more person yet accounted for. "My uncle! Oh, God. Agnes, go get him! Clark, help me with Ruslan." Dellis threw the door open to her cousin's room; already, the flames had reached the outer wall.

Clark grabbed Ruslan's arm and lifted him out of the bed with a heave, draping his arm over both shoulders. Dellis ran to his other side and took an arm, helping Clark ambulate the young man's limp form to the stairs.

The outer wall of the house was on fire, but there was a small, clear path down the stairs. "Let's try," she yelled to Clark.

"No, Dellis! Who knows if they're stable? We have to take Ruslan down the ladder."

She nodded, trusting Clark's instincts. "All right."

They walked back to the corner room; thankfully, Smith was out the window already, climbing down. Simon let out a loud groan and then positioned Ruslan like a child riding piggyback. Luckily, he was much shorter and stockier than his older brother, or it never would've worked.

"Will you be able to make it down?" The thought of Clark trying to take the rickety, rotted ladder with Ruslan made her stomach pitch; the darn thing barely held up when she climbed it.

"What choice do I have, lass?" Clark started out the window, his face red, his eyes bulging from exertion. Just as he got his feet onto the ladder, Ruslan roused, lifting his head.

"Cousin, be still," she yelled out the window, looking down at them.

Father, please, help them. A little divine intervention was needed right then.

On the ground, Smith held on to the ladder, his voice barely rising about the noise. "When you get halfway, just let him go. I'll catch him."

It wasn't a long distance, about eight feet, but if Clark could just get Ruslan part way, then he could manage the fall with Smith catching. Simon shook and groaned with each step he took until finally, Smith came up from behind and grabbed Ruslan. Her cousin, dazed but somewhat awake, helped the rest of the way down.

When she turned around, Agnes came rushing into the room.

"Where's my uncle?"

"He's coming."

Dellis heard yelling; someone was shouting, but she couldn't make out voices above the crackling and popping of burning wood. "Who's yelling? Is that my uncle?"

"I don't know." Agnes started to cough—loud, painful-sounding hacks.

"Go. I'll find my uncle." Dellis waved her friend off, rushing back into the hall, but Dane was nowhere to be found. Running down the hall, she checked the three other rooms, but all of them were empty. "Uncle Dane!" she yelled, but there was no answer. *He must have gone out one of the windows.*

Dellis ran back to the corner bedroom and climbed out, taking the ladder slowly. When she reached the bottom, she looked around at all of them, dirty and exhausted, lying in the grass. "Where's John?"

But no one answered, all of them wide eyed with fear.

"Where's John!" Panic squeezed her heart, taking hold with a vice-like grip. "He went in after Alexei and Will. They should be out by now."

Without a second thought, she rushed up the back stairs, but just as she reached the door, Simon grabbed her, pulling her back. "You can't go in there. The Captain will have my head if I let you go."

She pushed Clark back and went for the door again. "Like hell I won't. They're still inside."

Simon persisted, yanking her back. "Let me and Smith go; you and Agnes start getting some water. We've got to stop this fire from spreading to the trees. It'll consume the barn and spread to the neighbors."

"Simon." She hesitated long enough for him to grab the door and rush inside. "Be careful."

Smith ran up the steps past her, following Simon inside the inferno that was once her home. The familiar hallway, the one she walked day after day, carrying buckets and baskets down, the one where her parents used to kiss each other goodbye before they left, was consumed with smoke. All her father's journals and his treasured books were gone to Hell, and there was nothing she could do about it. The wood joists that held up the ceiling burned bright red, on the verge of collapsing, taking with them her father's dream of a perfect life. *Oh, God.* She chewed her nail, her body frozen, unable to move or form a thought beyond her beloved's name.

John.

Agnes grabbed Dellis's hand, using reason to bring her back to reality. "Dellis, pull yourself together; your Uncle Dane is still missing."

With steely determination, she rallied. "I'll find him."

"I'll start getting water. You check around front!" Agnes yelled, yanking Dellis down the steps.

"It's too late for water; we need to cut the trees and branches away so the fire can't reach them. It will have nothing left to feed on," Dellis yelled above the noise. "In the barn, there's an axe and a saw; grab those, and start there. I'll search for my uncle."

"Take something to protect yourself," Agnes warned, intuitively. "You and I both know this fire didn't start itself."

She spoke the words Dellis feared most. *But who'd do this to The Thistle?* "John's musket is in the barn. I'll grab it." She ran behind Agnes. John's Brown Bess was in Viceroy's stall, the barrel resting against the wooden frame. The damned thing was heavy and awkward, the long barrel difficult to maneuver. There was no way Dellis could aim and fire it accurately in a rush. She dug through John's clothes and found one of his smaller pistols, a British sea service flintlock. Grabbing one of the balls and his horn, she poured the powder in, rammed the ball into place, primed the flash pan, and then replaced the rod on the barrel.

When she ran through the barn door, she stopped to see if Clark and Simon had come out, but there was still no sign of them or John and Alexei.

Agnes was holding the back door open, yelling inside, an axe in her hand.

512

"Where are they?" Dellis asked, running up to the door.

"They've found the Captain and Alexei; they're just getting them out. Find your uncle!"

She bolted down the stairs and around the side of the house just as one of the windows burst, sending glass flying into the air in jagged fractals, bringing with them a rush of fire. She threw herself on the ground, just missing the sudden gust of flames, little pieces of glass embedding themselves in her palms.

Getting up, she dusted her hands off on her skirts and then rushed around to the front of the house. Just as she neared the corner, she heard voices rising above the crackling blaze. It was her Uncle Dane and another voice she knew all too well, her Uncle James. They were fighting, rolling around on the ground, exchanging vengeful punches. Not far from them, Will was lying motionless in the grass.

"My God." Dellis gasped and sprinted towards her friend. Landing on both knees in a thick patch of mud, Dellis slid up next to Will and shook her several times. "Will? Will?" She was unconscious, a large gash bloodying her forehead. Dellis examined the woman quickly, putting a hand to her chest, feeling it rise and fall rhythmically.

When Dellis looked up, Dane was on his back, James straddling his brother's hips, hand cocked back, poised for a direct hit. "This is it, brother; you go down in an inferno. A traitor's death. You get what you deserve."

Dane kicked and fought, but James pummeled his fists into his brother's face, subduing him.

"You brought this on yourself. It's by your conniving that Stephen died." Dane put up his arm to deflect a blow.

"No, you did this when you betrayed me. Now, it's time I finish it, once and for all." James grinned with pure satisfaction and then ripped a long, jagged knife from his boot, raising it in the air, ready to slay his youngest brother.

Fueled with adrenaline and rage so repressed it bubbled up from the deepest recesses of her soul, Dellis stood, pulled the pistol from her pocket, and aimed at her uncle.

"Release him!" she yelled, walking towards the two men.

James laughed, holding the blade to Dane's neck. "You won't fire at me, niece; you lack the courage. And it'll take more than one bullet to stop me. I've had a lifetime to plan this, and I'll have my revenge."

Dane glanced up at her, his eyes so blue she could almost see her father's precious face in the expression, that blank stare permanently etched on his handsome visage as he lay dying on a bed of autumn leaves. It wasn't fear; it was surprise and confusion. Devastation.

"Dellis, did Dane ever tell you how he betrayed me? Did he tell you how he and your father conspired against me? It's because of them all of this happened."

Her Uncle James's voice was raw and full of vitriol, but she barely heard it; time had stopped, and in a split second, she relived every painful moment in her life. One. More. Time. Dellis looked down at the pistol in her shaking hand as history replayed itself in all its horrific, beautiful truth.

"Mother, Mother, wake up."

"Get him down! Get him down! Stuart!"

"There will be no savage bastards from you, whore; how do you like that?"

"Wake up, Father, I'm here. I've come for you. Father, please, wake up!"

Her parents murdered, her brother scalped and tacked to a tree, and her own body ruined permanently, all because of a jealous man's vanity and the need to prove he was justified.

"Bring John back to me, Father, and I vow I will find the man that murdered you and Mother, and I will make him pay."

She swore she'd bring her parents' murderer to justice, an oath made in blood, and one she intended to keep. As if some otherworldly force yanked the strings of her hand, playing her like a marionette, she pulled the hammer back, cocking the pistol.

"You won't do it, Dellis." James hissed, his knife at Dane's throat, blood oozing from the wound. Then with brute force, James pulled back and plunged the knife into his brother's leg, twisting around until he screamed. "You won't shoot me!"

"You underestimate me, Uncle," she said, her grip full of confidence, courtesy of a steel ball and saltpeter.

No one will ever take from me again. No one.

Fingering the trigger, she whispered into the wind, "Look away, Father. Look away." Squeezing the trigger, the bullet made a *pop* and a puff of smoke as it discharged. Dellis watched it jettison from the barrel and whiz through the air in slow motion, its trajectory direct, its aim true, as the ball struck her uncle in the left breast.

James flew back, landing in the dirt, blood spattering from the wound in a stream of crimson. The same blood that flowed through her veins.

Her breath caught in her throat, a sudden rage blooming into a tirade, possessing her like a devil on the road to vengeance. With nerves of steel, Dellis ran to him, pulled out her knife, and held it to his face. "Now, it's my turn for revenge, and I get to claim your soul."

Dellis brought the blade to his forehead.

James gasped and groaned, blood bubbling up between his lips, making a red, sticky trail down his neck. He gurgled and coughed. "Mercy, mercy."

But she'd have none of it.

"Where was your mercy for me? What about my mother and my father? And Stuart? And John?" She brought the knife down, ready, without regret, to cut his scalp and take it. He owed it to her, and damn if she didn't want it. Never had she known such hatred, such fervent anger; it leeched from every pore in total possession of her soul. "You destroyed everything that I loved: my family, my love, and now my home. Why? Why?"

Tears brimmed her eyes, but she fought back, determined to finally say her piece. "For vengeance? For revenge? Did it make you happy?" She shook her head, tears finally breaking loose in a blinding downpour. She put the knife down and pulled her uncle's limp body into her arms. "My father loved you. I know he regretted what he did. I would've loved you. So would Alexei. All anyone ever wanted was to love you. Why wouldn't you let us?"

Dellis rested her head in his neck, years of tears and frustration pouring into the man that had devastated her life in every way, yet in the end, she couldn't hate him. She wasn't made that way. Her father taught her better. "I love you, Uncle. I love you."

He wrapped one arm around her, shaking and coughing; then suddenly, he fell limp in her lap. Lifeless. When she looked up, his great, fierce eyes stared up blankly into the night sky as he passed on into eternity.

Dane scooted over to her, his own eyes moist with tears, looking down at his brother.

"Are you all right, Uncle?" She turned to Dane and took his precious face in her hands.

"Yes, my dear." He nodded, but she could tell he wasn't. There was a knife buried deep in his thigh, blood oozing from the wound, and his ankle had an unnatural turn to it. "It's finally over. After all these years…" He shook his head. "So much waste."

Dellis brushed her Uncle James's hair from his face and leaned down to kiss his cheek lightly. "May you find peace, dear Uncle, wherever you go. I'll pray for you."

Just as she started to rise, her Aunt Helena rode up on a horse, Patrick and his father following close behind. When she saw her husband lying lifeless on the ground, she let out a howl and ran to him.

"Dellis, what happened?" Patrick asked, dismounting, his eyes fixed on the blaze that was once her home.

"It doesn't matter anymore; can you see to my uncle and Will?" Dellis pointed to the grass. "She's over there with a nasty bump on her head. Poor thing has had the living daylights scared out of her."

"What about everyone else?" Patrick asked, scanning the area.

Then suddenly, horror gripped her heart once again. *John.* Dellis rose quickly and raced around the side of the house, stopping abruptly when she saw Alexei and John lying in the grass, her friends hunched over the pair.

John wasn't moving.

Why isn't he moving?

Agnes was tapping his arm, trying to rouse him, but he was deathly still.

No. No! This can't be happening. He'll wake up for me. Yes, he was waiting for Dellis to return. She took off in a frantic sprint, her velocity so great she slipped on an unseen patch of mud and landed on her knees next to him.

"John, wake up, wake up." His eyes were closed peacefully, blood drenching his hair and the neck of his shirt. She shook him, but he didn't respond. "John! John!"

Touching the back of his head, she felt something wet and sticky coating her palm. Blood. Lots of it.

Tears flooded her eyes, bringing with them a blinding surge of hysteria. *No. Not again.* "John, wake up, damn you, wake up." She pounded her fists into his chest, but he didn't stir, not even the slightest tremor.

"Get up, Carlisle," she heard Alexei yell from over her shoulder.

John finally groaned, his head dropping to the side, and then suddenly, his body started to shake violently as if he were possessed by spirits, his eyes opening briefly and then rolling back. He hissed through clenched teeth, a thick, frothy foam forming at the corners of his lips.

"John!" Dellis screamed, releasing him, unsure what to do, the panic gripping her heart rendering her useless. "John!"

"He's having a fit of some kind." Agnes got down on the ground next to him, grabbing his flailing hands, trying to keep him from hitting himself.

It was a seizure. Dellis had seen one once before when she worked with her father; the strange, rhythmic motions looked almost like demonic possession. It went on for several seconds, though it felt like hours, her hands clenched at her sides, helpless to do anything but observe. When John finally stopped, his breathing was rapid and shallow, saliva spilling from his mouth down his cheek.

"John!" She called his name frantically, shaking him, but he was still unresponsive. "John! John!" His eyes rolled open for a second, focusing on her, and then they closed.

"No! No! No!" She wrapped her arms around him, drawing him to her breast. He was drenched in sweat, his body deadweight in her arms, an ominous reminder of holding her father's lifeless form. Fear held reason hostage while anguished, angry words spewed from her lips uncontrollably. "You don't get to leave me, John Carlisle. Damn you. Wake up! You don't get to leave me, too. You bastard! You scoundrel. I refuse to let you leave me. John!"

And then she screamed it again. "John!"

Burying her face in his hair, she wailed through sobs. "God, not him, too. No! You don't get to have him. Do you hear me? Do you hear me!"

Chapter Forty-Nine

The sunlight in his room was so bright, but his arms were too heavy to reach up and pull the curtain closed. Had he drunk too much the night before? Damn if he couldn't remember. John's head felt like the anvil on which a large mallet struck a piece of metal, pounding repeatedly with herculean force. His stomach pitched something awful, and he had a sour taste and a cotton-like dryness in his mouth so thick and sticky he dared not swallow. Yep, he must have over indulged the night before. Whatever he drank was utter shit, having never been hung so bad in his life.

No, he knew the sensation. *Opium.* He'd gotten into the herb. That was what it was. Only a combination of herbs and grain could cause such a sorry state of affairs.

Where am I?

John looked around, moving only his eyes, the stabbing pain in his neck making it near impossible to even tilt his head in the slightest. It was a large room, elegantly decorated, and the four-poster bed he lay in was draped with large, heavy curtains made of lush, maroon damask with gold fringe. No, it definitely wasn't his tent at the camp and not his room at The Thistle. It looked a bit like a brothel.

Damn, what have I done?

"John!" Suddenly, he heard a sweet, familiar voice say his name, and all was right in the world again. Fighting the pain, he turned his head, slowly, and looked into the most beautiful black eyes he'd ever seen. His favorite eyes.

"Dellis?" He croaked; his throat was parched and so very sore.

"Thank you, Father, thank you." She buried her face in his neck, and a stray lock of her hair fell into his face, smelling of lavender and sunshine.

She shook vigorously, slow-falling tears wetting his neck.

John slid his hand up the bed and then across his chest so he could cup her face. When she looked up, her eyes were red rimmed and puffy, tear streaks marring her porcelain cheeks.

"What happened? Where am I? I can't remember anything."

She sniffed, taking his hand in her own and nuzzling his palm, kissing it several times before she finally spoke. "There was a fire at The Thistle; you went inside to get Alexei, and my Uncle James hit you over the head. Simon and Adam got you out, but you wouldn't wake up." She sniffed again before another rush of tears came on. "You've been unconscious for days, and you had seizures. I thought I lost you, and you'd only just come back to me."

John nodded, though none of her story jogged his memory. The last thing he remembered was lying in bed with her; they'd just made love in the little shack behind her house, and she'd worn him out to the point of incapacitation.

Damn. "And here I thought you literally rode me limp." He shook his head, gingerly. "Your version of the story isn't nearly as tantalizing as mine. Perhaps next time you should lie to me. Yes, that's it. Just lie to me." When she started to cry harder, he deferred humor to words of love. "Don't cry, my love. You can't lose me; there's no place for me save by your side. And God sure as hell doesn't want me." Never were there truer words than the ones he'd just spoken.

She pressed her lips to his gently and then pulled back just enough for their eyes to meet, fusing them together forever in time and space. "I love you, John."

"Yes," he replied, drawing her down for another kiss; that time, she allowed him to slide his tongue between her lips and draw off her sweetness in slow, languid pulls.

"Enough of that," she said between sniffs, backing away. "It'll have to wait. You're not strong enough for such exploits."

Though his body said otherwise, arousal blissfully on the brink, John tended to agree with her. He was so tired, and everything around him was rocking back and forth, including her. If he shifted even slightly too fast the room would actually spin.

"Alexei? Will?" He glanced around, still trying to figure out where he was.

"They're both fine. Alexei was shot in the chest, but he's recovering. Thank God it missed his lung, or he would never have made it." She let out a little laugh, her eyes drying a bit. "Will is enjoying taking care of him. He's totally bedridden for now."

"I'm sure she is," he replied, wanting to laugh, but it hurt too much to try. "Merrick?"

"He's doing better. He jumped down the staircase and broke his ankle when he saw my Uncle James trying to take Will from the house. They fought, and James stabbed him in the thigh."

"So this was all James's doing." The picture suddenly made sense, though it was no clearer in his memory.

"Yes, he came to get Will. My aunt told me James made a deal with Lord Tomlinson. He shot Alexei and set the house on fire. You must've just come in when Uncle was trying to get away." Dellis choked up again, tears turning to sobs, her breaths short little pants of pain.

When she rested her forehead on his shoulder, John reached over and stroked her hair. "My love, don't cry."

"I shot him." She groaned out the words through sobs. "I killed my uncle."

"It's all right. He was a bad man." Nodding, John said, "He needed to go."

She chucked and then started to cry again. "I hated him for what he did to my family and you. And when I saw him on top of my uncle Dane, ready to kill him, something snapped in me. I wanted him dead. I knew it was the only way to end all of this."

"It's finally over." John managed to push out the words, though his head smarted with the slightest effort. He ached to comfort her, but he lacked the strength. Rolling his head towards hers, he kissed her forehead. "Climb into bed with me. I want you in my arms."

She looked up at him and sniffed. "I need you to hold me, John. I need to know you'll be all right. I can't go through this again. I'll go quite mad. You know it's in my family."

"Yes." He patted the bed, too tired to talk anymore. "Come."

With that, she did his bidding, tucking herself at his side, resting her head on his shoulder. "I'm afraid to let you go to sleep for fear you won't wake again."

That time, he couldn't fight back the laugh that forced its way out. "Again, I don't think God wants me; surely this most recent attempt on my life has proved this to you. So it would seem you're stuck with me, my love."

"Forever," she said more than asked, looking up at him with those great dark pools, drawing him into their fathomless abyss.

"Forever." And for his heart, that would never be long enough.

Chapter Fifty

"John, wake up." John heard Dellis's sweet voice in his ear, but he opted to ignore her. "John, please? You've been abed for nearly a week. I'm beginning to think you're milking this situation."

I absolutely am. He cocked a brow in suggestion but kept his eyes closed. She needed to work a little harder to convince him to even consider getting out of the warm, comfortable bed, where he had her at his beck and call. The sheets were like butter against his cheek, soft and decadent, and so very warm. No, he was most definitely not ready to get up. He rolled his back to her and pulled the covers over his head, enjoying her feeble attempts.

She ripped the sheets back, the bright morning sun sending a happy beam directly into his eyes. That did it.

"Bloody hell, that sun is bright. I wish people would stop hitting me in the head. A man can only take so much before he's permanently daft. Between your brother, Alexei, and now your uncle, I'm lucky if I have an ounce of sense left."

She giggled, leaning over him to grab the curtain. When he opened his eyes, her soft, pillowy breasts were right in his line of sight, and suddenly, he was hungry. Very hungry. "Breakfast," he exclaimed, reaching for her and then nuzzling his face in the little crevice between them. "Now, this is how a man should start his day, every day."

"There's nothing wrong with you," she said with an exaggerated sigh, tugging his hair. "Save being a naughty scoundrel with one thought on his mind."

"Food! Don't forget food." He looked up at her, smiled, and then set himself to the task of kissing her ripe, perfect breasts.

"Oh, yes, your stomach. I forgot about that." She shook her head with exasperation, yet she didn't stop him when he started working the synchs at the front of her bodice with nimble hands. "By the way, shouldn't you try feeding yourself now?"

"I'd much rather have you feed me." He looked up at her and raised his eyebrows suggestively. "Last time I had you waiting on me, it wouldn't have been gentlemanly for me to take advantage of it. Now that you're my wife, well... That's different."

He managed to open the front of her bodice, and pulling her stays and shift down, he found what he sought: a rosy-red nipple, plump and ready for his attention. Before he could have at it, she pushed him away playfully.

"My love, I'm a spy, and this line of work requires personal reconnaissance." Sliding her skirt to her knees, John said, with mock surprise, "Isn't there a little place up here that always makes you moan with pleasure and confess all your secrets? Now, if my memory serves me, and it's rather challenged at the moment, that little place is hidden under all these skirts. I just have to find it." He scooted down the bed, putting his head under her petticoat, his eyes feasting on her long, shapely legs and the nest of curls just barely visible between them. She giggled and shifted her legs, flashing him a mouthwatering glimpse of glistening, dusky pink petals. *Perhaps breakfast* can *wait.* He placed a soft kiss on her knee and inhaled deeply, his eyes focused on the intended destination. *My God, she smells delectable.* He could almost taste vanilla and lavender and a hint of her musky, womanly flavor on his tongue. "Wife, I find I'm suddenly famished for you."

He licked his lips and started up her thighs. One kiss just above her knee. Another right where her thigh met that lean, curvaceous hip. *Almost there.* He grinned and then slid his hands down her inner thighs, spreading them wide.

"Can you two save that for later?"

Wait. He knew that voice, condescending and with a hint of disgust. *Damn.* Arresting his pleasurable pursuits, he pulled her skirts from over his head, looking up at her. "What's he doing here? Can I not ravish my wife without her former spoiling the moment?"

"This *is* his house." Dellis pulled the front of her bodice together shyly.

"This is *his* house?" John asked with incredulity. "You brought me, your husband, a spy and competitor for your favors, to your former betrothed's house? Why would you…" He shook his head. "No, I don't want to hear the answer to that."

"Yes, I did." Her eyes were focused and full of conviction, though there was a bit of humor lurking in their depths. "There was nowhere else to take you, and Patrick and his father were kind enough to help. I certainly wasn't going to take any of you to my aunt's."

When John looked over his shoulder again, he found Armstrong standing in the door, Alexei just behind with his right arm wrapped in a sling. John looked back at his wife, admiring how she turned beet red from being caught in their compromising position.

"Later?" John mock-pleaded, mustering up such a desperate look she giggled.

"Later." And with a curt nod, she said, "Perhaps after supper."

"Dessert?" He liked that idea. He'd spread her out on the big, decadent bed and lick every inch of her like a sweet apple pie and then finish her off in several big bites. How he loved that evil apple.

Rolling over, John went to throw the covers the rest of the way off only to realize he had no clothes on. "My love, can you grab my leggings, or breeches, or whatever I'll be wearing today? I find myself *en déshabillé.*"

Dellis grinned, getting up from the bed. "How wonderful." He heard her whisper under her breath in a sultry tone.

"Once again, you've robbed me of my clothing, wife. And here I have things to do," John mock-yelled and then continued with a naughty grin and a wink. "What kind of game are you playing at?"

"Excuse me, gentlemen, I'll get the Captain something to wear." As Dellis walked out of the room, John noticed the seductive way she swung her hips; had he no audience, he would've dragged her back into his bed for a good slap to the backside and some proper treatment.

Saucy wench.

"John, how are you feeling?" Alexei asked, walking in behind Patrick, both men pretending they hadn't just interrupted a lover's interlude.

John shook his head, giving Alexei a sidelong glance. "Fifteen more minutes, and I would've been much better. *Much* better."

Patrick rolled his eyes. The man was just jealous, John decided. To his utter delight.

"Now, tell me what's going on?"

"St. Leger is still holding siege on Stanwix. Colonel Willet has made contact with General Schuyler; they're sending in Benedict Arnold and his troops to relieve the fort."

"How many men?" John asked, turning serious.

"Nine hundred, maybe," Patrick responded. "Can you tell us what you know about St. Leger's forces? Anything would help."

"Yes, of course." John nodded. Hopefully, his maps didn't burn up in Dellis's little shack; they'd be invaluable to Schuyler. "What about the Oneidas?"

"Two Kettles Together came to see us. A bloody hatchet was sent from Onondaga to Oriska; then a couple days later, the village was burned and their livestock stolen by Joseph Brant and some of the natives loyal to the King. After that, our men sacked Molly Brant's house and raided the nearest Mohawk village." Alexei paused, his brow furrowing with a pained expression. "The battle between our people has just begun."

"And Eagle Eyes?"

"No word of him, John." Alexei's tone was controlled and calm, but both men knew what it meant. While that Mohawk was alive, they'd both have to be on their guard.

"What of your village and Joseph?" John asked, changing the subject.

"We've heard nothing. But now that you're recovering, we should check with Joseph and Han Yerry. General Arnold will be arriving within a day. We should meet with him as a unified group."

"Agreed. Though I confess, I need another day to right myself. I've yet to be able to stand without the room spinning."

"You took a serious hit to the head," Alexei said. "It didn't look good."

John was painfully aware of that fact, the perpetual ringing in his ears and vertigo were only two parts of the fabulous trifecta of symptoms he was experiencing. Add nausea, and the whole nasty picture was quite complete.

Dellis pushed her way through the two men, throwing a pair of his uniform breeches at him. "I have a shirt and one of your waistcoats, too."

She handed him the rest of his neatly folded clothes and turned back to Alexei. "How is Ruslan?"

"Recovering."

"And your mother?"

"We won't speak about her or my father," Alexei said flatly, ending the discussion.

John pulled on his breeches quickly and then his shirt. Grabbing the bed post, he pulled himself up on his feet, using it to buttress while he stood. The room started to spin around him, a powerful wave of nausea starting again, but he pushed through. "Is there anything left of The Thistle?"

"Nothing, save the shack and the barn," she whispered, shaking her head, her eyes tearing up reflexively at the mention of her beloved house.

He didn't mean to dig in where she was still raw.

John reached over and gave her hand a little squeeze. "We'll fix it, somehow. I promise."

"I know." She nodded, though not convincingly. "You always keep your promises."

The Thistle was his home, too. His heart ached for the loss of his safe place, his peaceful shelter from the storm of war. At least her village still remained. They could rest in her cabin until they figured out what to do about The Thistle.

"Gentlemen, can I have a moment alone with my niece and the captain?" Merrick asked from behind, hobbling into the room, a black lacquered cane in hand to support him. Patrick and Alexei turned and walked out, though Alexei stopped for a moment, acknowledging his uncle with a curt nod.

Once the door was closed, Merrick turned, his normally youthful face looking aged and tired, fine lines forming at his eyes and bracketing his mouth. He wore relaxed clothing: a navy overcoat, a matching waistcoat, and buff breeches. Instead of boots, he wore a fine black shoe on his left foot, his right one wrapped tightly in several layers of linen.

"How is your ankle, Uncle?"

He nodded, tapping it lightly with the butt end of his cane. "Painful. It'll take forever to heal, but the cut in my thigh is much better thanks to your good tending. Mr. Armstrong was kind enough to lend me his cane so I can get around."

"Merrick, I'm sorry I betrayed you, but—" John started, but the older man interjected with a wave of his hand.

"That's forgotten. You don't need explain yourself to me. I know you had good reason for what you did." Merrick took a deep breath, looking down while he tapped the edge of his cane on the floor. "But there are consequences we must discuss. Ones that I'm afraid drastically effect both of you and myself."

John already knew to what the man was referring.

"I'd wanted to leave my title and fortune to you; it would be justice for my beloved Stephen to see his daughter inherit, but I can't do that now that you're married to a known traitor."

John nodded, looking at Dellis. She gave him a little smile and a wink of support.

"I fear you'll never be able to return to England. And if your Rebels don't win this war, you may still find yourself on the end of a noose."

The idea of not returning to England or Bristol didn't distress John, he'd long since given up his attachment to his homeland, but being caught by his former superiors and facing the noose, that terrified him. He was on the run. The forever burden of a marked man.

"But, I have hope that you'll have sons." Merrick smiled. "And to them, I'll leave my fortune."

Dellis smiled, her eyes softening. She ran to her uncle and hugged him. "Thank you."

Merrick held her close, his eyes meeting John's over Dellis's shoulder, understanding linking them. If they had children.

Pain like a knife tore at John's heart. "Thank you."

"There's something I want to do for you now. Your father's inheritance, there's still quite a bit left. I can give it to you so you can rebuild his home. I know that's what he'd want."

Dellis pulled away, kissing his cheek.

Merrick offered his hand to John, a shake between friends, family, and brothers in arms. "You two belong here, fighting the good fight."

John agreed. "After all, we're both Whigs."

"Yes," Merrick laughed. "Though don't tell the Duchess that. She'd never forgive me."

"Will you leave now, Uncle?" Dellis asked, grasping both of his hands in hers.

"As soon as I'm fit to travel, but first, I'll see things started on your house. John?" Merrick looked at his nephew. "I leave my boats and my house in Oswego to you. Perhaps, once this war is over, you can find something to do with my little business venture. It's quite lucrative, and I know how you love the sea."

John rolled his eyes and then shook his head with mirth.

"For now, I'll have my friend continue to run it as an inn. The income will be yours."

"Noblesse Oblige, Your Grace?" John asked, grinning.

"No," Merrick countered, his eyes crinkling a bit in the corner with emotion. "Love of family. Nothing more. I have so little of it."

"Thank you, Merrick." It was a place to start—though small—but it was more than John had five minutes prior. "Thank you."

Once Merrick had left, John drew Dellis into his arms, using her balance to help himself stay erect. "Perhaps I'll ask Alexei to help me start my own shipping business. I could give my brother a run for his money."

She shook her head. "I never saw the two of you being friends. Not for a minute."

"Neither did I," he replied on a laugh, but stranger things had happened in his life since meeting her.

Looking around the room again, John couldn't help but wonder something. "Do you suppose this is Armstrong's room? Or perhaps the wedding suite?"

Dellis followed his gaze, her eyes darting around the room, and then shrugged. "I don't know. Why do you ask?"

"What if I made sweet love to you all over this room? We could start on the bed, make our way to the desk, and finish against the dresser while you watch me take you from behind like a randy stallion," he said seriously, while his hips undulated against hers suggestively. "I'll make you scream my name with utter delight so everyone in the house can hear—especially your former."

Leaning in, John whispered playfully in her ear, mimicking her voice with a ridiculous high pitch that sounding *nothing* like a woman in the throes of passion, "Don't stop. Oh, God… It's so big! Harder, John, faster. Please."

"You're a rotter." Dellis slapped his chest, her cheeks turning as red as his old tunic.

"It would serve him right—"

"And your pride," she said and then burst into laughter.

"Touché, my love. Touché."

Dellis glanced at John, watching him fuss and struggle with his stubborn gelding. The horse was clearly not in the mood to do anything but eat and rest. Much like his master. "You know, Viceroy never gives me problems."

John gave her a sidelong glance, a grin tugging at the corner of his lips. He undoubtedly had a lewd comment to volley back at her but refrained due to their company. She heard him let out a sigh, once again pulling the reins of his horse, trying to control Viceroy. Even after a week, John was still so tired; his eyes were bloodshot and had black-and-blue circles wrapped around them like a raccoon's, and the back of his head was still bandaged with a piece of linen. *Thank God he's safe.* Once again, Dellis said a prayer of thanks to her father for protecting John, for surely only one who loved her so could've granted such a miraculous gift.

Alexei rode on the opposite side of her, Will seated in front of him, leaning back so she could whisper in his ear. He grinned suggestively and then kissed her ear, whispering something inaudible to her. Their love play brought a smile to Dellis's lips. So long she'd wanted her cousin to find someone; it was a dream come true to see him finally happy.

Agnes and Clark rode behind them. The whole group was together— homeless—but safe. Once they got to the village, they'd set up in her cabin until they could find a way to get The Thistle rebuilt. Her Uncle Dane had left her plenty of money to get started, and he'd arranged for his man Kent to come and oversee the project. That thought made her smile. Her father's home restored to its former glory, and her little makeshift family all together, living in one place. Nothing would bring her more joy, save John's child growing in her womb. In time. She had faith.

"Where's Smith?" Dellis asked.

"He went with Armstrong into town. Apparently, Walter Butler and some of his men started a ruckus at Shoemaker's Tavern. They went with Colonel Brooks and some of the militia men to investigate. We'll meet them later, not to worry."

She nodded, though anything to do with the war made her cringe. Finally, she had some peace in her life; she could do without the fighting for a while.

As they neared the village, Dellis looked around, taking in the forest that was her home. Everywhere she turned, there were shades of green and brown: olive, evergreen, russet, each one accenting the canvas in their own unique way. The ground was covered in ferns and thick bushes, the ancient trees hanging over and shading the road from the blistering summer sun. Amongst the giant oaks, maples, and beech trees, the spirits of her loved ones—her father, her mother, and even her grandmother—were welcoming Stuart home. Dellis could almost see his face when he was young, eyes bright and happy as they ran through the woods playing hide and seek with Alexei. That forest, her peoples' protector, was their homeland, and they'd fight for it. Yes, they'd protect it, and she and John would help.

Once the wooden pillars of the stockade were in sight, Dellis jumped down from her horse and walked up slowly, purposely taking her time. The tranquility of the forest was a welcome respite for her fractured nerves, and she wanted to savor every minute of it.

But as she drew closer to the village, she realized something was wrong. "Where's Ho-sa-gowwa? He should be on guard." Whirling around, her eyes scanned the trees fearfully. "There are no guards!"

John dismounted Viceroy, handing his reins to Dellis. "Stay here until I say so." He looked back at Clark, pointing to the three women. "Watch them."

Pulling out a pistol, John cocked it, heading for the village, Alexei just behind, covering the rear.

Dellis waited, her heart beating fitfully, threatening to bust a hole in her ribcage. Something wasn't right. Ho-sa-gowwa never left his post. The village was never without guards. Not since that day.

Panicking, she reached into her haversack and pulled out her pistol.

"Dellis, I'm sure everything is all right," Will said, walking over to Dellis and putting a hand on her sleeve. "They probably went to Oriska."

Yes, that was it. They were with Han Yerry and his men. It made sense, what with all that was going on at Stanwix. But there was something unsettling about the forest, the energy potent, tangible, menacing. She ached all the way down to her bones.

When John returned, the look on his face said everything and so much more.

"Tell me it's not true?" Dellis begged, her fear rising with the pace of her heartbeat. "Tell me it's not true!"

He stood between her and a view into the village. She pushed past him, but he grabbed her arm, pulling her back.

"Dellis." His eyes closed gently in acknowledgement.

"No!" Once again, she felt the all-too-familiar crack form in her heart, another wound to its already fragile, scarred surface.

He nodded, and when he opened his eyes, there were tears.

"I have to see them. I have to."

He stepped out of her way, knowing well enough that no one would stop her from seeing the truth for herself. It was the first home she'd ever known, the only family she had left through the worst, loneliest times of her life—her mother's family, Dellis's heritage.

When she entered the stockade, she let out a scream of pure, unadulterated horror.

All of them were dead. A massacre. The village laid to waste. It wasn't the first time she'd seen it happen, but it would be the last. There were no survivors left to rebuild.

Lying in the grass, scalped, was Rail Splitter, and next to him, Wind Talker, the great sachem who helped her interpret her dreams. Her cousin, Skenandoa, lay discarded, her clothes torn to shreds, a bullet wound between her eyes.

Suddenly, there were strong arms around Dellis, pulling her in close, but she couldn't tell who it was or what the person were saying. Loud screams of horror escaped her lips, like wails from a banshee. She was unable to control it, shock rendering her beyond thought.

"This was retribution."

It was Alexei; he was whispering into her ear, his arms like a vice around her. She sobbed into his chest, punching and slapping him, until finally she couldn't continue. "Oh God, Alexei. No!"

"They sent the bloody axe to Oriska. It was for turning against the Confederacy." Tears ran down his cheeks, his voice cracking with every word. "This was my fault. I led them to war. I did this. I did this."

Suddenly, Alexei pushed her away and started pacing frantically, like a feral cat. He tugged at his hair, the muscles in his hands flexing visibly. "I did this. It's my fault."

As the initial shock wore off and sanity seeped its way back into her brain, she ran to her cousin and wrapped her arms around him, this time offering *him* comfort. "No, Alexei. No. They had no choice. They had to fight. It was the only way to protect what was ours."

She looked over her cousin's shoulder at John; he was motionless, stunned silent. Their eyes met through tears.

"Where's Grandfather?" she asked. "John, did you see him anywhere?"

"No." He shook his head.

The breeze picked up, blowing leaves around them. A ray of hope came with the sun, peeking through the clouds. *Maybe he wasn't here when they came?*

Releasing Alexei, she ran to her grandfather's cabin, praying all the while. Surely God wasn't so cruel as to leave them without a leader. No. He wouldn't take her grandfather. Their rock. Their chief. But when she opened the door, her hopes were shattered. Hanging from the rafters, like a drying animal carcass, was Joseph. His big, dark eyes were wide open and lifeless. He'd been gutted and scalped, his intestines bloody and hanging from his abdomen, and most of his hair ripped away. Dellis gasped, covering her mouth against the nausea that overcame her, but she didn't cry. There were just no more tears. No more. Shock had stripped her of them, rendering her emotionless—dead inside.

When she turned around, John was behind her, his eyes closed, true pain creasing his brow. "I'll get him down," he said, but she held him back.

"I can't handle it now. Let's try and find the others."

They searched all the cabins and even the barn at the top of the hill, but there was no sign of Ho-sa-gowwa or Great Bear. Dellis's crew gathered up the bodies, lining them up next to each other, so they could say a prayer and properly bury each one. She stood quietly, numb, with her family at her feet. All of them dead.

"This is what we get for being brave. Brother destroying brother," Alexei said bitterly, tears starting again. "You were right, Dellis. You warned me this would happen. Why didn't I listen? Now, how will it end? When we're all dead?"

Dellis understood Alexei's painful words better than anyone: James against Dane and Stephen, Gavin against John, Rebel against Redcoat, White Man against Red Man, Man against Woman. Blood relations didn't stop war, it only made it hurt all the more. Was it just the true nature of man to destroy each other? Yes, she'd seen it coming. She warned her grandfather it would be the death of her village. But why was she not angry? Why didn't the need for vengeance seep from her soul and reach for the dagger at her waist?

It wasn't that simple. Were men not creatures of compassion and love, too? There were examples of their goodness all around her: Alexei and John once bitter enemies turned friends, her brave Oneida warriors fighting for their women and their homes, and John turning sides for the love of her village. All the men were protecting what was theirs with such love and ferocity that their struggles weren't empty or wasted. No, it wasn't simple. It was too easy to render their situation down to something as simple as man against man. Life was complex, and so were men.

"Alexei, they were brave and fought for what they believed in. This is our land. Our home." She took her cousin's hand in her own, squeezing it.

"And now, they live in this forest, watching over us. We must carry on, for them. So they didn't die in vain."

He nodded.

Searching for John, she found him on his knees outside the stockade, the discarded body of a woman lying near him. Dellis walked towards him and then stopped when she realized who the woman was. "Kateri?"

He let out a gut-wrenching howl, pulling the still, lifeless body into his arms. "She believed I'd protect her. That I'd come to help." John huffed out between sobs. He held her cheek to his own, cradling her face in his hand. "Some angel I was to her."

Dellis got down on her knees and wrapped her arms around him. "John, there's nothing more you could do."

"I should've protected her." There was true pain in his eyes, those sapphires turned glassy and red, he panted and struggled to breathe through anguished tears. "It all started with her. She was the first, the first one to believe in me, the first to trust me. I should've known they'd come here. I had dreams the other night. It was a warning."

Dellis's heart ached for him, the sight of his tears drawing her own forth. "John, there was nothing you could do. You were sick. We almost lost you, too." But she knew those were empty words to him; he'd go on torturing himself over it for the rest of his days. That was his curse. Not the one he believed her grandmother placed on him, for that was just the stuff of folklore and wives' tales, but the curse of his conscience. It made him a better man—a tortured one, but a better one.

"We'll bury her and say prayers," Dellis said, bending down to kiss her dear friend's cheek. "How about under the willow tree, near the river?"

"No," he countered with boyish angst. "I'll bury her. *I will.*"

John lifted Kateri carefully from the ground, carrying her in his arms back to her cabin. Dellis followed him, watching as he removed the necklace Kateri gave him from around his neck and placed it around hers. Then, he took her finest blanket from her bed and wrapped her with it, taking a moment to smooth and arrange her hair from her face.

When he was satisfied with how she looked, he carried her to the old willow tree and started to dig. Dellis sat quietly, watching him, hoping her presence would soothe his pain, but he was silent, never saying a word, just digging and digging until he was satisfied with the depth. Then carefully, he lifted Kateri's body and placed it in the little grave, arranging her so her hands rested in each other at her stomach. He brushed the hair back from her face, making sure it was neatly parted in the center.

Dellis leaned over, looking into the little grave, dirt packed around Kateri, neatly creating a sort of cocoon. Returned to the earth from where she came.

John closed his eyes, muttering to himself.

Dellis could tell he was saying a prayer while tears ran steadily down his cheeks, and then he spoke clearly, his crisp baritone and proper accent warming her broken, aching heart. "Your soul goes on forever, Kateri, though your body we commit back to the earth. Sadly, there's no chief here to relieve you of your worldly duties, so I'll send you on your way. I know you'll continue watching over us, and we'll honor you by living proudly."

When John was finished, he touched Kateri's lips with his fingertips and then stepped back and started to cover her. Dellis watched as her friend disappeared with each shovel of dirt, layers of sweet, brown earth covering her lovely face forever.

Once the grave was complete, John knelt down and placed the same two fingers that touched her lips on the mound of dirt.

"Goodbye."

So reverent was his love and devotion to Kateri, Dellis could do no more than watch in awe. Her eyes teared up, again, but she held them back. It was the moment when she needed to be strong for him, for Alexei, for all of them, though she herself lost just as much.

John rose and walked to her, grief like a mask covering his face. She took his hand, placing a kiss in his palm. "Kateri would be glad to know it was you who saw her into the next life."

"It was she who first saw good in me." His voice quivered. He stopped, drawing in a long breath and then finally started to speak again. "It's the women in my life that have changed me most. You. Kateri. Agnes. Your grandmother. All of you have changed me in some way."

Dellis sniffed back tears, watching his pained expression change to one of peace.

"I owe it to all of you to be better."

"You are John, you are. That's what all of us saw in you." Dellis reached out her hand to him. "That's what I saw in you."

Once all the bodies were buried, Alexei lit a small fire, pouring some of Wind Talker's tobacco into a pipe, and together, they sat, joined in prayer for the souls of their lost ones. They committed their loved ones to the great unknown. To Heaven.

"How will we ever go on? What do we do?" she asked, looking at Alexei and Will, sitting together, and then John. Everything Dellis knew and loved was gone. Both her homes. Her way of life. Those few people sitting around her were all she had left.

"We'll go on. For them." Alexei stared into the fire, his eyes so blue and fierce she believed him. "Joseph would want us to. Your father would want it, too."

Agnes sat quietly with Clark, holding hands, Smith beside them. Clark perked up and said, "We join this fight and honor this village with our lives."

"Han Yerry is at Fort Dayton. I say we meet him there," John said, taking Dellis's hand and giving it a squeeze. When she looked up, there was sadness in his eyes, but that sparkle, the mischievous one, it was there, too. "There are still St. Leger's men to deal with."

"Yes, we go now," Alexei said, standing. "We'll do this together."

Chapter

They rode silently together, all of them held captive by the events of the previous few days. There were no words for what John had witnessed. The specters, his perpetual company, had ceased to call for him. Why would they call anymore? Everyone was dead. No justice to be found, no one to be the benefactor.

He failed. He didn't protect them. How could he not have foreseen that moment? Of course the natives would take retribution on each other. He knew that, but why didn't he anticipate it sooner? *Why?*

John felt empty and disgusted with himself, such a waste of life. Innocent life. It wasn't their fight, but they'd been dragged into it, kicking and fighting back. And he helped. How was it they perished and he was allowed to linger to carry the torch of those who'd passed on? *Justice, you are blind.*

Upon reaching Fort Dayton, the militia was already gathering outside and, with them, several of the Oneidas. General Arnold with his First New York Regiment and the Massachusetts Continentals had arrived. But on first glance, it was obvious there weren't nearly enough men present to relieve Stanwix from siege. Another bloodbath was bound to ensue if they went down that road again.

"Alexei, Just One, it's good to see you," Han Yerry said, nodding to both men. Mounted next to him was his brave and noble wife, Two Kettles

Together, and beside her was Cornelius, Great Bear, and Ho-sa-gowwa.

"Uncle, how is it you're here?" Dellis exclaimed, her eyes lighting up at first sight of Great Bear and the young village guard. "They're all dead: Grandfather, Wind Talker, everyone."

Her uncle closed his eyes, his scarred, ancient face grimacing with pain. When he opened his eyes again, it was as if he'd aged ten years in a moment, the depth of the tragedy already taking its toll on him. "I didn't know that. Ho-sagowwa and I have been carrying messages from the fort to General Schuyler."

"We buried everyone, Uncle." Dellis nodded, fighting back tears. "You're our chief now."

He shook his head. "Han Yerry is our chief, and we'll support him. You're now all we have left of the matrons of our village." His words came out strong and proud, but underneath, John could hear the tremulous tones of devastation. Dellis reached over from her mounted position and linked hands with her uncle, their fingers intertwining. "The four of us—Alexei, you, me, and Ho-sa-gowwa—are all we have left."

Alexei shook his head, looking at John. "No, we have Just One, too."

Her uncle nodded. "And Just One."

"Thank you," John replied, his heart still too pained to feel any joy.

"What's happening?" Alexei asked. "What's our situation?"

"Honnikol died from his injuries. They cut off his injured leg, and he bled to death," Han Yerry said, stoically. All of them were silent, remembering the General that led them so bravely at Oriskany and paid for it with his life. He'd be forever remembered amongst their people as a friend and ally. "From what we've learned, some of the militia men captured Walter Butler, Han Yost, and other loyalists at Shoemaker's Tavern. They were threatening the locals to press Gansevoort to surrender the fort, or they'd set their natives loose on the town."

"What will they do with them?" Dellis asked.

John looked at her, marveling at her ability to seem so reticent and focused in the face of the recent tragedy. Was he not the trained soldier? Once again, she put him to shame with her strength.

"They've been tried. Walter Butler, as the son of Major Butler, will be sent to Albany for Schuyler to deal with. Han Yost is to be hanged here at the Fort."

"Han Yost is married to an Oneida," Alexei said pensively. "That won't bode well with our people."

Han Yerry nodded, a lock of his long black hair blowing into his face. "Arnold is hesitant. He doesn't have the numbers to overtake St. Leger and free Fort Stanwix. After what happened at Oriskany, the men are afraid to travel that same road to the Fort. Colonel Willet thinks Stanwix can hold out only a few more days."

"Just One, you've said nothing," Great Bear said. "What do you think?"

"Forgive me, my mind was…" John shook his head, clearing the fog that pervaded. He'd been listening to the conversation, his mind playing over each of the possible scenarios, knowing what he did about St. Leger's situation. "There was dissension in St. Leger's native ranks. I overheard two of the Seneca chiefs talking before I left. They were hesitant to fight, knowing their Oneida brothers were on the side of the colonists, and Butler promised the natives it would be an easy fight. They're surely angry with the outcome of Oriskany. If that flame could be further stoked, St. Leger would lose the control of his native contingent. We'd have the advantage if that happened."

"Good idea, Just One," Han Yerry said, giving a nod of appreciation. "I knew your word would be valuable."

"Thank you, my Chief," John replied, showing his allegiance for the first time to his new leader.

Han Yerry looked back at John, their eyes meeting in acceptance of his new role with his new people. It felt strangely right. Chosen by his own free will, not because of debt or out of necessity. It was his choice.

A sentry wearing a navy-blue tunic with beige facings, a proper continental uniform, came out of the fort to address them. "Oneidas, your presence has been requested by General Arnold. Your chiefs may follow me."

Han Yerry shook his head, the bright blue and red feathers at his crown billowing in the wind. "We bring our sachems and our matrons with us, or we won't meet with the General. That's how we negotiate."

"All right." The sentry nodded, boasting no disagreement.

John turned to his wife for a moment, taking in how lovely she looked in the setting sun, like a painting of the most beautiful version of Artemis. Dellis turned to him and smiled, perfecting the picture all the more.

"Come with us, my love." He wanted her there; she deserved to hear what would happen to her people. Had they listened to her, maybe Joseph and the rest of her village would still be alive.

Her eyes searched his face, so much going on in their dark depths John could only wish for insight into her thoughts—a crystal ball, a spell that gave him the power to read her mind.

"Yes" was all she gave up. Just one word. But she was thinking so much more.

"Clark, stay with the rest of the men and women," John called over his shoulder, waiting for his friend's nod of acknowledgment. The once second-in-command loyally followed John's orders as if he were still a captain. "Keep watch."

They all dismounted, leaving the rest of the Oneidas behind, while they followed their escort inside. As expected, the officer's barracks were simple, unadorned, with two sets of bunks, a desk, and a large stone fireplace. The decor mattered little; it was what sat behind the desk that deserved all their attention—the hero of Valcour Island, the rascal of Montreal and former apothecary-turned-sailor-turned-military giant, General Benedict Arnold. Looking up at them with his light-grey eyes, a furrow creased his brow, his long, dark hair pulled back, further accentuating his high forehead and strong features. Arnold stood and was just tall enough to look John in the eye yet be dwarfed by Alexei's impressive height, but the man was every bit a general—intimidating, tough, and dignified. He wore the blue uniform of the Continental Army with tan facings and sparkling gold epaulettes on his shoulders, recognizing his rank.

"Brothers, I've called a council of war to discuss the situation at Fort Stanwix. We've deemed our forces inadequate to deal with St. Leger's. Colonel Willet assured me that Stanwix can hold siege for a little while longer. I sent word to General Gates and General Schuyler requesting further assistance. I'd appreciate any advice you could provide."

Han Yerry stepped forwards; as chief and leader, he'd speak for the group. "General Arnold, I'd like to introduce you to Just One; he's formerly a captain in the Great King's infantry. I think you might find his information useful."

John was on—that was his line, his cue to take the stage. He took a deep breath, once again finding himself in need of his silver-gilded tongue to persuade, but would Arnold listen to the words of a traitor spy, formerly of His Majesty's ranks?

The General walked over to John, sizing him up, their eyes meeting. He threw his shoulders back, inducing a pompous stance of authority. Once a Captain, always a Captain; turning it on was a simple as lighting a candle, and just as easily, he could snuff it out. Much to his surprise, Arnold was intimidated; John could sense it in the cocked brow and searching blue eyes.

"Who are you?" the General asked, trying to look down his nose at John, though he was almost a head taller.

"I'm Captain John Carlisle, formerly of His Majesty's Eighth Regiment of Foot, Light Infantry, also a spy serving under General Howe; General Carleton; and most recently, General St. Leger. I'm also an Oneida. And to my credit, I'm also a proficient map maker and sea captain."

As John anticipated, his list of accomplishments impressed Arnold; it wasn't often one had an admitted spy with lofty connections such as John's to offer up advice. The General cocked a brow and inclined his head in respect to John's experience. "And why should I trust a former spy? How do we know you're not one of them still, come to lead us in a ruse de guerre?"

"You don't," John replied, confidently, almost arrogantly. "But you have little choice." He glanced at Han Yerry, then at Alexei, and then back at

Dellis, drawing strength from each of them. "And if you choose to trust these Oneida, then you'll trust me, for I'm with them. Han Yerry is my leader now."

A crease formed in Arnold's high forehead, his eyes narrowing curiously. "Why would a British Officer turned spy suddenly associate himself with a native tribe?"

"My wife is Oneida," John said flatly.

Arnold looked over his shoulder at Dellis; though his expression didn't change, John knew appreciation for beauty when he saw it in a man's eyes. "That's your wife?"

John nodded. "Yes."

"I don't believe a man turns sides just for a woman, even one so lovely as yours. If you're willing to serve and die for your country, it must be something deeper that leads you to turn traitor. Explain yourself, Captain."

John grinned. Arnold, a seasoned soldier, injured several times in service of his own country, understood the truth of the predicament. It took more than a woman, more than love, to make a man turn against his country. It was a question of honor. If one was willing to lay down their life for a country, one didn't turn traitor without just cause.

"You're correct in your estimation of my plight. While my wife is a delightful inducement, she wasn't the sole reason I turned. I've weathered my own storms in service of His Majesty, and it has cost me dearly: my respect; my honor; my conscience; and most recently, our home. A man can only lose so much before he takes up arms to defend what's his."

"So you're a Rebel now?" Arnold asked, throwing down the gauntlet. "A turncoat?"

"Not in the sense that you mean. I'm no Rebel. I'm Oneida. And where they go, I do. These are my people now; my home is with them. For now, they're friend to you, then so am I. If that should change, then so, too, will I." John put his shoulders back proudly, defiantly. "Again, if you trust these Oneida, then you can trust me. And if you don't trust them, you'll be knee deep in shit, for you and I both know that you can't win this battle without them and their intelligence."

"I could turn you over to St. Leger, trade you for some of our own officers. You're a valuable asset to them and an even more dangerous adversary being privy to such knowledge."

John nodded, trying to play it calm, though his heart pounded so hard it wore a groove in his ribcage. "You could do that, but my friends here might have a problem with such an action." He looked over his shoulder at Alexei; with a simple nod of support directed at Arnold, Alexei added to John's argument.

"General, we did this to the Oneida and the Six Nations. We dragged them into this fight, waging war on their lands and forcing them to break their peace to serve ours. Both sides are guilty of this crime, Rebel or Redcoat, it doesn't matter. The least you can do now is to show them respect. You have no idea what it has cost these people."

Arnold was silent for a moment, and then he clucked his tongue once before he spoke. "You're a fascinating man, Captain John Carlisle; when we have more time, I should like to hear your story. But for now, I must make decisions. I can't march my fighting force against the British. I lack sufficient resources. We must come up with a new plan. Stanwix will hold out but not forever. Tell me what you know."

John reached into his waistcoat and pulled out what maps he had left, unfolding them and placing them on the desk. "St. Leger is aware of the location of the magazine at Stanwix, as well as artillery. They'll likely build a siege trench to get to it."

"Do you know this for sure?"

"Yes, I drew the maps for him," John replied nonchalantly. "After I spent a few days in Stanwix as a prisoner, I figured out where all the vital locations were."

Arnold gave a look of appreciation. "You're a valuable commodity, Captain. These maps are excellent, and your knowledge is unprecedented."

"Thank you," John replied and then continued showing the General the maps. "This is how it's set up." He pointed to the map, showing the location of the military camps, the artillery, and the location of the native camps.

"During the battle at Oriskany, I understand Colonel Willet and some of his men raided the Seneca campsite as well as Colonel Johnson's Royal Yorker camp. They confiscated his maps, some of his letters, and many of the native's valuable goods. I have no doubt this infuriated the natives, and there was already dissension in the ranks, especially within the Six Nations. Major Butler was struggling to get the tribes to join; he made promises he couldn't keep. My suggestion would be to work on the natives."

"Interesting that you say that. While we await reinforcements, Colonel Brooks has suggested a potential idea. It also involves the natives."

Arnold turned to his sentry. "Get Brooks."

"What's your plan?" John glanced down at the maps. How strange it was to be devising a plan for the other side; not two weeks before, he'd helped design the Oriskany ambush. What a strange twist of fate he found himself in.

When Colonel Brooks walked into the office, he looked around at the group skeptically and then at the General.

Arnold nodded. "Tell them your idea, Colonel."

Obediently, the Colonel finally spoke. "There's a young man, Han Yost Schuyler; he's the nephew of General Herkimer and a distant relative of General Schuyler."

"He's well known to our people," Alexei replied from behind John.

"Our idea is to send Han Yost back to St. Leger's camp and have him tell the natives we're coming with at least three-thousand men. We'll send two of our Oneida scouts along to further support what he says."

John thought the idea through to fruition. It could work. The native scouts travelling with the prisoner would be the sticking point; they'd have to be convincing, spread the word around, and stoke up fear amongst the tribes.

"How do you ensure he says what you tell him to?" John asked. That was the biggest flaw he saw with their plan. If Han Yost betrayed them, it would all be a bust.

Arnold nodded. "Both his brother and mother have come to us to plead his case. I don't wish to send a man to the noose, especially one with such connections to our own ranks. And he *is* known to be feeble in the mind. We have his brother held captive. We'll offer Han Yost his freedom and his brother's if he'll do what we say."

"There are actually a few Oneida in St. Leger's ranks. They'd believe intelligence if they knew it came from their loyal brothers. We could send Anthony and Great Bear," Han Yerry said. "They're well known and trusted."

"What do you expect to happen?" Alexei asked. "The tribes aren't just going to run away and abandon St. Leger."

"No, Alexei, you're right. But Butler lied to them. He told the Seneca and some of the other tribes that they'd be able to just watch while the battle took place. He promised an easy victory. Now that their camps have been ransacked, and they've lost significant numbers against their brothers, they won't want to continue. It'll cause chaos for St. Leger. They'll question him." John smiled; his confidence bolstered with each passing minute. "Without his native warriors, St. Leger doesn't have the manpower to continue. That's when you can attack."

"Yes. It's brilliant," Arnold exclaimed, his eyes widening with the fervor of a man who sees victory in the distance. "Now, brothers, will you help us?"

Han Yerry nodded. "We're with you."

"All right," Arnold said, directing Brooks to the door. "Have Han Yost brought in. May God be with us."

John laughed. "Or Karma." She was much more tenacious and quicker with results.

Satisfied with the outcome, he turned back to Dellis, noticing how she grinned, her dark eyes full of mischief.

"What's that look for?" he asked curiously, walking toward her.

She hesitated, rolling her eyes skywards and then flashing him a look so hot it would set the fort ablaze. "Husband, I confess, watching you negotiate so bravely does things to me."

Then she let out a quiet little moan and dipped her head to the side, flashing him a suggestive smile. Her lavender scent wafted into his nose, drawing him into her world like a sweet incantation.

"What sort of things?" His eyes widened impossibly large.

"I leave it to you to figure out." She winked and then turned away, leaving him to watch her in awe.

"Captain, we're going to need your help," Arnold said from behind, reality busting through her magic spell liking a window breaking.

"Yes, sir," John replied, sternly, sounding very soldier like, though his eyes followed her out the door like a smitten fool.

At first light, John and two of Arnold's men dragged Han Yost from his cell, depositing him at the foot of the noose, a wooden coffin laid out next to it for him to contemplate. In the crowd, Han Yost's mother stood crying, a linen handkerchief in hand while she dabbed her eyes, watching him helplessly. It was all part of their plan to render Han Yost pliable and submissive so he'd comply.

John watched nervously as the feeble man trembled, his eyes fixed on the wooden casket that was doomed to hold his remains. It was unkind to play such a game on a sick man, but they had no other choice; desperate times called for desperate measures, and Stanwix would fall in a matter of days.

Colonel Brooks walked up to Han Yost, causing a hush from the crowd of onlookers; a hanging was quite an event for such a small village.

John stepped closer to the Colonel, pretending to be on guard.

"Han Yost Schuyler, before I commit you to the gallows, I offer you one last chance to save yourself."

"Anything. Anything," the man said frantically, lifting his shackled hands penitently to the Colonel. There was something reminiscent of Stuart about the pitiful man with his shaggy, dark hair, emaciated frame, and the absent look in his eyes that only the insane can manifest. Amongst the natives, lunacy wasn't a curse but a gift, something about the spirits on Earth. John was glad Dellis wasn't there to see how they manipulated Han Yost; it would've devastated her. So easily, that could've been her brother.

"Come with me." John's stomach churned in anticipation as he grabbed the slight man's arm and pulled him to his feet.

Once inside General Arnold's office, he put on quite a show; already a notoriously boastful and brash character, he used the full onslaught of his position to intimidate the fearful man. "We have your brother captive in our gaol. If you do as we say, I'll release him." Arnold leaned in, looking down his nose at his captive. "Your life, and your brother's, are in my hands, so think on your response carefully."

Bullied into submission, Han Yost nodded fearfully. "I'll do whatever you want, just let me go."

Arnold's eyes met John's, a nod shared between the two men. "Colonel Brooks, please brief the prisoner on what we need him to do."

John listened patiently as the Colonel recounted their plan, down to the most minute detail. Once finished, Han Yost's wide-set, dark-brown eyes glanced around, connecting with everyone in the room. "Believe me. I'll do it. Just let me go."

Arnold nodded, pointed one of his long fingers at Han Yost, and in a low, tremulous voice, said, "If you turn on me, if you even consider betraying me, I'll have your neck stretched, but not enough that you die quickly. And then I'll do the same to your brother."

Han Yost nodded repetitively, and so fast, it made John dizzy, his head still paining him from his injury.

"Captain Carlisle, have Han Yerry bring in the scouts who'll be escorting our friend here."

John opened the large pine door, allowing the chief, Alexei, and the rest of their men to enter, Dellis and Two Kettles Together following.

"Anthony and Great Bear will be escorting you," Alexei said, gesturing to the two braves standing next to him. Both men were shirtless and dressed in buckskin leggings with black and red war paint smeared on their chests; around their necks, they both wore gleaming silver gorgets they'd plundered from kills at Oriskany.

"Captain, with all due respect, you can't send Han Yost into a camp looking right as rain," Dellis said sweetly from behind.

"What do you suggest, Mrs. Carlisle?" Colonel Brooks asked with a quizzical lift of his brow.

"Give me his tunic and his shirt." Then Dellis turned to John, pointing to his belt. "Give me your knife and your pistol."

John leaned down and pulled his knife out of his boot. When she reached out to take it from him, he pulled it back, mischievously cocking a brow. "I want that back."

Dellis rolled her eyes. "Are you afraid I'll use it on you, Captain?"

John quietly mouthed, "You already have... Both of these." Then, snickering, he handed her his pistol.

Dellis and Two Kettles Together walked outside, carrying Han Yost's clothing. When they returned a couple minutes later, the man's green Royal Yorker tunic was ripped and littered with bullet holes, looking all the more convincing.

"Now he's ready." Dellis flashed Arnold a grin, which elicited a nod of appreciation from the General.

"Very nice. Captain Carlisle, your wife is as industrious as she is beautiful."

"Yes, she is." John glanced at Dellis proudly, noticing how her translucent skin flushed delicate pink. She was nothing short of brilliant.

The General walked up to the prisoner one last time, staring him down and offering up a threat. "Don't you dare cross me."

Han Yost shrank back in fear. "I won't."

Anthony and Great Bear each grabbed an arm and led the poor man away to tempt fate. It was a high-stakes gamble with thousands of lives on the line and the endgame unknown.

All they could do was wait.

That evening in their tent, John lay on their makeshift bed of blankets and furs, Dellis in his arms, the hard ground beneath them. It wasn't the haven of their bedroom at The Thistle with soft sheets and a warm fire, or their little hideaway in the village, but it was still perfect. He embraced the tranquility of crickets chirping and owls hooting outside their tent while she snuggled into him, trying to stay warm.

When she leaned up, her black hair tumbled over her shoulders, giving it the appearance of liquid silver in the moon's ethereal beam that had worked its way through the flap of their tent. "What is it?"

"I pray it works, this plan of ours," John whispered, cupping her cheek. He could think of nothing else, his mind replaying the day's events to the point of obsession.

"It will." She turned her face in, kissing his palm. "I'm so proud of you, my John. You're so clever."

He smiled. "You stroke my vanity. But let's hope ingenuity wins out where weapons have failed."

She tucked herself neatly at his side, her head resting on his breast. "Two Kettles Together said we can come to Oriska. They've invited us to stay, at least until The Thistle is rebuilt."

She was quiet for a moment, and then he heard her weeping, her body trembling against his. In all the time he'd known Dellis, she'd been a pillar of strength with an iron will to match. But even iron cracked under too much strain.

"You and Alexei are all I have left." She sniffed, burying her face into his shoulder. "I've lost everything: my parents, both of my homes, my brother, my grandfather. I almost lost you once; I can't bear the thought of you going off to war again, leaving me alone. If they find you… If you're captured…" She let out a gasp of unadulterated pain. "Oh, John, what will I do? I can't live without you. If anything happened…"

He shushed her with his lips, a long, languid kiss, silencing her fears. And his. Eventually, they'd be parted again, but he wanted to forget that for the moment. "Don't think about it, my love. I'm here with you tonight.

And no matter where I go, or what happens, we can never truly be parted." Slowly, he lifted her hand, letting it run over the braids she'd so lovingly given him long ago, a forever symbol of the ties that bound them together.

"I love you," he whispered into her lips; words that were once so foreign and acrid to his palate had become like a benediction, rolling off his tongue directly from his heart.

He made love to her slowly and then held her close, whispering more sweet words, just as she'd done for him through nights of relentless dreams that denied him rest.

When she finally slept, he listened to the breeze and the sounds of the night, waiting for the voices to return, their song to start anew, but it didn't happen. They never came. Their song forever silenced.

Morpheus denied John repose; he spent the rest of the night trying to devise a new plan for Arnold, something to replace the failed attempt. When blissful sleep finally came, and John's lids grew heavy, Alexei threw open the flap and said boisterously, "Get up, you two."

"I never went to sleep." John groaned, rubbing his sore, tired eyes. "Is there news? He rolled over, shaking Dellis awake. "My love, we must get up."

She ignored him, pretending to sleep, though a little smirk tugged at the corner of her mouth.

"A dispatch from Gansevoort just arrived. Stanwix is in trouble. Arnold is taking the whole battalion to the fort today," Alexei said, glancing at Dellis, who'd just curled into John's chest and pulled the covers over her head.

"I'll wait outside. Get dressed, both of you. We're leaving soon."

John shook her again and then planted a firm smack on her backside that made her yelp. "We have to get up, warming pan." Then he leaned in and whispered into her ear, "Though, I confess, I wouldn't mind spending a day lying under this blanket while you rode me limp. Tell me, my love, should we try that someday? We won't get out of bed except to get food and maybe a cup of tea. By the end of the day, I'll be misfiring, and you'll be saddle sore and full of my seed."

Dellis rolled her eyes up at him and shook her head, but what she said was contradictory. "I'll feed you, but only if you do a right, proper job. And if you don't, well, it's bread and water for you and plenty of drills until you get it right. If you defy me, you'll get twenty lashes with my crop across the backside."

His eyes widened like giant blue saucers but his lips curled into a smile. "You must make good on such a threat, woman. I can take no more of your teasing. Now get up!" With that, he snatched the covers off her and threw them across the tent, out of her reach.

She groaned a few times and then started to rise, her hair a delightful mess of tangles around her face, both her eyes still puffy and sleep filled. When she stood, he almost regretted exposing all that lovely flesh to his gaze, her full breasts impudent and proud, making his hands ache for a touch. "Oh, good Lord, I hate mornings." She gasped, scratching her head.

Her pitiful state made him laugh. "You're not suited for camp life, my love."

She shot him a look full of daggers and groaned her response to his attempt at humor.

Quickly, they both dressed and rushed to Arnold's office, the brisk morning air helping to further rouse them. Alexei was already waiting with Han Yerry, both of them looking wide eyed and reticent.

Arnold stomped in behind them and threw his hat down on the table, huffing out a breath of frustration. "We can't wait any longer. I sent word to General Gates. St. Leger has started to dig a siege trench, and there's concern about desertion amongst Gansevoort's men. I'm sending scouts ahead, if your men would be willing to take part?"

Arnold walked over to Han Yerry, their eyes meeting pensively. "You must come with us."

"Yes." The Chief nodded. "My scouts will leave now." Han Yerry turned to Alexei, giving him orders. "Send Ho-sa-gowwa and Henry."

"Captain." Arnold turned his attention to John. "Can St. Leger continue?"

"He certainly has the tenacity to do so, but again, I question the willingness of his native contingent," John replied.

His gut ached, the one cup of coffee he managed to suck down burning a hole in his stomach. Failure was the worst feeling. He'd been so sure the idea would work.

"I have a thousand men; it may not be enough, but it'll have to do." Arnold grabbed his hat and directed his guard to bring his maps and his things. "Gentlemen"—the General looked back at them and nodded—"we leave."

The drummers rolled out the march, and Arnold's relief forces started to move. The brigade was a thousand men strong, nine hundred men from General Ebenezer Learned's Continental Brigade from Massachusetts, four New York attachments, and a small party from the Tryon County Militia. John rode next to Han Yerry and the rest of the Oneidas, while four of their men scouted ahead.

The long, arduous march was something John was used to yet always found frustrating. As a light infantry officer, he and his men were trained for speed and agility, often ahead of the regiment, travelling in loose formations, scouting or taking part in skirmishes—softening up the enemy with sharpshooters. Taking his time and staying behind with the lineup was a test of patience, and as the sun rose and the sweltering heat of the summer set in, their snail-like pace was bordering on painful.

Not ten miles out of Fort Dayton, Ho-sa-gowwa and Great Bear emerged from the trees, a Mohawk warrior along with them.

"General, sir. We have news," Great Bear said, his eyes alight with excitement, in total contrast to his fierce countenance and the horrific scar on his forehead.

The Mohawk warrior looked around the group and then started to speak. John nudged Viceroy in closer to hear the news.

"Han Yost came to the camp yesterday and warned us of General Arnold's arrival. He claimed he'd been held captive, and that at least three-thousand men were coming to relieve the fort. The Great Father's men argued while my brothers picked up camp and left. We want no more of this fighting. It wasn't what Butler promised us. Too many of our men died, and now, we have to face the consequences of fighting with our Brothers of the Standing Stone. When I left, the army was headed towards Wood Creek. They were fleeing up the river."

John let out a sigh of relief, looking back at Dellis. *By God, we did it!* Their ruse worked.

She smiled and winked at him.

"Yes!" Arnold exclaimed, his grey-blue eyes alight with victory. "Those bloody backs are running back to Canada! Yes!"

"What now?" John asked, taking no offense at the denigration of his former side. It was almost an endearment. "What do we do?"

"We continue on. I want to see St. Leger's arse as we chase him away." Arnold boasted.

It took another day to reach the fort. Arnold sent word to Gates, dispatching a letter with a courier and an Oneida scout for added protection. As they neared Oriskany, they strayed back onto the Albany trail, following the same path through the ravines that Herkimer and his men had taken two weeks before.

John brought Viceroy close to Dellis and clasped hands with her for a moment, knowing that place would forever haunt her memories. Her eyes tracked back and forth, the horrors of war still on display; so many died in that ravine, their names and faces gone to the passage of time. Still littering the ground were the decomposing corpses of militia men left unclaimed, at least four hundred of them. John covered his nose with his hand, the stench enough to turn one's stomach inside out; bodies, purple and bloated, covered in flies, lay discarded and forgotten.

It was late in the evening when the relief force finally arrived at Stanwix. They were greeted by an abandoned camp, tents and supplies left behind for the taking. St. Leger's mortars fired a round with a loud *boom*, and the cannon from the bastions fired back, the cheers of the men carrying over the distance.

"We did it," Arnold said, turning back to his men. "Victory!"

The company let out a great cheer. "Huzzah!"

John proudly rode up next to his men-at-arms, Alexei to the left, Clark and Adam at the right. In front of John, also mounted, were Han Yerry and Great Bear. Behind them, Dellis rode with Will and Two Kettles Together.

"Thank you, Han Yerry, and thank you to your brothers," Arnold exclaimed with great adulation, shaking the Chief's hand. "I'm sending a small party of men after St. Leger. Can some of your men go with them as guides? We want to be sure they continue their flight back to Canada."

Alexei looked over at John and then Han Yerry; the two men nodded. "I'll go, and John and his men will come with us. Also, we'll bring Ho-sa-gowwa. He's our best spy."

"Good. We rest for the night, and then we must leave to deal with General Burgoyne. He's on to Saratoga, and we must stop him." Arnold smiled, giving them all a look of appreciation. "I envy you getting to see all those Lobsterbacks retreating into the forest. Make sure you get me a good description so I can send it back to General Gates and General Washington."

"I can draw you one," John said. "With pleasure."

"That would be wonderful, Captain." Arnold nodded. "You'll be quite useful to the Northern Army. I hope you'll join us."

John looked back at Dellis for confirmation; from then on, they were in it together. She nodded, already accepting their combined fate. They'd be separated again, only that time, he was with her people. "I'll join you. And I have some information about Burgoyne and Howe that might be of use."

"Excellent. Report to my tent when you return." Arnold gave the Oneidas the onceover and then walked away full of swagger and hubris. He went back to his men and started directing them to clean up the refuse left behind by St. Leger's camp.

"Shall we go?" Alexei asked, pulling the reins on his horse, ready to take off like the wind. "Have you enough ammunition? We may have company. I'm sure some of St. Leger's natives will be lurking about in the woods, looking for a fight."

"I'm ready." John looked up at Dellis again—his wife, his life—and grinned. It was his first victory with his new people. If felt right. It felt good. *Justice.* Not the outcome he imagined, but a different one, a just one. From then on, he'd serve no king, only his conscience and his honor.

"Husband?" Her sweet, sultry tone drew his attention. When he glanced at her again, she gave him a wicked smile and then slapped the leather reins of her horse against her palm several times, suggestion burning in her eyes.

He thought nothing of it and then went back to digging through his haversack, counting the number of cartridges he had. *Fifteen should do it.* And he had his tomahawk and his knife. Stuffed in his pants, he had one extra pistol to go with his musket. If his head would stop throbbing, he'd be ready for a fight. Actually, a little fisticuffs sounded pretty good; after his scuffle with Miles, John had gotten a fever for some hand to hand, just to loosen up. Yes, a fight would do him some good.

"Captain…" She called his name in that dulcet, suggestive way, drawing his attention. Once again, she was slapping the reins against her palm; only that time, she cocked a brow, her teeth biting into her bottom lip, turning it slick pink, evoking wanton thoughts.

Now? Right now? Her timing was rather inopportune, but try as he might, he couldn't fight the grin that formed, or the rock-hard erection that followed. Adjusting himself, he immediately found it rather uncomfortable being mounted with a swelling erection pressed into the hardened leather of his saddle. Viceroy fussed, sensing John's frustration.

She licked her lips, her eyes further darkening with want, all the while still using the rein on her palm, little red marks forming where she slapped; her thighs gripped the powerful mare's sides as if Dellis were riding him right then. With his eyes trained on her, unable to look away, he said, "Gentlemen, I must see the women back to Oriska, and then I'll join you. Who knows what ruffians will be lurking around, and I wouldn't want to put the ladies at risk."

Alexei rolled his eyes and shook his head, giving John a knowing look. "Fine, we'll meet you in the morning."

"Right, tomorrow morning," John replied, brooking no disagreement. He wouldn't be deterred that one indulgence before he rode off to battle.

When he was next to Dellis, he lowered his voice so only she could hear. "Wife, they're fully aware of my true intent, knowing I have no need to escort you back, for you're three of the most capable women. For my ego's sake, I better have trouble seating this horse tomorrow. I can take your teasing no longer."

She let out a laugh that caused everyone to look back on the moment's intrigue. "Yes, Captain Carlisle." With a loud *snap*, she slapped her palm with the reins and said, "I'm ever your dutiful wife."

The sheer ridiculousness of her words brought with them a roar of laughter that bubbled up from deep in his throat. "Don't start now, not on my behalf. I love your direct assaults, my Fennishyo, and how you make me worship in your beautiful valley."

"Touché, Captain," Dellis said, using his own words against him. "Touché."

Epilogue

Celeste watched as Lord Tomlinson impatiently sat back in his chair, running his left hand over the arm and then drumming his fingers on the wood. He was handsome, not in a boyish, arrogant way like John, but in a powerful and manly way. Tomlinson's long, dark, chocolate-brown hair was pulled back at the nape, the queue stretching all the way down to his shoulder blades and taped with linen. He had large, rugged features; thick, full brows; wide-set brown eyes; and a prominent nose that would've looked too big on any other man's face.

What was most striking about him were his lips; they were full and sensuous, the top one having no defined points. It made Celeste wonder what it was like to be kissed by him. He was wearing his officer's regalia, his crimson coat adorned at the shoulders by gold epaulettes, the royal-blue facings and cuffs detailed with fine gold cord that glinted in the candlelight. When Lord Tomlinson lifted his right arm, she noticed he had no hand, only a great wrapping of bloody linens with many layers of padding underneath. The wound looked to be fresh, the amputation only days old.

"Tell His Lordship what you know," Celeste said sweetly.

Mariah sniffed a few times, dabbed her nose with a handkerchief she'd stuffed in her fist, and then looked up to both of them with wide, glassy eyes. "My Lord, there was a fire at The Thistle, and Mr. McKesson was killed, but everyone else survived. After, they were all staying with the town magistrate, Mr. Armstrong-Jones, and his son, Patrick. I know because his servant is my beau." The girl glanced at Eagle Eyes, her eyes narrowing with anger and a tinge of fear. "There were three women with them: Miss Dellis; her slave; and a small, slight woman with light hair. Mr. Alexei and the Captain were both injured, but when they were finally well enough to travel, rumor has it they went to the fort to help General Arnold."

"I know the rest," Miles said, waving his hand—an order to be quiet. His eyes tracked back and forth from the maps on his desk to the floor, a flurry of thoughts brewing behind his dark eyes. *But what is he contemplating?*

Celeste waited with bated breath for his next move. What would it be? Since DeLancie was dead, and McKesson, too, Lord Tomlinson was her last hope, her last chance to get even with John and his Oneida whore.

Mariah cleared her throat and started again, but hesitantly. "Well, there is one more thing." She looked up at both of them through tear-speckled lashes with wide, glistening eyes.

"What's that?" he asked.

"My beau, Henry—that's his name—overheard something taking place at the magistrate's house."

What's she talking about? Celeste turned to the foolish girl and asked, "What did he hear?"

The girl blushed sheepishly, her cheeks and throat turning crimson. "It was Mr. Alexei, and he was with a woman."

"Doing what?" Celeste demanded.

"A lady wouldn't say, but you know what I mean." Again, Mariah blushed, looking up at Lord Tomlinson coyly. "He was with the little lady, alone, in her quarters."

He clucked his tongue, his hand curling into a fist, clenching the air with the energy and wrath of one ready to do battle. He slammed the stump, where his right hand used to be, on the desktop, a fresh surge of blood staining the white linen that bound it. But he didn't flinch, as if he were impervious to pain. "So, John has turned traitor, and McKesson has taken my wife."

"What will you do, My Lord?" Celeste asked, giddy with excitement.

"By now, word has surely gone out that one of our spies has turned and that the Oneidas have helped the colonists."

Eagle Eyes nodded.

"If they're with Arnold, I know where they're going. Burgoyne is going after Albany."

"What are you going to do with this information?" Celeste asked, unable to withstand the anticipation. "Remember, I helped you."

Miles grinned, showing even white teeth. "Yes, my dear, you did." With that, Lord Tomlinson stood and walked around the desk, offering his arm to Celeste with the gallantry of one walking into King George's court. She stood and nestled her arm in his. "You're the loveliest woman, even in your delicate condition."

She cocked a brow in suggestion, allowing her tongue to run between her lips, moistening them. "How kind of you, Lord Tomlinson. Just what a lady needs to hear, especially when her lover has left her to fend for herself in the world. Tell me, what will you do about John?"

Miles let out a chuckle, gently patting her hand. "We'll just have to get the traitor back for you. And *I* will deal with Alexei McKesson, personally."

"What a brilliant idea."

With that, the two of them glided out of his tent, ready to take the stage…

Acknowledgements

Rebels! Welcome back to the Revolution. When I started this journey, there was never meant to be a book three. The concept of The Turncoat didn't exist. As you all know, this was truly a counseling tool that the ever-brilliant Lorrie came up with to help me work through my dumpster fire of a life. But when I reached the end of The Traitor, I, like John, was frustrated that after all this counseling and soul searching, justice was still far beyond my reach. Here's a bit of brutally honest truth: my perpetrators had won, the real story was buried, and I was forced to move on with my life—never to be vindicated. Not the way it happens in the movies right? So, what next? I had many readers frustrated with the fact that John is forced to burn the proof that would've cleared his name at the end of The Traitor. Well, sadly, that's what happens more times than not. Just like John, when he leaves Fort Niagara at the end of The Traitor, he knew life would never be the same as it was, and he could never repair the damage to his career. I, too, stood facing the same grim reality.

Hence, we have The Turncoat.

I tried very hard, in various ways, to recreate the life I once had and found that I could never go back. Too many betrayals, too many lies and hurt feelings, and my stubborn pride that refused to face those who wronged me, my head bowed in defeat. Humpty Dumpty can never be put back on the wall, and John and I learned this together in The Turncoat. Acceptance was the journey of this book. Accepting that my dreams would never be fulfilled; mourning them; and finally, trying to find new ones. For John, the new dream was with Dellis and her people: the desire for a home, a family, and a life that was lived on his terms. I spent most of my life consumed with work and ambition, but when it was gone, all that was left was my makeshift family of friends and my husband. Through them, I found a new dream, a new life, and the ability to accept the loss of my old one. Not to neglect Dellis, in The Turncoat she learns to stop lashing out and constantly fighting everyone around her—especially those who love her and want to help. I was doing the same thing, always fighting to protect myself and what I felt was mine, only further damaging the relationships I had with those I loved. I, like Dellis, had to learn the very hard way that I was my own worst enemy. Failure is the greatest teacher; if we'll only listen, she has many lessons for us to learn.

I could've written a different story with more history, more facts, less story line, less relationship issues, more romance, and less sex, but that's not what these three books are about. This story is about tapping into the very core of complex human nature as I struggled to understand my own. A complete human experiences all these emotions simultaneously, and so was I as I sat behind my computer, day after day, crafting these books. The Rebels and Redcoats Saga is about people—yes, there's a war going on, and yes, we see the unraveling of the Iroquois Confederacy, not to diminish those important events—but it's really about how we, as humans, haven't changed that much. It's a wonderful thing that in this way we're linked to our forefathers, and we can look at their mistakes to help us understand our own.

Just because your life doesn't turn out like the one in your dreams doesn't mean it can't be just as fulfilling and later, become even better. I say this as someone who's living proof.

Now for my thank yous:

To my editors, Kathe and Jo: Thank God for you both. I'm serious. I would've thrown in the towel ten times over if I didn't have your support and patience. And thank you for seeing my vision and always helping me to refine it. You make my words beautiful.

As always, my amazing team that has stayed the course with me through these three books: Gaynor, Steven, Layla, Kelly Ann, Lorrie, Teres, Katie, Janine. To Renee and the Historical Romance Retreat cast of authors and attendees: you're all amazing; thanks for welcoming the brash Rebel into your elegant Regency/Victorian Hearts. The former Romantic Times Community, it was because of your support I'm published today. You're my idols, every freaking one of you!! The Indie Author community and the Once Upon A Book Community for welcoming this newbie into the fold. I have to give a shout out to Amy and The Historical Virtual Blog Tour for taking the Rebels and Redcoats Saga into their hearts and being so generous with their support. Also, to my research buddies I've picked up along the way: Amy; Morgan; and the freaking-fantastic Lorna, my Royal Navy go-to-gal. You ladies are the best!

Again, to the Oneida Nation, our first allies in the American Revolution. I hope I did your brave ancestors justice and shined a light on your incredible story that's so intertwined with the birth of our nation. Thank you to the staff and historians of Fort Stanwix National Park, Fort Niagara National Park, Fort Ticonderoga, Colonial Williamsburg, and The American Revolution Museum at Yorktown-Jamestown. You were all so very giving with your knowledge. I'm forever grateful.

To all the Rebel fans: Thanks for being readers, and I hope I keep rocking your world. I promise, what's to come is just as much fun. The Revolution is just beginning.

As a Chronic Migraineur, I take this opportunity to draw attention to this devastating disease that has affected my life and the lives of so many others. Every day is a struggle for me, never knowing when one is coming, living each good day to the fullest only to be stuck on a couch for weeks at a time unable to stand the light of day. The worst part for me is the cessation of my writing voice and fearing that it'll never come back. Thankfully, it always does, and I step into the sun, remove my ever-present sunglasses, and thank God for that one amazing day. I keep fighting the good fight, and I refuse to give up—neither should any of you. There's hope for all of us.

Finally, I send tons of love to my family and dear friends. Layla, my BFF and crit partner, you're just the freaking best, and I love you for it. Kelly, for being so insightful and always having my back... That's just awesome. Angie, my Agnes, my voice of reason, that's why I based the character on you. And last, but not least, if it wasn't for my husband and my sweet, yet-ornery cat, Mickey, I don't think I would've made it this far. I thank God this was the lesson I learned through all my trials and tribulations: never to take you for granted.

And finally, to John and Dellis, my muses. You inspire me every freaking day.

It is within these pages that I found justice, acceptance, and most importantly, love. Thank you.

Dear Reader

Thank you so much for spending your evenings with John and Dellis and for allowing me to take you back to the founding of our nation, the American Revolutionary War. I hope you fell in love, had an adventure, and learned a little about the wild Northern Frontier that's now Upstate New York.

As an author, I love feedback. I learn so much from hearing what my readers have to say about my stories and what little kernels of themselves they can relate to in my characters. It's because of my readers The Rebels and Redcoats Saga exists today, so I owe a great deal to your wisdom.

If you love my books, please leave a review wherever you picked them up. I encourage all your feedback, good or bad; it's what continues to fill the well of love I have for writing and recreating those unique areas of forgotten history.

Subscribe to my newsletter at revolutionaryauthor.com to keep up on all that's happening with T.J. London. I am also on Facebook at TJLondonauthor and twitter @TJLondonauthor.

Winter 2019, Merrick McKesson and the McKesson brothers' story is revealed in Man of War, the French and Indian War prequel to the Rebels and Redcoats Saga. Then, coming in 2020, The Rebels and Redcoats Saga Continues with book #4 The Rebel.

Rock the Revolution, Rebels!

About the Author

T.J. London is a rebel, liberal, lover, fighter, diehard punk, pharmacist, and author who loves history. As a storyteller, her goal is to fill in the gaps about missing history, those little places that are so interesting yet sadly forgotten. Her favorite time period to write is, of course, the American Revolutionary War (is there any other time period?). She also enjoys researching the French Revolution, the French and Indian War, the Russian Revolution, and the Victorian Era. Her passions are traveling, writing, reading, cycling, and sharing a martini (no more wine, I'm a migraineur) with her friends while she collects experiences in this drama called life. She's a native of Metropolitan Detroit (but secretly dreams of being a Londoner) and resides there with her husband, Fred, and her beloved cat and writing partner, Mickey.

48764353R00356

Made in the USA
San Bernardino, CA
18 August 2019